AN IMPERFECT TIME

BY
BRONISŁAW
WILDSTEIN

An Imperfect Time by Bronisław Wildstein
Translated by Mateusz Julecki and Christopher Zakrzewski

Cover by Jan Kostka
This edition published in 2019

Zmok Books is an imprint of

Pike and Powder Publishing Group LLC
17 Paddock Drive
Lawrence, NJ 08648
1525 Hulse Rd, Unit 1
Point Pleasant, NJ 08742

ISBN 978-1-950423-18-7 Paperback
ISBN 978-1-950423-23-1 ebook
LCN 219953595

Bibliographical References and Index
1. Historical Fiction. 2. Poland. 3. 20th Century

For more information on Pike and Powder Publishing Group, LLC,
visit us at www.PikeandPowder.com & www.wingedhussarpublishing.com

twitter: @pike_powder
facebook: @PikeandPowder

This publication has
been supported by the
©POLAND Translation Program

Wisła
Wybrzeże Kościuszkowskie
629
Canaletta
Le Royal
Meridien Bristol
Wiślana
Ogrodowa
Aleja Jana Pawła II
Ptasia
Ogród Saski
Zachęta
Narodowa
Galeria Sztuki
Topiel
Zajęcza
Tamka
Chłodna
Cicha
719
Grzybowska
Szkolna
Świętokrzyska
719
Solec
Okólnik
The Westin
Warsaw
719
Warecka
Foksal
631
Aleja 3 Maja
InterContinental
Warszawa
Złota
Nowy Świat
Chmielna
631
Prosta
Żelazna
719
Marszałkowska
Widok
Muzeum Wojska
Polskiego
Sienna
Złota
Pałac Kultury
i Nauki
631
Bracka
Książęca
Złote Tarasy
Warszawa
Rozbrat
Warszawa
Centralna
631
Novotel
Warszawa
Centrum
Hotel
Marriott
Aleje Jerozolimskie
631
Wspólna
Hoża
Nowogrodzka
Hoża
Wilcza
Mokotowska
Piękna
Koszykowa
Piękna
Piękna
Park
Ujazdowski
634
Aleja Niepodległości
Mokotowska
Koszykowa
2
E30
Politechnika
Warszawska
Centrum Sztuki
Współczesnej
Zamek Ujazdowski
Filtrowa
Filtrowa
2
634
Wawelska
Aleja Armii Ludowej
E30
Marszałko
Aleje Ujazd
E30
E30
2
Google
Map data ©2009 PPWK

AN INTRODUCTION

The flickering index of numbers on Adam Brok's monitor were taking an apparent nosedive, in free-fall. It seemed as if the computer had gone mad and wanted to throw off the virtual entities oppressing it. The screen filled with red. Adam instinctively glanced over at his neighbors' computer screens, visible behind the flimsy, purely symbolic partitions that separated them, and had the impression he was in a hall of mirrors. At dizzying speeds, in the grip of some nameless impulse, the machines were devaluing the transactions encoded in their bowels. The brokers' faces, turned to exchange incredulous glances with each other before turning back to their screens, all displayed the same astonishment, now tinged with panic.

It suddenly occurred to Adam that the computer screen was merely a thin sheet of glass. Beyond it, beyond the plunging index numbers next to the names of the corporations that moved swiftly across the tenuous surface, each accompanied by a little red triangle pointing downward – beyond that abstract world of numbers and letters and symbols, he saw unfinished buildings crashing to the ground, scaffolding collapsing, conveyor belts grinding to a standstill, stores closing, job centers filling up, lights going out, darkness descending on people and cities. Then everything went quiet; he found himself enclosed in a bubble of silence, all the more astonishing because the stock exchange floor was a perpetual roar of debilitating noise. The illusion lasted a fraction of a second. The roar returned with redoubled intensity. In the stock exchange all hell had broken loose. People were screaming at each other and into phones, or in many cases just screaming at no one in particular. The floor was an image of chaos. *Can we contain this?* Adam thought. *How did we keep it in check before? Or have we ever been in control of anything? Perhaps we were just riding time's turbulence, deluding ourselves that we were steering the waves?*

He may not have been alone in asking such questions: it was unusually quiet at "The Spouter-Inn." Somewhere in the back someone was shouting, while someone else was laughing hysterically; but instead of the usual buzz a heavy silence filled the restaurant.

"Why are we surprised? Why the hell are we surprised?!" Christina Lopez burst out at one point, expressing what everyone was feeling at that moment. "We've known for months it all had to come crashing down. It was a bubble, it had to burst, it couldn't go on forever! But we went on believing we could snatch a bit more, make a bit more – make money out of something that doesn't exist! We should be surprised it didn't go belly-up until now!"

No one contradicted her.

And yet it really did take us unaware, mused Adam as he left the restaurant after a few drinks and hailed a taxi. We're more than surprised: we're in shock. Shocked that something that was clearly going to happen, was bound to happen, finally has happened. He was still thinking about this as he let himself into his apartment and fished out a letter from Poland among the litter of leaflets and junk mail in the hall. An express delivery. The apartment was almost sterile – not like the apartment in Poland, he thought as he extracted it from the post office packaging. Nancy had cleaned up before she left. She didn't live with him, only staying there from time to time, but it was becoming increasingly clear that she was waiting for him to propose they move in together. Adam was in no hurry. He liked Nancy and they got on well, but there was something about the finality of the decision to live together that put him off. Still, sooner or later he would have to make up his mind. Nancy was going to present him with an ultimatum, that was clear. It was also clear in the end he would do what she wanted. The benefits far outweighed the costs. But Adam continued to put off the decision.

The letter was from his father. Adam plopped three ice cubes into a glass of pure malt, added water from a long-necked bottle, flung himself into a black leather armchair and switched on the television. As he flicked through the channels, every one of them was showing the scene he had participated in a few hours ago. The commentators, sounding very unsure of themselves, were all repeating the same warnings couched in phrases cocooned in layers of conditionals and dripping with caveats: that the markets might continue to fall and that a further downward trend might have grave consequences for the world economy. Beyond the windows, the lights of Manhattan continued to glimmer. Adam ripped open the envelope.

"I've decided to write to you, though I feel rather awkward about this. But then you can hardly say I'm badgering you – it is my first letter after all. I used to send you postcards; sometimes you'd even answer them. We both know perfectly well the grievance you hold against me – if that is what your deep-seated feeling towards me can be called. A justified one from your point of view. But in general? Except... is there an 'in general'? All my life I've exposed supposedly objective and impartial points of view to ridicule. The only points of view here are yours and mine, your mother's and mine. From my point of view... well, I've paid the price. But let's drop this general bullshit. That's not why I'm writing to you. I'm writing because I want to see you. I'd be glad if you could come home to Poland even for just a short visit. I can pay for your flight and cover the costs of your stay. I know you have money, you have a career after all, but if it would help... In any case I'm anxious to see you as soon as possible. In the eight years since you moved to the States I've seen you only a handful of times, and very briefly at that. The last time you were in Poland was four years ago. No, I exaggerate: almost four years ago. On that visit, you spent exactly twenty-three minutes with me. I know because I checked my watch and made a mental note of it. You were in a great hurry to get to some important meeting, or maybe just one that held some attraction for you. That's not a reproach. You might reply that before you left we didn't see each other that often either. That's true. It's been that way ever since I moved out twenty-three years ago and left you, you and your mother.

But I didn't want to be separated from you. It was your mother that didn't want you to spend much time with me. I can understand that – which doesn't mean I agree with her. But until you were fourteen we used to spend quite a lot of time together. Remember? After that… it was up to you. Your decision. Yours and your mother's. It was a question of emotions and politics. A volatile mix. But no point in theorizing. I just wanted to remind you of the facts. And maybe justify myself a little. This probably sounds pathetic. But I don't want to start crossing out and polishing and rewriting everything. I'm tempted to. I am a journalist after all – a columnist. But I decided to write to you the way I would talk. To talk to you on paper, if that's the only way.

You know I don't like to make a big drama out of things. But I'm asking you to come because I want to see you one more time. Maybe things aren't quite as bad as that, but you never know. I'm seventy years old. My father died when he was my age. I feel my time is coming. Of course, I'd like more time, but no one's going to ask me what I'd like. What more is there to say? I know you understand.

I'm waiting.

Your father"

Manhattan was lit up; it was like any other day. On television, they were talking of a financial crisis. The date was September 2008.

But that is not when this story begins. Perhaps it began a hundred years earlier. In a place called Kurow, not far from Pinsk, on the broad, forested plain, which at the time belonged to Russia (and before that to Poland, a country erased from the map over a hundred years earlier), there lived a Jew by the name of Baruch Brok with his wife Doba and five children.

All sorts of people lived there then: Russians, Poles and Jews. Jewish Orthodox, Russian Orthodox, Catholic. They did not always know who they were. They only knew they were *from* there. They knew which Catholic or Russian Orthodox Church they went to and who celebrated the services there. They lived alongside one another; sometimes they lived together. But the Jews were different. They knew who they were, and their neighbors knew they were different. They all lived under the same broad sky, which spread its brightness over them in daytime and glimmered with lights at night. Sometimes it clouded over or disappeared in fog, but the locals knew it was there and would be back. They had only to wait and it would reappear as always, in all its splendor.

The Brok family were not badly off. They had a pleasant house with a well-tended garden, a wagon and a horse. Doba looked after two cows and a large poultry flock. They lived on the edge of the village. Baruch was a merchant, trading in leather. But that was not his main occupation. He was a *tzaddik*; they called him a miracle-worker. He would disappear from home for hours at a time, sometimes for half a day or more. When Doba asked questions, he just smiled. Sometimes people saw him standing in the fields or in the forest, looking up at the sky. They said he talked to God.

Matwiej saw Baruch one summer day around noon. The Jew was leaning against a tree, looking directly into the sun. He stood there, quite still, for so long that Matwiej took fright and fled the scene. "Anyone else, it would have burned their eyes out," he said later, "but not him. He looked at me and smiled. His pupils shone as if the sun had moved and settled into them for good."

Piotr saw him in the little lake on the far side of the forest about three hours' walk from Kurow. It was spring. The leaves were a deep green and the flowers had bloomed, but the mornings were chilly. Baruch was standing in the water up to his armpits, looking up at the clouds. The morning mist was rising off the water. Piotr even stopped to ask if he needed anything, but then Baruch looked at him with that smile of his and said nothing.

Zosia saw him in a clearing in the forest. It had just rained and everything glistened; the world seemed newly born. Baruch was walking around in circles, arms in the air, his fingers snatching at the sun's rays. "Like he was dancing," Zosia reported in an unsure voice, looking at those around her.

Leon told them how he'd seen Baruch standing in the field by the forest when a wolf ran up to him. "It stopped less than a yard away then lay down on its belly like a dog. I thought it was a dog at first, I even came a bit closer, but it was a wolf, for sure. I swear. It leapt up, turned to me and snarled; then it disappeared into the forest. Swear to God!"

But the strangest reports came from peasants returning from the horse fair after the first heavy snowfall of the year. In the distance, on a hilltop under the blue sky, they saw a man climb down from his cart and leap into a snowdrift. He rolled about in the snow like an animal then lay perfectly still. His horse stood by waiting patiently. At first, they didn't know who it was. They drove up thinking something had happened. Then, coming closer, they saw it was Baruch lying in the snow, looking up at the sky, smiling. There was a crow standing close to him. Baruch turned to it, and the two eyed each other: man and crow. The peasants stood speechless and waited – a good while, by all accounts. No one spoke. There was only the steam rising into the darkening air from the men and their beasts and the creaking of the shafts as the horses strained against them. Suddenly the crow cawed and launched itself into the air. For a moment Baruch followed it with his gaze; then, noticing the onlookers, he grew serious and stared at them intently until they felt uncomfortable. At last, picking himself up, he greeted them, brushed the snow off his clothes, climbed into his cart, and drove off.

He healed both people and animals. He could set bones, ease sprains, dress wounds. He knew how to wash weak eyes and deaf ears. He could advise people on the treatment of chronic ailments, cure boils and carbuncles, drain abscesses, relieve pain. He stroked old Kuzma's hair until the pains clouding her mind went away. He cured Szydlik of the back pain that had left him virtually crippled. From the neighboring village, they brought him a young girl who had lost her mind, grown afraid of her family, and was tormented by evil spirits. Baruch clasped her to himself, though she struggled to break free. After thrashing about briefly in his arms, she calmed down and fell still; and so together they stood there for a long, long time, until at last Baruch kissed her on the forehead and let her go, while she ran to embrace her family. She was cured.

One night the miller brought him his little son. He had fallen ill a few days earlier and was delirious with a high fever. Old Mother Yevdokia's spells and incenses hadn't helped. Neither had the nettle and birch bark infusions. He only got worse. That night he drifted in and out of consciousness. The family gathered around him to pray. It was then the miller decided to take him to Baruch. The Jew stood looking at the boy for a long time; then he sat down beside him. He put his hands on the boy and there by the window he sat as the autumn night flowed past outside. You could hear the roar of the river. By morning the boy had revived. Soon he was completely well.

Sometimes Baruch would shake his head sadly to indicate there was nothing he could do. On those occasions, he wouldn't even try anything. It was useless to convince him otherwise.

He not only helped people from his village. Jews journeyed from far and wide to see him – to talk with him, seek his advice. The locals thought of him as their own. He never exacted payment. They gave him whatever they had, if they had it. Sometimes it was money, but more often foodstuffs: eggs, milk, cheese, flat bread, occasionally vegetables or fruit. Sometimes things they had made at home: cloths, blankets, bed linen. On occasion, he wouldn't take anything. "I have what I need," he'd say. "You may want it some day."

***

Somewhere far off the revolution was sputtering out. The losing side were strange bunch of people. They had wanted to depose our Dear Father Tsar and establish common ownership of property, women and children. The Russian Orthodox, who were the majority in the district, remembered others like them. They had claimed to be the true Orthodox. Only they truly loved God and therefore did not hold with the idea of private ownership. But they forced nothing on no one; and when people laughed at them and hurled insults, they ran away.

The revolutionaries, on the other hand, were set on remaking the world by force. People listened to them with fear and wonder, though sometimes they laughed too. Well, of course you could kill the Tsar, they knew that, he was a man after all, and such terrible things had happened before. But to live without any Tsar? The Tsar who kept order, who oversaw God's order on earth? That seemed not only a terrible thing to want but a stupid one as well. No wonder the army and police had put down the revolution. Could people be that crazy? Although you heard increasingly more often that it wasn't people but the Jews. That is what they said in the taverns and inns: it was a Jewish conspiracy, because the Jews wanted to rule the world. Learned people knew about a book that had been stolen from the Jews where it was all written down, how they planned to take over the world. When people looked at Itzhak or Tevya who had lived among them ever since they could remember, they found it hard to believe. But when they heard about Jews being God-killers, they began to believe it and anger welled up inside them. Word went around from tavern to tavern, from market place to market place.

Reports arrived that people were rising up against the Jews, assaulting them, beating them up, trashing their property. It seemed foolish to destroy perfectly good things. But you couldn't very well take them; that would be no better than stealing. This way they got their punishment fair and square. Though apparently some people did help themselves to things, because taking from a Jew, well, you could hardly call it stealing.

Direr reports began to circulate – reports of mounting violence, rage, arson. Then blood. Burning houses cast a lurid glow over the countryside. More blood.

Now they were killing Jews. In Bialystok, in Siedlce, the earth around their holdings became a blood-drenched mire. Twisted bodies protruded starkly from the mud around the charred heaps of what had been houses. Goose down from torn bedding floated in the air along with soot and the cries of the murdered.

But all that was still far away. True, peasants at the market in Konskie had beaten up some Jews, laid into them with their whips; and in Luckowice they had dragged out the innkeeper from behind his counter and beaten him unconscious then set on his wife when she came running to help him. By the time they were finished, all that was left of the inn was a pile of rubble. But that did not yet make a pogrom, although an air of dread now hung over the land. Winter refused to go away; the first rains hadn't come, and the earth was rock hard. They worried about the harvest. The sky was heavy, and the scud, unwilling to yield up its moisture, swept across it. The light emerging from behind the clouds had a dim, eerie quality.

How could it have happened? It was a question many later asked themselves but were afraid to voice aloud. Men from the neighboring town of Stryczkow had come to the Kurow market and chummed up with some of the locals. Together they went to the inn for more tipple, the out-of-towners standing rounds for the locals. Trading had been good, they said. Soon they got on the subject of the Jews. Something had to be done about them. Finally, one of the strangers said, "You've got one right here you're chummy with. Plays the saint, the slimy toad! That kind are the worst! He needs putting in his place."

"But he's a decent fellow despite being a Jew," protested one of the locals.

"You defending a Jew?!" said the stranger. "What's he done, dimmed your wits, or what? Maybe he's bewitched you? They say he's a sorcerer."

The strangers nodded assent. The locals felt ashamed of standing up for a Jew.

So how could it have happened that this group of strangers, armed with heavy gnarled sticks, left the inn and went with a few of the locals to the Brok holding? They shouted as they went, as if needing to nerve themselves up, though they formed a sizable crowd. They called on others to join them. "We're going to put the yids in their place," they cried. Some ran out after them; some joined the throng. Others locked themselves in their houses. Darkness was falling.

They stopped at the entrance to the yard. Brok's dog was barking madly. They smashed the gate and raised an uproar. Baruch came out of the house. He walked halfway across the yard and stopped a pace short of a man who had showed them the way. The man, cudgel in hand, stood uncertainly before him, as if at a loss what to do next.

"Quiet, Blackie!" said Baruch firmly. The dog hunched down by the kennel and whined. "What do you want, people?" he said, so that everyone heard, though he spoke softly. "Why have you come here?"

"You... Jew!" said the man in front of him at last, almost spitting on Brok. He made as if to raise his stick, but only lifted it off the ground. "Jew!" he repeated.

"Yes, I am a Jew," Baruch said calmly. "You know me. I've always lived among you. My parents lived here and my grandparents before them. There's always been peace between us, even though we pray differently. And you?" he asked, shifting his body as if to get closer to the stranger. With Baruch's gaze boring into him, the man seemed to want to step back. "I don't know you," he said. "I haven't done you any harm. It was anger that brought you here, that brought all of you. But we are not to blame. We've done nothing to deserve your anger. Think about it. Nothing's happened yet. Go away. Tomorrow you'll be relieved you did."

Such was the stillness you could hear their heavy breathing and the intermittent whines of the dog. Darkness closed in, though the people could still see each other.

"Thrash the Yids!" yelled one of the strangers in the crowd. Another, standing right behind the man facing Baruch, raised his club slightly and took a step sideways as if to go around Brok; but the Jew turned toward him, and he stopped. Then someone else in the crowd, it may have been a woman, for the voice was thin and high-pitched like a woman's, yelled, "Have done with the Christ-killing Jew! Kill him!" A clod of hard earth hit the window, shattering the glass. For a moment, no one moved; then the door of the house opened and Brok's wife, a child in her arms, ran out, desperately calling his name: "Baaruch!"

Brok turned abruptly. "Doba, go back!" he managed to cry out just before the man who had tried to circle around him lifted his club with both hands and brought it crashing down on his temple. In that sudden interval of silence the sticky smacking sound was plainly heard. Even before Baruch slumped to the ground, the man in front of him smashed him another blow across the face then leapt with both booted feet onto his body as it lay there thrashing on the ground. The crowd surged forward to reach him with their clubs and boots. They finished him off the same way they finished of his dog, which was tearing frantically at its chain. Several men had run up to it with their clubs. Pandemonium broke out in the yard. Doba screamed as she ran to her husband. A little girl that had run out of the house behind her raised a piercing cry. Louder still came shouts of "Thrash the Jews!" and the dog's appalling whines.

The clubs beat Baruch's still body into the mud. A man aimed a vicious kick at the place where his head had been. "Much good it did you, talking to God, eh?" he snarled.

Doba never made it to her husband. They struck her down with their clubs. Nor was her infant spared. Falling out of her broken arms, it lay writhing and screaming on ground while they finished its mother off. The child's screams drowned out the attackers' shouts, but then more boots and more clubs crushed the life out of it. The little girl, falling under a hail of blows, managed to get up and hobble away, squealing pitifully. More blows brought her down. Still she would not die. Now she was crawling on the ground, moaning in agony. For a moment, you could hear only her groans, for the howling of the dog, which they'd beaten to a shapeless pulp, had ceased, and the attackers' throats had grown sore from shouting. Breathless, they stood over her, as she tried to crawl between their legs.

"We need to finish her off... don't let her suffer," said one. A man brought a heavy hobnailed boot down on her neck. There was a crack like a dry twig snapping. The girl stopped moaning and lay still.

Again, there was silence. Again, you could hear the men's labored breathing. One ran inside the house; others followed, working themselves to a new pitch with their shouts. More sounds of shattering glass. Pieces of furniture came flying out the windows. But the excitement was wearing off. Someone ran out with an oil lamp, smashed it against a ledge and was about to light the oil when one of the locals knocked the flaming match from his hand. "You want to burn down the whole of

Kurow?!" he yelled. The wind was blowing up. "Thrash the Yids! Who's next? Let's go get 'em!" cried one of the strangers. But the cry was met with silence. They dispersed without a word. Each went his own way into the night.

***

The next day Abram, Baruch's younger brother, arrived in Kurow. He found eleven-year-old Jacob in the forest, frozen to the bone, together with his younger brothers Joseph and Adam, aged nine and three, whom he had managed to get out of the house. Anticipating trouble, their father had ordered his wife and son to take the whole family into the forest; he had been warned, it seems. But Baruch refused to run away. He told Doba to hide and not come back until it was safe. Doba took the children into the forest, but when she heard the shouts she turned back. She entrusted the children to Jacob and repeated the order to hide. But as she was running back towards the house, six-year-old Golda broke away from Jacob and flew after her.

Abram drove his nephews to the neighboring town and left them with a family he knew. He came back with two helpers. For some time, he walked around the farmyard, as if registering everything in a non-existent inventory. He stared vacantly at the bodies wedged in the mud. He did not pray. With his own hands, he loaded the bodies into the wagon. He had the dog's carcass buried.

He organized Baruch's, Doba's and their two children's funeral in a nearby town. He had their house repaired and redecorated so that no one could recognize it. Later he sold it. The new inhabitants expressed no interest in the fate of the previous owners.

A group of Jews came to the funeral. Even the old *tzaddik* from out by Baranowicze came. After the service, he went up to Abram and took him by the arms, but Abram, a big powerful man, gently removed his hands as though they were the hands of a child.

"Don't say anything, rebbe. I know what happened and what you want to say. I know it's always been like this and always will be. I'm not looking for comfort."

The *tzaddik* shook his head.

"Yes, it's always been like this, but I have a feeling it will get worse." He pointed at the leaden sky. "Bad times are coming. The Lord is turning away from us and we understand less and less."

Two of his students took him by the arms and together they shuffled slowly off. Abram turned away and stared blankly at the forbidding sky.

He'd left Kurow a dozen or so years earlier, when he was only eighteen years old. He got into the trading business with his brother, but quickly overtook him, collecting leather from all over the district and selling it far and wide – for big money, they say. He moved to Pinsk where he reportedly bought a two-storey house, and then a store on the main street. But that wasn't enough. Nothing satisfied him. He began traveling to Kiev then to Warsaw. He also ran commercial ventures in Berlin. He set up stores and exchange houses in more and more cities. He traded in leather then in gold and precious stones. His real money, however, he made in the weapons trade. Some said he did more than trade: he was involved in huge, illegal financial operations and had dealings with gangsters, selling their stolen goods. Others, or maybe it was the same people, said he was a sorcerer. He'd sold his soul to the devil. Though what would the devil want with a Hebrew's damned soul?

Abram Brok adopted his nephews as his own. He never married and he never went back to Kurow. The day he came for the bodies of his brother and family was his last time there.

No one in the village wanted to talk about it. People were not even sure which of the locals had joined the strangers – strangers, incidentally, whom they would still meet on market days in Stryczkow, sometimes at the Orthodox church, or on other occasions. The locals went on trading and drinking with them, but no one wanted to recall those events. In the privacy of their own homes, they said that among those who had helped to kill Brok were people he'd healed and even saved. Leon, whose horse he had saved, was supposedly there; so was the blacksmith's son whose chronic ulcers he had cured; and even Baruch's neighbor Stach whom he had taught to walk again. But who had really been there and seen the clubs falling on Brok and his family?

Some years later, a constable from Stryczkow let slip to a chance drinking companion in the tavern that a few days before the events in Kurow he had received a visit from his boss, the district police commissioner. He was ordered to put the fear of God into Brok. "But why him?" said the constable whose niece Baruch had healed. "He's a good Jew and has nothing to do with the revolution." "The authorities know what they're doing!" snapped the commissioner, flaring up; and, breaking off the discussion, he took his subordinate to task. Later he added: "It's the ones everyone likes that are the most dangerous. People trust them, and they wait for years, hatching their plans, biding their time, until one day they start stirring up the locals against the authorities. Maybe he is a decent man," the commissioner conceded, "but he comes from a poisonous tribe. He's got to be made to see he can't hide from the authorities. Everyone must be made to see that a Jew is a Jew."

The constable even got money for the job. He met with the wiliest of his underworld contacts, whose trade in stolen goods and other shady dealings he overlooked in exchange for information. He told him to see to it that Baruch and those who dealt with him got a good fright. Anatoly nodded. He understood. The constable never dreamed how it might end. Afterwards even Anatoly looked scared. But the affair soon died down. No one would speak of it. Only once, in a sermon, did the local Russian Orthodox priest say something about innocent blood crying out to heaven for vengeance and about the guilty and those standing idly around being called to account; and though he made no specific reference to anyone or anything, everyone knew.

That year spring refused to come. Persistent overcast shut out the light and the snowstorms went on until the end of April. The sun would not come out. A lean and hungry pre-harvest time beckoned. The heavens were closed from sight.

***

It was not until the doors slid open and Adam Brok emerged into the arrivals hall that he realized how much the airport had changed after the construction of the new terminal. His last visit to Poland had been over three years ago. Somewhat disoriented after the night flight, he stumbled along, staring at strange faces, watching people as they fell into each other's arms, hearing their cries of joy at being reunited. Something kept telling him he was here to say goodbye to his dying father and then arrange for the funeral. He tried to shake off this conviction which seemed to come from nowhere, but it was useless; the harder he tried, the more firmly entrenched the conviction became. He had a feeling of coming back. For eight years he had, without realizing it, been drifting away from his country. His visits only confirmed the fact: Poland for him was receding in time and space, becoming an increasingly fainter memory. Now it was embracing him again.

He had woken up in the plane while the other passengers still slept. On raising the window blind, he was dazzled by the sunlight, which glanced off the shapes piling up beneath him. Masses of cloud sculpted themselves into mountain ranges, hidden cities or fantastic buildings, which dissolved as the light hit them then re-formed themselves anew. On his first long-haul flights Adam would spend hours gazing at the clouds, the sun and the sky. But the novelty soon wore off and he stopped noticing them. Now, as he gazed out at the clouds, it took him a few minutes to realize the extent to which the sight absorbed and delighted him. He seemed to be seeing it for the first time. Over the Atlantic the sun was drawing the curtain back on the old world. The blue expanse was widening. Someone was bringing him back. He felt tension within him and he sought to make sense of the shifting shapes outside.

The strange feeling was still there when the plane landed with a jolt in Warsaw. In the chaos of the arrivals hall Adam tried to impose some order upon his impressions. Someone was watching him, but it wasn't any of the strangers in the crowd whose wandering gaze would settle on him momentarily and then move on. He realized he was returning to a past he thought he'd escaped for good. This past lay in wait for him even here in the form of this new terminal.

He recalled his conversation with Taggart. "It's actually perfect, works out very well, you know? We were thinking of sending you out there anyway. We appreciate what you did for us in Russia. Didn't work out of course... deal fell through, but you did all right. We want to get into the Polish television market. Not just there of course, but Poland's interesting and its potential's underestimated. Places like France and Germany, they've stopped developing, no prospects left, but Poland... why, anything could happen there. Europe as a whole you can..." – he finished the sentence with a contemptuous sweep of his hand. "But Europe's peripheries, that's different. Worth taking a look at. Besides, television these days is a lot more than just television. Not many people get that. Television's about ideas. And ideas – mused Taggart as he looked through the glass wall down on the New York cityscape – ideas are the biggest business there is. It's about what's important. Take pollution. Sure it's important to reduce our carbon footprint. But you have to explain it to people, you have to make them *see* it." Taggart was wading into deep waters, but somewhere even deeper inside him there lurked a roguish Puck. Many times Adam would come back to this conversation. "Now if we could get a piece of the new energy markets... that would really be good business. Crises are a great occasion for serious initiatives. They have a television corporation out there called WTV. Well regarded... seems to have cornered the market, but they overinvested and now they're looking desperately for capital. It's a great opportunity. We've done the preliminary research. Everything looks good. Digitalization opens new possibilities. So, what say we sign a tentative contract? We'll cover your expenses, and pay you on a profit percentage basis. Means more risk for you, but more money if you do well. So? Shall we hammer out the details?"

Adam walked slowly through the waiting lobby past strangers whom he might well have known once. His gaze passed over the broadly smiling face of an elderly woman. He turned away, but she was already running toward him with an almost youthful step. Only then did he know for certain it was his mother; and only when he felt her frail arms around him, the touch of her thin body, the kisses on his forehead and cheeks, which he had to stoop to receive, only when he felt these things did the full extent of the past, its images, sounds and smells, come flooding back to him. In his mind's eye, he saw an ecstatic little boy walking through a sunlit field hand in hand with his beautiful mother. He stared at the old woman before him and he felt a tightness in his throat. A nameless smell spoke to him of home.

The package-strewn trunk of the old rusted-out Opel Corsa would not accept his bulky suitcase. In the end, they managed to squeeze it into the back seat. The car interior looked no better than the exterior. During his last visit, he had offered to wire her money for a new one. She took offense. "As a gift," he said, trying to convince her. "In that case you can present it to me wrapped in a red ribbon; otherwise I won't take it. And if you try to send it to me, I'll send it back at your expense." She said this in a characteristic tone of voice, which could mean she was either joking or in deadly earnest; you never knew. The Corsa had looked a lot better then. Sending a car over was too complicated. He stopped thinking about it.

"So, tell me everything," she said, turning the key in the ignition and lighting a cigarette. The reek of nicotine permeating the car assailed his nostrils. It overpowered even the gasoline smell and the scent of his mother's expensive perfume,

"Oh, I forgot you don't smoke," she said, glancing at him and rolling down the window with difficulty. "A few puffs and I'll throw it away" There was a note of childish regret in her voice.

"It's all right, don't worry about it," he said. His head was spinning from the smoke, but he decided to suffer heroically. His mother inhaled with relief.

"Well, so how are things?"

"With me... well, you know... Everything's changing. It's like an earthquake. I don't know if I'll stay at the Exchange. I've had a few offers – one of them in Poland. For the moment, I'm taking a long holiday. I guess Father couldn't make it, eh?" Even as he said it, he realized he was raising the matter too soon. But it was too late. His mother's face contorted as it always did – as it had for twenty-three years. Those years he reconstructed and reckoned up much later, but he perfectly remembered the first time that grimace passed over her face. She had practically stopped talking to Adam. All he got from her were half utterances tossed out to be rid of him. Those long periods of apathy would alternate with effusive demonstrations of tenderness, embarrassing for a ten-year-old. It was from that time on that the very sound of his father's name, the very mention of him even in the most casual of conversations, would invariably bring the same grimace to his mother's face. Adam knew a pause would now ensue, a pause his mother needed before she could go on.

"Your father…? I don't really know. I think he's in hospital." After a moment she added, "I hope it's nothing serious. He was never a hypochondriac, I'll give him that." This last she said in a tone edged with unpleasant irony.

She might have got over it by now, Adam thought. The same niggling thought came to him every time he met his mother – and this for years. If she couldn't forget, she could at least come to terms with it. Face what had happened. No one was asking her to forgive, but she should stop this constant dwelling on it. As it was, she would with bat-like sensitivity pick up anything that evoked even the remotest association with her ex-husband and then obsess over it as though it were a thorn buried in her flesh. Her face would harden into a mask of bitterness and pain. This time she lit a cigarette.

"Your father could always fall on his feet. Let's hope he still can."

She's being unfair, Adam thought. She may have cause for bitterness, but here she's being unfair. Though maybe it's just what I like to think, he wondered, as his mother nervously changed lanes, provoking a furious horn-burst from a car coming rapidly up from behind. Maybe I just want to defend my image of my father, since there's so little left to defend?

"What about you? Are you still working for the same weekly? *Renaissance*, was it?" he asked, though he knew the answer.

"If you're asking does it still exist, yes, it does. I'm surprised myself. The weekly's still there. I'm still there. Of course, it's not like your father's *Republic*, which has become the main organ of our intellectual elite, the light of the salon. While we… we paid a monstrous price for that police informer, Stawicki, not to mention the ostracism… But I can see you don't understand. Our petty quarrels don't interest you. From the American perspective…" "She tried to impart a warmer tone to her irony. "I don't want to bore you. I'd much rather talk about things that really interest you. Much has changed in Poland since you were last here. Then again, who knows? Has anything really changed? A whole lot of farting and breaking wind and now it's back to the way it was. Pardon the vulgarism." She tried to control herself with her son who disliked her lapses into coarse language. "Back to the same old swamp. And I – we – we've been relegated to the sidelines. Increasingly more so. We're being pushed further and further out. Time's pushing us out too. Soon it'll have us out for keeps – out to the cemetery." She laughed drily and threw a defiant glance at her son.

When the idea dawned on him, it seemed as obvious as it had been sudden in coming. Adam felt ashamed he hadn't thought of it before. He should have done it years ago. He could afford it easily. In Florence on a recent weeklong holiday in Italy he had recalled his mother's fascination with the Uffizi Gallery. He was looking at Cellini's famous cast in the arcade opposite the museum: the beautiful youth sadly contemplating his trophy, the severed head of a woman-monster, which he holds in his outstretched hand. His mother had heard about the sculpture from her father, Adam's grandfather. He was on his deathbed, talking about his unfulfilled dreams and unrealized travels. He couldn't have been much older then than Adam was now. Gazing at the sculpture, Adam wanted to tell Nancy about it, but even though she listened politely, she didn't seem interested.

"Mom, here's an offer you can't refuse. As soon as I've checked up on Father… I'll talk with him and… you know, generally… see what's up… Right after that I'm taking you to Tuscany. To Florence. You've always dreamed of spending time in the Uffizi, if only to view Cellini's *Perseus*. There are other interesting places in Tuscany… Siena. I was there just recently. Passing through. I'll take you on a week's holiday. One week. I won't take no for an answer."

His mother turned from the steering wheel a moment. A young girl's smile spread across her lined face, a memory of bygone times.

"That's terribly sweet of you. I'm really very touched you should think of me. But you know I won't come. I've contemplated Florence enough. I could lead guided tours around the Uffizi… write a whole essay on Cellini's *Perseus*."

"You know it's not the same as the real thing."

"Of course, it's not the same. And that's why I know it's too late. There's a time for everything. Hard to explain… it's so obvious. If you haven't done it when the time's right, it'll never get done. People that go chasing after unfulfilled dreams make me laugh. I'm past the age of gathering impressions. I won't go to Florence. I'll stay here."

PART I

ZUZANNA

CHAPTER 1

She had never really got back to normal after her husband left her twenty-three years earlier. Perhaps because of the tragic death of her brother Tadeusz – "my little son" as she called him – which followed on its heels just four months later. He died in January. He had gone up to Gdansk, to take care of some Solidarity business. Irena called her a few days later, saying she hadn't heard from him. Susanna tried to calm her, but she felt icy fingers clawing at her mind, heart and soul. It was so unlike Tadek. She tried to put things in perspective. She realized her husband's leaving was taking a toll on her psychologically. All the more reason to keep her feelings in check. She had to look after Adam, go to work and carry on with her underground activity; and now she had to look after her brother's fiancée as well - Irena looked ready to fall apart at any moment. Susanna tried to be strong but could not control the trembling that ran through her body. She fought off panic attacks. "Not him, not Tadek, please not him," she kept repeating silently to herself. She prayed, but even as she prayed, memories of those mysterious murders and "unknown assailants" continued to oppress her. She kept seeing the bloody face of Father Popieluszko, the priest they'd killed.

The last time she had seen Tadek was on New Year's Eve, less than two weeks ago. She had picked Adam up at about ten from a children's party at the house of one of his schoolmates. Benedict had asked to have him for a few days, and also before that, for Christmas, but in both cases Suzanna had refused. Adam was in a fit of the sulks. For almost twenty minutes she plodded through the melting snow with him, trying in vain to cheer him with jokes. The jokes fell flat, and he went on pouting. When they got home, she felt no trace of the several glasses of wine she had drunk earlier. Luckily Adam was tired and fell asleep almost at once. Suzanna sat by him a moment longer, gently stroking his hair. When she was sure he was asleep, she went into the other room and sat down in front of the lifeless TV screen, vowing she would not switch it on. She ate some bread and cheese and washed it down with some leftover wine. As the alcohol slowly coursed through her body, she examined the tapes in the cassette player, rejecting Kaczmarski, then, one by one, Vysotsky, Kelus and Cohen. She paused for a moment longer at Armstrong before rejecting him too. She fiddled with the radio knob but found nothing to hold her attention. The wine was finished. She fought off memories of past New Year's Eves spent with Benedict. Times they'd spent together. Old times. Once again, she allowed her mind to dwell on what she detested about him. His pettiness, his cowardice. But as usual she realized after a moment; she was only poisoning herself.

She sat down on the window ledge. Outside, Warsaw loomed dark and indistinct. Here and there you could see the feeble flashes of fireworks. If it wasn't for Adam… something inside her said. But the thought was unclear. Her life was over, she was living its last embers, and if it not for Adam… She seized a bottle of vodka from the fridge and poured herself a glass. Then another, and another. The tightness inside her eased. But the ringing of the telephone brought it back.

"Happy New Year! We'll be by in fifteen minutes," shouted Tadek. She didn't even have time to reply.

She turned on the TV. People in far-off cities were partying in the streets. Next moment the screen was alive with the faces of Poland's communist leaders. She switched the thing off. Just then the door buzzer sounded. Tadek and Irena and a group of their friends burst into the room and kitchen. She just had time to close the door to Adam's bedroom.

"It was a good thing," said Tadek, hugging her and clinking his glass against hers. "He didn't deserve you. *He doesn't deserve you!*" he sang out. "But you knew that. Two worlds, one house… one bed. Well, it can happen, I guess, but to live together? You had yourselves a kind of Poland in miniature. The Solidarity activist and her disgusted husband, the regime's propagandist!" Tadek's laughter was infectious and Suzanna couldn't help joining in. Her brother grew serious.

"But he thwarted you at every turn, limited you, infected you with his… his…" – he groped for the right word – "…his skepticism, his disbelief, that suspiciousness of his. He wanted to destroy everything you believed in… what *we* believe in. His childhood trauma was supposed to excuse it all. The child in the cupboard! But what about us? I don't remember our father. They were pretty well done with him before I was born. After that he was just dying. I don't know if I really remember anything about him or if I've just built up a picture of him from the stories you told me. Can one salvage a two-year-old's memory? I think I remember the funeral and our mother crying. But that doesn't seem likely either. And Mother? What was her life like? It's thanks to you I grew up to be someone halfway decent. It was you that raised me when she no longer could. And he? After his 'trauma' only good things came his way. From age seven on he had a cushy life. So, they kicked him out of the university. Big deal! Then they tasked him with a job on the *Republic* so he could sing the praises of the Party, history's bearer of light and wisdom. He saved us from ourselves. Anyway, what kind of husband was he? You know he ran after every skirt he laid eyes on. And finally got caught by a canny young wannabee journalist. What a pile of schlock! To hell with him, that's what I say!... You know," he said, lowering his voice abruptly and whispering into her ear, "it's important, this trip to Gdansk. Very important. But now" – he was shouting again – "let's party!"

Suzanna yelled and sang with them. She almost felt good. They danced. Someone put on the soundtrack to "Cabaret". "*Life is a Cabaret, old chum, Come to the Cabaret!*" Suzanna screamed at the top of her voice.

"My wonderful sister," Tadeusz sang, hugging her. "Free at last. Young, beautiful, whole life before you. You can only be happy." Suzanna nodded.

When they left, she dragged herself to bed and sank into a leaden sleep.

***

Days passed and still no word from Tadek. Suzanna lived in semiconscious state. She went to work, did all she was supposed to do, and desperately sought some trace of her brother. Everything seemed to be happening somewhere outside of her. After consulting with friends from the underground she decided to call the police. They listened, took the photos she gave them and promised to put out a search for Tadeusz. The photos appeared in the press, along with a brief note about the missing man.

Benedict was less on Suzanna's mind too during those days, though she called him. She rang the editor's office.

"Ye-e-e-s?" said a hesitant voice.

"Tadek's missing. He's been missing for ten days. No one's heard from him. I'm afraid they may have arrested him. Your people." She didn't say the thing she most feared.

"My people?"

"Oh, give it a rest. You have contacts, influence. Try to find out something. That's all I'm asking."

"All right, I'll try. Though, despite what you think, my possibilities...."

"Just do what you can. I'll wait to hear from you." She put down the phone.

Weeks went by. Appeals for information about Tadeusz Sokol also appeared in the underground press. After a few days, she received a call from Jerome with whom she worked on the *Underground Weekly*. One of his colleagues from Gdansk had seen Tadeusz just as he was about to return to Warsaw. That was almost three weeks earlier.

They dragged Tadeusz's body out of the Motlawa River in early March. Her boss, *Portico's* editor-in-chief, called her to his office. For a moment, on seeing the two uniformed policemen standing next to him, she imagined they had come for her. Got to get through this somehow, she thought. Just as well Benedict can look after Adam. But then they asked her, "Are you the sister of Tadeusz Sokol?" and she felt the breath squeezed out of her body. They showed her a ghastly photo of Tadeusz's bloody face, beaten to a pulp.

Jerome drove her to Gdansk in his little Fiat. It could all be just a mistake. The thought thudded through her body as if it had been someone else's. Jerome pulled up on the side of the street opposite the red brick building of the Forensic Medicine Institute. He promised to wait for her in the café at the corner, but she, dimly conscious that he was speaking to her, did not catch the meaning of his words. She gave the man in the lobby her name. A man in a white coat and a police officer came down to meet her. They descended a flight of stairs. Paint of a nondescript color was peeling off the walls. At a signal from the white-coated man, the worker downstairs pulled out one of the huge drawers that lined the wall.

Tadeusz's body, oddly short, was covered by a sheet up to the armpits. It was as if someone had taken a piece of rubber and carelessly cut it into her brother's shape to brutalize it. The skin was greenish, the flesh seemed soft like custard. A broken bone jutted upwards like a spike through a deep gash in his arm. There were lesions all over his chest. Crushed and broken bones stuck out from what had been his face. Suzanna stepped forward, reeled, but managed to pull off the sheet. The legs were hacked off below the knees.

"What are you doing?!" shouted the man in the white coat, pulling the sheet back over the body.

"What... what did you do to him?"

"It wasn't us. Must have been the boats, the boats plying the Motlawa... the propeller blades... Death was by drowning. That much we've established."

He might have said more, but his voice trailed off. Suzanna made her way shakily to the door.

"Where... where's the..." Following the direction given her by the worker, she bolted out of the morgue, pushed through the door of the filthy restroom, knelt down and vomited into the toilet bowl. She wretched and wept in deep heaving sobs, choking on the bile. Her whole body wanted to dissolve in the dirt of that place, to be swallowed up in the spasms. It lasted a while. At last she got up, dragged herself to the dirty washbasin, splashed cold water over her face and rinsed out her mouth. When she returned to the morgue, she was almost calm. They took her back upstairs. She had to sign something, explain something.

Jerome was waiting. He asked no questions. "It was he," she said after a while, putting out the butt of another cigarette. "They murdered him."

The official version was this: Tadeusz Sokol fell into the Motlawa river in a state of intoxication on January 9, 1986. Death was by drowning. The severely lacerated body was sighted and fished out on March 6th. Injuries were sustained through contact with the propellers of passing boats.

The drive back to Warsaw took almost eight hours. They barely talked. The air in the car was thick with cigarette smoke; now and then Jerome had to open the window. They stopped a few times for gas and watery coffee and exchanged meaningless remarks. It was only during their last stop at a dingy old shack of a building called "The Warsaw Inn" past Plonsk that Jerome, finishing off a glass of some insipid drink, asked, "What are you going to do?"

They sat looking at the night and the lights of the cars swishing along the highway.

"I'm going to find everything out. I know who did it, but I need to find out the exact details. I'll do what I can."

"We'll help you," said Jerome.

CHAPTER 2

Tadeusz was her little son. That was what she called him when he was just a few months old and she had to look after him. She was ten years old, had a responsibility, and so she felt quite grown-up. Her father's health was worsening, and her mother had to spend more and more time caring for him while still run the house.

Zuzanna was pleased with her newly acquired duties. Looking after her brother was absorbing work and made her feel proud. She changed his diapers, bathed him, taught him to walk, tried to teach him his first words. She told him stories, which he seemed to understand, though all he did was babble. Or, he would fall asleep listening to them, in which case she was sure he took the stories into his dreams, populating them and taking part in them, for in dreams you could be anyone.

Even when she had to beg off play dates with her friends, when she arranged her lips in a sort of pout, the way adults do, and explained to them that she was looking after her little brother, the natural regret she felt at missing out on these moments of care-free play was more than made up for by the sense of superiority she felt over their childish games. They were merely playing at grown-up life, while here was she living it in reality. She suspected they even made fun of her, unwilling to admit they envied her for the serious tasks she was carrying out at her age. But she didn't care what they thought.

In looking after her brother, she felt she was doing something very important. She was fighting for her family; and so, she forgot the sadness that was increasingly filling the house, forcing out the joy of the previous year. Well did Zuzanna remember that time. How could she forget the moment heralding the happiest period of her life as a child? – that moment, a year and a half earlier, when her mother told her in a voice full of mystery, yet brimming with hope, that her father might soon be coming home.

Winter was almost over but wouldn't quite go away, though a warm breeze could be felt cutting through the chill of the streets and icy walls, rousing the trees and shrubs from their winter sleep. The few times Zuzanna had seen her father, it was through prison bars. A big man, a stranger, who awoke a strange mixture of emotions in her. He smiled, but his smile was so sad she felt she would rather he didn't smile at all. Her mother told her that Daddy had landed in prison by mistake and would explain it all to her when she got older. For the moment, she must be patient and not speak about it to anyone. That was very important. If she didn't say anything, they might let him out. If she did…

Zuzanna knew most children had two parents and it was better that way. Her home was a sad place. Not like other children's homes. Sometimes at night her mother would hide so Zuzanna couldn't see her crying. Zuzanna knew, but she didn't let on, not wanting to embarrass her mother. But the sadness infected her too. It was even sadder after Aunt Gienia got married and moved out, though of course there was more room to be had now. While her aunt still lived with them, Zuzanna had had to be very careful playing, and her mother kept having to move the sewing machine – a good, solid pre-war one – on which she sewed things in order to supplement her nurse's salary. The machine took up a lot of space in their one room. Zuzanna dreamed of having a place like other children's. She wished her father would get out of prison and come home, and her mother would stop crying. So, she tried not to talk about him to anyone. But when the Miedziecki boy at the next desk over made fun of her because her father was in prison, it was more than she could stand. She went for him, crying as she pummeled him with her little fists. "My father will get out. It was a mistake. And then… then you'll see!" The teacher pulled her off the boy, who was also in tears, and yelled at her. Zuzanna feared the consequences. She'd let it slip – spoken of her father. But a few days later her mother announced they were releasing him. On Sunday, she asked Zuzanna to pray for his return and this time Zuzanna tried to concentrate as hard as she could in church. She knew what her sins were, but she promised God she would mend her ways. She believed she would. Her mother was kneeling next to her, hiding her face in her hands.

The following Sunday her mother took her to the prison. It was the first time she was meeting her father in a room without barred windows. He lifted her up and threw her so high in the air that for a moment she felt frightened; but her mother's look of unrestrained joy calmed her fears. She looked at this strange man, her father. An odd man, tall and thin. His face was prickly when he hugged her. But Zuzanna didn't mind; she had never seen her mother so happy – her parents so happy.

A month passed, then another. The warm breezes had finally driven winter away. Trees in the streets and parks were bursting into leaf. Zuzanna was playing in the kitchen when she heard her mother cry out. For a moment she was frightened, but when she ran out into the hall, there were her parents, embracing. For a long time, they stood in the open doorway, clasped together, clinging to each other. Next day Aunt Gienia took her home with her. Auntie's belly was already showing, and Zuzanna knew she was going to have a baby. Uncle Stach went around the house whistling proudly.

Her parents came for her two days later by which time she was beginning to worry a little. Never did her mother look so lovely! Zuzanna felt a thrill of joy, but also a pang of regret that she would never look like her. Her father, too, was looking his best. He kept gazing at her and her mother with shining eyes. Mother fell into Aunt Gienia's embrace and for some reason they both burst into tears. That evening they sat by the open window. Huge industrial cranes could be seen standing idle over the building sites. Uncle Stach produced a bottle of vodka. Aunt Gienia brought out bread, butter and sausage, as well as pickles – cucumbers, mushrooms and plums, each item on its own little plate. Zuzanna liked the plums best, but she knew she shouldn't eat too many. Aunt Gienia wasn't drinking; bad for the baby, she said, glancing at Zuzanna. Mother drank a few glasses. The men finished off the rest; they talked little; from time to time, they slapped each other on the shoulder. Zuzanna accompanied her parents home. The spring evening was warm. They pushed their way into a crowded streetcar, laughing. Disheveled but laughing still, they extracted themselves from the crush and walked with a dancing step to the house. They moved Zuzanna's bed into the kitchen. This upset her a little, but she knew better than to make a fuss over it.

For her, those days were one long, unending holiday, even though she still had to go to school. It turned out her father also wanted to go to school – in his case, university. Before being imprisoned, he had studied architecture. He wanted to build houses. "We have to rebuild the world," he said to Zuzanna's mother, who would eye him with a radiant expression. He passed the qualifying examinations. When he came home with three tea roses, Zuzanna knew something good had happened. "Come and congratulate the future architect!" he said, presenting the flowers to her mother and hugging her. "I made it!" He seized Zuzanna and danced around the room with her. "Daddy's going to build houses! And not horrible ones like those over there," he added, nodding in a vague direction. Zuzanna knew he meant the Palace of Culture.[1] She didn't understand her parents' dislike of that building; it was huge, and she liked it very much. It had been the gift of "our Russian comrades" and was named after the now late, though immortal, leader of the progressive world, Joseph Stalin. A few weeks earlier Zuzanna had been on the top floor with her class on a school trip. Warsaw sprawled at her feet. She felt proud to be living in the capital. She didn't have to wait years for a special trip to visit Poland's tallest building as did people from other, less important cities – not to mention villages. She looked down upon the city, which the Germans had sought to wipe off the face of the earth. Yet here it was, rebuilding itself, clearing away the ruins, scaffolding going up everywhere – promising a radiant future.

"I'm going to build houses," her father kept saying, "and people will be grateful to me. I'll show them you can live in beautiful surroundings."

On Sunday Zuzanna walked proudly to church, hand in hand with her parents. She thanked God and begged him that it might be like this always.

Not long afterwards something happened that disturbed her. Uncle Stach dropped by in the evening. Her mother was doing her shift at the hospital. The men told Zuzanna to play in the kitchen and closed the door to the room. She heard raised voices, one voice mostly – Uncle Stach's. Her father's remarks were few and far between. They talked a long while. She could make out individual words and phrases: "Poznan... This time they can't just... it's now or... blood..." Her father was shushing her uncle and calming him down. The hot June night filled the kitchen, bringing restless sleep and anxious dreams.

In the summer, they would go to the country, to Granny Ola's in the Niemiry region. The buses were hot and airless. They would pull up at the stop with a screech of brakes and the grinding of gears and raise clouds of hot dust. The crowd rushed at them, shoving and shouting; children cried. They didn't always manage to get on. The driver would yell at the crowd to stand away from the doors, which he couldn't shut because the people outside were holding on grimly, pushing and shoving, bent

1. The Palace of Culture and Science – was a "gift" from the Russian people to Poland provided by Stalin and designed by Russian architects. It was viewed as a "Soviet" building.

on forcing their way into the mass of human flesh inside. In the end, they had to back away. Furious and exhausted, they stared at the departing bus, grumbling, cursing. Her father was left gasping for breath. Her mother tried to smile. Zuzanna wanted to cry. It would be hours before the next bus. A couple of times her father made a deal with a truck driver. Her parents rode in front, squeezed together next to the driver with Zuzanna on their lap. Still it was more comfortable than the bus where one had to stand jammed in a crowd in the suffocating, airless heat. Yet sometimes Zuzanna was able to ignore the discomfort and enjoy the trip. Once Warsaw's ruins and the suburban chaos of houses and building sites were out of sight, once the horizon receded into a sweep of green and yellow fields or was swallowed up by the forest, she forgot everything. Pines thrust up their heavy crowns; the sun flashed among the trunks, making the birches glow. But the best moment was when they reached their destination and she could jump out of the stifling bus into the clean fresh air. It was like plunging into cool water and feeling the dirt of the city being washed off.

To get to the village they still had to go through a piece of the forest. Though exhausted, Zuzanna enjoyed this part of the journey best, especially when her father carried her on his shoulders. She would wait for that moment. On being raised up, she shut her eyes and imagined herself floating in the air among the trees. She wished it would never end. But soon, always too soon, her father, panting heavily and yielding to her mother's anxious looks, would put her down.

By the time they got to Granny's it was dinnertime, and they were hungry. They each got a bowl of borscht with a generous dollop of sour cream. In the center of the table was a dish of steaming potatoes, buttered and dilled, which they would take and plop into their soup. After that they would go about their business. Her mother helped Granny and her aunts. Father worked with the men; but he would soon tire and go off to sit in the shade where he'd light a cigarette and have a coughing fit. The men would go on working. Zuzanna felt bad seeing him in such embarrassing moments. She knew he wouldn't wish to be seen just then. Father should be stronger. But Zuzanna understood this was only temporary. He *was* strong but needed time to get back to normal. Just as he had to rest after prison, so he had to rest in the shade after overexerting himself in the fields. The locals understood this. Sometimes they came up for a chat and joined him in a smoke. But Zuzanna didn't have time to brood over such things. Her cousins wanted her to come out and have fun. In the evening, worn out with play, they would run home for a slice of bread and sour cream sprinkled with sugar. The air turned blue and the sun hid behind the forest, leaving a red glow over the trees. The grown-ups sat and talked long into the night. You could feel a tension that never went away, even though the day's heat reposed in the darkness.

But it was beautiful – beautiful as never before, and as it never would be again. Her mother put on weight. One day, as she was walking arm in arm with Suzanna's father across the now harvested fields, Zuzanna ran up to them and touched her mother's round belly. "You're going to have a baby," she said with a sudden feeling of certainty.

"And you're going to have a little sister or brother," said her mother looking radiant, stooping down and putting her other arm around her. Zuzanna thought for a moment. "A brother would be nice," she said.

It was early September. The village was quiet. The fields and forests fell silent. Only the birds gathered in noisy conclaves, preparing for their flight south. Smoke smelling of juniper crept low over the earth. But the grown-up's night talk lost none of its intensity. It was Zuzanna's last visit to the village that year. Time to go back to school.

Uncle Stach found her father a job in the Zeran district. The tension of the night talks spilled out into the streets. Suzanna felt it even in school. The children played at being their parents. The Soviets would have to leave Poland, said one boy. The Jews wouldn't be bossing them about any more, said another. Gomulka would save Poland, said Karol. Zdzich took issue with him, insisting it would be the Primate –Wyszynski. The teachers were nervous and irritable. Even little cousin Ala's christening party ended with a scene – a heated dispute among the men. Zuzanna's father, who must have had too much to drink, was shouting angrily at everyone. They shouldn't be so sure, he insisted. Uncle Stach tried to calm him. Zuzanna and her mother took him home. "They're just like kids," he went on shouting. "They believe him. Have they forgotten he's a Communist?" Zuzanna's mother shushed him.

It was autumn. One evening her father failed to return from work. Mother fretted. Zuzanna came home from school to find Aunt Gienia there with little Ala in her arms. Uncle Stach hadn't returned either. Aunt Gienia tried to calm her mother's fears. Mother's face was expressionless, rigid and twisted with pain. "One uprising's plenty for me," she kept saying. Aunt Gienia didn't seem very calm either. But the men returned later that night. They seemed surer of themselves than usual and looked at their women with an air of tender superiority. After her uncle and aunt went home with Ala, Zuzanna had trouble falling asleep. An unusually loud creaking of her parents' bed kept her awake.

A few days later they took her to Parade Square in front of the Palace of Culture. It was like the day just over a year before when Zuzanna had gone to the May Day rally with her school. Unlike her mother, she liked that holiday. She loved the sight of the waving flags and great red banners. She enjoyed being part of a crowd; it seemed to make everyone happier. Now, just as then, people were converging on the parade ground, flowing in from the streets all round, strangers becoming neighbors – perhaps because a common purpose united them. Seizing her parents by the hand, Zuzanna knew they and all the others who had come together to form the crowd felt as she did. They were part of something greater than she could imagine. At the same time, she knew this was different from a May Day rally, and much more important. People seemed different, they moved and breathed and looked each other in the eye differently. She knew she was participating in an extraordinary event.

The streams of people became torrents, then a vast sea, which poured out onto the parade ground in front of the Palace. They waited. Excitement ran through the crowd; then came a burst of cheering. Zuzanna, who sat perched on her father's shoulders, soon realized the cheering had been prompted by the appearance on the dais of a funny looking bald-headed little man. When he spoke, he sounded as funny as he looked. But the crowd was delighted; they cheered, chanted, and applauded everything he said. Zuzanna gazed with disbelief at her parents; but they too seemed to be in a kind of trance. The crowd surged around her.

There was something odd about it all. The people were thrilled, delighted, full of enthusiasm. But all Zuzanna saw was a funny looking little man who seemed altogether disinterested in what was going on around him. At times, she felt they had made a switch: that someone from behind the scenes had substituted a strange puppet for the real hero of the hour, and that the dais was the stage of a puppet show – only the huge sea of people didn't realize this and was cheering someone else, someone who wasn't there, someone who didn't exist. Zuzanna wanted to tell her parents this, but they were waving their arms in the air, wild with joy like everyone else around them. She wanted to explain it to them, but it was impossible; she couldn't penetrate their enthusiasm. So, she began to delight in their happiness, delight in their joy, everybody's joy, here on Parade Square, in Warsaw, in Poland, everywhere. The late October air smelled of spring. She would remember it so later, returning many times to those events, though no longer sure what her childish experience had really been like.

The crowd wouldn't leave the square even though the funny little man and his entourage had left the dais. The people wanted to stay together, share in their triumph, warm themselves by it. But eventually they dispersed into the night, the air warmed by their fervor.

That evening would remain etched in Zuzanna's memory. But twelve years later, when she was running from the militia's riot sticks in the university courtyard avoiding the blows, and several days later, when she saw the same funny looking little man on television speaking in the Congress Hall of the Palace of Culture, and he was shouting, yelling out names and making threats in a sort of feverish trance, then images of that October happiness came back to mock her.

But this October day, as she walked home with her parents, she was happy. They were all happy. Her mother was well into her pregnancy. She was leaning on her father, who had one arm about her protectively and the other hand in Suzanna's. She could see his smile by the light of the moon that peeped out of the clouds.

Anxiety soon marred their October happiness. Several days later her father and a friend lugged home a big wooden green-eyed radio. Her mother helped them to connect it, and late at night they found the station they had been looking for. Her father glanced nervously around him. Amid the hissing and crackling of the radio, its green eye lighting up in sympathy with the noise, they could catch the words: "Casualties... in the hundreds. Soviet tanks fired on…" She understood. The army of our Soviet comrades was destroying the capital city of Hungary, which was fighting for her independence. Her parents sat with vacant expressions on their faces. "It's like the uprising," said her mother. Zuzanna knew she meant the Warsaw Uprising, which her mother had narrowly survived.

But everything was still quite lovely. She waited for her little brother with the same excitement as her parents awaited their second child. Her father was gone all day, working and attending university. He would return in the evening, eat very little then sit down with a cigarette and a cup of tea and gaze out at the darkness enveloping the city. One day, her mother being not yet back from her shift at the hospital, Zuzanna noticed her father asleep with his head on the table, the smoke from a smoldering cigarette curling upward from the ashtray before him. She put out the cigarette, which had been burning down to a pile of ash and woke him. For a moment he gazed wildly, uncomprehendingly about him. Something strange registered itself on his face. Only much later would Zuzanna, recalling that moment, know what it expressed: fear. It lasted only for the moment it took him to recognize her, then it was gone. His face lit up with a smile and he clasped her to himself while his other hand scrabbled for a cigarette in the pack on the table.

"I'm so happy," he murmured in her ear. "So happy to have you, you and your mother, and another child on the way... A little brother for you," he corrected himself under her reproving gaze. "Not many are so lucky. Yet there was a time when I thought..." – here he turned away from her to the window and took a drag on his cigarette, "... I'd never see you again." A violent fit of coughing seized him. His coughing fits were becoming more and more frequent. "But now I know the bad things are over. I have you." He put the cigarette down to hug her again. "And your mother – Terenia... You love her, but you don't know what a great person she is. You can only sense that she might be so. I met her during the war. Those were terrible times. But you knew what people were made of then, you could appreciate someone... like your mother... We were separated, but we found each other again after the war. Your mother was caught in the uprising. I was luckier. I'd had to escape Warsaw. If I'd stayed, I'd never have survived. She did, though the experience haunts her even today. But that's all behind us now. I'll have my degree in two years. Maybe your mother will too... She always dreamed of being a doctor. And I'll build. Warsaw was a beautiful city before the war. Hard to imagine now. But we have so much to look forward to, everything still ahead of us."

That Christmas was the best ever. Her father brought home a huge tree that reached up to the sky – the ceiling, that is. Zuzanna trimmed it with decorations she had made with her parents, paper chains and moons, a few glass balls and candles, as well as candies in bright wrappers. She knew they'd let her eat those candies on the last day of Christmas. At the very top of the tree they stuck a star made out of cardboard and covered in shiny silver foil. Under the tree Zuzanna found a doll. Never had she had one like this. It had hair, and when you lay her down to sleep, she closed her silky eyes and said the word "Mamma!" Father fetched a pack of Bengal lights, and when they switched off the light a fountain of sparks conjured up magical worlds in the darkness. Her mother sang out a carol and Suzanna joined in. In the end, her father joined in too, accompanying them in an uncertain voice.

In early March, they came home from hospital with baby Tadeusz. Mother let his sister hold him. Zuzanna was amazed. Though it understood nothing, this tiny little creature recognized her. She was sure of it. Its eyes rounded slightly, the mouth gave out a soft croak, and the little body moved as if it wanted to cling to her. This was her little brother. Her "little son".

***

Her father was ill. At first Zuzanna thought it was because he wasn't getting enough sleep. The noise and commotion around Tadzio at night was keeping him awake. This explained why he was still in bed when she was already off to school. But she soon realized this was happening too often. She recalled earlier signs of his failing health. The time he'd fallen asleep with his cigarette smoldering in the ashtray.

Those looks of her mother's. They'd meant nothing to her at the time, but in hindsight they expressed more than ordinary concern; and then the gaspings for air and the coughing fits and the long periods her father spent locked in the bathroom.

He was pale and getting thinner. At night, she could hear her parents arguing. One day her father came home early in a sullen mood. "Satisfied now?" he said to her mother, as if she were to blame. "They've given me medical leave… Now I'll have to start everything over from scratch… If ever I do get back to my studies. If..." His voice trailed off, and he gave an angry snort. Suzanna had never seen him like this before.

"But you knew you weren't able to keep up with your studies..." Her mother looked at him sadly. Her father made no reply.

Spring was breaking when her mother came to her at the school carrying Tadzio. "Your father's in hospital," she told her. "I have to spend more time with him, so you'll have to look after your brother for a few days. I've arranged it all with your teacher." She brushed off Zuzanna's questions with half utterances.

Her father spent over a month in the hospital. He smiled at her, tried to comfort her with stock phrases, but Zuzanna knew things weren't all right. She recalled her visits to the prison. His smile was just as it had been there. He gazed out of the hospital window as though it were barred.

When they released him, summer had arrived. Still he wasn't well. He stopped going to work. He was weak. He tried to look after his son but found it difficult. He had dizzy spells, and sometimes fell over for no reason. More and more often he stayed in bed. He wanted to read but found it hard to concentrate. He was in pain. Zuzanna could tell by the way he clenched his jaw and shut his eyes. Sometimes he bit his hand, no doubt so as not to cry out. Now and then she would hear him moan.

She spent the holidays in the country with Tadzio, Aunt Gienia and cousin Ala. When she returned at the end of the month, her father was getting up only for meals and to use the bathroom. They moved the radio to his bedside table. It was on almost all the time, though sometimes he turned it down so you could barely hear it. Occasionally he would talk to it or, more often, just comment on what was being said. Sometimes Uncle Stach came to visit. At first her father insisted on getting up and sitting with him at the table, but the effort exhausted him, and he soon resigned himself to his bed. Uncle Stach would sit beside him. They spent more time in silence than in talk. Sometimes they smoked a cigarette together, though after a while Uncle Stach avoided this. Zuzanna's mother must have said something to him.

Suzanna's father now left the house only for the occasional test at the hospital. Her mother always went with him. She had switched to working the night shift so she could be with him during the day. But it turned out it was nights that were hardest for him. So, she switched to days. She would run home at lunchtime and bring him food from the hospital canteen, but it was hard to get him to eat anything.

"Will Daddy… will Daddy get better?" Zuzanna finally got up the nerve to ask one evening when her father fell into feverish dream-like state resembling delirium. His sleep was increasingly fitful and shallow, full of cries and moans.

"Of course, dear, of course he will," her mother said robotically.

"But I want to know. I have a right to know, I'm his daughter… I love him and… you should tell me." Zuzanna would not back down. She spoke emphatically, and though she could not express what she felt, she plowed on: "I know it's not good. That's why… I want to know!"

Her mother looked at her as if for the first time. Something in her expression changed.

"You want to know. Of course, you do… Will your father get better? I don't know. He is very ill. He was ill when he came out of prison. The doctors can't understand how he managed to stay so well this past year. His internal organs were damaged. . . there… in prison… Liver, kidneys, lungs. Brain too… And yet if... if he's been able to keep so well all this year… then perhaps…" She turned away; and, covering her head with her arm, she sobbed in silence. Suzanna knew she was sobbing by the heaving motion of her shoulders. She went up to hug her – to quell the convulsions. She felt as though she were her sister. I should take better care of her, she thought. Then it was that she understood: her father was dying.

His dying dragged on for another year and a half. For the first time Zuzanna found herself wishing school would last longer, so she could get home later. Her father was slowly losing touch with the world. He moaned and cried out. Sometimes, overcome by nausea, he was unable to get up soon enough and threw up in bed. It all had to be cleaned up. Sometimes he was incontinent. Her mother brought home a bedpan and a bottle from the hospital. The smell of feces permeated the apartment. Suzanna could stay silent no longer.

"Mommy, why don't we take Daddy to the hospital?" she burst out.

For the first time in her life she saw real fury in her mother's face.

"Oh, so it's peace and quiet you want, is it? You want him to go and die in hospital and not bother you? Well, let me tell you: as long as I live, he'll stay here at home. If he's going to die, he'll die here, in his own bed. Under my care. And you... You can always leave, no one's stopping you."

Zuzanna was overcome with shame.

"No, I didn't mean… That's not what I meant. I… I only asked because maybe in the hospital they could… take better care of him…"

"No one can care for him better than I!" her mother snapped back. "He can take his medicine at home. Even the month he spent in hospital was unnecessary!"

Zuzanna struggled with herself. She could not pretend she wasn't wishing for her father's death. Better for him and everyone else, said a voice inside her. She reproached herself, but despite her attempts to suppress this voice, she was unable to. It's not me, she told herself. It's someone else talking to me.

Long before Father's death her home became a place of mourning filled with the odors of dying flesh and bodily fluids, with the moans of a mind losing touch with the world, with nightmarish dreams and moments of grave-like silence when her father would regain consciousness and quietly bear up to his approaching end.

Sometimes he asked her to read to him. Earlier, he had asked her mother. She agreed as always with a smile; but she was so tired she fell asleep almost as soon as she began reading. She awoke with a start when the book fell from her hand. She would have gone on, but her father stopped her, saying he was too tired, unable to follow what she was reading. A few days later he asked Suzanna.

He handed her the book to read – Benvenuto Cellini's *Life as Told by Himself* – and showed her where to start. She still remembered the place: page 34. There was a card with a picture of something vaguely plant-like on it, and she used it as a bookmark.

She read to him at irregular intervals. There were times when he asked for it almost daily and others when more than a week might pass between readings. They would not last long. He could not concentrate for more than fifteen minutes at a time. Usually he tired even sooner and signaled to her to stop. They never got even halfway through the book. The fact that he would often ask her to read passages over again didn't help matters. Much of what Zuzanna would read went over her head. Things that seemed clear suddenly became complex and obscure, hedged about with incomprehensible words and descriptions of bizarre situations. And yet the book drew her in somehow. It was like a mysterious, needlessly detailed and involved fairy tale.

"I always had a special interest in that period," her father told her, explaining his choice of book. "The Renaissance. The birth of our world. Florence was just a small town then. Smaller than a single district of Warsaw. But all the great figures of the age met there… the people who shaped today's imagination." He often talked like this after she stopped reading. He spoke in broken sentences. Only later did these fragments coalesce in her memory as a connected whole. "And Cellini. Before the war I studied a photograph of his *Perseus with the Head of Medusa*. It made an impression on me. The sadness with which Perseus gazes at his trophy and Medusa's face: the pain and the horror. I so much wanted to see the real thing. See if it wasn't just my imagination. The cast stands opposite the Uffizi Gallery – one of the world's finest museums, I'm told. There you can see the Middle Ages being transformed into the world as we know it today. The paintings take on depth and perspective. Because it's not true medieval painters couldn't paint perspective. They didn't need to. They focused on the essentials and didn't bother with the details that form part of our present view of things. An art historian in prison explained it to me. He taught me a great deal. I don't know where he is now or even if he's still alive. I so much wanted to see that sculpture. Others too. Michelangelo's. Verrocchio's. And the paintings. I promised myself I'd take your mother there some day. Your mother and you. We'd walk in their footsteps and see what they saw. But now… I won't be taking you. When I learned about this book – Cellini's *Life* – I just had to read it. I looked for it, but it was your mother that found it for me. She asked around and finally tracked down a copy in an antique bookstore. So, she bought it. That was just before Tadzio was born.

One day he asked Zuzanna to come and sit by his bed.

"I'm so sorry for spoiling this time for you... since coming home," he said feverishly, seizing her hand.

"Oh Daddy, don't be silly…" Zuzanna choked out dishonestly.

"You know, I thought… I really thought I could beat this. When I saw your mother and you, I felt as I'd never felt before. I thought there was still a life ahead of me and I'd achieve everything. I felt so strong… though I tired so easily. I hardly felt the pains I'd been experiencing for so long… since the interrogations. I feel ashamed somehow that I've not been able to overcome them and get better. Now I won't be taking you to Florence… Your mother deserved better. So did you. But I have loved you as well as I could and always will."

He died in early spring. Uncle Stach, Uncle Antek, Uncle Bronek, and one other man, whose face Zuzanna recognized but couldn't place, acted as pallbearers. Her mother, leaning on Aunt Gienia's arm, walked behind the coffin. Her face was ashen. Zuzanna suddenly noticed her hair was nearly all gray. It must have happened recently, and very quickly. When the funeral service was over and the coffin lowered, her mother sank down at the edge of the grave. Zuzanna couldn't tell if she had knelt down or fallen and broken the fall by propping herself up with her arms. But seconds later she righted herself and, still on her knees, tossed a clod of earth on the coffin. Tadzio, his hand in Zuzanna's, began to scream and wouldn't be consoled.

"Come," her mother said to her late at night when everyone had gone and Tadzio was asleep. "Come. I'll tell you about your father."

CHAPTER 3

Zuzanna met Benedict in the late fall. A dark, heavy drizzle was falling outside. She and Majka were sitting in the "New World," when Rafał came up to their table with a serious looking man, who seemed thirty or so. "Benedict Brok," he said, introducing his companion. They lost no time in getting on familiar terms. "Call me Benek," said Brok, smiling somewhat ironically. Zuzanna saw that he was scrutinizing her with a discreet although clear interest. He was wearing a greenish jacket and corduroy pants. He spoke little, but had a smirk, with which he didn't really seriously join the conversation made him even more interesting. It bespoke a mature detachment from current views and fascinations.

"So, you're studying the Renaissance," he said in a manner approaching seriousness. "But why exactly the Renaissance exactly?"

Zuzanna became alarmed as she always did when not quite knowing how to organize her chaotic thoughts.

"After all that's when… when our world was born. After all it's fascinating. But what interests me most is the question of perspective," she added more confidently.

"Perspective?" queried Brok, now seriously.

"Why yes. What does the appearance of perspective in Renaissance painting mean? It introduces another dimension, background, details. Everything that wasn't found in the Middle Ages. Which wasn't necessary then. But only in the Renaissance does man appear immersed in such an ordinary…human world… And you? What are you studying?"

"Me?" The irony returned to Brok's face. "Weber. Maxim Weber. Politics as the domain of the demonic. Venturing into the realm of power, and hence violence, is entrance onto devilish ground. Well, that's what Weber, who was a bourgeois thinker thought and didn't understand the sense of the dictatorship of the proletariat." His smile became clearer. "But that, which you say is really interesting. My topics. It turns out that sociology appeared along with the introduction of perspective to painting. That's very interesting." The irony resonated more clearly. They agreed to meet up to finish the conversation.

"Don't you know who he *is*!?" said Majka, genuinely shocked. "Our sociology's shining light. Professor Klein's assistant. Real hotshot…interesting guy. I'm not surprised they talk about his success. But, Be careful. His dissertation on Weber is on everyone's lips!" Pestered however on the topic of Weber, she wasn't able to say anything more.

Nor did Benedict much feel like talking with her about Weber. He asked questions instead, staring into her eyes, contemplating her beauty, until Zuzanna, who in any case liked this situation and felt a pleasant stupefaction, started to take on a somewhat more serious tone.

They went to see Fellini's *8 1/2*. Zuzanna was fascinated, although she wasn't really able to convey her impressions. Excited, she was speaking somewhat incoherently, when Benedict remarked with a sort of disregard:

"They have such problems..."

"What do you mean?" Zuzanna felt personally touched. Her enchantment began to evaporate. In the tight café, burned coffee, moisture, and cheap perfume, could be felt. "That we're supposedly what? Don't experience such matters? Don't have problems with... with... accepting ourselves... finding sense in...?"

"No. What I mean is that for us everything is more difficult, more serious. We feel the breath of history, we're written into a collective drama and we don't have time for such rummaging in our own innards... Maybe I'm wrong. Maybe I'm too much of a sociologist. Maybe I'm too much my father's son who was a leading figure of psychoanalysis already in Vienna and he disillusioned me to it completely.

Zuzanna, believed he lacked sensitivity, and for some time didn't let herself be appeased, but the story of Brok senior interested her. In the darkness, on a small snow-swept square not far from her house they kissed for a long time. She pulled away from Benedict completely chilled to the bone and returned home ossified, wondering, if she hadn't again fallen in love.

***

Memories coalesce. Zuzanna's memories and of those all, with whom she'll speak about those events, weave together penetrating and connecting stories. Their increasingly common memory will absorb everything they read, hear, and see. Experiences and discussions, images and reflections melted into an experience transcending the personal perspective of the human atom, which attracted and repelled by unknown forces, co-created the history of the time.

The university seethed. Under the cover of censorship and the "Small Stabilization", under the pressure of fear and daily pressure, the hopes of October were suppressed in the country condensed in universities. In heated discussions and debates taking place in student residences, cafés, and even in lecture halls, young people with no memory of the war or the UB were looking for a way out of an inescapable situation. Two years earlier, on the tenth anniversary of the Polish October, Professor Leszek Kołakowski had publicly and bitterly announced its demise. The deed cost him nothing more than expulsion from the Party. The universities were still virtual bastions of freedom. An increasingly more recognizable group of students – 'commandos,' as they came to be called – held public discussions. They went to official meetings and expressed astounding views: they spoke of the restraints on freedom, that the state of Poland is distant from the principles of socialist-democracy, of the lack of debate, which was so needed at universities. They threw organizers into a panic, and drove permanent student activists into a corner, who appealed to the student body to resist the *provocateurs* and place their trust in the Party's collective wisdom. In support of their arguments, the commandos were able to cite Marx, Engels and Lenin – sometimes even Rosa Luxemburg. They spoke passionately and looked, like they believed in not only, what they say, but that the reality around them is only a distortion of ideals, to which a return would satisfy the desires of the collective.

Suzanna attended these meetings as well. She was already identifying particular individuals. She turned her attention especially to one with wavy hair whose speech defect didn't hamper discussions. She was torn apart. She liked the commandos; she admired their courage, their fervor, their involvement, even the label applied to them. What didn't sit easy with her was their belief in the communist prophets they cited. Zuzanna understood one had to resort to the official platitudes and quotes of the ideological saints using them against themselves and the system, which they created; but she knew as well, and everyone close to her knew this, that Communism is evil.

She recalled the Corpus Christi procession of a little over a year ago which the police dispersed with riot sticks; her mother trying to shield Tadzio and she herself trying to pull the family into a safe place. It ended in fear and a few bruises. They were resting later in a small square where Tadzio took his distraught mother by the hand. "Mommy, why does God let this happen?" Zuzanna thought, that although she's grown up, she could've asked the same question.

"Evidently he wants to go through this," their mother said with a snicker, which was a sign of impatience, only Zuzanna wasn't sure with whom or with what: Tadzio, the world, God?

But Tadzio wasn't relenting: "God is good… why exactly is he making us experience this? After all we've done nothing bad."

"If only I knew, darling… if only I knew…" their mother said sadly, closing the conversation.

Nineteen-year-old Zuzanna realized, that her mother was an old woman, although she's a little over forty years old. She recalled her almost grey mother at her father's funeral. Not long after, snuggling her face to her mother's head, she noticed, that all of her mother's hair is already white.

Zuzanna breathlessly watched *Forefathers' Eve*. Benedict didn't have to tell her what getting the tickets had cost him; it was obvious, and she was boundlessly grateful to him. She was explaining, how much she wanted to see the performance to him earlier, which was to be shut down by the state in a few days. That's what the party decided. Benedict initially protested the decision, insisting they were dealing in this case with an experience of the collective. The object of that experience was of lesser significance, that is, the spectacle itself counted for little. But in the event, he yielded, as he put it, to the general fascination and watched the play with as much excitement as did Suzanna.

The drama was *about them*. It was about them that Mickiewicz wrote, which Dejmek faithfully transferred to the stage. The cheers and the applause were a spontaneous reaction, a response to what the bard was saying *to them*. He'd identified issues and images expressing exactly that, what they were feeling and experiencing.

"The shadows come and cover all the earth, / Men fall asleep…" Zuzanna heard declaimed on the stage; and she seized Benedict's hand, feeling a shiver, which connected them and the whole hall. Those, in whose name the prisoner was speaking.

"... full well I know / The kind of grace the Muscovite will show, / Striking the fetters from my feet and hands / To rivet on my spirit heavier bands!" the actor was saying this, but his voice resonated not just in the theater hall, but within the spectators as well; and that's why they responded, for he was speaking *for them*, and in their name. And when they heard, *"People! Each of you could, alone, imprisoned, by thought and faith overturn or raise thrones..."* – it awakened hope in them, it was bursting through the walls of the theater and was soaring over the city and the land immersed in winter. Pacing the stage was the spirit of *their* time cloaked in a hundred-year-old costume. There was a ball at the Senator's and the Warsaw salon, the national rite repeated itself. Did the duty not belong to them to break out of the circle of repeated time? The spectators were walking out of the theater feeling like old friends, or rather conspirators, exchanging knowing looks. The energy allowed them to not feel the cold that struck them as soon as they passed through the doors, not paying attention to the groups of figures, which were observing them from not far away. What they experienced allowed them to believe in the rebirth they carried within them.

It turned out, that their friends had tickets for the last performance on January 30th. The conversation started accidentally. In a small group, after class, they were in the university hallway wondering what was going to happen with the spectacle, they understood, that they're speaking about the most important things. They didn't remember, who first threw out the slogan to go before the theater or maybe try to go inside. It was crowded outside the National Theater. The crowed attacked the entrance, were held back by terrified ushers with difficulty. Finally, the group in which Zuzanna was surprised to find herself, succeeded in getting through to the foyer. Confusion reigned, but they were now inside the auditorium.

The bustle didn't pass and the performance didn't begin, although time goes by and the suspense increases. Finally the lights go out and the public on the ground floor and galleries jumped up, individual shouts could be heard, until finally everyone began to chant in unison: "In-de-pen-dence with-out cen-sor-ship!" and "Dej-mek! Dej-mek!" The Shaman comes on stage.

Finally, the spectacle was over. The curtain calls had come and gone; yet the ovations went on. Increasingly louder cries accompanied the steady beat of the applause – the same cries they'd heard at the start of the performance. The public spilled out into the street, formed a procession which marched in the cold night, warming themselves with their shouts: "In-de-pen-dence with-out cen-sor-ship!" Someone unfurled a banner. Only in the light of the streetlamps on the Krakowskie Przedmiescie Zuzanna was able to read the inscription: "We demand more performances!" They reach Mickiewicz's monument, where the banner was placed. Someone was still shouting something, but actually it's not known, what to do next, when out of the darkness emerges a line of police with riot sticks in hand. The crowd scattered. Zuzanna ran off with the others. She didn't know too well, how she made it back home.

***

After this, everything began to speed up. A petition calling for the resumption of performances began circulating through the campus. Zuzanna signed it enthusiastically, convinced that something at last, be it only a signature, might depend on her. Benek thought about it. "I'm not sure if you did the right thing," he finally choked out of himself.

A few days earlier Benedict informed her, that his father left the house for long trip. As they were climbing the stairs, Zuzanna now knew, what would happen now. What she'd actually decided a while earlier, though she tried not to think about it, was about to happen. It happened somewhat clumsily, almost unconsciously. And as if beyond her consciousness. When after everything Benedict slid off her and laying on his side, embraced her tightly, she felt that he had become someone unusually close to her, although she knew so little about him. They met increasingly more often. "I should be getting my apartment soon," boasted Benedict. Now they were at his place again. They were supposed to stay the night because his father went somewhere. Zuzanna explained to her mother that she was staying with a girlfriend so as to prepare for exams.

"You are wrong! This is not my indemnification!" He almost shouted. Zuzanna had never seen him in this state. He was nervous and uncertain. "I ... just ...", he choked and for the first time Zuzanna thought that he looks like a lost boy, like Tadzio, who cannot express what he feels, "I care about you and that's why I think ... if you did the right…"

Zuzanna embraced him. They were kissing and then found themselves in bed. The world enclosed itself within the confines of their bodies.

His father was screaming. He was screaming in his sleep and Zuzanna knew she should wake him up, but she couldn't push through to him during the night. Thick blackness choked her. She woke up a little unconscious, but the moans continued. It wasn't until a moment later that she realized that next to her, Benedict was thrashing and screaming on the bed. Scared, she turned on the lamp and was waking him up. It seemed to her that it lasted an awfully long time before he jumped up, gazing onto her with the gaze of her father, whom reality restored, when after returning home, in the kitchen he was falling asleep with his head on the table. Benedict for a moment longer was still recovering.

"I just have this," he answered her full of anxiety question. "It's from childhood," he explained somewhat later.

"For a few years of the war I hid ... they hid me. Then, when they took and killed my mother. I don't know how much time I spent in the closet. Maybe it was a year, or maybe even longer. It's hard to judge. They kept me in a closet and even gave me a bowl so that I would have somewhere to relieve myself. I was a few years old. Then they took me out of Warsaw. Towards the end of the war I was in a small manor house. It was much better, although I wasn't allowed to show myself to the locals. I was terrified. It somehow remained like that. I don't sleep well."

"My father was fighting then. They mobilized him as a doctor, an officer of the reserve in September. I was a year old. I don't remember anything. I have the impression that I remember my mother. But maybe it's just an image, a dream about a beautiful woman who takes care of me? After the defeat, my father got through to Romania. He transferred people through the Balkans. Then he was interned in

Hungary and given over to the Germans. He was lucky. He went to oflag. When he returned ... his wife and two brothers were already dead. I remember when I saw him for the first time. I was seven years old. It was already alright. I could go out, but I was constantly afraid. I was afraid of everything; I hid from people and every unexpected sound provoked a panic in me. I saw a big, dark man. It's hard to believe, but I felt that this was someone special. This time I didn't feel fear. He came to up me with a quick step, leaned over and took me in his arms. 'Son,' he said. He actually said just that, but I understood that he was my father and I wasn't even surprised."

Benedict wasn't effusive. Zuzanna had to try to pull it out more of him.

"My real name is Baruch. After my grandfather. We have such a custom. Along with his wife and two children they were killed in a pogrom in nineteen hundred and five or maybe six, after the revolution. My father and his two brothers survived. The eldest brought them out. After the war, my father changed my name, or actually translated it into Latin: hence Benedict. He wanted to free me from the burden of heritage." Benedict laughed sardonically.

It was Women's Day. The funny holiday of the red carnation, which her irritated mother brought, almost explaining to Zuzanna, that she wasn't capable of throwing flowers in the trash. Instead, she was clearly pleased to show off her tights, which nurses sometimes got "from an assignment". She usually smelled of alcohol, but although she wasn't drunk, Zuzanna didn't like this state. It was that day; a rally was held in the university courtyard. A few days earlier, two students were kicked out for organizing the demonstration after the last showing of *Forefather's Eve*. Zuzanna remembered one: it was that stuttering debater with wavy hair.

Tension was rising between those assembled. Also visible in the crowd were those clearly different from the rest of the faces, undercover agents. Someone was speaking about the breaking of the law committed by the minister, by expelling the students. The crowd shouted approvingly. Someone was whistling. A tall girl climbed onto the wall, saying something about freedom and censorship. In the confusion it was difficult to understand her. Larger and larger groups of somewhat older from those gathered, differently dressed men began to form a cordon around them. After a moment they started pulling people out. The crowd closed and tried to prevent them from doing it. Zuzanna, pushed from all sides, with difficulty was gasping for breath. She felt how the crowd undulates between anger and fear. Around people began to chant: "Tour-ists." Zuzanna screamed as loud as she could. Rage swept over her. She'd like to do something to men in herringbone coats or polyamide jackets, who pressed on them with evil faces. She saw how two were dragging out, taking turns to hit, a girl dying. Others were struggling with a boy, trying to free him from the group of students. She heard a woman's scream. "Do-yens" – was rising above the crowd a more and more widely shouted chant.

Finally, the cordon of advancing men crumbled apart and distanced itself. The students began to disperse when a shout suddenly rose from the gate. Only after a while did Zuzanna realize that the crowd was breaking up into groups and individual, escaping people, and in their direction, swinging clubs, speeds a line of riot police, assisted by packs of civilians equally ferociously smashing everyone they managed to overtake. The view paralyzed her for a moment. When in a she saw a boy falling over slowly who was overtaken by a few uniformed and undercover guys; white clubs rise above him and fall; everyone around was running away. A man in a quilted, polyamide jacket started at her. He was holding a baton in his hand. She threw herself into the escape too late. He ran in front of her, and the swing of an open hand, punched Zuzanna in the face on both sides. "You whore!" He yelled. She staggered and almost fell over. Something was exploding in her skull. It was more shock than pain.

She stopped understanding what was going on around her. She felt a jerk in her shoulder that accelerated her unconscious run. The secret agent managed to hit her with the baton on her back. She was running away like everyone else, trying to get past policemen and undercover agents. She was hit on the arm and back with a baton a few more times. She awakened outside Benedict's house. In her mouth she felt the taste of blood. She went to the second floor and, without thinking about it, started pounding on the door with both hands. Benedict opened a moment later. She saw his terrified face before her and then in the anteroom of his father looking at her in astonishment. She didn't really throw herself so much as fell into Benedict's arms and began to weep hysterically. She didn't want to, but she couldn't control herself. She doesn't remember how long it lasted, but it seemed endless. She was ashamed. She felt desperate humiliation: she wasn't in control of herself, she was nobody. She could be beaten, humiliated, insulted. Everything could be done with her.

Benedict took her coat off, led her to the bathroom, helped her wash up. In the mirror she saw a foreign face. Tousled hair, bloodshot cheek, swollen lip and eyelid. Benedict put her in an armchair and was calming her down. His father brought tea. "Calm down," he was repeating in a warm voice, holding her hand. "You're safe here. Everything's over." Zuzanna noticed Benedict's astonished look

It was already late when he walked her home. Previously, supported by his father, he was encouraging her to stay the night. Again, there was this surprised look which Benedict gave his father. Zuzanna knew, however, that her mother would worry. And she did. She was to them in the same moment she was opening the door. "Are you OK?" she repeated despite the reassuring assurances of her daughter. "What happened?" Tadek joined, who in pajamas, curious, unexpectedly leaned out of his room. His mother chased him to bed. "And who are you?" She asked only then, staring at Benedict, who was confused a bit.

"I...I'm a friend" he said unsurely.

"He's my boyfriend," Zuzanna said, provoking even her own surprise.

Only when Benedict said goodbye and left, after a moment's hesitation, kissing her on the cheek and accepting the subdued thanks of her mother once more, did Zuzanna burst into tears again, throwing herself into her embrace. Her mother calmed her for a long time.

"It's alright," she embraced her and stroked her head, "it's all over. That boy is pretty grown up" she allowed herself a joke when Zuzanna calmed down a bit.

***

The next day Zuzanna remembers disjointedly and the events were so mixed up that it was difficult to recreate the succession of events. More demonstrations were in different parts of the city. It's not known who decided about them having them, but information circulated among students. Large groups gather in the same place.

Shortly thereafter, militia and agents also arrived there. After a few shouts they had to run away. Everyone, however, had the feeling that they are participating in something unusually important. Zuzanna ran with a burning newspaper. They set them on fire in a group of a few people and now they were running with the burning sheets, believing that they'd burning falsehood itself and that from that moment it wouldn't be repeated as before. The howling of police sirens broke into their euphoria. The flames reach their hands. The newspapers had to be thrown away, they have to run.

A rally at the university. They appointed representatives. They gave speeches. They talked about censorship that must be abolished and freedom that must be restored. Everyone agreed. They talk about the ideals of socialism. Zuzanna understands that it's necessary to refer to official doctrine. Nobody after all, even dreams of regaining full freedom at this moment. It bothers her and probably others, but if socialist slogans would be a step toward freedom, then she could accept them. After all they're making a change of direction. They overcame fear and the feeling of hopelessness. They're regaining their dignity. From now on, nothing can be as before.

The fever of meetings, rallies and demonstrations - bewildering. Actually, they don't think, what's next. At the times when Zuzanna thinks about it, helplessness engulfs her. In the evenings she went to Benedict's. Evening meetings with him complete the fever of the day. They make love passionately, not considering, that his father is in the next room. Zuzanna doesn't even control her sighs, which could turn into a scream. Besides, Benedict's father clearly accepted Zuzanna. A few times, when she arrived while his son wasn't there, he invited her upstairs, offered her cigarettes, tea, and asked her how she was. He endowed her with a warm, understanding smile. Time with him calms Zuzanna down.

"Watch out for yourself," Benedict repeated, when tired, they fell onto the couch. It annoys Zuzanna.

"It's a special time," he says. "We won't let ourselves be driven to the hole anymore. From now we're really starting to live!" Benedict smiles indistinctly.

That day Zuzanna was at the Brok's. They were watching on television a broadcast of Gomułka's speech at Congress Hall. At times she stopped believing, in what she was seeing. She couldn't even imagine that something similar could still be said in public. Above the speaker's head, the banner read: "Each person has only one homeland." She heard that they were the enemies of People's Poland with whom the working class would set an example of and dispose of. Behind everything are Zionist inspirators, people with pimp morals, bandits from the anti-socialist underground. Memories of events from twelve years ago returned. The rally outside the Palace of Culture and the feeling that she couldn't express at the time, that the figure on the grandstand, and especially the enthusiastically greeted man, who now, twelve years later, throws threats and insults, that the man on the grandstand and the crowds beneath it exist in separate dimensions. But she was together with the people in the square. On the shoulders of her father, with her mother embracing him, who was waiting for Tadzio's birth, Zuzanna wanted to share their euphoria, feel one with everyone gathered around the Palace of Culture. Now a crowd of activists on TV chanted: "Wie-sław, Wie-sław!", "Ex-pose! Dis-close!" and Zuzanna wanted to cry. "Academic youth of Jewish origin or nationality," choked the gnome on the grandstand. "Zionism, Zionists, Zionist scheming," he repeated it as if he had the hiccups. And it wasn't until later that Zuzanna realized that he was saying it against her hosts, insults at Benedict, his father ... She looked at them and she noticed that they were exchanging strong glances. They're confirming what they already know. Zuzanna grabbed Benedict by the hand, putting out the other to his father. The men are looking at her.

A few days later, at a rally, they announced a strike at the university. Next to old slogans appear new ones: against racism and discrimination. The atmosphere kept getting heavier. A few days later, after negotiations with the university authorities, the strike ended. It was the last moment before the closing of the university.

"And what, the strike didn't succeed?" Benedict greets her. Zuzanna is overwhelmed with anger at his distance, which is only a mask of passivity, an effective excuse.

"What about you?!" she exclaims. "You didn't get involved or endanger yourself. You can afford peace!"

"I didn't have to get involved. It was others who engaged me. They weren't waiting for my decision. I've just gotten dismissed from the university."

Zuzanna became extremely sorry for him. She has a sense of guilt and defeat. She hugs Benedict and only up close can she see that his eyes are twitching nervously and something dark is lurking in them.

At the next rally, Zuzanna spoke for the first time. Breaking her stage fright, and stuttering, she said that, what - she knows well – she should say. She talks about racist criteria, the removal of researchers without even giving reasons, which isn't only an attack on the freedom of education but undermined the sense of the university's existence. She descended the stairs serving as a podium on rubber legs with an emptiness in her head, hearing some applause. She realizes, as probably everyone present, that the protest is burning up already. Only gestures remain. And waiting for the consequences. For the ultimate defeat.

A few days later he got a summons to the dean's office. She reads the paper handed to her by a stranger looking sideways: "Zuzanna Sokół, a 3rd year student of art history at the University of Warsaw ... struck off the list of students."

She had come to terms with it actually earlier. Now she's only bothered by how to tell her mother about it. First, however, she goes to Benedict. She waves the paper like a trophy.

"We're even. They also threw me out."

"Do you really think it was needed?" Benedict asks, destroying the further continuation of the speech planed by her and causing irritation. "Did it make sense?"

Her mother received the news of her dismissal calmer than Zuzanna could've imagined.

"Maybe it was necessary," she says, embracing her and making her a little girl again waiting for her mother's opinion. "Maybe ... You have to evaluate this yourself now."

They meet everyday in smaller and smaller groups, actually not knowing why, in the university courtyard. They informed each other about who was dismissed, who was arrested. Zuzanna notices that friends speak in ever shorter sentences, more and more nervously. Looking around at their sides, they lower their voices. Suddenly she realizes she was doing it similarly.

Some strange voices wake her up. Half-conscious, she clambered out of bed, leaned out into the anteroom, and sees her mother with a policeman and a man in civvies. The man pushes into her hands a summons for interrogation, today at noon.

"You just better go on time!" she repeats. Zuzanna sees her mother's frightened face.

She sat in a dreary, brown corridor for over half an hour before a gray man emerged from the next room and making sure, who Zuzanna is, with a gesture for her, to enter.

She tried to answer in small doses. She met at the university, she didn't recall the circumstances, she doesn't know them well, she didn't lead political conversations, she didn't know, doesn't remember. She tries to control her breath. At times, against her will, she smiles nervously at the man on another side of the desk. She's afraid, although she did everything to not show it, to gain distance, to not even admit to herself of her fear. The man growls, he ordered her to recall everything exactly, because if not...he looks at her glumly, lowering his voice. Zuzanna breathing in deeply, repeats as before.

"And what's this?!" The guy thunders, pulling out some papers. First, he throws them on the desk, then picks them up. He reads. Zuzanna Sokół, a 3rd year student of art history, spoke at a rally, attacking the people's homeland and calling for disobedience to the socialist state, propagated Zionist propaganda and disseminated false information about the racism of the party and authorities.

"Come on?! What do you think?!" The guy was over her, as if he intentioned to hit her. "You don't get out of jail for such things! The indulgence for people like you is over!"

Zuzanna explained. She spoke because she was concerned about the pointing out of the origin of Polish citizens. She tried to calm her paniced thoughts. If it's going to be prison, it shouldn't be long. It shouldn't be for more than a year or two. She'll hold out. Her father ... After all those times won't return... they shouldn't...

"You want to criticize the policy of the party, the government? You?!" The guy again leaned over her. Zuzanna was silent.

"And Benedict" the guy was dragging out the sounds, "actually Baruch, Baruch Brok, son of Adam, and his father Adam, son of Baruch, do you know them?" This time mockery is contained in the question. Anger engulfs Zuzanna, anger at herself, at her fear and rage at the person opposite, who crawled into her life, mocks the most important matters for her. She feels that she hates him, hates this place, this place, what people like him have made of her country, made with her, with her family.

"Ah yes, I know. Benedict is ...," she hesitates only a moment, "is my fiancé! And this is my private matter."

"There are no private matters here!" growls the guy. "She hangs out with Jews," he says quietly, looking next to Zuzanna.

"Excuse me?!" Zuzanna with difficulty throws this question out of her. She feels that she might explode, threw insults at the one at the other side of the desk.

"Nothing. So, what, do you want to return to college? You were unlucky, you fell into bad company. But after all it's a shame you should waste your life. You're young, talented from a working-class family. We could ignore these antics. The People's authorities know how to be forgiving. You'll sign this paper and we'll think about what to do next ..."

Zuzanna stared at the paper in front of her. "I am obliged to cooperate with the bodies of the Security Service ... I will inform you about everything I know ..." She calms down.

"I won't sign this."

"What do you mean you won't sign it?!" The guy jumps up again with a menacing facial expression. "I'm not asking if you want to sign ..."

"I won't sign!"

"This is your last chance. I'll leave you now for a bit. Then I'll come back, but not alone. And either the paper will be signed, or you won't get out of here. And it won't be nice."

Zuzanna was left alone. She already knew that she'll definitely not sign the agreement for cooperation, for being a stoolpigeon. She feels an internal tremble. Maybe it's only a few years, maybe they won't beat me.

The man returns, however, alone.

"So, what is it?" he leans over her. Zuzanna pushes the paper away without a word.

"You haven't decided? Too bad. It's your loss. Be careful, that you don't end up like your father. Nobody wins with us and who starts ... You'll now sign the interrogation protocol and a statement, that you won't say anything on this matter. We'll summon you soon. This isn't the end. Please be prepared."

Zuzanna reads and signs the protocol and the statement of keeping the details of the interrogation secret. She leaves. She feels a sudden weakness on the street. She had to stop. Her knees trembled, and the city, covered in rain, smudges even more. A truck passed along Rakowiecka Street. Under the tarpaulin, men holding flags and banners could be seen. One rolls open. "Root out evil!" reads Zuzanna.

At Benedict's, cuddling, she told him the details of the interrogation and cooperation proposals. She notices, that she's lowering her voice.

"They interrogated me too. I was afraid too," Benedict said grimly. Then he stared at her intensely. He was preparing to ask a question, which he doesn't ask.

"Well what?" Zuzanna asks in a whisper, cuddling Benedict even harder and staring into his eyes. He moved away from her for a moment. He looked like he had something to say but gives up. They started to kiss.

His father spent the days watching television. Once after Zuzanna came over, she becomes an involuntary witness of a sharp exchange of sentences, which she's never heard at the Brok's.

"Why are you torturing yourself?! Why are you gawking at this crap? After all it's well known, what they're going to say, who they're going to condemn, and in what words!" says Benedict in a raised voice.

"Don't you understand?" His father answers from beyond a cloud of smoke, and the voice flows from a distance, from a strange distance that is born between him and his son. "I have to get used to the situation again, which I already know from somewhere else. I have to get used to it, although I'm not surprised anymore. They sent me to retirement a year ago. After all you know why. They were cleaning out the army. They've just fired Henryk Weis. He wasn't fifty. He was a great cardiologist.

They do not have such there. But they threw him out."

On the screen under the inscription "Zionists to Dayan" some person in a fat donkey jacket holds a poster demanded "severe punishment of the enemies of People's Poland"

At home, her mother is yelling furiously at a scampering Tadzio. After pacifying the quarrel and sending her brother to his room, after a series of questions dismissed by her mother Zuzanna finally hears:

"They made us go to a rally. I wanted to get out of it, but that Party hag, Kwaśnicka, got me. 'Where're you going sister?' she asks. 'This is an important meeting. Failure to appear is a break of discipline. It's not just the end of the bonus.' I went. We condemned the enemies of the people. Those like you. We sent Jews to Israel. Well, no, not Jews, Zionists. That's what they're called now, but what am I telling you. After all you know them better!"

"Why do you say: them?"

"Because it's still 'them' for me, however. Don't judge me!" Her mother said, looking hard at her.

They agreed to meet on Constitution Square, from where they'd go by foot to the Brok's apartment on Koszykowa Street. The day was ending, but the springtime gusts were still shaking in the air. Zuzanna cuddled up to Benedict. On Independence Avenue from Jerusalem Avenue walked a small group of men, shouting something. A little drunk, they must've been coming back from a rally, because they were waving flags. In unbuttoned polyamide jackets, some in Tyrolean hats they looked like young workers: "Zionists away!" they chanted. "Zionists to Zion!" Two policemen, who quickened their pace toward them, relaxed and smiled. Zuzanna felt Benedict's arm stiffening. They were already passing close by: "Zionists away!" they shouted. Benedict curled up. She didn't want to look, but she noticed, how he's hiding his head in his arms. She looked at those chanting with hatred. "Well what?!" Said one provocatively, noticing her gaze and approaching them. "Well what?!" Benedict walked faster and pulled Zuzanna with him. Against her will, she remembered how he tried not to notice the anti-Zionist inscriptions in the shop windows; not notice the buses, used to bring demonstrators to the rally.

In the Brok's apartment sat an elderly, red-haired woman with a sharp face. She spoke loudly, not caring about Zuzanna's presence, to whom she nodded her head carelessly in greeting.

"Make up your mind! We should leave here. It's a matter of dignity. They don't want us here!"

"Why do you say 'they don't want'?!" Zuzanna couldn't stand it. All this is a campaign launched by the authorities. After all people aren't at fault for this!"

"They're not?!" The red-haired woman turned sharply to Susanna. "I think the young lady doesn't have enough knowledge and experience to interfere in our conversation! This 'campaign', as you were kind to call her, wouldn't have been possible without the involvement of so-called ordinary people. Someone shouts, 'Zionists to Zion!' Someone is cheering Gomułka. Someone smeared my door with dirt and points their fingers at me on the street. It is not the authority that hisses 'Jew!' at me. So, it's better that the young lady refrain from instructing me!"

"Krysia! A little calmer. Zuzanna wanted the best. She has right to speak on her behalf." Benedict's father speaks with the warm voice of a psychotherapist. Krystyna snorts and turns away from Zuzanna.

"Something important is going on in Czechoslovakia," says Benedict. "Maybe not immediately, but it will have an effect on us. It has to!" He looked like he was more convincing himself, than her. "One country of the Block cannot reform itself. It's a bit like dominos. Do you understand? If there can be another, better socialism, why not in our country?"

"And can there be a better socialism?" Zuzanna asked with doubt.

Sometimes with Benedict and his father she listened to Free Europe on a large solid Telefunk radio, which despite interference allowed one to understand words coming from another world. The radio was talking about that, which they couldn't find out from the official media, what was going on in Poland, but also in Czechoslovakia and elsewhere. But Czechoslovakia was the most important. In the elections to the extraordinary congress of the Czechoslovak party, pro-Moscow hardline candidates lost. "Prague Spring" - is a term Zuzanna was hearing more and more often. Polish media stigmatized Czech revisionism. The rallies were dissociated from the bourgeois, capitalistic tendencies that undermined the Czechoslovak party.

"We're going to Gdańsk Station to say goodbye to our friends," said Benedict, explaining why they must postpone meeting up. "They're leaving for Vienna, then for Israel."

"I'll go with you," Zuzanna declared, not thinking about it. And she insisted, although Benedict tried to dissuade her from this idea.

A spring night was starting. Cool shadows laying carefully on city. A group of a few dozen people was gathered on the platform. They stood close together, shielding each other from the world. Everyone knew each other. They repeated names, making sure of their presence. Benedict introduced Zuzanna. "My fiancée," he added. They said goodbye to the Stein family. Parents, nineteen-year-old daughter and sixteen-year-old son. Their faces were barely visible in the dim light of the lanterns. The daughter was moving away from the group and, ostentatiously knocking on her heels, was walking around, casting glances deep into the platform, on which stood a few groups of, indistinct in the night, men. They heard laughter.

The train left and they were still standing. Some woman began to cry softly. They were leaving in a large group, breaking away reluctantly, dividing into smaller groups casting nervous glances around, until finally Zuzanna was alone with the Brok's. Two men who had come up next to them, were looking at them impudently. "They have nice ..." one said, and the other laughed shortly. "Let's go," Benedict said, embracing her and heading for the tram stop.

A few more times with the Brok's she escorted their friends to the Gdańsk station. May was already ending, when she received another summons for interrogation. She had long ceased to come to the university courtyard. They stopped gathering there, and when meeting by chance, they had little to say to each other. A few of her friends were in custody awaiting trial. Many, like her, were dismissed from school. She was going to Rakowiecka Street this time with less panic than the previous time. However, she couldn't impose peace on herself.

The same ritual of waiting. A similar, though not the same officer he called her into the office.

"You're incorrigible," he began. "You got a warning, because this is what you can call deleting you from the list of students. You understand, this was warning is only," he bowed his face toward her in a slippery smile, "and now you are hanging out with enemies, Zionists. You're taking part in demonstrations at the Gdańsk Railway Station. Is that not true?

"I didn't know that they were demonstrations. I was seeing my friends away.

"And you keep doing your own thing. After all you're Polish."

"These are also Poles."

"Poles and they're emigrating from the country."

"Maybe they feel forced to do it ..."

"Forced?! Who's forcing them? You know that those are Zionist lies. Calumny against the homeland for which they'll be held accountable. So, you're saying that someone is forcing them?!" A threat clearly resonated in his voice.

"Maybe they feel that way?"

"And who cares about that?! So what? Will you still hang out with enemies, with Zionists?"

"I don't know that they were Zionists or anyone's enemies." Zuzanna calmed down. She had the impression that they're repeating the same issues over and over again, and the person before her is more bored of them than her.

***

"Daughter ... do you have to put yourself at risk like that?" Her mother had a hard time getting on to this conversation. "You know I didn't say anything, when you got involved ... well, you know yourself. Even when they kicked you out, though it's hard for me to come to terms with it. But now ... It's over. Why do you go to this station?"

"How do you know?"

"How do I know?" her mother laughed bitterly. "My senior manager called me in the hospital. There was a UB officer in the office. He was asking why you're hang out with Zionists, why you participate in demonstrations. He threatened ... Daughter, I know, what love is, but why these demonstrations? Are you needed at this station?"

"I think so. I think, that someone, who isn't... you know. This isn't for Benek. I'm doing this for myself. I feel that I should ..."

Her mother was looking at her in silence. She was nodding her head with a strange expression on her face and Zuzanna didn't know whether it was a sign of approval or confirmation of her mother's unspoken thoughts.

***

"Did you hear?! In Czechoslovakia they adopted two thousand words!" Benedict shouted almost as a greeting. Soon, however, he looked around uneasily. People on the sunny Krakowskie Przedmieście weren't paying attention to them. "It's a revolutionary resolution," he was now saying in a low voice, glancing at the sides. "It's the end of censorship, do you know what that means?" He leaned so close to her that she could feel his accelerated breath.

"But it's not in our country. And here?" Zuzanna made a gesture with her head. In the hot light people walked without a smile, without exchanging glances.

"Yes, but we must think in the long-term. In some time ...," Benedict slowed down. Zuzanna's gaze reached him, stopped him. The enthusiasm evaporated from his body, which stooped, bent over. "Maybe you're right, but we have to stick to something. Maybe however..."

He offered her an excursion for a two-week vacation to Solina. Her mother agreed unexpectedly quickly. A sultry, overcrowded train, in a crowd of angry, swirling, screaming at each other people, standing up, they dragged on to Rzeszów the entire night. Then they managed to cram into the back of the bus, on their own and others' packages, ignoring the shouting and epithets, with difficulty, despite the open windows, catching a stuffy breath in the stench of gasoline and sweat. In the afternoon, semi-conscious, they escaped into the air, which was trembling in the heat.

They lived in a room, in a railway vacation home, which Benedict's father arranged through acquaintances. The house stood on a lake at the edge of a forest. They rinsed off under shower in the bathroom in the hallway. And they fell asleep. They awoke along with the dying heat and driven by hunger, and bargained dinner from a complaining hostess. "Dinner is until seven-thirty, it's almost 8pm, this is only because you've just arrived," and then they set off on an unconscious walk through the forest at night.

They swam in a lake, walked around the woods, made love and fell asleep, to wake up and go on another trip or immerge in a book, constantly hungry, because the portions given to them from the kitchen were clearly shaved off by the hosts, and in the area it was difficult to find something to eat.

"It's just us," Zuzanna whispered in Benedict's ear, "only us, the forest and the lake. We're the first and last people. Around us there's calmness."

And yet every now and then she was woken by moans from Benedict struggling with nightmares.

They were able to forget the world they had escaped from. Even Weber, whose great volume in German - "I want to however complete this, what I haven't finished reading, they cannot forbid me from doing this," Benedict brought with him, situated their experiences in a different perspective. Benedict tried to tell Zuzanna about it. He made use of Jasper, whose book about Weber he also took. He sometimes discussed with him for Zuzanna's benefit, who had trouble catching the point of the dispute. She read Szymborska's poems to him. and shared her impressions of Konwicki and Brandy "I eagerly read about the times when men were heroes," she said without thinking in response to the question, did she really wanted to take two volumes of *Kozietulski and Others*. And she became worried, seeing his reaction. Benedict almost cringed, turning away from her. An awkward silence lasted for a moment, which he broke, turning to face her with a smile. "And do you know that a few dozen years later, during the November Uprising, chevau-léger's exchanged heroism for prudence?"

Two weeks passed and they had to return to Warsaw. Return to the world.

She already knew something had happened when she saw Benedict in the open door before her. He aged suddenly overnight and stared at her in a helpless and scared gaze. "Armies have entered Czechoslovakia. The army has occupied Prague." She could smell alcohol from him. "And our, Poles. A Polish continent. We have a share in it," he was barely heard. He led her into his father's room. Through the thunder of the jammers, the announcer from Munich reported on the progress of the Warsaw Pact forces.

"You were right. You just didn't draw the right conclusions. Changes in one communist country they are impossible, because these are the embers of revolution. Therefore, they should be choked," Benedict's father said it hard, without the usual smile.

It was already autumn when Benedict took her for a walk to the Łazienki Park. They sat on a bench, and he began with obvious uncertainty, stumbling over words.

"I don't know if I have a future here. I don't know overall, what I should do here. Apparently, I'm supposed to get some freelance work in the 'Republic' ... apparently. My father ... I didn't tell you, but they fired him a year ago. He was an army doctor, but such a reputable psychiatrist. They threw him out because he was a Jew. Now his friends are offering him a job in Vienna. You know ... he speaks German just as well as Polish. Besides he spent a lot of time in Vienna. He even knew Freud and his circle. He was a psychoanalyst, then he became disillusioned and returned to more traditional psychiatry. During the war ... I told you about it. He returned to find us. They offered, for him to stay in the army as a doctor, psychiatrist. He stayed. And now they fired him. It's amazing, but he still has a lot of energy. He wanted to work, and I ... maybe this PhD that I can't do in Poland, could I do in Austria? Take care of what I'd want and I think I'd be able to..."

"So what? Do you want to emigrate?" Zuzanna interrupted him, feeling that she has a problem with breathing and, despite the hot day, an icy chill is filling her.

"I'm deciding. The father is practically decided. And I..."

"And I? What place do you foresee for me?" Zuzanna asked in a voice that wasn't hers.

"Well, exactly. With this in mind I asked you to meet. I'd like to offer for you to come with us. Well, for this to be possible, before we would have to ... we would have to complete the formalities. Get married."

"Am I to understand that you're proposing to me?" Zuzanna felt a sudden relief and joy mixed with amusement.

"Well, you know ... I'm offering you a trip together, a life together, and marriage is after all a formality."

"Let me think about it, though." Zuzanna laughed almost in the voice.

"But of course. Of course. That's after all ... that's precisely the point."

But Zuzanna's joy, which suddenly appeared with Benedict's proposal disappeared just as quickly. For a moment she felt intoxicated. This great world of endless possibilities which up until that point she has only seen on a screen and seemed equally unreal, as apparitions evoked by celluloid tape, was to become hers. She was to cross through the screen and, with Benedict at her side, be on the other side of the fairy-tale reality. The perspective was breathtaking as was looking into an abyss, which frightens, but also attracts. Soon, however, Zuzanna remembered her mother and brother and felt the burden of responsibility.

"But you know ... It won't be possible. I can't leave my mother alone with

Tadzio ..."

"Yes, I know. I thought ... I thought about it. Because I talked with my father. We talked. As soon as we settled, quickly, I think that in half a year, maybe in a year, we'd be able to bring them. My father is going to earn good money there. I in truth don't speak German like he does, but I probably don't need much and I could ... In any case, it's obvious that we'll bring them here. We'll bring your family."

Zuzanna, escorted by Benedict, came home late - because, of course, the day ended in his bed - still joyfully dazed, but definitely less certain than when she heard the proposition. Something obscure bothered her, raised unnamed doubts.

Her mother was still awake and Zuzanna decided to attack her immediately.

"Benedict proposed to me. And he proposed a trip together to Vienna. His father will have a job there and Benek will be able to continue his career at the university. I could also go to college. And you and Tadzio we would bring as soon as we could, quickly ... "

Her mother looked at her without a trace of a smile, seriously.

"So, you've already arranged everything. For me? For Tadzio? I'm happy because of your happiness. I won't try to stop you, but I won't leave. And I think ... you shouldn't decide for Tadzio. When he grows up, he'll be able to decide himself, and now ... I won't give you my son and I won't leave his father. And he lies here."

"Mom, he's also my father. And I remember him. But he's ... you yourself know ... dead. I think he would have encourage you to leave. After all it's better. For Tadzio, for you mama. Benek's father is a doctor, he would probably help you find a job. If you'd want to. After all there's better conditions there. After all you still know German."

"Yes, I know German. I learned it in special circumstances. I wouldn't speak in it. I wouldn't want to live among people who speak it on a daily basis. You say that it's better for Tadek ... I don't know, maybe. I won't leave. And for Tadek ... You know ... I don't understand that much, I'm not so well educated. I learned in life however that this isn't the most important thing. We don't get to think through so many things and decide on so few ... I don't know why, but I know I should stay. I know for sure. I am sorry that I'm spoiling your joy. I know what it means when a beloved man proposes, but ... I can't do otherwise."

Zuzanna was unable to fall asleep for a long time. She was tormented in her sleep. She saw her father, Benedict, Benedict's father, then her mother repeated something unusually firmly to her, but Zuzanna wasn't hearing the words. In the kitchen, her father slept with his face on the counter and was shouting something in his sleep. Zuzanna tried to wake him up, but it turned out that it was Benedict with terrified eyes, who couldn't recover and is repeating something in a foreign language.

For three days she didn't meet with Benedict. She wanted to see him, feel him side by side right now, maybe even more than usual, but she had to impose discipline on herself. She came to him in the morning. She said that she has to think this all over and needs three days. Therefore, they won't meet during this time.

A few conversations with her friends didn't do much. "Leave, if only you can" that was the standard answer. Would they really leave so easily? She wondered. She was amazed at how much she missing Benedict.

Aunt Gienia gained weight. She already had three children, and the youngest,

Zdziś, was seven years old. Uncle Stach also became more sluggish and not as cheerful as he once was. However, at the sight of Zuzanna he became happy. He was asking, though, as she realized, he knew everything about her. He offered her a cigarette and puffing on it, was nodding his head sadly, not commenting on the situation. Then he went to the kitchen, where their bed stood, so that the women could talk peacefully.

"I can't help you much," her aunt said with a worried expression after hearing Zuzanna's story. "You won't convince your mother. I don't know anyway, if you should. She' might be the one that's right. I also wouldn't leave if ... well, you know. But you? You have a man, a future there, and here ... nothing is known. As always. Even if they started a war, will always come out of it well there, and us ... there's nothing to talk about. Well, it'd be a shame if you left. If the best ones leave, how will things change here? I can't explain it, but something doesn't feel right to me ... Don't be angry" she embraced Zuzanna. "I see that it's not easy for you. You should probably leave. What could happen to you here?"

Benedict opened the door immediately, as if he was waiting for her in the anteroom. He was unshaven and looked nervous. Zuzanna deeply inhaled the air.

"I've decided. I can't leave. Not now, anyway. I won't convince my mother and I can't leave her ... Maybe in some time. Because you know," she began to speak faster, losing the previously prepared wording, "I wouldn't feel okay somehow either. I love you, but it would be like an escape. They'd achieve what they wanted. We can't, we shouldn't ... In any case, I shouldn't. Because this is my country however ... and yours ..."

"I have to talk to my father, I have to," Benedict said uncertainly. He looked shocked. "I don't want to go without you. After all you know ... I love you." These confessions came to him with difficulty, even though he's already done it a few times. Zuzanna liked to repeat those words, make sure, get drunk with them. It was different with Benedict. "But I don't know if my father will decide to leave without me. And I ... I don't know if I could leave without you," he repeated helplessly.

Zuzanna felt relief and almost joy. Going to Benedict's, contrary to her will, all the time she was asking herself what she'd do if she heard the decisive: "tough luck, in this situation I'm going without you." Can he stick to her own and does she even want to stick to her own, even though she's definitely lying to herself? Will she not give in to Benedict? It turned out that he had succumbed to her. They agreed to meet at eight "Under the Galleries" on Marshal Street, between Constitution Square and Redeemers Church.

She came exceptionally early. She took a table snuggled into the corner of the cafe. Benedict came on time, a few minutes after her. In his hand he carried a tea rose. He was composed, freshly shaven and elegant. He smiled.

"These are for you," he said, handing her the flower. "I had a weird conversation with my father. I was nervous so a bit incoherently I started explaining your decision to him, but he interrupted me. 'I was beginning to guess that Zuzanna wouldn't want to emigrate,' he said. 'She's so Polish.' I don't know, what he had in mind, he didn't want to go further. This a bit ... pretentious. Unlike him. Well, but whatever. He pushed me not to decide on account of him. He has propositions for some unofficial consultations at the Medical Academy. In total, we'll manage financially. After all, he has a military pension. I'll finally find something too. My father also said: 'Once again, someone decides for us.' It wasn't a reprimand or resentful, which is why it surprised me. Especially when he added, 'Maybe it's good.' And, as usual, he explained nothing more. So, what, are we postponing our trip for now?" He smiled, stroking her cheek.

"I'm in the mood for something stronger," said Zuzanna. "I have to have a drink. Then you can take advantage of me."

They drank Albanian cognac. Already tipsy, Zuzanna felt that way anyway, they reached the Brok's apartment. It turned out that his father had been holding some whiskey in the liquor cabinet for a long time, which someone had given him as a sign of gratitude. Grimacing, Zuzanna drank some more good portions. She doesn't remember how she fell asleep. She got drunk for the first time in her life. She was twenty-one years old.

***

A few weeks later she spoke longer with Benedict's father. It was after setting the date of their wedding. Irritated, that Benedict didn't returning to the marriage proposal, Zuzanna asked him if giving up emigration also meant giving up on marriage. Benedict explained that after all he not only doesn't back down from anything, but he confirmed through his actions his will to live together, more than any ceremony could do. Marriage is only a formality for him. He stated that he couldn't get married in a church: he wasn't baptized and was a non-believer. They agreed on a civil marriage. A few days earlier, Zuzanna, who from time to time, officially, slept at the Brok's, was eating breakfast with Benedict's father. His son had to go somewhere.

"I was afraid you'd stop liking me," she began with naïve cunning. "You know, it's about the emigration. I stood in defiance of your life plans ...," Benedict's unclear account wasn't giving her peace. She wanted to understand.

"Do you really think so?" Adam Brok smiled as if he understood her intentions perfectly. "Or maybe you're just surprised that we yielded so quickly? You can understand my son. He's so hopelessly in love, for the first time in his life this way, but I ... Why did I yield so easily? Maybe I don't quite understand myself ... And you? Are you sure you understand your motives? Why are you giving up a better life and staying here? Maybe it's just a fear of the unknown, which you mask with big words? Or maybe however it's something else?" Adam Brok was smiling but looked sad. Zuzanna realized that he resembled her father, though he was so dissimilar to him. She always liked him, but for the first time she felt an incomprehensible closeness connecting her to him. He watched her with a hint of a smile.

"Would you like to understand? I'd have to tell you my whole life. We don't have time for that. I can only tell you that I was once a scientist. I wanted to understand man as a system of nerves, man-machine. Then: man as a system of conditions, reflexes. But the longer I live, the less I believe that the world and man can be understood, so that that we'd be able to understand ourselves. I think that our gestures mean much more, than we want to convey and we're able to visualize. Even your smile now, which is a polite statement: this old man should stop fucking around and say something to the point," the sharpness of the words melted into the tone of voice and a conciliating gesture, "only please don't deny it. We ourselves mean more

... maybe. And maybe the world is speaking to us, only we can't understand it? Or maybe I didn't deserve a trip? And maybe I didn't leave because I was just looking for an excuse not to start everything again? I've done this too many times and I'm tired. I'm too old and talk too much," he finished, waving his hand and looking at the window next to Susanna's head.

Her mother wasn't happy that the wedding would only be civil but didn't let it show. The wedding reception took place in the Brok's apartment. Her mother and Tadzio had already gone around ten. Her father-in-law disappeared somewhere and they were left in the company of their peers. Despite the efforts of Zuzanna and several friends, the mood was far from euphoric. Every now and then, a great drop of silence seeped between jokes, buzzing declarations and banter. They drank toasts for those in prison, for those, who left the country, for those, who didn't make it. They drank for themselves. It was then that Zuzanna got drunk for the second time in her life.

CHAPTER 4

The more than two years which passed since their wedding, Zuzanna remembered as a time of vague waiting, for what she didn't know, which passed she doesn't know how. In the Broków home, where she moved in, she was a refuge. She could experience moments of happiness there, though beyond the windows lurked an unpredictable and gloomy world. In truth the anti-Zionist campaign was burning out, and the newspaper, radio and television reported about rallies and demonstrations of condemnation and support less often, and less frequently those of questionable ancestry were unmasked, in order to remove them from their jobs and positions, their "real" names were less often discovered, but the threat was lurking in the air, in the humiliating, fearful gray of the city.

She was doing much better because Benedict's father was rich compared with her mother, and Benedict began to earn money. He was getting semi-official orders from the university, and later with the weekly "Republic", where he worked on some data, and sometimes he collaborated on an article under a pseudonym. Through all this these acquaintances, as he explained to Zuzanna with a specific, neither ironic nor disgusted grimace. His father's acquaintances and his old friend was Benedict's promoter, Bruno Klein. Zuzanna did not even feel the loss of her scholarship, but was only sure that she could not return to college.

The Brok's apartment was a social haven. A meeting place usually transformed into a drinking spree which barely anyone ended reasonably sober. It was Benedict's company. Zuzanna lost contact with her old friends except for two who sometimes came by. In their room - the other room was the shelter of Benedict's father - sometimes in a group of twenty-strong or more, pouring into the hall and the kitchen, drank vodka for hours, washing it down with tea brewed in glasses and listening to jazz, making unrealistic plans. Directors, without a chance for work, talked about their films and shows that will change culture; writers created great novels and made narrative revolutions before their debut; sculptors composed works revealing the secret of the world from cigarette smoke; sociologists, historians and philosophers sought to undermine the foundations of definitive knowledge. Because all, even the most ambitious projects, which were born on the third floor of Koszykowa Street, at the intersection with Niezależność Avenue, were infected with irony. Restriction of human potential probably never appeared with such obviousness as here. For that reason, each revelation had to be bracketed, adding a self-ironic comment to it, and articulating it with a joke. The world mocked them; hence it wasn't appropriate to approach it seriously. The solution against ridicule was to distance oneself from everything, especially oneself. In any case they knew, as their masters said, that every human idea, every accomplished effort solidifies into a dogma that binds people and life. So, irony was their weapon, the weapon of the powerless. They hardly talked about politics, a vile and cruel dimension which encloses them in a cage of darkness, in return they reserved helpless contempt for it. Sometimes the bearded and long-haired Bart joined them, called "the prophet" by his comrades of both sexes who showed up with him. He was a hippy. He shared this attitude of the world with Benedict's company, though he differed from them due to an almost religious fervor, which happened to erupt into impassioned speeches. He said one had to break the treadmill of daily obligations which captivated them, inhabitants of a technical civilization, gain distance, free ones self and feel free even in the gray world surrounding them, which then can reveal its true colors. He called out distant, if not mocking comments.

"It's much easier to weave flowers into your hair in San Francisco, it doesn't cost that much, and a policeman won't knock them out of your head on the first corner," summed up the unemployed philosophy graduate, Krzysztof Markus. "This is fun for darlings of this civilization, which gives them the opportunity to freeload and contest at the same time."

"Take this fun seriously, and then everything will be different" declared Bartek.

Soon after once being picked up by the militia, he got a solid beating and was sentenced to three months for resisting arrest despite the fact that no one who knew him could imagine it at all, and not just because of his doctrine of not opposing evil. Benedict summed it up by saying: "It's easy to proclaim an idea which you are doomed to."

After leaving prison, Bart's health category was changed. After changing the category from D to A, he was conscripted into the army for two years. It was then that they lost sight of him and never regained it.

Sometimes they hit the town in a drunken group only to fall into the first bar they came across. This didn't happen very often. The outside world was not friendly and even when drunk they could see figures circling around them. The night city was full of blurred shadows which could materialize and take the form as evil spectators preying on passers-by. Figures in uniforms made them sober, quiet, they tried to silently sneak past them. Apart from that, trips to the city were too expensive and devastated their limited and unstable funds. They sometimes went to concerts, to jazz clubs, to exhibitions, to the cinema or theater, but there wasn't much to watch.

Someone brought tapes of Włodzimierz Wysocki's recordings. They translated the Russian texts as they listened to them. There was nothing better to drink to than this hoarse voice shouting the hopelessness of everything in bold tales of an old age which could only be juxtaposed by the dignity of those that lost.

At that time, Zuzanna reminded herself that she was not planning anything, she was not thinking about the future, and she tried to chase away unpleasant thoughts. This was the only life which she could imagine for herself in this reality.

In September 1970, on Monday morning, Wiktor Czerniak, a visual artist, jumped out of the gallery of the store in the Central Department Stores. He was killed immediately. Last night in the Brok's apartment he was the soul of the party. He talked about conceptualism, shouting over the usual mocking Marcus.

"A work of art as an object has ended!" He cried out. "All the paintings have already been painted. All sculptures were made. How long can we paint mustaches on the Mona Lisa? And the museums are full, and no one can look at it anymore. We will democratize art! We will draw recipients into the creative process." It is here, at the Brok's, where a new museum-studio will develop. "Life becomes a creative process! We will not let it clot in any convention!"

"But we'll need a lot of vodka!" Marcus called out finally getting a word in.

According to witnesses, Czerniak, who was hanging around among clients, suddenly threw himself out of the gallery sticking out above the street, jumped over the barrier and fell on the pavement. Although no one knew the reasons for his suicide and there did not seem to be anything in his personal life at that time to push him, no one was surprised either. They drank in unique silence and only with time did the alcohol begin to loosen tongues. Would everyone's suicide be just as obvious? –Zuzanna wondered.

Benedict drank full glasses in a way which was unusual for him. He quickly became drunk. He snuggled into Zuzanna's shoulder, who was sitting on the floor in a group, talking in a characteristic, unsightly, digressive-alcoholic style. He was shivering. The next day he had trouble recovering.

About a week later, she ran into the kitchen through a crowd of shouting guests. On the counter sat Marian Balcerak, staring at the open and hissing burners. The stench of gas filled the kitchen.

"Have you gone crazy!" Screamed Zuzanna, rushing to the stove and turning off the burners, then pushing him violently to open the window. Marian was stunned, maybe because of gas, certainly because of alcohol. He tried to stop her, moving his head like a great St. Bernard. He spoke long, stretching words.

"But Zuza… think about it" he repeated. "This is pointless. Just like Wiktor… this is pointless. But if together...together we didn't wake up…these twenty people. And they would find us the next day…It would definitively change something. Don't you think, Zuza? It would have to change something!"

"You know Marian wanted to poison us?!" Zuzanna burst in like a storm, and her scream managed to attract the interest of almost all present, who, as always, were scattered into a number of groups in their conversations. Balcerak slowly stumbled into the room behind her. "He turned on the gas and said that our deaths will be a manifestation! It'll change something!"

Someone broke out in laughter. Others began to echo him. Balcerak managed to get a word in, to get through the laughter.

"But listen. It would be this. This kind of suicide. Like a group work of art…"

"Listen, next time you want to make a performance out of my death, ask me for permission" someone from those present exclaimed. "And don't decide for me so easily. I think it's a kitschy project." Throw in someone else. "Traveling to the other world is an expensive journey; ask if I bought a ticket" concluded Markus. More jokes broke out, and Balcerak started laughing to himself, nodding his heavy head. Zuzanna approached her exposed husband.

"He really wanted to kill us" she said. "We should throw him out."

"Let it go, it was only a stupid joke" Benedict managed to calm her down. He looked as if he still couldn't recover following the death of Czerniak.

She woke up with a hangover in the morning. She was beginning to know this state better. Sipping sour milk, which, barely conscious, she happily found in the third store she checked, and snacking on pickles, she tried to understand the events of last night. It wasn't going well. An invisible ring was tightening around her head, preventing her from thinking. Then suddenly Zuzanna realized how much she wanted to live.

"Didn't you think about the children?" her mother finally asked. This question hovered before her unspoken issues. Zuzanna was getting to it.

"No. Do those kinds of ideas have any sense today?" She replied with a question.

"They always do. Even in the worst times. If your father and I approached it that way you wouldn't be here today. Because times were definitely worse, and we had a war behind us, something which you do not forget, which cause people to think differently…worse."

"Exactly. No one invalidated that experience."

"But it's fun to live, right? It can be fun anyway. I was happy with your father and I can't imagine it not happening. And now? When I look at you, at Tadzia, I understand life. Because a person cannot live only for themselves. They don't know how to.

"We're somehow managing for now mom. Don't worry. We have each other, and I have you-all."

"You're weaseling out, but if you don't want to talk about it…" Her mother ended the conversation.

***

It was a December evening and suddenly Adam Brok burst into their room. "Come on!" he shouted. Zuzanna never saw him in this kind of state before. The radio was shining and rumbling: "the Provincial Committee building was completely burned down…the workers demand…freedom of press and religion…curfew… clashes in the streets." "It's Gdańsk, the shipyard is on strike," said Brok, oddly excited. "I don't think it will end so easily." Benedict stared at the radio, hypnotized.

Then there were days by the receiver. Police patrols were extremely densely roaming the streets of Warsaw. Sometimes large ZOMO[2] vehicles passed with a howl. It was hard to hear anything on mother's radio, even though its eye was pulsing spasmodically. However, "Elbląg, Słupsk, Szczecin" and then "Gdańsk" came from outside the wheezes and hums.

"We should do something" repeated Zuzanna "we should…"

"But what?" asked Benedict "You want to have a demonstration? How? You'll go out onto the street and start yelling?"

Zuzanna couldn't find a response. She however did not feel right. Benedict's skepticism divided their guests. She ran to her mother. She, herself nervous, managed to calm her down. She glanced uncertainly toward the corridor. Tadek wasn't there even though it was getting close to nine in the evening. The crack of the lock alarmed the mother who ran to the door. "What time are you coming back again!" she shouted.

2. Para-military police units from Communist Poland used to control crowds and enforce security

"What…look at you? Were you fighting again?" Zuzanna was already in the hall. In the dimness, Tadek's face looked terrible.

"I fought?! They beat me. The police. We were standing in a group, someone yelled "Long live Gdańsk!" We started yelling that. They drove up fast. We started running, but they caught me and threw me into the patrol van. Inside they were already beating a few. They beat me too. They then asked for an ID. "Just a punk kid, he's not even fourteen," said one of them. They threw me out of the van and gave me a few punches for a goodbye. But the way they were beating those inside…" he said, chocking up and sobbing.

"How do you look?" said the mother, looking at her sons beat up face.

"How I look? I'd show you my back and behind, then you'd really see how I look! But a samurai doesn't complain!" Tadek finished his declaration with a groan.

Unfortunately for Zuzanna, who embraced him, she began to laugh. She laughed completely, contagiously. A moment later Tadek joined her, and after a while their mother looked at them with a surprised indignation. They laughed loudly, feverishly.

That day in the morning Benedict brought an armful of newspapers. He threw them on the pile and in disgust laid them out next to him. The first pages reported about "incidents in Gdansk". "Provocateurs" which led to "hooligan pranks".

"It was enough to buy one. After all they can't differ." Zuzanna snapped.

"Sometimes a slightly different wording is information" Benedict explained unconvincingly. "But look. They had to write something. They were silent for two days. They couldn't for any longer. Something is happening."

"The latest news from Gdańsk: at the Tricity railway station, the army and militia opened fire on workers going to work. There are many killed and wounded. Fighting in Gdańsk continues. We will keep you updated on all information that comes to us ..." Between the howling and humming, the Brok family of three, a n gathered around the radio, suddenly heard the announcer's voice clearly. They looked at each other in silence.

On that day, Prime Minister Cyrankiewicz spoke on TV at 8pm. An elongated skull, a face made of clay, a mouth like a fish powerlessly catching air "The overriding state interest requires ... the use of force to restore order ... the emotions used by anarchist, hooligan and criminal elements, the enemies of socialism and of Poland... have become a feeding ground for the enemies of People's Poland...the working class under the leadership of the party gave strong opposition ... the working class which, under the leadership of the party, brought Poland out of the darkness of the Nazi occupation ... cast aside the provocateurs, do not listen to the troublemakers."

"Well we have our information" said Zuzanna.

"He said, that they're going to kill" Benedict's father summed it up.

"But they don't have control of the situation, that's why they say what they do. It turns out that the riots are still going on" commented Benedict. Free Europe spoke about fights and strikes in the Tri-City, Szczecin and Elblag.

At her mother's she met her aunt Gienia and her husband. With a bottle of vodka, they tried to understand the drowned-out message of Free Europe.

"And you know that in Szczecin they burned down not only the P-C (Provincial Committee) but also the villa of their first head, Walaszek" Asked her delighted uncle, pouring her a shot.

The radio reported that the order to shoot demonstrators had been suspended. Benedict looked at his father. "Are they yielding?" He asked uncertainly.

Something was happening. Zuzanna just knew it. She was sitting in a cafe with her friend, with whom she was finally able to meet up, looking at her watch and less and less interested in the heart problems of former acquaintances and the difficult situation at college. Finally, apologizing, she pulled herself away from the table. She made it just in time for the beginning of television's "Daily News".

"Today, due to poor health, the first secretary of the KC PZPR (Central Committee of the Polish United Workers' Party), comrade Władysław Gomułka, Wiesław, was dismissed." The speaker on the screen did not show any emotion. "The first secretary of the provincial committee in Katowice, comrade Edward Gierek, has been appointed to his position."

"The end of Gomuła, end of the gnome!" yelled Zuzanna, jumping up like a small girl.

"Let's listen to his successor. We still don't know what he's prepared for us." Benedict calmed her with a clearly pleased expression. Even his father looked at them with an unusual, radiant smile.

"People have been killed. We are all experiencing this tragedy" read carefully from a paper a man with a grey crew cut and a solemn face. "We can't help but wonder: why did this misfortune happen? It is the duty of the party leadership and of the government, to give the party and the nation answers to these questions." But the Broks didn't hear the answer. More rhetorical phrases stopped to mean anything. Zuzanna caught only the surprising, for an official speech, the statement about "ill-considered concepts in economic policy", and then the new one jumped headfirst into traditional gibberish.

"So now what?" She asked helplessly after turning off the television.

"They chased away the gnome, they admitted to the killings...Something must've changed. A crisis is beginning" wondered Benedict.

"It'll be the same in a new form. So, a little different" Benedicts father summed it up.

In the spring, Benedict came home with a large bouquet of tea roses. "I got a full-time job at the Republic!" He called, handing her flowers and embracing her.

CHAPTER 5

Many times, many years later Zuzanna wondered, when their relationship begin to fall apart. The appearance of Kalina, the existence of whom she only began to guess after some time, and about whom she would not know anything certain for a long time, finished their marriage. It could still last, she thought, it could be reborn, just as relationships could be reborn, which after conflicts and betrayals they regained an incredible, vigor of before. In any case, this was the story of several familiar couples from her perspective. This was also how their relationship could look, when, after quiet days, after quarrels, grievances and grudges, they were able to find each other, and a passion would be awakened in them almost like in the beginning. To onlookers, their marriage could also have the nature of a phoenix reviving from the ashes and only they knew that it was never a definitive revival, and the injuries remained, accumulated. Although they were able to fall asleep, be disguised in a sudden sense of intimacy with Adam, then a violent burst of love, which, however, happened less frequently.

Could their marriage be reborn? Could her and Benedict's relationship be revived, a relationship in which, over the years, they gradually separated from each other, so that sometimes it seemed that they were connected only by her son and maybe her husband's nightmares? Although as it happened the reflex of compassion and help, which, as usual, overwhelmed Zuzanna; when her husband's moans broke her sleep, they were accompanied by cold hostility, providing satisfaction while watching the man next to her tossing around in delirium. Could she rebuild her affection for her husband, for whom she felt so much reluctance and something unpleasant that she did not want to call it by name just because she did not fully understand her contempt? Then why was she going through so much with him leaving? But that was a different question. That, fundamental, in the moment of the break, as everyone said, of such a unique relationship, had peaked her disappointment with her husband during *Solidarity*, which, unfortunately, was only a confirmation of the act that took place three years ago, and which she never really forgave. That act was joining the party. Compared to it Benedict's previous affairs, before Kalina, faded, painful, but were of no importance. Maybe only this act of apostasy, confirmed by his attitude towards *Solidarity*, grew out of earlier events? Maybe what happened then was only a confirmation suspicions which she had pushed under the rug, which turned into certainty? This began earlier. With fascination bordering on terror, she found this moment was in the early seventies, three years after their marriage, when Benedict

and erotic freedom, were the most read columns of the magazine. Now he was clearly seducing Zuzanna, which pleased her, but at the same time she wanted to listen to what Benedict was arguing about among the most important figures.

"We dream of this democracy" laughed a little man with protruding ears and a bald, egg-shaped head "and you know, that God, wanting to punish sinners, realizes these dreams? Can you guess what it would be like? A bench ghetto, at best. And what leaders? Same as those who made the Warsaw Uprising, a Hecatomb. They murdered the city for their ambitions."

"Kaziu, you're not talking sense. What democracy are you talking about? This is a spectacle. Let's talk about how to educate our party elite. There is always some elite. We have our own and the problem, of how to convince them that one can remain socialist and develop...For the benefit of all ... Or that they move a bit to give us some space." Goleń laughed faintly, and a consistent, nodding laughter was confirmation from the gathered. Zuzanna wanted to puke.

"We must wake up the competition. We must somehow wake up the competition, so as to create a market. Socialist, of course..." Benedict introduced a new, almost fervent tone to the conversation. Goleń looked at him with acknowledgement.

"A socialist market? I thought it was a contradiction" Zuzanna blurted out unexpectedly. They all turned toward her. She felt as if she had said something indecent.

"These are just the standards. Socialism must also develop." Benedict looked at her angrily.

"You drink too much" he said to her irritably in the taxi driving them home.

"And you talk too much. I've had enough. You don't have to assimilate yourself with them so much."

She was liking Adam Brok more and more. When Benedict wasn't around or busy with something, she often had breakfast with him before going to work. She really wanted him to open up to her, but he was always coy. "Maybe I'll tell you later, maybe..." he repeated with an dour smile. Such a fascinating life, but it's like a closed vault, she wondered constantly. Pretty soon, she corrected her first impression. After meeting him, he seemed very confident and distant to the whole world. Now she saw in him a nostalgic, difficult to define, sadness, which she later recognized as the main feature of his character.

"I'm not a fan of his new company, those from 'The Republic'" he murmured once. "Maybe I'm not fair. They're doing sensible things. But their... chutzpah, that sense of superiority...Maybe I saw it too much. They are so pompous and so funny when they think they have pierced the spirit of time ... And one of their main authorities is Klein. Maybe he is even their spiritual mentor. They won't free themselves from this guy anymore," he finished by laughing.

"Dad doesn't like Klein? Zuzanna asked surprised. Professor Bruno Klein was a legend in the communities she revolved in. Maybe in all intellectual Warsaw. And above all Benedict was his assistant, he was writing his doctorate under him. When they threw him out of school, she asked, what his professor had to say about it. "What can he do?" he replied with a question, in which there was a sad understanding and maybe a little disappointment. It turned out however, that the professor tried to help Benedict. He was the one who arranged him a contact with 'The Republic' and probably introduced him to Goleń. Zuzanna never met him.

“After all, he was helping Benek…Got him a job, and later…” Adam Brok looked at her with an almost imperceptible smile.

“Yes, he likes to help. He always wanted to help me. I’m of course a part of his world, which he wanted to destroy. He was a friend of Sara, Baruch’s mother. A young, brilliant student of sociology. There is a tremendous amount of geniuses in college, but he retained it. He was an ardent communist. I remember his tirades over thirty years ago. Contempt for the Sanacja[3] run, capitalist, anti-Semitic Poland. That Poland was just a fragment of rotten Europe for him. The whole wormy, capitalist world that he condemned to destruction. He prophesized and called for it. And it came true. There is no longer that Poland or that Europe, that world. After the war, when I returned to Warsaw, I found Klein by chance... by chance? My dead friend said that everything happens for a reason. Bruno…Bruno Klein came to Poland riding a Soviet tank with a revolver at his side. He didn’t part with it for a long time. Then, in the forties, he always wore it, even for lectures, because he began to an instant academic career. Earlier, when he fled to the Union in ’39, he was locked in a camp by the Soviets as he was a Polish communist. He was lucky that they didn’t kill him, like they did his woman. Anyway, I don’t know exactly how she died. Then they put him in Berling’s army. And he returned to country and began to install communism. I avoided his help. Maybe I was a bit afraid of him? Once, however, I got drunk with him, as it happened to us then. He said he hated this intellectual sensitivity. He asked how after the war one could be overwhelmed with the fate of individuals. I did not ask how it was possible to implement communism after a Gulag. Though actually, what he was saying was the answer. He talked a lot about power, dialectics and history. He said that the war showed what beautiful spiritual exaltations lead to. And man needs elementary things: food, shelter, sleep and sex. He said that culture was founded on the suffering of an infinite number of human lives. For the aesthetic experience of a chosen few, the masses were dedicated to misery. Those who could not meet basic needs; he said they would provide it. “Civilization! Humanity! Sublimity! Art! Enough of these exaltations!” He shouted. He exalted terribly. I tried not to meet him later, and maybe because of him I escaped from the capital. But when I returned in fifty-six, I found him again. He no longer carried the revolver and was a revisionist. Such a careful revisionist. And a serious professor, of course. “You shouldn’t take me too seriously,” said Adam Brok one time. “I’m an acrimonious grumbler. I don’t like anything. My old friends, like Klein, whose help I still use ... They also like to help people like me ... their own. They didn’t think anything through. You know, when I came back, when ... I came back looking for Benedict and ... when I found him. I had a lot of friends from old times before the war. Not just Klein. Mainly left-wing...intellectuals. Doctors…Jews. They pressured me to stay in the army, but then for me...I didn’t really care, nothing really mattered to me...except for Benedict ... Baruch. He probably told you. I wanted to save him from Jewishness, as if a man could be saved from birth. I changed his name. And I...even signed up for the party, or rather they signed me in…but I agreed. I wasn’t blind, just indifferent. I saw the enthusiasm of those who wanted to change the world. They felt as if power was being pushed into their hands. I fled to Kraków first. Then farther on to Bydgoszcz. Maybe

3. Part of the interwar (1923-1939) government which was dominated by the military. Sanacja (Sanitation) took its name and ethos from Jozef Pilsudski’s hope to keep government “clean”.

not only because I saw evil and knew that it would end badly. Anyway, I had reason to fear. My brother, whom they killed during the war...I mean: he killed himself so as not to fall into their hands...That's probably how it was, I managed to reconstruct it that way. He was quite an important Bolshevik. He was in the Cheka. Do you know what the Cheka was? He escaped from Russia in the late 1920s. He described his experience in a diary. I read it ... Horror. Good material for a psychiatrist. Well, but I'm not talking about that...that was Stalinism. If they knew I was his brother... that would be the end for me and Baruch. Further away from the capital and in a smaller center it was safer. They brought me there in fifty-six. And then I realized quite quickly that they did not understand anything completely. Well, it wasn't easy... to admit it. I talk too much."

Virtually all Zuzanna's attempts to force Adam Brok to develop a barely outlined thread, to explain an issue that she could not understand on the basis of his passing references, all of these efforts failed. "I've already told you too much" he would answer as usual and dispose of her insistence with a joke or promise that he would explain later, though it was clear to both of them that it was only an excuse. All that remained for her was to wait until he was provoked by his thoughts and some unpredictable stimulus. He never told such stories to his son. Once Zuzanna asked her husband if his father had told him so much that now he does not want to repeat himself. Benedict laughed.

"Father? He said a lot? You must be joking. He doesn't say much."

"Maybe you're not asking him enough" Zuzanna said loudly. Benedict looked surprised.

"I've never thought about it that way, but you know, it's possible." He laughed out again.

"I've already gotten used to how it's not appropriate to ask father anything. All in all, you can reconstruct a lot from the half-words and individual sentences he gave me."

It was not history that Benedict's father dealt with. He wrote journalistic articles based on his observations in the provinces and data collected in the editorial office. He suggested greater independence for enterprises that would be able to compete with each other. This would, of course, involve the admission of other risky experiments, the possibility of bankruptcy for some, but Benedict proposed that this option be considered. Such a harsh thesis provoked discussion in the editorial office, but after nearly a month's reflection Goleń agreed that Benedict should include it in his article. Zuzanna tried to develop enthusiasm, even if related to her husband's involvement, but she was doing poorly.

"But I think you have more common sense than my son, ''Adam Brok replied to her complaint about herself. This happened after the publication of the article in which Benedict argued that socialism does not necessarily mean disregarding the laws of the market. It's just about civilizing and humanizing them. These theses were formulated on the high level of abstraction. Benedict got permission to quote a few bourgeois classics not published in the PRL which were by: Werner Sombart, Joseph Schumpeter and above all Max Weber. He was attacked unusually harshly in several dailies, which caused great anxiety in the editorial office. Many of its members had been grumbling louder and louder for some time that Brok's excesses endanger the weekly, silently adding that Goleń fell in love with the young intellectual, with which he probably compensates for his peasant origin. Now the ferment began to grow louder, and Benedict was worried. Goleń was nervous, though he tried not to show it. After a few days, however, at an editorial meeting with suppressed triumph, he stated that Brok's article was discussed in the Politburo and that "Number One" himself found it interesting, although controversial. Among the congratulations that Benedict received, no one asked the question that was puzzling everyone: who translated the article for "Number One".

Even this triumph Zuzanna received it quite coldly, which clearly offended Benedict, although he pretended to be distant.

"You have more common sense. These games...He's beginning to believe that he will rebuild the Polish People's Republic. It's sad, but as a specialist in mental mechanisms, I have to honestly say that there is a lot in this self-deception. Career is satisfaction. Success is not enough. You must have a sense of what you do. I can only say...You must understand: he will never fully come out of the closet in which he spent the war. After all, those nightmares still torment him. Am I wrong?" Zuzanna had to agree with him. Adam Brok frowned even more. "I often think that we deserve everything that happens to us. But not him. Not him, who was less than two years old when the war broke out. But I ... I have so much on my conscience. I can't even explain, I, a psychiatrist, that I am not to blame for what happened to my family. Because as absurd as it may sound, I am sure that I am at least partly responsible for it. For years of fear my son went through, which I couldn't prevent. But I'm glad, I'm so glad you're his wife." Brok said it almost tenderly, smiling at her in a way she didn't know. She felt touched.

Around that time, she began to think that she would like to have a child. Her child and Benedict's. Her mother's hints, which she had brushed away, had only strengthen her growing feeling. Sometime on Sunday morning, when they stopped making love and were laying there, exchanging caresses and looking at the spring light pouring into the room through the white curtains covering the window, she mentioned it to Benedict. He looked at her helplessly.

"A baby? I don't think I would have the courage. And anyway...Think. Why do we need it? We're mature people. We have to come to terms with our mortality, and the belief that children will take us into eternity is infantile. After all you don't believe, that we have a duty to breed. Duty to whom? And this way, look, how much nicer it is that nobody disturbs us. If you want, I'll make you coffee, bring breakfast to bed. Maybe then we will want to make love again. Don't you remember when you said, by Solina, that we are the first and last people? We are for each other. I believe in that."

A wave of tenderness swept over Zuzanna, but something was preventing her from fully enjoying the moment. Although there was almost everything which she needed for happiness. She was lying next to a loved and loving man, they were doing well and even the world outside the window did not seem so threatening any more. One just didn't have to think about it too much. Sometimes alcohol was enough. Zuzanna learned to dilute vodka with Coca-Cola, which showed up in stores. She even liked the taste. At work it was not so bad. Admittedly, a few days ago she was accosted by the HR director "And Mrs. Zuzanna did not appear again on the May Day parade..." he said passing by her in the hallway, leaning towards her with a crooked smile, and she did not even try to justify herself. "...I did not know that it was mandatory" she answered sharply moving away from him. "After all, we know that it is not..." his slippery smile almost touched her. "But besides duty there is loyalty. We are a collective and we should be able to rely on each other. And if someone distances themselves...The collective must rely on each other. Otherwise...I hope we understand each other" he suspended his personal voice, piercing her eyes. He stopped smiling now. "Do we understand each other?" He snarled menacingly. "Yes," Zuzanna answered automatically. This word left a disgust in her mouth that she could not rinse for a long time. Vodka and Coke didn't want to help either. We live a lie, a fucking lie, something kept repeating in her head. We apprehensively consent to it. We try not to notice the hypocritical rituals on television, not to look at the newspapers, not notice the signs adorning the streets with lies. We hide our heads in our arms and look sideways. Like the last cowards.

She asked Benedict, who had his mind elsewhere and returned from his next trip with a precise draft of an article about a small sugar factory near Lublin. She asked if he was bothered by the ritual of daily lies that everyone gives their approval for.

"Come on," he said peaceably. "There are always rituals. You are oversensitive. Sensitive, and as such, oversensitive. People don't do it, believe me. People want to live, earn, get rich. You...we are doing well, you don't feel these problems and you bother with trivialities."

She couldn't answer, though she remembered her mother. "Well, you know, she's a different case," she guessed her husband's answer. He would probably explain that they have a family tragedy behind them that changes their view of reality. Zuzanna sensed that their case, however, is not isolated and that the case exceeds family experience. However, she could not and did not want to argue with Benedict, who was smiling at her. Despite everything she didn't hold back and asked:

"And you? You devoted your time to Weber. You wanted to discover the mechanisms of social life, and now...You're fascinated by sugar factories?"

"If you only knew. I'm not a beautiful soul. Maybe I matured to that level. Our life was created there."

"Are you sure? And a guy from the Central Committee will close your sugar factory with one stroke of the pen."

"And this must be changed," Benedict said conciliatorily, embracing her.

In these new, so much better conditions, she painfully felt that she could not fulfill her life's dream, to see Tuscany. Earlier she realized that it was unreal, childish daydreaming. In this new situation, in light of Benedict's career, she almost believed it was possible. Benedict earned good money and approached her shyly submitted project with enthusiasm. They planned everything. It turned out that they would only have to borrow a little from father. Sleeping in collective rooms in youth hotels and buying bargain train tickets, they would be able to spend about ten days there. She swapped spots with Benedict, standing in queue for a few days to submit a passport application. Like all those waiting, they took turns, changing shifts every few hours, which they shared with other members of the queue, and wrote everything down in a notebook, making sure that no outsider broke into the line, breaking the spontaneous order. When, a few weeks after submitting the documents, Zuzanna got a refusal, for a moment she became a child who did not understand why they hurt her. The space around her shrunk, and she almost felt the boundaries closing around her. Benedict comforted her. He tried to intervene through, Goleń and the boss calmed them down with a smile. He told them to wait another year or two. "I think it can be sorted out later." So even the dream she had previously thought was unattainable loomed in the orbit of possibilities. All this returned to Zuzanna through a filter of sunlight lying on her body on Sunday morning, on the bed next to a happy husband to whom she could embrace.

"I'm almost twenty-six," she said, realizing at the same time that she didn't know why she was saying it.

"And I'm nine years older," Benedict said, kissing her. He probably assumed that despite everything, they had come to an understanding.

Shortly afterwards, his father invited them to dinner at the European hotel. They looked at each other in surprise. The invitation was almost festive. And they arrived at such a place for the first time. Everything looked strange. When they arrived at seven o'clock his father was already sitting stiffly, in an elegant suit with a thick knot of an old-fashioned blue tie under his neck.

"Choose something good," he encouraged. Only he did not eat. He only ordered a shot glass of cognac and coffee. Then another one. An hour passed, during which they ate, saying nothing. In the large, empty space between the words, tension grew. Zuzanna drank cognac and Benedict red wine.

"I'm going to the hospital tomorrow. I'm going in for surgery," said his father, smiling. Zuzanna felt fear.

"Couldn't you have said it earlier dad? Tomorrow I have a discussion about a script, I just got a proposal to write the script for a T.V. series...Never mind, but why are you just saying now this now dad..." Benedict got tangled up and Zuzanna looked at him furiously.

"You don't have to do anything. I've already taken care everything," said his father, looking at his son with an unreadable expression. She thought that Adam should be her husband, he should be a few decades younger and be her husband. This thought surprised her immeasurably.

"But...when do you have the surgery dad?" Benedict asked, rubbing his forehead.

"I wanted it to be tomorrow, but it turned out that they had to do some more tests at the hospital. So that I will have to wait a few days there. I've taken care of everything, you don't have to do anything."

"But what is it? What's wrong with daddy?" Zuzanna asked, probably for the first time speaking to him in this way. "What's the operation for?"

"I don't know very well." Brok laughed, puffed on his cigarette and finished his cognac. "For what?" There was irony in his voice. "I have some stomach problems. There's even a suspicion that it's cancer. In any case a tumor and they must try to remove it. That's all that we know." Benedict looked at his father dumbfounded.

"A tumor? Cancer? And dad only now..." he said in tone of a resentful child.

"Well, just don't make a scene," said Brok with a tone of impatience. "I invited you to wish me luck and to part in a good mood. I mean, to nicely say good-bye."

"Are you allowed to drink and smoke dad?" Benedict asked, as if not entirely aware of the situation.

"I don't know if you realize, but I'm a doctor. A psychiatrist, but I still remember something from general medicine. I had to remember it all the time. So just let it go" their father tried not to show annoyance. "Let's drink to my health again. I'm ordering cognac, how about you two?"

"Stupid situation," Benedict whispered in Zuzanna's ear after the lights were out. "But I'd like to ask you to take care of father the next few days. I didn't want to tell you until the case was resolved. I got a proposal to write, together with a professional screenwriter, a script for a television series a bit based on my reports. It would be a positive example, but without the discension; people who try to do their best in the conditions that they're in. The working title is *Managers*. And now I was supposed to go to the president. It was supposed to be a decisive meeting. It is up to him to start the venture. Do you think it's serious with father? Do I have to postpone tomorrow's meeting, or will you be able to manage yourself?"

"I can handle it myself. Sleep!" Zuzanna snapped, turning away from her husband. In the morning, however, Benedict changed his mind and started calling the station. "I postponed the meeting. We can go" he said.

"I told you it wasn't necessary," Father said calmly.

"But...if you want to." He was packed. There were two elegant briefcases on the hall floor.

"Father is going for a great trip..." Benedict joked awkwardly.

"Because this is a great trip. Probably the biggest," answered his father with a smile, interrupting Benedict, and added: "I'm kidding."

"Run away. Everything has been taken care of," he quickly drove them out to the hospital.

"You know, I feel foolish," Benedict said, staring at Zuzanna. They left for the hospital. The sun was shining on the street and it was spring. "I acted like...You know. It wasn't until today that it hit me that it could be serious. He is seventy years old. Yesterday...I talked...I talked like that...Not that I didn't care about this show. I care a lot. But I just can't believe that something could happen to him. He was always like a rock to me. So strong. Even physically. And now...I can't sort it out somehow."

Zuzanna realized that Benedict's father had aged a lot in the last few months. She was amazed that she had hardly noticed the metamorphosis of the man she liked so much and shared an apartment with him. She did not pay attention to the rapid transformation of a young, but confident, seemingly strong man into an elderly man. She was ashamed of her indifference and hugged Benedict.

CHAPTER 6

The date of the surgery, taken care of through connections of course, was set to be in three days. And again, through connections, outside of visiting hours, Zuzanna could stay in her father-in-law's separate ward almost without restrictions.

"You see, I take advantage of all the privileges that furiously disgust me in the land of the victorious proletariat. Typical human inconsistency," said Brok, looking at her with a strange smile. Zuzanna came to the hospital after lunch. She she took leave from the publishing house and stayed with her father-in-law until the night. In this respect, the PRL was priceless. Deadlines were arbitrary and nobody treated work too strictly.

Tests were done to Brok in the morning. During Zuzanna's stay, sometimes a doctor visited him, but it was more a social visit and a chat. Benedict came once a day, for about half an hour. Zuzanna was pleased. Her husband had a hard time getting out of the vortex of his job, and her father-in-law's stories drew her in more and more. When his son appeared, Adam Brok usually fell silent and fled into conventional conversation. Benedict did not seem to expect anything more. He was satisfied with his father's brief answers to questions about his health. He himself, with poorly hidden enthusiasm reported how his television adventure was developing, which was visibly taking on the shape of a multi-episode series. His father listened with a look on his face which Zuzanna found it hard to see anything but irony. He came to life when his son, not constrained by him, apologizing and justifying himself with television duties, disappeared.

"You are looking at my books. Yes, they accounted for a large portion of the luggage that shocked my son. Hölderlin..." he pointed to the stack of volumes on the metal table next to the bed, "he has been with me for over forty years. Although I dealt with it as a psychiatric case. It's actually a shame to talk about it. I was graduating, I even read a lot and suddenly one of my colleagues told me about Hölderlin that he was such a good poet and went insane. I knew about him before, I even read something, but then it suddenly hit me like a thunderbolt. Poetry, deep poetry, I thought at the time, is an expression of one's personality. The better the poet, the more he talks about himself. Nobody questioned the poetic greatness of Hörderlin. His poetry must be like a record of a developing mental illness that will finally overpower him. And I, a young, brilliant psychiatrist Adam Brok, will diagnose and describe the case of Hölderlin. This will be my pass to psychiatric immortality. Poetry, I thought then, is a game of associations more or less organized around a topic. I already knew the psychoanalytic method of free associations. The science of the master from Vienna fascinated me more and more. So Hölderlin was supposed to be my big psychoanalytic case. His example will allow me to capture the essence of mental illness." Brok grimaced with the smile of a caricature. "I looked at the poet with obvious superiority. I, wiser with some scientific discoveries, a step away from understanding everything I believed then, will be done…by myself and my special generation. I believed then...I wanted to believe in science. So, I thought that man could be diagnosed entirely. Be taken apart and know everything about it. And then put together again it in the revised version. Yes, I believed in science then. I had to believe in something."

Years later, Zuzanna will not remember whether this was the exact continuation of the monologue of Adam Brok, who for the first time spoke to her for so long, confided, related. Two days lying in bed and waiting for surgery, which had no chance to extend his life, as he probably knew, he stared at his son's wife for hours and told her his life story. At moments he stopped. He closed his eyes and gritted his teeth. He even turned and looked out the window. Something bothered him: suffering, shame, bad memories? It wasn't until later that Zuzanna found out how much pain he was in. Pain accompanied him for months at home, when he was sitting alone in a closed room and they didn't notice. When she learned of his condition, she wondered how he had been able to talk to her for so long these two days before the surgery. Or maybe it was the way in which he dealt with the pain and anxiety, saying goodbye to life? She remembered the cramps on his face, which she didn't pay attention to at that time, hand twitches, unexpected movements. At that time, it meant nothing to her, she didn't notice the signs, and only after all that these gestures returned to her and began to speak, after everything, when it was too late.

Or maybe what she now remembers as two days of storytelling lasted much longer? Maybe it was only later that she reconstructed and added coherency to the stories of her father-in-law from all those days that she spent at his bed before and after the surgery, in the face of impending death, deluding herself that everything could still turn around and reality will surprise us, as Adam Brok spoke about, though he didn't delude himself for a moment? Maybe only later from these ragged and unfinished stories was she able to shape the life story of a man she probably began to love then? Or maybe she felt real closeness to him later, two years after his death, when after Adam's birthday she realized that she was now connected to the dead Brok by something extremely specific, her son's blood, which is also the blood of his grandfather?

"He was my uncle, my...our guardian who saved us, brought us up, gave us everything he had...he was the reason why each of us looked for a place of our own on our own despite or precisely because he wanted to us to plant our feet so hard on the ground, and even though he was so strong…so strong that I have never met anyone in my life who could compare with him..." Brok fell unexpectedly silent. With time, he interrupted himself more and more, as if he were lost in his memories. Then, after surgery, he could fall into a long silence. Sometimes a quarter of an hour elapsed. He looked at the window and stopped seeing Zuzanna. Maybe he was fighting pain? That was when everything became clear. Surely for him as well. Sometimes, watching the clock hand, which had traveled almost half a dial, Zuzanna, unsure if she was doing the right thing, remembered her presence, and he returned to reality and sometimes even continued the story he had previously begun. But at home he could also take a break for a moment, lose himself in the past. At the time, however, these were only short moments.

My uncle, my father? He was a father to us, he wanted to be him, although I never thought of him that way. None of us thought that way. After all he adopted us, and maybe that's why he never married. His responsibility for us did not allow him to start a family. Maybe he was afraid that his own children would push us into the background, and he would not let that happen? It occurred to me later, after his death. After all, I am a psychiatrist, and then I was still...to some extent...I considered myself a psychoanalyst. After his death, suddenly so many events began to merge in my memories, seemingly forgotten under the dust of time, secondary things broke away, demanded attention and explanation...He had a guilt complex because he didn't save his brother. If we don't save those we love, guilt is natural, and the complex... Our father died when I was three years old. Then they beat him and my mother and my siblings to death...And I remember my father perfectly well, although I shouldn't, though I can't remember him so clearly...My mother in my memories appears vaguely, she is an aura of tenderness and atmosphere of my earliest childhood. With a smile, touch, the presence of a hand, home and its security, in which I believe, although from a perspective I already know how fragile it is. Sometimes I see her shiny eyes. In the background are the voices of my brothers and sisters, distant complaining of the youngest, her smiling face flashes, leads me through the garden of flowers and shows me, teaches their names, and then, behind the house, a dark forest rises. This forest will come back to me. It is night and Jakub leads me, in actuality he carries me, I walk only when he doesn't have the strength to carry me. Józef tries to help him, but he is still too weak, he is barely eight years old, but from time to time he takes me on his shoulders and with difficulty, wading in the soft soil, he carries me until he falls under my weight. I am afraid, I am terribly afraid, and I can hear my mother's scream from afar. Could I have heard this scream, or did I just imagine it? But I remember my father differently. I can see him precisely. I talk to him, although it's impossible. I can see him more clearly than my uncle. My guardian...Uncle...There was always a stranger. A large, broad-shouldered man with a short cropped black beard. After the war, he shaved it. 'Help yourself and God will help you,' he repeated, adding: 'Poles say so and they are right, but Protestants draw the conclusions.' My father comes to me from a time that happens in parallel, it is not before or after, but accompanies what is happening to me. Uncle Abram is the beginning of my conscious life. Its first chapter. The first, clearer memory associated with him is probably the earliest that has established itself forever in my consciousness. I am not yet five, it could be our home in Pinsk or Kiev. My uncle carries me in his arms, he is probably a little drunk, he used to do it from time to time, he is light-headed, but he holds me firmly, and I feel safe with him. It's already night. We walk along the wooden gallery upstairs. He probably wants to put me to sleep. But he says in a low voice, leaning into my ear, only to me: 'Your father was the greatest man I knew. And what? God looks at us from a distance. We don't know who we are to Him. Maybe pollen floating in the air? And our fate and suffering mean as much as them being moved emotionally? Alone, remember, we have to snatch up everything ourselves. Cut out your own path in this small space, where you have to fight with others for everything.' I didn't understand him at all, but I was impressed. Night, the smell of alcohol and tobacco, enveloping me with every word that I will remember many times throughout my life.

My uncle did not speak with us in Yiddish. Sometimes he dropped in some words, sometimes sentences. He did not follow Jewish traditions. Once, this was still in Warsaw, Józef asked him why they don't go to the synagogue. 'God can see us everywhere. But we will not see him in any temple. So why go there? We are Jews, we are circumcised. There is no reason to prove it,' he said, and then repeated it differently in different circumstances.

In Warsaw, the maid Marta took me to church a few times. I don't remember much of this except lofty mood and fatigue. In St. Petersburg, in secret before my uncle, the cook Nadia took me to the Orthodox Church. Uncle didn't really care. I remember the unending services, usually in the Spas-na-Krovi church, the temple of the Lord's Resurrection, although sometimes we went to an even more monumental, but not so beautiful, in any case according to my childish concept, Isaac's Dalmatyński Cathedral. I was stunned by the richness of the interior, candles, ritual and choirs that put me in an unusual, almost ecstatic state. But I didn't understand the ceremony and after some time it started to bother me, I wanted to run away. So, although I didn't protest the Sunday escapades with Nadia, I had an ambiguous attitude towards them.

In Warsaw, the household members were Polish, so we spoke mainly in Polish, also with my uncle, who switched from language to language with absolute naturalness, although everyone threw in foreign words. In St. Petersburg, we switched to Russian. In Zurich, we began to speak German over time. Together with my brothers, we sometimes began to speak French, mainly to annoy my uncle, who, however, took it calmly. He also managed in this language, although, to make us laugh, he butchered it unlike us, taught from a small age by native French women. 'Our place is accidental,' his uncle used to say. 'The home is just a fixed tent. We must be ready to move somewhere else at any time.'

I remember his quarrels with Jakub. It started in Warsaw, but this for me is still a blurry dimension of memory. We left for St. Petersburg when I was seven years old. From there we moved to Zurich after four years, a few months before the war. Uncle knew what would happen, and that is why he chose Switzerland. I don't know if he was more concerned about finding a safe haven for us or a convenient place to do business in a Europe in flames. Probably the second one. How did he know that war would not swallow Switzerland? How could he be sure it would break out? How did he even know so much? Jakub stayed in St. Petersburg, which they renamed to Petrograd. He studied history and was deeply involved in revolutionary organizations. Uncle did not interfere. He always gave us a lot of freedom. A lot. Maybe he wanted to teach us independence in this way, or maybe he could not otherwise, through constant journeys, when governesses, teachers and tutors took care of us? 'Does uncle know how much others have to pay for his money?! Is there no remorse?!' Jacob almost shouted a few days before our trip to Zurich.

It was right after dinner. We were all there. The three of us and my uncle. Everything seemed so idyllic, calm, we drank tea from a silver samovar and ate a cake from a matching decorative platter and the sun's rays arranged patterns on the white tablecloth. However, a few words were enough, and the mood collapsed. Jakub jumped from the chair and ran next to the table. Uncle did not move. He leaned back in his chair and lit a cigarette, following with his gaze the excited Jacob. His voice, the same as usual, strong, slightly hoarse, could be heard more clearly than shouting my brother: 'And do you know how much you're fooling yourself? Are you fighting for the good for others or for power for yourself? You believe that power for you is happiness for others. Like so many before you and so many after you. Only it never is. I listened to your agitators, I even looked at your books. Little about what this world will look like once you gain power. A lot about how you will destroy the one that is in power. It's nice to destroy. And then?'.

'Maybe those like you uncle need to be destroyed!' Jacob exclaimed.

Józef tried to calm him down, but the eldest was like in a trance. He shouted about the ruthlessness of his uncle, who breaks people, strips them of their dignity and pushes them away, because only money is important to him. For the first time and one of several times in my life I felt sorry for my uncle. I had the impression that Jacob's words touched him, although he showed nothing. Maybe I noticed something in his eyes?

He replied in the same tone as before: 'It's true. I am ruthless. Just like everyone. But I will never hurt you or your brothers. I don't like to hurt anyone at all. I have to fight. Like everybody. And in fights there are winners and losers. Do you think it's my fault that I win? How did your Englishman write in the learned book? Fight for existence? I didn't set up the world like that. You only want to destroy. You have beautiful excuses. But I know what is left of justifications. In general, I know what is left of beautiful words. I know they don't matter, but us. You, your brothers. For great words you want to destroy. Maybe you'd better stay here. I will not renounce you. But now it is better that we distance ourselves from each other for a while. Because we can reconcile. For me, you and your revolutionary companions are one of the species in the menagerie. God created you. I can even do business with you. But, you're just too predatory'.

Brok again stared into the past.

'As far as I know, they met only two more times. I was there the first time. Two years later, in Zurich. Jakub came to visit us. We were very happy. We had an extreme bond with each other. Only here, as before, our meeting ended in a row. It was worse than in St. Petersburg. We sat in the living room, from which we could see a lake through a large window, on which a sailing ship was moving along. It was so peaceful in middle-class Zurich, in the middle of Europe, which was dripping with blood.

'It's unbelievable,' repeated Jakub, 'you can believe there's no war.' He was calmer, but what he was saying was even crueler. He said that he could also afford ruthlessness, and if for the sake of the revolution it would be necessary to break family ties and trample on loved ones, he would. The party, since he joined it, is his family. Uncle clenched his jaw, but he spoke calmly. He said that in that case Jakub should not show up until he changes his mind. He added that it's only thanks to him he isn't in prison now, and his leaving the country is also owed only to him. Jacob started shouting that no one asked uncle for help, but he did not listen. He left, then returned and put a large stack of money on the table.

'This is for your trip back, and for your stay in Zurich until you find a train. As long as you feel that way, I don't want you living in my home' he said and left the living room. There was much more money than Jakub needed.

'I'll give him back everything,' he shouted after uncle left. He began to calm him down. We were torn apart. Jacob was almost a part of us. Next to him uncle Abram appeared like a stranger. Anyway, Jacob's ideals fascinated me, and I know that Józef was intrigued by them, although he did not follow them. The oldest, however, exaggerated.

'You shouldn't say that' said Józef.

'But it's true' Replied Jacob. For the first time I thought I couldn't accept such ideas. I was thirteen. For a long time I was tired of this contradiction between feelings and the hard consequence of thinking that one cannot divide people into close and distant. Finally, we convinced Jakub to take the money. 'They'll come in handy for the revolution,' he muttered mockingly, packing them into his jacket pocket.

In the evening, uncle sat in silence by the window and watched the coming night. I sat next to him. 'He doesn't even understand how much they need people like me,' he said more to himself. 'People can be helped. Sometimes. Single people. But when they gather in groups that are marching under some signs, it is too late. Then you can only do business with them.'

I quote you conversations and statements, although it is unlikely that I would remember them so well. And maybe I change them a bit, but I still remember. That past keeps returning. Now, when I'm in the hospital, I have the impression that it is getting more intense and I am also telling you about it in order to sort it out, to name it. I hope you'll forgive me," Brok said with a painful smile. "You will forgive me for treating you like a kid, but only a child instrumentally. Because I'm just telling you about it. I didn't even tell Baruch. Not everything, anyway. Maybe I feel more uncomfortable with him? You know, the time before the war appears to me much more accurately than later. The period after the war is hardly separated into months or even years by a series of murky, repetitive events from which I can barely catch something that I clearly remember. It's also certainly this lousy system that grinds people and deprives them of their memory. It wants to deprive us of everything, nationalize our privacy. And those years before the war formed me. These are stones on the path of my life.

Uncle probably never became someone really close to us. And although I loved him, although we probably all loved him, we felt admiration and gratitude to him, he always remained us of this dark man, returning after months, carrying foreign smells with him and the memory of dark adventures he never talked about. His loud laughter, which exploded quite often, was not cheerful, and he never really laughed.

Other experiences were also part of our lives. I remember Ksenia, a tall, beautiful woman who looked after me when I arrived in St. Petersburg. She lived with us longer than all the others, which, except for the servants, were exchanged quite often. She sang beautifully, often only for me, and she was my first childhood love. Probably not just me. I remember Jacob's eyes following her, although for me he was already grown up. At night I was awakened by the sob of Ksenia. It was heartbreaking. I ran to the room where it was coming from and wanted to enter. I was banging on a closed door. She didn't answer for a long time. The sobbing continued. Finally, calming down a bit, she asked me to go away. She didn't answer my questions. I succumbed. I couldn't sleep for a long time, hearing her muffled crying. I never saw her again.

'She left' my uncle said, brushing off my questions, adding that she would not be coming back and said to me goodbye. I saw the hateful way Jakub looked at him at that time.

Often, we didn't like his company. Strange characters, people with animalistic faces, screams, and quarrels that sometimes came from outside the closed door. He tried to isolate us from the excesses in which his life abounded. Drunkenness, and sometimes more than drunkenness, coming home from time to time, especially when he returned after long trips to the Balkans, and although he greeted us cheerfully, he carried a bad aura with him. 'I'm coming back from war' he answered our questions with a distorted smile. The servants tried to sneak past exceptionally noiselessly. Sometimes in the kitchen I heard the soft murmur of their voices. However, their drinking bouts were taking place in a separate part of the house, and the servants made sure that they did not get into the rooms we were in. It has not always successful. Once, several men who were fighting burst into the salon. I saw my uncle jump in between them, knocking two down and brandishing a revolver, calming the rest. They were afraid of him. Several times I heard the crack of shots. One or two squealing and shouting naked women being chased by undressed men ran out into the corridor. Even now I don't know if they were really terrified or just provoking the pursuers. I was nine at the time, so I was looking with fear and excitement. It was short-lived because my uncle chased in after them in the company of a servant, shouting: 'Go back or else I'll beat you!' And the company politely returned behind the closed door. I remember him standing at the top of the stairs, in only his pants, barefoot, with suspenders hanging to the ground and a torso that resembled a large barrel. He didn't look funny though. He was like the irregular figure of an idol or demon in the middle of a settlement that is supposed to frighten enemies. Once in the kitchen I heard strange moans and wheezing. I looked in. Facing me on the kitchen table was Sonia, a young kitchen assistant stretched out on her stomach, who appeared at our home not long ago. Leaning over her, with teeth clenched and a wrinkled face, my uncle moved violently. He pressed Sonia's face against the wooden table. Her strange grimace, which could mean both pleasure and pain, I later dreamt of it often. Uncle shouted that I should leave, he shouted a few times before I listened. I didn't see Sonia again.

Still others visited us in St. Petersburg. Elegant men with carefully trimmed beards arrived. I remember my uncle escorting one of them out. He walked next to him, a little above him, and in his eyes shined something resembling triumph. That one wasn't looking at him. He only turned to nod his head goodbye. His cool face was indifferent. Uncle bowed deeply, almost mockingly. One Sunday a beautiful lady came to him in a fancy carriage. They drank tea in the living room with the woman accompanying her. From under the brim of a green hat she smiled at uncle, who smiled back. He was more indifferent than usual, although his mouth twisted in irony from time to time, the sense of which I did not understand until sometime later. Officers, whose decorative uniforms made a great impression on me, visited him a few times. Gloomy figures with animalistic faces did not enter from the front door. They appeared from out of nowhere, like women who were brought in at night. But a few times strange people knocked on the main door: sloppily dressed, wrinkled and tired, and the butler led them to the living room, where with vodka they conferred for a long time with my uncle.

Sometimes uncle theorized, summarized events and human behavior. I was irritated by his blatant cynicism, but he also excited me. Jacob argued with him, Józef protested. I was too young. I could only remain silent. But he wanted to teach us, reveal the world, strike at our imagination.

When he returned to St. Petersburg, he showed us the city and talked about it. We used to ride a carriage along the Neva. A colorful detachment of mounted soldiers paraded in the square. Along the cloisters, in the light of the sun, women in long, bright dresses walked under white umbrellas, holding men's arms who are dressed in frock coats and high hats. 'You see? This beautiful world is ending. This beautiful, wormy world. I know it. You are a Jew like me, so you shouldn't worry about that. This is not your world. You will remain a Jew, even if you convert and renounce your ancestors. You will be one because others will always see one in you. They will want to humiliate you. And all you can do is control them, make them afraid of you.'

Once he returned from the Balkans in an extremely bad mood. Everything was as if normal. We talked and ate dinner. Only the servants were tiptoeing. Uncle sometimes told, as before, some irrelevant stories, something about the customs and cuisine in Bulgaria and Serbia. He had a few shot glasses of vodka. Which happened sometimes. This time, however, he did not put down the bottle. He kept drinking. My brothers went away to their affairs. Something was still holding me. It was getting darker. I wanted to turn up the lamp to make it shine brighter, but he stopped me. We sat in the twilight. He began to speak. Something like this:

'There are no selfless people. Or almost none. Your father was one. But he was saint. That's probably why they killed him. To do something, people must have an interest in it. Something must push them to make an effort. They want power, respect, women, feelings. They want to have something. Something of their own. Their own love, own children, own people, own things. And that's how it will be. Stupid people say you can't buy it. But you need to know how. You need to know how to move in between them and understand that these great ideas are a mask they put on to shield their true faces. Not to scare themselves when they look at a mirror.'

I didn't understand again, but the image, which was triggered his fantasies, stayed with me. As I walked to my room, I heard the whisper of figures who leaned in toward each other. Valet Warłam said that Fyodor would be gone. He looked around but didn't notice me in the corner of the shadowy corridor and ran his finger across his throat.

'The master got him, because he reportedly betrayed him,' he whispered so softly that I barely understood him. I remembered Fyodor, uncle's associate, who would come to us from time to time. The young, cheerful man felt almost at home in ours. He had something engagingly insolent in himself.

In Zurich, our company changed. Gray-clad men in bowlers came to us; sometimes, however, people came from another world, eccentrics, of whom I remember one long-haired man with a blue bow under his neck.

A short, bald man in a frock coat with a sparse beard also came to uncle. He is also someone I remember, whom I remember until today and I think I know who he was. Someone who left the biggest impression on the twentieth century. They shut themselves in for a long time. Outside the door came the angry tirades of the guest and of uncle's short, but definite answers. Soon after, two young men, vigilantly looking around with rapid movements and knocked on our door. The conversation did not last long, yet it was full of pauses and moments of silence. Both the host as well as the guests spoke firmly and briefly.

Several times a guest visited us, who we could not forget. He was tall as my uncle, but twice as stout, with a large bulbous head and a bulldog's face on which a Spanish beard grew. A large belly blew up under his jacket. He was always sumptuously dressed. I remember his navy-blue suit and colorful, velvet vest, always with a snow-white shirt, corset and cuffs, on which even I could see big diamond cufflinks. His watery eyes moved indifferently, but when I looked closer, I thought that nothing could escape his attention. They patted each other on their backs, laughing boldly, but I had the impression that in their every movement there was a concentration even greater than the everyday attentiveness of my uncle, which also did not leave him when he was drunk.

His lifestyle in Zurich changed a bit, where he became calmer. Although strange people and women appeared at night, but everything was quieter and calmer. Maybe the doors were closed more tightly? Every now and then, as always, women who were not servants lived with him. Usually a few weeks, but sometimes even longer. The green-eyed blonde Gerta lived with him the longest. She was cheerful and excited. She was all over the place. And like all the others she disappeared one day.

When Józef told him that he was going to study philosophy, uncle grimaced slightly.

'If you want," he said. 'Maybe it'll help you understand that life is what's most important. And life is made by me. I hope you will finally help me. You'll start working with me...What kind of subject is this philosophy?' He later asked rhetorically. 'Every philosopher starts from the beginning. Is there any progress from Socrates?'

'Exactly,' Józef grunted. 'There's something to think about.'

Uncle laughed out loud. 'We won't invent anything. We're able to make objects, we make our lives easier, only to finally notice that were complicating it. Well, we make it a little more comfortable and sometimes more pleasant. And that's all. We're not to be understood. We can try to survive somehow, but this cannot be understood.'

'Maybe that was the smartest thing he said?' wondered Adam Brok.

"He accepted my studies better, although without enthusiasm. 'At least it's something concrete,' he muttered. 'You will help people and yourself, that's always something.' Earlier he tried to convince me to participate in his business. This was back in Warsaw. We moved there after the war. I did my final high-school exams here. Uncle bought a villa in Żoliborz. He lived a more peaceful life than in Zurich. Maybe he was getting older? He was approaching fifty, although he still seemed the same as he was when he carried me in his arms, telling me about my father's death and about God. He shaved his beard, there was no sign of gray in his still black hair, and despite his powerful stature, he still carried himself softly like a cat. In the villa, my uncle gave me two separate rooms, so I didn't come into contact with him often and as usual, I didn't know much about his life. He still had various guests: during the day and night. For some time, a delicate girl, Weronka, who was not much older than myself, lived with him. She disappeared not long after my graduation.

Józef stayed in Zurich to finish his studies. Then he did a PhD and got a university position. Uncle continued to help him financially, even later, when Józef decided to transfer to a university to Marburg, to his mentor, with whom he was corresponding. Still in Zurich, uncle urged him to start work together with them. He promised to make him a partner, just like me, when I grew up and decided to work with him. He promised, though they were not precise commitments.

'You don't even know how much you can gain with me. How much can we gain,' he said strangely, half ironically, as if laughing at himself. Józef kept saying that he was not fit for it. Uncle's commented that only when we take up the challenge, are we able to prove ourselves, he proposed that he had already taken up his challenge, and that in the future...He lowered his voice, as if he wanted to deceive uncle a little, who, as never before, looked discouraged.

Józef passionately read Nietzsche at the time. Once, my uncle picked up the book that was on my brother's table. I think that's what Zarathustra says. 'Papers,' he said. 'They told me about this Nietzsche. If that's true, then you should burn those books and join me. With me you can test your...will of power.'

My uncle wanted me to join him in his ventures. On the second day after graduation, we went to dinner at the Bristol Hotel. 'I have a lot of interests in different places,' he said. 'I could leave you one. At first you would work with me. Then I would give you independence. There you will see what people are like. Not what they say, but what they do and how they do it, and therefore who they are. These will be your best universities. And when it comes to my interests, you really don't know much about them. This is certainly not a repetitive, boring job. I didn't bring you in because you were too young, and then...I think there is no point in entrusting secrets to those who do not want them.' He said it in such a vague way, giving me a typical, heavy look that would be softened by his smile. Except that the smile was not happy either. I was not convinced, though for a moment I felt stupid. Suddenly I saw my uncle like I've never seen him before. A tired man under fifty who expects his loved ones to help him. But he raised me. So, I answered firmly that I had already decided. I want to understand the man, and I didn't suppose I would be given such an understanding by my current interests by which, of course, I could learn the mechanisms of this particular game. 'Maybe when I finish my studies, we'll come back to this conversation,' I added in a conciliatory tone. Like a brother.

He looked at me and smiled cheerlessly again. "Well then, to your health and for your success," he said, striking a toast with shot glasses with me.

I was supposed to tell you about my adventure with Hölderlin, and I am talking about my uncle, but it is not just a distraction. I would have to start every serious story about myself with my uncle. He formed us. It was in relation to him, or rather in opposition to him, that each of us chose our own path. Maybe only our distant father weighed on us more. Just like on uncle. When they killed our father, his brother decided that God had abandoned us. And my story with Hölderlin is, contrary to appearances, a chunk of very personal experiences.

In '28 I went to Vienna. Maybe, like Józef, I was looking for a mentor, because I went to Dr. Freud, with whom I had exchanged several letters. In Vienna, I was to conduct Hölderlin's psychoanalysis, which wasn't working out for me in Warsaw. One of Freud's closest assistants offered me a visit to the psychoanalytic society. The mentor himself probably did not want to make personal commitments. I was already a qualified doctor, a psychiatrist, I worked at the Medical Academy and became more and more fascinated with psychoanalysis. At last, this was supposed to be the key that opened the casket with the inscription: human enigma. I was to explore the mystery of Hölderlin's disease.

At the same time, uncle decided to return to Switzerland. He mentioned this to me before. He was more impatient, almost unsure if I could think of Uncle Abram that way. When I decided to leave, he said it was a good idea. He made it clear that he stayed in Warsaw only because of me. This was also not typical for him. He said he did not know if it was final, just like he didn't know what would be final in his life, but he supposes that he would stay in Zurich for longer, though he hopes not forever. It will be better this way for his interests, he concluded. He bought a house in Zurich, in which I only visited him once. A beautiful house overlooking a lake, just like the previous one. Then I went to the cabaret with my uncle. I remember it very clearly, but strangely, like a nightmare. Jazz orchestra, burlesque dance group and clown master of ceremonies who led the performances. He danced with the band, told jokes, pulled an older guy dressed as a rooster on the stage, whom he introduced as a professor of history. He smashed eggs on his head that ran down a painted face expressing fear and suffering. Everything was steeped in greenish light against the backdrop of sharply collapsing expressionist decorations. It was deathly and frightening. The clown was calling out about a dumpster of culture. We watched it first drinking champagne, then vodka. At times the lights brought out uncle's face. It was grim.

Uncle wanted us, Józef and me, to meet him in Zurich, but it was impossible to find dates that would suit all three of us. I guess neither Józef nor I tried especially hard. I met my brother in '30 in Freiburg, where he moved after his hero. I actually got there because of Hölderlin. I was near Zurich. We could've visited our uncle. We didn't think about it. My brother told me about the visit of our eldest brother, Jakub, who escaped from the Soviet Union. Our brother, a communist...a former communist, was afraid for uncle. He was supposed to be in a terrible mental state. So Józef thought that these fears were part of Jakub's psychosis. He probably didn't use these words, but he did describe the symptoms of neurosis and anxiety. I couldn't believe it, Jacob...And as for uncle...As for him, Jakub warned him a year earlier, shortly after his escape. Uncle downplayed it. He was confident in himself, which was what Jakub said. As always. And as it turned out, he was right. Nothing happened to him that year. Nothing happened, so we forgot about Jakub's alarms." Adam Brok looked at Zuzanna and smiled uncertainly. Then he looked at the book on the table.

"I started reading Hölderlin in Poland. And gradually I gave in to him. At the beginning I was defying myself: one shouldn't melt over the patient's beauty or artistry. The underlying neurosis should be exposed. But it wasn't working out for me. I remember that at first, I was struck by the theme of ether, this non-existent element that played such a role in his poetry. I thought it was the key. In Hölderlin's time science was not yet able to answer the basic questions, and the rapacious mind of the poet tried to be ahead of his age. He wanted to solve puzzles that he could not yet answer. But was this how insanity was supposed to be born? It took me a long time to understand that there must exist a world that we do not weigh or measure, and ether is it, the divine element that connects things. I caught on to metaphors and sentences that will become famous. 'That, which survives, builds poets,' I read as a symptom of morbid megalomania, which over time must explode with a confusion of the senses. I haven't yet thought about my megalomania, which fantasized with possessing the key to understanding human secrets.

What's there to say: I wanted to decipher, therefore understand Hölderlin, to identify his madness. But the more I understood him, the more I lost my psychoanalytic distance to him and he subdued me. Originally, I imagined that the growing vagueness of his poetry was a testament to a growing insanity. However, the deeper I went into it to track down the underlying disease, the more I understood what the poet was saying to me, not a madman. He compromised my simple and ill-considered formulas in which I wanted to capture the world. Or in other words: I could understand Hölderlin only by rejecting the coarse tools with which I wanted to do his dissection, and giving up on them, I lost confidence, and my knowledge of the man turned out to be too conventional to perform treatments on his psyche. I swayed on the edge of the abyss, which the author Hyperion opened to me. I ran away and came back to hit. Hölderlin reached out to me, enchanted me and over time this poetry which speaks through him somehow began to make itself heard in me. I do not want to compare myself..." Adam Brok laughed aloud "I'm nothing of a poet. But Hölderlin helped me understand something. However, many years had to pass. I dealt with him in several stages. And now probably the last stage has come." Adam Brok looked at Zuzanna and fell silent. He nodded, wincing slightly. Then he said thoughtfully. "Sometimes I fear, that he's pulling me in, he wants to infect me with his insanity. I think every real psychiatrist must be afraid of mental illness. At least once. Anyway, I came to Vienna with a ready project to diagnose Hörderlin. My first attempts, my first reading of him failed. I explained it to myself through shortcomings in my psychoanalytical science. This defeat encouraged me even more to take on the Viennese escapade. In the very source of psychoanalysis, I finally acquired a certain amount of knowledge. Equipped with it, I will finally unveil the curtain of Hölderlin's case. Vienna..." Adam Brok fell back into his memories for a moment.

"Vienna seemed to me like Baghdad after the fall of the caliphate. Muffled, colorful and somehow meaningless. A big head that refuses to recognize the death of its dismembered body and lives on a borrowed life. My new comrade psychoanalysts became interested in the proposal to diagnose Hölderlin. 'Look at his childhood' they ordained like a doctor in the *Good Soldier of Švejk*, who prescribes castor oil for everything. I looked. And slowly I started to put together some weird charade.

The poet's father died of apoplexy when he was two years old. Hölderlin did not know him. He did not know him. He didn't know him consciously, suggested my psychoanalytical subconscious. Subconsciously, he could harbor guilt for his death. Especially if we consider his deep, intimate relationship with his mother, a relationship for which the father might seem an obstacle. Hölderlin's poetry arises out of a guilt complex that the delicate poet could not bear. His meeting with Apollo Christ before his last return home...he spoke of it from time to time in flashes of insanity...a meeting he had experienced in his imagination in the weeks before his return to Nürtingen, of which we know nothing, was a meeting with his imaginary father. And it was this imaginary meeting that forever destroyed the poet's unstable mental balance. There was no rescue for him, no psychoanalysis. I won't say" Adam

Brok laughed "my interpretations even aroused interest in the psychoanalytical headquarters. But they didn't satisfy me. Some elementary reflex of honesty stood up in me. I left Hölderlin alone.

I came back to him over two years later. Already with doubts as to psychoanalytical knowledge and its administrators, the lodge that was to rule the world, and whose members quietly but fiercely fought for influence and significance around their founding father. At the beginning I was promoted relatively quickly in this environment. I have passionately engaged in discovering the complexes and tracking the neuroses that make up our civilization. The prophet himself recognized me. I underwent psychoanalysis at the place of one of those who wore a gold ring with a precious two-tone stone offered to them by the prophet. It was a sign of belonging to a secret brotherhood that guarded the purity of doctrine. Under the patronage of Freud, it was founded by a Viennese evangelist, Ernest Jones. Adler and Jung's great apostasies, not to mention the lesser ones, made us watch over orthodoxy. I was close to the committee itself, in a circle that could directly lead to it. Only that the committee was already splitting at the seams. Psychoanalysis could not be mastered: it spread around the world in various branches, plunging into America. People did not want guilt and shame, renunciation and restrictions, they wanted to take advantage of the world that they thought they had finally mastered. They were eager to use themselves as they used their own items. And Freud was showing the way. Diagnosing civilization, he perfectly diagnosed himself. Subconsciously, he hated his father, the Jewish God, authority and guardian of restrictions. Although only his successors drew conclusions from his doctrine, he broke the seal and opened the gate. He was still in the bourgeois world, he still used the language of morality, although he stripped its foundations, although he replaced ethics with the medical technique of psychoanalysis. He didn't know that the method of mastering dark powers was magic. Freud believed that he was bringing enlightenment, and therefore, as he wrote to Ferenczi, psychoanalysts should rule the world to heal humanity. Only even psychoanalysis slipped out of his hands.

I did not understand all this at the time, although my doubts began to arise. My fascination with dreams, which we reported passionately and analyzed in the right ways, because a heretic like Jung, for example, would interpret them differently, and with time I began to suspect that he would have other dreams. So this fascination, which enveloped me completely, after some time aroused my suspicion that instead of discovering the world, we close ourselves from it, childishly and narcissistically isolating ourselves in an environmental greenhouse. This constant rummaging in one's navel, exaltation with pseudodiscoveries, this naive and perverse game in the circle of those close to us, ones who focus on their own psyche and its relations with the psyche of others. No, it wasn't innocent fun, just as there are no innocent experiments on oneself, when, like a sorcerer's apprentice, instead of mastering the demons slumbering in us, we release them and fall prey to them.

Neurosis and mental illnesses were spreading in my environment in Vienna. Was it because these games attracted mentally disturbed people or violated fragile, culture-built stability? Probably both. Suicides were an epidemic. Yes, it can be assumed that the instinct of death was revealed, finally discovered by the prophet...

Regardless of him, we could see how death arises from libido. Before she committed suicide, my...what to call her…love? Her name was Stella Meyer. Earlier, three close friends committed suicide. But it was just beginning. Kurt and Helga poisoned themselves. The illness of the chosen ones, those who were to heal the world, was just beginning to unfold. Doubts were just beginning to gnaw at my faith. So, I came up with the idea to go to Nürtingen, a place where Hölderlin had gone to already insane, and where on a bridge, by chance, his mother and sister met him, staring unconsciously at the current of the Neckar. From Nürtingen to Friborg, where my brother lived then, was close, so I could justify additional visits to my brother. Although Zurich was just as close from there, I didn't think about visiting my uncle.

We were driving Otto's car. Baron Otto von Holstein...Patron of artists, donor to the psychoanalytic society, one of the more colorful and scandalous figures of contemporary Vienna. My friend. My friend...could I think like that back then? Anyway, did we treat a category such as friendship seriously then? Stella Meyer was with us. Or maybe we were with her? Two years later she'll commit suicide. Then... who could have thought? A beautiful woman who ruled the world. Although...we felt that we were sailing the rough seas of id. And it was precisely us that were to master this element. Where id was, ego was to follow. But when we were going to Nürtingen, although we didn't admit it, it wasn't so good between us. Maybe this was the real reason for this escapade? Maybe I wanted to restore this extraordinary harmony that we felt at the beginning, although the word "harmony" probably isn't right, return to those few months, or maybe it wasn't months, maybe it was only weeks or less, when we found the fullness...only this word doesn't seem to fit...ecstasy? When Stella, Otto, I finally and others who appeared and disappeared, we were a complementary community of feelings and thoughts, and our days and nights changed into a series of elation...When we freed ourselves from the disease of possession, as Stella used to say, we crossed divisions dividing the world into mine and not mine, we got rid of the insatiable desire to gather and envy that comes from being unable to satisfy it. When even the objects of love could be shared with others and it only awoke another thrill of excitement in us. 'What is jealousy?' Stella asked rhetorically. And she answered: 'It's an extreme sense of ownership. We have to get rid of it and find pleasure in sharing. Then we will master the element of sex and transform it into art.' She repeated this so many times that I had to remember it.

So, we tried. In luxury apartments, paid for by Baron von Holstein, it was easier to free ourselves from the sense of ownership, and yet to achieve this state, we had to support ourselves with cocaine, mescaline, opium, and I don't remember what else, not to mention trivial alcohol. And maybe already then began the unnamed betrayals, despairs of rejection, for which there was no place in our dictionary, ambitious failures and depressions.

When we were going to Nürtingen, it was only three of us and it seemed that everything could be as it was before. The last night before our arrival, at a roadside inn, after dinner sprinkled with good wine, it was intoxicating. Although when we woke up...

But when I stood on the stone bridge on which the author of *Bread and Wine* stood, and looked at the river swirling under spans after the last downpour, I tried to guess what he saw, looking at the river in May, I knew then that there was no return or that there's nothing to come back to. I began to wonder what disease he had. Then suddenly I understood how arbitrarily the names we create are treated as formulas that allow us to capture and heal the world: schizophrenia, paranoia, such or any psychosis. Medicine and psychiatry aspire to the role of science, so we, its disposers, disregarding the bundle of symptoms with which we try to build finite quality, dazzle the profane, forgetting how defective this category is. And...we somehow help. Somehow...Is this not the status of science in general, squeezing itself into my mind, when we add theory to effects in order to free ourselves from uncertainty and find ourselves in the role of masters of creation?

The next day we arrived in Friborg, to my brother. It's weird that we've so rarely seen each other. We were so connected with each other and we were so happy to see each other again, especially in this first moment, and yet we found each other so rarely. Fate? At Józef's were two of his friends. The painter Franz Braun moved with difficulty, he not only had an artificial leg, but some hip injuries from a grenade explosion, which also deprived him of one eye. My friends saw his paintings and were impressed. I was to see them later. They also remained in my memories. Animal eyes sparkling in the jungle of colors. Fighting beasts lit by internal light. Expressionist metaphysics. Maybe I remembered them also because of their author and my conversations with him? I have even heard of the poet Gottfried Janzu. The appearance of these celebrities at my brother's aroused the unprecedented but evident recognition of my friends who were used to socializing with artistic grandeur. Earlier, we agreed to meet with Martin Heidegger himself, Józef's mentor. Braun and Janz came to meet him. They were more fortunate than us. They met Heidegger the previous day and stayed longer to get to know us. Heidegger canceled the meeting with us.

Almost at the beginning, Józef stated that a month earlier he had been visited by Jakub. We apologized to those present and left the house. 'He was in a poor condition. He refused to meet with them. He did not agree on setting dates and places,' said Józef, looking at me awaiting clarification. Only I couldn't explain anything. Jakub had visited Friborg a month earlier, but the shock it caused Józef was still visible. He had trouble naming and understanding his brother's behavior. He explained that Jakub's state required that his symptoms be treated seriously had his seriously treated his fears, which could very well be considered the beginnings of madness. Józef was terrified. 'I was terrified,' he repeated, as if infected from Jakub. 'After all he had always been strong before, and only uncle was able to upset him.' A month earlier, Józef's older brother behaved like a trapped man, resigned and burned out at the same time. 'As if he had survived his own death,' said Józef, and this I remembered. Jakub's behavior was all the stranger because he had fled from the Soviets the year before. His fears were arranging themselves into a paranoid nightmare. Europe was to be gradually wrapped in a communist spy network. Its agents were everywhere. They hunted him. Józef proposed to meet uncles in Zurich, but Jakub considered it an almost suicidal act. He was afraid of our guardian most. He claimed that uncle got into some shady business with the Bolsheviks, embezzling large sums of money from them, and when they figure it out, and in his opinion, it could happen at any moment, they would not forgive him. Therefore, soon after his escape, Jakub arrived in Zurich. He circled uncle's house, he obtained his address when he was still with the Soviets, he waited on him, and finally, when he was sure that nobody was following them, he accosted him in some locale. They talked for a long time, but uncle refused to escape and change his identity, which Jacob suggested. 'He hasn't changed,' said our brother with a kind of acknowledgement. He was still sure of himself. He explained to his nephew that he had prepared for this circumstance and that he had them in his hands. 'Only that you cannot have them in your hands' emphasized Jakub with a grimace, which could mean both irony and amazement of the guardian's naivety. As always, uncle offered him money. 'I didn't need it, I had the funds, I stole them. Looted goods, that's the revolutionary principle' said Jakub, choking in a strange chuckle, what Józef told me. He had never heard such bleak laughter. Jakub claimed that he was not afraid for himself. 'Almost' he added. He was afraid that they would catch him, and all that would precede death. 'You can't imagine what they are capable of, what I was capable of,' he kept telling Józef.

He said he had escaped from hell, where he found himself of his own wishes, from the hell, which he was creating. He showed the cyanide vial he carried with him all the time. He emphasized that he was not afraid of death, he came to terms with it when he realized that he deserved it a thousand times. He didn't really know what he was living for, maybe not to give satisfaction to 'the devil's servants.' 'He said so,' repeated shocked Józef. He wanted to write to me many times, but his commitment to his brother stopped him. Jakub was afraid that someone would intercept the letter. He explained to Józef that he doesn't realize the influence the communists had and the way they worked. Despite his commitment, Józef would have written, were it not for the knowledge that he would be able to tell me everything directly. Jakub told us about the deceptive pacification in the Soviets, which precedes, even more terrible convulsions. A calming, which is treated as a return to normality, although it arises from the suffering of hundreds of thousands locked in camps and building communist pyramids, from the tens of thousands killed and tortured, through hunger, fear and the enslavement of millions.

I couldn't recover either..." Brok sorted his memories, staring out the window. "Everything seemed unreal. We sat on a bench under the trees falling asleep in the early autumn twilight, it was getting quieter and calmer, and I listened to the recollections of my brother being pursued by oppressors and memories of my brother, who was building hell. While telling me all of this, Józef also looked as if he did not believe in his near memories. Small houses around. A sleepy town, Friborg was an oasis of harmony.

We ate dinner at a nearby gasthaus in a group of five. We drank local white wine. More and more wine. Janz turned out to be the soul of the party. The painter Braun spoke little, but aggression smoldered within him. He laughed noisily and made some unambiguous allusions to Stella, who with aristocratic distinction did not notice it. Józef calmed me with his gaze.

'Do you only paint animals?' Stella asked at the beginning.

'Unworthy human beings do not arouse my feelings,' Braun said with contemptuous expression.

I was drowning in Józef's story, I tried to imagine my eldest brother, whom I had not seen for fifteen years, and with difficulty I was finding myself in the gasthaus, in its noise and dim light, and participation in the conversation seemed unlikely. At some point, however, I began to listen. What they said became important and related to Jakub's story.

'An iron cage,' said the poet. 'An iron cage,' he repeated. 'This Weber had a gift of metaphors. Iron cage of rationality. We must finally break free from it, otherwise we will only vegetate. Not even the last people anymore. Less and less like people.' Janz spoke more and more excitingly, drinking more glasses of wine in one gulp. 'Why are you attached to this humanist fetish?' Braun interrupted. The alcohol was already affecting him. Although he spoke gibberish, which was the result of the same injury that he lost his eye, and the alcohol distorted his words even more, he accentuated them so hard that he could not be understood without difficulty. 'Fortunately, we're also animals. Animalness carries with itself sublimity. People are spoiled animals!' he chanted, hitting the glass on the table.

'Franz is a painter,' Janz laughed. 'He is allowed more. But I think that our mistake is much earlier, even earlier than it seems to Józef's mentor. Not from the times of Plato and the Sophists, but earlier. This does not mean, however, that I want to reject everything that man created: culture, even if a decadent worm developed in it, which in time will bite through it and poison it, so that the only thing left will be to throw it away. These are our sensitive, humane exaltations. And yet culture arises from suffering and misery that we do not want to recognize. How much did Michelangelo's frescoes in the Sistine Chapel have to cost, how much were the sculptures on the tomb of Julius the Second? How many people starved to death so that we could enjoy them?'"

Brok paused and stared out the window.

"I remember him perfectly, his bloated, but somehow inspired face and words that now come back to me. About which I thought often, especially during the war, I even dreamed of them.

'Franz is right when he speaks of the sublimity that lies in life, in animals and in this vital, animalistic element in man. We purposefully hurt ourselves, breaking away from nature, the only source of our strength. And we, our civilization...We are becoming machines, an addition to its mechanism... '

Stella and Otto looked at him fascinated, Józef nodded, and the tipsy Braun agreed with the tact of his words.

'We need a form that will free us from nihilism, from reification. A form of culture and a social form' Janz recited his monologue like a poem. I remembered the drops of sweat on his face. Then he began reciting his poems. Very beautiful poems. I remember that one was about the night that penetrates us, dilutes us until we lose ourselves in it.

'Your Freud speaks of culture as a source of suffering. Is psychoanalysis supposed to help man free himself from it' He turned to me.

'It's supposed to help him bear them,' I replied.

'Jewish talk!' he grunted. He checked himself immediately. He looked at Józef, at me. 'I'm sorry,' he said endearingly. 'It's just a saying. My point was that we should overcome suffering, not increase our weakness. We must free the will of power within us.'

Józef nodded. I can hear this conversation; I watch its participants as if it was happening yesterday." Adam Brok interrupted again with a strange grimace, in which Zuzanna would later understand as pain. He was silent for a moment, as if fighting with himself. Finally, he resumed: "It's autumn. Night is approaching, a cool autumn night, although the day was still warm. It was almost ten years until the war. In three years, Janz will already be the main Nazi poet. Braun will also be associated with Nazi art, but will soon be condemned as a formalist decadent, just like Janz."

Adam Brok fell into the past. It wasn't until sometime later that he remembered Zuzanna's presence and smiled apologetically, as always, when he felt that he got caught in the act of forgetting about her. He sorted memories for a moment.

"At the beginning of the thirty-three, a letter came to Vienna from Zurich, in which my uncle invited me to his place. It was strange and even disturbing. Sometimes he wrote to us, but it served rather to maintain contacts or to settle specific, our, not his, matters. He never wanted anything from us. Well, maybe except for the expectation that we will join him in his business, but I suppose, that in this case too it was more about us than about himself. Now he wrote: 'Come as soon as you can. I am asking you for the first time in my life.' I remembered this letter, or rather I recollected it to myself later, word for word, and I almost remember it to this day. Later, after his death, I learned that he had sent a similar one to Józef. He wrote that we had a lot to explain and more to settle. Anxiety hung over the folded lines of plain, untrained writing. I think so now, then...

At that time, I had a confused professional and personal life. I was stuck in conflicts with the psychoanalytic society and emotional dramas. A little earlier Stella committed suicide...I told you about that. At first, I was afraid that someone might be threating my uncle. Looking at the letter, however, I initiated however my professional instincts. I began to analyze myself and my anxiety. All the memories that attacked my head: people with animal faces, strange situations and even stranger guesses that I made, we speculated, watching the life of our guardian, all that returned to me in the words of his letter, I considered them the unjustified reaction of my exhausted nerves. I also remembered Jakub's fears, but found them to be outdated. They concerned matters from five years ago, and my uncle always did some risky deals. It should prompt me to react, but...after all, uncle did not write: come immediately! Even my uncle Abram is getting older, he's probably sixty years old and feeling the fear of old age, I gave him a diagnosis. It's unpleasant, but not dramatic. Uncle will not commit suicide; I acknowledged this time in accordance with the truth. You would have to come to calm him down, but you shouldn't give in to the emotional blackmail of an older man, I explained to myself. I convinced myself and I can't forgive myself to this day..." Adam Brok stared out the window, and Zuzanna remained with a series of questions she knew she should not ask.

"I wrote back to him in a tone of psychoanalytical advice. I will come, of course, as soon as I can, which does not mean, unfortunately, that in the coming days, but maybe in the next ones. Uncle should calm down a little. He has always lived unusually intensely, but there comes a time when you need to slow down a little. And similar nonsense. I sent this letter almost with satisfaction. Was it just about commitments that kept me in Vienna? Did I want to humiliate the one who seemed unbreakable?" Adam Brok snorted, contorting his face in contempt. "Enough of this self-analysis. I put down the letter and forgot about it. I told you that my world was collapsing in Vienna. It was consuming me completely. A few weeks later I received a telegram from my uncle. It contained only one word: 'Come!'.

The next day I was in Zurich. A hackney carriage took me to my uncle's house. To what was left of it. The fire was still smoking. A heap of bricks, metal scaffoldings, unburnt beams. The house stood in the yard. The neighboring buildings were saved. Inscriptions on makeshift scaffolding forbade entry. The people who bustled about it turned out to be policemen and magistrate officials. They sent me to the police station. There I was able to reach the inspector dealing with the case.

'I'm very sorry,' he said, which I was afraid of since I came to my uncle's home. 'Your father died in the fire. An unfortunate accident.'

I kept pushing. I wanted to see the corpse. He objected. 'They're quite charred,' he explained. To my question, on how do they know that he's my father, he replied that it could not be anyone else. Finally, he led me to the morgue. My medical title made an impression. The black, completely burned and distorted lump was the head, on which it was difficult to find places after burned eyes, a fold of the nose. A wide crack with several teeth protruding showed the place of the mouth.

'The house collapsed on him,' explained the policeman. The impressive stature could point to my uncle. I couldn't recognize the scraps of clothing, but I recognized the ring they found next to it. It was uncle's ring. It probably fell from a charred finger. A gold ring with an emerald eye. It was the only luxury accessory he never parted with. 'A souvenir' he repeated with a specific smile, probably of triumph. I examined it closely afterwards. Old St. Petersburg work, probably from the eighteenth century. A beautiful item. After completing the formalities, a week later a policeman gave it to me. Józef told me to keep it.

'He loved you the most,' he said when we were drinking vodka in a bar by the river. 'Although he was always fair.' I replied that I was the last one to disappoint him. I wore the ring on my big finger. It fell off the others, and on this one it barely held on. I wore it almost all the time. From snobbery? As a souvenir from uncle? I sold it during the war.

The same inspector questioned me. He made a note about the telegram and the letter. He repeated his version again. It was supposed to be an accident. There was only one servant in the house, apart from uncle. 'He claimed that your father liked to drink. Everything indicates that he fell asleep without extinguishing his cigarette. And when he woke up, if he woke up, you understand, carbon oxide, it was too late. The servant awoke from the acrid smoke. With difficulty, semi-conscious, he got outside. The house was already on fire,' said the policeman. 'You know, premonitions,' he summed up my doubts about the letter and telegram. 'It happens. We can't explain it. We cannot explain everything. And you said yourself that you haven't seen your father for almost three years. He missed you, maybe he felt worse, he drank a lot...'

For a moment I remembered Jakub's concerns that Józef had told me, and I wondered whether to share them with the policeman. For a moment. I pressed for the name and address of the servant. He hesitated, but finally it gave me.

I knocked on the door of an apartment in a tenement house for a long time. Finally, in the barely opened slit, I saw terrified eyes. Hearing my name, a man of indeterminate age and appearance let me in, but he probably fell into a deeper panic, if such a thing was possible.

'I'm very sorry,' he repeated. 'Such a misfortune.' It turned out that he was rarely alone with uncle. However, this happened that unlucky night. His nervousness suggested something more than a servant's guilt, whose negligence led to the death of his employer. He was shaking and sweating, but he repeated his version invariably despite my pressures and tricky questions: why didn't he make Abram go to bed undressed, especially since, as he testified, he had been drinking a lot lately? I repeated it in all possible ways, and he, still trembling, continuously answered the same way: 'The master was sick of company and forbade to enter. He told me to go to bed.'

The next day I talked to the policeman again. He took the address of my hotel. He was behaving slightly less confident. I sent a telegram to Józef. He arrived in two days. We did not know what was happening with the oldest, or even in what country he could be in.

'And what do you think about Jakub's fears now?' I asked him almost during the greeting. He replied that he did not know. He explained that the thought of it is natural, but it does not justify linking the death of uncle with our brother's fears. 'Three years have passed since my conversation with Jakub. And the matter went back many years before. Do you suppose they've been hunting him for so long? If they did, they would have found him earlier. We feel guilty. We have reasons. So, we want such simple explanations,' he said somehow as if he were pretending to be me, putting on my psychoanalytic costume.

'And if the Bolsheviks killed him, does it change anything?' I asked

He responded after some time. 'It does! It means, that we could've foreseen this, and we are more at fault'. He said almost with difficulty. He didn't look well.

We tried to arrange something at the municipality, but it took many days. We came, testified and signed without end. Uncle documents were incinerated, his will wasn't found.

In his spare time Józef went for long walks. He emphasized that he wanted to be alone. After a few days, someone knocked on my hotel room. Józef had left earlier. The inspector emphasized that this was an unofficial visit. We sat in a corner of the hotel restaurant by a palm tree. I remember because it was snowing on the street. The policeman had trouble starting. 'They took the case away from me, he finally said. 'Counterintelligence is dealing with it now, but I don't think they'll tell you anything.' That's why he decided to talk to me, although he feels a little out of order because he doesn't know if he's violating the rules. He dwelt for some time on the ambiguities of the regulations, because by telling me what he did, he did not break any rules. Fire specialists concluded that it is most likely that the fire occurred in several places at once, which excludes an accident. 'Do you understand?' He asked. In addition, a few days before his death, uncle went to the bank where he kept his money and took out almost all of them. Over half a million francs. 'I didn't know he was such a rich man,' said the policeman. 'Did you know?' I was sure that my uncle's estate was many times larger. Of course, I didn't confide in the policeman. Ultimately, these were only presumptions. I was confused. The words of Jakub came back to me, which I had never heard before. The policeman explained that he could have told me this, because the bank would have to tell us this sooner or later. 'Do you know why counterintelligence took over the case?'

After a while I said no. For a moment I thought whether I should initiate him, I felt a sudden surge of confidence and if it were not for the psychiatric training, which suggested that my state was caused by guilt, if not for this training, I would not have answered that I didn't know. He didn't believe. He tried to get more information. Finally, he said that the most sensational rumors were circling about my father. He was supposed to be an agent of German and Soviet intelligence at the same time. His handlers were to have killed him when they realized that he was playing both sides. The policeman was talkative. He mentioned uncle's shady deals. About relationships with people who were suspects, gangsters, but also subversives and communists. 'These rumors are extremely common, of course, in environments that deal with such matters. That is why I thought it would be appropriate to acquaint you with some of this gossip,' he explained.

I asked if I was guilty of anything for his involvement. He broke up. He said that I aroused his sympathy, and the matter is even more strange, because such a respected and recognized doctor, he said, he has...he did not know what words to use, and after a while said: 'such a somewhat adventurous father.' He immediately added: 'And your older brother is a professor of philosophy in Germany. The fate of your eldest brother is a little different..."he suspended his voice, but because he didn't hear anything from me, he continued: 'I know what it means to lose a father.' He repeated it several times, as well as about his sympathy for me. I began to doubt it. He clearly wanted to get something out of me.

Józef and I sat in a pub by the frozen river. We drank vodka. I told my brother about the policeman's revelations. He winced even more and fell into himself. We didn't know anything. We won't find out anything. Actually, we could hardly explain it to ourselves. We knew our adopted father so little, to whom we owed so much. Everything was in the sphere of understatement, unanswered questions, guesses. We had never helped him in anything. Has he alienated us with his strength and brutality? In the final situation, we completely failed."

Adam Brok was looking through the window. Beyond the hospital's window it was getting dark. Forty years and a few months earlier, in Zurich, it was snowing.

"Józef received the same letter. Uncle reserved telegram exclusively for me. In the restaurant by the river, Józef spoke a few sentences and stopped. He only looked at me sometimes, he was immersed in smoke. He was distancing himself. I remember: he smoked one after the other, in general we smoked a lot then. He said:

'I don't really know why I didn't come. I wasn't even very busy. Not enough to justify such a delay. Even under normal circumstances. But in these kind...'

We smoked. Every now and then we poured more shots into ourselves. We didn't have much to say. Not about uncle or ourselves.

'And you know, I think uncle's intentions were for us. It was because of us that he wanted to meet,' Józef said, what I was more and sure of. 'Maybe they were blackmailing him and that's why he took the money out of the bank? In any case, as always, he wanted to give us something. Leave something behind. He felt a threat or knew about it. And maybe he wanted to tell us about himself? Who would he confide in at last? We were his loved ones.' Józef drank and winced. He had lost weight, aged.

His cramps were so frequent that it suggested the development of a nervous tics. His lips formed an asymmetrical furrow. I haven't seen him for two years and I didn't really know what happened to him during that time. 'I'm sure,' he repeated.

He was bitter. I saw it. Not only because of uncle. He had already mentioned to me that he had just split with his mentor. Relations between them began to cool slightly earlier. It took him some time to understand the obvious for every outside observer. He told me later. His mentor did not want to have a Jewish student.

'Philosophy is a love of wisdom,' Józef told me in Poland. 'Sometimes we can become its medium for a while. Does it matter who becomes this medium? How lame or ugly he is? I have known this since I started occupying myself with philosophy. But then, in Germany, when the Nazis came to power, I felt it mattered. Revealing some fundamental falsehood. I could not continue my work. Even today I can't.' He told me a few years later. It was in Krakow. There he got a job at the university. I visited him. I saw that he wasn't doing well. He looked old. That's what it seemed to me then. He was forty but looked older. The gap in his mouth tightened even more. We sat in the "European" market. Pigeons swirled on cobblestone paths, suddenly, as a whole herd, they jumped up and unconsciously circled around and fell again onto the pavement. Krakow was spectral. It resembled Vienna. St. Mary's church, disappearing in the fog, seemed to be St. Stephen's cathedral. The day went away, consuming the Sukiennice, town hall tower, buildings around and the entire market square. Józef spoke nervously, puffing on a cigarette. I yielded to him and we drank vodka, although I mentioned that this could be his problem. 'Give me a break with these psychiatric talks,' he grunted. He repeated it several times.

I went to Józef after a conversation I had with my friend who lectured psychiatry in Kraków. He said more and more people were talking about the behavior problems, alcoholic including, of my brother. The university senate was not far away from taking an interest in it. It was said that during his seminars there was behavior that should not be taking place at the Jagiellonian University.

Józef only looked at me at times. He was looking at the market, which was plunging into night. It turned out that he's waiting for someone. He said working at the university was exhausting him, especially working with students. 'And to think that even ten years ago discussions with young people fascinated me the most.' In Kraków he had the impression that he was deceiving them, and this paralyzed him. 'I endure lectures somehow,' he said. 'I try to cover the thoughts of the classics, focus the discussion around them. I strive to watch myself and discuss from a safe distance those who had the ambition to understand the world. I try to classify their thoughts. But when it comes to discussion...Young barbarians appear. There are more and more of them. Nazis, communists. I am to convince them that the world has its measures, that there is good, truth and beauty. That we can come to the essential truth. Only I don't believe in it anymore! Although I know that the world will fall apart without these measures, I can convince them only if I can lean on the just foundation of existence. And I can't find it. I can quickly believe that we invented it to keep the beasts within us at bay, but chasing the truth, we came to how conventional our measures are. And what? I am to tell this to those defiant little shits, who want to overthrow the old world of pretense and put it in its place...it's a scam, of course! They will not raise anything! Listen to Jakub. He will tell you about the revolution. From the inside. A nightmare! Today, the same begins in Germany. These young people want to break free from the circle of banality that stifles them like the loop of this market at all costs. One time here, everything was in its place, and today there is nothing. It's just old decorations. It is only trivial, because its not sanctified repetition. And they feel it after all, because they don't know. To escape banality, they unleash the apocalypse. When this happens, as in Russia, it will be too late. Even if he, my former mentor, my former, fallen mentor...though maybe...smaller. And so, if he is right, that nihilism began when we answered the questions and reified the world two and a half thousand years ago...if even? Then what am I supposed to tell the young barbarians? After all, they would gladly agree that the essence of our western tradition is poisoned and that it brings with it nihilism and decadence. And so, I should deceive them that there is a hard and unchanging foundation of principles...I try. I try to deceive myself by using something like an ontological proof: if without justice the world falls apart, that is justice. Dostoyevsky is right: if there is no God, then everything is allowed, and so there must be God...But we know how arbitrary this scholastic evidence is. That's why I get angry when another young barbarian undermines the scaffolding of my deception, get irritated, I shout. And this is not allowed. I shouldn't have...' Józef interrupted his long monologue. I realized, that the young woman was coming up to our table, for whom he was waiting. He introduced her to me. He wanted me to meet her. It was his student. The conversation had to be ended.

A war was coming. Extermination was coming. We sensed it then in Kraków. But for the first time we felt it a few years earlier, in Zurich, after the death of uncle, looking at the snow falling outside the window, thrown by the wind. We left drunk and walked to the hotel through an empty city. In the whirlwind of the wind that tugged at us, it almost knocked us down so that we had to support ourselves, I heard the howling of approaching demons.

Earlier we were sitting in an empty hall. We wanted to reminisce about uncle. Celebrate him, just like it should be done. We knew that one should refer to the simplest tradition. We were supposed to reminisce him. He remained only in our memory. But we didn't have too much to say. We were trapped in a circle of our affairs. I was parting with psychoanalysis, parting with the years of Viennese life, my illusions and sins, which I did not even dare to name and sum up, with people whom I had hurt, who might have hurt me. It was similar with Józef. With uncle, our guardian, our adoptive father, we failed him to the end. What were we supposed to say?

"Lechaim! My brother said suddenly, raising his glass. 'To life!. It sounded stupid and uncomfortable in the empty room. 'Abram was life!' he felt obliged to justify Józef.

CHAPTER 7

They made an appointment with the doctor who carried out Adam Brok's surgery at 1pm. However, they had to wait for him in the corridor for nearly half an hour. When he approached, they felt that it wasn't good.

"Unfortunately, I don't have good news for you. It's very advanced stomach cancer. Metastases...it's harder to say where they are not. In such cases, an operation does not help, on the contrary. But we had to do it, we didn't know...we couldn't know, what condition he was in. I don't give him more than a few weeks to live. It only amazes me that he came to us so late. He had to suffer terribly. We sewed him up and we can do nothing more. We'll be giving him morphine. But what else can we do..."

They could not visit him until the next day. Zuzanna remembered the gray parchment-like face on the white pillow. He was sleeping when they came. But when they sat down quietly by the bed, he opened his eyes. He looked at Zuzanna and his lips twitched in an almost imperceptible smile.

"Sara" he whispered.

His eyes closed. He probably fell asleep from exhaustion. Zuzanna already knew that Sara was the name of Benedict's mother.

That evening, Zuzanna and Benedict were sitting by the open window, drinking vodka and Coca-Cola. May was ending, the night was almost hot, and the singing of birds filled the yard, separating them from the noise of the city.

"I can't imagine it," Benedict repeated with a helpless face. "It can't come to me that my father is dying. Although I should not be surprised. He's already seventy years old. I should be spending more time with him. It's you that acts like his daughter, and I...I feel guilty about not feeling enough. As if I'm not realizing it enough..."

Zuzanna looked into the night. Windows to the extensive yard were the attraction of this apartment. Large chestnuts and maples gave the feeling of asylum in the middle of the city. Benedict's father got this privileged apartment as an officer. "An officer with good contacts," he noted mockingly.

"The most difficult first step" - a female voice sang outside the window.

It was only possible to talk to him a day later. From then on, Zuzanna and Benedict began to spend their entire days together by their father's bed or in turns. On the next day, upon greeting her father-in-law, Zuzanna kissed him on the cheek, he smiled. She only dared to do so now. Earlier, they only had ceremonial kissing during weddings or family ceremonies.

"You remind me of Sarah, Baruch's mother," said Adam Brok, hinting that he remembered what had happened the previous day. "Though you are not like her. So what? Have they told you how much I have left? Months? Less?" He said nonchalantly. "They won't tell me, although they are friends, colleagues. You have to keep the patient in suspense. This is the power of the doctor. You can't even give up this ritual in the face of an ambiguous case like me. Patient-doctor. So?"

"What are you talking about father?!" as Benedict was unnecessarily outraged. "That's stupid. The father himself should know that in such complex cases it is not easy to make a diagnosis and give dates, but these...ideas..."

"Give it a rest!" Murmured father impatiently, turning away from his son, who was speaking more and more uncertainly and vaguely. "I hear voices," he said jokingly after a moment of silence. "Don't be afraid, I'm not going crazy. The voices of the past come back to me, important and deprived of meaning. In any case, I don't know which ones are which. My head hums with them in three, and sometimes four or more languages. They shout and argue amongst each other. I will have a terrible hassle, to clean up all of this" he was speaking very seriously. "Leave me alone. I have to deal with them and in that, no one can help me anymore."

It was one of the few times when he sent them away, uncertain whether to listen, but finally yielding to his authority.

At first it looked like he was getting better very quickly. He quickly began to get up from bed and, despite the protests of doctors and nurses, he marched to the toilet himself. Increasingly, he got up and sat at the table next to the bed. Sometimes he even walked a little in the hall. A more attentive look, however, dispelled hope. His eyes gleamed with an unhealthy glow. He tired quickly. He interrupted conversations unexpectedly. He looked through window. Sometimes, suddenly, he began to breathe violently, as if he wanted to saturate himself with air. His eyes were desperately seeking attachment. Sometimes he looked at Zuzanna for a long time, so long that she began to feel insecure.

"I wonder if you remind me of Sara just because you are the wife of my son, whose mother she was," he began, staring at her. He closed his eyes and spoke as if he were dictating a letter: "I married Sara in October of thirty-seven. Europe swelled with the threat of war. Six months later our son was born. Baruch. I remember this time as the happiest in my life, although sometimes I was overwhelmed with despair. I so clearly felt that our world was ending, so clearly that nowadays sometimes I can't believe it. My psychiatric soul reminds me of the mechanisms of projection, projection into earlier time, of what marked us later. But I have evidence. I remember my conversations with Sara and my friends. I remember our walk in the Łazienki Park. It was already September, we were walking along an alley chestnuts, and the hard fruit were falling around like hail. It was beautiful afternoon weather, but the sun was no longer scorching, so we could take Baruch in the open carriage. I held my hand over his head like a makeshift roof. I was afraid that a falling chestnut would hurt him. 'Don't you think that instead of multiplying, we should commit suicide now? We are happy. The threat of war is still far away. Now it wouldn't be so scary,' Sara said almost flirtatiously. She laughed, as if she were talking about something completely different.

Her words come back to me. The threat of war was close. And it is such that, despite all our premonitions, we could not imagine. If we did as she said, we would have spared her unspoken suffering. During the war she could think...she probably thought that Baruch had little chance. She didn't know if I was alive. I don't even want to imagine what she felt when she gave her four-year-old son to friends. I can imagine his scream. So what if she was gaving him to people she trusted? The war uneducated him. Thoughts about the child had to have tortured her, before herself... before they gassed her in Treblinka. Earlier, she assisted her loved ones in their agony. Her friends offered her escapc, but that would mean leaving her parents, her sick father, her lost, accustomed to care and prosperity mother.

When I think about my life since the outbreak of the war, then Baruch is its only rationale. And to think that through my fault we have never been able to be close, the closeness that should connect father and son. Finding him was such happiness, unbelievable and only one."

Adam Brok paused and closed his eyelids. It lasted so long. Zuzanna was alone with him. When she became worried, he began again.

"I met Sara a few months before the wedding. Less than a year. She studied German philology. The language das Volk der Denker und Dichter. She printed her first sketches about literature. I slowly recovered from psychoanalysis and Vienna. Sarah let me almost forget about it. Memories from there gradually transformed into a stranger's tale. Peculiar and not entirely clear. Nightmares were lost, which for years gave me no peace. I stopped dreaming that I was unconsciously flying down on my legs, which had turned into wheels, and could not break free from the tracks leading into the black pit below me. Or that I can't move, and behind me there are figures in the darkness that I can't see, exchanging hideous screams. And finally I feel...I know that one puts a huge nail to my head, and the other strikes it with a hammer and I wake up from tearing pain or fear of it. I stopped dreaming of Stella and Otto. Although still long after, I imagined, or perhaps dreamed, that I met Otto von Holstein in a black SS uniform. The specter of Otto in a black uniform returned to me during the war. When we saw each other for the last time, he declared that he was joining the Nazis. And radicalism and consequence could not be denied him.

'Maybe one had to go through all this decay to be reborn,' he said, looking around the cafe. We met at the Café Central.

It was not long after uncle's death. I decided to go back to Warsaw, although calling it a return to Poland is probably an exaggeration. In Germany the Nazis ruled and an extraordinary ordinance on the protection of the nation and state came into force. I wasn't interested in politics, but I knew it and I knew it was important, although of course I didn't know how important. The caretaker gave me a note from Otto.

'Maybe after all, we should say goodbye. I am waiting for you at Café Central tomorrow at noon. If the date doesn't work for you, leave me a message. Otton von H.'. He wrote something along those lines.

I showed up on this blurry noon. Spring still couldn't begin. I haven't encountered Otto since Stella's suicide. We exchanged bows at her funeral. Warm feelings turned into more than reluctance. I somehow blamed him for her death. He must have guessed that. Or maybe...Maybe he blamed me?" Brok hesitated and looked at the point next to Zuzanna's head. After a moment he returned to the story. Small finger movements helped revive the past, to evoke a vision that will remain in Zuzanna's memory as intense as her own memories.

"In Café Central, Otto was already waiting at the table that we had infamously occupied in our time. This cafe was a separate, closed world. One was overwhelmed as soon as the revolving door led onto the red carpet with the name of the premises. Even the light was special there. A blurry day from behind large windows intertwined with the illumination of ever-lit lamps, hanging from the ceilings and attached to the columns, giving a specific, gray-brown shade to the interior. Moorish columns, arches of the Viennese temple above round tables isolated from the city behind the windows. Maybe this, after all, was the real essence of Vienna?

It was an awkward moment. I join Otto, make a head gesture and don't know, too well, how to behave. Shake hands with someone who was more than a friend and now is...So we stopped at nodding our heads. I remember his words from the conversation. I think I said something myself, but I can't remember it. It probably wasn't that important...

Otto told us that we had created for ourselves an artificial and even grotesque world. A world where only our emptiness and suffering were real. He said this with such a contemptuously painful curve of his lips. He was always a little exalted. Such a distanced, ironic exaltation. But then...I remember exactly what he looked like and some of his issues. 'And this pathetic femme fatale...which turned out to be fatal mainly for herself. Poor bitch.' 'And you, who are you?!' I remember this response-question.

'You are probably right. I probably shouldn't be talking like that about her. But I say it between us. And we...well, we are worth the same' he said a little more, and then summed it up something like this: 'Maybe one had to probe this cesspool of culture to overcome it? This psychoanalysis...a Jewish idea at self-redemption. Reconcile us with the status of last people. I hope you don't have any grievance against me? Can you distinguish cultural recognition from our personal relationships? You are not only a Jew, just as I am not only a German, yet you are a Jew and I am a German. And that certainly means something.' He recalled a meeting with Janz, which left a large impression on him. 'We need form, and the führer offers us form. These pseudo-cultural games are as shallow as Art Nouveau swirls. Time to end this. Time to get real courage.' He was saying something else, but I don't remember exactly what. I don't remember who got up first. Maybe we did it together? We knew that this was the end of the conversation. We didn't shake hands.

Vienna I extricated myself from this for a long time. Because it's not just Otton, Stella and our small group. It's also my fellow psychoanalysts. I attempted explanations to the prophet, which even to a certain extent I got caught up in. In Warsaw I left it slowly. I severed myself from psychoanalysis, and I didn't reconcile with classic psychiatry: as always, I stood a bit to the side. I was separate. Sara changed my life, let me love it. For this short period.

It was an extraordinary era, these three, less than three years before the war. A covetous time. I have the impression that we wanted to squeeze everything out of it, feeling how threatened and limited it is. Our happiness had a specific, bitter taste. I remember waking up at night and looking at Sara sleeping next to me. I touch her gently so as not to interrupt her peaceful sleep. And I think that this beautiful woman and the child dreaming in the corner of the room, our son, immersed in the glow from behind the window, is more than I could ever have imagined, and therefore it cannot last. When I walked home from the clinic and looked at the city, which I liked the most of all, and saw smiling people, I thought these were the last days of such peace and joy. The last days of this beautiful city. I intoxicated myself with walks around Warsaw, which is gone. Because now it is a different city. Only a lot of greenery remained, as then. But back then, I have a feeling, the city was choking on it. Spring was endlessly passing into summer, and in the fall it was still long. Young, joyful people on the streets, as if there was still hope. I know that various unpleasant things were happening then, how it is between people, but what did it matter compared to, what happened next? Maybe memory drains that which is bad...Because in perspective that evil turned out to be so insignificant, it became nothing in the face of the apocalypse that came, and the abhorrent world that came later. I remember the tension that sometimes appeared among my friends. Anti-Semitism...I remember Klein and others like him, for whom that world was the bottom of degradation. This, they declared and shouted. They were even partially right. But what came, monstrously evil, made us see everything in other proportions.

And then, about a year before the war, my brother Jakub came to us from France. It was the beautiful last autumn I was telling you about. An agreement was signed in Munich. Baruch was six months old. 'I prefer to be here in the same country as you. I won't be saved anyway. I hope that at least you...' Jakub suspended his voice. He came to my clinic. 'A guest from France' he was announced by a porter. 'He said you couldn't remember his name, but you know each other well.' I started to feel something. I left the office. An elderly man sat with a worn face on the bench in the corridor. I shouldn't have recognized him, I last saw him when he was twenty and I was thirteen. And yet. He looked at me in suspense. I came on soft legs. 'Jakub?' I asked.

Sarah was bustling, she made dinner. We were renting a flat on Jerozolimskie Avenue. He tried to smile. To Sara, to Baruch, to me. He tried to play with the little one. His face was changing, relaxing a bit, but I saw a specific contraction in it, a mask that is made of deepening injuries, which turn into neurosis. He spoke little. He demanded that we talk about ourselves. He was captivated by Sarah. At one point he asked if she would be offended if he pulled me out for vodka, men's vodka. I suggested the "Ziemiańska", I thought I would show him a fashionable place. He refused, wanted something small and out of the way.

'Do you remember how we escaped from Kurów?' He asked, after we emptied half the bottle in silence. 'You can't remember,' he told himself. I remembered. He was carrying me. 'I've been running away for almost ten years...though maybe I've been running away since always? In any case, for ten years I haven't really known what I'm living for.'

'None of us knows,' I replied.

'But we don't think about it. And I have been asking myself for ten years why I am alive, because I know that I deserve to die, I deserve everything that will happen to me, and more. While still with the Soviets, when I began to understand what we had done, I realized that we would not create a new man...and fortunately we will not create him, we would only be hurting and injuring existing people... When I understood this, I understood that I deserve to die, and began to think about escape. At first, I lived to create communism, and then to escape from it. When I ran away, I thought I had survived, to give testimony, to tell about what we did, what the communists want to do. I published a few articles in the émigré press, some in the French press. The end. French intelligence offered me a consultant job. I accepted it. All this turned out to be senseless and meaningless. I wanted to save uncle. It failed…'

Jacob said, that reviewing the documents of the Central Committee, unofficially, actually, as someone like an illegal GPU controller, he figured out that at some point, millions of dollars intended for a secret operation leaked out. And they disappeared. Amazing money then. It was the beginning of the twenties. The cavalry proved itself very well during the civil war, but after the end of operations, the number of good horses drastically decreased, they died off, and were eaten. Breeding stallions were lacking especially. And Bolshevik Russia was under a blocked. The case was solved by a trusted comrade from international relations. Substituted brokers were to buy Argentine stallions to Sweden, and in fact transport them to the Soviets. Between a few mentioned brokers appeared uncle's alias, who used it in these types of deals. The trusted companion disappeared abroad along with the money, and the only trace of him remained exclusively in the committee's archives.

'If it had been earlier, I would have transferred the case to the Cheka,' Jakub said grimly. 'If it had been earlier, I would have initiated an investigation that would have led to the death of uncle, which would have been preceded by terrible things, to the death of my educator, adoptive father, the man who saved and raised us.' I would've denounce him. I know that. But then the world around me was beginning to collapse. I hesitated. I stopped. I didn't do it'.

It turned out that uncle was involved in this, as well as in a variety of other grim affairs. He confessed to Jacob when he found him in Zurich after escaping. 'Did I have the right to condemn him?' My brother asked. He repeated that uncle was an angel compared to him. 'I killed people, tortured and tormented them. You can't even imagine what I was doing. It's hard for me to believe in it. I was building hell. My intentions don't justify me in the least. I didn't save uncle, I didn't save anyone. I constantly wonder why God saved me...'

At first I thought it was a rhetorical phrase, funny coming from the mouth of a former Bolshevik. But my brother said it again. 'Maybe this is the most important thing,' he said, 'to understand why God still keeps me alive. Is this the way I should repent for my sins? Although I know that what I have done cannot be made up for, and only God can let me be reborn.'

'So you believe in God?' I asked uncertainly, laughing a little, although the conversation was not a lighthearted one.

Jakub wasn't laughing. 'I'm starting to believe. I'm trying'. This was probably after two bottles. However, he spoke soberly. That's what it seemed to me. I think about it more and more often. Then Jacob said he wanted to leave me his diary. He asked me to read it and to consider, whether or not to publish it. He said it was important to him. But maybe only for him. The three of us met with Józef only once. It was not a happy meeting."

When Zuzanna will later recall her father-in-law's monologues many times, when they come back to her unexpectedly with some distant association or without reason, they will never just be the memory of Adam Baruch's voice. They will be her memories, a series of experiences and images that will be accompanied by his voice. Perhaps she will be able to visualize these memories, which she will later look at, like albums from Vienna, the Café Central, texts about places and cities in which her father-in-law lived. Photographs of Romania from the late 1930s, Bucharest and the Carpathians on the borders of countries. Sometimes she looked for books that might contain them, and sometimes she came across them by chance if it was by chance, if something in life is by chance. Photos from there will recall Adam Brok and his world, his last memories. His voice was losing strength, but he continued to speak. With apparent effort, closing his eyes, he reports what he could not prevent.

"Then there was the war. I was lucky. If you can call it that. If it wasn't the other way around. I was mobilized. I said goodbye to Sara. I was at the front. Near Lwów I was caught in the German-Soviet pincer. They cut us off from the command staff, we didn't even have anything to fight with. Unexpectedly, as the only officer, I became the commander. I dissolved the unit. I said I was going to Romania and that they could do whatever they wanted. Just hide their weapons so that they can find them later. Wandering a bit through the wilderness, overcoming steep slopes, I walked to Slanice, a small spa town, where our government was interned. Picturesque mountains rose all around. I met some friends and it turned out that, contrary to appearances, I had something to do. There's probably always be something to do. Romanian border guards were trying to take away a suitcase with gold coins from the governor of the Krakow province, which he had confiscated just before leaving from an exchange office doing illegal business. A fight broke out on the border, in which Polish policemen beat Romanian guards and left with the suitcase. They handed it over to Slanice, and the Polish authorities decided to send it to France as soon as possible. I became one of the few couriers burdened with this responsibility. Partly on foot, partly by rail I got to Bucharest. Autumn was hot and sunny. The city's rhythm seemed peculiarly joyful, which deepened the sense of alienation and pain. Broad, tree-lined streets carried crowds of walkers. Eighteenth-century Orthodox churches leaned on new, tall buildings. Everything seemed calm and indifferent. I arrived at the embassy and, accomplishing the impossible, met with the terribly busy ambassador. I gave him the money.

I was involved in moving soldiers from the Romanian border further to France. I made my last trip in the winter of '40. At the border I was waiting for a group that I was supposed to lead through the mountains. I settled in an abandoned hut, which smugglers' friends showed me. They said that the family there had been murdered and since then no one had the courage to stay in it. During the day, through the snow, I wandered to a familiar inn, where the people entrusted with me were to appear. The inn was the property of smugglers. I even got books from them, which breaking through the mountains various travelers left there. At night I listened to the wild wind or tried to read by the kerosene lamp. The storm was falling apart into a pack of individual voices. Although I got used to their howling and wailing, sometimes unexpected thumps woke me up. The house lived and moaned in the wind. I tried to read. It was white during the day. There was snow around the hut, and in the distance, rounded mountains with dark clouts of forest. It was beautiful, but my existence was accidental and superfluous. The overwhelming state of unreality did not want to give way. Earlier I was able to feel it in Vienna, when I realized that all our efforts are worthless and even funny, and we are like children who are playing, not realizing what is happening around us. However, those were moments. Then... well, but it was later, after the war. Then, in the emptiness of the winter mountains, in the inhuman whiteness, the sense of unreality on the border of loss of existence continued and increased. It hurt. Sometimes I was saved by Virgil, whose volume in Latin I got from smugglers. I spent there I don't remember how much time. It could have been two weeks, it could have been more. Finally, when I lost hope, a slightly reduced group appeared. We decided to go through Hungary. There we were captured and interned.

First, I was in a Hungarian camp. Then I was transferred to an oflag in West Germany, and although I was dying of anxiety about my relatives whom I had left in Poland, nothing special happened to me. It was hungry, gloomy, and hopeless. It was possible to live. We were liberated by the Americans. I had to return to country, to my loved ones.

In Poland, my life became tracking down the dead and reconstructing their deaths. Existence became meaningless. So overwhelming, even physical, that at times I wondered if it could only be caused by the loss of loved ones. The loss of a nation...If it wasn't for Baruch, whom I renamed Benedict, if it wasn't for him, I don't know...Because I was very lucky to find him. And if it wasn't the hospital where I lost myself in, just like in alcohol. I still had a sense of danger because I knew that the communists could discover me. I was becoming aware that Jakub did not fall into paranoia, he co-created it.

One day, when I realized that my hands would not stop shaking, if I didn't drink my dose, I decided to give up alcohol. After a few attempts it succeeded. After a few years I could even drink a shot. I wondered what I was living for. But these are not questions that we can answer. Life conceals its meaning from us. If there is any sense. Like annihilation, annihilation in which my relatives and whole nation died. I was trying to reconstruct their deaths, what had happened before...their ending lives...I wanted, even for a moment, to feel their escaping breath... For hours without end, I endlessly imagined their last journey. Sarah's path...I couldn't stand it anymore, I hid in vodka, into mad work...I ran away, so as not to imagine how they were only transformed into fear and pain, they became shaking meat. And then, as these images moved away from me, the feeling of guilt returned. And again, I tried to recreate their suffering again, participate in it...I envied their death. That they no longer have to suffer anymore. And then I thought it was a punishment...that was why I was spared, and actually not spared. Left alive. Sometimes I think, that busy with the dead, I devoted too little time to Baruch. I owe him too," he once said frantically, grabbing Zuzanna's hand when Benedict moved away for a moment "and I pay for it. But... The entire time I kept wondering, if I have the right to live! I asked myself...I didn't have...the right to live and if it wasn't for Baruch...Only, do we even have the right to live after what happened? Live as if nothing? Love, breed, accumulate things...in this...cemetery?

My relationships with people were impermanent and shallow. With women... Whenever I got a little more involved, I felt guilty, guilty about the dead. Every moment of peace and pleasure was a sin. Everything positive and good I squeezed out of my life like parasites trying to breed in it.

I met someone...a woman. Suddenly I began to feel, that she's close to me, she was noble, beautiful and I could spend my life with her. I consciously destroyed this relationship. I couldn't betray Sara, the memory of her...Now I think I did wrong, I hurt people, but all in all I was right. You can't betray the dead...Sara. When I stopped drinking, I realized that I would only live my life. I will have to raise Baruch, and during this time I should help people, focus on work in the hospital. I will never make up for my sins anyway. At times I asked myself: Am I doing right, helping people? Do they deserve it? But I immediately understood that I could not answer this question. Only who would answer them? Anyway...I needed this. I needed a job, the hospital. Also because I wanted there to be less and less of me. For me to dissolve in what I'm doing. That my pleas, judgements, and opinions would disappear. My usurpation. For me not to think: me. I tried to stop thinking and feeling. I aimed to become only a reaction, an answer only, answer...as I should..."

He looked at Zuzanna intensively. He tried to tell her something, explain an extremely complicated issue that is so difficult to translate into words. After a while he gave up. He lowered his eyes.

"I quit my life. The memory of the dead returned by itself, it penetrated, though not as violently as before. I was falling into nothingness. The emptiness grew inside me, hurting me from within. I understood that I could never fill it with anything. I realized that the void I felt, which, to tell you the truth, I still feel, was not just the loss of those I loved, with whom I was tied to, almost everyone...This emptiness returned when the pain after losing them faded. I felt like I was sinking into a dark funnel. It grew in pain after Sara, Józef, Jakub, and others. It was there before..."

One day, the summer was hot, they were surprised to see Adam Brok, who was lying under a blanket with his eyes closed and whispering something. Zuzanna thought her father-in-law was praying. However, he opened his eyes as if he had heard her thoughts.

"I once told you about a meeting with Józef in Friborg. In autumn, probably in '30. I was there with Stella and Otton and we talked with my brother's friends. This conversation, the words of that poet...Janz. Even then I felt aversion to them...to him. Otto reminded me of him. It was even worse. Then there was the war and I could only think of it with revulsion. Did those who murdered my loved ones recant his poems? But albeit, do we not silence disturbing thoughts too easily? We turn away from the uncomfortable truth, because it can provoke bad consequences? Some things, which he said...

There are fewer and fewer of us. The more we build around us...we design ourselves in things, we seduce. Maybe that's how it must be. It's like the law of conservation of energy. The more we create, focus on the outside, the less remains of us. We are becoming an addition to the built world. What happens in communism is just a caricature. These sculptures on the MDM (Marszałkowska Housing District), next to the Palace of Culture, people as additions to drills and pickaxes. But it's not just communism. If there is nothing outside us and the world is a biological machine, maybe we can even make it better...but then we will become dispensable..."

He was spoking less and less. He was laying longer, staring through window with glassy eyes. Zuzanna wondered if it was the influence of the morphine, which was being injected more and more intensely. Perhaps only to break the silence, she asked him why he became a psychiatrist. He turned and looked at them with a sober gaze.

"I thought about it many times. Did I want to understand people or heal the world? I am a child of madness. I was born in the screams of my parents being killed. We wanted to treat the disease and plunged deeper and deeper into it. Those in Vienna who translated moral norms into medical techniques turned them into shamanic spells. I saw how from the madness of freedom, which becomes chaos, a madness of order is born, which becomes a prison. My older brother organized madness, which we will be the victims of for a long time. When will we rise out of it? Now in Poland and around, it has entered a mild phase, it has lurked, but the world we live in resembles the brain of a schizophrenic. Schizophrenic normality, which may again explode or lead to ultimate dementia and withering. Will we experience a shock that will cure us of this insanity? Can we still really be normal? Or maybe I unconsciously understood that the history of people is insane? If there were something under the further attacks of madness, under wars and revolutions, if there were something permanent and repetitive, which we can go back to when the next spasm ends...Was I one of those who wanted to understand the spirit of history, the zeitgeist, the structure of the disease, believing, that reason manifests in itself and we can control it...I was punished..." Brok fell silent and closed his eyes.

This was a few days before his death. He spoke more in interrupted fragments, in shorter sentences.

"They're coming back to me and I think they want something. We are always guilty in the presence of the dead. Stella, my uncle, Sara, brothers, everyone, to whom I gave so little...Then living in abjection...how to survive in this stench... When they were dying...When they were afraid, when they were waiting for death. Their bodies...burned or turned into soap, leather...hair. Words...we have to speak, but we can't say anything. When they were suffocating in the wagons, before they were suffocating in the gas chambers...when they were finishing them off with clubs...were they still human? Because if there's nothing, in their pain they were like animals, in final fear and suffering...If they were mortal, then they are gone...nothing remains and there's nothing to remember...It's difficult to reconcile with their death, with one's own. You are moving away from me. I try... to remember one more time...her face... was...was it?" He fell silent.

When they came the next day, he just grimaced at their greeting. Maybe it was supposed to be a smile. He didn't say anything. He also tried to answer their ritual questions with an indistinct smile. Then he turned his head and looked into the summer light outside the hospital window. They sat still. Suddenly Zuzanna jumped up and grabbed her father-in-law's hand. It was cold.

CHAPTER 8

"I didn't know you well father. Not well enough" said Benedict. The night was steamy. Funeral attendees have already said their goodbyes. At the cemetery, well-known and self-assured doctors, trapped in black clothes and tightly tied ties, or in military uniforms, were struggling to catch their breath in the hot air. Under the downpour of the sun, they transformed into a group of elderly and helpless people who looked at each other in search of support. Disheartened, they made their way back to the Brok apartment. They raised clumsy toasts, ate herring and sprat sandwiches - these fish were the only things Zuzanna managed to buy along the way. They were reminiscing but no one was able to say anything interesting. Someone congratulated Benedict on his career, and a few people joined in. They left uncertain, once again declaring their condolences. At the cemetery, a man of difficult-to-determine age stood out, short, somewhat clumsy, bald, with a grayish bristle protruding on his head and the same kind of beard. He moved nervously and violently. Everyone saw him, but he hardly noticed anyone. He walked over to Benedict and shook his hand. Then he reflected, approached Zuzanna.

"My wife" Benedict introduced her.

"Yes, I assumed," he replied carelessly. "Klein. Bruno Klein."

"I can't free myself from this man anymore" She remembered her father-in-law's words.

"I was Adam's friend," said Klein, drinking vodka and leaning towards Zuzanna. "Before the war, I was friends with Sara, his wife, Baruch's mother. He grimaced clearly. "That world is passing away. Fewer and fewer of us from that Atlantis. It is a pity that I visited Adam so rarely." Zuzanna did not remember any of his visits. "An extraordinary man. With such broad interests...But maybe a real psychiatrist must be like this? Only that today specialization is reducing us" his words moved everyone present "and those like Adam are departing..."

"None of them knew him properly," Benedict said, neither to Zuzanna nor to the open window, where they finally sat down alone, drinking vodka. "And I... how much did I know him? Now, when it's too late, I'd like to ask him so many things. It's so trivial...But I remember a lot. I remember how we lived in Bydgoszcz. In the beginning I went with him to Warsaw. City of ruins. I had the impression that smoke was still coming out from under it then. My father had nothing to do with me, so he took me to the hospital. Not in his unit. He didn't want me to watch mental degeneration. He was right. I came there accidentally a few times. Joining my nightmares was the image of deadly terrified, helpless people circling behind a window. Someone was having a panic attack, screaming and throwing himself at the closed door. The nurses dragged him somewhere. I usually sat in the nurses' station. When they had time, they played with me. I asked about my father over and over again. I was afraid he would not come back. I was constantly afraid. They calmed me down, but it didn't last long. If the weather was nicer, I played in the garden. I started going to school. Then we moved to Krakow for a short time. Later, for longer, to Bydgoszcz. I went to school. I went to his hospital for lunch. I stayed to wait for him. When we were going home, I smelled alcohol on him. Actually, he always carried that scent with him. Sometimes he played with me and told me strange fairy tales. Many years later I realized that he was altering the classics for his own use, Greek myths, pieces of the Bible, Iliad, Odyssey, Aeneid, Shakespeare and even Kafka. About a man who woke up as a beetle, or about a village doctor. These stories fascinated me and filled me with fear. More and more often my father read books with me: in Polish and German. He went out when he put me to sleep. I couldn't sleep but I pretended. I didn't want to sleep. I was scared of dreams. After all, you know, I have it to this day. Well...a bit. But then I had to pretend. My father became irritated when I wasn't able to fall asleep for a long time. I knew I couldn't keep him, and I was terrified by loneliness at home. More than just sleeping. That's why I tried to fall asleep. I knew my father would come back and at the same time I was terrified that I would not see him again. I was shivering that someone would come for me. I will hear the thump at the door. That they'll drag me out of my hiding place. Anxiety took my breath, filled the house, changed the shape of things, raising their voices: creaking, peculiar sounds. The terror was usually objectless, not specific, but all the more intense. The figures who would come for me had no faces. I hid in bed, under the covers, but it didn't help. In desperate situations, when I was ready to run out of the house, into the night, I hid in the closet, wrapped myself in a blanket and I could stay like that for a long time and even fall asleep. A few times my father found me there. I remember the first time his screams awakened me. He was thrashing around the house trying to find me. He was drunk and furious. When I got out of the closet, he swung but didn't hit me. 'That's how you play?!' he shouted. I was shaking and couldn't answer. He realized. He took me in his arms, began to rock me and calm me down. He sat by the bed, stroking my head until I fell asleep. Then a few more times...But then he didn't get mad at me anymore.

From that time nurses and other women who made something to eat and cleaned began to visit us in the evenings. Sometimes they stayed until morning. My father came home drunk, well…under the influence of alcohol." Benedict laughed joylessly. "He often picked me up and staggered around the apartment slightly and sang songs. 'Your mother's name was Sara. Remember it. She was the greatest woman in the world!' He repeated. I noticed that when he put me to sleep, he sat down and looked at the dark window, sipping from a glass. A bottle of vodka stood beside him.

Sadness assailed me. A thick, unspeakable regret that I did not understand and did not know what caused it. However, I felt that it filled me and the whole apartment with bitterness. I desperately missed my mother and tried to remember her. With no effect. Then a young woman appeared, Katarzyna, Kasia, who stayed with us for longer. I'm became very attached to her. She lived with us for a year. I could have been ten years old. In the evenings, my father did not drink that much. He was even capable of laughing. Their relationship quickly began to fall apart. I remember a night when they came home. I think my father was already drunk. He pulled out a bottle. Kasia struggles to embrace him and urges him to stop. Father breaks free with anger. He keeps drinking from the bottle. I remember a few similar scenes. I'm terrified and desperate. I'm afraid for my father, for Kasia, for us all. I'm afraid. Arguments start to break out between them. One wakes me up. I get out of bed and go to their bedroom door. Father is almost screaming. I remembered the words, although I didn't fully understand them at the time. They often came back to me: 'We can sleep together, you can even live with me, but you'll never be my wife! Understand! I have a wife, although she is dead!'

It was probably after that that Kasia moved out. Maybe it still went on, but not for long...one night, shortly afterwards, a racket woke me up. I jump up, terrified. I was afraid of noises. I dreamed of war. You know, without end I dream about war. I remember: my father stumbling and closing the front door with difficulty. He bumps about it, staggers, finally falls on the doorstep of the kitchen. He's unconscious. Drunk to unconsciousness. I drag him into the bedroom with difficulty. He's so heavy that I can't move him, and yet I try. Finally, I push him into the bedroom, but I'm unable pull him on the couch. I cry with anger, fatigue and fear. Finally, leaning against him, I fall asleep. I wake up when my father starts to lift himself. It's already gray. I remember his unconscious gaze, which slowly begins to comprehend the situation. He hugs me, caresses me, takes me in his arms and carries me to bed. It was after this that he probably stopped drinking. I saw him drunk a few more times, but these were such detached cases. He's changing. He becomes so, as you knew him. A noble, distanced to the world, elderly man. Although I understood how old he was when he was hospitalized...as a patient. The first and last time."

***

It was autumn when the phone rang during breakfast. Even in the receiver, Zuzanna could hear the terror in her mother's voice. Tadzio wasn't at home at night. It was already before the dawn, when mother began to call from the telephone booth to the emergency services and the police. She found out nothing. She and Zuzanna were frightened. Benedict promised to take care of the matter. At work, Zuzanna sat as if on needles. Around noon, Benedict called. Tadzio was in custody. After a few hours, together with Benedict, they found themselves at police headquarters on Malczewski Street. The captain already knew who he was talking to. He was a little embarrassed by the mess of his small room, covered in paper scraps, to which he probably quickly tried to bring some order to.

"The case has already been referred to the prosecutor. It can't be retracted, there's going to be a trial" the policeman said, as if explaining himself. "The officers captured young people during a brawl. Tadzio wanted to run away, but attacked the policemen. Chances for avoiding a reform school seem unlikely. The prosecutor has already issued a sentence and Tadzio will be in custody for the trial."

Benedict showed initiative. He calmed his slightly shaken up mother-in-law.

He visited Tadzio's school. Using his editorial contacts, including Goleń's personal contacts, he met with several judges and prosecutors. The process was accelerated. Instead of a month it took place in a week. An earlier date was not possible due to Tadzio's state.

"Just don't get startled when you see him," Benedict said to her the day before the trial. "And prepare mother. He got a beating. You probably know, that those who mess with the police end up losing."

In spite of everything, the sight of Tadzia shocked her. Beside her, she could hear her mother's increased breathing, as she was trying to control herself. Her brother's face was half black. In the dimness of the court corridor, no details were visible, and the spots from which Tadzio's eyes emerged differed only in intensity. He smiled a little crookedly at them and greeted them with an almost cocky gesture.

"Remember. You panicked. You wanted to run away. There was a commotion. You don't know what happened," the attorney repeated in an undertone, leaning forward.

"Who would have thought" he grunted.

"Remember!" The lawyer spoke sharply. "If you don't want to spend the next years where you spent your last days."

The trial proceeded without surprises. Tadzio recited his text reasonably well, though without special enthusiasm. The court assigned him a probation officer and released him.

Benedict invited the whole family to the restaurant "Budapest". They ate Hungarian pancakes. Zuzanna wondered if they really eat something like this in Hungary. Mother was almost happy. Zuzanna also returned to her old self. Benedict clearly decided to make up his parental obligations.

"You should be more careful next time," he said with artificial seriousness. Zuzanna wanted to laugh.

"Yeah, I should get better at running away" agreed Tadzio.

"I didn't mean that," Benedict continued in a more serious tone.

"You should thank Benek" mother said before Tadzio could reply. "He pulled you out of juvenile school or even from prison. Assaulting a policeman is a serious matter and they could've convicted you like an adult. You are already sixteen."

"Thank you," Tadzio mumbled without due respect.

***

In the winter Zuzanna's mother began to feel unwell. She called, asking her daughter to visit her after work. Something in her voice worried Zuzanna.

"I'm going to the hospital tomorrow," she said. She claimed that it was nothing serious and, despite repeated pressure from Zuzanna, she refused to refer to Benedict's contacts. "I am a nurse. I also have some connections. Certainly not like your husband's," she said with clearly felt irony, "but it's enough for me. I'll be back soon anyway".

However, weeks passed, and the prospect of returning was not approaching. Mother's condition was getting worse. She did not complain, but despite the subsequent drugs, the test results were increasingly alarming. With increasing difficulty, and with increasing rarity mother got out of bed to sit in the chair in which at the beginning she spent most of her time. Without informing his mother-in-law, Benedict contacted his father's old friends. However, what the doctors in the hospital were saying was confirmed. Actually, it was not known what was happening to Teresa Sokół. "Blood test results are so bad that a bit more time, and leukemia could be suspected. Terrible weakness of the body. And these heart problems..." the doctors complained. Over time, some kind of infection caught on. Mother was rarely able to get up from bed anymore. A dried, gray old woman. Zuzanna realized that her mother was not yet fifty years old. Her contemporaries from Benedict's company acted like young women.

Zuzanna became close with her brother again. Not only did he often sit with her next to mother, but from the hospital they usually went to the Brok apartment and talked long into the night, or just sat side by side, looking at the darkness outside the window. Sometimes Tadzio slept at their place. She was surprised by his maturity. Benedict often visited his mother-in-law, but, as usual, he was rarely at home.

Tadzio passionately absorbed his mother's memories. Never before, maybe except at night after the death of her husband, when she told her daughter about him for several hours, did she say so much. Mainly about her husband. She wondered out loud with her children, what his escape from a Soviet camp might've look like. Once again, she was convinced that he could've gone to the West, but he stayed in Poland to find her. Their romance began in '41, when mother was seventeen and he was twenty. In '41 he was already an officer in the AK[4], they sent him east to the Wilno region. During the negotiations, he was captured and imprisoned by the Soviets.

"Father didn't even want to tell about what was going on there, what they were doing to our people, but at last he mentioned a few things," mother said with difficulty, breaking through the old trauma. A few months later, the uprising broke out in Warsaw. Father only found her a year after the war. Shortly afterwards they got married and Zuzanna was born. Father began to study architecture. They arrested him two years later.

"Do you know that the one who interrogated, beat and humiliated him, was a Jew?" Mother said once, staring at her daughter. Zuzanna felt pain and shame.

"And what? And how many pure-blooded Poles were there?!" Zuzanna could not spare herself irony.

"You're right. Many. And yet I precisely remembered him."

One day, mother awoke from the lethargy in which she was immersed in more and more often. She looked more closely at her daughter. Tadzio was not with them.

"I told you about the uprising. Enthusiasm in the beginning. Joy that is hard to describe, although people were dying around. We were regaining freedom and capturing our city. We were regaining dignity. Then there was more and more death and hopelessness. And suffering...Our city was being destroyed; we were being destroyed. So many of my friends were killed, people whom I loved, and yet I can't condemn it, say that it wasn't necessary to fight...I will never cross it out! Despite what happened...What happened to me...I never told you what happened after, when I was escaping from the Śródmieście through the sewers...It wasn't yet a camp, but

4. The "Home Army" – the underground that fought the Germans

they locked us in a few houses. A bunch of Ukrainians or whoever else was keeping watch over us. Of course, Germans were also there. Some week I don't remember much of or don't want to remember. They started drinking in the morning. They were even capable of being nice then. Only later...At noon they were already drunk. They began to hunt women. I remember, as if this was all just a dream. Such a nightmare that haunts me in my sleep...I don't really know what actually happened and what I imagined. What they did to me...what they did with me...Some women saved me. They took me to this kind of improvised infirmary. I laid there I don't know how many days. Then I ran away. Sometimes I wake up terrified and with relief realize that it was a dream. Only that these dreams repeat what happened then. I imagine that these are also dreams, only earlier ones. But they were not dreams, although I do not exactly remember those events. I didn't tell anyone about this. I had to tell you."

Zuzanna recalled her mother's scream, which awakened her from her child's sleep several times. Immediately after, mother was at her bed and was calming her down. Now Zuzanna thougth that maybe she was also calming herself.

For his seventeenth birthday, Tadzio brought a bunch of white roses to the hospital.

"Thank you very much for bringing me into the world. All in all, it's pretty good here. There are some many things I couldn't try if it weren't for you" he said jokingly, but it could be heard that he was moved. Mother was also touched and she got out of bed for a few moments.

"Tadzio is almost grown now," she said when they were alone.

"I feel a little at peace. You're an adult. You have a good husband. You can help your brother. I can leave now."

"What mom?!" Zuzanna almost became angered.

"Come on. We all have to die. And I don't feel good here after Janusz's death. When you were younger, when Tadzio...but now you can do it. And I..."she reassured her daughter with a hand gesture "I know that I am dying, but...I do not despair. Since Janusz died...I won't say, it was even nice. I also found good people. I helped someone. And above all there's you two." She grabbed Zuzanna's hand and pulled her close. "Actually, I only regret that I don't have a grandson, that you...I mean, I regret so many things, but they are beyond us. That, what's happening in our country, which they took from us...But we...You're twenty-seven years old. I don't know why we live, why God ordered us to suffer so. But you have it better and... Tadzio was right. Surely, you probably don't regret, that you're alive. Without you my...anyone's life would have no value. Somehow it is this way. If we don't extend life, everything loses its meaning."

She died not long after. They buried her next to her husband.

***

"Benek?" She heard a playful female voice.

"With whom do I have pleasure with?" She asked in sudden confusion. Someone laughing on the other side hung up.

"Some woman wanted to talk to you, but she hung up when she heard me..." Zuzanna started to speak in Benedict's direction, who was just leaving the house. He looked at Zuzanna like a schoolboy caught red-handed.

"I don't know who it was, I have to go now," he said uncertainly and too quickly.

On the tram to work, Zuzanna remembered her last meeting in the company of "The Republic". Pieczycki flirted with her again. It was beginning to take on the nature of a ritual, although he was dismissed so many times, he still had hope. This time he had a lot to drink.

"Sławek, give it a rest" Zuzanna was tired of it "you're friends with my husband."

"I am not offering you marriage," he said, leaning toward her, "maybe we can just refresh your relationship. Benek is not so prudish..."

"What are you trying to say?" Zuzanna snapped, who decided that Pieczycki was going too far.

"No, no...nothing" he got scared and walked away.

Now those words, to which she didn't give much weight, began to mean something. She remembered the wives' glances sideways at her, which could carry information tinted with mockery. From memory smirks returned, which she noticed out of the corner of her eye, more and more ostentatiously. She thought then that it was a reflex of jealousy. Benedict's career was soaring. In a few months, the series *Managers* was to be broadcast, widely announced as the first television film that bravely tackles Poland's problems. Benedict was everywhere: in newspapers, on the radio, on television. Envy of her husband could seek compensation in the mockery of the cheated wife. Now, however, the signs formed a single pattern, in which all elements matched each other. I'm paranoid, she tried to calm herself down at work, but she could not think of anything else, and suspicions turned into certainty. Benedict was having an affair. Earlier unimportant details, her husband's strange behavior, the sudden reduction of his temperament and, above all, the more frequent stays outside the home, arranged themselves in a more precise story and her attempts to question it seemed to be useless.

"Let's face it. Supposedly things are changing, but Jurek needs to order me decent cosmetics in London. And these aren't any luxuries, God forbid, just Western, even lower standard..." Julita chattered. Zuzanna probably liked Podlecki's wife the most of all the female company of 'The Republic'. She did not find in her this special pretentiousness or that specific, salon sophistication, manifested in a constant, ironic game that kept her from others. Maybe Julita was just more stupid and that's why Zuzanna made an appointment with her for coffee? "We are wives of journalistic stars, yet we live at the level of German workers or worse..."

"So, everyone knows about Benek's affair?" Zuzanna interrupted.

"So you...you know..." nearly mumbled Podlecka. "I mean, I don't know anything...Only everyone..."

"Everyone knows!"

"Everyone says, that it's now serious, but I…"

"So that means the ones before weren't serious?"

"I don't think so, I mean, I don't know anything, just...that's what they say..."

"Why is it so serious this time?"

"You know...It's been going on for so long... they say that with the same, this actress...you know anyway."

That evening, Zuzanna moved to her mother's apartment, which Tadek now occupied alone. She left Benedict a card. "I'm leaving. I do not want to act as a reserve at home and babysitter. Your lies humiliate me. Maybe it will be more convenient for you too. You will be able to self-fulfill yourself"

Despite a loud party, her brother received her heroically. He assigned her the kitchen, from where he chased away the guests. After a few shots of vodka, smoking a cigarette from a cigarette and intently listening to the noise outside the door, Zuzanna thought that it hurt less than she feared and that she would not bat an eye. She woke up, knowing, that she could not imagine her life without Benedict.

He called her at work. He started in an almost accusatory tone but interrupted him. "Do you want to lie to me again?" He hesitated and began to inaccurately explain something. Zuzanna hung up the phone.

It was a few dizzy and painful days. She dreamed that her husband would come and justify himself and she would say everything she thought about him and throw him out; she hoped that everything would turn out to be a series of misunderstandings that he would explain, and in this scramble of thoughts and feelings she only knew that she wanted him to come and she did not know how she would behave.

He came after three days, when she came back from work, again not knowing what to do with herself. When she heard the long bell, she was sure, it was him. He came with a huge bouquet of tea roses.

"I would like to apologize to you very much, I'm a fool. That everything is finished and will not happen again. I'm an idiot, but I know I love you so much and I can't imagine my life without you. I would love to erase all the crap I did. It's all because we are somehow moving away from each other lately. In thinking, feeling... No, I don't want to justify myself, I'm just describing. Believe me, it doesn't mean anything. It's just like you said by Solina. It is only us. But we will have a baby. If you want to. Because I would love to."

***

Adam was born in the late spring the following year.

"If it a son, could we name him after my father?" Benedict asked timidly. "It's a tradition with us, but if you..."

She agreed immediately. The offer even made her happy. She often thought of Benedict's father, who, before his death, had become an extremely close person to her. It wasn't until later that she remembered her father and felt a twinge of remorse.

Zuzanna endured the inconvenience of pregnancy unexpectedly well. Aunt Gienia helped her a lot and looked after her. This life, however, which was glowing in her, helped overcome rebellious physiology, anxiety attacks and depression. Pains and nausea, waves of sexual excitement and disgust to herself, feelings of helplessness and unexpected, despite her surroundings, sense of abandonment - all this was dominated by pride and confidence in herself. She was a mother. The discomfort of everyday life, the dullness of the city and the country, the insolent lies of the propaganda and a sense of powerlessness, which was heard in the aggression of passers-by and passengers, in the arrogance of people in offices from the saleswoman to the director, everything decreased to the buzz of the moment. The child to be born took Zuzanna into the future, a different and better time, and allowed her to gain a distance to the miserable era. With affection she thought about her parents, about Benedict's father, and at times she had the impression, that she feels their presence next to her.

Benedict was tenderness incarnate and Zuzanna could think, that things are getting better between them, if not...If not for other matters that had not spoiled anything, but left an unpleasant residue, which in time layered itself until it poisons their relations. But then it seemed to her that she could go over it on a daily basis as if it were the stumbles of a clumsy child. Her husband became a little older son, who deserved to have much forgiven and his future watched over with concern.

With great hype, television began broadcasting the series *Managers*, for which the script was written by Benedict. Every week, sixteen episodes in turn, four months. They were separate, hour-long films, although sometimes in following episodes characters from previous ones appeared. Each episode told the story of an employee who was promoted, to managerial and sometimes CEO position. Full of enthusiasm and new ideas, it collided with the conservatism of the environment and even superiors, but thanks to party connections it found allies at higher levels, who not only helped him implement his ideas, but promoted them, and the hero convinced most of his former adversaries to his projects. Incidentally, love and friendly intrigues took place, but everything ended well, although sometimes the final result of the hero's actions was suspended, and the film cut out when waiting for the result. There was even one episode without a happy ending. The hero broke down and gave up, but the filmmakers suggested that his place would be taken by another enthusiast, with whom viewers had already got acquainted. Zuzanna was struck by the show's schematic and ostentatious didacticism. However, Benedict began a preventive conversation.

"Maybe you shouldn't watch these movies," he went on playfully.

"They're not for you. This isn't supposed to be great art. But, film journalism, such an intervention. They're supposed to encourage. Encourage people not to be afraid to fight for change and decision makers to invest in it. After all it's worth it."

"Does that have to be so...so flat? They're perfromance" Zuzanna broke out.

"Well, you are exaggerating a little," Benedict replied, somewhat offended, trying to maintain an amusing exterior. "I said they are not great works. I did not claim to be an artist. As you say, these perfromances nevertheless have a task to fulfill. Maybe more important than many artistic manifestations. Originally, the scenarios were slightly different. The heroes did not always win. I wrote them based on my own reporting experience. However, they convinced me that they should look different."

"They convinced?" Zuzanna asked against her will, because a quarrel with Benedict was the last thing she wanted to have in her current state.

"They convinced." Benedict kept his head and was still smiling. "Not only pressed, but also convinced. It's all about effect, honey. We know very well that this system is not perfect. But there are no perfect systems. These films are didactic, but is that bad? There are always those who know how to gain power and those who understand reality. And the point is for the latter to be able to convince the former to do the right thing. Besides, the first effects of the film you can already try out. The car you drive doesn't make you angry?"

Zuzanna had to agree on this. The Fiat 125p, which Benedict purchased for part of the fee, beyond the queue that would have postpone the purchase by years, was the source of her endless satisfaction. And she would rather not think about the series. Maybe something will change thanks to him?

The "Teleneta" program was considered the most significant journalism of Polish television. Despite her fears, Zuzanna could not resist watching it.

"I would like to thank the current party leadership not only for that, in the conditions created by it, the series *Managers* could appear on TVP, but mainly for the fact that the problems shown in it can find their happy end" said Benedict with deep seriousness at the end. Aunt Gienia looked at Zuzanna with a hard to name expression on her face.

"Did you have to say that?" Zuzanna asked Benedict in a tone in which, as she realized irritably, sounded like the complaint of a resentful child.

"It's a price," Benedict explained. He spoke quickly, as if he wanted to guess, anticipate her further accusations. "They agreed on it with me earlier. I know how it sounds" he calmed her outrage with a gesture "but understand, this is a part of the whole game. You have to caress them, appease them, convince them to do what we want, still believing that they're decide."

"What do we want?" Zuzanna asked, surprised.

"What do you mean what? It's obvious" Benedict was taken aback. "Within the limits of possibility...well...to liven up the economy, for people to have it better. To introduce market mechanisms...absorb new technologies...Well, what am I telling you...it's clear!"

The question, does Benedict still believe, in what he says, Zuzanna did not ask.

The reception in honor of the team of *Managers*, and therefore Benedict, was organized at the Palace of Culture. To Benedict's anxious questions Zuzanna expressed her willingness to participate, although the large belly in which the child could arrange wild frolics, did not put her in a playful mood, and her attitude towards *Managers* remained unchanged.

The first part of the ceremony took place in the conference room. There was a screen behind the pulpit, and the speeches were pointed out by fragments of the film. Comrade Alojzy Walaszczyk from the Political Bureau spoke first and talked about how important it is for comrades, artists and journalists, to carry out their plans with excess. "Because and you all, comrades, remember, you have your task in the national production front" he said. Zuzanna looked around. On unmoving faces there were no smiles to be seen, maybe in the eyes...Maybe.

Next was the minister of culture. Then the president of Radio committee and editor Goleń, who had already managed to become a member of the Central Committee. Benedict was the fifth consecutive speaker. It was a clear honor because he appeared before the director of the series and a critic who praised the film's production qualities. This part of the ceremony lasted only a little over an hour and a half, and its time limit, as she heard later from regulars, was a symptom of positive changes and a gesture to the creators of the series. In addition to gratitude to the party's leadership, government and television, next to plans, tasks, socialism, a people's homeland, capitalist crisis and progress, Goleń intertwined comments on reform that allows one to think of real socialist competition. Benedict thanked the authorities relatively sparingly, while more, although quite vaguely, he talked about the need for a new one. The director thanked the authorities that enabled the synthesis of art and social activity. The critic dwelt on how thanks to socialist patronage, new content gets artistically interesting expression.

The banquet took place in the next room, where the participants went, dignified at first, and then speeding up the pace and crowding at the entrance. The tables were richly set beneath crystal chandeliers, and the waiters kept bringing subsequent plates and bottles, those gathered emptied them with passion.

Zuzanna, could not drink alcohol, she ate only a little mayonnaise salad and fish, which she could not associate with anything. What's important is that it's tasty, she agreed with herself. She came up toward the commotion whose epicenter was at the corner of the table. Lech Sopel, with a red face, embraced by Podlecki, who whispered something in his ear, drank another large shot in one gulp and, breaking free from the friendly embrace, shouted:

"Don't you see it?! This is the end of life on credit! The disaster is just around the corner. They won't lend to us forever. And we won't pay them with our trash made according to socialist norms! It's finiiiiiiished, you understand! We're drowning."

Suddenly two men appeared on both sides and led him out so abruptly that he virtually didn't get a chance to protest.

"I wanted to calm him down. This could end badly for him." Muttered Podlecki.

"He's been drinking too much for some time. I don't think I can protect him" snapped Goleń angrily. "And in such a moment!"

"Well, yes, Benku, such a success" Podlecki stammered with admiration and envy.

"Yes, just it's not turning out the best for us. We're trying in the *'Republic'*, Benek even more and what? What are the effects?" Said almost defiantly a drunk little man with protruding ears.

"What are you talking about, Kaziu?! Did you think there would be a revolution?!" Goleń directed all his anger at Niecnota, who had to sit down.

"No, Władek, I know what it means that you are on the committee, but you know...this all goes so slowly. After all, we won't avoid increases in prices, and how will the increases be ... you know. Workers can...you know..." Niecnota hung his voice. Zuzanna could not stand it.

"Why are you talking like this? How did you get such a feeling of superiority?!" Niecnota glanced at her, stopped his gaze and chuckled. Others joined him. Zuzanna was taken by fury, which for a moment didn't let her get a word out.

"Your involvement is nice, but..." Goleń soothed her, embracing her, "but a little, don't be offended, naive. Work has its dignity, workers are the salt of the earth, but...you don't know them."

"I...don't know?" Zuzanna freed herself from his embrace and regained the ability to speak. "My mother was a nurse from the village, my father was a worker, although he wanted to study. My family...I know them as I know you all. I don't see you being better!" Everyone around laughed. Even Goleń could not remain serious. Zuzanna wanted to cry.

***

"They took us to the stadium. The buses rode furiously and delivered new people. There was a crowd. Mostly they were party members, but they took some like me to fill the stadium. There, activists were already spreading banners and waving them. The next ones to the microphone condemned the troublemakers from Radom and Ursus. It was stupid. Although Szymek took half a liter and in three of us that we would drink from the bottle, to endure it somehow. The heat was sweltering. They already brought crowds of people and it became stuffy. It seems a little funny, Szymek was telling jokes, we were laughing, but it was a mess anyway. As if we were eating shit."

Uncle Stach sat down, and with a grim face was looking around the kitchen. His wife embraced him and he buried his head on her breasts. He returned grim from work, which ended in a rally at the 10th-Anniversary Stadium. Zuzanna and her one-year-old Adam sat at aunt Gienia's. Busy with the child, she did not follow what was happening in the country. Only the information about the increases in prices awoke her curiosity. News of strikes broke through the jammers from Free Europe.

"Did you hear?" She asked Benedict. He heard about it and was concerned.

"You know, raises in prices are inevitable. We live on credit. Money ceases to have coverage. There won't be anything in stores soon."

"And now... What's there?" Zuzanna drawled out.

"Exactly...You have to make prices more realistic, because even that which we have will be gone."

"And who caused this?!" She shouted. "They didn't ask us for an opinion. Let them deal with it now!"

Benedict shook his head. He began to explain He did not defend the government's economic policy, but since it was adopted, its consequences must be borne. Otherwise everything will collapse. Zuzanna hated these arguments and such discussions with her husband. Maybe because she could not beat his arguments, and passionately felt that she was right. Benedict's consistent reasoning, which convinced her that the distances between systems were smaller than it seemed, and he argued that sometimes worse order was better than chaos, caused confusion.

"We idolize, that which we do not have" he said, and Zuzanna was losing her support and stopped understanding the world around her.

The price increases were canceled. The strikes died down. In Radom and Ursus people were hunted down. They were beaten and arrested. Television was full of condemnation of the "troublemakers". Zuzanna felt humiliation. Benedict agreed.

"It shouldn't be like this," he affirmed. "You can't act so brutally. But anarchy cannot be allowed either...especially in this geopolitical system, with Russia at its head."

Zuzanna screamed. Finding no arguments, she hurled insults at her husband. He fell silent and she felt ashamed. Agreeing was pleasant, but she did not want to bring about a situation where it became necessary.

The establishment of the Workers' Defense Committee, of which she learned from Free Europe, and immediately afterwards mentioned it to her Natasza in the publishing house, caused another discussion.

"It's a suicidal initiative. And dangerous," said Benedict, and anticipating her outburst, he added: "I'm full of admiration for the courage of these people and I understand their intentions, but...you know what hell is paved with. Weber theorized this. The consequences need to be thought of."

"This mean, that we can't lean out?! Are we to live like rats?! In the closet?!" Zuzanna choked on the words that carried her. And only after speaking did she understand the meaning of her last issue. Benedict winced, put his head between his shoulders and turned away from her.

"I'm sorry. I didn't want to. It just came out like that," she explained, embracing him. This time they made peace very easily, but Zuzanna had the feeling that something bad remained between them.

It was another party of the "Republic". Zuzanna had conflicting feelings. She was irritated by the editors, journalists, their wives and mistresses, who were full of superiority and arrogance. At the same time, it was also her world. She only had occasional contact with her colleagues from the "Portico". Outside the circle of the "Republic," stronger ties connected her exclusively with her family: Aunt Gienia and her relatives as well as relatives in the countryside. She liked them, but she was unable to talk to them about many things, and even when she did, she seemed to be trying to translate herself into a language she did not have complete control over. That's why sometimes meeting with them could be tiring. Sometimes she wondered if her interlocutors felt the same. There was also her brother: someone so special in Zuzanna's life like Benedict, but he was only nineteen. Among the annoying figures in the circle of the "Republic", she felt at home. She joked around with them in a more sophisticated manner, where ironic approaches became a kind of art. The cynical distance that allowed one to tame the world, almost invalidate it, was almost amusing. Reality ceased to be dangerous. You could not remember how close the border is to what is allowed. Reality was that which was allowed. One could even play with it. Only sometimes did Zuzanna discover that nothing but Benedict's work connected her with these people, and even that she's able to feel aversion to them that turns into hostility. However, when she did not see them for a long time, she began to feel the need for contact. Maybe it is a way to relax, focusing on her son and being closed at home, escape between people, into a world where problems are lighter...- she tried to explain to herself.

It was another party at the Goleń apartment, which, although unique, ceased to make an impression on Zuzanna. She got used to similar standards. This time, quite spontaneously, the meeting evolved into a debate on the KOR (Workers Defense Committee). The host himself attacked the initiative with the support of those present.

"Immature little shits!" he yelled.

"Some of them are older than you" someone noticed.

"And what about it?" Goleń fired back.

"But wait, Władek" Niecnota interjected, to whom alcohol added courage.

"It's not bad. They're building a strong opposition. Against this background, we look moderate. They'll get thrown into jail and we'll be the ones they'll talk with," he chuckled.

"Just shut up, Kaziu. When you say something..."Goleń snarled, and Niecnota fell silent, terrified of his own courage.

"Do you have to be so cynical?!" let out Zuzanna, who promised herself that she would not speak. Indignation and alcohol broke the barriers. "You think you are so important, but you jump when they tell you to. You don't have anything to say!"

"Watch out, you're talking about your husband," Pieczycki said in an undertone. Zuzanna heard. Humiliation took her voice.

"I was sure that our protester would speak up" the host said with good-natured sneer. The entire environment had managed to notice his atypical understanding of Zuzanna.

We want to do something, not demonstrate and close ranks, in accordance with our worst tradition. With bare chests against tanks. We must overcome this romantic curse. From Somosierra to the Warsaw Uprising. Mountains of corpses and what? What do we have from these beautiful symbols?" Goleń's gesture hung in the air, as if afraid of its meaning. The host lowered his voice: "I know many of those who make up this committee. They seemed reasonable and decent people. But they were carried away by our passion for self-destruction. If they want to die...too bad, but they drag others with themselves, everyone, the whole nation. And that's why I'm protesting. The hard-liners already say that there was too much of this freedom. Here comes the information...you know where and you can imagine, what kinds are being returned via return mail. Everything we've won can be damned."

"And those people, whom they're beating up there? Those they're locking up, what about them?" Zuzanna snapped.

Goleń looked at her disappointed. Others exchanged glances with barely hidden disgust.

"Every country must punish criminals, even if the city's demolition and shoplifting take place under a political banner."

"But they're not locking people up for that in Radom or Ursus."

"Do you know for sure? Investigations are ongoing over there. There may be mistakes, but we can't throw accusations without evidence. Free Europe is propaganda. And those from KOR? After all they're instrumentally using workers."

Zuzanna wasn't able argue with him. It wasn't until she returned home that she spoke to her conciliatory husband: "People are being persecuted there. You get over it too easily."

"But Zuza. Do you think they didn't steal when the opportunity arose? These feelings of yours for the workers is a modern workermania. You keep saying, that you're one of them, but do you at least know them? Have you seen what they are capable of? After all, this system grew out of a silly cult of the worker!"

"I know, what they're capable of. But I know, that there's something else in them. They're like my family, I would want to help them. But those in the Party... even your friends from 'The Republic'...At times I think, that there's nothing else in them beyond these...games. Their intelligence serves only to justify that, which they do."

"Zuza, that's endearing," Benedict spoke to her like a child, embracing her and starting to kiss her. He was already very drunk. "Someone else might think that you only play, and I know you are like that...and that's..."

"Give me a break!" Zuzanna broke free. She didn't let herself be appeased. Her anger at the company of the 'Republic', at everything around her, she finally focused herself on Benedict. She was amazed by the resentment she felt towards her husband.

Tadek was accepted to study philosophy. For several years it was possible to study it again in a normal fashion. His joy spread to everyone, and even one-year-old Adam looked excited about his uncle's stories. They celebrated with wine at "Fukier".

"So, what now? Will we just interpret the world or change it?" Said Benedict, striking a toast with Tadek.

"It will have to be changed, so as to be able to interpret it," Tadek replied in a similar tone.

He came to them to listen to Free Europe and talk about philosophy with Benedict. But their intellectual conversations increasingly turned into political quarrels.

CHAPTER 9

"Impossible," Zuzanna heard. Filip Madej stood on the street, staring at her and the pram she was pushing hard through the soft mud. In the early afternoon, we found a free table at the 'Hortex'. Madej was one of Benedict's colleagues, a member of a group that met with them a few years ago and finally broke-up. He was a sociologist, a few years younger than Benedict, who was thrown out of the university with him. He finally got a job at the Polish Academy of Sciences. He returned to his doctorate.

"I don't think anyone thought Benedict would have such a career," he finally said, hiding in cigarette smoke. His sarcasm was ostentatious.

"He turned out to be a positivist," Zuzanna answered, slowly arranging her sentences and promising herself that she would remain cool headed. "We don't always agree, but I think his choice also makes sense."

"Oh, not only sense" Madej almost laughed. "It's confirmed by his subsequent gratifications. The world manifests the correctness of his path."

Zuzanna thought that she should leave. Loyalty to her husband required it. In any case, she must protest. Meanwhile, overcoming her anger, she felt helpless.

"What you say is unpleasant. He's trying to do something. Are you accusing him, us, of not starving?"

"God forbid!" Madej became serious. "I didn't mean to offend you, especially you. I just want to be honest. His positivism borders on propaganda. Benek probably has the best intentions, but...what can be improved in this way? We sell the illusion that we live in a normal state! But let's give it a break, I don't want to talk about politics..."

"Then tell me, what else can be done? What more can be done?!" Zuzanna almost shouted. Madej looked at her closely.

This is how Zuzanna's cooperation with KOR began. She started using the car more often. Benedict was pleased that his wife was leading a more social life. She carried packages of the "Information Bulletin", reams of paper and parts for the copier. She received directions from Filip and met unknown people from whom she received something to pass on to the next. She remembered some of them. She learned surveillance recognition techniques. Overcoming fear and tension, she felt something special. She was afraid, but she finally faced what surrounded her, what took her breath away while causing her to feel ashamed every day, but not knowing what for. With tension and anxiety, she felt that something unusual was happening. A gasp of oxygen in the air of the city, choking like the stench of a dirty rag that absorbed dirt and invisibly spreading between people, percolating sweat and fear, despair and stupor, waste of the day and nightmares. In the capital of the communist country, which was denied hope, she felt a fresh blast, and then a surge of fear. She swayed on the edge between fear and excitement.

"Maybe you'll live differently" she whispered to Adam "Maybe..."

She was able to withstand the pressure of the crowd of sad and tired passers-by better, whose humiliation could break out as aggression against anyone as they crowded the stores for meat scraps and shoddy clothing; they stood in endless queues, waiting for something that could be delivered; they fought for a place in suffocating buses and trams. It was easier for her to bear the grayness of the city, the ruined walls disfigured with ideological slogans, dirty streets lined with stinking paint and the lies of the newspapers. Sometimes she had the impression that thanks to her commitment she could free herself from the pressures of everyday life and the trap of history. She saw herself pushing the pram with Adam on a dirty street, the walls of the houses surrounding her, the city and country from a different perspective, from a different point of time and space that gave peace and understanding which was difficult to put into words...

The mud of autumn turned into the mud of winter, and the puddles turned into snow sludge, which slowly melted, revealing the droppings of the past year. It was early spring. A dirty spring began. Zuzanna decided to tell her husband about her involvement. He was shocked. At first, he couldn't find the words. He looked at her helplessly. He stood up and started walking around, puffing nervously on his cigarette.

"Why are you telling me this just now?"

"I didn't think I needed permission. And I really wanted to spare you the anxiety. Finally, however, loyalty...you understand it yourself. In the end I use our car, in fact, more yours..." Zuzanna wanted to give the conversation a slightly lighter character, but Benedict did not acknowledge the convention.

"You must not know what you're getting into! Do you think they'll tolerate you for long? Have you ever wondered why they do it? Maybe it's a provocation? Maybe they're flushing out all those desperate individuals, raking them into a sack, to lock them up and intimidate everyone? Don't you think about that? And about Adam?"

Zuzanna was overtaken by anger.

"Do you want to take away any hope from me? Even my rebellion? And I tell you: nobody controlled me or those I know. Maybe they'll lock us up, but I don't feel like living in...a sewer. Maybe you are deluding yourself? You repeat: we've achieved.. and I ask: what have you achieved? Yes, you have a car, you earn good money, and I am with you...Only...sometimes I am ashamed!"

Benedict looked her in the eye and for some time stopped and stared. He put on his coat and left the apartment. Zuzanna wanted to stop him, even apologize, but everything happened too quickly. She sat by the window and took Adam on her lap. She smoked a cigarette, trying to blow the other way, and she rocked him, humming some improvised song. One had to watch carefully to see the barely appearing buds on the branches behind the glass.

She woke up in the night. Her husband was laying down next to her. She felt the intense smell of alcohol. She turned on the bedside lamp. Benedict watched her and tried to smile, but he did not succeed.

"You know what I think about your involvement. About KOR. But I know you well enough that I won't try to dissuade you from this. You are my wife. We have a son. I…I love you. We'll have to live with it somehow." He leaned in a little awkwardly to her. It was a rush of feeling. She embraced her husband.

Soon after, Benedict came home with a bouquet of roses and an uncertain smile. Zuzanna felt that something bad had happened.

"I signed up to the Party," he said after a casual chat.

"Whaaaaat?" Zuzanna thought she had misheard. Her husband took advantage of her bewilderment by saying that this decision is a consequence of the strategy he adopted when taking up a job in the "Republic" and that one should try to act in such conditions as exist, and one should not worry about signs, just...

"You must not believe in what you're saying! She interrupted him. She was stupefied and embittered. He started explaining again.

"I don't want to hear it!" she screaked "I'm ashamed for you."

Her husband looked at her with a gaze which was bitterness mixed with embarrassment. She took Adam and left.

She had to decide. If she stayed with Benedict, she must at least partly believe in his explanation. After some time, pushing the pram in front of him blindly and subsequent collisions with passers-by she realized that her husband's joining of the Party was in the logic of his actions. The fact that she had to interpret this act in this way was understood many years later, in different circumstances, after parting with her husband, when she was thinking about her life once again. At the time, in 1977, although she recognized that Benedict's decision was within his sphere of freedom, just like her involvement in the opposition was, it was another painful disillusionment. She would never really be capable of forgiving her husband. Feeling sorry for him will build up, bore in her, and transform into aversion appearing more often and stronger than before.

It was a May evening. The doorbell was persistent. Benedict almost jumped out of his chair. Zuzanna noticed that he had been reacting a lot more nervously lately. He looked at her in alarm, as if he was waiting for her to open it. Her brother stood in the doorway.

"Zuza!" He shouted, embracing her. She knew something important had happened. "We went because a friend from Kraków called that something's happening. You know, it was about the demonstration of mourning during the juwenalia's, after the murder of a student, Pyjas. There was a crowd of secret agents at the station, but they weren't looking for us. Besides there was a lot of people. I managed to pass. We went to mass at the Dominican church. People couldn't fit in, a large group had to stand outside. But the sermon was heard through megaphones. A beautiful sermon. The priest was talking about the wall, the living wall that we're building. He proclaimed that the death of Pyjas meant something, and he himself became a rock, a speaking rock on which the community would rise. Then we formed a procession. With mourning flags, we walked across the market square to Szewska Street, where Pyjas's body was found. Candles were burning in front of the gate, a lake of candles. The walls were covered with information about what happened. Some shaggy student, supposedly his friend, read a leaflet about the murder and calling for a boycott of the juwenalia's. He called us to an evening manifestation. We knew something had to happen. The juwenalia were dying out. There were still some disguised clowns, but hardly anyone paid attention to them. Someone on the juwenalia stages was trying to organize some fun, but that was a margin. Students walked around the market square, next to the streets, reading information about Pyjas's death, calling for a stop to the fun and calling everyone to Szewska Street for the evening. After dark, after eight, we were able to get there with difficulty. On the street we were packed like canned sardines. Suddenly, it turned out that the exit to the market square was blocked by the UB's, who took each other by the arm and created a multi-row dam. Before they succeeded, a group with black banners, which opened the procession, broke into the market. Then the UB phalanx tore apart the crowd, and the street outlet was closed off. To those who got through, others joined in at the square and the demonstration of several thousand went to Wawel. I know because one of ours got through with them. There they announced the establishment of the Student Solidarity Committee. Meanwhile, in a packed crowd we were choking on Szewska St. Then that shaggy one, who read the obituary, began to shout to turn the procession over, go out to Planty Park and get to Wawel that way. We pushed through and went through the dark alleys. Others joined us. At the head I saw two tiny girls, almost children. We walked with candles in silence and darkness because the lights went out; they gradually extinguished the lanterns before us. The UB's were redeploying, chasing us along the trees, but again, there were thousands of us, so they only accompanied us, followed us at night. We were crossing the street; someone ran out and stopped the vehicles. Finally, we came to Wawel. A lawn of candles was burning under the wall. Kudłacz read the declaration about the establishment of the Student Solidarity Committee. He didn't have a microphone and only single words came to us. Then someone else, probably an actor, with an expressive, somewhat monkey-like face read the same, louder and clearer, but it was no longer necessary, after all we already understood everything. The point was that we were no longer lonely like Pyjas. There are people who don't want to be silent anymore. They revealed themselves. They provided their names and addresses, like KOR. Now it will have to be done in Warsaw..."

"That's weird," he continued after a moment. "A painful and dreary affair. They beat our colleague to death, and I feel optimism, but at the same time I feel sorry for him...That's how it is. We were capable of protesting and we won. These were the first demonstrations that the police did not break up."

"And how do you know, that UB's killed him?" Benedict broke the silence.

"How's this from? Tadek seemed surprised. "Everything points to it. The circumstances. They received anonymous letters saying to take care of him. They began to work intensively. The authorities did everything to present death as an accident..."

"And how do you know it wasn't an accident?" Benedict was inquisitive. Zuzanna noticed that in conversations like this he could be extremely calm.

"What do you mean how?" Tadek was beginning to get upset. "But everything... They were in the dissecting room. They saw a bruised person."

"Who were they?"

"His friends!"

"And that's enough for you? These are specific witnesses. Are they specialists who can distinguish one injury from another? Think it over. They're his friends. They were in a state of heightened anxiety..."

"What are you trying to say? That this all was a misunderstanding and that we should apologize to the authorities?"

"No, I'm just trying to understand the situation. Sine ira et studio, have you learned this yet?"

Zuzanna hated the tone Benedict was using. She saw that her brother could not answer him with calm reasoning. He was looking for words, arguments, but he was in a losing position under an onslaught of skepticism, and Zuzanna could only oppose it with the feeling of justness deprived of argumentation. Without a word, she came up to Tadek and embraced him. She looked at Benedict with reluctance.

***

She was waiting behind the wheel on the inner street of Ursynów. She was looking around for someone who was supposed to drop off some materials. He was supposed to throw the packages in as soon as she stopped and then disappear, and she was supposed to leave immediately. She had done it so many times and each time different characters appeared with boxes and evaporated like shadows. For the first time, however, no one came, and Zuzanna's impatience turned into anxiety. Still, she waited, more and more uncertain. Five minutes passed, which dragged on terribly long, seemed like hours, and Zuzanna decided to leave when a breathless Filip jumped into the seat next to her.

"Drive!" He commanded. He led her through the thicket of streets, ordered her to do a loop, and only when he was sure that no one was behind them did he start talking.

"They went after us. All the young members of KOR are locked up. They locked up Kuroń, Macierewicz, Chojecki, Lityński and others. They threw Michnik in as well, who just managed to fly in from Paris. In total, several people with sanctions are waiting in custody for a trial. The printing house where you worked fell through. I don't know if this isn't the beginning, that they won't lock me up too, although I hope that they don't know about me. After Kraków, they decided that they would no longer picket. Stay low for now. We will continue to do our job. Those, who will stay. I will visit you at the publishing house as soon as I know how the distribution network works. I will give your contact to someone trusted in case they lock me up. He'll say he is from me and...it concerns the paper about the suicide."

At home, Benedict looked at her strangely. On the table lay the "Republic" with an introduction by the editor-in-chief of "Silence Above this Casket". Goleń was indignant that the human tragedy, which was the death, even if a bit of a reckless man like Pyjas, was used shamelessly as a pawn in the political game. "To what level of wickedness must one drop to, to present an accident as a crime exclusively to advance ones own political interests?" Goleń asked rhetorically. The article was long but did not go beyond this simple message revolved in all possible ways and decorated with all available decorative rhetorical possibilities. It was about 'extreme cynicism', 'insolent gossip preying', 'taking advantage of naivety and gullibility'. The text ended with calling for those who "broke all the principles of not only socialist, but also of civilized civilian coexistence", to be inclined to taking responsibility for their actions and "that severe consequences would be brought against them."

Zuzanna threw the weekly. "And what? Is this what you fought for? Is this what you've achieved?" She asked with a contemptuous laugh, though her own voice sounded strange in her ears.

"Of course, you understand...They said to Władek that we must take a position..."

"And you took it!"

"It doesn't matter that much..."

"And that, which you write about your sugar factories does?"

"This is different. That's a proposition, hard fact, and this...this is a kind of ritual, not that important..."

"I don't know if it's that important, I know, that it's vile. This call, to destroy people who dared to say aloud what everyone knows...For example Tadek...And you...you work in such a tabloid?" Zuzanna tossed a copy of the weekly to the ground. Benedict jumped up upset.

"So what…should I quit? Not do anything? Isn't it better, that I'm trying something? I didn't choose this system, none of us did, it doesn't depend on us…so now what? Should I hide in an internal emigration…disappear?"

"I don't know, what you should do. I do know, that I'm ashamed for you…and for myself! I need to get some air." She took Adam and spent a long time walking around the city.

May smelled of melting asphalt, dirt of a flaky city and lilacs. Drunk people staggered down the street. Birds, trying to shout over them, rose their mating trills to the navy-blue sky. A sticky night was watching over the city. Zuzanna was looking at the lights outside the windows.

Freelance writers fulfilled orders. In the shallow patches of lamps, refreshing themselves with alcohol, they wrote about the superiority of socialism, the wisdom of the party and the intelligence of its leaders. They chuckled, bragging to each other about how they would be rewarded for the slop flowing from their machines. They bid on who would write the biggest absurdity. Editors and then censors checked whether ritual gibberish would sound ironic, whether something that reluctant readers might not read properly should appear. Are they able to, from among the selected information arranged in a different reality, bring out an element of truth? The censors checked it again. They corrected texts with guidelines, which were of course supplemented on a regular basis. One need to keep track that the name of someone who has just been removed from the list of people who can be mentioned did not appear. Even editors were not always able to keep up with swelling catalogs of people and things that one could not write about. The tired censor, from a pile of recommendations, struggles to dig out information whether it is allowed to record an accident at an aluminum mill in which several people were killed. It wasn't allowed to write about an increased number of leukemia cases in a region or to record deaths caused by it, nor was it permitted to record a plague on cattle that killed them off in the area. But about an accident? The censor is careful. He writes a note. He recalls the scandal that happened when his colleague did not take care of the next edition of the book on Polish contemporary literature, from which the name of the writer convicted for disobedience to nonexistence was not deleted. The book had to be withdrawn from bookstores. What costs. And the colleague lost his job. Where will he find one now? He will probably have to go to a factory. A lot of work left, because there are still tapes with programs for tomorrow's radio broadcast. The censor carefully moves the glass with cooling tea over the counter covered with printer's copies. One can't trust anyone. They mostly make mistakes from stupidity and sometimes even from zeal. If it weren't for us, the proud censor, were it not for us, it's scary to think what would happen. And are we appreciated? One is moved a bit. Do they know that our work requires more responsibility than a policeman's? Do they know how much they owe it? Our store...some say is that stocked no better than miners in Silesia - funny. However, the censor knows that's no time for getting emotional, especially since it can lead to such dangerous concerns, and the morning editions are waiting.

Zuzanna returned when it got quite dark and Adam was already asleep. Benedict explained. He explained that he did not like the tone of the main article. He suggested that they just drop the subject.

"We won't drop it!" Zuzanna stated.

That night, for the first time since they lived together, they slept separately. Zuzanna was woken up by a wail. Benedict was wailing in the next room, struggling with his nightmares. She stopped her reflex. For the first time, she did not hurry to help him, she did not calm him down. She listened with pain as the moans slowly faded away, and he fell into a restless, bad sleep again.

During the day the house was full of silence. At night, her husband's laments woke her, causing Zuzanna a growing sense of guilt. After a week, or maybe a little later, pulled out of sleep by Benedict's screams, she ran into his room to wake him up and calm him down. With effort he tore his eyelids open, freeing himself from the phantom's trap, and his unconscious eyes changed rapidly at her sight, they became filled with relief. He embraced her. Then, however, there was the day. Their daily interaction did not returned to their former closeness.

He personally appeared at Madej publishing house. Some time passed and he reconstructed the broken distributor's network. Zuzanna received further assignments.

On July 22, a holiday of lies just like the entire Polish People's Republic, an amnesty was announced. KOR members and the last workers kept there for over a year were released, even though some of them received ten years. Madej triumphed. He invited Zuzanna for vodka. His mood spread to her. She felt a sudden relief. One will be able to return to a normal life, give up activism that could have ended up in an accident, in prison, unknown endings. Only after drinking subsequent shots did she realize how deep the tension of recent months had been. His measure was the relief that overwhelmed her and turned into a bliss when the stress began to thaw, steaming and evaporating in the noise of the pub. So one will be able to go back to a normal life. Philip embraced her.

"They backed off, they've broken! Maybe they are afraid of an international incident? Now we have to follow up with another blow. Establish a new institution. We will slowly create an informal opposition. Brick by brick we will tear this wall apart."

So this isn't the end?! Filip's words showed that this was actually the beginning. Anxiety combined with excitement enveloped her. Maybe this is a great opportunity given by history? Maybe this is the opportunity that cannot be missed, she thought, confused by the subsequent doses of alcohol, trying to overcome the strikes of anxiety. And then Philip kissed her. He tilted her head and began kissing harder and more passionately. After a moment of bewilderment, Susanna began to return the kisses. In the dim, hazy light pulsating with drunken shouts, no one was bothered with the kissing couple.

Zuzanna finally decided that it was time end the evening together and she refused Filip's suggesting about going to his place. However, they exchanged kisses and caresses all the way to Zuzanna's apartment. She only pulled herself away from him at the door of the tenement house. Benedict was waiting at home with an open bottle of wine and dinner. He looked at his wife sadly, and she realized that she was drunk and that she feels stupid.

"You know, we were celebrating with friends, you understand..." she explained herself clumsily.

"Of course. There's a reason for joy. I thought we would celebrate it together...I wanted to say that you were right and apologize to you..." he said more resentfully than jealous. Zuzanna, however, avoided continuing the conversation. She barely had time to wash up, after which she fell into a deep sleep.

She refused Benedict's offer to go to the seaside. She didn't even agree to a trip to Niemir, which she liked so much. She stopped going to 'Republic' parties. Autumn came suddenly and ended abruptly. New magazines and the NOW publishing house appeared, the literary magazine "Write" and the Scientific Courses Society were created, and Zuzanna had more and more work, which Filip commissioned her to do. Sometimes they had private meetings. Which ended in kisses and caresses. She came to his studio for the first time in February, she actually came by to warm up. Everything was happening almost beyond her will and awareness. When, after everything, they lit cigarettes, Zuzanna thought that her sensations in Filip's bed, though pleasant, could hardly be called ecstatic and could not be compared with the elation she was able to experience with Benedict. "Maybe one day," said something inside of her. Recently, their erotic meetings had almost died out and this was because of Zuzanna.

She looked at the unknown room and the naked, unknown man wandering around it. She understood that she had cheated on her husband and felt rotten, though she explained to herself that he deserved it.

"Get dressed!" she snapped at Filip, who stood by the bed happily.

"I didn't presume you to be so shy," he bit back, clearly abashed, laying down next to him and struggling to embrace her. Zuzanna however got up.

"I have to go now" she said firmly, interrupting his persuasions "Don't escort me back. The less we are seen together the better"

Despite Filip's efforts, she visited him no more than once a week. She learned to derive satisfaction from their rapprochement, but then a hangover always seized her which she couldn't shake off. She bore the feeling of guilt, which she fought by remembering her husband's betrayal and insignificance. In effect, she felt worse, although her dislike of Benedict grew. They lived side by side more and more, only sometimes at night, woken up from sleep by his wailing, she woke him from nightmares, calmed him, and tenderness could turn into passion. Then, however, a gloomy day crawled out, an edition of the "Republic" lay next to the bed, and in

Zuzanna the long-standing reluctance made itself heard. They met less and less often. They were replacing each other with Adam, so they were rather passing each other than being together.

It was late spring. The smell of flowers blossomed through the sticky smell of the city, and the birds sang in the cacophony of voices. Probably for the first time Zuzanna remembered herself this way in Filip's bed. She experienced endless elation and the world finally drifted away, leaving them in the abyss of spring, which elevated itself above human settlements, cities and thoughts, rules and prohibitions. Then they smoked cigarettes and talked about everything at once, not remembering what was happening outside the walls of the studio on the third floor of Odyńca Street.

When she left, in the approaching, warm dusk, which made the dirt and smell of the city bearable, and the figures of passers-by seemed almost transparent, she felt a sudden desire to return to Filip's the apartment, to his bed, to him. With difficulty she managed to control this impulse and got scared. She tried to understand and organize the thoughts and feelings that did not allow themselves to be arranged into a coherent whole.

"You were supposed to be back over two hours ago" he muttered. Adam threw himself into her embrace.

"I'm sorry, something unexpected came up" she excused herself carelessly.

"Mama, story, story!" her son demanded. Benedict took him from her embrace, kissed him all over, and gave him back.

"Now you take care of him."

She returned to the room when Adam was already asleep. Taking a puff of smoke, Benedict looked at her from under his eye. A lamp on the wall was lit, and circles of light plunged into darkness, leaving the table and the figure sitting beside it in dimness. Zuzanna immersed herself in it. She sat down at the table, lit a cigarette, and after a while she threw out:

"Shouldn't we get divorced? Haven't you thought about it?" Benedict winced, for a moment he was silent.

"Have you thought about Adam?"

"Will he be the only reason for our relationship?" Benedict was again silent for a longer time before he answered:

"I was thinking about it. It's obvious that things are not going well with us. Maybe you think that I do not accept your activities? It's true, when there was the amnesty, I wasn't happy just because they released these people. I was glad mainly because I recognized that KOR, after completing their tasks, will disband and you will come back home. And I won't be afraid anymore...for you, for all of us...I soon realized that this was not the end. Maybe the opposite. Only I accepted it. You believe that your...your activities will change something; you don't believe in mine. I...But we have to deal with it. I accept this. Adam is not the least important matter either. This is a very important matter. But it's not just for that reason that I want us to be together. How many times do I have to tell you that I love you and I don't know what I would do without you. And that's...virtually it."

"You know, I have to think about all of this. But now I'm going to bed."

Before falling asleep, Zuzanna leaned over her son who was tossing and turning in bed. She gently brushed her finger against his cheek and suddenly realized that she saw Benedict's features in him. He was leaning out to her through their son's face. Then she thought she saw Adam Brok in him and her own father, though they were so unlike. She fell asleep, dreaming about all those who are dead.

Filip protested moderately. Zuzanna was disillusioned. She had been preparing for this meeting for a long time. She thought through all the issues and her answers to her lover's hypothetical arguments. In a large measure this proved unnecessary. In truth, Filip said how much he would miss her, he gave up relatively quickly. He accepted her terms: they will work together, but he will not make any attempts at intimate relations.

"Try to forget about this!" Zuzanna stated and at the same time realized the pretentiousness of her issue.

"I certainly will not try to do that," said Philip in a tone of mockery.

Returning home, Zuzanna could not get rid of the heavy thought that she wasn't anyone particularly important to Filip. For her, the decision to break up proved to be more difficult and painful than she had previously imagined. She felt emptiness and hopelessness as she walked through the night in the fumes of the steamy city. Her world will once again be confined to her home. Her future was drawn in predictable and conventional shapes. A world of unlimited possibilities, elation and passion closed behind her. She felt an apprehension toward Benedict, to the flat on Koszykowa Street, to herself. She was thirty-one and her life has practically ended. She already knew how she would spend them and with whom. To the end of her days she will be sentenced to his fear, nightmares and daytime compromises arising from them. She will grow old with him, she felt her body dying, the passion in her going to sleep, which was awakened in her meeting of Filip. Her life will fade, shrink, disappear. Already a few years earlier she realized that her body, which was previously one with her, was beginning to alarmingly become independent, lagging behind, not keeping up with her expectations. She no longer felt the strength within her that could cope with everything. Muscles and tendons, unnoticed, began to be automatized. Internal organs communicating with arteries of blood sent signals of their independence. Mysterious processes that will one day tear the body from its will and make it a prison for its former owner, these processes began to sink into the cells of her body and, like social conventions, registered her in one and the same role from which she will no longer be able to free herself. Even dreams will die out inside her. She will bring up Adam and will renounce herself for the sake of her son. There will be less and less of her. She felt regret and anger. Is she supposed to remain only a wife and mother making extra money in the publishing house just to justify her existence? Will he be correcting pseudo-books that shouldn't be out, be able to correct books that don't need her anyway?

A drunk guy got in her way. He was babbling about fucking. That he wants to fuck her. Zuzanna pushed him away, and he waved his hand as if to hit her, but the hand soared in a hopeless gesture that could evoke only compassion. A helpless attempt to capture something in an empty space. The guy staggered and kept walking.

Poor fool, Zuzanna thought. A pathetic asshole who needs to be drunk to gain the courage to face a woman. I don't want to remember who he is or rather who he is not. Polish streets are full of such cases. And I? Do I, by lecturing myself about the platitudes of responsibility, run away from my dreams? Am I not lying to myself?

Maybe I also hide in the closet of my fears? I'm not capable of living, of burning, blazing in such a way as to feel that I'm alive, just like a few days ago in Filip's flat above Warsaw, communism, my obligations? Maybe life is only for the brave, for those who are able to risk everything and for others remains vegetation? And I chose vegetation? I'm less and less attractive, Zuzanna thought. My time is running out, my short time. I love my son, but do I have to renounce my life for him? And Benedict? Do I feel more for him than sympathy?

"Do you have something to drink?" She asked her husband who waiting for her.

They drank vodka with cola, and Benedict tried to be funny. He could be brilliant and charming, even in such moments. Zuzanna had to admit it, she struggled to be fair, nevertheless her husband only irritated her. Finally, the alcohol blurred reality and freed her a bit from her memories. Then Benedict carried her to bed despite her faint protests. She woke up on a wet pillow and with a wet face. She didn't remember herself crying. Washing herself and drinking tap water that tasted of rust, she realized that she would have to get used to Benedict and his old life again.

CHAPTER 10

"They arrested Ala, they're accusing her..." Aunt Gienia's short sobbing was preventing her from speaking "they're accusing...of theft..."

The panic on the phone was conveyed to Zuzanna. She very much liked her twenty-two-year-old cousin. Her diligence and ambition which had more than invoked Zuzanna's recognition, and admiration was mixed with envy. After graduating from high school Ala went to work and consistently began to take evening college classes. Gradually she was promoted, and recently she became an accountant in a large furniture factory, which was a real achievement. The participation of this cheerful girl in a criminal scandal seemed unbelievable. Everything became clear when her parents came to the Brok's in the evening.

Hardly eating, over a bottle of vodka, they spoke about this matter chaotically. Recently, their daughter has changed so much, she had lost so much humor and joy of life that finally her mother forced a confession out of her. A few people from management offered to let her join the black-market sale of part of the factory's production. She was supposed to help falsify accounting records and get a lot of money in return. She refused. Then the same people began to blackmail her: if she did not turn a blind eye to their activities, or try to cover them, she would be accused of fraud. It will end badly, and only for her. Ala did not bow, even though among those pressuring her were the personnel director and secretary of the party organization. She promised silence, provided that she didn't have to deal with scams. Those negotiations were ongoing but now Ala was arrested. She was accused of embezzlement and falsification of documentation.

"Do you understand, do you understand this?" Aunt Gienia was crying. Zuzanna tried to calm her down. Even Uncle Stach, usually calm and cheerful, looked devastated. Benedict showed the most energy.

"We won't leave it, don't worry. It's just bad luck. You'll see, everything will return to normal, and Ala won't just get out of jail. She will be acquitted of everything. You'll see." Benedict was confident. His attitude calmed the guests down a bit. After they left, he told Zuzanna that he was taking everything on himself and did not need her help. She felt satisfaction. However, days went by, and nothing changed. Ala was in prison and only Benedict lost his original energy and confidence. He became bleak and resigned. Finally, he could not dismiss his wife's questions.

"It's more serious than I was afraid. These guys from the factory have some special arrangements. Everyone is afraid of them. I don't know if I can do anything." Again, he became the Benedict that Zuzanna couldn't stand.

"There are difficulties, so you put your tail between your legs? Is Mr. Editor changing our reality?" She snorted, not thinking about her words. In his gaze there was resigned reproach and maybe the feeling of guilt.

"No. I didn't say that." Something like determination awakened in him again. "Alright, we won't let it go. We'll fight for Ala!"

Zuzanna put a hand on his. She felt closeness and a kind of pride.

The October evening was relatively warm, when they heard distant cries outside their windows. They quieted down but returned. There was joy emanating from them. From Free Europe, through the clatter of the jammers, information about the election of Karol Wojtyła as pope was met with enthusiasm. Subsequent waves of ovation reached them from outside the window.

"The Poles are happy" said Benedict with a specific smile.

"What are you talking about?! After all, you are a Pole as well and you should be happy just the same!" Zuzanna shouted at him.

"Well yeah. Of course, you're right" Benedict agreed without conviction.

***

"You have a guest" Natasha informed her. In the hall of the publishing house sat a young, unknown man.

"Jacek Rojek" he introduced himself. "I worked with your cousin. I am the personnel director at the Furniture Production Factory. I would like to talk about Ala."

***

The sluggish light of autumn plunged the empty cafe into unreality. Pale items without consistency, the pale speaker on the other side of the table.

"Your husband is asking a lot of questions, he's doing a lot of digging around in Ala's case. This could end badly..." the man from the opposite direction smiled indistinctly. The coffee was sour. Zuzanna winced.

"Is that all that you wanted to tell me? You dragged me out here for this?"

"Nooooo. You know. I am the personnel director..." Only now Zuzanna realized what everyone was quietly repeating.

"You want to say, that you're a functionary? Or…"

"I don't mean anything by that. Like I just mentioned. I would like to warn you, that making a buzz around the case can only hurt Ala."

"My husband is a journalist. He believes, that the case needs to be publicized because a terrible injustice has occurred. After all we know perfectly well, you and I, that Ala is in prison innocently.

"That's the decision of the prosecutor's office. Apparently, she had evidence. I just wanted to say, that Ala can be helped. Everyone can have a slip up. You and your husband slipped up in sixty-eight. And now...you are doing great. Ala has been in jail for over two months. The process won't start so quickly. I am a lawyer by profession and additionally I have some experience. At earliest, the trial will be in a few months. I think, that Ala will get another sanction, they will prolong her detention for another three months. It would be best if she confessed to these...irregularities. She doesn't have a record. She'll probably get a suspended sentence. Not big. They will release her. And she will find a job at another plant. She will be able to continue her career. Do you understand Mrs.?"

"I understand." Zuzanna with difficulty held out to the end of Rojek's speech, on whose face wandered a pale smile the entire time. "I don't know what your arrangements are, that you can promise something like that. I know, that Ala will not confess to a crime she did not commit. And I know, that those, who committed them should be responsible for them and for setting up Ala. And we will bring it about. I promise you," she said emphatically, leaning across the table and staring at him ostentatiously. Rojek didn't even pull away. His smile became filled with boundless contempt.

"Who are you to promise me that? You have everything switched in your head! But we can bring you to order. Do you want, because of your fault, for an innocent girl to suffer? This is your business. You're not capable of offending me. I'm only warning you. My offer is valid, but for a time. And don't believe so much in the influence of your hubby, Goleń's pet. His abilities have limits. Anyway, I think he's already gotten too hot. Give him my blessings. He'll know what it's about."

Rojek went away, and Zuzanna sat dazed for some time, swallowing the sour taste of coffee.

"That son of a bitch, Ubek " Benedict blurted out when she told him about the meeting. He jumped up and began to roam the room. "But he shouldn't kid himself..." Benedict slowed down. He lit a cigarette. "Only what can we actually do?"

"And you're saying this? The famous journalist? Author of the most recognized weekly on our side Europe?" Zuzanna couldn't hold back the sarcasm. In her husband's gaze she saw all the hopelessness of party corridors, the ugliness of smoky offices and again corridors leading to court rooms, arrests, prisons...

"I'll try," he declared without faith.

After a few days he returned sullen.

"I talked to the prosecutor, with Karczmiarz. And..." he again looked at Zuzanna with the expression she knew so well, too well, arousing in her aversion and feeling, against which she defended herself and did not call him "and I do not know myself. This Karczmiarz is a scumbag. It seems that he not only knows the case perfectly but is initiated into the machinations of Rojek and his team. As if he were one of them. He suggested that Ala confess, and God forbid that she accuse anyone, because it would only increase the sentence and another sentence for libel. He said that because the trial could not be done in the timeframe, he would be forced to extend Ala's imprisionment. He will be forced...he almost said it with mockery. Unless... here he hung his voice. He made it understood that if Ala confessed, she could leave. I also spoke with a lawyer, Majski. He said he feels the clouds gathering over Ala. And the judge will make such a verdict...you know. Whatever they'll tell him to give. In this situation...it maybe better..."

"So nothing else can be done?!" She shouted with rage and despair. Benedict looked at her helplessly. "Try to write about the case. Maybe it will change something!" Benedict nodded. He didn't look convinced.

The article did not appear, and Ali's detention was extended for another three months. There was hopelessness in the Kowacki house. Zuzanna forced herself to visit them with difficulty. They stopped asking her, though their gaze was one big question. Aunt Gienia was emaciated, her husband became slouched, twenty-year-old Ewa looked at her cousin with a grim expression, and her brother, Zdziś, who came back beaten up after another fight, just said: "And you? You won't do anything?!" And without waiting for an answer he locked himself in the bathroom. Aunt Gienia, pressed by Zuzanna, moaned through her tears "she's so dejected" and she didn't want to say anything more about the visit to her daughter. After returning home, Zuzanna attacked Benedict with fury. He was explaining himself, turning his head and lit a cigarette nervously.

"Goleń said I don't realize what I've gotten into. He's told me this before, but never so definitely. My article will come out heavily censored or not at all. He said that even then it's still a great act of courage on his part. He can release the text if there are no references to the place or the case. It will be a story about an anonymous girl who in time did not realize the irregularities of the company, was accused of them and is now awaiting trail with a second sanction."

"But it's senseless. And...a great fraud!"

"But it's always something! This publicity, a signal, that we will not leave it...that we can come back to the matter.

For the first time the Kowacki's didn't invite them over for the holidays. Anyway, and for the Brok's they went along under the mark of her cousin's case.

Ala was pale and emaciated. Zuzanna saw her for the first time in almost half a year. Visiting options were radically limited. In the visiting room, she didn't immediately recognize her cousin huddled in grey denim. She tried to breathe optimism into her but wasn't finding it within herself.

"I read it in the 'Republic'. Can such…such a general article help at all?" Ala asked with doubt. Zuzanna saw the devastation that five months in prison had made in a cheerful and resolute girl.

"I don't know what to advise you. This Majski is a good lawyer. He will explain to you because...you will have to think about what to say" she said despairingly.

"I want to leave, I want to leave!" Ala repeated, staring into her with grayed eyes.

At the trial, she did not admit anything, but did not mention what she stumbled upon at the factory. The Prosecutor Karczmiarz demanded six years. He spoke about the exceptional demoralization of a young woman who, at the first opportunity, tried to appropriate state property. He noted that an important symptom of this demoralization is the lack of remorse, of which would signify an admission to quilt. The sentence was three and a half years.

"A nice girl," Zuzanna heard, passing the young judge Jolanta Biesiada who was chatting with the prosecutor when the worried Ala was taken out of the room. "She'll sit no more than two years. 'A year isn't a sentence, two years is like a brother'" the judge laughed coquettishly.

Both parties appealed against the judgment. The Kowacki's, although invited, did not show up at their place in the evening.

"You know, these are some cracks. Goleń had suggested it to me before, and recently he said it almost directly. These window dressings are just fragments of a big breakthrough. A matter in which important Party members and UB's are involved, hence this Rojek. They must have silenced her."

"They must've?! What are you talking about?" Zuzanna could not recover from the indignation.

"From my perspective. Otherwise it would be too big a scandal. Poor Ala... they want her to confess. Then they will shorten her sentence."

"And what? Are you behind this?"

"I do not know. Three years is a very long time. We know she is innocent. In any case they do too. What will change if she confesses? I'm not sure, if for abstract principles, to force her to suffer so much time..."

"And you? After all you were supposed to take care of everything! You promised!"

"I know. I believed, that I could. I'm sorry. I feel so horrible and I feel such pity for her. I didn't know, what sits behind this matter."

"And this is what you've achieved?" Susanna sneered near tears. She was drinking in such a way that Benedict was looking at her anxiously. Now, however, he himself drank his diluted vodka in one gulp.

"You're not going to want to hear, that which I have to say. In light of Ala's injustice this will sound cynical, but..." Benedict fell silent.

"Talk!" yelled Zuzanna.

"Maybe it's better that they started stealing? Not just, as they have so far, using the country and everything that is in it, but simply stealing, appropriating it, transforming it into their own property. Because they will have to begin to legitimize and consecrate this property, so they will start to burst the system. They will want to pass something on to their children, possess something definitively, not be condemned to constantly making arrangements with companions. And in this lousy way they'll humanize the system, that is, they'll destroy it."

"What are you talking about?! And the prisons will be full of honest people who won't want to agree to this, like Ala?! In order for such scoundrels would take over everything?"

"Yes, unfortunately. Their predecessors, idealists in leather jackets, like my uncle, shot those who hindered them in the back of the head, like your father. And if they let them go, it was only for them to die outside the prison. They don't want to risk too much. You can get along with them. They'll leave us some scraps, if we don't bother them too much, they'll let Ala go if she confesses. And they will give us more freedom, and then we may slowly regain it as much as it overall exists..."

"What you say is atrocious. You're becoming repulsive." Zuzanna was drunk and furious. Shc hated her husband.

"Me? I'm only trying to understand the world. And draw conclusions from it. Is it atrocious, that I'm trying to see thing the way they are?" Benedict was sad.

She went to Aunt Gienia uninvited. Earlier, her aunt demanded that Zuzanna visit them all the time. The after a time she stopped inviting her. Zuzanna carried a feeling of guilt without cause and that is why she wanted to explain herself to her aunt, uncle and cousin even more. To talk with them honestly. They were close people and she wanted it to stay that way.

Uncle Stach looked at her without a smile. Together with auntie and Ewa, they sat without a word over the tea brewed in glasses.

"We tried almost everything..." Zuzanna began hopelessly, who did not know how to explain the failure and what to say in light of the next trial, which was to take place in a few weeks. The hosts looked at each other.

"Doesn't seem like you've made that big of an effort," Eve murmured reluctantly.

"Why do you say that?" Zuzanna scoffed. "We've done everything we could."

"When Tadek had to be pulled out, Benek was able to," Eve continued in the same voice. It was evident that she was saying the thoughts of the whole family outloud.

"Because it was different matter..." Zuzanna wanted to explain, but her uncle interrupted:

"Of course, the shirt is closer to the body." They looked at her without sympathy. Zuzanna began to feel unusually miserable.

"But that's not true. We did everything, that we could…"

"And what did you do?" Ewa asked persistently. Zuzanna thought that she could name Majski's settlement and his fee, but at the same time she realized that the well-known lawyer did not help.

"Such a famous editor and he can't do anything? He can't help an innocent girl?" There was no irony in her aunt's voice, only bitterness. Zuzanna said her goodbyes quickly.

The snow melted away. The earth was laid bare and from under the grim of the past year, demure sprouts started to come out. The rain was drizzling. At the appeal hearing, Ala confessed to negligence that could have cost the factory significant losses. This was somewhat hard to understand, because the losses could only be associated with selling products under the table, but the court did not delve upon the matter. Ala's verdict was lowered to two and a half years. She left after another ten months, in February. Zuzanna visited her in prison, but she had the impression that in addition to the bars, an invisible barrier had fallen between them. Ala didn't really want to talk with her.

As soon as she learned about her cousin's departure from prison, Zuzanna ran to the Kowacki's. The hosts greeted her coldly. Ala was seated at the table. She answered questions with half-words, looking at her with an unreadable expression. Zuzanna did not finding the lively girl with whom she parted a year and a half earlier.

"But it's only been a year and a half," it escaped her almost without thought, but she felt obliged to continue. "You're twenty-three years old. I wish I had that much."

"Would you like to go prison for a year and a half?" Ala asked sneeringly. "It can be a lot. A lot to survive, think, understand. Maybe I left something behind going there? Something which I didn't find after returning?"

That was her longest statement. She answered decisively that she would not be finishing college, where she was kicked out, landing in prison. Anyway, she would have to start them over again.

"You didn't finish yours either, right?" She threw the statement at her sarcastically, then lit a cigarette and stared at the wall. The visit was over. As she was leaving, Zuzanna thought that, among the many other things she didn't realize, the prison deprived Ala of the chance to meet the pope - eight months earlier.

***

"Let Your Spirit descend and renew the face of the earth...this earth," said the man in white.

When Zuzanna found herself in the crowd on Victory Square, feeling a common tension and anticipation, it crossed her mind that these were only naive illusions, hopes that could not be fulfilled. She thought ironically about herself, a mature woman clinging to faith in words that can overcome violence. And then suddenly she wasn't just herself anymore. She felt and believed together with everyone there, whose hopes focused on the man in white in the middle of the square. It was beginning to fill her with strength that gave peace.

Zuzanna's faith melted as she grew older. It faded after her father's death, which she felt as if it were an undeserved punishment. She became lost when she thought about his life, about the fate of her parents. Over time, religion ceased to be important to her. It evaporated from her area of interest. In truth, Adams' baptism was something obvious to her, but it was not tied to any further consequences. God moved beyond the horizon of her affairs, and the Church was a nice but increasingly distant and exotic attraction. She accidentally entered the sanctuaries, feeling their exoticness and incompatibility with the world around; she even prayed, but it was like returning to ever more distant memories, which she had left behind at the doorstep.

Now she felt the same, as she did eleven years earlier at the showing of *Dziady*, only much more intensely. "People! Each of you could, lonely, imprisoned, with thought and faith overturn and raise thrones," Zuzanna recalled, looking at the man in white who's raising his hands to them, to heaven and indicates.

"Let Your Spirit descend and renew the face of the earth ... this earth," said the man in white. "It is necessary to follow in the footsteps of what, or rather who, throughout generations, Christ was for the sons and daughters of this land. And not only for those who openly believed Him, who confessed Him the faith of the Church. But also, for those seemingly standing nearby, outside the Church. For those doubting, for those in conflict." Zuzanna understood that the man in white was talking to her. "If it is right to understand the history of a nation through every human being in this nation, then at the same time it is impossible to understand man other than in the community that is his nation. It is known that this is not the only community. However, this is a special community, probably most closely related to the family, the most important for the spiritual history of man. And so, it is impossible to understand the history of the Polish nation, this great millennial community, which is so deeply about me, about each of us, without Christ.

It is impossible to understand this city, Warsaw, the capital of Poland, which in 1944 decided on an unequal fight with the invader, a fight in which it was abandoned by allied powers, a fight in which it lay under its own rubble, if one doesn't remember that Christ the Savior also lay under the same rubble with his cross in front of the church in the Krakowskie Przedmieście."

Zuzanna already knows that she must have heard these words, because her mother must have heard them, who now hears them thanks to her. Her mother, who survived the uprising, but not entirely, something of her died and was buried under the rubble, something she only mentioned to her daughter on her deathbed. And the daughter is only now beginning to understand that the suffering of her parents makes sense, although she can not yet fully understand it.

"We are standing here near the Tomb of the Unknown Soldier. In the history of Poland, ancient and modern, this grave has a special meaning. Special justification" says the man in white, and Zuzanna feels that her life, her problems and pains are inscribed in a longer sequence of events that gives them meaning, just as her son's life justifies her existence, allows her to approach understanding. The fact that she is here with those who were and those who will come allows one to rise above the lonely jungles full of pain and darkness.

"I knelt at this grave together with the priest Primate to worship each seed, which, falling to the ground and dying in it, bears fruit. Whether it be the seed of soldier's blood shed on the battlefield or a martyr's sacrifice in camps and prisons. Whether it be the seed of hard, everyday work in the sweat of the farm, at the workshop, in the mine, in smelters and factories. Whether it be a seed of parental love that does not shy away from giving life to a new person and undertakes all rearing efforts. Whether it be a seed of creative work at universities, institutes, libraries, and workshops of national culture. Whether it be a seed of prayer and service for the sick, suffering and abandoned. Whether it be the seed of suffering itself in hospital beds, clinics, sanatoriums and homes: 'everything which constitutes Poland'.

Let Your Spirit descend!
Let Your Spirit descend and renew the face of the earth!
This land!" Said the man in white.

***

"Why were you not there?" Zuzanna asked her husband, full of enthusiasm when she arrived home at night. She had the feeling that everything was different, and she did not quite return. The papal retinue left, but they were still standing at Victory Square. The words of a man in white were combining, rising in a unified breath above the city. They did not want to disperse, and only when the echo of the voice melted into the stones of the square, the walls of buildings, and the hands of clocks kept going, taking nothing into account, they slowly moved in the direction of their affairs. Individual people broke away, at first a little insecure and shy, and the melting crowd moved smoothly towards the Krakowskie Przedmieście. They were still breathing in unison and everything was in its place, so Zuzanna was not surprised that someone caught her in their arms and that someone turned out to be Filip Madej. He emerged from a group that was linked collectively, and Zuzanna was glad that in this way she could express her elation. Filip was just one of them and Zuzanna didn't even feel jealous when she noticed the girl clinging to his shoulder. They walked slowly into the disbursing crowd, which finally, spontaneously in a group enter the church of the Holy Cross, where Zuzanna equally unwittingly began to pray, and actually a prayer almost without words freed itself in her and allowed her to remain outside of time in the peace of the church. She awoke from it when the night came and by herself, she walked home unexpectedly coming back to life in Warsaw.

"Why weren't you there?" She asked with a sort of sympathetic reproach, dancing with her son in her arms around her amused husband. Adam squealed happily.

"I saw everything on television" replied Benedict.

"You saw? You only saw? You couldn't have seen this! This wasn't to be seen. You had to experience it! You weren't able to understand this, looking at the television!"

"But I don't like crowds" he explained with a smile.

"You don't like?" Zuzanna stopped her disappointed and set her protesting son on the ground. "Maybe you are afraid of him?"

"And even so," Benedict answered seriously. "Maybe I am scared. One should be afraid of him. Read Le Bona. The crowd is an unpredictable animal. Do you remember March?"

"Then the commies set them against each other. They can be different." Zuzanna knew that she doesn't know what she should do. Her elation was mixed with disappointment as she looked at her husband.

"Exactly. As I said. They're unpredictable. Let's avoid crowds."

"But this wasn't a crowd! This was something different…I can't name it, but something good…"

"Zuza...It's beautiful that you experienced joy there, but...I don't want to offend you...in these conditions emotions easily change. However, this was a crowd, a great number of people strangers, connected by sudden passion...Understand, the crowd is unreflective..."

"This wasn't a sudden passion and strangers," Zuzanna said, turning to take Adam to bed. She stopped wanting to talk to her husband.

Many times, she regretted that she did not follow the Pope. She followed his pilgrimage desperately censored by television and listened to Free Europe, which gave information. Even on the streets of Warsaw, summer brought a fresh breeze. Passers-by looked differently at each other. She saw more and more smiles. Something must come about from this, something must happen.

However, eight days passed, and the Pope said goodbye to his native country. And again, everything was as it was before.

"Sorry, it's a bit naive," Benedict explained. "What did you expect…did you expect? That the communists would convert, and Moscow would withdraw its tanks? Such national religious...feelings" he found the word after a moment's hesitation and reflection "although they give a sense of community, they can be ambiguous. Especially in such a situation. It is difficult for them to build something, so they must, in a sense, be directed against those who do not share their views. I think our experience of war and communism should teach us something. It all starts beautifully...Collective ecstasy, a reality which surpasses us, to which we try to adapt man. And then you know how it ends, our parents experienced it, and we..."

Zuzanna did not answer. She did not agree with Benedict, but she didn't have the strength to argue with him. Anyway, she could not find any arguments and was falling into depression, which began to fall on her with the coming autumn. She tried not to give up; resist the hopelessness of autumn Warsaw, the depressing sense of the passage of time in which nothing changes, only the body and everything around it is aging, and dreams and thoughts become sterile, lose themselves in the misty air. Everything was just like before. The authorities announced false, optimistic economic results, in which they only slightly processed and adapted the false reports from the workplace to the beautiful whole. Factory directors collected data from managers only slightly correcting reports of foremen who tried to guess the expectations of supervisors in order to best complete the reports on which their fate depended. The lie flowed from top to bottom and back again. They after all expected it and set the measures.

The world was becoming grayer, a bigger lie and more hopeless. It was harder to predict; it was harder to believe that you could buy that which is necessary. To untangle yourself from the loop of efforts to survival. Queues were swelling and aggression was increasing that could only be unloaded against others in the same situation.

Zuzanna was more involved in conspiratorial activities. She demanded further tasks from Madej. At night she couldn't sleep and read *Marquez's Hundred Years of Loneliness*. The chronicle of an imaginary city that becomes the Latin American Book of Genesis waiting for its *Book of Exodus*, consumed her. It occurred to her that Polish experiences should result in denser and richer works, which now, when it is possible to print underground, may finally begin to arise? Sometimes she went to churches. Only then did calmness embrace her. In truth, she didn't really know if she was praying. Sometimes she tried to remember the words she once knew long ago. Sometimes they came back to her by themselves. She didn't however know how to focus enough to stay in the church longer. Sometimes she would take Adam to mass on Sunday. The boy was becoming impatient, and Zuzanna wasn't able to calm him down.

Once again, she refused to participate in a social meeting organized by employees and friends of the "Republic". Benedict excused himself that he could not break off contacts with people he not only worked with, but also is trying to do something more serious with. Under Zuzanna's ironic look, he did not develop this thought.

***

In March Zuzanna was arrested.

The police stopped her car, but when the functionary ordered Zuzanna to get out, a brown Fiat with three men inside stopped. One approached them. They ordered to open the trunk stuffed to the brim with leaflets reminiscent of the anniversary of March. The policeman ripped open one of the packages and nodded sadly. She went to the police station on Wilcza in the back of the police car.

"You've gotten what you've asked for," said the man in the brown suit with concern. "And this is the wife of such a famous journalist. It'll be difficult, but you still have the chance to disentangle yourself. You just have to tell us everything and write it down."

"I refuse to answer" Zuzanna choked out this learned issue through her throat so vaguely that not only the man on the other side of the table did not understand her, but she didn't either. She felt ashamed. She had discussed it so many times with Madej. She repeated it so many times that she's capable of not testifying. Now she was afraid.

"I refuse to answer!" She now said loudly and clearly. Then through several hours of shouting, persuading and threats she repeated the same thing, despite the fact that the two interrogators were switching off, not giving her a moment of peace. After some time, she almost stopped understanding the words. She sank into a strange lethargy, staring at different objects: a gray radiator, a brown table leg, a darker border on the wall, a meter from the floor. Every now and then, when a more sharply formulated question came to her, she would repeat her mantra.

"We're going to lock-up," the officer finally said in a weary voice.

"I must inform my husband. I was supposed to pick my child. Someone has to do it!" she protested angrily.

"You should've thought of that before!" The UB officer grumbled. "We can still go on our way if we start to treat each other like partners. If you answer a few questions, you'll be able to pick your son up in person."

"I refuse to answer."

The cell was thick with foulness and smoke. Someone was grunting, somebody was babbling. The door slammed shut, and for some time she couldn't catch her breath in the dark brown gloom. For a moment she thought she would suffocate. She remembered Ala. Is it possible to spend a year and a half in such a place? She could not sleep between the heavy bodies of drunk prostitutes struggling with the night.

The next day she was called again, but the interrogation lasted shorter. The UB's gave up.

After two days, in the evening, when she got out of prison, breathing in the air of rotting winter and spring, which did not want to come yet, across the street saw Benedict puffing on a cigarette and leaning on his car.

"How did you know, that I'm here and at this time?"

"They called me the first night. I started looking for you. You know...I was nervous. On the second day they interrogated me. I said that I didn't know anything. They threatened a bit. They said they're keeping an eye on you. It's not over yet, they warned. They gave me the car. But they did a search at our place. They took some illegal books and prints from you. You shouldn't keep it at home, they'll take it. Have you really thought about all of this? Have you thought about Adam?" Benedict looked helplessly from above the steering wheel. The wipers smeared the wet twilight on the windshield.

"We've talked about this!" Zuzanna answered more sharply than she intended. She dreamed of taking a bath and her son. About seeing him, touching him.

"You smell funny," said Adam, moving away from Zuzanna when she instinctively caught him in his arms. Out of the corner of her eye, she noticed the frightened look that the girl who was taking care of him gave her.

Exiting the tub, she felt a tiredness that overwhelmed her. Benedict was waiting for her in bed. He said something about love. Unexpectedly, tenderness enveloped her.

Five thousand złotys paid to the police court exchanged for three months of detention Zuzanna received for "actions leading to littering of the city". But the grim characters who staged the parody of the trial did not provoke laughter. Filip gave her the money and invited her for vodka.

"We have to drink to your baptism. None of us are really conspirators anymore. They also caught me and held me several times for two days. Now they want to disciplinarily throw me out of PAN. I was just about to defend my doctorate," he informed her with a smile.

A large group from the apartment of Igor Stawicki moved to Danka Brak's apartment. They sang Kelus' songs. The gray-haired, powerful Wojtek Roski, an underground printer, did not leave her. Targeted by the security service and monitored all the time, he knew how to break off and disappear from the previously prepared den, where he and his team were able to not leave the basement for two weeks, working a dozen or so hours a day. Food was brought to him and subsequent portions of prints were collected. Then he recovered, drinking for several days, if the furious security service did not lock him up for two days to repeat it several times in a row. They beat him hard a few times. After several week's bouts in a hospital, he appeared ready to go. He started his war on communism towards the end of elementary school, when he and his friends began planning a resistance movement. It ended at the planning stage because the security service caught the small conspirators. Beaten terribly, he spent several months in prison. He was thirteen and had a lot of luck because he was released. He was eighteen when he organized a conspiratorial group with his peers. They disarmed several policemen and robbed the district branch of the PKO. It was 1955. Captured, he got hit in the face. He was waiting on death row, but he was lucky again. A year later, on a wave of the thaw, his sentence was changed to fifteen years. He left in 1965. In sixty-eight he was caught in the demonstration area and got three years. He left in '70. He volunteered as soon as he heard about the establishment of KOR.

Zuzanna struggled to brush off his courtship. He took her hand and looked into her eyes. She had to keep him in line in the strongest terms. Maybe because of, or maybe under the influence of alcohol, he was getting more and more sullen.

"It's fun now, believe me," he repeated. "They'll really get on our case soon. And then it will turn out who is who. Who will endure and remain firm. Because after all we will not win against communism, the system, the empire. What this is really about is not letting yourself get broken. Now here at wolce, and then in prison. Because we're behind bars, only the keys give us some freedom. For now."

Several times on the street, officers dressed in civvies stopped her, put her in a car, and took her to the office, where they unsuccessfully tried to interrogate her. She was afraid of them. Then they put her in custody for two days. One time they started talking about Benedict.

"You are very tolerant," said the, smiling, pale fishy-eyed man. "You endure all of your husband's girlfriends..." She felt disgust. As if he was trying to put his hands under her skirt. She didn't say anything. "This one now, Halina, looks more serious than all previous ones. But you probably know about it best" he continued, wincing his face in a faded smile. "So now what? Does your husband do it with your consent?" She didn't respond. The character said something more on the same topic, he tried to make some vulgar jokes, but, finding silence, gave up.

She marched back to jail again. As always, she had no way of contacting anyone, and as always, Benedict was waiting for her when she left police headquarters. He tried to smile, but he was only able to make dismal smile. Zuzanna's smile didn't seem convincing either. She couldn't help thinking of what the UB officer had said. The rain was drizzling. Everything around was sticky and slippery.

***

The director, Łukasz Alski, called her at work to his office. A well-maintained, caring about his looks, middle-aged man pointed her to a place behind the desk, glancing sideways, as if checking if someone else was still hiding in an empty office. He asked if she wanted coffee.

"Of course you know why I invited you," he began hesitantly, turning over the papers on the desk. Zuzanna was almost certain. The UB's threatened that if he did not want to cooperate with them or even talk, he would lose his job and can say goodbye to his dream of any job. As she went to the director, she was getting ready to be fired, but now, stirring the coffee the secretary brought in, only to disappear immediately, she noticed that the teaspoon in her fingers was trembling a bit. She began to calm down, observing the director's nervousness. She looked around the office. She was here for the first time. Marx, Engels and Lenin stared sternly above the shelves with 'Portico' books. From the wall opposite with an ingratiating smirk hung its gaze on them a much smaller comrade Gierek, with even smaller images of Jaroszewicz and Jabłoński.

"Of course I don't know, Director," she replied almost provocatively.

"Please, don't joke around!" The director took on a bit more menacing expression. "You are well aware that in this situation you cannot work here anymore. By the way, I expected a bit more loyalty. You can't complain about the bad treatment. And you…"

"I what?"

"You are acting against the state, against your homeland...And against us, against the 'Portico'! Do you know what problems you have exposed us to?" The director paused, looking uncertainly from side to side. He continued more calmly: "It's not just recklessness, it's...very inappropriate behavior. Do you know that I should let you go for disciplinarily reasons?"

"For what?"

"What do you mean what for? For failing to appear at work without notice and without justification. And several times, for two days at a time."

"I was arrested."

"Don't kid around, this is supposed to be an excuse? You know, I'm still wondering whether to give you this disciplinary dismissal. It all lies here!" The director raised the paper and waved it at Zuzanna. "If it wasn't for your husband... He is a very intelligent man and...It will be a gesture towards him that I fire you in the ordinary way. I hope you will appreciate it. Do you understand what you've brought down on us..." he looked around again "of course we have nothing to fear, but the possibility of misunderstanding...I think you are aware of the importance for the Polish culture of our publishing house. 'Portico' is ... well, you know it, and now...I mean...appropriate people have to review our publications once again, ah and this and time, and...You should apologize to us!"

"I lost my job," she told Benedict with a smile. He replied with a similarly, only slightly more forced.

"You didn't have to do all this to give up your work. You could've just walk away. I earn enough ... And this way, you had to provoke the entire country...You didn't give them a chance."

Zuzanna thought she was in a particularly privileged position. Once again she felt ashamed.

They watched her. She learned to identify the guards. She no longer transported underground prints by car, but only helped those who needed it to move around. In this way she also met the leaders of KOR. A few times she took Jacek Kuroń somewhere, who invited her for coffee. He explained that what they do has meaning.

She informed Benedict of her new tasks.

"Why are you telling me this?" he asked with resignation. "If you want, you can take the car. It's also yours. After all I'm not able to explain anything to you."

"I can explain much to you either" she replied. She shook her head with a vague smile.

"You must know how much this costs me? No, I'm not complaining on my behalf" he stopped her reply. "It's about you, Adam, though...as far as I am concerned, I will not say that I'm completely not afraid of them." He looked at her sadly. They sat by the open window, behind which the deepening night filled with the abundance of spring. Strips of steam from subsequent cups of tea were cooling in the dark. "I can see them after all. They come to our door. I'm afraid that they will come inside again. This apartment...My father's apartment...I thought it would be my, our refuge. They profane it. Even in it we can't take refuge! And this is supposed to be your choice! Have you ever thought about how Adam would receive it? Does it seem to you that he's indifferent to it? That he doesn't feel what's going on around? What will be next? Clearly, they're not going to allow what you're doing! They will corner and choke you. And if they throw me out? What will we live from? Władek talked to me recently. As a friend. You don't believe in our friendship? He always speaks well of you. He believes in your best intentions and admires your courage. But he always thought you were like children. They will torment you gradually, and one fine day they will tear your heads off. They will throw you in jail for many years. They'll destroy you. He warned me that pressure was already on him to throw me out. On account of you. He is still able to defend me, but he doesn't know for how long. What shall we do then? Have you thought about Adam?"

"That, what you're doing, is blackmail. Can we depend on nothing anymore? Do you want to build everything on fear?"

Benedict fell silent. He looked at her with the gaze of a hurt child. Zuzanna realized that she was attacking him more often, the more she wanted to overcome the growing fear. She thought her husband might be right. And when they throw him out of work ... She felt tired, more and more tired. The fear that they might approach her on the street and take her to police headquarters, arrest her, caused increasing tension. Uncertainty was rising from between the houses, boiling up from the streets. She saw it in the faces of passers-by, in figures behind her back. Everyone that looked on her, raised her anxiety. She didn't tell Benedict about it. She was closing herself off to him. The more fatigue she felt, the more he irritated her with his fear, which showed itself in nightmares. He was irritating with his passivity, depression, which he brought home. They were separating further apart, though sometimes they unexpectedly found moments of old passion and tenderness. At that time, Zuzanna thought she was unfair to him, and tried to make it up to him, but at the same time the words of a UB officer came back to her: 'Now this one, Halina, looks more serious than all previous ones", and it was difficult for her to overcome the feeling of hurt and sorrow although she explained to herself that the UB officer probably lied. Something in her said though, not this time. It was understandable, actually. Even sex happened with them less and less often. At times she thought that Benedict's betrayals are, or should be, indifferent to her. However, the truth was different. Although she knew that this time she was not going to interrogate friends from around the "Republic" with whom contacts had truthfully died a natural death.

"Why are you cheating on me?" she threw out once unexpectedly for herself, after one of those increasingly rare moments when tired they came back to reality, touching each other with their naked bodies and lighting cigarettes.

"What…what are you saying?" Benedict was recovering, bewildered and afraid. "Where did this thought come from?"

"But it's the truth," she said with unpleasant confidence. She felt disgusted towards herself, but even more towards the husband who was again a stranger. "Just please, don't lie, don't deny it. Do we have to go back to our conversation from a few years ago?"

Benedict tried to embrace her, but she broke away, stood up and began to dress. He looked with the familiar to her eyes of a lost child.

"Listen, even if...even if I did come across something, it doesn't matter. An accident...after all you know that it has no effect on what is between us..."

"And I? What if something came across to me? It wouldn't have an impact either?" Benedict said nothing.

When she returned after a few hours walk with Adam, he was waiting for her with a bouquet of flowers. She took them.

"I don't want to talk," 'she said, ahead of his pre-prepared matter. She went to the other room. She realized the banality of her own situation and was overcome by anger.

Slowly, relations at home returned to normal. To Zuzanna's surprise after a few days, they found each other in bed. Quickly, however, she freed herself from Benedict embrace to light a cigarette and look at the night outside the window. He was laying calm with his eyes half-closed, and she thought they would no longer be able to overcome their detachment.

Her new colleagues did not ask how her husband reacted to her involvement. The exception was Igor Stawicki. But he was really no exception. Despite his connections with the opposition, he was still able to keep his university position. Perhaps he was somewhat protected by the fame of a young genius, which he strengthened with a brilliant doctorate on Husserl. He was unconventional, giddy and picturesque. Zuzanna liked to meet with him. He allowed her to forget about the dullness of the world around, about the threats. He only annoyed her when he inquired about Benedict, but only she was only ready to forgive him.

"And how does your husband tolerate this?" He inquired waving his hand with the cigarette. They sat in the 'Crossroads'. Igor could hardly sit in his chair. He gestured and looked around as if he already wanted-wanted to get up and set off somewhere. When they met in the apartments, he almost never sat in one place. He moved nervously between the walls that stopped him at the last moment. He sat down for a moment only to rise up again and run the few steps that the small rooms allowed. And he talked, talked all the time.

"Clearly they're pretending to be the opposition. This Goleń and his team, your husband...Such a licensed opposition. They can criticize mid-level directors, call for more rivalry in the framework of socialist competition..." Igor was choking with laughter. "They must hate us. Since we appeared, it's difficult for them to play their game of appearances..."

"Give it a rest. Don't bore," Zuzanna grumbled, and she started to get irritated. Igor laughed.

"Do not get angry. I don't want to make you sad. I just wonder...Because maybe I'm in the wrong? Maybe they want to be a more serious opposition and you're a liaison? Admit it!"

"Stop talking rubbish! We're finishing this thread or this conversation!" Zuzanna sharply brought him to order seeing that he was in the mood to continue.

***

She kept waking up for a long time, feeling short of breath and dryness in her throat. Struggling with the hot daylight falling on her through the open window, she struggled to tear her eyes apart. Benedict was sitting by the bed. He was smoking a cigarette. She noticed his strange, worried look. Overcoming dizziness and nausea, she dragged herself to the bathroom. With difficulty she rinsed the previous night from herself. She was kneeling beneath shower, trying to remember the chaotic events of a few hours ago.

Stawicki's two small rooms were, as always, densely filled and immersed in twilight. It was a time when team talks ended, some of the guests were gone, and alcohol made everything possible. Sonny Rollins was coming from the speakers. Some girl wanted to unsuccessfully dance. Wojtek Roski got to Zuzanna again.

"You are so beautiful...so beautiful. And this is all ending, ending...Soon we will go to the cell. And there...Our life closes...The last flame..." He embraced her, but she broke away with anger.

"Life is an experiment!" The host shouted, raising his shot glass. "Have a drink, Zuza. There are no more roads, because we only told ourselves that they were marked out for us. We disenchanted the world and we see only the wilderness. And there we can mark every trail. We can tell any story because they are all worth the same. We are free!"

"An educated snowman!" Growled Madej. "He's getting exalted! Are you free under communism?"

"Yes, even here, even here we can be free!" Stawicki yelled defiantly. "Are we not able to?"

"I didn't feel free in custody. They probably rarely locked you up, Igor, too rarely" drawled out Danka Brak.

"Good," the host succumbed. "We must push off communism to fight off a space for ourselves. We, at the university, do not have it bad. But I understand, I understand...You have to fight for more...Maybe we are lucky? We will build everything again..."

"What is he talking about?" Danka wondered. "After all we have to restore the measures. But when? When?"

From close up Michał Bogatyrowicz looked into Zuzanna's eyes. It was dark and stuffy. Everyone said something different, and Zuzanna stopped understanding. She drank subsequent shots with random people and tried to follow the trail of the saxophone, which melted into the panting of the double bass, to rise again in the passages of the piano, break free from the stuffy cubicle and soar into the hot night. The couple entwined on the couch moaned. Madej escorted her home by the night bus. They were probably kissing at her door.

This happens to me too often, she thought struggling with a hangover and staring into the mirror in order to pat on another layer of cream into her tired face. Bruises under the eyes loomed even after intense makeup. Nausea did not want to pass despite the second tea. I'm getting old, she thought, looking in the mirror. A hung-over balance sheet of thirty-three years. I feel tiredness and old age. More often hopeless returns home, heavier hangovers. Our collective martyrdom. Without redemption.

"Maybe we will go with Adam for a walk?" Benedict asked. She almost automatically wanted to refuse when she saw her overjoyed son at the door of the room. They left the car on Ujazdów Avenue and walked around the Łazienki Park, animated like every sunny Sunday in June. They passed other families, and Zuzanna was starting to feel better. Dizziness and nausea subsided, nerves thawing in the light of the sun.

Two men with characteristic handbags attached to their wrists were looking towards them. She realized that she had been seeing them for some time. They followed in their footsteps, keeping the same distance the entire time. She remembered the story of Benedict's father about walks in the Łazienki. These memories came back to her so often that Zuzanna wondered if she was the one who composed them from her father-in-law's words. He builds the distant past of his son. He remembers the rapacious time before the great catastrophe. Adam Brok told her what her mother only mentioned and her own father did manage to tell her. She looked at her husband, remembering his father's face and feeling a surge of tenderness.

"Your father told me how a year before the war you walked around the Łazienki. With the whole family" she said unconsciously. Adaś looked at them with interest.

"No I...I don't remember," Benedict replied, frowning.

"How could you?! You weren't even a year old," Zuzanna burst into laughter.

"Dad wasn't even a year old!" Adaś gladdened. Zuzanna hugged her husband. Two men stood under a tree, closely watching them.

***

It was Tadek who brought news of the strikes. Shortly after the increase in meat prices, they began to explode here and there and just as quickly go out. And then they appeared again somewhere else. The tension trembled in the July air. Passers-by were breathing heavily in the city heat. The melting glue was unable to hold propaganda posters that slid to the ground and covered the pavement. In the evenings they listened with Benedict to the radio in the everpresent company of Adam, who desperately protested against attempts to put him to sleep. They captured the facts through wheezes and gurgles. The strike from Świdnik moved to Lublin and took over the city. Authorities extinguished the strikes with wage increases, and they broke out again, elsewhere, even stronger.

Madej was letting everyone know, that they needed to be ready. Nobody knew exactly what for. The party at Danka's happened in two capacities. Next to the music, which as usual at some point was replaced by choral singing, next to conversations, jokes and flirts, tensions rose. They were waiting for what Jacek would say. He claimed that now it would be finally possible to force concessions on the government. Strikes must be converted into institutions, free trade unions. "Maybe we don't realize how crucial this time is!" he finished. They believed him. They wanted to believe. But when they dispersed and went home, uncertainty returned. Even alcohol didn't release her from this. Outside her house on an empty street Zuzanna saw two figures again. She quickened her pace, but they fenced her off the tenement door. She stopped helplessly. One leaned in so close that she could feel his breath on her face.

"And now what? Do you want to shout, call for help? Give it a try and we'll take you to the cell and give you such a fucking beating that you'll remember the Russian month! Now what, whore?! You think you can let yourselves do all this?! And I tell you, watch yourself, because as soon as you jump up, no one will help you. And your fucking hubby. We'll take him care of him too. Just try something on us!" His index finger swayed almost at the height of Zuzanna's nose. She fought with herself so as not to fall back, not to run away. She stood still in the same place right in front of him.

"This, you whore, is last warning, remember!" He said, stepping away with the other who was staring at her glumly. She couldn't stop trembling as she entered the apartment. The alcohol evaporated from her and left her body weak and thoughtless. Benedict was standing in the foyer.

"Something happen?" He asked anxiously. She dismissed him.

"A strike broke out in the shipyard!" Tadek announced from the door a few days later. Everyone was waiting for this strike. They believed that it was only the shipyard that could make a breakthrough. Was it only about the memory of what had happened ten years ago? Tadek packed up and went to Gdansk. The tension in the streets of Warsaw was stiffening in the heat. Their oppositional net was busting. Some were arrested and awaited trial in prison with prosecution sanctions. Some were locked up for two days and released in order to beyond the doors of the jail lock them up again and again. Some hid. Zuzanna finally came to Stawicki. Nervous, he walked around his room with a cigarette in his hand. He didn't know much either. He informed Zuzanna that Madej was locked up and Roski had hidden. He asked her to let him know what was going on. He would like to help.

On the street, Danka Brak took her arm. They roamed the city for a while to see if they had a tail. Danka needed help. They were to provide leaflets to FSO in Żerań. The Brok's car was out of the question, it was certainly watched, anyway Zuzanna saw the guards, even Benedict noticed. They were supposed to take the tram the next day.

She left early. Two men showed up unexpectedly beside her and led her by the elbows to a Fiat standing nearby with a driver. His face seemed familiar. The interrogation ritual was shortened this time. She was warned that she was being investigated, which could be turned into an investigation against her and they threatened her with very serious charges, including an attempt to overthrow the system, for which even the death penalty could be obtained. This time, after a 48-hour lock up, by the office where she picked up her possessions, three officers were waiting for her. They showed the search warrant, put her in the car and drove her home.

In the opening doors of the apartment Benedict greeted them holding Adam by the hand. He couldn't hide his nervousness. Their son, who threw himself into her embrace, stopped abruptly in front of her, but she scooped him up, thinking that maybe this time he would withstand the stench that beats from her. He bore them bravely. Slightly less the presence of strangers in the apartment. After a short fight with himself, he burst into tears. Zuzanna tried to calm him down, but it was not easy. The search lasted several hours and ended up with nothing but the gigantic mess that paralyzed the inhabitants. For a long time after the officers left, they looked at each other helplessly.

"Listen, these aren't trifles" Benedict began to say shaken up, but Zuzanna interrupted him and locked herself in the bathroom. Showering herself with water, waiting for the bathtub to fill almost to the edges. She immersed herself in water and steam. She melts. It puts the stress to sleep. She almost forgets the fear and tension. But when she finally leaves after more than an hour, her husband waits for her, puffing nervously on his cigarette.

"I spoke with Władek. He warned me. This time this is going too far. These strikes...they're preparing to deal with you. Have you seen what's happening?! I, I also...I don't want our house to change into a UB parlor!"

"And this is my fault?!"

"Whose then? If you provoke a dog, then he'll bite!"

"I'm tired. Give me a break. This conversation is over."

"But don't you understand that it's already different?!"

That evening, the television daily 'Dziennik' announced that a government commission headed by Deputy Prime Minister Jagielski had begun talks with the Inter-Enterprise Strike Committee.

"See?" Zuzanna shouted to Benedict. "Everything is changing! They won't take us to prison anymore Understand?! This is our chance! Now, precisely now we can't back down!"

"You are…you're all naive! Do you think this is serious? It's just a game. And it will end badly."

Zuzanna went out to the other room. She did not want to talk to her husband, who came after an hour, proposing that they did not return to politics. She didn't react when he suggested that they together with Adam go for a few days to the countryside, to Niemir.

That week was hard, stuffy and full of tense feeling. Zuzanna didn't really remember how it passed. She constantly listened to Radio Free Europe. But it was Benedict who brought the message.

"I wouldn't want to jinx it," he said impatiently, unusually for him. Władek said that they were to come to an agreement with the strikers."

They were looking at the TV screen. Zuzanna could not believe her eyes, but at the same time a wild enthusiasm was beginning to envelope her. She tried to visualize: free trade unions, the release of political prisoners. Free unions...knows what that means. The wall is cracking. Through the gap lights breaks through. A man with a mustache with a pen decorated with a buńczuk signs the agreement. Zuzanna grabs Adam, who looks as if he understands everything. She embraces Benedict, who looks uncertain and scared.

"We've won" she sings.

CHAPTER 11

Zuzanna will always remember the time that followed afterwards as something extraordinary, incomparable to anything she experienced before or after. Perhaps it was announced by the man in white, over the hours in Victory Square, which smoldered for a long time in the dim light, only to wake up in the next few days and connect with those on the square and those at the ends of the country. Maybe it's something related to what the nine-year-old girl sensed in front of the Palace of Culture in the tension of all of those gathered...Now, however, it was a magical spectacle of days that were difficult to separate, transforming into weeks and then months. She was young again. She mainly lived on coffee, tea and cigarettes. She almost didn't need to sleep or eat, she didn't need rest, like everyone around her, like her old and new friends finding a community, which will survive everything, and when they meet after many years, full of regret and resentment, unfulfilled and embittered, even then, in short, unexpected moments they will be able to recognize the splendor of that time in themselves. It's difficult to cram these memories into later written biographies, calendars and dates. Events were an explosion, lasting side by side and it was almost impossible to sort them into threads, put them in an orderly chain of causes and effects. Even the division into days and nights became something conventional and irrelevant.

The memories of those experiences will also be specific. They weren't her property. They transcended the person of Zuzanna Brok nee Sokół in order to give her something more than the experience of a specific woman thrown into a specific time and place. Her personal dilemmas and unfulfillment, regrets, ambitions and longings became unimportant, faded into an experience that went beyond the existence of an individual lost in the river of occurrences. After many years, with the consciousness of lies, injustices and betrayals, she will be able to come back to those memories to purify herself, to feel pride.

A meeting at Jacek Kuroń's, a meeting at Igor Stawicki's, at Danka Brak's. Everyone knows that an opportunity is opening that takes one's breath away. They talk and talk, shouting over one another without end. No one can embrace the meaning of these events, although everyone is aware that some kind of breakthrough is happening. Perhaps Kuroń is the boldest in his interpretations, as always. They argue continuous, trying to name all their ways for hope. No one even imagines how big the opportunity is opening before them is or how much time they have, but everyone agrees that they are finally creating a future, they're building their own history. Now it has taken the form of a trade union, which consists of the uncountable number of people who find solidarity in it. It must manage to get stronger, become a force that can be used to oppose communist violence. They argue about tactics.

Antek Macierewicz organized the work in an apartment on Bednarska Street. Crowds of people topple over one another and sway in a small room, not really knowing what they want, or rather knowing clearly, but are unable to translate their desires into possible actions. Macierewicz and a few colleagues are trying to organize the chaos. Structures are waiting for newcomers, which are then to be used to find each other, of the organization. The newcomers are watching them. Many do not have the courage to fill in the boxes and sign their names. Some come back and with determination enter their details. Others, after a while, with despair blur them.

It was then that Zuzanna realized that she's smiling at strangers, and they return her smile. They understand each other. This has not happened before. Strangers did not look into each other's eyes, and a smile could be a provocation. Now it connected them. The hot September rushed through the streets, bewildering people with new possibilities. Zuzanna feels that she is beginning to no longer be afraid of those who might be following her.

Great matters consist of individual fates, although they move past them, and Zuzanna hears from her friends that she must return to work, regain her lost job, which has become a battleground. She appeals to the labor court, just like everyone expelled for political reasons. But when she returns home, Benedict reports that there was a call for her from the 'Portico'. The director has sent her an invitation.

Alski is glad that he will be able to take her on again. For the second time Zuzanna drinks coffee and looks at the round, smiling face on the other side of the desk, under the weight of the reluctant glances of the communist trinity on the wall above him. He reflexively looks at the opposite and empty spaces where the photographs of dignitaries once hung, which no one has filled up yet.

"See how well it turned out!" says the delighted director. "All's well that ends well. Let's leave the labor court" he calls full of optimism. "You are writing an appeal and I will accept it. You don't even know how happy I am that we will be working again, that we are creating normalcy." He pauses for a moment and looks at her seriously. "I'm really happy, although I guess you don't have to believe me. Earlier...I...after all I had to...it wasn't only about my position, it was about the publishing house. After all it's so important. You have to defend the culture, even at a price...And that's why your return today makes me so happy!"

When after a week Zuzanna enters her room in the publishing house with a sense of triumph, after a few minutes its space filled up, and she became the center of it. A crowd of employees gathered around her, whom so far, she had known mainly by sight. They are waiting for her to establish a union there, the name of which they did not decide on. And so suddenly Zuzanna becomes the chairwoman of the Factory Founding Committee of the Free and Independent Trade Union, which in a few days will get the name Solidarność. Zuzanna listened to this news in the swirling crowd in the smoke-dense room of the Inter-Enterprise Founding Committee at Szpitalna Street. It's brought overjoyed emissaries from Gdańsk along with the most important information: a single, nationwide union structure will be created. Zuzanna screamed with joy, but her voice was lost in the chorus of enthusiasm. Someone grabed her in an embrace, then she embraced someone, whom she kisses. The joy is not confined in the tight rooms of the office, but it bursts them open, exploding over the city.

Regaining her job and an unexpected union career was another chance for Zuzanna to participate in the rapid stream of events, a deeper immersion in a great movement in which she is already deeply involved. She drove to different workplaces, where employees who are determined to act awaited her. They know what they want, and her role is to connect them with others, break the sense of isolation and integrate into the common front that was engulfing the country. They treated her as an emissary, someone who would explain the status of the new union in the thicket of bureaucracy, which would propose overcoming the obvious contradiction of their venture with the system to which they were condemned; she would come up with solutions. Zuzanna crams in the labor codex at night. She herself is surprised by the enthusiasm with which she approaches the endless, incoherent, bureaucratic records. She's learning self-confidence. She had a conversation with Madej, who explained to her what she had intuitively known before.

"You need to be confident in yourself and convince others that we know everything, that we can break the system, destroy it from the inside. And we must not yet speak this openly, but we must make it understood."

Zuzanna sees the faces of unknown people but not strangers staring at her with an almost childish trust. He must lose the jitters, fear, that she cannot live up to their expectations. In another time it would be impossible. She wouldn't be able to face hundreds of strangers, usually only men, and tell them what to do. In another time, even if she memorized the labor codex, just as she did, she wouldn't be able to cope with these detailed questions, explaining the matters of leave and meal breaks, to answer the doubts of men of her father's age - if he lived, if he was not deprived of what was currently happening – people, who have behind them a life of harm, shame and disappointment. She could not make contact with those who are young, violent, full of anger and hatred. Now it's different. She reflexively smiled at them. The hundreds of faces she sees in front of her are no strangers, though she didn't know them before. She understands them, though for so many years she lived in a different world. She knows them: and those of her father's age who make her think about him, and those of her brother's age. She doesn't have to simulate anything. She tells them what she feels and thinks. Her confidence grows from a sense of closeness, from that, she can finally publicly share with them that of which everyone knows and propose a way out of a situation which everyone would like to change.

"We have not chosen the system in which we live and, unfortunately, we still cannot get rid of it (she suddenly remembered that she was saying Benedict's words, and cheerfulness overwhelms her). But it depends on us on how we live in it. We're able to change our country so that we can feel almost at home in it. It will not be the country of our dreams yet, but we will not be ashamed, looking in the mirror in the morning. We will feel that we are even partly working on something that belongs to us."

Not all of those from the factories she visits receive her with the same confidence. She sees faces numb in everyday humiliation, ironic and withdrawn faces, but she can accept it. She can withstand the reluctant glances or remarks made in an undertone by young workers who demonstrate what they could do with her. Overall, she's able to not worry about it, especially since such behaviors are only a margin and if they become more visible, the dangerous intervention of the community puts an end to them.

Fatigue burned-out in the fever of the day falls on her at home. It falls on her after her return, late at night. In fact, without agreeing on anything, Benedict took on the responsibilities related with Adam. Sometimes in the morning or evening they exchanged a few sentences about it, and her husband agrees to everything. Rarely, when Zuzanna returns extremely late, she sees his worried gaze, but she no longer has the strength, nor for that matter the desire to ask about the cause of his worries, which she of course can guess.

The time of agitation, speeches in workplaces, participation in the election of founding committees quickly cames to an end quickly. Her life moves to the premises of a new union, to offices, to rooms in various places of the city and apartments, where they meet to agree on what is most important. In the clouds of smoke, they talk, argue, jump at each other's throats only to reconcile later.

***

Everyone whom she meets now, becomes close to her. And that is why it will be so difficult later to face their misappropriation, betrayals, meanness, and their own defeats. After many years, when she encountered those she has not seen for a long time, joy will be her first impulse. Only a moment later memories and reflections come, which will percolate in her, depress her, and bring her back to the present day. To some, her fate will be associated for a long time or forever, with Jerome Jano. A small, gray man who did not finish law school, but spent two years in the army. He never really talked about himself, and therefore later, even many years later, Zuzanna would have to force out single memories of him. He didn't seem to have a personal life.

Then, also unexpectedly, she finds friends she lost years ago. From the times of the open house, ten years earlier.

In the headquarters of "Mazowsze" someone gives her a hug. She releases herself with difficulty from the hands of a laughing, stout man in his forties with a well-lined face.

"I know that I have changed, but it's me, Leszek Jurczyński" he helps her startled memory. Zuzanna remembers their last meeting, fifty zlotys, which she pressed into his hand so that he would leave her alone. His indistinct smile when he talked about being fired from the Academy for the happening "Multiplication". She's looking at him now and feels embarrassed, but he lets out a hardy laughing at her.

"You haven't changed at all and I...I don't drink anymore. I haven't taken a drop of alcohol in my mouth in a month. Solidarity. I figured I had to meet you here..." He stops and Zuzanna knows, how this sentence was supposed to end.

She also met Krzysztof Markus. Jurczyński found a job in a children's publishing house, and Markus became a warehouseman at the Rose Luxemburg Works. At night, after leaving the "Mazowsze", Zuzanna went with him to the 'Melody', a crowded place opposite the Central Committee complex. Marcus pointed out some windows to her that are still glowing. "It would have been impossible just a few months ago. At this time comrades were resting. We're taking their sleep away." He smiles with satisfaction.

"These colleagues around, previously strangers...I was also someone else to them, now they are my friends. There are no barriers between us, understand? I stopped being this apropak, as they call people like me. Quite witty, this is a propos... Maybe we're really such apropaks, we don't know how to be internal, and only a propos...But now it's different...And with you. You've always been beautiful, but now you're beaming..."

Zuzanna suddenly realized that in the morning she does not gaze into the mirror, as she did before, tracing the signs of time for longer and longer: folds swelling on her forehead, furrows running from the nose above the lips and sharpening facial features, a network of wrinkles in the corners of her eyes...She does not touch her skin with her fingers to feel the sagging lurking under it, which will soon reveal itself on the outside. She has come to terms with her appearance, or rather does not take care of it, just as she does not take care of her metrics and perspectives, which seemed to close with each moment, with each day where her unspecified dreams drowned... Now she relishes the rush of history, melts into it, is a part of it, and so she does not hopelessly fight for her individual status, which suddenly turned out to be part of something bigger.

The National Coordinating Commission decided on a one-day warning strike. Zuzanna is in a group that has already called for it before. She meets people who talked about what was happening in the provinces: intimidation, beatings, blocking the operations of the founding committees. Those who came asking for help did not have confidence in them. Even in the bravest person could feel anxiety, sometimes one could see plain fear. It was necessary to react, to strike, to use the wave of enthusiasm which carried them, to push away the still lost and uncertain disposers of violence.

However, when the decision is made, she feels tension which was mixed with excitement. She comes home late at night. In the cool last days of September, the dark landscape of the city forms into well-known shapes, it leads her steps, promises support.

Benedict isn't sleeping. He's probably waiting for her. He's sitting by the window, smoking a cigarette.

"Do you really know what you want to do?" he throws that out almost without an introduction. "Do you know what another strike can mean?"

Zuzanna is tired. She would want to go to sleep, but she hasn't had a conversation with her husband in almost a month. She sits across from him and lights a cigarette.

"I was his spokesperson."

"Of course. I should've guessed!" Benedict snorts with a kind of smile. "My fearless wife!" He looks at her for some time, wondering whether to say something, and then suddenly throws out: "But do you know how you're plying? Like children. You perform a spectacle of steadfastness, rebellion, collective purification, but you are a toy in the hands of someone else."

"I understand that Goleń directed us" this time Zuzanna cannot free herself from the irony.

"Different people direct. Consider, why they did not crush the strike in the shipyard? And now? More important than your decisions are shifts in the Politburo. And...just so you know! Władek's role is...You don't even know how much you owe him..."

"You know what? I'm just not capable of talking with you. I know, that nobody directs me. And you know it. However, unfortunately, I know what directs you. I won't say it because it would be too unpleasant. And at the same time you suggest that you are the lords of history..."

"Who are the 'we'? What are you talking about?" Benedict was extremely hurt.

"Clearly you talk to me like that too. In the plural. So, if we're 'we', then there is also 'you'. It doesn't matter. You are such an intelligent man. And you use all your intelligence to justify your...well, never mind. You know what I mean." She thinks she has said too much. Benedict lowered his head and rested his forehead on his hand. A trail of smoke from the cigarette covers his face.

Four days later, Zuzanna came to work an hour ahead of schedule. The few trams she saw did not take passengers. They rode with Solidarity stickers and were decorated with national flags. The city was withering away in suspense. In the "Portico" they gathered in a large hall. They sat almost in silence, sipping coffee or tea brewed in glasses. It was only after over an hour that the first information about the scale of the strike began to break through the busy and overloaded telephone lines. The country stopped. Despite expectations, the scale of success was staggering.

Zuzanna didn't stay long at the publishing house and after a few hours she ran with a couple of people to the headquarters of the union. The building was already surrounded by a crowd. It was impossible to get inside the crowded rooms. Enthusiasm was buzzing. It melted the October chill. The hustle and bustle came out of the building, flowed over the city, became its rhythm. Someone was shouting through the megaphone subsequent information confirming that, what everyone knew. They relished in their success. In the following days information from the country began to flow in. From distant places, towns, far away workplaces. Excited voices said that it was now different. Party governors and UB's backed off. They felt their strength. And they, the people of Solidarity, stopped being afraid.

That evening, after endless conversations with consecutive people who became acquaintances, after mutually basking in their triumph, the foundation of plans that they made in the next dense rooms, on the streets, squares and tram stops, when she finally arrived home and put her son who was waiting on her to bed, Zuzanna who was semi-conscious from fatigue, but also on a wave of enthusiasm that released her subsequent energy, she began a conversation with her husband. She wanted to finally talk with him, to share what was most important. By not participating in the same experiences, they became more and more strangers to each other. These feelings downright hurt physically. Zuzanna felt them, when she returned home and at times thought that Benedict must feel them similarly. His agreement to take care of Adam carried with it something distressing.

"Have you not noticed that you have always been wrong?!" She did not want to demonstrate the advantage, but to share the victory, infect him with it, so she did not choose words. "You were against the opposition, which was to end in a catastrophe, and its existence was to be, in your opinion, a great provocation. Then there were the strikes, and now there's Solidarity, which, although it's such a success, is winning...exactly, what is it in your opinion?"

"Why are you talking to me like that? As if I represented the communist authorities to you. I also want this system to disappear. Like any reasonably intelligent person."

"Then why don't you get involved in what we're doing now?" Why are you standing next to, maybe even...After all, if we had listened to you, if I agreed with you, we couldn't do anything...Gierek would still rule, there would be no Solidarity, we would live in a walled-up world at the mercy of the authorities..."

"Are we not dependent on it? Are we not condemned to expect that they will take the army to the streets or that they will summon the Soviets for help? After all, your successes are only the result of their calculations, the fact that, it's not worth it for them..."

"And if it's true? It's not worth it to them because they don't want to risk it, because it would be too much of a risk?"

"And if they're just preparing, in order to hit harder and more accurately? If this is just the beginning, to knock this nation's head off?"

"Don't you understand that this kind of a position is capitulation before the fight?"

"But maybe differently. It's the proposition of reason?"

"What reason? Fear. Fear rules you. And the only thing you believe in is the ability to convince, or maybe not, rather to please these sons of bitches in power..." When the words came out, Zuzanna realized that she had exaggerated. On a wave of excitement, she said what she was thinking, but at the same time she realized that Benedict would close himself off again. As usual, he will hide in the lonely closet of his traumas. This time, however, he reacted quite differently. He looked into her eyes and began to speak as quickly and violently as she did.

"Fear...Maybe you're right. Maybe it's fear...But isn't fear a good adviser to the weak? And we are weaker, you must realize this! Were our national uprisings a good solution? The Warsaw Uprising? Shouldn't we study it? Fear...Isn't that another name for the instinct of self-preservation? At times it seems to me that you are deprived of it. It's even fascinating, but in the long run...This isn't a way to survive...Sometimes I think that those like you have infected the whole nation with your bravado and you are in a frenzy. You have lost your natural, reflexes of self-preservation...And responsibility? Also, for us, for our son and family?"

"Responsibility...Is it the synonym of fear? Actually, if people listened to you...nothing would not depend on us."

"But exactly, it depends! By putting everything at stake, you...you take responsibility for the disaster that comes. It is you who will owe her!"

Benedict was almost flushed. Zuzanna thought her husband was screaming in his sleep. Her husband, a stranger trapped in his fear. She felt fatigue and even compassion. Foreign, cold compassion for other's loneliness.

She doesn't remember when she brought home the first larger group of Solidarity members. At the beginning it was a few people. Then, however, it was possible that twenty or more guests were able to gather in the apartment. She stuffed them into one room, remembering the meetings and people from over ten years ago. She barely recalled that incarnation. The memory of him did not carry nostalgia. They were so much younger, but the hopelessness of their existence overwhelmed the memories. In fact, their lives only made sense from their current perspective. And that's why her meetings with Leszek Jurczyński or Krzysiek Marek were so unusual. The latter came to her place entangled in a group of several people. He greeted Benedict, looked at Adam appreciatively, looked around for a moment at familiar corners, as if trying to remember something. He was sad for a moment. Zuzanna also remembered the death of Wiktor Czerniak. Unexpectedly, she saw again the face of Bartek, a hippie she had never thought of and who got lost somewhere. There was nothing to go back to and only one thing spoke clearly and sharply. Then as never before she and Benedict were one. His father, Adam Brok, lived in the other room, and she and her husband understood each other almost perfectly...Benedict's father was no longer alive, and only playing with their son was she able to find closeness with her husband. Sometimes, unexpectedly, in the moments of physical contact, when he smiled at her so that for a moment, she knew everything about him and was sure that he understood her like no one else, the aura of those times returned. She fell asleep in her husband's embrace, immersed in their love. But then she would wake up, drag herself from sleep, wash herself, do her morning beauty routine and make breakfast, she looked at him, and unspoken questions and replies hovered around them. She thought about the content of her days, about the matters of all of them, and disordered images, dreams, thoughts formed on their common experience, and thus Solidarity, which permeated her thoughts about the future of her son. And, trying to organize her experiences, she realized that her husband, who is outside their orbit, beyond the most important experience of her life, soon will turn to the editorial offices of the "Republic", and she asked herself what they were doing in one house.

Contrary to the promises she made to herself, each week she read his articles word for word. She wandered through Goleń's vogue editorials, who wrote about a dangerous anarchic element, so typical of Polish culture, which makes it impossible to recognize reality, does not take into account realities and leads to missed opportunities facing the country. "Instead of working out our future prosperity, just as Western European countries have done, we demand their achievements without offering anything in return. Instead of working for the common good and investing, we demand another day off from work," wrote Goleń.

Pieczycki wrote with irony. He juxtaposed communist moralizing efforts with church appeals; Stalinist masses "with Solidarity demonstrations; calling for a national awakening - with communist slogans." Against this background, Benedict was moderate. He wrote about excessive claims that undermined the economic balance. He called for economic reason. He was afraid of egalitarian attitudes.

Initially, Zuzanna and her guests got momentum at home, continuing the discussions started somewhere in the city. Then she began to invite them home. Sometimes Tadek joined them with his colleagues with whom they formed the Independent Student Association. Benedict greeted them, listened to them for some time, and after uttering a few sentences, went unnoticed with the whining Adam to the other room. Sometimes he asked questions. He asked so that he could be considered a voice in the discussion, which, however, disappeared unnoticed. Zuzanna often thought that only she could hear and understand him. Only she picked up the intention of the question: how do they know the goals of the authorities? They were dismissed as naive and she knew that the question was aimed at their fundamental certainties.

Those gathered argued about tactics and even strategy, about what was to be done tomorrow or in a few months, but they did not ask each other such questions. They had to lean on some certainties.

Benedict's presence caused a specific tension. Everyone knew who he was, and even more so towards Zuzanna's husband and their host, they tried to maintain correct but cool politeness. A blister of alienation seemed to stiffen around him. Tadek collided the most sharply with Benedict, who quickly fell into anger.

***

It was already cold, late November, when someone informed Zuzanna about an important document that was sent to "Mazowsze". There was more tension than usual on Szpitalna. People came together and leaned over the dozen copies of an official document. It was a print of the prosecutor general Prosecutor Lucjan Czubiński, "Remarks on the current principles of the prosecution of participants in illegal anti-socialist activities." The document, addressed to the prosecutors, urged them to act towards the preparation of trials against Solidarity activists recognized as "participants in illegal anti-socialist activities". He talked about gathering evidence, and suggested its fabrication, called for harassment of "participants", for searches, investigations, and arrests.

Piotr Sapeła, an employee of the copy room of the Prosecutor General's Office, showed it to his father, who in turn was a Solidarity activist, Krzysztof Łoziński, who gave the document to Jan Narożniak. Zuzanna met Narożniak few years earlier through Madej. A shy and endearing boy, he was active in the underground publishing house "NOW".

They already had a registration crisis behind them caused by the changes that the court made in the association's statute. Tension was building up. Strike readiness was announced. The authorities backed off. But now everyone knew the matter was more serious.

At the beginning there was a search in the headquarters of "Mazowsze". This message touched Zuzanna especially personally. Worse than when they first entered their apartment. She knew then that it was possible. Now she hoped that they had built a fortress that they would not dare to break into. They dared. The next day they arrested Narożniak and Sapła.

"Today Narożniak, tomorrow you!" posters and leaflets proclaimed. This exclamation mark expressed what they felt. The date of trial was coming. The next few days melted into a moment of concentrated tension. Zuzanna remembered Benedict's shrunken face, who, looking at her, gave up on what he had to say. Tadek visited their place, shouting that everything was about to be resolved. Readiness for a general strike had been announced.

"Mrs. Zuzo, what will happen?" Alski leans towards her, who is clearly waiting in the corridor to talk to her. Up close, Zuzanna sees the beads of sweat on the director's face.

"Director, calm down. We will win" she says with certainty, which she feels that others share with her. They pushed their tension deep down, though it smolders at the bottom of their convictions. Maybe they still haven't got used to the feeling of strength, or maybe it was just faith which they were not completely sure about?

"Bratkowski brought them to Ursus. They're free" he hears in the crowd around "Mazowsze". It is already late at night when he found himself dancing at the Ambassador. Out of a large group only a few people were left. Zuzanna, a little drunk, finally agrees and dances with the young Solidarity activist from Ursus, Cześko Biela.

"We'll chase out the reds and we'll make justice" Biela whispers in her ear, and then he begins to speak in a whisper. They raise subsequent toasts; it's not even known who's putting up for them. "We will chase out the reds and we will make justice" Zuzanna begins to sing. Biela kisses her, and she gives in, she returns his kisses, which becomes an element of their rising passion. This passion brings them both out of the "Ambassador". They walk in an embrace, warmed by it through the cold of Warsaw. They stop an out of place taxi, and Zuzanna did not consider what was going to happen. There is only a slight resistance to the increasingly intense caresses of Biela. She was calm and having a good time. The taxi stopped. After negotiating Biela scoops out his last coins. They climb the stairs of a dingy tenement house. Zuzanna does not mind the strange, even somewhat rancid smell that overwhelms her when she enters the tiny anteroom, from where Biela guides her to his room. They fall on the divan and Zuzanna only remembers Benedict for a moment, although she tries not to think about him, which she succeeds when she is overwhelmed by a wave of bliss that allows her to forget the particulars, because she is a small part of their joint victory.

She is awakened by a dryness in her throat. It's still night. She rinses her mouth and brings herself together in a dirty and quite disgusting bathroom. Four o'clock is nearing. Her host also wakes up, encouraging her to stay, but Zuzanna firmly cuts off the discussion. Biela heroically decided to escort her. They wave cars passing by. Finally, someone stops and for a fee of thirty złotys, agrees to take her home.

"Oh, come on," Zuzanna interrupts Biela's excuses, who has no money, and his declaration that he would accompany her. For a goodbye she kisses him briefly, decidedly pushing him away. Through the taxi window, looking at the receding, shrinking figurine, she thinks that the guy is her brother's age.

He had called the "Portico" a few times. She asked him not to do it. He approached her at Solidarity headquarters.

"We need to meet, even to talk. Why are you behaving like this? I did something wrong?" He was panting in her ear.

"Give it a break. I have a husband, a child. I'm a lot older than you."

"But still...we were...it was...amazing..."

"There was nothing. You're having delusions," she said jokingly, just as she turned Tadek's bizarre ideas into jokes.

Biela looked at her with the gaze of a resentful child. Walking away, she glanced briefly at his unmoving form. He stared at her direction the entire time. For a moment she felt sad and thought she was losing something.

***

It took some time before Zuzanna realized that in this exposed community, currents and vortices began to stand out. Environments and societies are emerging. There are those who know each other better, understand each other, and others who cannot or do not want to understand the obvious. Those who are nice and those who are harder to like. Those who understand the allusions and jokes of the environment, and those who are surprised by them. People gather in more and more regular groups, which gradually become societies, and although movements between them and infiltrations are still intense, one can slowly distinguish the variable circles centered around people or environments. Zuzanna realizes that even she is in the field of interest of those who are trying to convince her who she is and who should be who in their one big enterprise. Surprised, she discovers that delicate remarks are supposed to orient her in the changing landscape of their joint activities and to inform who is worth how much. She begins to realize that she has been hearing this information for weeks, she only needed time to understand that the tips given to her make up the competitive images of their movement, in which everyone has internal leaders and opponents. Conversations that seemed selfless begin to suggest a goal. Joyful exchange of feelings and thoughts permeates the tension of the struggle for power. Malicious remarks, ironic shots, harsh comments, just as well gestures of approval, and even admiration, are not only used to express emotions and insights, they become part of a collective game in which the majority participates unconsciously.

Zuzanna noticed all this more clearly since she was elected to the administration of "Mazowsze". Therefore, she was in the very center, doomed to make choices, preferring some over others. At times she thinks that this is a mistake, she should not have taken on a function for which she was unsuitable, but at the same time she realizes that it's a responsibility that one cannot shrink away from. Sometimes the game starts to pull her in. She understands those who explain that this annoying Antek and his whole group must be finally marginalized. More ideas and actionable projects appear in which he reveals his his true nature and compromises him. Then suddenly she began to distance herself from him, to those around, to her friends.

There is disappointment and disgust. She involuntarily sees more and more hidden moves that she would not like to know about. Intrigues sometimes seem even without reason, violent conflicts break out for no reason, resentments swell suddenly and are venomous. She hears unfair judgments, slander, unsubstantiated insinuations. She sees activists who are trying to organize, find full-time jobs, comfortable sinecures, positions, stability, recognition. Discouragement overwhelms her. However, she gets rid of it immediately when she sees the same people completely involved in specific operations and becoming lost in their joint venture.

In the evening, they met at Solidarity headquarters, exchanging views on the concentration of Soviet troops near the eastern border of Poland and movement of units in East Germany and Czechoslovakia. In the growing anxiety, somebody finds it hard to make a joke and she looks at the face of Konrad becoming more serious, explaining something to Paweł who was nodding his head, the same person he was making fun of the day before, she sees that something deeper connects them, and inevitable conflicts bubble along the surface of their bond. Focused faces lean towards the reporter talking about the conference of Warsaw Pact countries in Moscow. They look in the direction of the troops gathering at the border. Their every gesture, every decision becomes fraught with consequences. It's hard to tear your hands away from the table to report, to vote. They are in the gun sights of those behind the border barriers, whose wood will break like a match under the weight of caterpillar tracks.

It is not fear, although surely more than once each person feels its touch. Every once in a while, Zuzanna has trouble breathing, the air escapes from between her lips. She feels shortness of breath and her heart began to pound harder and harder. She must calm down, bring things to order, looking at those around who must endure what she has to. She remembers her son, and then a sense of responsibility comes back to her that weighs on them together. They all know that so much depends on them, though maybe not at all, whether foreign troops will enter our borders again. Maybe it's already decided, but they are responsible for what will happen next, what will happen to them and the country. The responsibility overwhelms them, its importance loses itself in the nights of the coming winters and summers, which will come. After all they dared to take it on themselves. They believed that they could lift it and face all those who were lurking on the borders and inside the country. To those who now in the most magnificent edifices of the state, in the light of fluorescent lamps, are leaning over plans on how to destroy them - suppress Solidarity. At the headquarters Security Services lists of those who are destined to be interned are readied and subsequent names are added to them. The future camps are designated. In barracks, officers receive more sealed envelopes. And they are sitting in the middle of the capital, wondering how to prepare for a confrontation.

"A Soviet tank has entered Warsaw!" Tomek called from the end of the table. The noise of voices stopped. In the room stiffened from smoke, it is a still silence, Tomek continued: "He stopped before the Supreme Court. He submitted a petition for registration of an Independent Self-Governing Soviet Union. Judge Zdzisław Kościelniak refused. The PZPR's leadership role is not mentioned in the constitution!"

The room shook. They roared with laughter. They patted their knees, hit their shoulders, rocked in their chairs, shouting: "There is no party leadership role!"

Zuzanna laughed with them. They laughed so loudly that they could be heard across the borders, their croaking made its way to Moscow, where the old men covered in medals looked west with astonishment.

Zuzanna saw the laughter in the faces of those who were shaking off their tension. Laughter was their defiance. She loved them for it. And that is why it was so difficult to come to terms with the fact that the next day they will talk about unacceptable things to each other, they will get along then marginalize someone, and promote someone, to fight out a position or a full-time job. This dark current, inseparable from human affairs, afflicts even Solidarity, she tried to convince herself. People would not free themselves from their ambitions, and their passions will wash away the noblest goals, she explained to herself. She wanted to talk about it. She returned tired and, as once before, instinctively, began to confide her doubts in Benedict, when she suddenly realized that she shouldn't be doing it. She paused suddenly.

"I didn't understand. What did you want to say?" he inquired.

"Actually…I don't know myself. I'm tired."

"I don't blame you. You do a lot already." He said warmly.

She turned toward the window. She looked at the frost on the branches made visible by the light cast from the lanterns, and the first snow icing over outside. The sky was without the stars and the moon was black. Frost was coming from the east.

The clouds will float away, and the sky will be blue-grey, she thought. If I have control myself, what I can tell my husband, if I have to watch myself before him...a strange voice tapped in her head. Benedict was smiling at her as if to encourage her, but she didn't manage to say anything. Maybe she was too tired.

"In a couple of days! Let's arrange a meeting in a couple of days", explained Madej, when she accosted him in the Solidarity headquarters. He had dark circles under his eyes and looked unconscious. He was running somewhere. He was an activist and expert, functioning at the epicenter of ongoing activities. Stawicki, who she came across in the same room in a moment, agreed without hesitation. Although he was not only on the board of the university branch of Solidarity but filled the function of an advisor for "Mazowsze". They walked along the cool and dark street for a moment. The cafe attracted with warmth and human presence. Stawicki sank into a chair and, closing his eyes, sank into a cloud of cigarette smoke.

"You're charming," he laughed. "What did you think? That we will transform into another species of man? Without any flaws, personal ambitions? The workers will free us? Have you already forgotten how similar beliefs ended?"

It was crowded and loud. The sounds clustered into a uniform noise. In the indistinct light, human figures lost their identity.

"I'm not that naive. I just wanted to share my woes with someone, but..." As always, in such cases Zuzanna's intuition turned out to be too difficult to translate into precise sentences. She was surprised to discover that the spoken words became murkier than the thoughts behind them. "Why are you talking about workers? After all, Solidarity...We have overcome these class divisions...In the shipyards the workers demanded freedom of speech!"

"For certain?" Stawicki stared at her from behind the glasses slid low on his nose. "And I think these are just illusions. We will have to face these egalitarian tendencies that are already growing. And this can be no less dangerous than the party. You will see! This time the workers really want to rule us. It's no accident that you are concerned. The time of the masses is coming. We'll have to defend ourselves against it. Then alliances will have to be changed! We'll be surprised yet..." Stawicki waves his hands, his face contorts a strange smile.

"But I'm worried about something else! These threats have nothing to do with these...divisions you are talking about. You feed off of them, have prejudices against them, against workers...like...my husband. And I mean something completely different. That...we don't measure up to what we create. Can't you see that something amazing is happening? These people...we...are better. Earlier we were pulling each other down, now...it's just the opposite...they, we are crossing each other...Solidarity has somehow raised us up and that's why when we can't measure up to it...It's sad."

"You know, your exaltations can even move someone. However, they do not make it possible to recognize reality. In any case, it's extremely difficult from the inside...I know something about it. And yet I am able to analyze what you are saying and see all the assumptions you need to make to fund your faith. You must believe in history that is just coming true, in the god of people, which we have turned out to be, and the spirit of the community of which we are only elements. My dear, this is dangerous collectivism..."

"And you are a fucking apropak, " Zuzanna interrupted.

***

Zuzanna literally doesn't remember how winter passed. Only that the holidays came out of it as a different, special time. The white of the snow unexpectedly covers the city, obscuring its dirt. Feverish meetings at the headquarters of "Mazowsze", which moved to private apartments, sometimes to their place on Koszykowa St. The rhythm of the discussions that are capable of turning into quarrels only to unexpectedly become an agreement. And the sense of closeness which connects her with these people, the community from which individual people can be replaced by others, but the sense of identity and community remains.

They spent the holidays together with Tadek and his girlfriend, Irena. Zuzanna sent her brother to aunt Gienia and her family, especially Ali, with invitations. Gienia and her husband visited them on the second day of Christmas. Ali and her sister excused themselves, and Zdzich, who had his first leave from the military, got lost somewhere.

Tadek brought a Christmas tree, which they dressed together with Adam. Irena helped Zuzanna. They prepared dishes for the Christmas Eve feast and the festive table. The products were obtained by men, especially Benedict, who being an editor, got a huge package with food not available elsewhere. This time Zuzanna refrained from comments. The holidays, as always, were to be a unique time, an oasis of light and warmth on the winter night, free from politics and conflicts. Irena accompanied only Zuzanna, who, as always at Christmas, returned to the everyday neglected art of cooking. As a little girl, she learned from her mother, then practiced under her careful tutelage. The holidays were special. Therefore, she was able to prepare the Christmas Eve feast, which evoked the genuine enthusiasm of those present. Perhaps the enthusiasm was all the more honest because Benedict, who had Christmas Eve dinner at noon in the editorial office and had already returned slightly tipsy, to avoid disturbing the women, he took Tadek out for a traditional shot at the nearest pub. They returned to sit down to Christmas Eve dinner in good spirits and friendship, which meant that they had kept their word and stayed away from political topics. The dinner met traditional requirements. The scent of cabbage and mushrooms permeated with dried fruit and nuts and the sharp smell of fir needles from the Christmas tree, miraculously somehow intertwined harmoniously and created a unique Christmas aroma. Toasts made with frozen vodka helped digest the huge amounts of food and improved the mood. Adam, who found a small army of plastic soldiers under the Christmas tree and could, scattering streams of sparks around the room, burn a packet of Bengal fire miraculously obtained by his father; he was happy. When Zuzanna brought him to bed, he did not whine at all, but almost in his sleep he asked: "Mother, why can't it always be the holidays?" "Because then they would not be special" Zuzanna answered automatically and only then began to think about her son's question and her reaction.

Sitting down, she stroked Benedict's hand, who kissed her palm, looking at her with a smile. We are in an exceptional time, when the good in us is released, spoke a voice in her that wasn't entirely hers. We are in a special time for our country that brings hope, allows us to be better. But every year God is born, she thought. If I said it out loud, it would sound ridiculous, but it's true. We don't understand it, but we feel it. That's why we can meet every year, freeing ourselves from our anger and grievances, from anger and sorrow. We enjoy this moment, with our presence and even the food tastes different, not only because I've put so much time and effort into preparing it. It doesn't bother me that Benedict is horrible when singing a carol, that he doesn't believe its words, because really, do we truly know what we believe in? She held Benedict's hand, and her thoughts fell asleep in her, they melted in the candles' flames on the Christmas tree, in their reflections on the glass behind which the winter dreamed.

The next day, together with Irena they were preparing a late breakfast, Tadek entered the kitchen. He hugged her and kissed her.

"You know, I still think I'm very lucky. We are" he corrected. "And now when I am at your place...I always liked Christmas at your place. But it's different now. I'm sure you can feel it. We are being reborn. It's funny that I, a brat, ten years younger, am telling you this. But that's what I feel. After all I'm already graduating. And I see how people have changed, those, whom I thought I had earlier gotten to know. It's simply unbelievable. The conformists took on dignity, the indifferent took on passion. If I wasn't involved myself, I would ventilate something false. But I see that it's different. I don't know for how long, but now it is. And I myself...After all, I was also getting tired of everything, and now...And you...You've gotten even more beautiful. You know, I remember my parents. I can't remember my father, but I have the impression that he remained in my memory. I see his face and form. A tall, thin man. So, I think it wasn't given to them. They only got the October scam. Now this euphoria we're experiencing is also for them and that is why we can't screw this up, understand? You surely understand this better than I do!" Tadek answered himself, embracing her. In the open doors of the kitchen far from them stood Benedict with a sad expression on his face.

Gienia and Stach came with a pot of impeccable cabbage stew. They tried to be cordial, but Ali's imprisonment left a shadow over them. Between the hosts and guests and the efforts of Zuzanna and Benedict it did not help. Perhaps her uncle and aunt had the least resentment toward Tadek, who honestly laughed at his jokes and hugged him spontaneously. Despite everything, the Kowacki family tried to overcome the trauma inside of them. Tadek might not have even noticed it, but Benedict was sure. "They don't believe that we did everything in our power to help their daughter. Can we blame them?" He asked Zuzanna after they left. She agreed. She had asked about Ala before. "She will never be like she was before," said her clearly saddened aunt. Her husband just nodded his head. Zuzanna pulled him out to talk about Solidarity. He was a member of it. "That's how it should be done!" He announced in a firm voice, slightly glancing at Benedict, who started playing with Adam. "But isn't that unusual?" Zuzanna wondered. "Well yes, but it's just the beginning. Everything is yet to come. That's how it should be done, but this is only the beginning and nothing is certain" he said firmly.

"It's a shame," Benedict said. "It's a shame they can't forgive us. And additionally...I would like to tell you..." He looked at her, desperately searching for words. "I of course understand your enthusiasm. And I would give anything for you all to succeed...although...I have concerns. I'm a sociologist and I know a little about the nature of such movements, but" with a gesture he stopped her answer "that's not my point. I'm afraid of what this might lead to, but now I'm saying, just so you know, that nevertheless I'm with you all too. Although we are different. And I don't want to argue." Zuzanna understood how much it must've cost him and felt moved. She hugged him.

But the holidays passed and the daily fever of that time began. The fight for free Saturdays was just an excuse. This is how Zuzanna saw it, who, together with her friends, treated the next clash as a turning point, an attempt to force the party to make concessions, launching a process that they however did not know how to use, and were afraid to imagine. It was supposed to be a series of events at the end of which threatened taking power away from them. The tension grew with the awareness that it was a fight for every inch of the office, every record and decision, a fight in which there is no ceasefire. Sometimes at night, while drinking a shot of vodka, Zuzanna felt her neck muscles loosen, and her body contracted as the tension unwound. But Benedict treated the matter of Saturdays, like everything else, differently.

"Don't you understand that this is the time to roll up your sleeves, not in idleness?" He snapped.

"As for me, you know well that I don't even have Sundays off" Zuzanna fired back.

"Yes, because you devote them to getting others Saturdays off."

"You're becoming a doctrinarian. Of course a huge part of the work in this country is fiction. With slightly better organization, our economy would benefit from free Saturdays. And you act as if you were solving equations and weren't participating in life. Where is your sociological passion?"

"And you became a union dialectic. The less we work, the more we will achieve. Indeed, that's union logic."

In these moments Zuzanna interrupted the conversation. There was no point in continuing. Madej said what she had to, in her soul, agree to.

"At first, they built the fiction of Poland as an almost normal country, where almost normal economic mechanisms rule" he was becoming furious, brandishing a copy of the "Republic" with another series of texts pulverizing Solidarity, which was initiated by Goleń's editorial "and then from this perspective they attack Solidarity as a union full of demands that prevents reform and development. It's a multi-stage hypocrisy, but they must do it to defend their integrity. This Goleń! New Greater Poland, which wants to do so much for Poles, because he knows that he's not capable of doing anything with them. A false dick, who must justify the vileness committed for a career. I'm sorry that I'm saying this to you" Madej said.

"Why? I'm not at all associated with Goleń" Zuzanna declared with irony, which was supposed to be light but cost her more than she thought.

In February, General Wojciech Jaruzelski was appointed Prime Minister. Exceptionally, both in Zuzanna's and Benedict's environment, the nomination was received rather positively. Just like Jaruzelski's message about ninety days of peace. They were already tired. In "Mazowsze" they wondered if anyone, who emerged from under the Soviet wings and spent his whole career in the communist army, if patriotic feelings could rise up. Zuzanna felt distrust. Benedict tried to explain to her that the duffer Pińkowski would be replaced by a resolute and rational person. She didn't believe. A man with no spine needs to keep himself extremely straight, it occurred to her as she was watching the rigid figure of the new prime minister delivering a message on the television screen.

It quickly turned out that calls for peace were a propaganda operation. The tension was rising again. The turning point was approaching. Zuzanna was sure. The time of trial was coming. They were waiting for it. The situation became difficult to bear.

***

A person was screaming. From the cacophony of human voices and unclear sounds, the desperate cry of the massacred man stood out. Others shouted, moaning was heard, but this voice rose above and dominated. Sometimes he floundered, he choked, someone was probably strangling the beaten, blocking his mouth, but then again the scream was heard, which suddenly stopped. The clamor still continued, terrified voices were exchanging indistinct words, and then, all at once, everything went silent. The cassette finished. They sat in silence for a while. An indistinct March morning full of clouds and humidity was gathering outside the windows. In the dim light, tired and gray faces stiffened in determination.

"No, we won't let this pass!" Someone said. No matter who, because they expressed what everyone felt. "It will finally be settled. They will have to pay. This will be a breakthrough. We'll do a general strike and push them to the corner. This will be the beginning of their end!"

***

The phone woke them up at night. Benedict looked at her in paralyzing fear. Zuzanna answered half-sleep, but what she heard woke her up immediately. "Rulewski severely beaten, Łabentowicz and Bartoszcze were also beaten. But Rulewski is in serious condition. ZOMO and SB entered the room of the Provincial National Council in Bydgoszcz, where Solidarity and country activists were invited. They told them to leave and beat them hard. Rulewski..."

Despite the night, the headquarters of "Mazowsze" boiled. It was clear to everyone that the only answer would be a general strike. Their ultimate weapon.

When Zuzanna returned to those moments, and she returned often, they remained a breakthrough event in her mind, a moment when their fate was decided, and the current of reality took a certain direction. In the internment camp, in the gloomy years that followed, trying to find a way out of the deadlock situation, they would be returning to the time when everything still seemed possible and the course of destiny could be reversed.

At the headquarters of "Mazowsze", successive versions of the story of events intersect, repeated without end, enriched by the question of who is behind the provocation, because nobody had any doubts that this was a provocation. They argue whether it was organized according to the central authorities or one of their factions to harm another. In the yellowish light of lamps, immersed in a sleeping city, they shout over and threw out more arguments. In one area they agree: one cannot give way, step back. One couldn't leave this matter.

Before the morning someone from Bydgoszcz brought in a cassette. They sat at a table. Silent. Every now and then someone jumps up, takes a few steps only to return to their place. Sometimes someone curses, but they listen in silence. They listen to the screams of a beaten man.

Remembering those days, Zuzanna has the impression that she didn't sleep at all. If she fell into a short, restless nap, it was only to once again relive the events of the day.

A resolution is coming. The union's authority, the National Coordinating Commission, breaks off talks with the government and calls for strike readiness. The Bydgoszcz region stands for a few hours, but it's just a test. Zuzanna along with others wonder how to react if the authorities introduce martial law. Rumors on this subject are becoming more common. People gathered at Szpitalna St. repeat them to themselves first with disbelief, but because more and more new people pass it on to others and no one knows anymore who or what their source is, they become more and more likely.

"Clearly we know it comes from the party to scare us!" exclaims the redhead Roski, who appears unexpectedly at "Mazowsze"

"Even if it's from them, it doesn't mean it's false," says the irritated Stawicki.

"It means that they want us to think that way and be afraid" adds Roski.

But then in a moment, in a few hours, in a day, these rumors are reinforced by information about the decision of the Russian Politburo, which decided that a general strike would be the reason for intervention of the armed forces of the Pact on Polish territory.

Another meeting of the Solidarity authorities with the government team led by Goleń's friend, the new deputy prime minister Mieczysław Rakowski, is flabbergasting. Rakowski attacks. Shouts. Solidarity heats up the atmosphere, which will lead to Soviet intervention, it repeats. Negotiations are broken off. The official media shiver with indignation at Solidarity's troublemakers who threaten not only stability but also the country's existence. Information about the prolongation of the Warsaw Pact troop maneuvers becomes the main news. Suggestions from concerned presenters and commentators whose eyes are suspended tensely on their viewers after presenting the issue so that it is understood.

"We can't lie to ourselves," Madej says. "An intervention is possible. Just as it was possible in August or autumn" he says calmly.

They crowd Zuzanna's room. They sit on all the furniture, on the floor. Despite the chill of the March night, the windows have to be opened because the smoke of cigarettes makes it difficult to speak, scratches at the throat and squeezes tears from the eyes. Benedict said hello, but soon, using weariness as an excuse, withdrew into the other room.

"And what's supposed to come from this?" Jurczyński casts a question for all of them. "Should we be afraid?"

"No, we should be getting ready!" Madej answers what everyone thinks. Almost everyone.

"Wait, but we can't fight!" Stawicki looks more unconscious than usual. "We have to deliberate on how to avoid this."

"We can somehow fight, though not with a gun in hand." Madej is calm. "And the certainty of safety...we would have such safety if we dissolved Solidarity and joined the Party.

They look at each other. Stawicki looks as if he wants say something when Jurczyński bursts out laughing.

"We'll join the party!" He calls. "And we'll be safe!"

Laughter raises them. The Brok flat, the highrise, Warsaw, the country, all laugh. The laughter is listened to by the anxious figures in muffled offices surrounded by edifices of plain clothes agents. Above the rows of phones they look at each other in silence.

When everyone finally leaves and semi-conscious Zuzanna tries to collect even a part of the cigarette butts which are strewn everywhere, Benedict enters the room.

"I'm sorry, I'll try to limit these incursions," Zuzanna says instinctively.

Benedict looks at her in suspense. He wants to say something that is not easy for him. She would like to help him, but she is too tired to even ask. She needs to take a breath. He goes to the window and looses himself in the humid chill of the night. He moves slowly and is unable to formulate the sentences. With difficulty she turns and looks at Benedict, who finally decides.

"I'm not going to convince you of anything. It's probably too late. I'm afraid that a bad time is coming. We may not even realize what can happen. We argue, we differ in opinions...However, I want you to know one thing. Whatever happens, we are family and you can count on me. It is simply inappropriate that I say such obviousness things, but I want you to know that you can have absolute trust in me..."

Not knowing why he made this declaration makes Zuzanna extremely angry. She wants to answer but doesn't know what, so she waves her hand and goes to the bathroom. She doesn't even have the strength to take a bath. She washes herself quickly. Falling asleep, she thinks that she enjoys privileges that none of her friends have.

The meeting of the National Coordinating Commission in Bydgoszcz took place four days after the beating of Rulewski. All major Solidarity centers participate in it. They focused on telephones which called every ten minutes or more often to communicate the current state of affairs. The crowd at Szpitalna St. went silent when their representative picks up the phone in order to later report on the state of affairs in Bydgoszcz a bit inaccurately. When he finishes, its hard to describe the racket that breaks out. Everyone wants to share their remarks. The noise calms down a bit only to break off when the phone rings again.

"Wałęsa blocked an immediate call for a general strike."

"A team has been appointed to conduct negotiations, which will take place in two days."

"If they don't yield, a four-hour warning strike will be conducted. If they do not react, an indefinite general strike will begin on the last day of March."

They look at each other. Decisions were made. A confrontation was coming, but they know it is necessary. A state of tension cannot be kept up indefinitely. The breaking point is coming. They know that they will win. It will be a turning point. They will regain their country.

Rakowski shouted again. He's grotesque. Watching his marionette on the TV screen, those gathered at Szpitalna Street make unfunny jokes. Everything is decided, as they previously thought. They hear talk about some of Wałęsa's strange movements, but they do not take it seriously. Gossip and innuendo are a UB weapon. Walesa is not predictable, but now he has been bound by official decisions. The strike can only be canceled by a decision of the NCC, and there is no chairman among the negotiators.

A crowd besieged the headquarters of "Mazowsze". There was a four-hour warning strike. Warsaw is standing, the country is standing. The country that is Solidarity. Telephones connect. They are informed about successes. In the headquarters, timid officers sum up data and pass it on to the central headquarters. A general with a swollen face calls the prime minister, who is also a general. The country is dying, skulking. The Prime Minister General taps his clawed finger on the map spread on the desk more and more nervously. They are still not ready yet. Not yet..."

Zuzanna returns home extremely tired. Maybe mostly from anticipation. She must sleep if she can, if she can fall sleep. Tomorrow is their day. A general strike began. Benedict runs into the room.

"Come on, come on!" he almost pulls her in front of the TV, where the tired and downcast Andrzej Gwiazda reads the text about the suspension of the strike. Zuzanna doesn't believe her eyes. She doesn't pay attention to Benedict's carefree joy. She's unconscious. He goes to the phone and dials several numbers in turn. They are all taken. Everyone's trying to understand what happened. The phone rings and Zuzanna, without really identifying the voice, hears: "It was Wałęsa, he arranged it all! We fucked up!"

They sat at Stawicki's and drank vodka. There was no ordinary fuss. Sometimes only someone would break free and throw out a vulgarity. Another told a joke. Just yesterday at the same time they were ready for everything and capable of everything. Now they felt as if the air had escaped from their lungs. They were just exhausted.

"It couldn't have been done otherwise. Wałęsa blackmailed us. "Madej rests his head on his fists. He is semi-conscious from fatigue. "Without agreement with anyone, he undertook the talks himself. We later learned that only his driver was with him. Funny. Nobody knows him. I don't remember his name. I think Mietek. Strange face" Madej frowns "disturbing, insolent mouth. Doesn't matter. What's important is that Wałęsa himself, without agreement, went for talks with the government and established a new agreement with them. And then..." Madej downs a shot "appeared unexpectedly at the administration. He stated that he took care of everything. We began to protest, everyone, most probably Karol, Andrzej. Then he stopped and asked: "Do you want a war with me?" Or something. "Do you want me to tell people that you are trying to deprive me of the power they gave me? Do you want that?" I don't precisely remember the words how he put it so. I asked later. Nobody remembered. We were too agitated. But he certainly said that. Only, just as Wałęsa, not quite precisely. However, the message was clear. Who will go to go away in such a situation when the reds want to jump down our throats? For people, he is Solidarity. And that's why you had to give way.

"It's fucked-up," Jurczyński said. "Such pressure. Everything was possible. And this way...We turned tail, we retreated. They already know that we don't have balls, that we can't afford a real fight.

"Don't exaggerate!" Madej was getting angry. "This isn't good for various reasons, but nothing decisive. They also backed off."

"This must be considered a success." The host, as often, went against the tide. "After all they mainly gave way. In actuality they fulfilled all our demands. Sometimes we have to go back a little, so as not to drive them to the corner, where they can only bite. After all, we don't have tanks."

Someone responded sharply. A discussion ensued. They talked, calmed down. They forgot about what had happened. They were preparing for the next days.

Zuzanna said nothing. She had a sense of defeat. When she remembered that moment so many times, she already knew the events that would follow and confirm her intuitions. Only did she really feel them then? Maybe everything will start to mean something only from a later perspective: statements that indicate signs of failure, signs that can only be read after a year. When the real defeat comes, she will return to this moment, feeling that this was when they began to slide down the slope. People struggled with the everyday hassle, striving for survival, which became more and more onerous, they couldn't withstand such a long mobilization. Once again, she analyzed that moment, listening to the words of Zbyszek Bujak a few years later: "I am convinced that it is the Bydgoszcz conflict that was rooted in our defeat. The great Bydgoszcz stress, then the cancellation of the strike - took people's power away, disarmed them. At that point we lost our weapons." All around them lingered the lethargy of martial law.

But then, on the first day of April, Zuzanna woke up with new strength. Brushing her teeth, she spat out in disgust, rinsed herself off in the shower, explaining to herself that nothing decisive happened, and even that it's difficult to unambiguously assess Wałęsa's compromise. At breakfast when Benedict, sensing her uncertainty, smiled and asked: "So what else did you expect, what more could you achieve?!" It was difficult for her to answer. After all, the government declared that local authorities violated the law and norms of political action. An investigation was to be carried out and the guilty punished. So maybe it was a success?

That day, everything still seemed possible. The hope of spring was stirring in the strangest of places, in Poland surrounded by hostile armies waiting for the decision to break through its borders, although foreign troops were already inside. Even though the commanders of Polish soldiers were waiting for orders from Moscow and were asking the Kremlin to approve their plans and help in the event of failure. The night before, a stone fell from their hearts. They were not ready yet. Help from the authorities in Moscow did not seem so obvious in a complicated international situation. They themselves did not have the strength to suppress a general strike that would paralyze the country. Now they returned with relief to their plans and maps. They entered more people on internment lists. They prepared detaild strategies that would spread widespread confusion and lead to a loss of confidence in Solidarity. They wrote down additional provocations. They were storing food, which was increasingly scarce.

***

Spring was in full bloom. Zuzanna reviewed the typescript of a book on the birth of perspective in painting. The function of the president of the union in "Portico" exempted her from professional work, but sometimes, taking advantage of free moments, she tried to come back to them. The publishing company stopped printing the obligatory rubbish. Ambitious plans were directed towards translating contemporary classics so far not present in Poland and creating publishing cycles composed of items ordered from Polish authors, which were to address basic aesthetic issues.

Perspective: see through and see clearly. In two dimensions reveal the three-dimensionality of the world, show depth on a plane. We are building an illusion that better captures reality - she wondered - we are building mathematical formulas to better mislead the eye. But mathematics is not enough. Two eyes and a head in constant motion. Every, even the slightest change in the position of the viewer changes the image, eliminates the distortion of one position. Brunelleschi developed the scientific concept of visual deception, Masaccio used it in his frescoes, Alberti theorizes. And yet perspective is not a technical matter, to which it is brought by those who cannot understand that behind every technical innovation there are meanings. She remembered her father's voice from over twenty years ago. She sees his face as if pressed into cement. "It is not true that medieval painters could not paint perspective. They didn't need it. They focused on what was most important."

Zuzanna remembered the paintings, copies of the paintings she saw, led by the voice of her late father. She returned to one of her favorites, Madonna of Chancellor Rollin by Jan van Eyck. In the foreground, the chancellor kneels before the Holy Mother with the Child, and then, behind the columns of the large window, the infinite world extends. On the terrace, where the peacock and magpie walk, two figures with their backs turned, leaning on the balustrade, contemplate the earthly landscape. A city with a crowd of human figures unrecognizable from this distance, with a river partitioned by an arched bridge that meanders among fields and green forests with villages hidden among them and escapes beyond the reach of human sight into the land of blue mountains with white peaks. But all this endless reality makes sense only because God's blessing hovers over it. It is this grace that the governor of this land contemplates, immersed in prayer in the dense colors of the foreground.

Earlier there was only the first plan. That, which is important. Mapping the secondary landscape was not worth the effort. Anyway, its reflection would draw attention away from what is important. Then masters like van Eyck began to show also what the eternal and sacred history radiated. Their successors immersed themselves more and more into the deceptive multiplicity of the world outside the window. Staring at the amusing eye, the flickering diversity, they stopped seeing anything else. The hole in the wall absorbed them. They forgot about what was important, what was happening in the foreground, about the truth that had completely preoccupied them before. Not remembering, they were still immersed in it, this is what soaked their world with meaning, created its order, but gradually evaporated, escaping to leave a series of unrelated events, a mosaic of colors and shapes which did not mean anything anymore.

Zuzanna tried to understand the evolution of perspective, put it in a meaningful way, but something disturbed her thinking. Only after a moment did she realize that it was a growing clatter. She wanted to wait it out, but it grew more powerful, it approached the door of her room, filling the space. She had not yet managed to identify its character when the door opened and someone rushed in with a scream: "They've killed the pope!"

A crowd gathered in the church. A kneeling crowd filled the room of the Basilica of the Holy Cross, leaning toward the floor in silence. The room whispered, prayed, offered its requests and promises. Zuzanna closed her eyes. The man in white comes back to her: his words on Victory Square, his gestures. For a moment she thought that if he had offered them Solidarity, freedom in an enslaved country, then maybe he had to pay for it?

Since August she appears more often at church. Listening to the audience, she remembers the words of prayers. She tries to take Adam to Sunday masses, although the constant lack of time prevents them from being regularly present. Still, Adam was getting used to it. He was getting used to the church.

Now in the Basilica of the Holy Cross, thinking of the man in white who is struggling with death, knows that she feels exactly the same as everyone else. She melted in common prayer, and pain and fear give way to a sense of something that surpasses them, an elation in which there is trust.

"How could this happen? Who could've done this?" Benedict repeated, walking around the room and relishing cigarette smoke. It was night. More and more clearly it was breaking through the fading buzz of the city with the voices of birds, breaking into the apartment through the window open at this time. Zuzanna was calmer since she heard in the 'News' that the Pope would probably live.

"What do you mean 'who did it'? Soviets!" She said with a certainty that astonished herself.

"What are you saying?!" Benedict was offended. "Maybe they would like to, but they're not stupid. This is some absurd. They wouldn't take that risk! After all, the matter would soon become clear."

"Soon? Clear?" Zuzanna spat out the words. She was choking on them.

The Pope was slowly recovering.

She met with Goleń for the first time in a few years at Balcerak's gallery. "Marian asks you to come," explained the embarrassed Benedict. "He came to our office, he did not know how to communicate with you. I think he cares more about your presence than mine."

The painter surrounded by a wreath of adorers spotted her instantly. He pulled them apart and threw himself at Zuzanna, embracing her.

"I'm so glad you came," he repeated. "I hope you forgive me for the happening in which I wanted to cast you without asking for permission. The ultimate happening."

"I've forgotten about it. Many important things have happened."

"Yes, but sometimes I think it was my best idea. Maybe it was worth it, huh Zuza?"

"It's hard for me to agree, my son wouldn't have been born then."

"You know, that's an argument. Maybe the best I've heard. I need to think about it. I've always had trouble with it." Balcerak kisses her on the cheek and let himself be carried away by a group of admirers who surrounded him to drift further.

"Well, my rebel." Goleń moved in her direction, extending his arms. Zuzanna stepped back.

"My dignitary. I don't have the boldness." Avoiding his embrace, she reached out a hand, which the surprised Goleń shook. Remembering this over many times, she felt the need to wash her hands.

"So What? We won't be able to talk anymore? Politics will take over everything?"

"It's such a special time...You say: politics...We live in it. And anyway... Don't pretend. You chose it yourself. It's everything to you."

"However maybe not since I want to find a common language with you. I've been doing it for a long time and you're a neophyte. Maybe that's why it's pulled you in, so that you can't talk to old friends...

"Big words. But we're talking." It is only at this moment that Zuzanna noticed a special, somewhat clumsy figure with a large, bald head decorated with two tufts of unkept hair. The figure moved toward her. The gray-head with the small beard continues in her direction.

"I also wanted to talk to you. I've heard, I've heard a lot. And you're after all the daughter-in-law of my best friend and the wife of a student, also a friend. I remember how we met at Adam's funeral. Such a beautiful, nostalgic girl...It would not occur to me that I would see you as a revolutionary." Klein shakes his head, smiling thoughtfully.

"A revolution? I'm a bit afraid of these word games."

"But words count, my dear." Klein looks up at her. "And I have experience with the revolution. Ash is always left behind after it. Everywhere. Around and in us."

"But does it appear to me? It's you gentlemen who defend the orders that grow out of the revolution. We want to change them. And without using force."

"Don't kid! After all you understand" Goleń chimes in, leaning towards her. "That revolution has already burned out. We are slowly building normality. You are the true revolutionaries with your maximalism, romantic idealism, this new national-Catholic ideology" he raises his voice. "Don't you realize that? You don't build scaffolds just because you can't. Without the use of force? You don't have it yet..."

Looking at his contorted face, Zuzanna thought he was a little right. In fact, amongst themselves, they often, half-jokingly, noticed that the ideology of nonviolence was adding to necessity. Watching Goleń, who waved his hands in front of her, she wondered if she would feel pity if someone decided to take care of him. Aversion began to grow in her. Sophisms that she couldn't oppose irritated her more and more.

"So what? Is every appeal to value dangerous?" She snapped.

"Oh, yes," Klein observed sadly. "Of course I'm not accusing you of bad intentions. And we" You don't even realize what idealists we were. Like sacrifices, ready to burn ourselves. And what? You know very well what the effects were. Or rather, you don't really know it. It had to be experienced. And that's why when I look at you all...So what if you wave different flags? There were also different banners then, and under each there were determined idealists! You may have the best intentions, but the effects are always the same. We want to cleanse the world, and because it can't be done, we're looking for the guilty ones. First those on the other side, and then, when we get rid of those, those in our ranks...The logic of the revolution."

"The iron laws of history?" Zuzanna tried to utter virulent sarcasm to herself.

"The most elementary sociological principles" Goleń was genially mocking again. "Perhaps you'll agree that there are."

"I hope that you're not fighting about politics?" Benedict emerged from the crowd and embraced her.

"No. We're talking about historiosophy. The discussion carried me away, but we probably should go back to Adam." Benedict looked at her alertly and understood.

"Ah yes, of course. We got carried away a little."

They were driving around, bypassing the center blocked by Solidarity. A column of union cars filled the intersection of Marszałkowska and Jerozolimskie Streets. The police stopped them the previous day despite prior consent to the demonstration. They refused to return. A string of trucks and buses blocked the center. Warsaw froze in tension. Benedict looked at her from above the steering wheel.

"Does this make sense?" He asked.

"But does it make sense to give consent for the manifestation and then to block it? Inviting for negotiations and then torpedoing them?" Zuzanna said. The conversation broke off.

In a nearby office in a closely guarded building, a stiff bird-shaped man received reports at his desk. "People are getting tired of it," said the stout general. Relief could be detected in his voice. "It's good because you can't save the country without it," declared in a studied voice from behind the desk the bird-shaped man.

***

August rolled over them intensely and again Zuzanna did not have time to go to Niemir despite encouragement from her husband and her son's sadness. *"In full sun in the middle of summer / Among the gentle waves of greenery / The work was coming along fast / I put the boat on dry ground"* she sang to Adam, sweeping him away to dance. *"Build an Ark before the Flood / Draw all your strength for it / Build an Ark before the Flood / Even though the crowd would mock your work / That which is most valuable must be saved, and yet there's so much of it here."* As part of the broadcast from the *First Review of Real Songs*, she heard this song on a radio station in the new headquarters of "Mazowsze", Mokotowska St., and then on one of the tapes, which were distributed by any means possible. Jacek Kaczmarski was a star there. Zuzanna heard him for the first time about two years earlier. She was swept away by *The Walls* and *The Source*. She thought then that the voice of the young generation was coming: violent, angry, pathetic. So different from their muted, ironically nostalgic Janek Kelus, whose recordings have been running between them for several years, and sometimes they listened to him. And they sang along with him at concerts held in their homes.

"Build an ark before the flood / Ours over the fate of tears / Build an ark before the flood / For the first and last baptism." The melody carried her off and captured the text, although she did not fully listen into it. The song was a warning, so therefore and hope. They were built a living arc in an encircled country. When she went as a delegate to the First Solidarity Congress in Gdansk two weeks later, among hundreds of people who made immediate acquaintances and friendships, together with others she felt the strength and certainty that at this moment they are

throwing out the final challenge to those buried in their fortified headquarters, scared and pushed to defensive. They felt it, voting on "A message to Eastern European working people." They knew that the eyes focusing on them were not only from Eastern Europe. They embodied the expectations of all of those in the camps, behind the wires, behind the barriers of borders separated from the world by entanglements and kilometers of plowed fields with watchtowers, on which machine guns equipped with optical sights scoured the ground. They were their hope. They knew their voice would sound far and long.

CHAPTER 12

A bang on the door pulled Zuzanna out of the bathroom. She had just washed off her makeup and, barely seeing her reflection, applied a thick layer of cream on her face. She came back late. Adaś was already sleeping. Benedict was reading Karl Mannheim. He had recently been trying to convince her that it would be worth trying to finally translate and publish his *Ideology and Utopia*. She listened inattentively.

That Saturday, she was at the Solidarity headquarters until late sitting with a group commenting on the ongoing proceedings of the National Commission in Gdańsk. In five days on Thursday on Victory Square, for the eleventh anniversary of the Gdynia massacre, a great rally was going to be held, a protest against the attempted passing of extraordinary powers for the government. The sketchy anniversary was an excuse. They agreed that there was never enough rememberance of communist crimes. Ceremonies commemorating, that what everyone knows in private, but that they do not even think they can talk about out loud, changes awareness. This time, however, the main goal was a response to the authorities that attacked, provoked, and brewed conflicts. There was a student strike. Ten days earlier, the strike of cadets of the Higher Officers' School of Fire Fighting in Warsaw was broken up. With delight, the television repeatedly showed the attack on the college building combined with the helicopter assault, with the handcuffed students being dragging out. The commentary, as usual, talked about radicals and troublemakers against whom the authorities must use force, because, contrary to the calculation of various political players, there is fortunately still enough of them to bring order. Immediately afterwards, the National Commission met in Radom. Properly trimmed materials from these conversations went to the radio and television, and then were reprinted in the newspapers. This took place directly after the decision about the rally done by "Mazowsze". It was not known how the tapes got to the authorities: whether it was wiretapping or whether any of the participants recorded the proceedings. The rulers created the atmosphere of omniscient. Eavesdropping seemed unlikely or even impossible, the image of an agent inside the National Commission was difficult to accept. They argued about this on Mokotowska St., at the headquarters of "Mazowsze". And at the same time, they repeated what had leaked. Some expressions reflected their mood. "This will be their last fight" said Karol Modzelewski. The leader from Silesia, Andrzej Rozpłochowski, put it more clearly: "Gentlemen, we have to fuck them up so bad that Kremlin chimes play Dąbrowski's Mazurek." They felt that they could do it. They knew they were changing history. The tension swelled and the final confrontation was coming from which only they could emerge victorious. Anger grew in them. More and more often activists beaten by "anonymous" perpetrators appeared at the "Mazowsze" headquarters. "Soon it'll be the end of your fucking Solidarity," they heard from the attackers. The confrontation was approaching and could only have one result. The anxious Zuzanna returned home through the frost and densely falling snow.

The thumping was increasing. Zuzanna ran out of the bathroom in a bathrobe. Benedict stood pale in the corridor like a wall. He wasn't approaching the door. She thought she saw her husband shivering.

"Who's there?!" She shouted in a voice that gave off confidence.

"Police! Open up!" She heard. She tried to control her panic. A confrontation was starting, she thought. It could be dangerous. We will win, but it could be dangerous.

"It's after midnight. Please come in the morning" she still drew her strength from firmness.

"We have a warrant. Open up or we'll break through the door!"

"I am on the board of Solidarity! You will answer for this!" Her own voice seemed high-pitched. At the threshold of the room, Adam stood in his pajamas, terrified, rubbing his eyelids.

"If you don't open in five seconds, we'll break through the door!"

Benedict moved his lips but didn't make a sound. Zuzanna felt sympathy and rage. She ran up to the door. Dark figures swirled in the peephole. Someone seemed to be putting a crowbar under the door frame.

"I'm opening it," she called. "Take care of the child," she said turning toward Benedict, unscrewing the latch.

They poured into the anteroom, throwing her against the wall. Uniforms in blue, fat uniformed police and civilians with raised collars on quilted jackets. Someone was holding a metal bar in their hands. The chaos of characters and voices filled the apartment. She heard Adam's scream. She wanted to rush towards him, but the character in civvies strongly grabbed her arm.

"Zuzanna Brok?!" He wasn't asking nor stating, leaning towards her.

"Please let me go!" She shouted, trying to break free and run towards her crying son, but the character held her tight, and the police blocked the way from both sides. She could hear Adam's crying but could not see him. Surrounded by heavy figures, she did not know what was going on.

"By the power of the declaration of martial law you are being interned. Indefinitely."

There was a tussle going on in the anteroom. She realized that Benedict was trying to force his way in her direction with Adam weeping in his arms.

"Please let me through! I'm a reporter. I have to find out what this means. This lady is my wife."

"Calm down, sir," he said in a bored voice. "Or for resisting the authorities and being under martial law it's punishable by up to and including the death penalty, we'll throw you in jail and take the kid to an orphanage. Well then? Will you be backing off?"

"Benek! Calm down!" Zuzanna called desperately. "I'll go with them, but... you'll see, this won't last long!" You have to take care of Adam."

"Yes, yes," the character laughed. "You have three minutes to get dressed and take the necessary things. I warn you that it is cold. And if you don't hurry, we'll take you in your bathrobe."

"On what grounds are you want to take my wife?! I demand documents!" Benedict said it in an almost imperative tone, all the while trying to calm his son down.

"Based on the martial law decree. Here it is." The character thrust some paper towards Benedict. "Don't touch!" He screamed, taking it out of the reach of his hand. "Here is a list of people to be interned with addresses. Your wife is here."

"Give it a break" Zuzanna repeated in a calmer voice. "Explain to Adam that nothing is happening. It's only until tomorrow." The character laughed mockingly.

This could not be true. This is their last spasm. They'll pay for it, Zuzanna's head was banging when she grabbed a few things from the closet and locked herself in the bathroom to change her clothes. Her hands were shaking. Everything seemed unreal. Adam kept screaming.

"Calm down, son. Mum must leave, but she'll be back soon," he whispered, embracing and kissing him. Benedict had to help her free herself from her son. She kissed her husband with a forced smile. "From now on, it's all in your hands. However briefly. Anyway...You're used to it."

On Wilcza, a crowd of friends swirled among the blue uniforms sifted with figures in civilian dress. Drunk, with bound hands, Paweł was yelling that they would pay for this. He got hit with a truncheon. Danka had a hard, shrunken face, Agnieszka was pale. They were locked in a separate room which was divided by bars. The officers rushed off somewhere, they were shouting and advising each other. They were prisoners in the middle of a great battle. Officers dressed in uniforms and civilian clothes ran before them as if on stage.

"It's the only moment they can enjoy!" Danka croaked. "They'll have to explain themselves tomorrow!"

After a few hours in a group of five they are loaded into police trucks. Shaking with cold, they go to Grochów. In a large nine-person cell, bunks were arranged in three levels. There was no light or water. Huddled up on bare, dirty mattresses and wrapping themselves in coats, they try to fall asleep. Only when muted light began to pour in through the blocked windows do they get bedding, blankets and a bucket of snow. They could wash their hands, faces, and cracked lips. They were able to suck on the snow. It is not until the evening do they got a liquid to drink, in metal cups, that has an aroma of grain coffee. They also got a dark grey liquid, which seems to be a soup, and a thick, loaf of bread each. They eat everything.

A headache. The next morning, Agnieszka vomited into the toilet. In the corridor there was yelling and unrest. Rollcall. A guard with a bayonet enters the cell. "Good morning," he says and counts them. Then they brought in a bucket of warm water. They could wash themselves. It was the happiest moment since their arrest. The radio was turned on. They could finally compare their theories with official propaganda. Up until now they only knew that they had struck at the head of Solidarity. They arrested its leaders. Everyone, whom they managed to capture. There would be strikes and a confrontation. Now the matter would be resolved.

The shapeless form of the sectional ward appeared in the door and informed them that they could write appeals. They get paper and pencils. They wonder if such an appeal is not an indirect acceptance of the situation. They argued. For now, they decided not to write. The guards took them out for a walk. The walkway surrounded by a high wall - five steps in width, seventeen along - was covered with snow. The sky disappeared in the grey-blue coolness of the air. They got so much water that they could wash the floor and the sink.

Bread with marmalade had a delicious taste. They could write to family and filled out package vouchers. They could order products from the canteen.

The sectional ward woke them up with the gray dawn which leaked through the windows with difficulty. Based on the news coming from the radio box hanging on the wall, which is shaking, they tried to understand how widespread the strikes were. There were calls for students and apprentices of the medical schools to help in hospitals sounds worrisome. There were stories of anarchic elements that were attempting to agitate the citizenry, breaking this work was countered by hostile elements, as well as wild strikes inciting hope which were controlled by law enforcement. In the canteen they managed to buy toilet paper, tooth powder, sanitary pads and playing cards, as well as ten smelly cigarettes each. Their smoke filled the cell, heating it. Food could not be acquired. For lunch there's watery cabbage soup with potatoes. They're hungry.

The days pass by playing cards and reflecting on how the situation will develop. The radio on the wall played lively music. In the evening, news about the death of seven miners during the pacification of the strike at the Wujek mine, as well as about the breaking up of the strike at shipyard in Gdansk. There are wounded there too. Maybe deaths. Maybe there are many more killed. Maybe the news of seven killed is only a declaration that they are killing and will kill, and the number seven is only a symbol, as Danka states. They looked at each other in silence for some time. A sharp hysterical female scream is heard from one of the cells: "Murderers!" They join in. The prison is screaming. They chant in an incoherent chorus: "Mur-der-ers!" Nobody answers. Finally going hoarse, they stop. On the radio they talk about troublemakers. They ask: who are the excited and aggravated, what dirty misdeeds do those who impersonate worker's leaders and who now have blood on their hands want to settle?

They're starting to get sick. The skin on Zuzanna's fingers begins to crack. The warden comes in the evening. For now, there are no opportunity for packages. They must prepare for transport to a camp. For a long time. For a very long time.

Agnieszka looks bad. She has stomach problems. None of them feel good. Agnieszka confides that she is pregnant. She talked about it, but nobody cared. They started calling them forth from cells for questioning. Anka and Danka say they refused to answer. They call on them again. Agnieszka is silent. Zuzanna is also summoned at the end the evening. She went under the supervision of two guards who led her through an protected passage into the corridor. From there, to the office door covered with green artificial leather. Behind the desk sits a man who checks something in the papers. Without looking, he indicated her place on the other side.

"Mrs. Zuzanna Brok..." he makes sure. And how do you enjoy jail?"

He looks up at her and smiles faintly. “I know it’s not nice,” he enters her prolonged silence. “You’ve only spent eight days with us. You’re young. It’d be a shame to waste your next years. Because in the camp it will be years. Don’t you miss your son? What’s his name? Adam?” He smiles faintly again. And likewise, without waiting for the answer that does not come, he continues: “You’re lucky. Good friends. That’s why you’ll get a chance that others won’t. You should sign this” he puts a form towards her with a pen across it.

“I hereby certify that today I have read the letter of the head of the Office of the Council of Ministers of 17 December 1981 and I fully confirm my knowledge of the fact that I am obliged to follow the principles of the people’s rule of law. I undertake to strictly comply with martial law and socialist rule of law in force in the Polish People’s Republic. “

“Well, you should hurry up” says the officer impatiently. “Sign it and you’ll spend the holidays with your family.”

Zuzanna hesitated. She heard something about declarations of loyalty, declarations of withdrawal from the union and cooperation with the authorities. They do not demand anything like that from her, it was only a confirmation of the current state of things, to which she must agree anyway. If she brokes their law, she’d go to jail, no matter if she signed the paper or not. That, which they call the law, these paragraphs of theirs apply to everyone. While going to university or to work, she also signed some declarations of loyalty to the socialist homeland, which she did not even read. Everyone did it. It couldn’t have been otherwise. They only demand formalities from her. And she would so much want to leave, to embrace Adam, go home and see Benek...

“Will I be released if I sign this?” She makes sure with a surprisingly infantile voice.

“Like I told you. But please hurry up. I don’t have time” the officer now said it in a sharp, determined tone.

Zuzanna signed. The guy frowned in an inscrutable smile. He took the paper and put it in a cardboard folder, which he took under his arm. He got up, opened the door and called someone in the corridor. In a moment, the guards entered and took Zuzanna away. She was stunned.

“But when I…”

“Please wait. We’ll summon you” he replied with a smirk. Then the doors close behind him.

“What’s with you?” Anka asks.

“I got angry. They told me they could let me out. That someone is trying on my behalf...I guess my husband...I couldn’t say, I would like to go out for Christmas. My son is six years old.”

“And they didn’t want anything?”

“No... Actually nothing. I was surprised myself.”

At night, Zuzanna could not fall asleep. The longer she thinks, the more she knows that she made a mistake. They will not release her, and they have a declaration of loyalty in their hands. Agreeing to it was breaking under pressure. She turned over on her bunk. At the time of trial, she gave up. How could this happen? She tried to understand. She feels almost physical pain and disgust to everything, the world around her and to herself. The cold night takes the breath away, it spreads out on her chest.

After breakfast she is summoned again. The same man is sitting in the office, who is looking at her with the same indistinct smile.

"But you were supposed to release me!" Zuzanna exclaims.

"Yes, yes, of course," the officer repeated in a careless tone. "Of course, we'll release you. However, there are still a few formalities."

"What formalities?"

"I must interrogate you."

"I don't know anything. After all you're holding me here."

"Well yes, but you were in the very center of everything before. We want you to tell us how you were preparing for martial law, which you then called a state of emergency."

"We weren't preparing at all!"

"You're kidding me. Clearly, there were plans. Tell me what the organization of the union was supposed to look like under new conditions. Well, under the conditions of martial law."

"What are you talking about? There were no such plans, just..."

"Just what?"

"Nothing. We didn't prepare anything."

"Ma'am please, because I will lose my patience," a threat sounds clearly in his voice. Zuzanna was silent. She looked at the SB agent with growing rage.

"Well alright" the guy changed his tone, softens it. "Let's assume you don't know. It's about the formality. You must tell us something." Zuzanna is silent. "Do you want to leave?" Without waiting for an answer, the officer repeats it more sharply: "Well, do you want to leave or not?!"

Zuzanna wants to very much. She misses her son, her home, and as well, unexpectedly, Benedict. She hates prison, the closure. At night she realized that they might not let her go, she thought she couldn't take it anymore. Despair enveloped her. Now, however, she began to understand that this was a game, which she is losing along the entire line. She must hold out, understand that she will not be released. Come to terms with it.

"But you promised me..." she repeated.

"Well yes. But I have to interrogate you. I have to have something in the report. Please just tell me such general matters. Who was the most active in planning... trade union activities?

Zuzanna is silent.

"I'm really going to get furious now!" growls at her. "You signed that you would cooperate..."

"I didn't sign anything of the sort!"

"You signed that you would observe martial law. And this imposes on you the obligation to cooperate with the authorities. Do you not understand?!"

Zuzanna is silent.

"Don't you understand that if your comrades see your declaration, you will be burned anyway? Are you aware that they can...? And I just want a basis, anything."

Zuzanna doesn't reply.

"Well alright. I will go hand in hand. What can you tell me about union activity before your internment? Well, come on, anything."

Zuzanna tries to forget that she can get out and spend Christmas at home. She already knows that she will return to her cell and she will share the same fate as the rest. Why would she deserve different treatment?

"Well tough, you decided yourself. Please say goodbye to your family and son. I don't know when you'll see them."

In the cell, she sat on the bunk and began to bite her lips from pain, humiliation and sorrow. She tries not to cry, although she knows that tears are falling from her eyes. Krysia hugged her.

In the afternoon she was summoned again. The guy placed a white sheet of paper before her.

"Alright. We'll compromise. You will write me something about your actions before the imposition of martial law. Something, which you can write."

Zuzanna looked at him and pushed the pen away.

"I won't write anything."

"You won't write anything?"

"Nothing."

"Well back to your cell then."

However, shortly after returning, the doors open, letting in the oval form of the sectional ward.

"Zuzanna Brok. Pack up."

She exchanged hasty farewells and in the company of officers moves towards the duty room. She tried not to think or imagine anything. After all nothing is certain yet. She got her documents. She signed a receipt for the return of her money and personal belongings. Another gate opens and Zuzanna was finally standing on the snowy street in the falling dusk. On the other side she sees Benedict, who ran up to her, embraced her, kissed her and led her to the car. Driving, they passed burning braziers, next to which uniformed figures warm themselves. Next to them stand, armored cars, sometimes tanks. Twice a military police patrol stopped them. Young officers look into the trunk, check documents. Benedict showed his documents, freely explaining. A few hundred meters from their house stood a tank. Adam was waiting for her at the door.

Zuzanna left the bathroom after losing track of time. Melting she is continuously replaced the hot and steamy water, she wanting to rinse off arrest from her, its stench which saturated the cells of her body. When she finally pulled herself out of the lethargy, she immersed herself in the bathtub and forced herself to leave, in order to once again rinse herself with the shower, she felt that she still has not completely freed herself from that tiring odor. Wrapped in a bathrobe, she goes to the room of her already sleeping son. She put him to bed earlier. Now she only touches his restless face through which the shadows of dreams fly. Adam murmured something, picked up his head and opened his eyes. He sees his mother and calms down. He embraced her and fell asleep with a blissful expression. Benedict waited, smoking a cigarette, and smiling at her. They sat as usual under the window, closed this time. By the light of the lamp, the snow reflected the light of the moon.

"So, you pulled me out?" Zuzanna finally asks, enveloping herself in smoke, which is in no way reminiscent of prison cigs.

"Well...I tried." Benedict is embarrassed. "Władek got involved. And finally, they said they would release you, if I promise that you won't do anything stupid..."

"You promised for me?!"

"Don't worry, it's just a formality. I was only talking about my...obligations. Anyway, these are obligations. I repeated, that you were an adult, independent woman. And I... Anyway after all you had to promise to obey the law..."

"Wait a minute!" How do you know that I've committed to anything?"

"Because they said it's this kind of necessity. A formal necessity. Otherwise they can't let you out. After all, anyway, we still have to obey their laws, no matter what we think of it..."

"They told you, that I would have to sign a statement of loyalty?!"

"Loyalty, loyalty! You made up a name for yourselves. After all, it's a scrap of paper on which you confirm the obvious. You live in this country and even if you don't recognize it, you are subject to its laws. Would you rather be in jail?! Would you prefer that Adam torment himself without knowing what was happening to his mother on Christmas?"

"Don't bring him into this. So you made a deal with them that I had to sign a declaration of loyalty and then I would be released?!" Zuzanna is furious and Benedict resentful.

"What do I have to provide for you? They said that it's a condition and they're doing it only for me. They made it understood, that it's actually about Goleń. You would be released for Christmas. Others are staying."

"You could've at least talked with me!"

"But I couldn't..."

"You know what, I have to think all this through. I shouldn't have signed it. But it's also your fault!"

"Give it a break." Benedict tried to embrace her, but Zuzanna broke free. She went to the window and looked into the night. Her head is all confused, but she knows perfectly well that she shouldn't have signed anything. She's ashamed, and therefore maybe she blames Benedict even more. She tried to stand back from the situation, understand her husband, but she cannot lose her anger. Suddenly, the house was filled with a strange, intense noise. It came from the other room. They ran into the room, but something is happening outside the window. They approach the window. A column of tanks was going especially fast down the street. The caterpillars seem to tear at the pavement, which is desperately failing. They stood next to each other for a moment. Benedict makes a gesture as if he wants to embrace her, but Zuzanna turns her back on him and walks away. She sits down at the table alone. After a moment's hesitation, Benedict goes into the room, turned off the light and went to bed.

"Do you know what's going on with Tadek?" Zuzanna asks Benedict who was unconsciously puts on his glasses while he is still waking up the next morning.

"I was at his place. He seems to have escaped. They went to get him; they even broke down his door. I saw it. I know nothing more. He didn't reach out. I even visited the Kowacki's once, but they didn't know much. Anyway...I was busy with you, that is with the attempts, for you..."

"Maybe its exaggeration" replied Zuzanna, getting dressed.

"Where…where are you going?" Benedict finally asks.

"I have to find out, what's going on. Check what Tadek is doing. That he is well and such."

"Maybe I should go with you...to help..."Benedict suggests uncertainly.

"No. I prefer to do it myself. You've already helped enough," she throws it out, feeling that she's unfair. But she can't fix it. "Can you give me the keys and papers?"

Benedict fulfills her request in silence. He looks at her for a long time. Suddenly he explodes.

"Have you not forgotten that you have a six-year-old son?!" He yells out unusually violently for him. Zuzanna stops in the anteroom. For a moment she doesn't know what to do or say.

"You can look after him some time! Perhaps this just might be the best occupation for you!" She exclaims with passion and runs out, slamming the door.

This day passed by for her with fruitless searches. Despite the cold, a group of people gather near the headquarters of "Mazowsze" on Mokotowska. Several friends among them. "Yesterday they dispersed people here, beat a few hard, even women, they arrested them..." someone begins to tell. The wail of a siren is heard, and a police car comes up on one side and a ZOMO unit run up the other. People begin fleeing. Without thinking Zuzanna also beings to run. They're chasing them. They're chasing her. Behind her, noise and screams rise. She turns into a side street and realizes that no one is after her anymore. She looked carefully from behind a wall and at a distance of about a hundred meters she sees several officers beating a man and woman with clubs and pulling at them. The woman fell over and one of the policemen began to kick her. The man breaks free, she didn't know whether he wanted to run away or throw himself to her aid, but they knocked him over, kick and beat him with clubs while he's wreathing on the ground, and then they pulled them by their clothes on the street, helping each other at times, and throw them into an arriving police paddy-wagon.

The door of her former apartment, Tadek's apartment, is loosely pushed into the door frame and taped up. Zuzanna looked at the ruined entrance to the house where she spent the first twenty-one years of her life. She came into the world here, then her brother, from here her father and mother departed, a place filled with memories, a shelter that Tadek took over, now devastated by strangers. She wondered if she shouldn't go in but felt that she didn't have the strength. She descended the stairs. On the floor below a door creaks open, and the elderly man whom Zuzanna recognizes as her neighbor, Mr. Zenek, who places a finger on his lips, he invites her inside with a gesture. He sits her at the table and his wife makes tea.

"Zuza…I'm sorry, Mrs. Zuzanna…"

"For you I will always be Zuza" She interrupts "Please tell me everything, that you know."

"It was a terrible bang. It woke us up. We were already, you know, I'm sorry, you know...at this age, not what you, young people, we were sleeping at this time. But the bang was terrible. In my pajamas I looked past the staircase. I heard screams, but already that team: ZOMO's, UB's, devil knows who else were screaming at people, for them to not look on if they did not want to go to jail...and they led Irenka, Tadzio's fiancé..."

"They were so boorish..." interrupts Zenek's wife.

"Jadzia, let me finish. So only after we talked, you know how it is among neighbors, each person saw something different. And Lewandowski saw the most, on the very same floor. Because they were screaming, yelling at Tadzio through the closed door, for him to open it, because they would break it down, he slipped out through the window. They were breaking down the door, that took them a while. And Tadzio is agile, he was always agile, I remember how many pranks he would pull, so it helped him. He probably let himself down the antenna like a cat, jumped down and fled. That's all they saw of him. So, they were screaming at Miss. Irenka. They pulled at her and took her away. We don't know what happened to her. And they sealed the flat. We asked around to our neighbors. Nobody knows anything more."

No one is answering the doors at her friend's apartments. Zuzanna stood on the third floor of a tenement house on Odyniec Street and rang the doorbell of Filip Madej's door endlessly. Just in case, she says loudly: "It's me, Zuzanna." But from behind the door, she's responded to by silence thick with memories and fears.

She returned home at dusk. Already in the anteroom a joyful Adam runs up to her.

"Dad bought a Christmas tree!" He yells, throwing himself into her embrace. Benedict, embarrassed, smiles, pointing to a tree put up in the corner of the room.

"You had the right to forget that tomorrow is Christmas Eve, but Adam's waiting. I hope you'll make a Christmas tree from this fir. I brought some food, but I also don't know too much about what to do with it..."

Zuzanna walked up and embraced him. She really didn't want to cry, but her body shook with spasms. She pressed herself tightly to her husband, hoping that in this way she'll calm down, especially since Adam is pulling her by her hand. She hid her head on her husband's shoulder, feeling that against her will something is flowing from her eyes.

Benedict promised that he would do his best in Irena's case, but especially during this period the matter was difficult. He even went somewhere and brought a message that they would check whether Irena is in jail or not. But the information will only be available after Christmas. "If there will be," he added gloomily.

It was a sad Christmas. For the first time in her life, Zuzanna forced herself to dress the Christmas tree and prepare dishes for the holiday table. Although Adam was cheerful and, as always, made a ballet of Bengali fire, and Benedict feigned delight at her culinary art, she knew that even the dishes that came out weren't her best. Anyway, the Christmas Eve table was exceptionally poor. Adam quickly sensed that Christmas was missing something, and the mood was definitely not festive.

It was Christmas Eve by the radio. However, they did not look for carols on it. They quickly got up from the Christmas table and sat down near Adam Brok's receiver, which was turned on all the time to the drowned garbled voices and beats of Free Europe, from which became a clearer voice only from time to time. They switched the radio to the BBC, then to the strangely not jammed France Internationale, only to plunge into the noise and rumble of Voice of America and Deutsche Welle and to return Free Europe again. When they listened to everything in Polish, especially from the little information, which the stations had at their disposal, was repetitive and the interpretations remained hackneyed and predictable, Benedict began to look for news on German and English stations. He translated them immediately for Zuzanna. Everyone was talking about Poland. Adam probably understood the importance of the matter, because he sat beside them calmly and lasted that way for hours in silence, moving around the soldiers on the floor. Benedict moved the arrow to subsequent programs: Russian, Czech, French, which he hardly understood, and then Zuzanna was turning the knob, continuing to listen to information that they did not understand at all, as if they were hoping that they could find some encoded message in them, a code allowing them understand, read something new from them. They drank vodka, hardly speaking with each other. Semi-consciously, only rinsing her mouth, slightly staggering, Zuzanna moved in the direction of the bed. It was far away and didn't promise peace.

The next day Benedict drove them to church.

"Why don't you come in with us?" She threw out as they left the car, surprising herself. It seemed to her that even Benedict hesitated. He was smiling helplessly. Characteristically for himself, she thought. Characteristically in our relations, because she hasn't seen such an expression on his face in other situations, she told herself.

"Well you know…I can't…"

"Why not?"

"Well, after all you know...I'm circumcised," he tried to turn the matter into a joke.

"All the first Christians were circumcised...even Christ," she partially accepted the convention.

"But I'm not a Christian."

"There's no ban…"

But Benedict already decided. He smiled a little more confidently.

"Give it a rest Zuza. Tell me, at what time should I pick you up."

It became cold. Zuzanna didn't continue the conversation.

The church was crowded and gloomy. As if it's not Christmas, something told Zuzanna. Everyone's eyes turned to the manger in which the Holy Family, animals and shepherds leaned over the Child. Does everyone, like her, in the illuminated by brown light stage try to see the symbol of Solidarity? The priest tried to raise their spirits by saying that it was a holiday of hope, because even the massacre of the newborns missed the Child-God whose mission is to save the world. Despite the heavy mood, the feeling that they were feeling it together added strength. As they exchanged the sign of peace, she realized that everyone was greeting each other with the sign of victory.

Actually, the matter seemed clear. Solidarity lost this battle. Did it lose the war? Even the facts were uncertain. It wasn't known how many were locked up. Five, ten, twenty thousand, maybe more? The information about what was happening to them was contradictory. A heavy burden of uncertainty fell upon her. What happened to her friends from the cell?

It wasn't known how many were killed. From the Wujek mine, information said it was about nine. A report about pacification appeared in Free Europe. Zuzanna already knew about the shooting at miners. Now the biggest impression was made on her by reports of the ZOMO's throwing wounded out of ambulances, about tormenting them, beating doctors and nurses.

Many activists were in hiding and were trying to organize a resistance movement. At times, Zuzanna clung to an unconscious faith. It was known that there was still a strike at the Piast mine. The miners went underground. They could not be taken by assault. Maybe this bonfire will spill out into a blaze? Zuzanna thought. Further strikes will break out in Silesia and then throughout the country. But these were only flashes of hope. Then she imagined this strike: surrounded by darkness, in a dim light and thin air, without communication with the world, losing the sense of time...How long could one last?

She was increasingly worrying about Tadek. Various thoughts about him, imagining what might have happened to him, didn't let her sleep. Before dawn, after the first day of Christmas, she fell into a dark sleep. There was a war. Characters in uniform threatened her. She heard a desperate cry from afar. Tadek was the one shouting. She tried to break through to him but couldn't. Then she was surrounded again by scary, laughing figures. They didn't let her approach the massacred corpse of her brother. She woke up screaming. This time it was Benedict who calmed her down.

Someone rang at the door before noon. Zuzanna jumped up first, trying not to see her husband cringing and freezing. In the viewfinder she saw an unknown bearded face. Opening the door, she felt unease.

"Mrs. Zuzanna Brok?" A young man stood in front of her with a large canvas bag over his shoulder. A small pin was connected in his fur denim jacket. "I am a friend of your brother's, of Tadek," he added. Zuzanna was still observing him. So, he added: "Well, the samurai. You were his love."

She began to laugh. She was twelve when her mother brought home The Love of the Samurai directed by Wacław Sieroszewski. She was fascinated by this exotic, tragic romance full of the clash of swords and the smell of blood. She summed it up to her, still not understanding anything, brother. Although was he really not able to understand anything then? Then she turned her fascination to the films of Kurosawa and Kobyashi. She also summarized them to her brother. She played samurai legends with him. This became the reason of their family jokes and built codes understandable only to them.

The visitor came in and broadly gestured at the wall, and Zuzanna answered him with a helpless spread of her hands. Eavesdropping was possible. They went out for a walk.

"Tadek is hiding" said Jarek Rolski. "We started a publishing house, i.e. us from NZS. Tadek prints. Now it probably wouldn't be good for you to meet. You may have a tail. They could've let you out to follow you" the boy went straight to using 'you' with her. The news about Tadek awakened a sudden wave of optimism in Zuzanna, but despite the desire to see him, she had to agree with Jarek. It turned out that they had released Irena the next day. She went to her family.

"You walk with such a bag?" Susanna pointed, puzzled, at the sackcloth on his shoulder.

"It's empty. It's a rule. Anyone who can, should walk with a bag or backpack. Then it's difficult to identify those who are carrying something" he laughed.

"Maybe I can be of use for you for something," she said. He promised that he'll reach out. He was in a hurry and couldn't even stop for a cup of tea.

"The crow will not defeat the eagle, it'll sooner fucking fall dead! He said for a goodbye, kissing Zuzanna on the cheek.

"You look as if you've returned from a meeting your lover," remarked her husband with a sneer.

"Tadek is safe. And...and maybe everything isn't lost" she replied suddenly regaining hope.

Benedict looked at her in suspense, as if he wanted to explain something to her, but said nothing. Then, next to the radio hopelessness fell upon them again.

Immediately after Christmas, came up an equally gloomy Sunday. The next day it was announced that the strike at the Piast mine was ending. Workers are going to the surface. The last strike of a free Poland collapsed. She felt something dying in her. It leaves her. It leaks out of her like spoiled blood. She was weak and nauseous. She thought that she would never want to leave the apartment. This was no longer her country. He was taken from her. Now it was their wife. They could do whatever they want in it. It was their property again. And even in this, once her own flat, she cannot hide. If they want, they'll come in, break down the door, take her, separate her from her son and husband. She felt powerless hatred.

She had to hear that song later. Janek Kelus sang it, although the text was written by someone else. When this time comes back to her, she will always be accompanied by *The Last Shift at KWK Piast*. It expressed everything that Zuzanna could think at that time. *"Authority in your disguised uniforms / And bandits dressed as authorities / Again at Parade square at the top / They lead soldiers in the oath. / Only honor is yours, those in solidarity / A lump of coal as Polish conscience. / It's your time...Leave the mine! / Free Poland - pushed underground. / Order and peace, and work on the surface. / There are still individual cases... / A free country. What holds you in this hole? / Time to gather. Time to get in the cage. "*

They spent New Year's Eve alone. Zuzanna strongly refused Benedict's suggestions to visit or invite someone. She was already drunk before midnight. Her husband took her to bed.

CHAPTER 13

She was waiting for this summons. Everything repeated itself, only worse, she thought, taking a deep breath and entering the director's office. Alski looked weird. He was irritated, but there wasn't that uncertainty in him which she saw the previous time, almost two years ago, when he handed her the dismissal. However, he started similarly.

"Mrs. Zuzanna, do you know why I asked you here?" She wasn't in the mood for games this time. From above a cup of coffee she looked him straight in the eyes.

"Of course, I know. I hope that the dismissal won't be disciplinary." Unexpectedly for her, Alski smiled.

"I have to have an admonishing conversation with you. Because you know... There's martial law. Trade union activity is suspended. I am responsible for order in our establishment...In our publishing house" he corrected himself. "It somehow seems to me that I picked up the incorrect language," he almost laughed. "As such, I must tell you everything. Do you understand? In truth I have no influence on what you do outside of work, but I am also obliged to remind you of the current legal order."

"That means, I haven't been dismissed?"

"No. I don't want to say that it wasn't talked about." Alski looked around alertly. "But we've come to the conclusion that actually...well, you can stay."

This time he walked her to the door. She was beyond the doorstep when he decided:

"Mrs. Zuzanna, would you let yourself be invited. I would like to talk less formally."

The interior of the "Under the Arkady" seemed to be immerged in the darkness of martial law. There were not many guests, and the conversations were spun dimly. Alski was telling about how an SB officer was at his place, demanding her dismissal, but he refused. He was very proud of himself. They've already drank bruderszaf.

"I know that I shouldn't, but maybe we could move to a less formal footing?"

After subsequent shots he decided to confess everything.

"I said that I can't fire you. I have no reasons. I was surprised by my courage." He laughed joylessly. "I was terrified of him. I began to explain that this is an artistic publishing house and nothing political can be done here, and I'll keep an eye on you, so that there won't be any agitation. That dismissing you would only bring unnecessary hype and make you a martyr. By the way I added that after all you will have something to live off of, so, you understand, I suggested to him..." Zuzanna looked at his glistening with sweat, smiling face and gave up the sharp words that were pressing on her lips "and I added that the previous dismissal didn't help anything, and if you work, you'll have less time...You understand"

They drank after another shot. One had to hurry. They were closing the local soon. Curfew was approaching.

"I want to be truly honest with you." Alski raised his solemn wet face suddenly at her. "I don't know what would've happened if he really pressed me. After all, the 'Portico'...What problem is there to firing me and appointing one of their bureaucrats. They're already come. Personally, I know a few who are in line for my position and are doing everything to do me dirty. I know them. That would be the end of the 'Portico'. The one who would replace me wouldn't even need a suggestion. He would sell it. Not only you, half of the editorial staff would not be there second day after his arrival. Therefore, if they had pressed me...I don't know..." Zuzanna wasn't finding the words. After a moment of silence, Alski continued: "I know one thing. Now it's different. Then...You know, I feel guilty...For firing you then. It didn't occur to me that it could be done differently. It probably wasn't possible. If I tried to oppose them, I would already not be there. You were a small group and it didn't make sense. Now it's different. Even under martial law...Although hopelessness comes over me from time to time..."

***

The snow was still laying on the sidewalks. The dirty gray heaps began to melt. Zuzanna left the "Portico" and started towards the tram stop, tearing her shoes out of the gunk with difficulty and anger. She thought with a kind of unpleasant satisfaction, that today is Benedict's turn to buy food cards and trying to get through the queues for hours. Last week, she left from work at noon, spent her five hours in the grocery and meat stores and didn't manage to use her cards in the liquor store.

She got stuck in a kind of snowbank. A man in a fur hat knocked her hard and looked at her askance, muttering a curse word under his breath. For a moment she wanted to tell him something, but she gave up, avoiding another argument. Fatigue collapsed on her, which suppressed humiliation. Even the air was dirty, thick and not breathable. One had to wade through it like through mud. The few hundred meters to the stop didn't seemed possible.

"You don't recognize your friends?" She heard next to her. A passerby, a short middle-aged man in a worn overcoat and a beret with a nub on top provoking so many jokes in its environment, was smiling at her. It was Jerome Jano. She became glad.

"I'm glad to see you. I didn't know what had happened to you. Escort me to the stop."

"Let's take a walk," he said.

"You also chose a time to take a walk!" She groaned.

"I was waiting for you by the publishing house. Nobody is watching you. Not now, in any case. We're making an underground magazine. I would like to draw you in."

He explained that this is now the most important thing. It re-integrates people: those who do and those who read. It documents the state of affairs. It allows one to prepare for more resolute speeches. They agreed that someone would be bringing it to the porter's lodge and will leave a manuscript for her. It covered items from art history, contained materials with information that she would have to compile and form a chronicle of the week with a specific number of characters. Over time, they may also send her other materials for development and editing. On an established date someone will receive it from her at the tram stop. They agreed that she would always carry a large bag with her.

"If you're going to have a matter for me, leave the courier information. For Gray. Don't forget: Gray. I will find you. And remember, this is an important thing. A lot of people work with us: authors, editors, computer scientists, printers and distributors. Everyone is threatened with quite a few years. If such projects intersect, it's easier to be exposed. Therefore, do not participate in any others. And don't tell anyone about ours. Even to those whom you trust fully. The less people know, the better. People have a tendency to share with those close to them. That's how information wanders. Our magazine is called 'The Underground Weekly'.

When she got on the tram, saying goodbye to Jerome with a gesture, she realized that she was waiting for such an offer. It was looking for her. Actually, she didn't feel fear, just something along the lines of stage fright; uncertainty if she will fully manage with the task. In the crowded streetcar she realized that she was not overwhelmed by the usual, which changed into disgust, aversion to the crowds of passengers pushing by and crushing her. She took a deep breath. She felt a sudden surge of strength.

At home, Benedict was reading, *The Story About the Iron Wolf*, to Adam. Zuzanna took over the reading and then later offered a joint staging of it. Adaś was happy. After dinner, when they had put him to sleep, and she wanted to tell her husband something optimistic, he beat her to it.

"'The Republic' will start publishing again in two weeks," he said, hiding in a cloud of cigarette smoke. A chill permeated her.

"And what?"

"Exactly. The first issue will be released without the input of the editorial staff. Discussions are ongoing. It's not known who'll stay and under what conditions..."

"And you?"

"I what?"

"Don't pretend. What'll you do?"

"Well exactly, I'm thinking about it. They asked me to be one of the select few. I mean...you understand that I would fulfill a certain function. This is a matter for the future, because first...I told you. Only Władek will be in the footer as the chief. And the texts will be signed. It's been an issue for some time. A few months, half a year. Maybe later..."

"A function you say? What kind of function?"

"Well..." The cigarette burned out. Benedict crushed the cigarette butt, which was burning his fingers, in an ashtray with passion and impatiently dug out the next one. He focused on this unexpectedly difficult activity. "Well, Goleń's deputy, vice-director."

Zuzanna laughed. She was surprised by the sound of her own voice: screeching and foreign.

"You are getting promoted. Martial law came in handy. I will be the wife of the vice-director of a major weekly.

"Give it a break. After all I haven't decided yet. I'm talking with you."

"And on a job at the 'Republic' have you already decided?"

"Give it a rest. What do you want? For me to quit my job?"

"Yes, I want you to quit your job! I can support the home for a while. Then something will come around. With your qualifications…I'm sure!"

Benedict lit yet another cigarette and violently blew out a gulp of smoke in her direction.

"You're going to support me?! That's Ironic! Do you know why you have a job? It was Władek who defended you. They can fire you, just like that" he snapped his fingers.

"And therefore, you must be in the 'Republic'? And in the party? The party that organized martial law? And the 'Republic'...Do you know what kind of magazine it is? What kind of meaning it will have? After all we probably both realize what it was before. And now? It will be an organ of martial law, of Jaruzelski!"

"Don't exaggerate! Władek promised us that this wasn't any propaganda, but an intellectual magazine that would try to look for new directions, of course with awareness of the conditions..."

"New directions! With an awareness of the conditions! What are you fucking talking about! You were a voice of the regime! An intellectual voice. Now you will be a voice of martial law! An intellectual one of course!" Zuzanna realized that she was running around the room, shouting and waving a cigarette. Benedict also sprang up.

"Indeed, an intellectual conversation with you is difficult. But what do you imagine? An uprising? With Russia on our neck? A boycott of the state? How do you see this at all?"

"I see that you can only imagine collaboration! There are other options."

"What kind? You're kidding yourselves. The party won. I knew about this from the beginning, but I'm not happy about it at all. You don't know Goleń or people from his environment. You don't want to know them, and these are also Poles. They're looking for ways out. You have to save what you can. Then, step by step, rebuild normalcy."

"What normalcy? Rebuild the PPR, and that's denial of normalcy! Ways out are being sought by those, who are now organizing resistance. They're rebuilding Solidarity, publishing little magazines, creating a resistance network, sitting in prisons, hiding..."

"You're naive. How long can this last? Even if you manage to strike for a few days...You saw how it ended in December. Demonstrations? And what? They'll disperse you all. Maybe you will even burn a few committees, a riot will last for a few days. What's next? People want peace."

"People want other things as well. It's you who explain to them that nothing is possible."

"You so much don't like Władek, but it's thanks to him they let you out..." Benedict finally choked out.

"Then maybe you shouldn't have been gotten out! That would've been the best. Then you'd be able to save the country without obstacles." Zuzanna can't control herself.

"Listen. I know very well that we won't come to an agreement on this issue. I've already stopped convincing you. I would just like to urge you to be careful. Can't you accept that each of us will do what we think is right and possible? We can't even establish such a status quo among ourselves?"

"Yes, there will be a status quo and symmetry. We must tolerate each other. We must recognize your right to imprison us."

"I'm, I'm locking you up in prison?!"

"You justify those who do it."

The conversation broke off. Zuzanna had the impression that they had told each other everything. She felt antipathy towards her husband. What am I doing with him, something inside of her asked. He looked at her as if he wanted to say something more. He sighed, waved his hand, and went to bed. Zuzanna made her bed on the couch.

***

Sometime later, Krzysiek Markus visited them, and then Leszek Jurczyński with several people. They sat over tea brewed in glasses and tried to reconstruct the state of their surroundings, Solidarity, the country. Igor Stawicki also came by without notice. He said he was hiding for three months. He realized that they were no longer looking for those whom they failed to intern, so he returned to his home and to work at the university. After a moment of reflection, he added uncertainly that he didn't know if they wanted to intern him at all. Jurczyński burst out laughing. In a moment everyone was laughing, including Stawicki. And he agreed that Solidarity should be rebuilt.

Benedict greeted them politely, exchanged a few sentences, then usually walked away to his room.

The first issue of the 'Republic' appeared after the break. The editorial written by the chief editor, who justified the imposition of martial law, was dreary. Goleń wrote that in the defense of fundamental order sometimes one needs to resort to extraordinary measures. In this case, it was necessary to tame the anarchized element of Solidarity, which had to lead to the destruction of the state and referred to the worst Polish traditions. At this point, Goleń referred to the theoretical text of the "great modern thinker" Bruno Klein, who agreed to publish his latest essay in the 'Republic'. The text was entitled *The State or revolution?* Klein pointed out that revolutions arise out of utopian thinking about justice and from the faith that it can be realized in the human world. Because every human order is imperfect and therefore not entirely fair, the supporters of revolution will always find enough arguments to undermine it. However, undertaking the fight for impossible to realize justice, they destroy the order that protected the space of private life. They demand that man submit to great ideas. The state, however, even if it grew out of revolution, must rely on the order that leaves space of freedom for individuals. That's all Zuzanna understood, besides she didn't want to analyze the text more deeply.

"I've never read a more anti-Marxist manifesto!" Stawicki laughed. "And how perfidious he is. He defends the PPR by fighting Marx."

Another important article referred to by Goleń was the text by Podlecki *Next to the Brazier*. The author described his discomfort caused by the view of soldiers at a brazier right under his window. Meanwhile, his 10-year-old daughter reminded him that it was cold and proposed to bring them tea in a thermos. The soldiers received it gratefully. The commander stated that although he agreed to break discipline in this way, it would be difficult to endure otherwise. He winked understandingly at Podlecki, who noticed that one of the soldiers was puffing on a cigarette hidden in his sleeve. This was also against regulations. Meanwhile, the Podlecki's felt a deep chill and took refuge from it, gathering themselves with the members of the guard to the brazier. Podlecki clearly realized that life goes beyond tight regulations and ideologies. Understanding is the most important thing. *"Let's not ask too much of people,"* he appealed. *"Those, principally who settle accounts, look for sinners, demand purity, no matter from which side, are the greatest threat. If we understand this, we are capable of getting along. Our possibilities are limited, we are not a particularly large or strong country, but we are able to arrange our life inside. Our real and therefore private lives of specific people. And we should focus on this. Let us not become crazy about great words, great ideas, great politics. Young soldiers were on duty. They did what they had to do. One had to understand them. They gently pointed out that the curfew was coming. Does it really bother us so much? The soldiers stayed with the brazier, and I returned to write the article for the 'Republic'. Everyone has their responsibilities."*

Benedict's article said that the current phase should be used to build healthy economic relations, which should be the basis for the revival of the economy. He wrote something about the realization of settlements between workplaces, which would be involved their independence, but the jargon that followed then made Zuzanna feel aversion to it. Besides she didn't know why she should read the text to the end.

"You know, I told Władek that I wouldn't be his deputy" Benedict said proudly when everyone had left and Zuzanna was closing the window after ventilating the smoke-filled room.

"And what? You don't regret it?" Zuzanna could not help herself from acerbity. Her husband looked at her disappointed.

"I'm probably not thinking about it in these categories. It seemed to me that I could have more opportunities in this role, but maybe I'm wrong, and you are right. In any case, it's no matter."

"Unfortunately, I'm afraid it is" Zuzanna sighed, wondering if Benedict really doesn't understand what's going on.

Stawicki, who unexpectedly came to the Portico just before the end of the work day, dragged her to his place. While making tea, as usual, he talked about several things at once, conducting simultaneous polemics with himself and occasionally bursting with contagious laughter. The cigarette in his hand drew Art Nouveau ornaments.

"You know I'm moderate, but the resistance must be maintained. Without madness, but consistently, although it's other forms can also be considered. I mean, I'm thinking of trying to build up this free space that WRON is leaving us. Well" he prevented her protest "I know that it seems to us that this isn't so much, but maybe it is about finding something intermediate...No matter what, I've decided to get more deeply involved. Only that our company broke up. Danka is in jail; Filip is hiding others..."

"It's good that you want to get more involved. Against the sad times" Zuzanna laughed. She wondered if Stawicki could be turned into a decent conspirator. In any case, that wasn't her task.

Spring was floundering in the melting snow, which was turning into slick mud. It suddenly erupted in April and changed the city within a few days. Then Zuzanna saw a large inscription on the wall for the first time: "Your winter - our spring".

The sight of a large, almost gray-haired man surprised her. Roski smiled at her engagingly. The publishing house, which was visited by a lot of people, was a good meeting place. Roski offered to escort her home.

"I do what I used to do," he told her after a series of compliments. She wondered how much it was his convincing, but seeing his gaze, she believed in it. On the street, girls have already changed their outfits and walking style. Liberated from their winter cocoons, they blossomed in the shapes of female bodies, stretching out, they absorbed the spring and men's gazes. Am I still one of them? Zuzanna wondered, while also felt the bewilderment of the waking world. "Maybe more conspiratorially," Roski continued with a smile. "And you, don't you think about the conspiracy a little?"

"You know, I have a job," she replied enigmatically. Roski looked at her inquisitively but did not ask questions that hung in the air.

"I spoke with Stawicki recently. He's looking for an outlet for his suddenly awakened, conspiratorial passions" she remembered. Roski clearly became interested in the information.

It was a time of meetings. Jagged relations were slowly rebuilt, people started to find each other.

"Zuza" she heard a familiar voice. She stopped and looked around uncertainly. The sun was shining, and people were rushing to their businesses. When she heard him a second time, now close to her, she was sure. Though she only saw him when he caught her in his embrace.

"I missed you," Tadek repeated. "I had to see you. I think I've kept all of the rules of a conspirator." Unprecedented optimism burst out of him. "You'll see. The crow won't defeat the eagle! Our spring!"

They walked around Warsaw, and he told her the story of his last months. They already had a magazine and publishing house. They recreated the NZS net. They have contacts with Solidarity, with "Mazowsze".

"You'll see what'll happen on the streets of Warsaw on May 1! In just a few days! Will you come?" She didn't have to answer. "Actually, I just feel stupid because of Irena. They roughed her up, frightened her. She spent the night in prison. She doesn't have any ill will to me. Although if I stayed, they would've taken me and done nothing to her."

It was a great May Day demonstration under Solidarity standards and banners. Participants greeted each other with a victory sign. The city was theirs.

The police tried to block the side streets but was withdrawing from the main streets despite the arriving of reinforcements. They walked in an endless procession, tensely watched by police lines backing into smaller streets. Clouds of leaflets flew from the roofs of the houses, from windows onto the procession. Sometimes they spurted out from the center of the demonstration. The crowd chanted: 'Long live Solidarity!', 'Free Lech!' and they heard the same cheers from the buildings. Streets and houses chanted; the city was filling with freedom.

Two days later, after an independence mass, she left the church in a sublime mood. However, as soon as she was outside, a terrible clatter hit her ears, and then an intensified scream. The events took place violently and unconsciously. The crowd around waved and started thrashing in all directions. The people almost knocked over Zuzanna, who was only prevented from falling down by the crowd, and then snatched her, carried her with them, forced to run. The momentum turned into a spasmodic flutter. She heard incomprehensible voices from which single words were being torn out: "They're beating us!" and a moment later: "ZOMO!" Suddenly, a few meters away, she saw a line of officers in helmets, with shields and large clubs that beat everyone in front of them. Those that fell twisted on the ground under the impact of steel-toed boots. Along with the crowd, she threw herself to the back, but from there the others were pushing. She begins to lose her breath and feels like she's about to lose consciousness. The ZOMO's were almost on her. Someone bent under the strike of a baton. In front of her she saw a helmet with a plastic visor mirroring the sun's rays. The baton rose. The blow, however, missed her. The crowd seized her, separated from the ZOMO's and carried her somewhere to the side.

Zuzanna finally breaks out of the thicket of people and rushes into a side street. She can finally breathe. Panting heavily, she runs farther and gets to the square. A crowd is already gathering on one the side, and police cars are coming in from the other side. She hears the bang of shots. She stops, paralyzed for a moment. Soon, however, she realizes that these are explosions of tear gas grenades. Firecrackers fall into the crowd and explode in a thick cloud. People throw back some, someone a few meters away from her caught a smoking tube in his hand, which exploded at that moment. A cloud of smoke stuns Zuzanna, pushing her breath back into her throat; furious pain and burning eyes blind her. She runs blindly, unconsciously. Only after some time and in a different place does she manage to get a handkerchief out of her purse and wipe her sore eyes which water endlessly. At a distance of several dozen meters, the crowd clashes with the ZOMO unit. Zuzanna doesn't understand why people aren't running away. It is only after a while that she sees a group of men with metal trash bins and poles attacking the ZOMO's who, after a moment of struggle make a run for it. Men are building a barricade at the end of the street brought from all directions - benches, trash cans, and hard to identify objects. But almost at the same time, armored cars break into it and the barricade falls apart. Behind the cars, a line falls onto the rubble pile, onto which stones and broken bricks prepared in piles are spilled.

Zuzanna tries to get out of the turmoil, return home, but she is semi-conscious, and the whole city turns into a battlefield. She tries to run. She only slows down to catch her breath. Zigzagging around the streets, escaping from the charges of ZOMO's, from the blows of batons, struggling to get out of the clouds of tear gas, trying to avoid the streams of water that throw people off of their feet. Ultimately however, she is struck by a blow of water from a cannon, a few meters from her. She falls over and rolls on the pavement, and when she finally manages to get up, she sees that she is completely covered in blue goo. Only after a while, when she notices blue dyed people being picked up and packed into police wagons, she understands what's going on. The scenes pass in front of her: a group of people driven to a wall, from where there is no escape, crouching under furious hits of clubs, they're pulling someone on the cobblestones and throwing them into an arriving car, someone breaks out and runs away.

She doesn't know how she managed to get home. Beaten, covered with blue paint, tearful, with smudged makeup, agglutinated hair and in a torn dress she looked terrible. Benedict looked at her in horror. She locked herself in the bathroom. She tries to wash her hair, which is difficult because the blue paint holds firmly. Her eyes are still watering, but she starts to see a little better. She notices bruises on her face, though she can't remember what might've caused them. She's all beaten up and bruised. She has a scrapped-up knee. In all, nothing dangerous. She throws her damaged dress and underwear into the corner of the bathroom. She comes out in a bathrobe. Benedict is waiting for her upset.

"Are you OK?" He asks with concern.

"Ah, nothing. I survived. They didn't lock me up and didn't even beat me solidly. You see? They've only roughed me up a little! Those people of yours are gracious!"

"But, honey...Everywhere in the world the police disperse illegal demonstrators..."

Zuzanna explodes. All the humiliation, sorrow and powerlessness melt into the rage she turns against Benedict. She screams.

"What are you fucking saying! Illegal Protesters? I was at church, do you understand me, you fool?! In the church, fuck! Your guards of order got me, all of us, as we were leaving after mass! Do you understand, you dumbass?!" Suddenly she realizes that Adaś is standing in the doorway to his room, who looks at her in amazement and frightened. She runs over and grabs him. "Don't listen to what mom says. Mom was showing, what not to do!" He laughs and cries at the same time. "How heavy you are." She turns to her husband. "You know that I almost took Adam to mass. Do you realize what would've happened then? I wouldn't have run away from them! Do you know what could happen to Adaś?" Benedict is silent.

***

"Do you have an intention to keep hiding?" She asked her brother a few days later. He came to the 'Portico'. On May 3rd they captured and arrested Jarek Rolski. Apparently, they beat him hard. Tadek managed to escape.

"I'm not in the mood to fall into their hands. Although, if it were possible... Sure, I'd love to come back. And begin to function normally. As much as it is at all possible. Because I allow myself to be normalized!" He declared cockily.

Zuzanna decided. In the evening she went up to Benedict. She didn't know, how to begin.

"Maybe your relations will come in handy for something..." Only at that moment did she realize her voice sounded sarcastic. Her husband looked at her anticipatively. "It's about my brother, Tadek."

"I'll try, but I can't get engaged…"

"But I know," she interrupted.

She just came home with Adam, whom she picked up from kindergarten, when Benedict fell in like a storm. She felt it had succeeded.

"You can tell Tadek to come home. Władek vows that nothing will happen to him" he said with pretended nonchalance. "I'm sorry that it had to take several days."

It was a small family holiday. This time they let Adaś sit with them until late. He stared at his uncle with fascination and never stepped back. Tadek clearly enjoyed the admiration of his nephew. Zuzanna had the impression that she saw in Benedict's gaze a shadow, when he was observing them.

They drank vodka. They didn't talk about politics, although Tadek talked about his conspiratorial-underground adventures. A funny scene was followed by an even funnier one, separated by another joke about WRON, which her brother remembered an infinite number of. Benedict joined the jokes and even tried to sing with them *Green Crow, December Ballad or Hymn of Interned Extremists*. When Zuzanna was carrying the half asleep, but still purring something cheerfully, Adam, she thought that only he could completely sink into momentary happiness. Between jokes and bursts of laughter, she saw Tadek's face becoming tense. She understood him perfectly. Deep under their joy was humiliation. Just as if they signed another declaration of loyalty, she thought. When she returned to the table, Tadek raised a toast.

"Benek, after all I must finally honestly say it. I thank you, that thanks to you I am with you all now. You obtained a sign for me from the authorities. Not everyone is lucky that their sister is so connected. Come on," he restrained Benedict's almost angry protest. "I'm really grateful to you. After all you didn't introduce martial law. And that our authorities can be gracious...In this way they also strengthen their power...And we, well...We're trying to live in this filthy world somehow" he frowned, putting down his shot glass.

CHAPTER 14

"You know, Bruno would really like to meet with us. Well, Bruno Klein" Benedict began the next day, as usual, he had a little uncertainly, when approaching her with what he considered controversial. There are more and more of such matters, Zuzanna thought. At the time, however, she was grateful for his intervention in Tadek's case. Maybe he consciously wanted to take advantage of it?

"With us?"

"Yes, Yes. I even think more so with you. He's taken a liking to you" he laughed hard. "Maybe we could invite him over?"

"Couldn't we meet on more neutral grounds?" She didn't feel sympathy to Klein. Maybe mainly because of what Benedict's father said about him, or maybe because of his article in the 'Republic'? "Then maybe we'll go over to his place?"

Klein occupied a villa on Lekarz Street. Less than fifteen minutes away from their apartment. Zuzanna had never met someone before who had a house in the middle of Warsaw at their disposal. The spacious, one-story villa with an attic was a bit cluttered, but Zuzanna quickly realized how purposeful this disorder was. The dissonances were planned, as was the juxtaposition of the folk figure of Christ standing on the floor and a reproduction of Kandinsky on the wall above it. The real chaos of multilingual books and newspapers scattered on several tables has been reduced to a few separate spheres. The whole is precisely composed.

Zuzanna had to admit to herself that the interior was impressive. The deliberate maze of books and works of art could be fascinating. They sat at a heavy, wooden table from a century ago, too big for the three of them. The white tablecloth did not cover the entire top. The middle class wins, Zuzanna thought, amusingly remembering the story of Adam Brok about the destructive appeals of their host during his rebellious youth. The maid, Mrs. Józia, served the table and disappeared unnoticeably into the kitchen. They ate roast beef, sipped red French wine, whose taste Zuzanna tried to absorb and remember, as well as the name which the host repeated with care: "Chateau Desmirail Margaux." After Benedict's proposal suggested by Klein, which Zuzanna could not refuse, they transferred over to using 'you'.

"You remind us of ourselves from fifty years ago, well, almost fifty." Their host laughed and the brushes above his ears moved. "Well, I don't mean physical resemblance, although and among us there were beautiful girls...Sara, Benk's mother... It's about this passion, infatuation, faith. Yes, faith above all. We were followers, we believed that we would change the world. Just like you now. Therefore, when I look at you, I remember...In addition, you are actually someone from the family. My friend's wife, my friend's daughter-in-law..."

"Interesting..." The alcohol released an unrestrained malice in Zuzanna. "I have the impression that in my father-in-law's recollections did not include same tenderness."

Klein, who had been speaking earlier in a deepening trance, swaying and closing his eyes, woke up. The stubble above his ears bristled, the pins of his pupils sank into Zuzanna.

"Really? What did he say?"

"I do not remember exactly. Nothing specific. Oh, an example of your commitments. And maybe a bit, because of this reason, to you..." Benedict looked at her tensely. Klein leaned on the arm of the carved chair. He loosened up.

"And... yes. Indeed...He already had his faith behind him. He experienced revelation and disappointment with his prophet in Vienna, with Freud himself. That's why he fascinated us then. Besides, he was much older, experienced. Yes. And later, after the war...It was something quite different. He could even dislike me. I survived, it's my fault. Fact. You won't understand this. But then...Anyway, less about Adam's attitude towards me, towards us. I think he was more complicated than you think. For me, the closeness that I feel to you, to you both is important…I know that it is impossible, everyone must live through their experiences to the end, but I would like to somehow, even a little, spare you our disappointments..."

"That's nice, but you probably exaggerate a little with your fears." Zuzanna thought her irony sounded too ostentatious. "We are not like you..."

"Do you really think you're discovering new human experiences?" Klein's voice was again in the tone of involved sermon. "And in this you are exactly the same as we are! We were discovering new faiths, and in reality, just like you, we were constantly recreating the same script, still the same drama of humanity in ever new decorations."

"Only we're not convincing ourselves that we are revealing new worlds. We want to return to what has been proven. To a few truths, falsified and banished by the creators of new faiths..."

"You want to tell me you have no religious and patriotic fervor?"

"Maybe there is fervor, but there is no pride," Zuzanna announced, realizing at the same time that she had overdone it. "I'm sorry...I didn't mean to...offend you both."

"No, no. It's fine. That's exactly what's endearing about you, that you're so honest."

Klein looked at her with the smile of the Cheshire Cat from above a crystal glass of amber liquid. They have already moved on to dessert, i.e. chocolate mousse and coffee. The host personally, with celebration, brought around a flat, carved, triangular shaped bottle of Armagnac. He dwelt on the advantages, which clearly, in his opinion, far outweigh cognac.

"Of the same class, of course," he added. "As a historian of art..." he turned to Zuzanna.

"...would-be," she remarked, but he continued:

"...you should contemplate this taste and smell as a work of its own. Feel into it!

Can taste and smell be a work of art? Zuzanna wondered, obediently trying to succumb to the charm of the alcohol, of which she liked the most the unusual, dark gold, almost bronze-like and glistening with fiery shines of color. She tried to find the sun of ripening grapes in it, the light of Gascony, which she had never seen, but knew so well. Generations rake up the ground, spread out wooden scaffoldings supporting young grapes that will wrap around them to grow into large bushes. Pale green fruit will swell up on them, absorbing the juices of the earth and the warmth of the sun sailing over the ocean. Then for years they will mature in oak vats and take on their soul, listening to the stories of the farmers at night. Zuzanna tried to sense it from the thick aroma of the liquid in her hand-shaped glass. Is this already art? she was wondering, looking up simultaneously at the shimmering golden fish from Paul Klee's sapphire black abyss. Can art fulfill in itself, when after all it always sends beyond itself, like a mythical naval battle, which against monsters from the depths of time is fighting a warrior on a boat with hair tied in a bun in another Klee painting next to it?

"And us? Were we discovering something new? We wanted justice, the abolition of violence, the communion of the human community...That, what you now..."

"We want very little…"

"It appears to you. You want everything. That's why you don't compromise ... As we did then."

"We want it to be like then. We want to rebuild the world you destroyed."

"And do you know how it was then? Anti-Semitism, violence, street clashes. Have you heard of razor blades in the clubs of nationalists? The humiliating of women at university? Have you read leaflets calling to striking Jewish face's with brass-knuckles, which talk about humanitarianism? You want to recreate that?"

"No, we don't want that."

"And you think that the great ideas that you love so much: nation, homeland, justice will not turn against decisive, and therefore real people?"

"I don't understand you!"

"Exactly. Because I don't share your faiths, I'm already a stranger to you. Solidarity is everything for you. What about those who do not want to unite? Following in a common procession?"

"But we want to give them that chance. So that they would not have to participate in May Day marches."

"Now it's not the May Day marches that are dangerous. That ideology is dead. You're creating a new, passionate and therefore dangerous one. Now we are threatened by national-religious processions."

"We're not forcing anyone."

"That's what's said. At the beginning, when you don't have power.

"So, what are you proposing?"

"Let communism die peacefully. It will gradually evolve towards a relatively normal state. A kind of imperfect, not entirely fair, weak, one that will not interfere in anyone's life."

"Just like that?"

"Just like that. Because what is this all about?" Klein's question hung in the air. Benedict looked as if waiting for it. He was observing the discussion tensely in order to join in at the most convenient moment."

"Yes. That's what it is about. We all really mean that: you, me. Before ideologies and religions possess us. To have the right to build one's own life. I wish I could study Weber and his contemporaries freely. Share this with students. Raise Adam together with you. To say what I think without fear. Avoid the humiliation of offices and queues, to be able to meet our elementary needs without superhuman efforts. And just like my colleagues in the West, be able to take my wife to Florence from time to time. To Uffizi." He smiled at her. Zuzanna felt touched. And yet something was wrong. She wanted the same thing, and yet...

"Can you not see that this is all related. These queues, everyday humiliation, it's clearly communism...

"We can see it perfectly. Bruno did it and he knows it" Klein nodded sadly "and that's why he's been trying to fix it for almost thirty years. Only it's not that simple. It's not so easy to make eggs from scrambled eggs. That, which you propose is equally as dangerous as what you want to fight. Don't be indignant. No one is accusing you all of bad intentions."

"But I don't agree with this..." Zuzanna repeated, who couldn't say much more. She was already involved, and two men were explaining things to her as if to a child. In fact, she didn't even know what she didn't agree with, except that they were unfair to them, to Solidarity.

"That means what? Happiness is locking oneself in at home?"

"But of course not. We should visit each other. Like you're visiting me now," laughed Klein. "Can there be anything better than meeting with friends over a good meal and alcohol? Well, maybe some lighter French music. It will match the liquor." He switched from Mozart to Edith Piaf.

Zuzanna thought that this interior and the host were disarming. Actually, she didn't really want to talk about politics; she wanted to taste the aura of this room like the aura of the Armagnac. Braque's woman was still playing solitaire on the wall. Leaning on her forearm, slender as a flute, over a bottle of xeres she stared into the future, which didn't want to free her from sadness.

They were leaving into a warm night, even having their host say goodbye on the doorstep. Benedict embraced her and she hugged him confidently. They walked through a calm city that percolated through by the aroma of Armagnac. Zuzanna hummed *Rien de rien*. They turned into Independence Avenue and almost collided with a three-person ZOMO patrol. The characters in uniforms barked. They demanded their documents in a sharp tone. Zuzanna rummaged through her purse, looking at them with hatred. She can't help but notice that her husband quickly, perhaps too quickly, willingly giving them his ID, adding even though not asked: "I'm a journalist."

"Where do you work?!" The character in the helmet in the light of the flashlight, which shines over them another, compares the photo with Benedict's face.

"I told you. I'm a reporter."

"Where?!"

"In the 'Republic'"

"This weekly?" asks the one who is probably the commander.

"Yes...weekly..."

The one shining the flashlight directs it straight into Zuzanna's face.

"Documents!" he barks.

She retrieves her ID angrily and almost pushes it into the officer's hand. The commander looks again at Benedict's document and gives it back.

"Everything's in order. You live close. So, go home. Good night." The officer with the flashlight, who took her ID, looks at her again, then gives it back.

"Thank you. Goodbye" adds Benedict hurriedly. Zuzanna moves away. They return home next to each other. In silence.

Probably from that moment she had an imaginary dialogue with her husband. She had it for many years. Sometimes it spoke up in their disputes when she wanted to show him that his rationales were only a construction protecting him from fear. When the discussion, which became an argument, broke off, Zuzanna was able to keep it going further in her soul. She also returned to it later when she had only regret and resentment to her husband. And later, when she sometimes tried to understand him because she wanted to understand her son. Finally, after many years, Zuzanna's thoughts began to take a specific shape. However, she constantly revised them and tried anew against further doubts. Only once she will close them in a finished argument, speaking to her seventeen-year-old son, who probably didn't understand much. And Zuzanna will return to them, struggling with consistent formulas of her opponents, who will encircle her all her life, and she can only oppose them with a vague sense of right.

***

The days went by with their own rhythm. Every now and then Warsaw was surrounded by clouds of gaseous smoke, water cannons firing upon the crowd, and police pickett lines were hitting the demonstrators. Then the city changed into an area of hunting, chaotic clashes, escapes, chases and the tormenting of the captives. Zuzanna went to the demonstrations with determination in order to, along with others, shout out that which they weren't allowed to say, chant their opposition, then run away into the crowd, to hide, to avoid a beating and getting arrested. She was most concerned then about her brother, who was packed himself into the very center of the street riots, but still managed to get out of them in one piece. After the first attempt, Benedict gave up his endevours to persuade her to stay far away from street brawls. He waited for her upset, smoking cigarette after cigarette sometimes on the street in front the house's gate.

In September, Zuzanna walked Adam to school for the first time. When she bid him farewell, leaving him in a new environment, she felt emotional and soon after anger. She understood that she was giving her son to the world, their bonds will never be the same as before, they will be loosening up more and more, because this is the way things are and it's good this way, though sad. Her son's life will develop, and hence become more and more separate from hers. Thinking about it, she recognized the abnormality of the world, in which nothing is as it should be, and school will accustom her son to lying and hypocrisy. She felt nauseous.

She became involved in the *Primate's Committee for Aid to Persons Deprived of Freedom and their Families* at the church of St. Martin. She helped unload and sort transports from the West. She made packages and wrote letters. She consulted this with Hieronim, who came to the conclusion that the scale of the phenomenon excluded surveillance of all volunteers, and in Zuzanna's case such activity is quite obvious. She had the impression that slowly the rigors of the conspiracy are loosening.

Initially, in the columns of the 'Republic' Benedict published only economic articles. He assessed the economic ideas of martial law quite negatively, although he did not express this directly. Criticism resulted from articles that had a simple postulative character. With time, he wrote more and more often about the classics of sociology and economics. He particularly analyzed the thoughts of Schumpeter, pointing out that modern capitalism is a myth, because it has very little connection with the economy of this type described by Marx, and that modern democracy can take various forms.

"I see that they delegated you to the section of deep theory" Zuzanna could not refrain from malice. As usual, he looked at her with sorrow and resentment

"But you know that this is my appropriate field and passion. Anyway, are you questioning the importance of theory? Even today?"

Zuzanna snorted.

In November, Tadek invited her to the farewell for Jarek Rolski. Zuzanna barely recognized him. Emaciated, with a broken nose, which had coalesced in a strange way, despite the dim light he did not take off his dark glasses. Zuzanna already knew that on one damaged eye he hardly sees, and with the other he has problems

"After all, France is the homeland of enlightenment, maybe they will do a rationalist miracle with me," he struggled to joke around, but he didn't sound happy. He was nothing like the human, who at the epicenter of martial law was optimistic. In detention, they shrugged their shoulders over his condition. Nothing could be done. The trial sentenced him to several years in prison. He accepted the proposal to emigrate after six months in detention.

In a group of young people, Tadek's peers, Zuzanna felt somewhat out of place. Nothing, however, was in its place. The young people were dreary. Only alcohol improved their moods or rather released energy from them. They listened to traditional blues. Then someone turned on a record of 'Perfect'. They sang *Autobiography* in chorus. Zuzanna joined when they chanted, *I would like to be myself*, which in the collective performance turned into *I would like to beat ZOMO*.

"And what? I'm supposed to stay here?! Let myself be beaten at demonstrations or to submit humbly?! Fight for toilet paper, toothpaste and sanitary pads as for treasures and to tear them out from others in need? Risking the birth of a child in a dirty hospital? In the name of what? I am twenty-three years old and I think I have the right to life. Here I am left with vegetation full of humiliation!" shouted the girl right next to Zuzanna.

Tadek objected, he was arguing, but his sister didn't see the old conviction in him. After a while, he explained to her that his peers more often were leaving or did everything to leave. And it's those who are the most entrepreneurial.

"Normally, it's hard for me to accept this. This is really a retreat. They want that from us. But in the case of Jarek..."

Suddenly Zuzanna remembered the events of fourteen years ago. The Gdańsk terminal, to which she was accompanying friends of Benedict and his father's friends. Will these situations always recur? Then she was younger than those around her. So many years have passed and it's only worse. A meeting with Agnieszka Pelikan a few weeks earlier returned to her. Her child died shortly after birth.

"They screened me in a boarding school. I explained that I was pregnant, that it couldn't be done. But they didn't care. They released me a few weeks before I gave birth. I hate them. I will never forget what those motherfuckers did!" Agnieszka's delicate face shrinks in an almost animal grimace.

They arrested Tadek in the beginning of December. The magazine and publishing house fell through, in which he probably played the main role. She was struggling around the apartment painful powerless. Opposite her was only Benedict. He couldn't do anything and represented them. She couldn't not fault him. She attacked with fury.

They only organized Christmas for Adam. He probably felt their inauthenticity despite all the props that appeared in the right place and time: Christmas trees, gifts, Christmas carols from the tape recorder and the Christmas table which was even better stocked than a year earlier. Only the mass in church was real. Zuzanna felt the Christmas spirit and it seemed to her that Adam found his true element there. Returning home with her husband, who picked them up after mass, she thought that she had to make a decision. If she stayed with him, she should somehow tolerate his choices. She must make up her mind, although she is not completely sure of anything. She tried to smile at Benedict. He looked surprised. At home, she hugged him and kissed him. Adam looked at them with embarrassed joy.

And yet nothing was ever just as before, although sometimes they could believe that their feelings could be excluded from the world, locked in a sanctuary of their shared apartment. These were just moments. Every now and then, despite herself, Zuzanna exploded. She wondered if she should stay in a relationship whose only reason for being is Adam. All in all, she didn't know if that's how it truly was. After all, despite moments and even periods of strangeness, her husband remained someone special and maybe closest to her.

Tadek got three and a half years. She observed the bored young judge, who chatted lazily with the prosecutor and indifferently moved his gaze around the room, over the barriers, the over benches filled with SB-guarded audiences, over Tadek. She decided to remember his name: Marek Pietrzak.

Not long before Tadek's trial, Wojtek Roski was arrested. His trial took place two weeks later. They came in a small group. UB's in grey suits pressured them in the benches, they looked insultingly into their eyes. Only hatred suppressed Susanna's anxiety. When she heard the sentence - five years in prison - she refused to believe it. She counted the years that Wojtek has served so far: twelve, thirteen, more? She heard his words: "It's fun now. Soon they will come after us for real. It's only about this, not cracking. Because we're behind bars anyway."

They're separated by the bars of barriers. A big, heavy figure - Wojtek towers over two policemen leading him in - turning towards her. A familiar, somewhat coarse face smiles. Roski greeted her with his cuffed hands. She will remember that nostalgic smile of the man disappearing behind slamming doors. There was regret in him for what had not happened. The doors close and it's too late for a gesture of consolation that Zuzanna forgot to make, for some words she could not find.

"Please leave," she heard, and under heavy gazes of UB officers she leaves the room.

Sometimes, they went to Niemir with Benedict and Adam, where they could even stay for two days. She had the impression that she was regaining her strength. They waded through the snow and the silence of winter day settled on them. They watched the buds of leaves glistening after the rain, which stretched out on the trees in an endless number of drops and in the flickering of the sun repeatedly duplicated the shapes of plants. They breathed in the heavy smell of a hot summer which bewildered and made one lazy. They walked in the woods and for a moment forgot about the world around. For a few hours, even for the day and then night.

In Warsaw, they usually pulled themselves out for a walk around Łazienki or Wilanów once a week. Then as well, but only for a short time, they could not remember, what had infected their thoughts and bodies. Over time, they went out for family walks more rarely, and the moments of purification were becoming shorter and more uncertain. They were less and less with each other, immersed in each their own separate world.

On July 21, 1984, amnesty was announced. An act of grace of a communist state on the eve of a communist holiday. Tadek came out on the same day. They were standing on the street, on the other side, a little further. It wasn't allowed to stop the car too close to the prison gate. Leaning on the hood, they smoked cigarettes without saying a word, observing the slammed shut metal wings. They grew out of a wall that dragged on in both directions topped with barbed wire, a twentieth-century invention. Threads of smoke trembled in the July heat. Passers-by walked indifferently, with difficulty catching the hot air, which was filled by the stench of melting asphalt and of desire, squeezing through the walls. The small metal door next to the gate opened and Tadek came out with a large backpack on his shoulders. She called and threw herself in his direction. Benedict grabbed her arm at the last moment. Right before Zuzanna with a screech, struggling to break, rolled a truck. From the cab a driver leaned out a still threatening them fist and the last of a bouquet of curses flew in. Tadek waved and walked toward them with a loose, almost dance-like step, smiling with all his face. Without looking at the sides, he crossed the street and snatched his sister into his embrace.

***

This time a slightly larger group of people gathered at their place. Zuzanna observed her brother. She looked anxiously for signs of pain, sadness, resignation in his face. And with ever greater satisfaction she ascertained that they weren't there. Tadek was full of energy and optimism.

"And what? They have to let us out! And its's probably difficult to consider me re-educated!"

Those present laughed. Even Benedict laughed. Adam, who, despite parental orders, got out of his room again, was looking at his uncle in joyful delight. Almost like Irena, who held Tadek's hand and didn't let it out of her sight, staring at him with glistening eyes. At one point her brother became serious. He took Zuzanna aside.

"Do you remember Wojtek Roski?" He asked. And without waiting for an answer, he added, leaning into her ear: "He ripped open. He ripped open terribly. He's snitching on all his friends. He's to be a witness of the prosecution in another, large trial"

Zuzanna didn't believe it. It's impossible. Anyone but Wojtek.

"It's almost certainly the news. I would say that it's sure, but I learned extreme caution there," added Tadek, before he moved among the other guests, with his existence hinting that he had not died yet.

The information about Roski was confirmed. And finally, after some time Jerome answered her questions in the positive, Zuzanna lost hope. What could happen? She wasn't finding an answer. Nobody could explain it to her, anyway.

It was September. In the 'Portico', a sealed envelope with a wax seal was waiting for her. Inside was a hand-written letter from Wojtek Roski and a typescript of his statement.

Zuzanna. I write very officially, because I know that in this situation I am not allowed otherwise. I am sending a statement to everyone, especially to the people who were my friends like, I hope, you. Maybe you'll be able to and consider it appropriate to disseminate it. I explain as much as I can. If you would like to verify the truth of my statement or find out something more, I'm leaving a phone number. You can pass on what you deem appropriate to whoever answers. I'll come where and when you want, if you'd want, you only have to give me a few hours' notice in advance. Goodbye. Wojtek Roski.

The phone number adjacent was in figures twice as large as the letters in the letter.

The statement was written on a used-up machine. Some letters were almost invisible.

I, Wojciech Roski, declare that in prison I behaved dishonorably. I became a witness to the prosecution and disclosed to investigators and the prosecutor's office of many matters that I under no circumstances should've disclosed. I have put my colleagues and our common cause in great danger. I have hurt valuable people and my loved ones. That, which I have done is unforgivable. I do not find any mitigating circumstances for myself. I declare that it was not alcoholism which was the cause of my behavior, which does not change its assessment.

Jerome got an identical text. He was sure that it came from Roski. He didn't explain from where. They decided to publish the statement in the "Underground Weekly". Zuzanna didn't call the number provided. She destroyed Roski's letter.

It was another autumn. The joy of her brother being released from prison was diluted in the drudgery and the dangers of everyday life, it became commonplace. Zuzanna was walking down the street and with wonderment was observing the leaves turning yellow on the trees. It seemed, that they were changing color before her eyes. Someone was calling out to her, but not loudly. The slim man in the military jacket was smiling. Zuzanna couldn't identify him, though she knew she should be able to.

"I've changed," he said, rather than asked with a joyless grimace. It was a much older and changed Czesiek Biela, someone similar to Tadek with whom she spent, or it seemed to her, that she spent a fragment of the night after the release of Janek Narożniak.

"What a coincidence..." she said thoughtlessly. Who told her that they don't believe in coincidences?

"It's been four years..." she began to justify herself, but he waved his hand.

"I have the impression that it's been twenty. The July amnesty embraced me. I was in jail because of a strike since December. Two and a half years. I was lucky. I got six. Well, not only did I get a sentence, but what's there to say..."

They stood opposite each other. A moment later, Zuzanna felt ashamed that she didn't even invite him in for coffee. He was looking expectantly.

"What's going on on your end?"

"Same as always." Biela was looking at her as if he wanted to say something. Finally, he decides. "I got married. In prison. My girlfriend was pregnant. The kid was born when I was in prison. And she's pregnant again. I want to leave. To go West. Those UB's approach me and propose emigration. They've already proposed it in prison. But now? Apparently, I got some shitty job. But it's too little to support us. Justyna is desperate. I want to leave so badly..."

"And you?"

"Me? I don't know myself. I don't even have family here. They're in the countryside. Justyna's parents help, but how long can they? On the other hand,...to run away? Admit that these motherfuckers won? I don't know myself. What do you think?"

"I don't know, I can't answer for you. You understand..." She felt helpless and wanted him to leave already. For a moment they stood without a word, passed by discontented passers-by.

"Well so what? It was nice to see you. See ya!" he said, reaching out his hand. As he was leaving, she realized that he was clearly limping.

The leaves were dying off exceptionally quickly on the trees. They twisted in colors of agony under the streaks of continuous downpour. Nothing was changing in the country. It was already late October, a foggy evening, when the phone began ringing unusually obtrusively. She finally answered. Benedict was not there as usual.

"They kidnapped Father Popiełuszko!" she heard Danka Brak's voice in the handset.

The Church of St. Stanisław Kostka was filled up by a dense crowd. In the congregation it was breathing heavily with the same desire. In whispered silence, it prayed for the priest's life and return. Zuzanna had been here several times before. Danka brought her to a mass led by a young priest. There was something unusual in him. Not only because, that he spoke uniquely explicitly about the oppressions of the communist authorities and the need to regain freedom. Faith radiated from him. It was giving them a sense of strength. Each time she left after the mass celebrated by Popiełuszko, she felt cleansed and ready to face the world. Now, kneeling on the floor, she heard a whisper, the begging of those gathered for the recovery of the priest.

She came here almost every day for several days. At home, she especially watched the TV news, in which until recently there had been calls to deal with the defiant priest, and Urban, who always seemed to her a caricature of the system, embodying both its perfidy and ugliness, talked about performances of hatred, which were supposed to be masses celebrated by Father Jerzy. Now, veiling their faces in seriousness, the announcers talked about the progress of the investigation. The ober-policeman Kiszczak himself, announcing that three perpetrators of the abduction had been arrested, sadly shared with the viewers the fear that the victim may not be alive.

"Here's your world!" She threw out to Benedict, who was also staring into the screen in suspense.

"But listen, it can be a provocation against the authorities..." he began frantically.

"What nonsense are you talking about?! Kidnapping, or maybe murdering an important opponent of the authorities is aimed at it?"

"Well, after all in this situation, the blame will fall on it. We said in the editorial office that it might be pro-Moscow..." Zuzanna left the room, slamming the door with a crash.

Popiełuszko's massacred corpse was fished out of the lagoon on the penultimate day of October. In November, his funeral drew hundreds of thousands of people. It seemed that all it would take was a call, for the sea to move and wipe out the regime. ZOMO's, SB's, police hid in fear at the gates. "If they don't stop, there will be no rescue for us," choked out the terrified head of the repression forces to a shaky supervisor with a bird-like profile. "We will have to evacuate." The general in dark glasses tried to keep military appearance. "Will the helicopters be on time?"

The helicopters weren't needed. Terrified Church leaders called for peace. The guards of the Church and Solidarity leaders also called for peace. The crowd slowly dispersed. Anger poured into the hopelessness of autumn.

***

These were premonitions that suddenly became concrete. Zuzanna realized that Benedict started avoiding her. She didn't remember a similar situation. Maybe it was heralded a bit by events from eleven years ago. Almost a year before Adam was born. Then she moved out to her brother's. But from that time eons have passed. Now she wouldn't decide on moving out with her son. She would sooner demand that from her husband. Meanwhile, their strange relations relaxed more and more. Meetings became more and more fleeting and her husband avoided conversations. Everything was becoming clear. He had someone and it was a serious affair.

It surprised her that the matter could hurt so much. She struggled to analyze her condition. Wounded ambition? The feeling of harm done? How much emotion was there still in it? And what is this, feeling?

She attacked. Benedict retreated. He tried to turn the matter into a joke and even let loose on Zuzanna. He spoke about the divisions between them and about his wife's unfairness that hurt him so. He twisted away from answering. He fell silent. She couldn't stand it.

"Why aren't you saying anything?!" She screamed so loudly that she probably was waking Adam. It seemed that she hears his sudden movements.

"Do you want to wake him up? Do you want to make him a witness of our fights?" Benedict asked angrily, and she felt humiliation that could only for a moment overcome pain, anger and despair. A moment later, without worrying about anything, she exploded again. During these scenes, when she screamed unconsciously, not even realizing the words being thrown out, Benedict was getting dressed and going out.

She was left alone. Adam was separated from her by a closed door and his childish dreams, which she did not want to interrupt at any cost. The night fell on Zuzanna in thick silence.

She couldn't sleep. She was rolling on the bed, shivering. She fell into restless dreams of phantoms before dawn. She woke up too late and unconscious. She tried to gain distance to her situation. To see it against the backdrop of events in the country. To compare her state with the condition of people locked up in prison, awaiting sentences. To assess one's pain in the correct proportions, recognize its banality against the background of the history of the community that was fighting for survival. Find it in the community that determined her fate. She tried to work more, in the publishing house, in the "Underground Weekly", in whose editorial she had already gained a significant position and participated in determining the shape of the entire edition. She wanted to sacrifice herself and forget about herself. However, she couldn't focus on anything.

In the least expected moments: at work, she could become weak on the streets, she almost stopped seeing and it seemed to her that she'd fall. Long minutes passed before she recovered. She couldn't eat. She forced herself a few times, but it ended in a series of vomiting. She was vomiting more and more often. She was getting skinnier. She looked bad. Getting worse. She wanted to do something with herself, but she did not know what. The advice of her girlfriends, Danka, Agnieszka, was prosaic. "Put his suitcase outside the door and change the locks. Then he'll be beaten. He'll be apologizing to you, and you don't let yourself be appeased so easily. And even better, chase the bastard away!" Danka almost shouted. Curious, how much of herself does she apply to such advice? The thought slipped through Zuzanna's head. But immediately her own matters filled it. If she could throw him out of the door and if he came back with a bunch of tea colored roses, would she accept him? Wouldn't everything just be for him to humble himself and understand his mistake?

She recalled all his cowardice and insignificance, she was molding a nasty figure out of them, which deserved only contempt, but soon, almost at the same time, she remembered the tenderness and understanding that gave their life meaning, and above all she realized that she didn't know how to live without Benedict. And if she could.

He finally admitted to it.

"Yes, I have someone," he said at the time of her next outburst, in response to the umpteenth time of her question. "Yes," he stated, hiding in a cloud of cigarette smoke. "Only do you really have reason to be outraged? Through the last years, and these were long years, has it been going well between us? I was coming home as if to a battlefield. A person expects peace in his own home, and I continuously had to face you, respond to attacks in which you could deny me honor and faith. I was a representative of the world of oppression for you, the hated regime...it's actually I that should be asking you: what are you doing with me? How can you live with me? In this situation, are you surprised that I am looking for at least some acceptance?"

Zuzanna did not know what to reply. But after a moment anger broke through the layer of uncertainty.

"You could always talk! You're after all an intellectual, a dialectic! You've always been able to justify your vileness and anxiety! You are a mendacious hypocrite to the bone!"

"If you think so, what are we doing with each other?!" Benedict threw it with unknown to her confidence.

"Well, exactly! Move out!" She shouted in a voice that embarrassed her.

"You're right. I'll move out. I should. Allow me to do it in a little bit. However, I must...we must agree on certain issues. I'll leave now. I'll return in a few days and pack up," he said calmly.

She had the impression that it was taking him hours to leave. She wanted him to be gone and at the same time she desired to call out, for him to come to his senses and think it through. After all they can reconcile themselves and find themselves again. To understand, that it's only them and their son in an evil world, which breaks in through open windows with distant, angry voices. But she knew she wouldn't say it. As always, Adam woke up at the wrong time and came out of his room. He stared at them frightened.

"Nothing is happening, son," she struggled to speak calmly, though her voice broke and she choked, swallowing her words. "Dad must leave suddenly. Do not worry. It happens."

Benedict, who was finally ready to leave, stopped. He hesitated. He came up to his son. He ruffled his hair and kissed his forehead.

"Listen to mom," he said in an uncomfortable voice. Then he looked at Zuzanna. He stood for a moment, as if waiting for some words. Then he turned and started for the door in a slow tempo. He stopped at the door once more. "Bye," she heard a strangled word. She doesn't know if he answered, embracing her son. The door closed.

Then there were unconscious months, of which she did not remember much. She gained peace, which cost her immeasurably when with Benedict they negotiated the terms of separation. She had the impression, that huddled in her own pain, she was observing a strange, cool woman settling with her ex-husband when he would meet their son and how much time he would spend with him in a week. They determined financial matters. They set dates and conditions for the divorce. He was also quite sure and determined. It was only after everything was done that he began to speak in a helpless way, familiar to her.

"I know it's not time, but...I would like to tell you that...and it's not just about Adam...I would like to say that I am grateful to you for so much and so I wish we could...stay friends...anyway remember, you can always count on me and if only..."

"Stop it!" She snapped. "This is pathetic." She managed to say it with sarcasm, although the real, huddled in a cocoon of pain, Zuzanna, silently, asked him to think about it and return to her. He made a gesture as if he wanted to reach a hand out to her, but she turned to the window. Out of the corner of her eye, she saw him leave, pausing for a moment in the open door. Then he turns and disappears.

For months of the passing year, she wondered why parting with her husband hurts her so much, it overwhelmed her with despair, paralyzed her with hopelessness. She thought about the words. Love. Passion. The longer she struggled to analyze them, the less she understood them. The threads of suffering remained from them. Everything was dominated by a deep sense of undeserved harm. And yet, if he decided to come back to her...asked her to forget, after all she would accept him, forgive him. She tried not to think about it, free her from hope, of whose deceptiveness she was perfectly aware of. She didn't count on anything. And yet when she woke up unconsciously, she looked at the phone, wondering if it wasn't his ring that had wrenched her from a feverish sleep, she cooled off for long minutes, waiting for him to contact her.

And now even worse came, though she thought that nothing worse could happen to her. Tadek's death came. She contemplated it all, looking through the dirty window of the "Warsaw Inn" at night torn by the lights of cars.

"We'll help you" said Hieronim.

***

Hieronim brought Zuzanna to the apartment on Koszykowa around midnight. Benedict phoned in the morning.

"Do you know something already?"

"Yes, I know. You've killed him."

"What are you saying?! Zuza…"

"I know exactly what I'm saying. No, not you. You have clean hands. You're only justifying them!"

"Listen, I could come over…"

"For what?"

"Maybe help you something. Maybe it would be better if Adam stayed with me a little longer. Maybe you need help with the funeral..."

"I don't need anything. I want Adam to come back today. And you...Why don't you do an investigation in your weekly?"

"Sure, that we can do, although, as you know..."

"I know perfectly well. It was a joke, understand? A joke!" Zuzanna laughed dryly. "Tell Adam to come to the 'Portico'. I will take him home from there."

PART II

ADAM

CHAPTER 1

An elegant, shapely woman who was approaching through the hospital corridor stared at Adam. Up close, she turned out older than she originally appeared. With a provocative smile, she came close and causing him to be confused, kissed his cheek.

"Well, do I have to introduce myself so that you would want to meet me? Have I gotten so old? Indeed, we haven't seen each other for a long time. It's me, Kalina, your father's second wife, the evil stepmother."

"No..." Adam stammered, "no..." he hesitated for a moment. They haven't talked to each other for almost twenty years. They were using the familiar 'you' before. "You don't have to introduce yourself to me. Nothing...you've changed little" he added, wondering what connection with reality this small compliment has.

"Ho ho! Not only handsome but also an elegant young man. It's good that you came," she added in a completely different tone, losing her smile. "I would like to tell you something about your father. The daily rounds are still going on, then there'll be procedures. Let me invite you for a short coffee. They have a pretty nice cafe here. You've been gone for so many years...You don't know how quickly we are Europeanizing, "she said, laughing again.

The hospital bar did indeed look better than the images of similar ones, which were appearing from Adam's memory. Outside the window, they were sitting next to, was a cloudy day. The dense pack of leaves were still colorfully dying on the trees. She was watching him from up close. The same brown and oblong eyes were now surrounded by a network of wrinkles, droopy skin, and although the outline of the face remained what it once was, this was the face of an aging woman. He noticed this with satisfaction.

"Your father is dying," she said. The pause was prolonging. Adam already knew previously that his father would only summon him in a serious situation. It occurred to him, that he could be dying. That's why he came from America. But such a decisive delivery of the matter provoked panic in him. Emptiness filled him.

"It's cancer," Kalina said after a moment. "I talked a lot with the doctors. I think they're telling me the truth, not just as a wife..."

"Wife? But you divorced him!" Spat out Adam angrily. Kalina looked at him closely.

"Ah yes...I forgot. But here I presented myself as his wife. Somehow, they accepted it. Especially since they can recognize me."

"Indeed. You're a known journalist."

"Not even that. I asked the editorial health specialist to call the doctors in this hospital and make sure they have a friendly attitude toward us. So therefore, they probably speak honestly with me. It's in a terminal stage. They don't know how long he has left, but at most months. I persuaded him to write to you. I wanted him to call. He refused."

The silence dragged on again.

"You didn't take an interest in him…"

"You want me to feel guilty?"

"You were always the most important to him!"

"Not enough, for him to have stayed with me!"

"With you? He wanted you as much as possible. It's was a story between him and your mother."

"And you. Give it a rest! You didn't stand him for long either."

"Me? What does that have to do with anything?"

"Nothing. I've stated the facts."

"You don't know the facts! You don't know what was between us. "Kalina looked angry. "Or maybe he left me? And yet I'm here! And this isn't the first time. Your mother wasn't here...No... Forgive me" she stopped his sudden gesture with her hand "I shouldn't have. I just...I just feel very sorry for him. So lonely here..."

"Maybe he earned it?"

"Him? And you say that, his son, the most important person for him...I think you should at least try to understand him...He would have so much to tell you. Maybe things he didn't tell anyone...You know, he could still make a career. I met him in ninety-five. We had a government and Kwaśniewski became president. People were needed. For various positions. He refused. They offered him a television program. It would've been great. He didn't accept. I asked him: why? He was still healthy, really in good shape. "You have to understand that we've lost," he said. I don't know what he meant. We didn't lose then for sure. And today...I don't feel like I've lost."

"I believe it!"

"Ah yes. I don't have that self-destruct gene in me that seems to be in your father. Maybe it's not a gene. Maybe it's what he survived as a child...he got out of the war...Maybe and I would be different. You should understand this better. You are his son. You should..."

"And you...do have children? Because your knowledge on these topics is clearly deep."

Kalina froze, looking at him strangely.

"I understand that that's supposed to be a joke?"

"Why? After all I don't know anything about your life."

"No, I don't have children. And as you can probably guess, I won't have any."

"You can adopt."

"I'm not planning on it." She looked at him coldly. "I'm fine as it is."

"And you're suggesting that it's my father who left you…"

"I'm not suggesting anything! I'm saying you have no idea about this. And you're old enough that you could refrain from making easy judgments. Fuck! That you can't smoke here either..." Adam realized what the gestures of Kalina meant, which she from time to time seemed to mechanically slip her hand into her purse.

"You know...you were the main topic of our talks. It upset me then...He didn't show it, but he felt terrible when your mother restricted your contacts with each other...and later...when you refused to meet him...when you became infected with dislike to him..."

"I didn't get infected with anything. I started growing up. I put the facts together."

"You, constantly with these facts...He acknowledged that you believed in his responsibility for the death of your uncle."

"Responsibility...big word. He was only on the side of his killers."

"What are you talking about?!" For the first time Kalina looked as if she was about to jump up and leave. "If this was your mother, but you...After all, it isn't known if this wasn't an accident, and I, all in all, think it is was."

"Even the Rokita commission stated, how very unlikely that version is."

"The Rokita Commission...And did it say anything specific? I'm a journalist and I deal with unbelievable events every day. And even if he was killed by some morons from the security forces...what did your father have with it..."

"He was on their side..."

"How can speak like that?!" Kalina was outraged, choking on words. "Your father even wanted to involve the 'Republic' in this matter. He wanted us to do a journalistic investigation!"

"And what? Did you do it?!"

"You can make jokes! You don't know those times. Your father...It was a terrible risk on his part..."

"For what? Did he pay for it?"

"They saved him. But...You still don't understand anything. If it wasn't for those like your father, martial law would have been different. They would've broken your necks...I'm sorry, not yours...You're only involved because of the family...If it wasn't for those like your father, there wouldn't have been the Round Table and I don't know myself where we would be. He just didn't understand what happened after. He thought, it was a revolution. Populism will come, Peronism with this mustached half-brain at the head; hunting for those like him, like your father, for everyone in Poland who wanted to do something and not just pray or curse Moscow. The mob would start, anti-Semitism would break out! He didn't understand that intelligent people from both sides can get along...he blamed himself unnecessarily...But let's leave politics. We won't come to an understanding. You have a good, American perspective..."

"Indeed, let's give it a break. Tell me about my father."

"I can't add much. Stomach cancer. He suffers. You can find out the details from the doctors. What do they matter anyway? They even stopped giving him light therapy. This is the end. And that's why...You are the most important person for him. You could..."

"What could I?"

"I think he would like to tell you a lot...explain...explain himself..."

"I should go to him now."

"Yes, you're right…You should."

Adam stood up and quickly moved away from the table with a gesture of farewell. As he was leaving, he looked at Kalina out of the corner of his eye. She sat facing the window and was going through her purse with her hand.

***

Kalina entered Adam's life twenty-three years earlier. It was because of her that his parents split up. But she appeared before. Long before he saw her figure, and brown eyes looked into the depths of his pupils. He couldn't even point out specific scenes that heralded that things were going badly at home. Maybe his mother stayed up alone exceptionally long at night, smoking cigarette after cigarette. Perhaps the silence between the parents became even more impenetrable and sometimes broke out in nightly quarrels, which did not even end in temporary reconciliation. He heard the strange, high-pitched scream of his mother and the silence of his father, which was interrupted by the question: "Why don't you say anything? Well say something!" His mother's question again became a scream. Perhaps the unusual gestures of his father, who came up and suddenly began to ruffle his hair, looking intensely, as if he wanted to say something. Adam waited in suspense, but everything, as usual, ended in silence. Once, as many times before, he was woken by his father's scream at night. This time, however, the moans and wailing continued. Adam realized that for the first time since he remembered, his mother was not waking his father from his nightmare, although she's there and can't sleep. Shouting and wheezing desperately, his father extracted himself from his night alone.

Suddenly everything became obvious. His parents were separating. Adam cannot reconstruct the chaos of feelings that swirled in him and exchanged at a dizzying pace. There was even a sort of excitement between them of a new adventure, perspectives that were opened by his parents' breakup. However, everything was dominated by compassion for the mother, with whom something very bad was happening, anger at the father and disbelief that their life up until now may ultimately fall apart. Until the end it seemed to Adam that this entire painful confusion was a great misunderstanding, and his parents, whom, in the end, one could always rely on, will explain and rebuild everything that was. But his parents separated, and his father moved out.

"Father has already found himself another family, we don't need him," said his mother. "He treated us like you do your toys when you get bored of them."

His father, for an exceptionally long time, explained something different to Adam: "We'll always be family, and you can always count on me, just like your mother. Now mother is bitter. She has the right. Maybe only sometimes she says things that she hasn't thought through to the end. And you will always be most important for me" his father repeated with a strange expression on his face.

At home it became empty and quiet. Then, in accordance with his parents' agreement, Adam visited his father's new apartment. He was supposed to spend weekend there. Then for the first time he saw Kalina, for whom he knew that his father had left his mother.

She was young and very pretty. Younger and prettier than his mother, Adam thought, and he felt ashamed. Kalina came over with a smile and looked into his eyes. "I hope we'll become friends. In any case, I will do everything to make it happen." Small fires flickered in her pupils. She was cheerful and offered more and more new games, but Adam felt insecure. He couldn't lose himself in the joy, plunge into the pleasures of the day that his father wanted to devote to him. The memory of his mother returned, which permeated every pleasure with a sense of betrayal. His father probably felt his son's attitude and the time spent together more and more often changed into moments of uncertain silence.

However, when Adam returned to the apartment, in which his mother unconsciously sulked, he felt like fleeing to his father. It was sad and hopeless. He wanted to cry. After moments of anger at his mother, at the world, Adam realized that everything was his father's fault and it would be best never to see him again. Maybe then he wouldn't miss him so much and the meetings that paralyzed them both.

The ambiguity of meetings with his father deepened. They both wanted them, but when they came, they couldn't take advantage of them. The joy that Adam felt at seeing his father was answered by the echo of the feeling of guilt towards his mother who was immersed in lonely despair in the empty apartment. The son's uncertainty was passed on to his father.

Only meetings with Uncle Tadek extracted him from the hopelessness of that time, who for Adam simply became Tadek. His uncle treated him as equal. They went over to 'you'. With Kalina, at her explicit request, he also switched to 'you', but he tried to avoid direct contact with her.

It was different with Tadek. Uncle told him about serious matters: about the homeland, democracy, communism and independence. He talked about Solidarity waging its underground battle, which it must finally win, and Adam remembered one of his first such clear memories. An endless sea of human figures and heads. Heads, because he's high up, on the shoulders of his mother who laughs and screams with everyone. His mother looks young, although she couldn't bc that young anymore, wonders Adam. Of various, calls chanted from time to time, he remembers the loudest, from time to time absorbing the noise; when the crowd chanted with one voice: "So-li-da-ri-ty!". Some tall, strange man takes him from his mother and sits him on shoulders, and she, after a flash of uncertainty, helps him with a smile. They scream to understand each other because the uproar is rising, everyone around is yelling, chanting and cheering. Now Adam is probably up the highest. Beneath him, people moved by one impulse swim, sway, dance, and he hovers high, feels confident and safe. He's part of their enthusiasm. Around spread a late, cool autumn, steam hovers above the crowd, and those gathered rejoice as if spring has arrived. The man said something to him which Adam didn't understand but remembered one strange sentence: "You will tell your children about this!" Finally, the man takes him off of his shoulders and gives him to his mother, whom he kisses on both cheeks. They laugh together. The crowd slowly begins to disperse and suddenly breaking out from the crowd a familiar voice is heard. Through the throng, calling to them, Uncle Tadek pushes through. He reaches them and throws himself into his mothers embrace. They grab Adam onto their arms and dance, tossing him up.

He also remembers previous images. His parents stare at the TV intently. Tension draws him in front of the screen. The announcer, as usual, says something incomprehensible. At the elongated table sit variously dressed people. Adam's eyes are caught by a strange mustached man who writes something with a large, colorful pen equipped with a wonderful tail. Suddenly, his mother jumps up with a scream and embraces his father: "We've won!" She calls. His father doesn't look as he's overjoyed the same.

A little earlier, Adam remembers some confusion at home. He remembers his father's nervousness and lack of his mother. Then his mother, who smells strange, is again at home, and with her many men who walk back and forth and look in everywhere. Adam doesn't like them and begins to cry. His mother calms him down, and then they stand over the mess that turns their apartment into a foreign and fascinating landscape.

The time that followed, Adam remembers as extremely turbulent, tangled and not entirely clear, but at the same time as interesting as never before or later. Maybe because all the tensions, nervous crises, bursts of anger and joy that filled those days were immersed in an unusual aura. He couldn't name it then, but he was feeling it in the air, at home and on the street; he saw it in the faces of his uncle, mother and her guests, who crowdedly flooded through their apartment, so that it seemed to him as if they were almost never alone. Only after years did he realize that it was hope. It was that which gave off such an extraordinary intensity and color to those experiences, it enlivened people and made them more beautiful.

Only at night, from time to time, Adam was dragged from his sleep by his father's screams. Then he heard moans and his mother was already saying something, reassuring his father, whose voice was turning into a loud, spasmodic breath.

Then also, in times of hope, Adam discerned the least of it in his father, who sometimes tried to explain something to his mother. She reacted angrily. He remembered the tension between them as a constant feature of his parents' relationship, so that he couldn't imagine almost living without it. It was also for this reason that Christmas was so special when his parents avoided quarrels and even discussions, which usually ended abruptly anyway. Then, by the light of candles flowing from the Christmas tree, they displayed only tenderness to each other.

Everything changed one winter night, though nothing heralded it as unusual. Adam went to bed at the usual time. At night he was woken by a racket. He didn't want to hear it, he hid his head under the pillow, believing that the bad noise would pass. However, he heard his mother's unusual voice and knew that nothing could be calmed down. He jumped out of bed, ran out and saw his father standing motionless in the anteroom and his mother looking at him strangely. It was she who a moment later opened the door behind which chaos swirled. Chaos pours into the apartment. Terrifying figures in uniforms and in civilian clothes divide his parents and surround his mother, whom Adam loses sight of. Despite his attempts, he couldn't fail to explode in screams. His father grabs him in his embrace and unsuccessfully tries to get to his mother. Gloomy characters corner them. Fear takes Adam's breath away. He feels through his body that his father is just as afraid. Everyone is shouting something which he isn't capable of understanding. Finally, his mother shuts herself in the bathroom. She comes out dressed. She kisses him and breaks free, because Adam doesn't want to let her go, but together with his father they unravel his embrace and the mother surrounded by a crowd of heavy silhouettes disappears behind the closing door. They are left alone with his father in a peculiarly empty apartment.

Dark, hard days without his mother approach. In the morning instead of "Teleranka", a bad character from the puppet theater appears on the television dressed in uniform. His name is General Jaruzelski and he announces a war. It's he who locked up his mother. His father disappears and leaves him with unknown women who even try to be nice. Yet it's best when it's grandma Gienia. At night nightmares haunt him. Monsters take his mother and he can't find her, sometimes they take both parents and chase him.

A few days before Christmas, his mother returned. Adam is happy. His father too. His mother put Adam to sleep, who sleeps almost without bad dreams.

Nothing, however, returns to normal, and Christmas don't resemble previous ones. On the second day after her return, his mother only plays with him briefly, and then dresses rapidly. His father tries to stop her. The dispute turns into an argument. His mother runs out, slamming the door. During the day, his father buys a Christmas tree and, in the evening, when his mother returned, his parents reconciled.

Adam dressed the Christmas tree with his mother and was happy that the next day will be Christmas Eve, and everything will be as it was. However, nothing is the same. The table is poorer, and his parents are sad. They don't sing Christmas carols because they want to understand what the choking and wailing radio says to them. The supper ends unusually quickly anyway. His parents move to the clamoring box and drink vodka. The radio talks in various incredible languages, but mainly wheezes and moans like a tormented creature, like his father at night, when nightmares overtake him. Adam fell asleep restlessly.

Even in the church it's somehow sad and different than during other Christmases or even whenever else.

Then at home the radio, which Adam begins to hate, begins its endless concert of clamor, from which it is rare to pick out understandable fragments, sometimes only sentences or single words. All that's known was that bad things are happening. Someone hurts people, locks them up, beats, sometimes kills. Then his parents moved the knob and the radio spoke incomprehensibly again. Foreign languages were changing, and his parents were searching constantly, and although Adam doesn't understand a word, he knows that they are talking about the same thing, nothing changes and the help that his parents are looking for isn't showing up and wont. He sees it in their faces, in the reflexively leaning toward each other figures. Before bed, his mother explained to Adam that Uncle Tadek must hide from the evil people who have conquered the country. She comforted him that they only managed to do it for a moment, but she was so sad that it's hard for Adam to believe her. There's no indication that the evil would depart quickly.

Quarrels broke out between his parents. Adam didn't understand what the cause of them is. He feels sorry for his father who his mother yeld at. He answered something helplessly. Then he goes somewhere. He returned in the evening and for a long time tries to explain to, or actually calm down his mother. Arguments exploded from time to time and spoiled the atmosphere in the home, which should have been a shelter from the evil world. Because winter had fallen on the country. The unusual aura that Adam remembered so well evaporated completely. The walls that Solidarity posters decorated - Adam could tell them apart at first glance - become uniformly gray. People scurry in panic. Shapeless figures in uniforms and helmets walk the streets. They warm their hands at the braziers, looking around scornfully and hatefully. The city is filled with cold, sadness and fear.

At the beginning of a new era the house is practically empty. Usually one of his parents stayed with Adam. It is only after some time that his mother's friends begin to appear. They speak in lowered voices. Their faces are bleak and restless.

Spring did not change anything, although sometimes people would gather in the streets and it came to clashes with uniformed officers. Sirens howled; puffs of pungent gas enveloped the city. Hatred and anxiety were felt.

Adam studied politics at an accelerated pace. He wanted to understand most importantly how adults lived. He already knew that Jaruzelski, carrying out Moscow's instructions, deprives Poles of their freedom. Solidarity was to restore it to them. Now it lost the battle, but was not defeated, although it was forced to hide. His mother explained it all to him. Adam understood. After half a year, his uncle could stop hiding. Father took care of it. It was all weird. Father was someone important. He knew bad people who had made martial law, locked up his mother and were chasing his uncle. And it was his father who had his mother released and then defended his uncle. Maybe the bad guys were afraid of him? But his mother in an incomprehensible way resented his father because he was someone important. Adam didn't know how to ask for clarifications. It was a secret of adults, when he tried to ask them about it, they dismissed him.

"Thank you for this intervention," said his mother with slight irony, kissing his father's cheek when she learned that bad people would no longer chase their uncle. His father smiled in a way his son didn't remember for a long time. Then they quickly put him to sleep and disappeared into their room, although it was not late.

The next day, uncle Tadek came. He kissed his mother, tossed him up, unusually cordially shook his father's hand. His father as a matter of fact also looked at him as a friend. Adam looked somewhat furtively at his uncle: a fighter who came out of the underground. It was one of the more beautiful evenings he remembered from his childhood. The adults drank alcohol, told jokes he didn't understand, but overall, he didn't mind. They sang funny songs. Father was especially funny.

Since then, the uncle began to come to their place again. He once asked Adam about dreams. He asked him to tell them to him. Adam tried to be precise. He remembered the dream of a crowd as large and as joyful as when he floated over it on the arms of his mother, and then this unknown but familiar man; only that in the dream the man fell over. In the fear which took one's breath away, Adam fell into the crowd, which was overcome by panic. The wail of sirens was heard, and people sought shelter. In black uniforms, the Hitlerites were approaching with weapons ready to fire. Tadek caught and saved Adam a little above the ground. But fear remained. Ranks of dark figures were approaching. One could hear shots. People struggled to hide. His uncle and mother pulled Adam one way; father showed them to run elsewhere. Dark figures were getting closer and Adam woke up sweating with fear. He asked Tadeusz why he needed his dream. His uncle, asking for discretion, explained that he was making an underground newspaper. They come up with the idea to collect testimonies about martial law, even as fleeting as dreams.

Since that time, his uncle took Adam's political and historical education upon himself.

Parents were able to clash as violently as never before.

"You support those who break our necks, take away our freedom and dignity! Do you really understand what you are doing?!" Cried his mother at night, forgetting about the presence of her son who, unable to sleep, was rolling around on the bed in the other room and remembered this clash unusually accurately. They lowered their voices every now and then, but soon they forgot about it. In any case, his mother forgot, because his father rarely raised his voice. Even at this moment, when passion and trauma rang in his words, which his son had never heard before.

"And do you understand...do you all understand what you are doing?!" He said in a low and voice changed beyond recognition. "Do you want blood to flow through the streets?! What a pity that your mother can no longer tell you what an uprising is, what such surges of national dignity lead to! Do you think our son, his generation, will settle your accounts based on your intentions? Who gave you the right to pledge his life?! I, squabbling over trifles, am trying to build a future for him. You exalt yourself with great ideas...I know what they can lead to. I know what a nightmare is that you can't even imagine..."

"And that will always be an excuse for you? You want to build everything on your fear? You never came out of that closet. And you want to propose such a life to your son? In the closet?!"

His father fell silent. He went out to the other room. Adam imagined to himself, that he's flipping through books, unsuccessfully trying to read them, as he did in times of agitation. His mother remained in the kitchen, smoking cigarettes in silence. Then she entered his father's room. Adam heard her low voice: "Don't be offended. I didn't want to hurt you. After all I can guess what you're feeling. Me too..." The voices faded; the light went out. And as usual at night, when Adam was woken by his fathers screams, he almost at the same time heard his mother reassuring him. In her words was the lost during the day, was tenderness.

And then they locked up uncle Tadek. They locked him up for underground activity, Adam already knew that exactly. His mother told his father that she was taking Adam to his uncle's trial. "Did you really think this over?" He asked. His mother shrugged her shoulders. His father didn't sleep the night before the trial. Nervous and excited Adam, waking up from time to time, heard him walking in the kitchen.

In the morning he decided: "I'm going with you" he said.

"For sure?" his mother's tone was different. His father replied with a gaze full of resentment. Adam was pleased. He liked it when they went together, especially since their father drove them in a Polonez, which made Adam's peers envious. Policemen checked the ID's of those entering the courtroom, and a group of civilians alongside pushed them. The police officers protested against Adam's presence, but his mother firmly stated that she had no one to leave her son with, anyway there was no ban on the presence of children at the trial. Fed-up, they waved a hand. They looked at his father, who paled and curled up. Adam felt ashamed and turned the other way. His mother waved at Tadek, who was being led into the room. His uncle repaid with a smile and perky movement of his bound hands. He also smiled, making a head gesture towards Adam, who felt pride and sadness. His uncle received a prison sentence of three and a half years. Adam had the impression that his face twitched as the sentence was being read. Then it returned to its former state. He smiled at them once again.

In the evening, his mother shouted at his father.

"Now what?! Are you still going to be on the side of those who locked up Tadek?"

His father struggled to embrace her, but she pushed him away.

"Don't touch me!" she yelled, leaving the room.

Arguments between his parents broke out more often. Though they extinguished just as suddenly, the tension lasted, thickening in the apartment, made breathing difficult. Sometimes his father came with flowers. He was whispering to his mother. "...after all we love each other" Adam heard "we have to understand that we see it differently, we have to achieve minimum tolerance..." Usually his mother answered so quietly that the son could no longer hear. But once he remembered her raised voice, almost a scream: "And my friends? And Tadek?! Those who they beat, who are sitting in jail? What about tolerance for them? Have you thought?"

His uncle got out after a year and a half. His mother was happy. She organized a small party at home. A few of Tadek's colleagues came. His father was there. They drank vodka and sang *Green Crow* and Kaczmarski's songs. In the morning, his parents looked at each other as they had not done with each other for several years. For some time, it was better.

Sometimes they went to the countryside, to Niemir. The walked as a trio through the woods. They waded in the snow, between the tall pines that supported the blue-grey sky. In the spring they saw the leaves burst open on the trees later perched on by coniferous crowns, and the smell of juices penetrating the stems and trunks made them dizzy. In the summer the sun laid on them in a thick patch, and the smell of forest ground cover intoxicated. And then came the time of dying, blending into the ground in the sour aroma of rotting leaves.

At night, adults drank vodka, following up with bites of sausage, and talked about past times and those who were no longer alive. The children overheard them, trying to understand complicated stories and meanings which were not obvious. Sometimes, at dusk, the adults lit bonfires for children to bake potatoes. Strong, burnt fragrances drilled into their nostrils and squeezed tears from their eyes.

In Warsaw, his parents took him to Łazienki or Wilanów. Adam liked the stories of his father who knew everything about these places. His mother looked at them with satisfaction. His father told him the history of buildings and the equipment that filled them. The world had another, invisible dimension. Under the things that could be seen, a dizzying and mysterious depth opened up. Those who lived before them appeared in his father's stories. They erected buildings that the living now used and admired, and thus also created their current world. They continued after death. Adam felt that they were with them now, though invisible and in a large part forgotten, they accompanied and spoke to them, although it was difficult to understand them.

It happened that later all three of them found a place at a cafe and Adam could eat, from a tall cup, ice-cream covered with dark chocolate. He noticed that his parents' gazes met above him and softened. But it was enough that at home one, usually his mother, said something and the fumes of resentment built up again. Adam was afraid of those moments. His mother's outbursts, his father's silence. And he waited, for them to go to the countryside again and to Łazienki. And yet, despite these tensions, it was possible to somehow live, and even, this Adam understood many years later, he was happy then. Everything collapsed, when, which he also later understood, then the invisible Kalina entered into their family.

After his father moved out, the house seemed foreign. His mother conversed with Adam less often. She locked herself in her pain and he, though he wanted so much, couldn't help her. The person who could bring some life to their home was Tadek. He came often. He tousled his angry mother, finally making her laugh. He boxed and wrestled with Adam, sang Kaczmarski's songs and allowed for the foreignness of the walls to be forgotten. Then, however he left and sadness fell over the flat. Adam thought it was so bad that it couldn't be worse. He would soon find out how wrong he was.

Uncle Tadek stopped showing up. His mother was not only grim, she was getting more and more restless. She dismissed his questions. "Uncle had to leave," she told him for him to leave her alone. Undetermined anxiety and even fear overcame Adam. He remembered the dream he had dreamed a few days later when Tadek visited them for the last time. He was walking towards the sea, although he didn't want to and was more and more afraid. There was night all around. From a distance he heard a desperate scream. The scream grew. It was so terrifying that it busted open Adam's skull. He thought that it was his father again, whom his mother wasn't next to and because of that he couldn't wake up. When he realized that it was Tadek's scream, he awoke.

Adam spent the weekend with his father. He knew that something disturbing was happening, something that could be worse than he could imagine. This time his father didn't really want to talk with him. He was exceptionally, somehow differently, uncertain. Kalina also appeared and disappeared without her usual spontaneity. Something very bad was happening beyond the borders of Adam's understanding.

He was sleeping fitfully. Nightmares were waking him up. He went to school sleepless and semi-conscious. Around one o'clock he was called to the teacher's room. His father sat at the table looking strangely. He took Adam to lunch. Normally he would've enjoyed this intervention. A nasty dinner in the canteen will be replaced with an attractive meal in the company of his father, who additionally freed him from a few hours of school boredom. This time, however, everything was different. Adam had no appetite, and his grim father did not know how to express what he had to say. Finally, seeing that his son had only pushed his food around, the father, who ate almost nothing, pushed his plate away and lit a cigarette.

"Uncle Tadek is dead."

Adam thought he had heard wrong.

"Uncle? Tadek? That's…that's…impossible."

His father moved closer to him with his chair. He embraced him.

"I understand you. For me it's unbelievable. He was so...full of life...He was only twenty-nine years old. He could've…could've...You know, I'll take you to your mother, to the 'Portico'. She asked for it. She needs you. I think you understand..."

Adam didn't understand anything. How could Uncle Tadek be dead? But it meant that he would never be able to see him or talk to him again. He will not come to their place and he will not be here. Just like that.

During these few days, his mother clearly changed, although Adam would have trouble describing what had happened to her. When they went to her, to the publishing house, he got scared that his mother would cry. Maybe it didn't happen often, but maybe even more so her son couldn't stand her tears. In the study, he saw her still face. He understood that his mother would not be crying, but it didn't relieve him at all. She got up from behind the desk, saying to his father: "Thank you," and she embraced her son. He felt her dry lips on his forehead.

"Do you already know what happened?" Adam nodded his head. "I still have some work, look at the albums," she said, and inadvertently, looking his father over, who was still standing in the doorway of the office, repeated: "Thank you."

"Maybe I could…"

"No, thank you."

It wasn't until evening at home that he dared ask:

"But what happened, mom?"

"The communists killed him. Just like Father Popiełuszko" his mother said calmly and to Adam it seemed that her lip twitched for a moment. He wasn't sure though.

"But why?" Asking this question, he realized that it's silly.

"He was probably bothering them too much. He learned something, but maybe...maybe they just recognized he's too dangerous for them. I'll try to explain it."

She sat next to him when he laid in bed to go to sleep. He pretended to be asleep for her to leave. He couldn't fall sleep for a long time. At times it seemed to him that in the other room he heard something like a moan, but it could be an illusion. He woke up in the middle of the night screaming. He was crying. He couldn't control his tears, he was overcome by them, when his mother burst into the room. She embraced him and began to calm him down. He fell asleep not knowing when.

There were a lot of people at the funeral. They followed the closed casket. Then they poured soil on it. His mother and Irena, dressed in black, received condolences. Adam stood next to them. Some approached him, shook his hand, caressed his head. He had the impression that he was observing everything from the outside, from the crowns of trees, from which from time to time flocks of cawing birds rose. Strangely split in two, he had the impression that his cramped body was choking him. The air was like lime. At one point, his father approached Irena. He embraced her and kissed her. He approached his mother, who reached out her hand. He squeezed it and stopped, maybe he was about to say something, but his mother turned toward the man who had just come and embraced him. His father stood a moment, then hesitantly started to walk away.

A large picture of a laughing Tadek, girded with a black ribbon, his mother placed on the bookcase.

CHAPTER 2

"I told him, I repeated, for him not to go" Irena, who was drunk and had her makeup smudged up, was crying, hitting her head on the table, on which leftovers of food, dirty dishes and shot glasses, and above all ash and cigarette butts were laying around. They filled everything. Adam had the impression that he's wading in ash, which rose to the ceiling, mixed with cigarette smoke and the odor of vodka, and solidifies into the dark jelly of air. It filled plates and glasses, eyes and lips, settled on the skin and penetrating it. It poisoned everything. Adam thought he was drunk. Finally, he really understood what adults felt, wobbling on their feet and staggering, unable to finish sentences, losing one's thoughts and not recognizing reality.

He lasted until the end of the wake. The chaos of the event prevented his mother from enforcing appeals directed at her son about going to bed. After a threatening sentence, someone separated them, strongly lecturing his mother on something, pulled her somewhere, despite the fact that she was trying to free herself of them, and the pageant of the characters shouting over each other, kissing and raising toasts which continued to be triggered by an invisible mechanism.

Most of the funeral participants went to their apartment, bringing bottles of vodka with them, and even obtained: blood sausage, liver sausage and yellow cheese from several stores along the way. Adam was amazed at the age range of the guests. Among them were people younger than Tadek and much older than his mother. The apartment was cramped, dense and gloomy. Then alcohol loosened up tongues. The guests began to jostle each other, shouting their regrets and opinions louder and louder, and finally bellicous voices and singing. The night fell on the city and the apartment boiled. Somewhere the reason for meeting was lost, which was only disclosed on the face of his mother and maybe Irena, sometimes with sudden, awkward glances at some of the newcomers. Adam had the feeling that something extremely wrong, painful, simply terrible was happening. His uncle was reduced to a small plot in the cemetery and photographs with a black ribbon on the wardrobe. It was upsetting him, leading him to confusion, the screams and laughter occurring more and more often. Adam wanted to cry, but the confusion that seized him did not allow him to even focus on his own pain. Someone was constantly approaching and embracing him, caressing his head, and even, despite the boy's resistance, tried to kiss him. Adam felt ever growing disgust.

The party looked like it wasn't going to end, even though the vodka had just run out. Discussions continued, for who's going to the shebeen for another allotment. It was proposed to start a collection and only the strong opposition of his mother, supported firmly, but calmly by her friend Hieronim Jano, destroyed this plan. His mother, who also did not look sober - had a red, angry face – insisteted on ending the event. Suddenly everything calmed down, saddeness set in. Guests, lingering a bit and exchanging farewells in the anteroom for a long time, as they began to leave in groups. The stragglers were shown the door by his mother, who was accompanied by Hieronim. The last ones, already very drunk, told how much he could be counted on, with the help of a friend, but she simply pushed them out the door. After a while Jano left as well, receiving the silent consent of his mother, who shook her head when asked if he could still help. Adam watched him. His mother's friend looked sober and, as always, was different. He seemed lost. He never raised his voice. His gaze sought points of support. A small man without expression entangled in a world too big for him. When he left, Adam was still hiding behind the door frame. He couldn't even imagine falling asleep.

His mother looked around the corners, around the table, looked into a few bottles and glasses, but inside there was only ash. She sank into a chair and only then looked at Irena, who continued her litany which wasn't directed at anyone specific. She was resting her face on a dirty tablecloth. She was pushing around the dishes with her hand. His mother was looking ever closer. She listened to her words.

"He was explaining that he knew something so important...that I couldn't tell anyone. He thought he knew who the snitch was among those top experts. It's all my fault!" Irena was sobbing. "My cousin, my aunt's daughter, we were so close, she married a police officer. An important one. Once, Tadek and I went to my parents, in Radom. We came across a family party. And that husband of Marysia, Heniek, got drunk. He argued with Tadek. We separated them. And then he came after Tadek again. He was insulting him. He was laughing that they had them, us, like on a fork. They have their people everywhere. They pulled him away. The next day, Tadek said he wanted to apologize to Heniek. It was strange and unlike him. I called Marysia. She invited us. Tadek asked me to take her away at some point, that he wants to drink with Heniek. And that's how it was. We brought a bottle, Marysia took out another. I've never seen Tadek like that. He was listening to all the bullshit he was chattering. He didn't agree with all of them, but they echoed each one. Rather, he pretended. That officer was getting tanked. Tadek sometimes objected, but not too strongy, and was filling his glass up constantly. Marysia wanted to protest when her husband took out another bottle, but I took her to the other room, with the children. They already had two. I kept telling her to leave the guys alone. They have to drink and talk it out. Then they will reconcile. She broke free when she heard a noise. Heniek fell off of his chair. Tadek didn't look much better. But when I was leading him home, he was laughing. Unpleasantly. He was mumbling that he found out what he wanted. Now he would have to check it. And this is what happened later. He went to Warsaw. He was going around, questioning, investigating. He was putting everything together. I knew that it wasn't good. "What do you want to achieve?" I asked. 'Do you believe you'll learn something by playing detective? Alone? He was dismissing me. We argued. He argued with everyone. And finally, he went to Gdansk...And now he's gone..." Irena was saying something further, more unclearly. Adam stopped understanding, and his mother who noticed him made a fuss that he was not sleeping yet. Then she had to pull Irena out of the bathroom because she fell asleep on the toilet. It was dirty. Everything was dirty, even the air.

***

Weeks went by. Adam came to the 'Portico'. His mother had a guest, it was Hieronim. As usual in such situations, she gave Adam an album to look at. She was speaking more animated.

"He went insane, right?" She snorted. "He went insane and that's why he died.

"I repeat what our people have said." Jano walked around the desk where Adam's mother was sitting. "He claimed that he's almost certain, that in the immediate entourage of the TKK there are snitches and that they're so important that they can control the union. He swore that he knew about one, the most important one. At the beginning he tried to get along with the management of 'Mazowsze'. He later sent a letter. And finally...He wanted to reach Wałesa himself. That's why he went to Gdańsk...as if he were undermining the sense of what we're doing..."

"Because there are snitches? Because the commies are trying to steer us? After all, it's obvious to anyone who can connect the facts. That, what we're doing makes sense in spite of that...And we can't see it..."

Adam missed his uncle. Sometimes he spoke to him, in emptiness, he asked questions that he could not ask his mother, let alone his father. He missed him; his smile, spontaneity. Sometimes he could cry alone, remembering Tadek. His death strengthened the feeling that the world was an empty, painful void. His parents were no longer with each other, and each of them alone was not even a fraction of what they had been when they were together. At times Adam felt as if he was living next to, but not with his mother. He could miss his father desperately so, that even he was surprised by the strength of this feeling. However, when he would meet with him, after a moment of joy which would wake up from time to time, a feeling of guilt and aversion to him which he heard, poisoning their every conversation, every meeting.

Adam didn't like school, but sometimes he preferred it than going back to the emptiness-filled home, to his overfilled with grief, sorrowful mother. Although when some man visited them, and the shadow of a smile from the past strayed on his mother's face, the son worried even more. His mother was supposed to be the guardian of the past. That's how it was, and moments of smiling were flashes in her life.

It was different when they went to Niemir. Then his mother became someone else. At times she could even be joyful and free layers of vitality that surprised her son. He also liked the countryside very much. He liked his cousins, uncles and aunts, as well as long lonely treks in the woods, which became travels to different times and lands, and he changed roles in them which marked the fates of the worlds. Once in a while he walked with his mother, who told him about so many and such interesting things that she never mentioned elsewhere. She talked about trees, but also about painting. About how landscapes are painted. She explained that a real image is always something more than a reproduction of colors and shapes. As he listened to the elders talking in the sleepy village in the evenings, he thought that what they're saying is more than just the meaning of their words. He listened to the melody of their voices, he stopped understanding, and their conversation became the basis for closely undefined dreams leading somewhere into indefinite, dreamy heights, which Adam was sure one day he would understand. However, they rarely did this and for brief amounts of time went to the countryside.

Visits to his father were always associated with a basic inconvenience. It was his father who was guilty for the breakup of their family, and although his mother could be unbearable, mentioning him with dislike and sneer - his father never did this - Adam felt that he shouldn't forget what he did or forgive him. He hurt his mother. He destroyed that which was the best, their three-person intimacy, which seemed would have survived everything.

He missed his father and felt guilty for the aversion he felt toward him. He wanted to visit him and felt opposition. This confusion of feelings filtered through the guilt he felt because he believed that hurting his mother meant that the wall that separated him from his father was becoming tighter. He couldn't, did not want to tell his father about his problems, he couldn't play with him or devote himself completely to the attractions offered to him. Kalina troubled him. He couldn't hide from himself that he liked her and was the source of his erotic fascinations. This angered him. He dreamed of a meeting with her, she could disarm him, and immediately he was throwing away his emotions and trying to arouse aversion to her. When he accidentally grazed her hair or skin, he felt shivers. At home, he found himself imagining her touch. He brought himself back to reality with difficulty. Sometimes, when his father embraced Kalina and she was returning it with affection, he was discovering a sudden surge of jealousy in himself.

He categorically only liked theoretical conversations with his father. His father transformed into a mentor, a little impersonal, wiser teacher who revealed the intricate drift of the world to him. He explained the secrets of economics, which at first seemed boring, but a closer look revealed its fascinating depth. Gray, uninteresting port docks hid a hectic, impulsive life. This was where the boldest projects were organized. Heroes prepared ships and set off into the uncertain seas, looking ever more for a new Golden Fleece; explorers settled in unknown lands, built cities and roads, clashed with forces of nature and wild tribes. The stakes were the highest: victory or defeat, life or death, then they became smaller, though still important: dominance or dependence, wealth or poverty, profit or loss. Father explained that wars, clashes between states and ideas would disappear, reason would win, which would dictate the best solutions. Big quarrels seen as unprofitable would die and competition would remain between the best ideas for faster travel, more comfortable housing, better computers that would provide all necessary information; the competition of subsequent entertainment technologies, spatial images indistinguishable from reality.

This world was fascinating, but barren in some way. Adam found it difficult to name the cause of his discomfort. Is it only because the real fight ended, which was brought to playing with holograms, and risk can be taken only behind a desk, staring into a computer screen?

***

His father explained how much pain and suffering people would spare themselves in the new reality. Adam understood. After all, he knew about the Holocaust. His father told him, or rather recalled how he was able to survive the war.

His mother, Adam's grandmother, was killed by the Nazis. These were all terrible things. His mother, previously his uncle, told how their father was tortured to death. Tadek's death also belonged to the cruelty of politics. His mother said it simply: the communists killed him. His father avoided such explicit statements. When his son demanded an answer, he started: "You know, your mother needs to understand, she couldn't come to terms with her brother's death, but we're not sure...After all, it could have been an accident and in fact everything indicates it..." And when Adam recalled the death of the priest Popiełuszko, he explained: "You must understand the complexity of this matter. It wasn't the authorities that killed him. Yes, officers did it, but most likely it was a provocation against those in charge, who knows how far-reaching..."

Probably the biggest outrage that Adam caused his mother, was repeating what his father said: "But we do not know if uncle was murdered..." He said it when he was unexpectedly irritated by his mother's usual tirade against the communists, who were guilty of all evil, and the doubts sown by his father did their harm, so he repeated: - "...we don't know if he was murdered..."

His mother jumped up from the pile of papers which covered the table. "We don't know, we don't know..." she repeated, unable to find the words. "I know! Everyone who wants to know knows! Those who don't know, are those who don't want to know, who are afraid of knowing. Like your father! He's intelligent enough to be able to justify any excuse, any smallness and rascality! Do you want to follow in his footsteps? Do you remember those who killed Popiełuszko..."

"But they were clearly tried. The government did it, and the whole thing wasn't beneficial to it..."

"It wasn't? How do you know? Your father, who can call any interpretation a conspiracy theory, in this case, without a trace of evidence, develops hypotheses that reach Moscow. Popieluszko was murdered by the UB's. We saw them. We saw what culture they come from. These are communists, that's how communism is. Urban was their ideologist. He gave them justifications. And your father's 'Republic'? It creates a favorable climate for them. It supports Jaruzelski and his clique. These are the principals of the killers! Those that carried it out protect them. And that's why they'll be out soon, and they'll have it good. You'll see!"

Adam heard about all evil and harm in the world, especially in Poland. However, his father showed reality from a different angle, he complicated the picture, caused anxiety.

***

He didn't remember when he first heard about the Round Table. It was winter. Dirty snow laid in the yard and on the streets. Unexpectedly, their home became a place of unceasing meetings. Earlier, they were also often visited by guests and they were able to argue about complicated matters of the country until late in the evening. Now, however, the apartment was transformed into a club that commented and supplemented the meetings, which were taking place a few kilometers from them, although, as he already knew, the most important ones were taking place in the guest house of the Ministry of the Interior among the trees at the edge of a village with the graceful name Magdalenka, twenty kilometers south of Warsaw. There, the host was Czesław Kiszczak, a person with the face of a dangerous dog.

His mother seemed skeptical; some were enthusiastic. Sometimes they came to them and those directly participating in meetings with the government, like Filip Madej. To Adam he seemed like his father at times, though he couldn't identify the features that made that impression. Mother and Madej were connected by peculiar relations in which there was closeness and tension.

Sometimes, when the house was empty and his mother was overcome by reflexive tenderness that irritating her son, she tried to explain something to him. One evening she let out in that snappy tone, which her son hated: "You know, we are involved in the negotiations almost through family. Your father's friend, Władysław Goleń, plays an important role in them. And in the team that advises him, as far as I know, your father is the main character."

The echoes of the Round Table even reached school. Teachers hinted at it: some with excitement, others with noticeable aversion, almost fear. During breaks, the Round Table became the topic of their talks. Maciek said it's treason, that instead of fighting the communists, they're getting along with them. Real patriots will be hung out to dry as always. Staszek objected, he said its hope: Poles are finally getting along with each other and only then can they be strong. Nobody defended the communists. The boys exchanged rumors and their impressions. His father also looked moved: "You know, maybe this is a chance?" He repeated. "We'll come to an agreement and that which needs to be done, will."

"Don't you realize that it's like a next edition of August?! We'll get our time again and move forward. Like then!" Madej almost shouted.

The leaves started to bud on the trees, and the birds outside the window did not want to finish their songs as night fell much later. The Round Table ended. Spring began to fill the city.

His mother was running more often to Constitution Square to the "Surprise" cafe. Inside it, crowds poured through in clouds of cigarette smoke. People harangued, argued and reconciled, arranged and organized. Adam felt the growing excitement. This was a time of trial. The elections were coming, which were to decide...Actually, no one knows what, because after all the communists would remain in power, but how much will they have...From the wall, Sheriff Will Kane, Gary Cooper, gazed firmly at this circumstance without revolvers. Adam promised himself that he must see *High Noon*, which his mother told him about. "Gazeta Wyborcza" lay in heaps, and the posters of the next candidates shaking the hand of Lech Wałęsa, several of whom hung in view, leaning against the wall in thick rolls. Leaflets, stamps, stickers - the arsenal of their army - were issued to successive flocks of aroused newcomers. One of the candidates was Filip Madej.

Several times, Adam enthusiastically participated in poster campaigns, hung placards in indicated places, but smaller ones wherever it was possible. He glued posters over every piece of wall, every piece of gray space in the world that they were to send back into oblivion. They were only electing one-third of the Sejm, but they were electing them. This couldn't be without consequences. The Reds were stepping back step by step. Adam remembered that, half-memorable, perhaps more imaginary time from eight or nine years ago. Himself on the shoulders of a strange but a familiar man, a young joyful mother, Tadek, who's celebrating with them. That hope seemed to arise in the burgeoning spring.

One night his mother came into his room. It was already late. He just put down the book - it was *Moby Dick* - and turned off the light.

"Are you asleep?" She asked in a dramatic whisper. He turned on the lamp. "I saw the light was on a moment ago," she justified herself. She was tipsy, as usual, with a cigarette attached to her lips and a small ashtray in her hands. He hated when his mother was in this state, which happened far too often. Although now definitely less often than after the departure of her husband and then the death of her brother. Then in the evenings she could have trouble getting to her room. Adam would wake up and thought about whether he should help his mother, hearing her collide with the furniture. In the end it turned out that it wasn't necessary. The next day she took a shower, prepared breakfast, and although her son could see the fatigue of the previous night in her face, she behaved energetically. She was going to work. But now she looked completely different than before. Her face did not contract into a mask of suffering. She seemed excited, almost happy.

"You know, I wanted to tell you, you can ask...You can probably guess that I work for an underground publication. I'm in the editorial office of the 'Underground Weekly'. And we decided to make it an official publication. It means going to the surface. It will be a weekly and will be called 'Renassiance'. I think I'll take a chance and leave my job, at the 'Portico', and I'll completely involve myself in this endeavor. It's kind of crazy. I'm forty-two years old and want to start my life again. But I have the impression...the hope that the whole country begins it...and therefore...Do you agree?"

Adam felt the lack of his father unexpectedly painfully. Together they were able to experience things even more profoundly, come to an agreement with each other, make decisions together...

***

On the day the results were announced, after an improvised victory celebration at the "Surprise", his mother came home with a large retinue, which continued the party. The fourteen-year-old Adam then drank his first official shot of vodka. Joy pulsed in their apartment for a long time and filled the night. Through the open windows it leaped out over the city, hovered above it and kept it awake. Adam remembered a similar joy, or he thought he remembered, from nine years ago. The last guests who left, singing and shouting, were accompanied to the door by his mother with an amused look. Adam couldn't remember seeing her like this for a long. Then, watched by her son from the other room, she went to the bookcase which Tadek's photograph stood. She looked at it for a long time. She leaned her forehead against a shelf. It took Adam a moment to realize that his mother was crying silently.

His father, whom Adam visited two days later, did not look so pleased. Adam was struck by the different atmosphere in both apartments.

"This victory is too unambiguous..." repeated his father, walking around the room with a cigarette in his hand. "I hope that the current Solidarity leaders show common sense. Geremek and Mazowiecki look like those, and Wałęsa seems to listen to them. They better not lead to an inflamminf the situation now. They better know how to back down...Stay cool."

Suddenly Adam noticed Kalina's gaze, who was observing her husband coldly from the couch in the corner of the room. For the first time he saw that expression in her. Until now, the looks she gave his father only made Adam jealous. Now irony seemed to flicker in her gaze. Adam decided.

"I would like to speak with you…"

"But we are speaking" said his father surprised.

"It's okay," declared Kalina. "I was about to leave."

"I'm already fourteen years old," Adam announced, and he thought it sounded funny. They were now alone, and his father looked as if he wanted to continue his current monologue.

"But I know." His father was more and more surprised.

"I think it's time to end the dates of my visits. You shared my time with my mother when I was little. That has passed. I think I can decide for myself when I will come to see you. After all, you see that we often postpone these dates..." His father came back suddenly from the world of great politics. He was looking at his son with a hard to name mixture...surprise, sorrow?

"Are...are you saying that...you're not going to visit me?"

Adam started feeling sorry.

"No, I didn't say that. Only these dates... You know, I already have my own life. After all, it shouldn't be that I put you on a timetable...We have telephones. We can make appointments.

His father picked up his glasses from the cabinet. He removed them from the case and began to thoroughly clean with a felt cloth.

"There are no dates, as you call it, you know yourself...After all, we see each other less and less often. Each of us has our own affairs. If there is no such external framework, our relationship will diverge. After all we don't live together.

"But why? Is this my choice?!" Adam said it sharper than he wanted. His father fell silent. He was looking through the window.

"Yes, you are right. We have to bear the consequences of our decisions. But...I would like...After all you know. You're older now. Even if I did not behave as you expected...as I should've...Now it would be easier for us to come to an understanding. I have...I think... a lot to tell you..."

His father agreed. Actually, he didn't have a choice. When they said goodbye and he embraced Adam extremely awkwardly, the boy felt more responsible. His father was helpless. It occurred to him that adults were often helpless. He felt sorry for his father. At the same time, he reminded himself that it's his father who's at fault for everything. Anger filled him. When he was leaving the house on Ursynów, he felt relief. He was becoming an adult.

CHAPTER 3

When Adam remembered that time later, he invariably realized that this was the most political period of his life. He experienced successively: induction, recognition and disappointment.

It started with enthusiasm. Smaller and bigger regrets caught up with us, but the euphoria dissolved them, blurred them. The quarrels were hot, but they did not divide us yet, this attested to their involvement. An exceptionally passionate dispute flared up in their home a few days after the election, when it turned out that the leaders wanted to agree to the demands of the communists and accept the changes in the Round Table contract. Adam slowly began to grasp the nuances of the national list and the rules of the old and new regulations. Breaking through with this knowledge at first tired him, but soon became a source of fascination. It was like discovering a new, complicated game.

"And what would happen if we didn't give in!" My mother called out. Michał Bogatyrowicz, who came to their place with Madej and Stawicki, jumped up from his chair.

"Do you want to bet Poland at the roulette table?!" he burned out. "What will happen?! What can happen! Have you forgotten about martial law?! That they have an army, police and that Soviet troops are stationed in Poland?! The Round Table was fought by Jaruzelski with his team under the threat of resignation. Do you think their hardheads will agree to everything? We've gained so much, and you want to sacrifice everything for your uncompromising attitude?"

Those present seemed convinced. Besides, his mother wasn't even able to oppose Bogatyrowicz. Adam realized that his father could say the same.

"She used to be a nice ass. Now she's just a bitter hag of the revolution" he heard almost from behind the door. It was probably the voice of Bogatyrowicz, which was accompanied by the laughter of Madej and Stawicki.

"I don't like that Bogatyrowicz," he threw out when he was left alone with his mother.

"He's a great figure," she laughed. "But what? Do you have any reasons? Come on, say it!" She was jerking at his head.

"I have the impression...I'm not sure..."

"Say it already..."

"I think he was saying something unpleasant...about you...When they were leaving."

"To Filip?" His mother grew serious. "What did he say? Say it!"

"This way, to Madej. He said...I think he said...that you've gotten old..."

His mother looked at him closely, and Adam felt himself blushing against his will. Anger and shame came over him. His mother was nodding her head and, lighting a cigarette, sadly laughed.

"And you think I'm getting younger? Well...Men say that about women. Often. I hope you'll be different. She caressed his head and walked away to her room.

Summer was growing with the frenzy of expectation and hope. Warsaw was soaking in the heat. Adam joined a KPN demonstration, which was marching through the center of the city, raising shouts against Jaruzelski. ZOMO units attacked them not long after. He was running away with others, got hit with a baton a few times. He was proud of himself.

Another quarrel similar to the one he witnessed in June broke out over a month later. His mother attacked Madej, who tried to minimize the importance of Jaruzelski's election as President of Poland. Those present looked at them in suspense.

"After all that was the deal," Madej explained. "Why are you all surprised? This is still a communist country in which we break-up spaces for freedom one day, but only one day, leaving them only the facade, which we will demolish at the right time. And Jaruzelski's election? It's just a formality. Confirmation of the status quo, which we cannot change yet."

"What's happened to you all?" His mother asked in a raised tone. "Have you stopped understanding the value of symbols? And it's you? Do you not understand what meaning this has to ordinary people?"

Madej got angry. He tried to speak calmly, but Adam saw how much it cost him.

"You have to see things in proportion. Just yesterday we had only symbols. Today we have realistic politics. The art of the possible. We're really changing the country. And you want to risk it for a gesture! And besides...if we're talking about values, compel agreements."

Stawicki word laughed but herson became serious. He bent over Adam's mother. "Exactly!" he emphasized every. "Already now we must start building a state that follows the rule of law. Respect for commitments. Do you understand?! In this way, we're breaking communism most effectively. We're building a new order!"

***

A month later on the TVP news they watched material about the nomination of Tadeusz Mazowiecki for the position of prime minister. Adam tried to sort out his thoughts. Did that mean that they're taking over authority? His mother embraced him suddenly and started kissing him.

"Do you understand, what's happening?" she shouted, "Do you understand?!"

It was the time of television. Although fascinating things were also happening in the streets. Small stalls sprouted up like mushrooms after the rain. Temporary, mounted on metal frames, they filled the pavements and transformed the city into an oriental bazaar. Peddlers cried out, customers, and often ordinary onlookers crowded around, loudly commenting on exhibited goods. The city became dense and cramped. The strangest things could be bought at the stalls. Random, all sorts, becoming more expensive by the hour, but they were there and there were more and more of them: food and underwear, toiletries, clothes and books, toys, jewelry, electronic gadgets of unknown purposes and even furniture. The choices stunned people. Adam and his friends were looking at "Świerczczyki", pornographic magazines, which began to turn up at improvised counters. The sellers wouldn't let them be picked up. They were too young. Only from a certain distance, from behind the backs of those looking at them, sat the still unreachable objects of their desire: women with whom everything could be was done. Some of his friends bragged about their first successes with girls, but probably even they didn't believe them. The stories themselves were important, were probably repeated by those older than them who already had something to boast about. The art of narration was important, the ability to perform, which made it possible to imagine and absorb someone else's experiences substituting one's own unrealistic desires. They experienced them. They gathered around the narrator, forming a circle and leaning towards him. The air was thick, emanating physicalness.

Summer was booming, and women hovered above the pavement in thin dresses sticking to their skin in the heat, in skirts that rustled against their thighs, women more fascinating than the most sensational politics. They walked with a dancing step, aware, flourishing in their gazes, but ignoring them. They walked by them, through them, not touching them, inaccessible.

Money lost its value. The subsequent zeros printed on them meant nothing. Banknotes had to be spent immediately on anything. Coins stopped functioning. Everything was happening faster and more unconsciously.

The last, unnecessary class of primary school began. They grew out of it over the summer. Teachers lost their confidence. Nothing was obvious and guaranteed anymore. Only two people caught the wind in their sails. A young history teacher and a much older geography teacher. An excited historian was waving his hands and was showing real and potential events on a map. Even putting together analogies, he could still somehow stick to the subject, although he mainly exposed them as frauds that were ordered to be taught in the communist school. He made plans, or rather dreams about their country, which was going to soon surprise everyone. The geography teacher actually waved her hand at her subject. She told about a time before the war, the rebirth of Poland, which was destroyed by the aggression of two criminals. She told together and seperately about the war and ruin of their country, which, however, survived and was able to be reborn after each disaster.

However, this was mainly the time of television. Even before that, Adam was watching the grim reports from China that accompanied our victory. It was on the day of the electoral success in Poland, on June 4, that tanks ran over a group of students in Tiananmen, the Square of Heavenly Peace in Peking. The corpses were carted away under the cover of night. A hunt for rebels began. They were dragged away with their heads bent toward the ground. This image will remain in Adam's memory, he'll even dream about it and it'll emerge from his memories like a personal experience. Just like the image of a man who alone stops a column of tanks. This was happening even before the order to attack. The tanks hesitated. A few days later, the soft barricades of bodies were no longer a barrier. Steel vehicles crushed them more easily than wooden barriers.

"Remember Tiananmen!" Stawicki shouted many times when they were arguing about the limit of the concessions of Solidarity. "Do you think that there are no tanks in Poland, not even Soviet ones?"

Shortly after starting school, Adam and his mother watched the swearing-in of Mazowiecki's government in the "Daily News". The prime minister with the face of a sympathetic turtle stretched out his hand in a gesture of victory. An ovation swept through parliament. His mother who had tears in her eyes raised her hand with two fingers straight. She noticed her son's gaze and started laughing. She caught him in her embrace. Suddenly returned the time when everything was in its place and on his mother's face one couldn't see that which marked it later. "What, I'm funny?" She was laughing. "I am, and I don't mind it at all."

He watched crowds of Germans on television from brotherly East Germany crowding trains, which were traveling to Poland, Czechoslovakia and Hungary. It was especially from the latter country that people wanted to flee to the West to take refuge in the evil state of their revisionist brothers. Hungary opened their border with Austria to them. When the leader of the GDR, a small man with a foxlike smile, tried to block the trips out, demonstrations spread throughout the entire country. Demonstrations, rallies appeared in an increasing number in the countries of the communist bloc. They were blowing it up. The riots began to haunt the Soviet Union itself. They were spoken of on TVP, although they didn't manage to film them. Individual photos found themselves on television, which for a moment froze on the screen, becoming a sign of the era.

Summer became lost in the momentum of history. The leaves, violently breaking away from the branches, swirled unconsciously in the air. Rain was pouring. Adam remembered winter eight years earlier, weeks by the radio, which he hated. Incomplete and jagged information about disasters which came together to become defeats which were perilously breaking out from the howling of the deafening machines. The events that this autumn brought were reflected on the TV screen, restoring the world its right measures. Only eight years earlier, they listened to the radio with his father.

The demonstrations were moving to Czechoslovakia. Then the night came, which became a symbol. The crowd threw itself at the wall dividing Berlin, dividing Germany, dividing Europe. People were tearing it with their hands, smashing it with hammers and crowbars, chisels, hammers and files, whatever anyone had. The wall had no strength to last. It gave way, cracked, gaps were opening up, crevices, holes, it moaned, broke down, spilled over, ceased to exist. The night flashed with fireworks, firecrackers, flares, bundles of lights that wrote in the sky the end of the Communist prison. Adam watched it with his mother, with the whole capital, Poland, the world. A chorus of cheers of joy rose beyond the windows. In the dark space of Warsaw bolder and bolder fireworks were blowing up. Adam was looking at his mother. She was happy.

A week later, in the early afternoon, Adam with a group of colleagues stood in a crowd on Dzierżyński Square, or rather on Bank Square, because the square was returning to its old, pre-war name. The monument of the executioner, creator of the Soviet repression apparatus, the pride of Polish communism, Feliks Dzierżyński, was being demolished. When the crane hooked the steel ropes around the neck of the monumental statue, the crowd froze. The viewers looked in suspense. Nobody was sure what would happen. They talked about the durability of the monument. Their opinions where that cranes were not strong enough, some said that there was no equipment that could topple it. Dzierżyński will have to be blown up, which could endanger the entire square and all the houses around it. The tension was rising. Meanwhile, the monument came off of the pedestal amazingly easily. Iron Felix soared smoothly up, and individual shouts changed into a choral roar. Dzierżyński was hanging. He was rocking on the ropes. And suddenly it began to crack. "Tear his head off!" Someone in the crowd yelled and at the same moment the stone head of the hero of the revolution broke off and fell from the high above onto the cobblestones, splashing into pieces. People picked up this cry, screamed and went crazy. Risking, under a monstrous concrete block dangling on the ropes, they were collecting the stones from the cobblestones, into which the head of the hero of the revolution changed. A moment later the rest of the monument fell into two parts, the other of which fell to the ground. An unrecognizable fragment of the body hung on the ropes, an anonymous lump of stone. On the orphaned, foreign pedestal, a piece of stone shoe was left that looked as if the owner, fleeing in panic, had left it. As a group they besieged the stone platform, climbing onto its surface, they were singing the Polish anthem.

Adam came home full of joy. Unexpectedly he remembered, Tadek, Uncle Tadek. His lungs squeezed themselves and for a moment he couldn't breathe. He felt a strange feeling, almost pain, which broke into his euphoria. It's so unfair, it was constantly in his head, after all, Tadek, like no one, deserved to see this victory. The image of his mother staring at the photograph of her brother returned to him. He was alone. He didn't have to control his crying. But after all he was happy.

Cold winds brought the first frosts of autumn. At Wenceslas Square, Vaclav Havel, who had been conditionally released from prison a few months earlier, spoke to an immense crowd that densely filled the largest square in Prague. Wenceslas Square, Adam realized, does this mean Havel Square?

Autumn was ending with freezing rain. Winter hit with the cold of snowstorms. Sidewalks were covered with ice on which pedestrians were sliding. An armed revolution began in Romania. There were gunfights in the streets. The marriage of the Balkan satraps who tried to escape was captured and after a strange, short trial, shot. Blood stains solidified on the gray pavement on the TV screen.

On the second day of Christmas, when many guests came to their home, a quarrel broke out. After a few shots his mother began to remind Madej and Stawicki of their inaction in the matter of the security service their burning files. They belonged to a group of advisers, and Stawicki had an important position in the Office of the Council of Ministers.

"Don't you understand that they're destroying our past?! There will be no documents that can reveal what happened behind closed doors during communism. There won't be any evidence!" His excited mother said. Madej tried to calm her down:

"Don't you have the impression that you're focusing too much on the past? Now something else is more important. We're making fundamental economic reforms. This is most important. Only in this way will we change our country. And you're still about that past and its testimonies. Tear yourself away from it! Don't you understand that we overthrew communism?"

"You're saying that the past is unimportant? What happened yesterday isn't important?"

"Yes, this is exactly how it must be approached! Do you know how many problems we have now? Heavy industry, unreformed agriculture, unregulated finances. And you want to occupy us with settling accounts," Stawicki intervened. He was excited as usual. He couldn't keep up with getting rid of words. He was throwing them out with the speed of a machine gun, but to Adam's astonishment, they always formed correct sentences that resulted in another, surrounded, and deprived of the opportunity to answer. "The reds are good for us. They want to cut themselves off from the past. They want to cooperate in the reforms. And you want to antagonize them? Now we have a problem with workers who defend their outdated plants, with peasants who demand the purchase of their products, which they complained about during communism. This is a nation which we have trouble with, not with the communists."

"Why do you oppose these matters?" his mother got nervous. "After all, our situation arises from the past. Do you want to cut yourself off from it?"

"Yes! It would be best to burn these papers!" Stawicki threw out. "You don't even know what's real in there! Anyway, why do we need it! 'Let the dead bury their dead.' You don't remember the Gospel?" He laughed in a strange high voice.

"Only such documents say something about the living," Jerome interjected. "And they are not only with us. They're definitely in Moscow. And God knows where else. I wouldn't lose my head that those who burn them, don't burry the more interesting ones somewhere in their backyard. So, we won't know about it...but others? And you think they won't make use of it?"

"Give it a break with these conspiracy theories" Stawicki got wound up and perorated with passion. "Moscow has so many problems that it cannot deal with itself. Other communist intelligence services no longer exist just like their leaders. So, what's going on? To mess around in the muck that they produced? Do you know what is dangerous? I'll tell you! It's Solidarity that's dangerous today. It wants to take over the function of PZPR. Only that that one is dying. And Solidarity is young and craves power. Everywhere. In workplaces and in the state. And it has a ready, national-Catholic ideology. It wants to take the place of the party. That's the way of things. Don't you see this threat?"

There was a moment's silence. Adam knew that many present were still involved in Solidarity and had important functions in it. They were stunned by Stawicki's attack. Madej intervened.

"You know Igor. He doesn't pick at his words. But after all he indicates a real danger. And we have to think about it so that it doesn't become concrete. Any of you who licked a bit of sociology or made some observations can identify the mechanism which Igor points out. And can bring up such a threat from their own experiences.

"Wait a minute, wait a minute. After all, Solidarity guarantees these reforms...If it wasn't for it..." Marcus shrugged his shoulders.

"Still. Don't you know about the constant pressure to make a cadre revolution?!" Stawicki didn't let his arguments be beaten. "They demand constant changes, the resignation of professionals to replace them with ours..."

"Something strange, these professionals are exclusively from communist stock..." someone noted.

"And if it is that way? You have to use them, and not dig into their past."

Adam realized that the quarrels were getting more and more serious, they're settling into memories, starting to weigh on relationships. When Stawicki and Madej were leaving, that first one brought up the fanatics. Adam heard this word for the first time, which since then he will hear more and more often.

Discussions tired and disappointed him. He believed that they had won, and everything would finally become easier. In the meantime, it turned out that the number of problems was increasing, those who should be together are arguing, and he doesn't even know who to agree with. He would instinctively want to stand by his mother's side, but he was tired of her eternal dissatisfaction, bitterness, which consumed everything and poisoned all the joy that he wanted and had the right to feel. The communists lost, and in Poland it should finally be as it should be. Meanwhile, his mother was looking for a hole in the assembly, as she busied herself with contemplating the past, she was complaining. She was constantly complaining. Adam desired someone to finally organize his world. To explain, as in the past, which side is right. Only who was supposed to do this? He felt a growing distance from his parents. And Tadek was dead. He missed him so much now. His mother talked about the theft of state assets by old commies. When they were still coming over, Stawicki and Madej, because they had actually stopped appearing for some time, explained that it's impossible to avoid the anatomy of revolutionary changes.

"Would you want to supervise everything?! To control it?! After all it's neither possible nor sensible. Freedom and the natural processes that are its consequence come to the surface with its dirt! Do you want to sterilize them? They'll die!" perorated Stawicki.

"No, I want to introduce some order, elements of justice!"

"You're constantly going off about justice. A Robespierre in a skirt. You want to go in that direction?"

His mother was getting annoyed and wasn't finding the right words. Sometimes Jerome supported her.

"Is it because corruption exists that you want to sanction it?"

"No. I want to see it in a reasonable perspective as a margin. And dealing with the margin cannot overshadow the essential matters. And you are all into your "Rennaissance", with this affairmania...Don't you understand that we should accelerate and not slow down market processes? Only in this way will we boost the economy, and you all want to justly share poverty..."

A war came to the upstairs and the whole group of former guests stopped coming over. Adam's mother along with him were happy that he got into high school, but he felt that other matters were absorbing her. He even felt a kind of sorrow, though he explained to himself that he was just as sure of his competence as she was.

His father, whom he had not visited for several months, had clearly aged.

"You know, I would want to buy you something," he said awkwardly. "A present. Do you want a bike or maybe a computer?" Adam chose the computer. "I understand, at your age, you would want things to be simple. Only they sure as hell aren't" his father spoke exceptionally rapidly for him. He walked nervously, puffing on a cigarette. It was somehow empty in his apartment. Adam wanted to ask about Kalina, but something stopped him. "We should somehow get along, all of us, try to rebuild this country together, and not settle our alleged or even real faults. So much evil has risen here. Let's try to free ourselves from it, not multiply it."

Mother watched the election in the editorial office. She came home quite late, tipsy.

"Are you happy that you took care of Mazowiecki?" Adam said angrily. His mother did not look delighted.

"I'm glad he got the red card. But the fact that that UB shaman from Peru overtook him disturbs me. It's their fault too. Those friends of ours whom you have recently seen here, and it seemed to you, or at least to me, that we know them so well. It's them who led to it, that people have become cross wired in their heads and are looking for saviors from another dimension, and they no longer see who has adopted them."

The second round of elections ended in an obvious way. Adam wasn't able to enjoy it.

"You rarely visit your father lately," said his mother later with a strange smile. "Maybe you should," she laughed unpleasantly. "He's lonely. It bothers you. He's getting a divorce, or rather his wife is divorcing him." Adam felt ashamed for his mother.

In his father's home, which was usually so orderly, a mess broke out. Adam came without notice. The first snow had just fallen. His father was probably drunk. Unshaven, in a stained, wrinkled shirt, on which he pulled on a felt, sweater buttoned in the front, he was thrashing around the apartment, as if he wanted to get out of it. Adam couldn't remember seeing him in a state like this before.

"Oh, well...Nice to see you, son. You don't remember me often. I should be glad that you do at all. So I'm happy, I'm happy... '' His father stepped up to him with an almost dancing step, embraced him, kissed his head. Adam was embraced by the smell of nicotine and alcohol. "Your mother won. And I...I probably deserved what'll happen to me. Because there'll be an acceleration of things, right? Those like me they'll fire. After we've earned it. They'll dissolve the 'Republic'. Or maybe... maybe court proceedings await us... Maybe rightly?" His father was hiding his head in his arms, making strange sounds which could imitate laughter. "I don't fit into this new world anyway. I have too much doubt. I'm myself doubt. Anyway...It's difficult to classify me as a real Pole."

He was saying something else, but Adam stopped listening. He wanted to leave as soon as possible. Under the unbearable irony of his father fear reigned. He had the impression that his father's hands were shaking. For a moment his father had trouble with lighting a cigarette. Adam felt a violent aversion towards him, which involuntarily turned into contempt for this shaky, old man. He was looking at his face. Against his will, with some unpleasant malicious passion he saw him transform into his own caricature. His nose was lengthening, his lips were bulging. He felt dislike toward his father and was ashamed of himself. He had enough of his parents: a panicked man and his mother, an aged woman, consumed with sorrow and resentment. Almost without saying goodbye, he ran out of his father's apartment, who tried to keep him. He unconsciously walked the streets for a long time. People indifferently rushed to their affairs, they were unfamiliar and unpleasant. Aware of their power over men, girls in groups chirped and laughed. Couples snuggled up conspicuously. Behind the glowing glass of the cafes, groups of friends always played out the same performances. Adam felt aversion to them all. Unrecognized by anyone, he lonely carried the feeling of his own worth. He was a stranger here. He had never felt his own individuality before this way. Thrown into a world averse to him. Even the winter air chased and cornered him. He returned home late at night, cold and tired.

"What happened?" His irritated mother kept asking him.

He dismissed her and locked himself in his room. He couldn't fall asleep for a long time. Loneliness had the taste of rust.

***

And then everything accelerated even more. A new prime minister, new parties and new people appeared. His mother didn't look victorious. Political normality turned out to be noisy, vague and unpleasant. The adult world was a hypocritical game of power and profit. His mother was right. But what about it, was she right? Politics had become dirty and repulsive again. The adult world was alluring, but also repelling. His mother had little time, but even Adam didn't really want to enter into deeper conversations with her. Perhaps his father and mother's former friends who stopped visiting her were right, and in any case they did it less and less often? She became bitter and could not overcome her resentments. Perhaps his father understood the basic thing when he claimed that there was no need to deal with politics, which was reduced more and more, would remain a game on the surface, a clash for a smaller and smaller sphere of power, and the important things will be happening somewhere else?

Adam's longings, thoughts and dreams were filled with women. Those from movies and television, from stills and commercials, as well as from pornographic films that he watched together with colleagues. Unattainable women, although it was so easy for others. There were also girls from class and school. They attracted and repelled. They aroused fascination and aggression. He was starting to date them. Breaking through his shyness, he had his first kisses and caresses on a park bench or in the late stages of a party, which began to really start up, and couples were being lost in the dark, in the corners of the room, on couches, armchairs and couches. He dreamed of gratification, but the girls slipped away. Sometimes it seemed so close to the final moment, but it slipped out from his hands. He dreamed of satisfaction, so that he would not have to do it with himself. He promised himself that he would quit this degrading addiction, but after a few days, after a week the promises would break under the pressure of his raging organism. Every now and then he was struck by female beauty beyond sexual desire. Face, movement, gesture. He saw slender fingers, and his skin waited for their touch, which didn't carry with itself any other promise and was a goal in itself. Beauty became tenderness and understanding, a dream of transforming the world.

Second grade of high school was beginning. The September evening was still warm. Opening the door, Adam felt something unusual was happening.

"Come, come quickly" his mother called him.

The ashtray was full. His mother and Jano sat at the table covered in papers, over already empty tea glasses.

"Listen," his mother said with a clearly changed voice not just because she was trying to give it a solemn tone. Something seemed to bother her words. "You're sixteen now. You should know these facts. After all, Tadek...uncle Tadek was clearly someone close to you..." She probably wasn't waiting for a confirmation, because she continued: "Here's what we learned from the Rokita commission. This is what the police files say: March 5, 1986, at 18:10, someone called the MO police station in Gdańsk. In Motława at the Ołowianka heat and power plant, there was supposed to be a naked corpse of a man in the water. The MO documents, in the case file, there's a report that a telephone call was made by a technician working at the heat and power plant, Lech Zapolnik. Nobody of that name worked there. What's more, after reporting by phone at 18:10 policeman Grzel arrived at the scene of the accident at 17.00! Over an hour earlier. You know" his mother turned to Jano, lighting a cigarette "it is amazing that they cared so little about the details. They must have felt very confident. Of course, this corpse was..." his mother's voice vibrated alarmingly, she stopped, but after a while continued "was Tadek. Your uncle. And what else I learned... Tadek was butchered...I saw him after all. I read the description of the injuries...There were more of them than I managed to see in time. Doctors from the Department of Forensic Medicine of the Medical University of Gdansk deemed that Tadek drowned. Supposed bloating of the vesicles in the lungs attested to this which is characteristic of this type of death. All wounds were to be inflicted by the screws of ships sailing on the Motława River. It's they that were supposed to rip off his clothes, because he was found naked. It is on the basis of these data that the prosecutor's office discontinued the investigation on April 25 that same year. They were in a hurry. Tadek arrived in Gdansk on January 11. That was when he was last seen. There are rumors going around that he drank and while drunk fell into Motława on the night of that same day. Such a version, as hypothetical, appears in the prosecutor's decision. January was freezing cold then. The Rokita Commission checked. The Motława was definitely frozen until the end of January. By what miracle would Tadek have drowned in the channel on which skaters were sliding on at that time? He would've sooner frozen on the ice. It is amazing that they don't want to give the Commission SB documents. They are still covered by state secrecy. Two years after the fall of Communism, in a supposedly free Poland. It's all unbelievable, but we'll snatch it out from them even if we have to make a revolution again!" His mother's face shrank into a cross grimace, but Adam was captivated. This was the mother, whom he loved.

However, weeks and months passed, and in Tadek's case nothing went forward.

The next parliamentary elections came and there are negotiations about who will become prime minister. Adam stopped being interested. His uncle's case stood in place. It was a June evening. He was escorting Angelica and, as usual, they were making out in front of her house. They've been dating each other for about a month. She'd been flirting with him for a while. She irritated him with her recklessness, empty cheerfulness, and laughter for no reason. Sometimes, however, when he explained the hypocrisy of the adult world, and she listened to his tirades, beneath her gaze he sensed a depth that was hidden on a daily basis. Her beauty could not be just a mask. Anyway, even her cheerfulness could be endearing.

They stopped in front of the gate. It was late. They kissed for a long time.

"I'll still come inside," he suggested.

"But my parents are there..." she objected uncertainly.

"Only for a moment," he insisted, himself not really knowing why.

"And...you are," remarked Angelica's father, tearing himself away from the television for a moment. Her mother was also staring at the screen in suspense. "It's good that you escorted Angelica home."

"We still have to go over tomorrow's history test," she murmured, leading him into her room. Her parents didn't pay attention.

"Oh, Walesa came!" Her mother called out. "They're recalling Olszewski now."

Someone proposed a motion to postpone the vote. On the screen, in the parliamentary room, a fever was rising. The deputies shouted over each other, someone tried to get to the rostrum, and the marshal tried to control the ever-growing chaos. Adam casually glanced at the television, which his hosts had their eyes glued on, and gently closed the door to the room behind him.

"Don't be so sure..." it came to him as he was turning Angelica on her bed "Olszewski can still take it..."

Angelica barely defended herself as he slipped his hand between her thighs, pulled her panties off, catching the sounds coming from her parents' room. Olszewski was speaking now. Angelica grunted quietly, not knowing whether in protest or approval...

"I believe that the Polish nation should feel that among those who rule it, there are no people who helped the UB and SB keep Poles enslaved. I believe that former collaborators..."

Angelica moaned louder. Adam, concerned, covered her mouth with his hand. He was already in her and everything was so obvious...

"He's right," came the voice of Angelica's Father, "after all it's obvious."

"Well yes, but he ordered to print more money..." the woman was explaining something. The world was flowing away from Adam...

"How do you know?"

"I saw it in 'The Word'"

"Well, unless so..."

They pulled apart from each other.

"You must go now," Angelica whispered, brushing his face with her lips.

"Good night," Adam announced.

"Goodnight. Look they recalled him."

"Maybe it's good. Finally, this row will end."

Adam had the impression that he was floating above the streets. He couldn't remember how he had walked the entire way. In the apartment, his mother, with an unmoving, pale face, stared at the dead TV.

"Catastrophe," she declared.

CHAPTER 4

So much time had passed, and everything changeed beyond recognition. Repeatedly things happened that, which couldn't happen. The world, which was to finally, once and for all follow a specific path, once again surprised and rushed into the unknown. Everything was cloaked in new shapes, it was transformed so much that it was difficult for Adam to believe in the reality of what happened in his youth and in himself in the chaos of that era. All the more so he was trying to decipher the sense of events that shaped his existence and the meanings of his choices, which would appear less and less obvious over the years. He wanted to understand himself from that time, the teenage and then twenty-year-old Adam Brok, who desired to shape his fate, excitedly use the freedom he gained rapidly or something that he then labeled.

His mother was tiring him more and more. An increasingly greater hostility was created by the repeated and intensifying over time, of the longer and longer litanies of greivences towards old friends, which she poured out on her son, or rather in his presence which for him seemed only a pretext for something else. The allegations piled up. Conformism, weakness, environmental chauvinism and egoism were only the foundation on which his mother-built edifice to condemn the apostates, those who were recently so close to them. Their faults became proportional to participation in the creation of a new state, which his mother did not recognize as her own. Adam couldn't listen to it. He couldn't believe that comrades in arms would change so much after victory, that for incomprehensible reasons they would go to the dark side of the force, at that moment, when it was defeated. Conversation with his mother became almost impossible. Adam reacted only when he couldn't stand it anymore, when the accusatory speech rose to its apogee. Then he exploded.

"Everyone's guilty, just not you! You are the only saint among sinners! And you're always right!" He interrupted her, almost shouting. His mother was surprised and she dropped her rapture, falling silent for a moment only to attack him a second later with passion, as if he represented all of her former friends who had left her alone by the holy fire of their once mutual fight.

"What do you know!" She called out. "They hate competition. They deny us not so much the reason as the right to exist! They go into sleazy deals, and they call every criticism hate speech! They humiliate us on a daily basis and want to exterminate us from the public sphere. They offer us such tolerance! And the mindless herd prefers to repeat after them rather than confront themselves with the painful truth. And you're joining this choir?!"

The once crowded house slowly emptied. Only a handful of the old guests remained. Jerome was always there, less and less often Krzysiek Markus. The group from "Renaissance" came: Ela Patkiewicz, Witek Kuźnar, Tomek Bąk, sometimes someone else. Sometimes Danka Brak or Agnieszka Pelikan would drop in. From time to time his mother's former boss would visit from the 'Portico', Łukasz Alski. More and more rarely came those with whom his mother's conversation was interrupted by longer and longer moments of hard silence. Igor Stawicki would still come by, whose disputes with his mother turned into stormy quarrels.

Adam was more and more convinced that he was only a mirror for her monologues. It irritated him additionally, or maybe above all. The contraction of his existence to excuse was offensive, and his mother began to resemble the objects of common jokes, examples called foolish, funny and dangerous characters. Her lips twisted into a neither ironic nor painful grimace with an inseparable cigarette, contemptuous snorts with which she commented on television reports, statements of experts and commentators, and newspaper articles. After all, everyone could not be wrong, the monitor could not be only a screen behind which the powerful were playing their games. Poles overthrew communism, took power into their own hands. Was it to give their fate to those same characters in new costumes?

The leitmotif of his mother's monologues was the case of Tadek, Adam's uncle. The unexplained death, which his mother considered a homicide, which nobody wanted to take on. Only the 'Renassiance' published an article on this topic. Adam read an analysis of facts that his mother had told him earlier. The prosecutor's office explained that the inaccuracies in the reports were due to confusion in the PPR police.

"Confusion in the militia!" mocked his mother. "The discovery of a corpse was reported by a non-existent man an hour after it occured, and Tadek was drowned in frozen water."

His mother's investigation showed something else. Tadek went to Gdańsk with his friend and colleague from the underground, Andrzej Molnar. His mother found him.

"He's was agent," she said firmly, lighting another cigarette. "We've been looking for witnesses for years. We announced it in the underground press, and then in the above ground press. He never came forward. I learned recently and actually accidentally that he went with Tadek. I got a hold him. Of course, he's doing great. He's the owner of a thriving publishing house. He made a big deal of seeing me. He didn't hide his irritation: 'What are you accusing me of? I've never talked about my stay in Gdansk because it was not related to the case. I knew Tadeusz Sokoł well and therefore, when it turned out that each of us had something to take care of in Gdańsk, we went together. He didn't confide in me what he was going there to do. It wasn't fashionable at the time to ask about such things.' His mother mocked Molnar's voice furiously: 'I never talked about it because it was not related to your brother's death. We just went together. We returned separately. I mean, it turned out that I came back.' Cold son of a bitch!" She wheezed, ignoring the convention's dear to Adam's heart, in effect at home.

The prosecutor's office did not want to go back to the investigation. The Interior Ministry refused to release the files. After further prompts, 'Renassiance' received the answer that release of documents in the possession of the ministry would not bring anything to the case. Formerly, influential friends refused to intervene in it. "We have a state that follows the rule of law. After all, we can't just put pressure on independent institutions because it concerns one of us. In this way we will ruin what we are building, a new, in our state!" His mother spat at those quotes: "ours, ours!" she almost sang, quoting Madej or Stawicki.

She had the right to be bitter. The investigation was not move forward. Did it however pass sentences too quickly? Did her pain not dictate hasty interpretations according to which law enforcement agencies generally avoided explaining the dark sides of the Polish People's Republic? "Conspiracy theory" his colleagues would say if he explained his mother's interpretation. He thought that this term made a choice and allowed one to refuse to connect facts and dig deeper into them. Did it not, however, also protect against immersed in endless associations, falling into a past that could not be changed anyway, and therefore dealing with it does not make much sense?

"The world is so complex that we can always juxtapose different events and treat them as an illustration of arbitrary combination" explained his father. "Yesterday I saw the Jaguar of my former editorial colleague, Kazik Niecnota, who was the spokesman for the general parked in the area of Redeemer Square, but he made his real career now, in free Poland, now he's a millionaire, editor and owner of the magazine 'In the Face'. So, at the same moment where Niecnota's Jaguar was parked, I saw Bogatyrowicz, who was walking in his direction. It was already dark, and I didn't notice if he got into the convertible which left immediately. Of course, one could draw the conclusion that they wanted to meet up. One could start comparing articles that appeared at that time in 'The Word' and 'In the Face', noticing their similarities and differences, consider the strategies that editors took to carry out their ideas and write it out in their titles, and always such relationships can be found and acknowledge since discussions with each other are constant. But it could've been, and probably was, just a coincidence. Bogatyrowicz passed by the car, or maybe just Niecnota, who stopped there for other reasons, offered to give him a ride. They had a meaningless chat in the car. A coincidence and that's it. How many incredible coincidences happen in our lives? Look at these people."

They sat in the garden of the "Literary' Café", observing crowds of passers-by strolling in the spring afternoon at Castle Square.

"They look at each other, look around and position themselves in regard to each other. Men stare at women flirt with them or keep them at a distance. You don't need a lot of imagination to trace the intrigue under these inadvertant gestures and looks. Look at this forty-year-old with a camera. You can immediately see that he is a foreign tourist. He's gawking at that attractive girl who sometimes returns his gaze. The guy wonders whether to approach. He hesitates. She gives him a look. Coincidence, provocative? Earlier, she was exchanging sly glances with a young man who was watching them while they were leaning on the balustrade over the W-Z Route. Look. The girl is slowly moving away. The tourist follows her. Filming. The young man moves away from the balustrade. He walks a little to the side, but maybe so no one realizes that he's following them. Nobody, except the girl he's in league with. Maybe they are hunting rich tourists?" His father laughed. "And after all those figures will lose sight of each other as soon as they leave our field of view." And this German or American will remember the girl only after watching a movie from Warsaw. Or maybe it'll be different?"

Adam couldn't remember his father being in such a good mood. He's always happy when his son visits, but it seldom provokes in him such a good mood and almost never did it last for so long.

The 'Renassiance', which his mother co-created, functioned only as an object of jokes among Adam's peers. It was "pathetic" and could only be invoked with compulsory irony. It was a hollow publication, people immersed in the past who could not understand the present, were still conducting battles with non-existent communism and arguing about past matters. Gray-haired, unshaven bearded men in stretched sweaters and old, unkempt women with faces shrunken in resentment, with a cigarette with their thin and still contorted lips. They were surrounded by the smell of bad perfume and cheap tobacco. Actually, his mother's perfume was good, even though it was dominated by and fought by the smell of cigarettes. She tried to look good, although she didn't always remember to and certainly didn't follow fashion. Well, and she was getting older, which was hard not to notice.

While the opinions expressed by his mother were the object of mockery in all the environments in which Adam found himself. Then he had to come to her defense. He provoked amazement, disbelief, indignation, and all the more provocatively defended her not fully thought through judgments and assessments. He quickly realized that, despite his fears, he was not in a hopeless position. His opponents, peers, and even teachers, voiced with absolute sureness their opinions, in whose defense they could only cite their obviousness. He was surprised to discover how poorly justified these universally accepted truths are.

Sometimes, amazingly, he realized that he was indeed finding himself on his mother's side. On television, he saw old acquaintances and had the impression that something had transformed them, fundamentally changed them, although they looked the same at first glance. They said they're defending fundamental values. They were getting upset responding to unsubstantiated allegations. They thundered at populism, xenophobia and hatred. They stigmatized hypocrisy. Their gazes were strange, their movements had an almost mechanical character, something alien was creeping into the gestures...Adam saw it in the film *Invasion of Body Snatchers*. Unknown beings entered people and took control of them. Characters that seemed and behaved as before were no longer the same people, or even human. They were members of an alien swarm nested under their skin. Something difficult to grasp, however, distinguished them from people whose bodies they colonized. Adam had the impression that those whom he had recently so admired had a similar transformation. He explained to himself that his feelings were caused by his mother's accusations. She maintained that former friends had fallen victim to their own hypocrisy and perversion, which led them to crossing the furthest border, to betrayal. Maybe that's why Adam couldn't free himself from looking at them in a specific way. Despite the efforts he made, a sense of abnormality remained.

When they sometimes appeared at their home, Adam could see this change even more clearly. It was abnormal. He couldn't capture what provoked his impression, but it was getting stronger. Maybe it was the looks he sometimes caught, a little surprised, maybe contemptuous, different? He never had the courage to talk about it with his mother. He was afraid of an explosion of further accusations, perceptions that didn't explain anything to him, but only deepened his state of confusion. He wanted to run away from it, and his mother irritated him more and more. Their disputes turned into quarrels, especially since she instantly reacted aggressively to his opposition.

"They made you already! Huh! Your father explained to you that everything is as it should be in this best of worlds? And if we believed him, believed just like him, then communism would still last. But now...We live in a lie. We overthrew a dictatorship to sink into a lie! Falsehood is comfortable, warm...I can see that even you are starting to get bogged down in it..."

He hated that tone of his mother's, of screaming and anger. Especially since he wasn't able to answer otherwise. Unexpectedly, he realized that he was raising his voice, screaming. At such moments he ran out of the house. And his mother was more and more depressed, more and more gloomy and grumpy.

He started senior year of high school when the post-communists won the parliamentary elections. His mother was shocked. For Adam, who was now no longer interested in politics, old passions echoed. He felt regret, almost pain. The situation was simply unimaginable. How could Poles choose those who deprived them of their freedom and dignity for decades? And despite these feelings, his mother saying the same thing out loud caused irritation.

"How's this possible?!" She repeated, waving a cigarette and running around the house. "How's it possible that can they forget after less than four years!"

"You all fucked-up at your own request!" He reacted, maliciously repeating that, which he had heard somewhere. "After all, the Commies won only twenty percent, it's you who ruined the chance, scattered into so many parties..."

"You're right, but to a lesser extent!" His mother snorted. "In fact, such as Bogatyrowicz, Stawicki, Madej, your father as well are responsible! It's them who explained that the post-communists are a normal party..."

Everything repeated itself even more severely two years later, after Kwaśniewski was elected president. This time his mother was brought home by Hieronim. She was drunk. Hieronim partly walked her and partly carried her into their home, casting embarrassed and apologetic glances in Adam's direction. Dangling on his shoulder, he dragged her with difficulty into her bedroom, after which he backed away, muttering vague farewells and explanations. The strange pair, which Adam saw through the opening door, caused him to instinctively go to help. However, he stopped halfway there. A cold fury swept over him. At such moments he could hate his mother. Without saying anything, motionlessly he watched Hieronim's struggles. After he left, he stood at the door of his mother's room. He was looking at an old, drunk woman scattered on the futon, on which she poured out the contents of her purse in order to dig out a cigarettes and lighter from it. She looked unconscious. The tousled hair around her head gave her a gorgon-like appearance. She was saying something to herself. Then she looked at her son. Her gaze became more conscious.

"Everything's fucked-up!" She threw out to herself.

He went out to his room. He lit a cigarette, then passionately crushed it against the lighter. He isn't going to smoke, he decided. In England, where everything was in its place, people smoked less and less. He'll reject the addiction that united his parents. Actually, a lot connected them, although they're so different and so deadly divided. They were entwined by a strange knot, he thought. He actually wanted to talk to his mother about what happened, but when he saw her, he lost the inclination. It was probably impossible anyway, and now his mother is already sleeping in a heavy drunken sleep and he'll have to check if she didn't leave a lit cigarette somewhere.

A few hours passed since midnight and he couldn't sleep. He felt an internal shiver. It surprised and upset him even more. Everything happened at once: his mother's state and the earlier quarrel with Anka.

It was still evening, and no one knew who had won. They were sitting over beer in an indifferently humming pub. Adam confided that he's more than he would've ever supposed concerned about the outcome of the election. Perhaps because he would never before have thought that Poles could elect a communist as president. In the middle of his monologue, Anka said in an amused tone:

"I voted for Kwach."

"Whaaat?" For a moment he didn't know if the girl was provoking him, or maybe he misheard…

"So what? I was supposed to vote for that country bumpkin to be president for the next five years? I don't want to, but I have to..." she was mocking Walesa's intonation.

Only after a moment did Adam find the words. He let out an angry mockery. He called Anka an idiot. He was almost shouting that such chicken brains, having no idea what they were doing, were destroying elementary principles and introducing chaos. Only then did the astonished girl regain her voice. Now she was shouting that she didn't ask for such a tone and that he was the idiot, the true son of his mother. He ran out of the pub and finally on the street, walking home, did he realized how much he hoped that he would take Anka home and that they'd make love, indifferent to the whole world and the result of the election. Then it was only worse. The first returns were still giving Wałęsa the victory, but over time the candidates began to get closer to each other and around midnight everything was already clear. Kwaśniewski won.

Above a subsequent cup of tea in the kitchen, Adam stared at the blurred outline of the trees in the autumn night outside the window. Everything was losing its meaning. Poles could've chosen a communist creep because of a few marketing tricks, a blue shirt and talks about how everything can be easy, pleasant and trouble-free. So maybe the solemn memories of Solidarity and national uprisings were only youthful exaltation? He should get out of here. Leave the country that scoffs at itself, break away from stupid compatriots, stupid like Anka. He looked once more into the night: truthfully nothing connects him to this country except resentment. He'll leave his parents behind, Anka, the triumphant commies. Free, on an island he will depend only on himself and will only settle accounts with himself.

He opened the window. A damp chill crept into the kitchen. Adam felt as it permeated his body. He beheld the night of barely drawn shadows, which he knew so well. Chestnuts, maples...his mother taught him about them, how to recognize trees. He had trouble with that. But he remembered how chestnuts and maples looked and distinguished them everywhere. They once looked at them together with his father and mother. They've always been there. Since he was born. And earlier, much earlier. They accompanied his parents. They were witnesses of their relationship. The relationship which he was reconstructing, although in reality the relationship was reconstructing itself in his consciousness beyond his will. This knowledge spontaneously developed, expanded, filled gaps. The memories enveloped him in the autumn aura, settled on his skin, seeped into his blood. They circulated in it like microbes, poisoning him. He should free himself from them, cleanse himself. Then he'll be capable of great things. He'll create himself again. The land of freedom was opening up before him on the island. He'll leave behind a frozen past that forever traps him in its dead cocoon. Freed from it, directed to the future, not limited by anything, he'll finally be someone else, that person whom he wants to become. He'll be like Robinson Crusoe, because the colorful, anonymous crowd around will not tie down or limit him in any way but will only be material that he'll use to chisel out his fate from it.

He visited his father the next day to confirm his decision. He wanted to see his satisfaction and strengthen his dislike for him, for the whole of Poland. But at his father's, as usual, nothing was so obvious. Listening to him, despite himself, Adam found compassion. From the beginning of the nineties - since Kalina left him, something combined in Adam - his father seemed even more torn and lost. He was clearly aging. He could stop caring about himself, which had never happened to him before. Even during the day, his son could clearly smell alcohol on him. In the discussions that broke out when several friends gathered at his place, and which he enticed Adam, he became a more frequent guest of the apartment in Ursynów, where his father was more often a listener. In truth he was able to actively take part, but usually his energy faded quickly, consistent with tangled arguments, fell apart and died. A sudden surge of vigor quickly vanished.

His son's visits always pleased him. He was smiling, trying to fill the role of host, although when there was no one else, they usually went to a cafe or restaurant. There was rarely enough good mood in his father for the whole meeting. When it was approaching the time to go, he got sad, remembered about some not-so-important matters, of which he wanted to share with his son, and Adam wanted to suddenly run away. His father looked at him almost helplessly.

"Yes, you're right, I voted for Kwaśniewski, although I must admit that before placing an x next to his name I hesitated. I did it because I couldn't vote for Wałęsa. Do I have to explain why? I know Olek and actually I like him. I worked with him. But I felt the indecency that he could win, become president. Will it really be reconciliation? Will those like your mother accept it? Even though she doesn't accept anything. After all she has never come to terms with reality," said his father uncertainly, hiding in the cigarette smoke.

"But she changed it!" He threw out, again against his will as embedded in the role of her defender, her son.

"Yes, you're right to a certain extent. Although it wasn't so simple and even one such as Olek, I'm sorry, the newly elected president also took part in it. I know that I speak incoherently, but I wonder...I'm fifty-seven years old, and again I'm not sure...I don't even know why the result of these elections doesn't please me as it should..."

In the evening he reconciled with Anka, although the first attempts almost led to another, even more violent row. In truth, the girl apologized for her comments about his mother and he for the epithets about her, but actually none of them withdrew from what they had said the day before. They didn't truly make up until they were in bed. But while Adam was kissing her goodbye, on the doorstep of her apartment, he felt an intense anxiety again.

He returned home late at night, so he didn't see his mother until the evening of the next day. She was sitting in the kitchen with her back to him, looking out the closed window and smoking a cigarette. He wanted to tell her something, talk with her, but he had no idea how to start. He didn't know exactly what he wanted to tell her. He stood behind her in silence for some time, after which he returned to his room without a word.

***

He never knew how right he was against everyone and everything of his mother's. This position tormented him and over time made it for him more and more difficult to bear. While he rarely saw his father, he never tried to convince him of anything. Directly anyway. They avoided political topics. His father acceptanced Adam's historical passions, bought him books dealing with his son's current fascinations, but discreetly offered other texts as well. He told a tale of economics as the queen of sciences, which would dominate the rest. He suggested to his son that his historical passion was an extension of him playing with soldiers, which with age was transformed into lonely dramas acted out in the forest surrounding Niemir, where, waving a multi-functional stick, Adam incarnated himself into successive roles in dramatic heroic scenarios he invented.

It was hard to disagree with his father. Adam discovered history as a fascinating, multi-dimensional film in which he could participate, tracking the never-fathomed to the end secrets. Getting to know the past events was becoming a continuation of the fun adventure, or actually, the next fun adventure, incomparably more interesting and more thrilling. He ran around in the woods, taking on more and more new roles, changed epochs, fought battles and concluded treaties, escaped from conspirators and plotted intrigues which eliminated enemies, he sailed, built cities and burned them, stirred up revolts only to suppress them.

The father the first guide to the land of history was his father. He told about the places where the three of them went: Wilanów, Łazienki, and Warsaw museums. These were Adam's greatest memories: his beautiful, young mother staring at his father who knows everything and unfolds the worlds hidden behind the shapes of the present, conjures them with hand gestures and guides them, embracing them with care. The world opened up not only in time but also in space. Sobieski fought with the Turks, who were coming in masses from Asia and the Balkans. Bearded men with shaved, turban wrapped heads or clothed in high hats on their heads, with only a strand of hair on the left, coming from the east and south, shaking spears and crooked sabers. Under green flags they conquered cities and defeated Christian states. In a battle with them the Polish King Warneńczyk fell, who stopped the Turks, but the betrayal of his allies led to defeat, and his head was brought to the Sultan. In the defense of Hungary their king, another Jagiellon, Ludwik was killed. The Turks are moving further, besieging Vienna. It's saved by the charge of the winged Polish cavalry, the hussars. Sobieski breaks the power of the Turks, then chases after them. He seizes loot, wonderful tents, banners, ornate weapons. In Łazienki, a hundred years later, they're already in another era, and the stone Sobieski, who trampled beaten infidels before its entrance, is only a historical memory. Poland is weak and King Stanisław August is trying to lift it from collapse. His mother protests: "He was a weak king, who betrayed" but his father explains that this was not always the case and history is complex. His mother just resisted too much to give way. Adam is fascinated with her unusual behavior. He prefered that his father not go deep into the complications of history, which on a closer look turn out to be an almost incomprehensible charade. From his father's stories images are left to him, and not complicated connections between events. The winged riders fly from the hills above the city, the Turks flee in panic.

Adam is glad that his parents are not arguing as they did at home. In the matter of history, his mother leaves the final word to his father. Only sometimes did she describe the appearance of places and explained where their shapes come from; which completes Adam's vision.

His father buys him colorful history books. They take turns reading fragments of *The Knights of the Cross* aloud with his mother. Adam tried to explore the book himself, discovering the complex relationships of words, sentences and meanings. This is where he learned to read. The novel was fascinating, although sometimes terrible. The Teutonic Knights nest in the snow-covered stone strongholds. They are like ruthless birds of prey falling on the local population. In underground dungeons they keep those who dared to resist them, they torture them, kill them. And finally, there is a great battle that will break the power of evil, and the black and white coats will cover the earth. Colorful knights' triumph under a banner with a white eagle. On television, Adam saw the movie that illustrated the book and delighted his eyes. He also watched adaptations of other Sienkiewicz novels: *The Deluge* and *Colonel Wołodyjowski*. He learned how huge Poland was then, and maybe that's why so many enemies attacked her. This great country could nevertheless deal with them. It stretched from the snowy, dark backwoods of Samogitia, where Kmicic's company raged, to the sunburnt steppe, on hot stones where Nowowiejski, sick from the desire for revenge, hunted for Azja.

Adam read *The Trilogy* by Sienkiewicz and immediately after it Tolkien's trilogy *The Lord of the Rings*, from which he also couldn't tear himself away. At times it seemed to him that Mordor was ruled by knights with black crosses on white coats. Only that the Teutonic Knights were real, he explained to himself the return to history. He had already read illustrated history books. The fascination with the ancient East came from there. At the same time, he sailed with Sinbad on the seas of the *Thousand and One Nights*. It drew him in, the foreign and the unknown. He watched winged bulls and demons. Lions, full of arrows, dragged their paralyzed bodies across the ground to fall prey to the spears and swords of Assyrian rulers. Nineveh's glory rose so high that it would soon be incinerated, bursting into flames in the night sky for the last time. Earlier, however, it reached west, into the secret world of the desert, where thousands of years ago the largest buildings of that time rose up, which were to be the shelters for the dead. Between them, between their sands and the two rivers of Mesopotamia, the refugees from Egypt built their little kingdom around a city with a temple in the middle which was to become a secret center of the world, changing its shape. God chose a small in number, insignificant tribe to tell it the truth. And it is in this tribe that God will be born. He came into the world to a chosen nation, becomes human, dies and rises from the dead - the vortex of secrets opens into the abyss, over which Adam prefered not to lean. He prefered to accompany Cyrus, who coming from the east occupies almost the whole world, to die in an endless steppe at the hands of elusive barbarians. Then Adam will jump ahead two hundred years, he'll negate them, in order to follow a young Macedonian hero who in ten years conquers everything that could be conquered, and dies in Babylon aware that with him the dream of one kingdom of all peoples is lost, although his companions in arms will stand to a bloody showdown between each other, trying to tear it up for themselves.

Over time, he'll be interested in more recent epochs and lands. From the battlefield of Cannae, where the triumphant Hannibal seemed to throw Rome on his knees, to only fifteen years later bear the final defeat at their hands, from Rome falling under the blows of barbarian; from William, who leaping from a long boat, thrust his hands into the sand of England, crying: "I take possession of this land and just someone try to tear it out for me", after that the characters on revolving stage of the French Revolution, successively depriving themselves of their heads like puppets at the Grand Guignol.

His choice of college as the Warsaw School of Economics surprised everyone, and partly Adam himself. The decision matured in him for a long time, but he made it quickly and almost at the last moment. He rejected history, just as one closes the door to a child's room full of fascinating games and toys, which, however, should not obscure or even replace reality. We leave them with regret, but with the clear awareness that one has to say goodbye to the childhood era, the carefree constant mask ball in a world in which things are weightless and meaningless. This is how Adam gave up on history, which he considered a game, although it has seemed to everyone, since forever, his future profession. He realized that it was just a staged play in an unchanging shape, which no one can change in any way.

The exam went well for Adam. Besides he never feared it despite the chilling stories and the intimidating number of candidates for one place. Challenges excited him. Mathematics never presented a difficulty for him. It enticed him like a complicated game that he wanted to face and knew that he could meet it. Economics became his second subject of interest since his early childhood, when his father presented it to him as a fascinating tale of hidden spells that could change reality. Later on, in these ramblings, Adam's later college advisor, Professor Sławomir Mucha, initiated him at his father's apartment. And after all, just before the submitting the application, going to college for economics didn't seem real to Adam. It was not even about the fact that he would have to give up for it the fascination that accompanied him since childhood, which culminated in the profession of a historian, more sensational than the work of a detective. Dreams of tracking the secrets of the past, revealing its successive layers had already begun to fade and reveal their illusoriness. At the same time, however, Adam realized that changing his studies and profession was a fundamental shift in the reversal of his life. He had been considering this fundamental metamorphosis for at least two years. He entertained himself, imagining the consequences, but did not find enough conviction to make it, and probably didn't even believe that he would do it.

Economics was abstract, universal, mathematical. It existed beyond history and allowed it to tear itself away from it, enabling it to break with the land that bound it, rooted in the never-ending past. His change of studies was the first stage of leaving the Poland which was full of his mother's sorrows and his father's fears.

His father had a part in Adam's choice, but the final decision - once again he realizes it after so many years - was due to the need to free himself, escape from the world in which his mother and father fought their inexorable battle over him. The ruse of his father was that by giving him a chance to get out of the hopeless fatalism of the past, in which his mother was imprisoned, he overcame her. He won. Although he too was immersed in this reality, engrossed in it completely. He's only unsuccessfully trying to distance himself from his involvements, Adam thought sometimes. Maybe that's why he wanted to spare his son this? You are not doomed to anything, he seemed to say to Adam, though he never said it directly. You can shape your life and free yourself from the ghosts of the past, he whispered silently. And Adam followed his suggestions, although he felt that in this deep, dispute with his mother not named by his father, that she was right. She was right, but what came of it? He could ask such questions to himself then, though he could not justify them: neither why he was admitting that his mother was right, nor why it had no consequences.

Those things which his father did not say, Bruno Klein proclaimed extremely eloquently and directly. He was probably always his father's mentor, who he introduced to Adam while he was still in high school. The famous intellectual fascinated the boy. His words freed up stunning viewpoints. Maybe that's why Adam's father didn't have to convince him of anything?

For vacation after the second and third grades of high school Adam went to London. His father arranged a language school for him. England exhilarated him. As in a trance, he roamed the city on the Thames, losing hours and thoughts. He had the impression that everything was in its place when it was exactly the opposite in Poland. London was colorful, crowded and joyful. It was a fulfilled world. It was only from this perspective that he felt the provincial abnormality of Poland. He confided this to his mother, realizing while saying that the answer would be at most a joke. But his mother smiled warmly.

"So what? Are you going to build normality for us?"

Her question was rather a statement and didn't contain the trace of irony so characteristic of her. He didn't answer. He thought that his mother's proposal again chains him to the burden of the past, from which he would like to finally break away. It links it to Poland, which, as Klein used to say, he should overcome in himself. His mother tried to bind him to this country, and he wanted to be free. He'll be free on the island.

Sometimes his mother would say things that would shake Adam. He felt he should get involved. Then, when he regained the distance that helplessness gave, he realized even more clearly that he had to leave, so as not to get bogged down in the hopeless responsibility he could not cope with, which would finally destroy him like his mother.

"I met my old friend," she began as they bumped into each other in the kitchen making tea. Adam noticed that his mother was shocked. This time, she really wanted to tell him something, not just weave her monologues of pain and resentment.

"I met my old friend," she repeated and paused for a moment. To Adam it seemed almost that she was embarrassed and touched her face with her fingers. "I knew him first in Solidarity, Czesiek Biela. I found out about the case through our newspaper. His wife was desperately looking for some contacts. They locked him up..." His mother inhaled some smoke, trying to sort out the story. "He just got out. I talked to him for a few hours. I'll write an article that they will of course ridicule in 'The Word', if they notice it at all. But let's start from the beginning. I met him... but it doesn't matter..." She looked uncertainly at her son. "It was this extraordinary time. Immediately after the release of Janek Narożniak. Well...in the fall of nineteen eighty," she said a little irritated, noticing the surprise on her son's face. "Never mind. Such a young, dynamic worker, very intelligent, though without any education. Somehow, he reminded me of Tadek. Then I met him in the mid-eighties. He just got out of prison. After two and a half years. I'm ashamed of this meeting until today. I didn't even offer him coffee. Finally, he confessed what he really wanted to talk to me about, but he didn't have any money to invite me anywhere, and a conversation in the middle of the street was virtually impossible. I didn't think about it and in general I wanted to run away from him. I didn't even ask why he was limping. They beat him so bad that they damaged his spine. He's a little crippled. He used to be such a strong man..." mother interrupted again. "Then he hesitated whether to emigrate. The UB's pressed him, his wife pleaded. They had two children and had nothing to live on. But he persisted. He decided to stay. Somehow, though with difficulty, he supported himself and his family. Another child was born to them. Toward the end of the Communist times he started to do some businesses. And he was somehow managing. They moved to a small town, where his wife is from. And finally, not long ago, together with their colleagues, they bought a bankrupt state slaughterhouse. They renovated it and reportedly made it the most modern plant in the region. Czesiek even now lights up now when he talks about it. They got into debt, but their prospects were enormous. And then the prosecutor got involved. Czesiek served a year in custody. They released him, it seemed that they'll release him from the charges, but the slaughterhouse went bankrupt. And they went bankrupt. It looks like the matter was organized by their competitors. Czesiek and his partners were not from their organization. From the start, they began pressure them to sell the slaughterhouse to local tycoons who made them an offer. Czesiek says that the prosecutor actually even told him that it was a condition for him to have a truce. He didn't agree to it, and so he went to prison. Now, after that year, when I talked with him, he looked worse than after those almost three years in prison. 'After the overthrow of communism, in my free country,' he repeated sarcastically. I didn't know what to reply to him. He said that the city was run by a post-communist clique. He explained the details, I believe him."

The article on this subject, written by his mother, appeared in "Renassiance" a month later. Not much later, the district prosecutor's office on behalf of Prosecutor Materak, who was one of the characters in the article, sued his mother and the weekly for slander. His mother's trips to subsequent court sessions began, from which she returned increasingly furious. In 'The Word' appeared a article, "Buddies...Above the Law", which clearly showed that 'Renassiance', and especially Zuzanna Brok in the name of combatant loyalty defended her colleagues without worrying about what they did. This leads to attacks on the judiciary, as soon as it dares to treat former Solidarity activists in accordance with the law. Legal and sociological authorities looked at the matter with precaution, recognizing that this is perhaps the most disturbing phenomenon in contemporary Poland: disregarding the law and attempting to create an adversarial classification in order to gain from a privileged position.

His mother and 'Renassiance' were found guilty. The fine was considerable from their perspective, and the apology they had to publish in the weekly was humiliating. His mother said nothing. She was sitting in the kitchen, with a lit cigarette, staring deeply through a closed window at the barely visible trees. Adam sympathized with her and didn't know how to show it. Maybe because he wasn't in the best shape himself. He and Anka were breaking up. He felt helpless and knew that nothing could prevent her. Maybe only run away, leave, start everything over again. To disentangle himself from the vague sense of responsibility that he could not bear.

"I'm pregnant" Anka said it too calmly, playing with a straw with which she was drinking juice from a tall glass in front of her. The cafe was empty and the people at the tables were busy with each other. The girl raised her face and looked into his eyes. Only then did Adam realize that she wasn't joking. She seemed usually different. She didn't flirt, didn't look around to comment on the events and laugh at their participants. Adam fell into a panic. He thought that this is how people who expect something look. They count on a reaction. They want help, advice which is supposed to be support, they desire understanding, acceptance and forgiveness. They always want something. And Adam knew nothing and wasn't finding the strength to do anything. Even his thoughts did not want to form exchanges that he understood. Vague questions flew through his head: about the likelihood of what happened with the contraceptive measures that Anka takes; about that which can be done in this situation, what can he do; he suspects that the girl is playing him; the image of a trap slamming shut on his life, transforming it into vegetation...

"And what...what do you intend to do?" he was putting the words together slowly.

"What do I want to do? I wanted to ask you" something unpleasant sounded in the girl's voice.

"I...I would want to say, that...it's your choice after all...I'll...I'll accept it."

Anka laughed with a voice not her own.

"And you wouldn't accept it?"

"No, after all it's not about that..."

"Sure, that it's not about that. I'm going to have to go now. I have class."

He didn't stop her. The memory of that moment would come back to him. Anka made a gesture that stopped him from getting up and bent forward as if she wanted to kiss him, but only for a moment bringing her frozen face to him and turning away, walked away quite hurriedly, not looking back, although close to the door she slowed down for a moment, or it only seems to Adam, maybe something was blocking her path, because a moment later, that lasts long, far too long, she energetically stepped out of the cafe. They didn't meet until a few days later. She didn't have time before.

It was at the same café again, "Telimena" in the Kraków suburb. A sleepy afternoon. Anka gave him a peck in greeting.

"I've decided. It doesn't make sense. I'll abort it" she said almost without introduction. Adam felt relief. Anka was sure. He realized that he should say something.

"Have you thought this through?"

"What do you think?" She looked at him ironically. This wasn't the girl Adam was used to. "After all I've told you."

"You know…If it's about the operation itself…"

"Give yourself a break. I've found out what's needed. I want, for you to pay for half."

"You know…Maybe you need more…"

"No. I want you to pay for half."

His father didn't ask Adam what the money was for. He gave it to him the next day. And the relationship between Adam and Anka began to break down. They ultimately split up half a year later.

"You're not meeting with Anka anymore?" asked his mother.

"We broke up."

"I guessed. When she was here the last time...I felt that she had resentment toward you. You probably know I never really liked her. But at that moment I felt sorry for her and felt...that she might be right..."

"But you don't know anything about our break-up, just like you didn't know anything about our relationship! Why…"

"You're right" his mother interrupted his angry tirade. "They were only meaningless impressions."

He saw Anka later a few times but decided not to approach her. He came across her by accident, meeting friends when he was visiting the country three years earlier. He was glad, just as she was. That's what it appeared to him then. They agreed to meet up the next day. He went to the meeting strangely uncertain. He felt that it's the result of an unnecessary reflex. She kissed him as a greeting, but he had the impression that he noticed a similar reserve in her. Maybe it was a projection of his state. He noticed the ring on her finger.

"You have a husband?"

"Clearly you see" she replied almost flirtatiously, raising her hand.

"And children?" he probably asked involuntarily, immediately feeling the inappropriateness of the question, which, moreover, Anka's look made him aware. It wasn't friendly.

"No, I don't have any!" she almost growled. "And you?"

"Neither do I," he answered hurriedly, as if he wanted to blur the impression of his question.

Something, however, grew between them, but perhaps the meeting was simply a misunderstanding. Anka perfunctorily talked about her career at the cosmetics company. She even asked a few questions about Adam's life story. She didn't seem interested. Despite the similarity, this is another person, he thought, looking at the cloudy physiognomy of the woman on the other side of the table who pouted as he tried to talk about himself in a playfully interesting way. She took advantage of a pause which was to increase the tension.

"I'll have to go now. I have classes," she said, rising and leaning towards him as if she wanted to kiss him. She didn't do it though.

CHAPTER 5

"Our reality is fluid," said Klein with a specific singing song. "It's slips out of our hands. It causes fear. For the first time on such a scale all permanent forms of our existence, all points of support, faith and rules have dissolved. We're desperately trying to grab the substance of life that cannot be grasped. We sink deprived of the land of certainty. The drowning person would give everything as a point of anchor. Hence the sudden, new careers of old illusions, strong identities, the search for community, order of existence, and natural law. But this is gone, and it cannot be rebuilt! There is a liquid world. Rivers of transubstantiation. We can convince ourselves that somewhere there are permanent points of support that the current of existence has ripped out from under our feet. However, these are delusions that save us from despair, but not drowning. Relishing the current of existence, we'll believe that there is a hard land somewhere that carries salvation, a ground of unshakable certainties. But there is one rescue. To learn to swim in the foamy current of life, learn to live in a world of post-modern risk. Old beliefs give the illusion of shelter. Even a makeshift marina can be built on their impermanent foundations. However, the inevitable and imminent catastrophe will be much worse, it is hopeless. Meanwhile, the current of life opens before us new, stunning perspectives. Swimming with it, we begin to really live in it. We are free, detached from everything, without any ready form. Nothing is the ultimate truth, so everything is possible. We create ourselves and our world. Our life becomes an aesthetic act, a work of art. Beyond religions and ideologies, identities and identifications, beyond hierarchies and standards, we achieve freedom that allows us to live our lives like a mystical act, to unite with it. Awareness of death's finality allows us to overcome it. To annihilate time. We regain dignity by coming face to face with our own destiny. Without illusions, cheats or excuses."

Once, while still in high school, impressed by Klein's tirade, he began to repeat it in his own words to his mother. He wanted to provoke her, but she looked at him with a special, unusual for her, almost warm irony. She was making him more and more upset.

"To live" he repeated "to live!"

"Like flies" she added.

"Why like flies?" Amazement overcame his anger.

"Because they also live only for a moment. They last one day; every moment is final for them. And they're not connected with anything, nor are they aware of their form."

"What are you talking about? After all this is absurd!" Adam became furious at his mother's simplicity. "It's awareness that allows us to overcome our limitations. Try to understand that."

Adam's mother looked at him with a mixture of amusement and forbearance.

"You know, I also know Klein. I talked about him with your grandfather, after whom you're named, your father's father. He didn't really want to admit to the friendship Klein so likes to refer to him. But no matter. He also puzzled me with his sophisticated arguments. Together with your father they confused me. That's why I thought about it for a long time. Actually, I think about it even now. I'm trying to understand: are all my instincts wrong? They can deny them so eloquently. Or maybe there is fundamental falseness in what they say and how they think? The more I think about it, the more I'm convinced of it. They are important, influential, they impose opinions. It took me a long time before I realized that although they were so smart, they understand very little. The world for them is a dead lump of matter, a prison. They don't realize that if they really live, then the world must somehow live. That is why they change so easily from extremes to extremes. From building a completely new world, writing one's own book of *Genesis*, to withdrawing, recognizing that one should focus only on oneself, and every community is dangerous and oppressive. Of course, except for their own enlightened community of those who know better" his mother's voice sounded old, scornful. "One should strive only for self-fulfillment, self-realization, self-creation. There is always this emphasis on the self. As in masturbation. I know that they wouldn't agree with this interpretation" she added, when Adam snapped at both his mother's mockery and the vague string of her associations "neither Klein nor your father. It's after all about freedom and free relations between people. As they say. But who are those people invented by them? Who are these disinherited from everything and brought to sheer possibilities as individuals? Once again, they invented a man who isn't there. Once again they are trying to be gods only to become animals."

Adam didn't understand his mother's speech, especially her points, but as soon as she finished, he stopped worrying about it. He decided that there was nothing to understand. His mother opposed Klein's thrilling visions with gibberish. Her limitation caused him shame. He quickly forgot her words. However, it turned out that he did not entirely. After years they'll come back to him and cause anxiety.

***

Adam met Bruno Klein at the end of his sophomore year of high school. His father arranged this meeting, enticing his son with information that he'd be able to meet someone extraordinary. Adam, however, demanded to be given the name of the mysterious guest, making it dependent on his arrival. The revealed identity impressed him. The meeting of one of the more powerful Polish intellectuals, a philosopher and essayist translated into so many languages, was an honor. Adam had already read a lot about him. That's why, he looked with fascination at the strange, seemingly ageless, small and busy figure with a big head and a vivid, frowning, almost monkey-like face. The small white beard attached to it was searching for an object towards which the owner was to make his tirade. Adam found it difficult to believe that this man was the same age as his grandparents. His passion was disarming. Klein asked about everything: school, his mother, whom, it turned out, he also knew well and spoke of her by name, finally about the boy's views. He invited him to his place.

Adam visited the Villa on Lekarz St. at the end of his junior year. The house in the middle of Warsaw was a world in itself, a strange maze denying the order of the city. It made an even bigger impression that it was so close to Adam's apartment. Klein knew how to measure the introduction of his sanctuary. At first glance, the house gave the impression of being neglected and cluttered. It wasn't until the host, as if casually pointing to individual objects, revealed his hidden order, or rather the multitude of orders that governed it, the complex relationships between the objects that fill it.

"Reproduction can also be a work of art," Klein pointed out, pointing to Dürer's Christ-like self-portrait, who was staring intently at the viewer from the wall above the fireplace. It was emerging from the dense, dark space in which his long hair was entwined. The slender, almost spider-like fingers gripped the fur collar of the jacket and made a vague sign. The gaze penetrated the viewer, looking for something in them...But Adam didn't have time to think about what, because the host inattentively brought attention to a large French album of natural history, which stretched on a Rococo table under a copy of a Miró painting. Shining starfishes immersed in the sea from the photo in the book are reflected by tiny creatures flying in the blue space of the Catalonian painter. Klein goes further, passes a carved Gdańsk wardrobe, next to which on the wall hangs a wooden Christ hidden is his suffering of an anonymous country carver, and then from a colorful, violent abstraction a Kandiński knight is trying to get out. In any case, this is how the host explains the image to the stunned Adam, adding in an almost exalting tone: "And always this melancholy...Finally..." he says it casually, without actually referring to the side wall illuminated by a small lamp on the exposed spot of a small graphic by Dürer; gloomy, winged melancholy over the emaciated greyhound between objects scattered in disarray, in hopelessness that even the joyless cupid does not revive "alchemy, the philosophical stone, formula of salvation...Our beautiful and grim illusions. Leave only disorder and ash" Klein says sadly, leading him into the depths of his maze "but let's now leave these human ailments. Let's go further."

The man only walked a few meters to a table next to the elegant cupboard, from where the host extracted a flat bottle.

"Armagnac. Another work of art. This time original", he explained, pouring dark gold liquid into the shot glasses.

The taste of Armagnac will forever be associated in Adam with the villa on Lekarz St. and the maze of books that grew out everywhere. They stood on shelves reaching the ceiling and were protected behind the glass of the library; they laid on tables and end tables, on cabinets, dressers and couches, and even windowsills. The books corresponded with each other so cleverly that Adam wondered if it could only be the intention of the host to build new qualities from their combinations, or simply that human works must ultimately enter into meaningful relationships with each other.

Adam's every visit to Lekarz St. was ceremonially arranged before and no one else ever accompanied them. Larger meetings took place in his father's apartment. It was precisely Klein, and then subsequent guests of his father's and their debates that attracted Adam, made him become a more frequent guest of the apartment on Ursynów. One of its regular guests was a professor at the SGH, a well-known economist, Sławomir Mucha. The radical provoked with his vision.

"We'll finally break free from this mess! A new era is beginning!" He hovered, throwing his lean, nervous hands. He was stringy and broken like a tuning fork. "We'll break with this romantic babble, our parochialism. Europe will impose new measures on us and will end nationalistic foolishness."

Mucha's radicalism fascinated Adam, which he couldn't fully accept. He let it carry him like a sinful passion, sinking into which, he betrayed his mother, dead uncle, his greatest memories, the crowd of close people forming his life up until now.

Dislike for Polish identity was Mucha's obsession. In his diatribe it became the main obstacle to the modernization of the nation, which should fall into the European sea and finally dissolve in it. Disgust for the Polish backwater permeated Mucha with faith in the arrival of the kingdom of rationality, personified by the European Union. It was it who was to introduce a reasonable model of the functioning of humanity. It was to end history and by nature unruly politics.

"Mathematics is the structure of reality. Do you know the story of Einstein? His first model was a closed end spherical universe. This view reigned then and Einstein didn't have the courage to question it, although his calculations told him something else, they suggested that the universe was expanding. If we accept the static cosmos, the Einstein equations showed that it would have to collapse, melt to a single point. Einstein – he's not the first one anyway - added a term with a constant that balanced the model to his equations. Einstein called it a cosmological constant. It resisted the strength of gravity and allowed the universe to last, or rather allowed Einstein's model to last. Its author failed to draw final conclusions from his own calculations. And that's why it wasn't until a few decades later, when empirical research confirmed it, that it was possible to announce that the world was expanding. It's a fact. No matter if the theory of the Big Band, an initial explosion is true. But mathematics is truth itself. If Einstein had let it lead him, he would have overtaken experience. And this is how it is with everything. We can build a mathematical model of economic activities, an algorithm that will reduce the unpredictability of the world and enter it in our projects. We can create the basis for rational action."

"Watch out, you're introducing metaphysics through the back door," Klein added, with a frozen laugh on his face. "Are you aware of the consequences of what you are saying? You assume the existence of a fundamental order, the consequence of which would have to be some natural law. Do you know where this can lead you?"

"I don't deal with metaphysics. I'm just talking about the rationality of the world, our world, from which we should draw conclusions. Fortunately, the time of Europe is coming, a common Europe which is a rational project. We'll free Poles from their nap for a separate purpose. We'll modernize them completely so that they won't be able to recognize themselves" Mucha laughed diabolically.

Once, while still in high school, Adam wanted to show off for his mother and began to tell her about mathematics as the queen of sciences. From a distant, long-term perspective, he'll reflect on his attitude towards his mother and his striking ambiguity. On one hand, he felt superior to her. His mother was not equal to his father or him. She didn't understand the present, the new world and its rules, imprisoned in the past she wasn't able to disentangle herself from it. At times it seemed that she could not reason abstractly. On the other hand, she was a point of reference for Adam. He wanted to provoke her, amaze her, bewilder her. Every new fact, every interpretation he juxtaposed in his mind with his mother's probable reaction. In his imagination he argued with her, convinced her, forced admiration, although he often didn't have the courage to attack her in reality. When he referred Mucha's issues to his mother, without referring to him, he felt pride. She looked at him with interest.

"I don't know mathematics, but if what you are saying is true, we have proof of the order of the world," she said at one point with an unusual smile. "Is it not the same as the existence of God?"

Adam was almost dumbfounded. Such conclusions could not to be derived from Mucha's arguments! He was grabbed by the passion of negation.

"God?! This god?! The God of old women begging him to remove their calluses?" He didn't provoke his mother and it made him even angrier. She answered calmly:

"Exactly that. Do you think that from his divine perspective, your sophisticated ideas and mathematical arguments are so different from the naive prayers of a woman like me? Has it occurred to you that from his distance the distance between your sophistication and my ignorance is almost non-existent?"

Sometimes he didn't fully understand what she wanted to tell him, and he gladly accepted that she didn't know it either. However, uncertainty remained. He found that he wasn't always able to answer her. Then he wished that Mucha was with him so he could drive her into a corner. The economist hated ignorance, crowds, holy masses and Solidarity.

"We cultivate these collective ecstasies. A rush of sheep. Collective prayers and spells, our national voodoo. As if at the end of all these elations there was no hatred for a stranger, others, a Jew or a fagot. All this is a manifestation of senselessness. Magical thinking, conjuring reality. Another edition of Polish stupidity."

Sometimes Igor Stawicki, also now a university professor and his mother's former friend, joined them. He has just published the work *Rebirth of Fundamentalism*. "The Word" said it would be the Polish philosophical book of the coming decade.

Stawicki's book dealt with the rebirth of fundamentalism in the West, the United States and Europe. It was supposed to have a fundamentally different character than Islamic or Hindu fundamentalism and was only in a certain way a reaction to it. According to Stawicki, those were a disease of the age of maturity, a hopeless and generally harmless attempt to defend their own identity in a globalizing world. They were taken advantage of as an excuse by some Western centers to maximize their power. By contrast, fundamentalism in the West is the rebirth of nationalism supported by religion. It was a reaction to a subsequent, this time the last cultural and political revolution of Western, global civilization. This revolution ultimately sealed the death of community replaced by society, but a new type of society, already cleansed of the atavistic remnants of identity that survived in it to this day. The new society was only a temporary, fluid, orderly system of contracts, a group of fully independent individuals. It offered freedom that man has never known before. Freedom that awakened fright and before which man tried to escape to identities belonging in the past. An attempt to resurrect them in the long run was doomed to failure, but it evoked dangerous passions that could explode with the most terrifying shocks, including civil war. The new conditions more and more divided Western societies into the contemporary era of dynamic individualities, mobile and adaptable to new conditions, and lost masses which react with fear and aggression to inevitable, postmodern processes.

Stawicki lavishly cited Klein, in the work of *Myths Which Devour Us*, which was printed in the eighties and the recently published *Liquid Identity*. The author of *The Rebirth of Fundamentalism*, however, went further in his conclusions and suggested that the elites should take control of social processes. He called it postmodern democracy. It was about installing fuses in the political system that would forever prevent these fundamentalisms from emerging which would blow up our civilization. Anyway, that's what Adam, from reviews and talks at his father's place, reconstructed from the contents of the book, which he got from Stawicki with the dedication "To a young friend, son of friends, in the name of freedom." Despite promises made to himself, Adam never read it.

Its author ceased coming to their apartment on Kosz Street, so he visited his father from time to time instead. Adam noticed that most of his mother's old friends, or those he recognized as such, stopped coming over. Now he was finding them in the circle of his father and of "The Republic", of which they were radically critical a few years ago. On behalf of his mother he felt this as an injustice, deviation even, but he had no one to talk to about it. His mother and father were on different sides to this dispute, moreover, Adam was not sure of his intuition and could not give them a rational shape.

"So, you suggest that Kalos kagathos, good and beautiful, take over all power, and under the banner of democracy? You however don't write this straight." Klein grimaced as he ran around Stawicki, who pleased drew lighted figures with his cigarette.

"You see, in this one I can be a Straussist. I don't share his other ideas, but I agree that the esoteric elements are useful in writing. Those to whom it is addressed will understand. Others don't have to, or maybe even they shouldn't. After all, they're supposed to be unconscious actors of the spectacle and participate in the building of the system that will actually deprive them of their voice. If they understood this, I don't think they would agree."

"This is very sophisticated." Mucha stuck out his protruding nose at the shaky, thin face of the fakir. "And I would suggest a bid bond. It would be calculated exactly at the price level of the cheapest bottle of vodka. To the penny. Such a price wouldn't tell you anything, nor am I able to give it to you, but among a large group, I vouch, it would automatically bring to mind the bottle that they would have to renounce when going to vote. The bid bond would be returned after a few days. But who of them would renounce a bottle of vodka right away to get it back in some time? They live in the moment. Then all populisms, solidarity and self-defense would end..."

"I'm sorry but I can't help but react," Adam interrupted unexpectedly for himself and others. "After all you can't identify this. Solidarity, Self Defense is...it's quite different. It's not fair, you're insulting..." Adam paused. The flow of swirling, contradictory thoughts did not let him finish. He saw amazed faces of Mucha, Klein, Stawicki, his father turn to him...

"I'm sorry too," Mucha began, looking at Adam carefully. "I didn't mean to offend anyone, but as the ancients used to say, my friend Plato..."

"You're exaggerating!" Benedict Brok interrupted firmly, causing perhaps more astonishment than his son before. "You can't identify everything with everything. I was critical of Solidarity, but comparing it with the Self Defense..."

***

"Uncle Stach has died," her mother said. "The funeral is in three days." Adam felt silly. For some time already, his mother mentioned that uncle was ill, he's in the hospital. Adam promised her and himself that he would visit him, but more urgent matters, those which all kinds were, meant that he was postponing the visit for later. Now there is no later, and he'll never make up the neglect.

He didn't know Uncle Stach well. Sometimes they saw each other during the holidays and met in Niemiry a few times. He was actually a great uncle, his wife, Gienia, was the sister of Adam's grandmother. He felt instinctive sympathy for his uncle's family and their children, although they were people from another world.

There were a few dozen people at the funeral. An old man, grandfather Antek, aunt Gienia's brother came from Niemir. Uncle's daughter, Aunt Ewa, came from the States. The young and well-groomed woman contrasted with her sister Ala, who with strands of long gray hair seemed a generation older, although they were separated by a few years. Adam's father, notified by him, also came. He made a move as if he wanted to approach his mother, but chilled by her gaze, he merely exchanged bows.

The widow, aunt Gienia, was extremely calm. It seemed that she was in a different dimension and had little interest in what was going on in the cemetery. She didn't cry and even a few times silenced her daughters' sobs. Ala had the hardest time controlling herself. All this time, Aunt Gienia was assisted by her son, Zdzich, the youngest of the siblings, a massive man with a shaved head, in a black suit and a white shirt without a tie, under which a thick gold chain was visible. He embraced his mother, reassured his sisters, carefully looked after everything. He reminded everyone of the invitation to the wake, which took place in the nearby restaurant "Malwina". It was he who rented a country-styled room and paid for everything. Long wooden tables were covered with plates with appetizers, bottles of wine and vodka. The waiters served hot dishes.

Zdzich was a gangster. There were legends in the family about him. In the eighties he was imprisoned several times. In truth back then it wasn't known who's in jail for what, but Zdzich had reportedly already then made his first robberies and printed fake currency. It was told that when the locals came to him for payoffs, he smashed their heads, and then with a few colleagues found their bosses and demanded a cut. He made a lot of money when Communism collapsed, the transformation process occurred and the duty on alcohol trade was removed. Trains with tankers filled with high-grade liquors were already waiting over the border, and on the roads, there were long lines of trucks transporting them to Poland. Of course, Zdzich wasn't in the forefront of those who made a lot of money then. They were former officers transformed into businessmen, supervising the legislative process, collecting from the still state-owned banks, managed by comrade-professionals, loans for the gigantic operation of purchasing, transporting and distribution. Zdzich only distributed alcohol locally and got a percentage of it. It was then that he also gained the right connections. In the nineties he was arrested only once and for a short time. He bought some shops and restaurants.

Now he came up to Adam.

"So what? Want to have a drink, cousin?" He offered a large, full to the brim shot of vodka to him. "For memory," he announced.

"For memory," Adam repeated, and realized that next to him in a black dress his mother was standing.

"That man..." she began, nodding at the tall man without age and expression, who was looking around as if he wanted to say goodbye "I have the impression that I know him..."

"Because you know him. Oh, Zuza, Zuza..." Zdzich nodded neither with admiration nor with reproach. "He's a big businessman, Jacek Rojek, Ala's employer and a bit, but a little bit" Zdzich showed on his finger "my partner. Only, I think you knew him before..."

"It's that Rojek?" His mother's face contracted.

"Well..." Zdzich filled the shot glasses. He moved a plate of appetizers in their direction.

"And you…tolerate him, invite him…"

"Yes, we tolerate…Ala invited him. I told you, that he's her employer."

"But earlier he put her in prison, ruined her life…"

"I don't know if he ruined her life" muttered Zdzich, drinking a shot and glancing to let Adam know that he should do the same. "I know that nobody helped her then." He looked hard at Adam's mother. "And when it wasn't easy...in the late eighties, he offered her a job. He remembered her. And Ala doesn't have any resentment toward him, quite the opposite. Give it a break with this past. As a matter of fact, I have the impression that he would like to talk to you. Maybe he'll explain to you..."

His mother looked like she wanted to say something, but gave up, winced in a grimace feigning a smile, and walked away. The man in question approached her. He explained something, smiling faintly. They sat at a small table in the corner of the room. Something forced Adam to watch them, spy on them. This meant that he couldn't focus on what Zdzich was saying. He tried to guess the conversation his mother was having few meters away. Even though that Zdzich provoked curiosity.

"So now what, cousin?" He asked, pouring more shots. "Your mother...is a nice woman, but too... principled. She can't forget...And yes...what are your plans?"

"Plans?" Adam repeated surprised.

"Yeah. Plans. After all, college is just the beginning. The beginning of what in your case?"

"I don't understand you. Of work."

"And now? Maybe you would like to work already? Earn Real Money?" Zdzich moved closer to him. Adam had the impression that he could smell sweat.

They drank again. Adam's cousin's unambiguous suggestions aroused satisfaction and confusion. He glanced toward the table occupied by his mother and tall, indistinct man. She looked in his direction. In the dim light it could only seem to him that he saw the tension in her gaze. They looked at each other through the room, restraining their moves...Adam looked from up close at Zdzich's narrowed eyes. He held his gaze for a moment. Finally, he laughed.

"Come on! I'm not proposing a heist to you. I have way too many candidates for that." Adam didn't know if his cousin was serious. "I have money, which needs to be invested. You're an economist. Good" he reacted to Adam's snorting "you'll be him. But you're ready for it. You're good. I know it. I know people. Psychology is the foundation of my profession. And you're family. So I can trust you. I could hire you... For good money..." Zdzich bit a gherkin and poured again. There wasn't much left in the bottle. The face opposite was a few centimeters away. Adam could see drops of sweat squeezing through the skin on Zdzich's forehead and cheeks. His propositions impressed him. They were an invitation to another reality, the fascinating world of men. That where other, simpler rules obliged: the risk paid off many times or ended in defeat...At the other end of the room his mother jumped up from the table. The man opposite her was explaining something. She wasn't listening.

"Take me home. I want to go now!" She said, suddenly appearing beside him.

"Zuza, come on, I haven't talked to your son yet." Zdzich was effusively hospitable. "Then I'll order you both a taxi and bring you home. Did something happen?" He changed his tone suddenly, noticing something specific in the face of Adam's mother.

"Nothing happened, but I have to go!" His mother said angrily.

"Because if he..."

"Him nothing. He's not here" his mother shrugged her shoulders.

They spent the time in a taxi ordered by Zdzich in silence.

"I hope that you didn't promise Zdzich anything?" His mother neither finally asked nor state.

"Nothing" he replied.

At home, undressing for bed, he heard something from the neighboring room. Led by a vague impulse, he went to the door. He needed some time to realize that his mother was crying. He hesitated. She was lying dressed on the bed. Her small body, now Adam noticed how she lost weight lately, quiet spasms shook, from which only sometimes louder sobbing was heard. Her son embraced her.

"Mom...What happened? Why are you crying? Don't cry anymore..." His mother leaned on his shoulder.

"You know...They've gotten me. They've finally now gotten me," she said in a quick voice that she was struggling to make sound normal. She dug a cigarette out of her purse and reached for the partially filled ashtray on the night table.

"What are you saying? How did they get you?"

His mother inhaled a cigarette. She was almost calm.

"During martial law, I signed a loyalty paper. I mean, not quite a loyalty paper, a paper, that I will obey the law. I shouldn't have done it."

"A paper that you'll obey the law?" Adam didn't get it. "After all, that's obvious. It's not relevant."

"You don't understand. It was wartime law. I shouldn't have done it. They came to me. Now they'll use it" his mother became silent. She turned her unmoving face away from the window. She looked at him thoughtfully.

"I would have to explain a lot to you. Maybe I should. I don't know why in this 'Malwina' I agreed to talk to Rojek. Curiosity? The desire to understand? As if there was something to understand. In any case, I sat down at the table with him. And at one point I had the impression that these almost twenty years evaporated. Because we've already had a similar conversation. Eighteen years ago. He came to me at the publishing house. He was a personnel officer at the plant Ala worked at and a UB officer. They set her up in their scams. I once mentioned this to you. And he explained to me that Ala would take the blame and they would take care of the matter. And that I should give it a break. He was saying something similar now. As if only the premises had changed.

Adam didn't remember this account as his mother's story. He'll put it on what he saw in "Malwina", the image of a blurry man, and he heard him as if he was standing right next to him and listening to the matters of a former SB officer.

A pale face with an indistinct smile was leaning over the table.

"I hope you don't have this long-standing dislike of me. It's been so many years...Because I feel sympathy to you. After all we are bound by a piece of the past. This builds good contacts. You know that even enemies from times of war can get to like each other. And after all they are divided by their blood and their past hatred. We should overcome old injuries. I after all somehow like and respect you.'

"He paused," said his mother. "He was clearly waiting for my reaction. I said nothing. We looked at each other. He resumed again."

'But I'd like to talk about something specific as well...' he lowered his voice. 'Why are you still getting into it? I know that I won't convince you. Just as I couldn't convince you twenty years ago. And I was right. And because of your stubbornness your cousin suffered...'

'It's you who destroyed her!' I almost shouted. Earlier I promised myself that I would only listen. I won't talk with him or discuss. I couldn't stand it. He was probably glad that he provoked me to reacting, although he nodded his head sadly.

'And you keep doing what you've always done. We, you...What does it matter? What's important is the result. That was the world, if it wasn't me, there would be someone else, and besides...I gave you and your cousin a chance...You didn't take advantage of it. You should feel guilty. Do you think that if Ala knew that it happened because of you, that she'd forgive you? And your husband? Did it not surprise you that he withdrew so quickly? Or maybe he had his own reasons? But this is a thing of the past. Those matters are so distant to me...I have children your son's age.'

"He remembered everything. His knowledge paralyzed me" his now composed mother was already analyzing her behavior.

'I have a pair. A boy and girl. I want the best for them, like you for your son. And after all we live in one country. We should care about its future together. I care. You probably as well, but you are dragging these corpses of the past with you. Mrs. Zuzo...Give me a break. Where does this stubbornness in you come from? After all you won't bring your brother back to life. And even if you proved that we killed him?

So what? Do you believe you'll find those responsible? That you'll sentence them? Free advice...Our camp was just a device. After all, it's known whose commission we acted on...These are now people worthy of respect. You know it yourself. The trial in December? It's a mockery. Everyone can see it. And then fifty people were killed. Those who did it are national heroes. Look at the surveys commissioned by the 'The Word'. But I'm not interested in all this. I choose the future. I'll do television. Good T.V. Only sometimes I think you underestimated us. That Roski who somewhere there drank or starved...Everyone turned away from him. It's hardly surprising. He spilled so pathetically. He came to our side, became a witness to the prosecution. You must have been surprised. Such a tough guy...You underestimated us. Although it must be admitted that someone among you also helped us, was helping, without such people we could do little. Intelligent people mediated between our worlds, connected them. They should get rewards and they'll get them; they work in new conditions. It's they who create democracy, the free market...And you? You're not so steadfast either. You signed a loyalty paper. After all you don't want to settle accounts. Please only realize...'

"Then I got up and left. He said something behind me, but I didn't hear. He knew about the loyalty paper; he was blackmailing me actually. And Wojtek's case. You don't remember him?" Maybe it's a suggestion, but Adam had the impression that he remembers a large, heavy man, although he can't recall his face. "Indeed, I learned about his death recently. I haven't seen him for many years, since they locked him up a dozen years ago. Although not" his mother draws smoke and looks deep into her son's eyes "I saw him a few years ago. I was passing by on the street. He was standing against the wall. He looked like a prisoner. Still big, but hunched and emaciated. He saw me and smiled. I didn't recognize him at first, although he seemed familiar to me. I slowed down and he took a step toward me. Then I realized who it was. I accelerated. And now that son of a bitch UB was bragging that they broke him. At Uncle Stach's funeral...When I think about all this..." his mother looked around as if she was looking for support somewhere. She lit another cigarette. And finally, she looked at Adam again. "I'm not happy with myself. Maybe I should've given Wojtek a chance. Nobody took care of him. He wrote a statement to the underground press in which he took the blame. And he left me a letter with a phone number. I never called...It all came back to me. Maybe that's why I started crying so much" his mother smiled miserably "the loyalty papers case, Wojtek's death, Stach's funeral and that Rojek in the place of honor, Ala's employer...Listen!" His mother's hallow eyes fixed on Adam. "Don't hang out with this Zdzich. He is a dangerous man. Someone who doesn't respect his own life will not respect someone else's. After all you know I don't interfere in your affairs. This one time promise me you won't hang out with him." She stared at him in suspense. Adam promised.

Zdzich accosted him several more times. Adam wriggled out due to lack of time and explained that he had other activities. One-time Zdzich smiled and patted him on the shoulder.

"I understand. Your choice. I respected that."

Zdzich was shot and killed in early autumn 1998. The funeral was picturesque, slightly opera-like. The broad-shouldered, black-clad men with bull's necks and with blondes attached to their arms in big ringed hands held large bouquets of flowers.

From beneath their jacket sleeves tightly wrapped around their forearms protruded from snow-white cuffs and the shadows of hidden tattoos. Gold shimmered, and sometimes cufflinks shone with precious stones. Arranged in a line, they expressed condolences and kissed Aunt Genia, who seemed to understand nothing, surrounded by her daughters supporting her. The casket was almost invisible under a mountain of colorful flowers. When it was let down into the grave, they were moved away. Wreaths with sashes emerged from under them. "To Zdzich - we will not forget" and "To Zdzich - colleagues" proclaimed the writing. Some of the flowers fell into the grave. The earth buried them. Still, the tomb looked like a flower mound.

The gathering took place in an elegant hotel in the city center. Somewhat accidentally, the four of them found themselves at the table in the corner of the room: Zdzich's sisters, Adam's mother and him. Ala looked a bit drunk.

"He lived well!" She stated clearly provocatively to Adam's mother. "He lived well! And what of it, that shortly?"

"You really think so?" his mother asked.

"But what do you mean?" Ala drank another shot. "About that he didn't live long or that he broke your law?"

"Give it a break!" Eve looked at her anxiously.

"Why should I give it a break? So as not to offend Zuzanna, the great lady editor? Adam is already an adult." She smiled at him. "At his age Zdzisiek had already had his first time in jail behind him. And you know what?" She turned to his mother again. "For Solidarity, for leaflets and such stuff. He sat in jail, they threw him out of work, threw our father out too, although he worked there all his life, because he also got involved. It was the same with Ewa and me. What, you have already forgotten, Ewka?"

"I haven't forgotten anything"

"Ewka and her husband left for the United States, they were pressed by UBs, and overall they did them good. Look what a stylish woman and she has two children. And we somehow had to manage. Our father sold vegetables and fruits. Zdzisiek met some people in jail and started hanging around with them. He helped us. What? Was he supposed to be worried about martial law?"

"That was then..." his mother probably said reflexively finishing her vodka.

"Then, now...That the difference? Those who live well have beautiful words in their mouths. Those who ruled still rule. That prosecutor who accused me and knew that that was all a farce, was in the previous government, now he's a famous lawyer. I saw him on television. He talked about human rights. That judge...who convicted me, also knew everything, now she is in the Supreme Court or the Constitutional Court, I don't distinguish. And Rojek is even much better off than then. I anyway won't let anyone say anything against him. He found me and got me a good job. Others didn't care. Do you think it changed because they took you in? Because you fought out a place for yourselves next to the manger?! On our backs?!"

"Ala, calm down!" this time Ewe was almost yelling.

"Alright, alright. After all I don't want to offend our nice cousin, always full of promises and pretty sentences." Ala grimaced at the caricature of humbleness. "Zdzich lived a short life, but just as he wanted. I wish that for everyone. At the cemetery, this length becomes meaningless. Our father lived twice as long. And what, was he happier? Our brother lived so long that his life could be divided among others. I regret one thing... I can't do it like him...I can't afford it..." Ala cut off. She put her hand in her mouth and began to bite it.

"Resentment speaks through you. I understand" his mother was bleak. "It's a shame, that I didn't know that you had such a difficult situation in the eighties. Maybe we could've..."

"Just as before...Better not anymore." Ala jumped up and ran into the depths of the hall.

"I'm sorry" said Ewe and went after her.

They left. They walked in silence through the still warm autumn Warsaw.

***

Adam made his first contacts with the Polish branch of the large American R&B Corporation thanks to his father. He graduated and, despite the offer of the position of assistant and work on his doctorate by Mucha, he was looking for something else, especially for something that would lead him out of Poland. He soon ceased to be interested in the academic debate between Keynesians and neoliberals. Mucha spoke of it with contempt.

"It's clear that in the seventies, Keynes' model suffered a defeat. However, it functioned well for thirty years. All in all, it was a fairly simple formula. Add money during stagnation to boost demand. And here it turned out that entrepreneurs didn't get caught once again on the same trick. They understood that increasing the money supply was only reducing its value, they automatically raised prices and stagflation appeared. Keynes's fundamental mistake was that he tried to build an all-encompassing model, and this was only a time-limited project. The free market is also needed so that such models almost hatch naturally from the cooperation of groups and enterprises that will test their algorithms in practice, bearing the associated risk. We'll build subsequent equations, capturing in them unruly reality, or maybe rather, it should be said, extracting from it hidden order. So, we will be able to control it. Step by step, the strongest minds. Those like you, Adam."

Adam understood Mucha's reasoning in his own way. All-encompassing theories must be left behind. To occupy oneself with the empirical, to practice, take risks, live. He decided to leave academic economics and enter its living matter.

He signed his first contract with R&B for three months in his last year of college. Then there was another contract and finally a three-year contract. Associated with it was a several-month trip to the company's headquarters in the United States. Adam felt that his real life was beginning. He came back flying. He wanted to show off to his mother, all his friends.

At home, his mother, Danka Brak and Agnieszka Pelikan sat over a half-empty bottle of wine. He sat down, thanking them for the glass. Agnieszka smiled brightly at Adam. For a moment he thought she was still an attractive woman.

"I saw you recently on television" his mother recalled.

"On T.V.?" Danka said surprised.

"You looked very beautiful at Goleń's funeral. Almost as beautiful as my ex-husband. Were you carrying a wreath?"

"Even if...Maybe it's worth honoring even one's opponent, if we see the class in him" Agnieszka declared warily. "You have the right to resent Benek, but that shouldn't be..."

"It's amazing," his mother continued, as if she was explaining something to someone that she herself could hardly believe. "The speech over his grave was given by Filip Madej. An outstanding, well-known, media professor of sociology..." his mother was parodying someone's voice.

"Give it a break, do you want to chase them beyond the grave?" Danka was full of disgust. "Filip's speech was really good."

"Oh...with certainty...And how much truth was in it?"

"A lot. He said a little on our behalf, that we didn't have to agree with Władek, but we remember his honesty and civic involvement."

"Honesty, civic involvement? Am I dreaming? Władek? Are you talking about that son of a bitch who built the rationale for martial law? Did he participate in the most beautiful head-busting in our history?"

"Somehow he didn't bust them. You take everything to extremes. It's about being able to appreciate one's opponents. This is a beautiful and rare feature" Agnieszka interjected.

"Appreciate one's opponents? After all these are your real allies! Almost ten years now. How you forgotten? Goleń became a Władek for you. And can you appreciate your current opponents?"

"You know what, it's getting harder to talk to you" Danka was already clearly angry. "I understand your resentments, but are you not exaggerating with this hatred?" After death!"

"It's not about hate, but monuments. It's you who put them up for them. And it's you?!" His mother turned to Agnieszka. "You who promised you would never forget what they did?"

Agnieszka became pale. Adam had the impression that her lips were trembling.

"Don't exaggerate...Don't drag it out..." she said in an uncomfortable voice. But his mother was already taken by anger.

"You don't remember, what they did to you?! What they took from you?!"

"You...you...I don't want to call you names with your son..." Agnieszka jumped up shouting: "I hate you! Those kinds are the worst. You don't take anyone or anything into account. Other people's wounds mean nothing to you! I hate you! I don't want to know you! Never!"

Adam stared in amazement at Agnieszka running out when he realized that Danka was also heading out. She tried to control herself, but said in a shaky voice:

"Don't you realize that it's simply impossible to talk to you anymore?! Then you're surprised that people turn away from you! We were the last to talk to you. Everyone said that you went crazy. They told about what had happened to you. They were right."

Danka left. It became incredibly quiet in the apartment. His mother became petrified. Adam wanted to say something but couldn't find the words. He remembered the story of Agnieszka's miscarriage, of which he had heard years ago. It took a moment for it to come back to him, why he had come. He had to repeat it a few times for his mother to realize that her son was going to America.

CHAPTER 6

He returned to Poland two weeks after the election triumphantly won by Leszek Miller. It was prophesied by everyone that the Post-communists were to rule the country for the next twenty years. Adam thought that he didn't care much anymore. Less than a month earlier, planes hit the World Trade Center towers. This day and the next tied him to the States. He felt a growing distance to Poland and its political vicissitudes. Actually, he was only sorry for his mother. A year earlier, Poles chose Kwaśniewski for the second time, this time in the first round. Adam was then arranging papers for a trip to the States. He felt something like masochistic satisfaction. Nothing bound him to this country anymore. Now, when he came for a short time, the satisfaction demonstrated by Sławek Mucha irritated him.

"This is the end of solidarity movement!" Repeated his college mentor. His thin face shimmered with grimaces of satisfaction. "This populist chutzpah has ended. It landed where it should've. In the dustbin of history..."

"You know what, I can't listen to this!" Adam interrupted him.

They sat in the large hall of the 'Hortex', where even a large number of guests always gave the impression of being lost. The white October light was pouring in through the high windows. On the other side of Constitution Square, years earlier there was the 'Surprise' cafe, the seat of the Solidarity civic club's electoral staff. The restaurant was closed quite a long time ago. It was in 'Surprise' that Adam experienced his political initiation. Twelve years earlier. In another era. Now he was elsewhere. While still in the States, he was summoned by a representative of the R&B board. They probed his knowledge of Russia. The company's corridors talked about a great Siberian contract that R&B was to negotiate with a powerful international company. Apparently, the matter was currently being decided. This was Adam's next chance. He'll go to Russia. Then he'll come back to the States. That country with his sad mother and lost father is moving away like childhood. Adam felt old and burned out. That was twelve years earlier. Twelve years of his conscious life. The astonished fakir opposite him gestured to calm the snake who stopped listening to his flute. Adam felt anger and contempt.

"How can you rave about how power being taken over by those who lead an irresponsible economic policy, the reverse of what you yourself would normally propose? After all, Kwaśniewski vetoed the reform of public finances and re-privatization. Resentment speaks through you. To put down those you hate. That's all you're interested in. But why you hate them, you've never explained to me. Say it now! Maybe I'll understand something."

Mucha stared at him helplessly. He was moving his lips, but no sound was coming from them. He looked like a scared child.

"I'm fifty-four years old," Adam's mother was telling him two days earlier. They were sitting in the kitchen over a bottle of wine. Night was falling. Autumn was starting. Adam thought that he associates Poland with autumn. "I'm fifty-four years old," said his mother. "I still don't understand anything. Supposedly we've won. Communism fell. But did it fall? What's happening with this country? What's happening that young, entrepreneurs like you want to run away from it? If no conclusions are drawn from evil, and scoundrels are wallowing in profits from their villainous deeds, they set the measures, then...can we be surprised of anything?" That was one of the longest speeches she made. She demanded that he tell her about his life in the States. She herself said little. "After all you know," she concluded. She was right. He knew.

They sat in silence, sometimes smiling at each other. Adam looked through the glass at the already brown trees. This view accompanied his life. He can return here for brief periods of time. He'll come visit, but he knows that this won't be his world anymore.

Thoughts about this came back to him when the fakir in the 'Hortex' at his table, his mentor, university professor Sławek Mucha recovered and began to spell it out. Adam wasn't listening. Single phrases reached him: European Union, nationalism, transformation, modernization. He interrupted the flow of the speech of his former professor. He apologized politely. Then he walked away. The fakir stayed at the table. He was saying something else, as if he had to end the speech, even though the conversation partner had already left. His gestures faded slowly in a foreign light.

"Supposedly I could be happy, but I'm not truly happy." They were sitting with his father in the 'Literary' by the window. "Supposedly we've won, and this IPN not only exists, but is beginning to distribute its papers more and more widely. These UB abominations will still poison us for a long time. I'm not happy because something is still wrong. We didn't burry our valley of grievances and resentments. I haven't reconciled with your mother" his father spoke extremely quickly. He hit his fist against the table. Adam wasn't recognizing him. "Maybe now, right now something should be done...But I myself don't know what. And they have businesses, great fortunes. They triumph. They don't think about burying anything. Besides how could they do it? Renounce what they have? I'd like to forget...to disentangle myself from it." His father calmed down. He was staring hard at Adam. He spoke with difficulty. "But how to disentangle oneself from one's own life? How to forget it?"

***

"I'm preparing a new book," Klein explained.

For the first time Adam realized that his host is an old man. He had the impression that the hands pouring Armagnac into bulging glasses were shaking. The disorder of the villa at Lekarz St. seemed less controlled. A vague, unpleasant aura emerged from the landscape of objects that the host was no longer able to control. Melancholy, Adam remembered. He had previously mentioned to his mother about

Dürer's graphic, which he had seen at Klein's place.

"And has he shown you Saint Jerome?" she became interested. "Those two copperplates: Melancholy and Saint Jerome, Dürer planned and sold as a whole. They only parted later, distorting the creator's thought. Saint Jerome is a study of harmony and happy order. Confident immersion in divine order. Melancholy is a wilderness in competition with the Creator. Two concepts of wisdom. It's probably not by chance that Klein only has Melancholy" she laughed.

Adam wasn't able to trust her intellectually. A few times his father mentioned to him about her "ideological" tendency. He heard about the ideological attitude of 'Renaissance' and people associated with it at every turn. His mother knew about art, but aren't her explanations based on ideological assumptions? Adam didn't know. It didn't interest him much. Now however, his mother's seemingly forgotten words returned intensely.

"I have something for you." Klein proudly placed a wooden figure of Christ before Adam.

The almost half-meter wooden Savior was dying, putting his head on his shoulder. There was no tragedy in it, rather a gesture of resignation, a distance to people who didn't want to accept him. Jesus was closing his eyes, he no longer wants to look at this world, he distances himself, dies. The simplified statue had distinct features. His hair tangled into a thorny crown; his hands were clenching on nails.

"It's still from the times when folk art existed in Poland, just like folk music. This is a true work of art." Klein stared at the figure in suspense. "Here. A belated birthday gift." Almost with regret he moved it toward Adam. "I'm actually starting a book about fear. I've already written about it, but only a little. I'll write about two types of fear that accompanies us today. One is the infantile fear of our condition, a refusal of understanding our own mortal status, a childish fear. The latter is the fruit of our maturity. A rational song of experience. It makes us aware that all firm identities, coherent, consistent ideas and holistic concepts must lead to totalitarianism. Therefore, we should watch for them, hunt them down, exorcise them; build a security system at the level of language, so that the hydra of metaphysics is not revived, which will never be satisfied with a piece of our existence and will always strive to dominate us completely. We need to build a strategy of slipping away, dodging, escaping from stronger principles, ties of community...You know, I realized that one can reach for Blake's antinomy: song of innocence - a song of experience. Of course, it'll have to be reworked anew..."

Adam was in a hurry. They agreed to meet for a longer conversation in a few days. In the evening, his mother for a long time looked at the wooden Christ.

"A beautiful sculpture. It's funny" she laughed "you received Christ from Klein."

"I received a work of art."

"But its Christ!" his mother summed up.

In the evening 'News' information appeared that the outstanding Polish philosopher Bruno Klein found himself in the hospital in serious condition after a stroke. Adam visited him the next day. "The old man won't dig himself out this time," he heard in the corridor, passing a crew of journalists.

Klein was laying alone in the room with his eyes closed. He looked like a mummy with an artificial, unnecessarily attached white little beard. The table was filled with vases of flowers. On the floor stood another two buckets full of them. An intense fragrance rose everywhere, penetrating with the smell of urine, disinfectants and the indefinable smell of the hospital. Up close, it could be seen that Klein's lips were moving.

Adam was only allowed to enter for a moment. As he was leaving, he exchanged bows with the Podlecki couple whom he knew through his father from 'The Republic'. They were carrying a large bouquet of flowers.

The next day, Klein recognized him. His hand, pulling away with difficulty from the comforter, made a summoning gesture. Adam pulled up his chair, leaned over the old man. Klein's eyes opened wider. Dark, empty cavities in which fear trembled. The clawed fingers gripped Adam's wrist extremely hard.

"Don't leave me, don't leave me, Baruch..." Klein whispered. Adam thought he was confusing him with his father. "Don't leave me with them! They're only waiting...I have a home, you know, I'll leave you everything in my will, just don't leave..."

"Give it a break, Bruno. Everything'll be alright. We'll still drink a lot of Armagnac at your place," said Adam without conviction.

Klein closed his eyes. His hand wasn't letting go of his guest's hand. After a while, his eyelids rose again. His gaze was more conscious, though fear was still creeping in him.

"Thank you for coming, Adam. You're so much needed...so much needed..." Klein fell silent. He seemed tired of speaking. His eyelids were closing, so that in a moment they could jump up with a sudden impulse, his pupils were dilating in fear. "Adam, be with me. I don't want those people. They're strangers!" He quieted again, closed his eyes and opened them again. "Look, I have no one for whom to leave what I have. And I have a lot. It's not just that villa on Lekarz St. The things inside are worth a lot more, works of art... I didn't make a will. I was always afraid...I didn't want to think...You have to organize this all, bring paper, arrange it, well, a notary or someone else...I'll leave everything to you..."

"Bruno, calm down. A time will come for everything," said Adam almost instinctively, ashamed that Klein's proposal had caused such a vivid reaction in him. A vision of possessing a villa in the center of Warsaw and works of art of great value filled his mind.

"You have to take care of this, because I will soon..." Klein's hand again clings to Adam's hand.

"You better think about the book you're going to write." Adam tries not to think about what he should do to settle the formalities related to the will and free himself from the questions of how to start discussing it again with Klein.

"Book? What's the book for? There will be no more book. And besides there's too much of this all..." His eyes close and open again. Dark crevices lead into the abyss of fear. The old man's hand convulsively clutches Adam's hand. "Don't leave..." Saliva seeps from his mouth, his lips are limply sagging. His hand relaxes.

"It's nothing," reassures the doctor. "He must fall asleep or faint, it's hard to distinguish in this case. The body should rest if it is to gain strength. If it gains it."

"Interesting. I've known him for so many years, and I don't know anything about his family," his father wondered. They were sitting in his apartment over cognac, which he took out to drink to Klein's health.

"It should be an Armagnac, '' Adam noted, but his father had only an opened a bottle of cognac that someone from the 'Republic' had given him.

"My father told me about that Klein had a wife or fiancée before the war, I don't remember. Then in the Soviets they sent them to a gulag. He came back without her. I don't know if she died or if he was looking for her. My father didn't like him, and Bruno always talked about him only in the best words. And about my mother he spoke of as if he were in love with her. At times I have the impression that everyone, including you, was a foster family for him. Although he was always talked about family ties quite ironically. 'Atavism of offspring,' he used to say. 'The illusion of overcoming death, we should finally grow out of it,' he repeated. All in all, I don't know if he had any children. Probably not. Suddenly I realize that I know so little about him. Maybe this is the case with everybody when their time runs out." His father was in a reflective attitude, and the bottle which was being finished had an additional influence. Adam wanted to tell him about the proposal of a will from Klein, but in this situation, seemed to him tactless, moreover, he was ashamed of his, suddenly awakened greed. "Unexpectedly, it turns out that our knowledge of those leaving blends into lumps of banalities. A few dates and events that we vaguely remember, and which mean so little..."

On the next day, Klein looked better. He even managed a smile when he saw Adam.

"I feel like I've gotten a little better," he began cautiously. Then he remembered: "I think I told you about my will last night." Adam couldn't pretend that he wasn't waiting for these words. "I was a little unconscious. But it's probably a good idea. As for Polish items, I have a lot, but not only Polish. I should make this will. You'll have to help me" Klein suspends his voice. Adam refrains from continuing this thread. Suddenly Klein closes his eyes. His face shrinks violently under a lash of...pain? fear? After a moment, his eyes open and there is only a void of fear. He grabs Adam's hand with both hands. Incomprehensible gibberish comes out of his mouth. The strength of the grip is amazing. Adam wants to run out, call the staff, but he's unable to free his hand.

Klein died the next day.

"All that's left behind for you is Christ" noticed his mother.

CHAPTER 7

The last time Adam came to Poland was almost four years earlier. In truth it came to him from time to time to visit his mother and his country, but the sheer volume of events and ventures caused him to forget about the desire that was not particularly strong and fit rather into the sphere of holiday projects. The state of affairs was changed by his mother's letter.

I really miss you. Now exceptionally. I feel lonely even though my loyal friends remain by my side. Although even their number has become smaller. We decided to reveal Igor Stawicki's political past in 'Renassiance'. I'm sorry, outstanding Polish intellectual, philosopher, Professor Igor Stawicki. Yes, Yes. You remember him well. My old friend, almost close friend, once our frequent guest. He turned out to be an extremely sleazy scumbag. We wrote about it in the weekly. I mean, I did it. I wrote the article and signed it. It was my initiative and decision. But we discussed the matter as a team. After all, the whole weekly takes responsibility. We knew what we were doing, we guessed the reaction that would come. And yet it did not occur to us what could happen.

It became hell.

In my darkest dreams I wouldn't have imagined that the "Word" would write, that I was a collaborator. I.E. no one used that word, but a large part of the "article" devoted to me deals with the "loyalty paper" I signed and collected the testimonies of all those who at that time did not sign anything. They're very outraged at my "capitulation" and juxtapose with the heroism of the environment. They don't deal with Stawicki's informing. Of course, the constant chorus is that the steadfast do not settle accounts, only people who want to cover up their own weakness deal in it. In the "Republic" (yes, yes, in that weekly, in which the withers away my ex-husband, your father) an interview with Stawicki appeared. The snitch became a media hero and it must be admitted, he used it brilliantly. Intelligence could never be denied him. So in this interview (and not only in it anyway) he gave me credence. He noted that his "ex-friend" is trying to compensate for her lack of courage in a difficult time by labeling apostates and traitors, when it doesn't cost her anything anymore. He declared that he has sympathy for me. That scumbag feels sympathy for me.

We have a trial. I mean, I have a trial and the weekly has a trial. Supposedly we have all the information, all the materials from the Institute of National Remembrance, but the Polish justice system, the justice system of the Third Polish Republic...I already have experience.

Well, I won't whine anymore. I got what I asked for. Only that I've never discouraged you from your ideas, even if they hurt me. Your emigration - because, let's be honest, this is emigration - it hurt me not only because it was distancing me away from you. I was worried that you were lost to our, still constantly our country. You, my only son whom I gave to another world. It comes to me as a guilty conscience. I think of my dead family, about your uncle, Tadek, my (almost) "sweet son". You know, debts with the dead are a lot more difficult. The simpletons don't get it. It's true that we've entered a simple phase of our culture. Never mind. Now, for the first time, I'm started thinking that you might've chosen well. Good for yourself.

Well, but enough of that brooding. I kiss you and don't worry about my stream of consciousness. I needed to let this out. You've always fallen victim to my dangerous tendency. I saw that it irritated you and tried to control myself. I did not succeed enough. So I'm sorry, and for this letter too.

I hope you remember: I can't be killed so easily, so don't worry.

Mother

It took Adam five days to get vacation time and to freeze or transfer cases he was working on. During this, he pulled out articles on the Polish media from the Internet. He was increasingly worried about his mother.

"These papers..." she said. "I didn't immediately realize that it was Stawicki. Snitches in UB documents appear under pseudonyms. We get copies of such documents from the IPN. It takes time to find out who is who. You have to submit an application, wait...I did it all, especially since it wasn't only about the secret collaborator whose nickname was "Stawrogin"..." his mother stopped. She looked at Adam with tension. They sat in the kitchen as usual. The still bare trees stretched their black fingers toward them.

Adam asked his mother to dress warmer and opened the window. He could no longer stand the cloud of smoke, which took one's breath away, and distanced them from each other. His mother gave a surprised look. They uncorked a second bottle of wine. Adam always brought a few carefully selected pieces. His mother liked wine and clearly wanted to know about it. Her financial capabilities and the assortment of Polish stores, and in any case a combination of these factors, made it difficult, if not impossible. However, she could talk about wine perfectly. It seemed to Adam that these were rather literary fantasies, but whenever he remembered, he sent his mother a case of good wines and cheeses, which, according to specialists, suited each other. What he brought this time, his mother probably enjoyed too pretentiously. We co-create our passions, and then we believe in them, we cherish them, he thought, staring affectionately at his mother who played before him a spectacle in the pleasure of tasting wine.

"But I realized who 'Stawrogin' was before the IPN confirmed it. And it was the grimmest. The way in which I found out. Do you remember how I opened up ten years ago? It was after the death of Uncle Stach. The conversation with Rojek. It's striking how everything is tied together. The UB scared me with my loyalty paper. He bragged about how they broke Wojtek. You know, I'm guilty of it a little. Maybe more than a little?" Adam's mother stared deeply at him. She tilted the glass and drank as if she didn't know what was inside.

"I found some reports on this topic. "Stawrogin", mentioning me, makes contact with Roski. I identified Roski for him. I suggested that he was doing something in the underground. It was I who associated Roski with "Stawrogin", who turned him in. And they broke him. I'm responsible for this." His mother was silent again. She clenches her lips. "When I was reading these papers, everything became clear. These were the first months of martial law. Stawicki was always around me. He was saying that he wanted to get more involved. At the same time Wojtek offered me cooperation. I was already involved in the weekly. I recommended Stawicki to him. I recommended..."

His mother looked into the coming night.

"I understood that "Stawrogin" is Stawicki. He chose a non-coincidental nickname. Viciousness worthy of an intellectual.

His mother was laughing stiffly. She emptied the glass. "It was then that I started to dig around Roski's case once again. Actually for the first time. Earlier..." His mother puffed on her cigarette and looked past her son's head. Then she turned to him. "Earlier...I ignored it like the others. The snitch and degenerated died. Then I sort of found something out, but it was still not enough. And now...I tried to reconstruct his story, its last chapter. I don't really know what for. I didn't think about any article. What could be in it anyway? I knew that I owed to him, that I have to...I delved into his world, among people who like him, lost. It was more and more gloomy. Among this human debris I was finding former, brave Solidarity activists who mentally broke down after the fall of Communism, they became alcoholics...Finally I reached his last partner. An old, scary hag. I bought her a vodka. We were drinking together. She didn't really tell me anything. But I remember her words. 'He died,' she repeated. 'He died. I feel sorry for him. Sorry for people. But he was already weak. He was useless. He had to die. He talked about you all. You left him. You left him like trash.' She screamed at me. 'And he remembered you all. You were everything to him. And you! He was probably in love with you!' she threatened me. 'So your name is Zuza, right? Do you know how much he talked about you? And you? What did you do for him?'"

His mother stopped. Again, she looked into the blind darkness outside the window. Adam had nothing to say.

"Remember, I told you that I met Roski shortly before his death. I didn't come up. I ran away. I didn't care about the traitor and degenerate. Well yeah. Let's not slobber over it...I came up with the idea to write a joint statement about Stawicki, for us to destroy him together: the 'Word', us, still someone else. I know how naively it sounds from today's perspective, but it seemed possible to me then. I was under the impression of all these matters. I thought that we could do at least that much. Publish in a few papers a consistent declaration of former activists, friends of Stawicki, cut off from him and at least in this way do justice to those like Roski. Well, I wasn't so naive so as to suggest it to 'The Republic'," she laughed again.

"I couldn't talk with Bogatyrowicz. Too much has grown between us. I made an appointment with him, and still, as it seemed to me, sometimes writing to 'The Word', friends: Danka Brak and Filip Madej, Professor Madej. I invited them to my place, to our place. We sat here. I think also over wine. They accepted my invitation in a distinct way. That they seem to ignore what happened between us, what divided us. They're so generous not to remember what I did. I tried not to notice it. The matter was more important, and they somehow represented the environment from which the 'Word' grew out. I was hoping that at my place, with wine, some of the old atmosphere would come back, that we'd be able to agree on important matters, overcome deepening differences to behave decently...God, how stupid I was! After a few sentences I realized. I saw their faces contort in a grimace of irony. Actually, a caricature of irony, contempt. I thought then that they were parodying Herbert. Do you remember how it went in *The Power of Taste*? 'To grimace, strain out mockery.' Only that the 'priceless capital of the body' was not to fall for that, but they would be rewarded with the applause of the salon, the ones that the author of *The Power of Taste* considered crazy; they will be rewarded with applause and all the profits that follow it. I understood that every thought could be perverted. I realized what a devilish trick this is. To bend nobility and dignity and replace them with their caricatures. I looked at the faces of old friends. They were once beautiful. Now they looked like their own caricatures. They were them. Mouth poisoned with a sense of superiority. But I kept going. I tried to explain to them, though in the depths of my soul I knew it was hopeless. I didn't want to, I couldn't give up."

"They raised doubts. 'How are you sure?' they started. 'If it's true, it's terrifying, but how do you know it's true? Do you know for sure? That, what you say, is circumstantial, and in the civilized world there is a presumption of innocence. You accuse Stawicki of a terrible thing, the ruining of man' they said. 'And all on the basis of receipts from the Institute of National Remembrance, UB papers...Do you suddenly believe them?' They reminded me of the case of Marian Lew, a rector, professor... You probably remember. About a year ago, a terribly loud affair broke out around him. The former chief of 'The Currier', Wilczycki, published documents that Lew was an agent. Then he lost the trial, which means nothing to me, but even the investigator from 'The Currier', who was in charge of the case, a Czułno, admitted that it was rigged. Wilczycki could not defend himself. They fired him and condemned him. He himself is quite a questionable figure: A guy from Bogatyrowicz's stable. Then he emancipated himself a little. Maybe it's a game between them? In my opinion, it is worth returning to Lew's case. He was officially acquitted. He became a symbol of oppressed innocence, an authority to nth power. But he didn't explain himself of anything, and the documents seemed solid. It's unnecessary digressions anyway. I remember those cases when they referred to Lew's incident. Although I didn't treat it as a warning yet. Madej and Brak raised doubts, but in fact everything was obvious for them. Stawicki's case should not be touched. 'Igor can be irritating,' Madej said at one point, 'but he was one of us. If you believe in these revelations, then break off contacts with him. That which was leave it alone, however. If we did the matter as you want, it's a bit like we wanted to spit on our own past.' I understood what he wanted to say. When I realized it was Stawicki...I felt...I felt so lousy, almost like your father leaving me again. But what am I going on about your father?!"

Adam's mother looks at him in suspense. "After all, this universally pompous Stawicki was no one to me, nothing connected me with that snitch, I haven't seen him for a few years. And yet...Then I fought it quite quickly. Breaking my disbelief, I tried to convince them. 'We owe Wojtek this,' I announced and at that moment I realized how weak that argument was. 'Him?' Madej asked with an ironic expression. 'The guy who wanted to put us in the slammer? This is a fact, not your presumption about Stawicki.' 'But he paid for it!' I probably shouted. 'He paid for it?' I don't remember anymore who said that. 'He drank himself to death and that's it.' 'What's with you going on about Roski?' that's certainly Madej. I noticed how differently they pronounce those names: Stawicki, Roski. The name of the first one was pronounced normally. He was one of them. They talked about the latter with a probably reflexive contortion of the lips. As if they were saying an indecent, foul word: 'He always drank, caved in, lost. You cannot blame communism for everything. There are losers in every era. There are always losers.' I knew now, that I wouldn't be able to change their attitude. I stopped understanding myself what I meant about Wojtek. I started in a different way. Stawicki informed on everyone. On me, on them. 'And I don't give a damn," Madej announced. 'I can afford it. Let's assume you're right. Let's suppose Stawicki was a snitch. What will be the consequences of our statement in this matter? Well, I can tell you. All of our opponents, and there are a lot of them, and also in your editorial, will announce that KOR were collaborators. Those who have never risked anything will settle accounts with us. Maybe Stawicki was an agent. After all, we know that those kind existed. Fuck it. What does it matter now? Now other matters are important. You give ammunition to fools, last hour workers who want to distinguish themselves with fundamentalness.'"

"That hurt them, and only that interested them. They were yelling at me. And I? I was helpless. I started without conviction about the truth. 'Why are you so principled and heroic?' I don't remember who among them said it: 'It's time to get out of those trenches. You're like that Japanese soldier who was fighting World War II in the Philippines in the 1970s.' They spoke in turns. They attacked. They began to bring up my past, my life after the fall of communism. 'Why is there so much resentment and bitterness in you?' They asked. 'Are you doing so badly? You're a vice-president, and you chose what you write about. We understand that your personal life isn't going as you'd like, but...' They were subtle enough that they didn't get into the matter. 'You yourself joined these frustrations. And yet you had the same chance as we did. Now you are starting to become like those driven by resentment...You're led by resentments, you're constantly attacking someone!' I returned the favor. We parted in anger. They barely said goodbye. And that was a foretaste of the whole matter. Then it only became worse" she laughed joylessly.

They finished the bottle. His mother rested her head on her hands, and sank into the night filling the kitchen. Adam wasn't able to say anything, he could only accompany her.

The next day, he had a meeting with his father in a cafe. After the greeting, some brief questions and information, he asked him if he knew about his mother.

"Do you mean Stawicki's case?" his father confirmed. "Your mother got into it unnecessarily. She doesn't ask for my opinion, but I would've advised her against it. For her sake. And besides...those UB portfolios...It's not known why they became for your mother a revelation of truth itself.

"Dad just give it a break with those eristic tricks. We both realize that the UB's were not misleading themselves. I didn't get involved in this earlier, but because of my mother...I'm simply amazed that in Poland this whole anti-lustration strategy is so shoddy and so dominant...It's such a trivial relativism, tricks with which you can challenge any action, any judgment...And the success of this strategy..."

"This isn't about relativism" his father was extremely moved. "You don't understand this. You're far away, far away from our affairs. It's easy for you to make judgments. In addition you're too young to really remember those times and understand them. Because the point is not that the UB's mislead themselves. Do you know what kind of recruitment methods there were, how they forced people to cooperate?! For you, an agent is an agent, and they were completely different people. Some tried to behave decently, even when they signed the paper, others...It was like living under Communism. Do you want to condemn us that we were born under bad circumstances?! Not when and not where we were supposed to?!" His father spoke in a raised tone, waving his arms. At the next table someone turned in their direction. His father lowered his voice. "Everything is black and white for your mother."

"But that's not true…"

"Yes? But I spoke with you…"

"About what?"

"Well..." His father seemed confused. He put the half-smoked cigarette into the ashtray and took out another one. "I mean about...Tadek's case."

"She mentioned that she has new leads. She also talked about an interview with Stawicki that appeared in your paper."

"So what? Was it not supposed to appear? It's a standard after all."

"To give a snitch a voice?"

"To give a side a voice."

"I read that interview. You treated Stawicki very gently. There was no interview with my mother. And after all that's, in your view, the other side."

His father was abashed.

"Yes...You're probably right to an extent, but...I don't have that kind of influence in the 'Republic'...however, I managed to block the report about your mother." He looked at his son with a sort of triumph.

"Maybe that bad. Maybe it would be good for such a report to appear!"

"Are you kidding" Have you read the article in 'The Word'?"

"So only those about my mother can appear?"

"Give it a break! The world is, as it is."

They exchanged a few more sentences. Adam's father wanted to learn about his life, but his son responded laconically, ostentatiously looking at his watch.

"Excuse me. I'm going to have to get going."

"But after all…We barely talked…"

"I'll call."

***

A few days later the first hearing of the trial that Stawicki brought against his mother was held. It was classified at the plaintiff's request. Adam had to wait in the corridor among reporters, operators and photographers who bet on the verdict and talked about the latest soccer records. The vast majority bet on Stawicki's victory. Adam chatted with Hieronim and Elizabeth Patkiewicz, a friend of his mother from 'Renassiance'. They waited with him, angry that they couldn't smoke. Patkiewicz even ran out into the street. "Only for one," she explained. The short dress revealed her skinny and crooked legs. Hair dyed red and gathered in a bun with strands breaking out. Close to the skin they were gray. Patkiewicz managed to come back a few minutes before his mother left the room in the company of a lawyer. Stawicki followed her in step. He recognized Adam. His welcome gesture and smile faded, and reporters fenced them off, flooding the heroes of the trial with a barrage of questions that fell at the speed of a flash. Adam pushed through the cordon and took his mother's arm. She leaned on him. It seemed that only he discerns her inner tension. The reporters were mainly interested in what his mother would do if the court agreed with Stawicki, and how she imagined compensation for injuries made to him. His mother replied a bit automatically that she wrote the truth and has proof of it. Questions to Stawicki were milder. He smiled and explained that he believed in the court, because we live in a country that follows the rule of law, in which he also has a modest share in fighting to bring it about.

The group of four sat down on Koszykowa St. over wine, which Adam bought in a greater amount on the second day after his arrival.

"It doesn't look good," stated his mother.

"Sons of bitches! Sons of bitches! Where the fuck do we live, where do we live?!" Patkiewicz repeated furiously, tossing her head as if in an epileptic seizure. "Is it possible to lie, to lie with impunity?!"

"It's possible" Hieronim said in a calming tone.

"The funniest thing is that Stawicki's defender was Zenon Karczmiarz. You know him, former minister, in the Third Republic. I first came across him almost thirty years ago. The UB system accused my cousin of scams that they were doing in the plant where she worked as an accountant. Karczmiarz was the prosecutor and cooperated with them. He urged her to take the scandal on herself and then she would be released from prison. She disagreed, so she served her sentence. Now...the figure at the bar, the moral authority is an attorney for the snitch in the case, which I will probably lose" his mother laughed almost amused.

"Some things are coming together," she said when the guests had gone. "I learned a lot from the Institute of National Remembrance. And Lew's case that I told you about. If the revelations about him were true, it would mean that the security service had an agent among the most important Solidarity experts, those who could basically influence the direction of its politics. After the death of Tadek, his fiancée, Irena, told me how through her family contacts...this is a surprising, but typical for those times story" Adam remembers the funeral and the wake; sobbing Irena, her endless monologue, the story that is only now beginning to mean something to him, a perspective beyond the picture and the ash filling everything "so thanks to drinking with his almost brother-in-law Tadek finds out who was the snitch in the Solidarity authorities or associated with them. Nobody wants to take him seriously, so finally Tadek decides to go to Wałęsa himself. He's already targeted. I told you about, how many years ago when I found a man named Andrzej Molnar, who together with Tadek went on his last trip to Gdańsk. He didn't report, despite all the summons that appeared in the unofficial and official press. Then he arrogantly explained to me that he had nothing to say. Documents at the Institute of National Remembrance confirmed that he was an agent. Not many of his reports remained, but precisely this one, in which he writes that he managed to establish a joint trip to Gdansk with

Tadeusz Sokoł. And one more thing. Strange, but I was the most moved by it. A few days before Tadek's departure to Gdańsk, Lt. Col. Jacek Rojek was delegated there. Do you remember this individual at the funeral of Uncle Stach? We've talked about him lately. A vague, hard to remember, though tall figure, distant smile. He was delegated to Gdańsk for three weeks. Time to settle the matter and clean it up." His mother wrinkles up in a strange grimace.

"Then I tried to reconstruct his story. In the same year he's promoted to colonel. Two years later, in eighty-eight, he leaves the ministry. You know, I've already made some connections in the Institute of National Remembrance." His mother walked around the room nervously, with a cigarette writing unknown words in space. "There's also a prosecutor's department there. I'm trying to interest them in Tadek's case. My capabilities have pretty much ended. From old influential acquaintances, no one wants to help me..." His mother looks at him in the way she seems to only allow herself in the presence of her son. There's helplessness in it.

Adam quickly realized that he could only help his mother with his presence. Everything in him rebelled against passivity. His professional reflex ordered him to treat reality as a set of tasks to be solved. Playing with her was complicated. She never brought ultimate victories. Successes became new challenges and new problems, ineffective methods had to be replaced by others. In Poland, however, he quickly felt that he and his mother were standing in front a wall.

Through the Polish branch of the R&B, he found himself in a reputable lawyer's office cooperating with them. He was accepted by one of the more talented consultants, despite the young age of the board member, Marek Lecki. Through the windows of the glass building on John Paul II St., the fenced, impressive constructions at UN Rondo were visible.

"This isn't about the quality of legal services." Adam had the impression that the certainty of his host faded a little. "I'm saying heresies now which I am not allowed to speak as a lawyer. Especially from the American perspective, which you represent, and I know something about it. This however isn't America. Here, some matters are not to be won."

"But my mother is right. She has documents, testimonies..." Adam himself was surprised by the naivety of his desperate interpellation.

"Sir, now you are speaking heresy. What does it matter? As well in America. Each of us is a little right or a bit wrong. It has nothing to do with the case. Only in contrast to America with Poland, some things are insurmountable. And so it is, unfortunately, with your mother's case."

He came to the journalist of 'The Currier' Monika Gaj through old friends. She was recommended to him as a specialist in difficult cases, brave and aggressive. Despite her young age, she was already quite known. They made an appointment by phone at the 'Modulor' at Three Crosses Square. The journalist was supposed to have a newspaper under her arm, but as soon as she arrived a little late with a characteristic, dynamic step, Adam thought that he would recognize her right away. Do people assimilate to their professional stereotypes, or are particular occupations attracting specific types of people, he wondered, waving to the woman. With a certainty, which she did not need to specifically demonstrate, Gaj approached his table.

"You didn't have to give signs. After all, I saw immediately saw you, an American businessman in Poland" she laughed.

"I don't think you'd expect consolation" they transferred to 'you' after a few sentences "so I will say it honestly. The case is lost. Nobody will get involved in it."

"And you, your paper, 'The Currier'?"

"Me?" She looked at him with bright eyes. "It's funny you found precisely me. Anyway, to whom else could you go? Only I have bad experiences in these matters. 'The Currier' isn't my newspaper, I just work there. Of course it won't get involved in anything. It's still licking its wounds after the Wilczycki scandal. So even if I decided to do something about your mother, my bosses would not agree. But I still wouldn't agree to it."

"Why?"

"That evidence from the IPN...You never know what's in it."

"You mustn't be telling the truth. After all they're reliable documents, you can check them anyway..."

"The truth, the truth. The true son of your mother! I'm sorry" she stopped his reaction with a gesture "I don't want to offend you. I even somewhat respect your mother, but...she's a character from...from another world. I would say from a heritage museum, but you might be offended. That weekly of hers... Do you know how it functions in the media environment? As a synonym for shame. I don't want to say that it's fair. I don't want to use these categories. You repeat after your mother: the truth. I wonder, do you say that in America? Everyone has their own truth. It's about reaching people with it. Somehow, 'The Rebirth' can't. They call it 'The Dying.' After all we know Polish courts. Your mother will lose and everyone who takes her side will lose. Because it's not just about the courts. Do you want to be offended at the world? I have the impression that your mother did that."

"Cynicism? In such a young, beautiful girl?"

Gaj started laughing, looking at him ironically.

"Why cynicism? Are you analyzing me Why not start with yourself? Maybe you should see in yourself, for example, pride, the conviction that you with your mother are the depositors of the whole truth. And after all we know that it's unavailable to us. Sometimes we can only have a small part in it" the girl said it in a different, almost solemn tone, as if she were quoting someone. Immediately, however, she started laughing contagiously.

"Do you remember the motto for *The Captive Mind*? If you're fifty percent right, that's good, if sixty then you're happy, and if you're seventy-five, it's very suspicious. Not to mention a hundred percent. This was said by a wise Jew from the Subcarpatians. Is this in no way close to you?" She was clearly provoked him.

"You're one hundred percent right. Only, then, what do you do as journalists? Because I understand that it's not seeking the truth..."

"Good question. We're trying something, on a small scale, but why immediately eliminate significant figures of our culture? We don't have too many of them."

"Maybe that's why."

They bid farewell, promising each other another meeting. Golden flames flashed in Gaj's green eyes. He invited her to New York. He wanted to run away from Poland already. He couldn't do anything about his mother's case, and the role of support and confidant irritated him. His mother didn't try to stop him. Only his father by phone asked for another meeting. Adam politely got out of it. He was in Poland for two weeks.

CHAPTER 8

He didn't see his father for over three and a half years. Now he was standing before Adam. A few meters away. An old, emaciated man with the remnants of gray hair on his head. His father. Blue striped pajamas leaned out from under a checkered brown bathrobe. Adam's father moved uneasily towards him. Everything seemed undeveloped on him. The gesture of the hands that protruded towards his son stopped before came into contact; his movement slowed down, froze; his lips opened, but they didn't say a word.

Adam came up to his father and embraced him, surprised that he's so much taller than him. His father insisted that they go to the hospital bar, where Adam left Kalina a few minutes ago.

"I'm in the mood for a trip. The furthest that I can afford now" he joked. He was weak. He shuffled slowly, grabbing his son's arm to support himself.

Kalina was gone. Adam breathed a sigh of relief.

"Kalina's visiting you..." he said more than asked.

"Oh, yes...Someone's visiting me..." The continuation was suspended in an understatement. "Do you live with your mother?"

"As always."

"And you flew in…"

"Today."

"Thank you because...I think...Did you get my letter?"

"I came to see you."

"Thank you."

"How are things with you?"

"You probably already know."

"I don't think anyone knows that."

"Give it a break. It's clear. They've even stopped treating me."

"But..." the voice stops in Adam's mouth. His father raises his head. In the net of wrinkles, his faded eyes slide into the depths of time.

"I'm seventy years old. My father died at this age. Of cancer. As I now."

"You say that as if you were prejudging..."

"Give it a break. You act towards me like I did to my father. Thirty-five years ago. He was a doctor. He was getting upset. Now I'll get rid of this unnecessary calming ritual. I was hiding behind him. Your mother was braver. She was always braver. Maybe that's why she was closer to my father than I was. Especially before death. Have you spoken with her?"

"A little. You know, I didn't have much time. I flew in. She drove me home in her Corsa. It's starting to be an intense experience. I took a bath. And I came to you."

"And her…"

"She probably doesn't know, what state you're in…how serious…"

"I'm not asking that. I know she didn't come." His father's face collapses, he starts to break down. "I'm asking…if she didn't talk…about me..."

"I think she doesn't come because she doesn't know about your condition. She thinks it's a conventional ailment..."

"And if she knew…"

"Then she'd probably come," Adam declares firmly, at the same time thinking that he doesn't know what his mother would do, what else she'll do.

"You know, I think I have to finish this trip. I need to lay down."

Adam helped him take off his robe and to lay down on the bed. His father laid down with his eyes closed for a moment, breathing heavily. He looked at him with a mixture of tenderness, regret, and helplessness. His father was passing. Part of Adam's life was closing forever, along with the unasked questions, the white pages, a whole book of white pages that would now never be filled. His father opened his eyes.

"Tell me how you're doing."

"How I'm doing?" Adam asked and was surprised that he had nothing to say. Eight years have passed, and he doesn't have much to talk about.

***

He climbed the career ladder at R&B, became acquainted with its mechanisms and methods, with which they were to master the world. They brokered transactions that created huge international enterprises, liquidated some to replace them with others, took jobs from thousands, and gave them to thousands of others. They associated with people who did not know about their existence, and together they multiplied their own capabilities, built teams from them, allowed them to make arrangements to eliminate the arrangements of others. They assisted companies to grow, become powerful, increase production and employment, and to push to the defensive, and sometimes bankrupt, other companies. Supported by them they grew, hired new employees, opened up opportunities before them, allowed them to get rich, buy things, fill up bank accounts, become someone else when their competitors fired employees, who landed on the moving sands of unemployment, so as to in suspense search for a place for themselves, selling things, giving up subsequent habits and getting into debt, to discover that they are now someone else. They analyzed the work of businesses and the teams operating there. They tracked unnecessary, multiplying links, dead cells in which unnecessary employees were stored, and crossed them out with one stroke of the pen. They sold goods whose production hadn't even begun, and services that haven't been invented yet. They discovered algorithms that were to minimize the unpredictability of the world, and thus the risks that accompany it; they entered equations in the bowels of computers that Sławek Mucha never dreamed of. And it seemed that they had finally found the formula of subdued subjugation, a virtual perpetual motion machine, which once set in motion will endlessly multiply profits, and everything confirmed this belief, confirmed them with certainty until yesterday, until September 2008. Adam saw how his bank account was growing with satisfaction, which he invested in subsequent ventures. Money, which he didn't know, how he would spend, multiplied, piled up, only to shrink up, evaporate and show up only as an electronic phantom, a few days ago.

He traveled the world. Sometimes he flew to the other end of the globe for two days and didn't even feel the change in time when he was back. Waking up at the hotel, he tried to remember if he was already in Seoul or still in Singapore. Looking from the windows of the hotel room at the great bay with clean whitish sand swept by waves, he tried to remember whether it was San Francisco or Dubai, and it wasn't until the great, flat-topped mountain in the middle of the city, which he saw, going out onto the balcony, he realized that it's Cape Town. When he recalls the many places that he has been in, his memory displays before his eyes a moving film stopping every now and again in an image that he's not able to identify, assign to the place, and the film turns out to be a chaos of senselessly stuck frames outside time and space; unnamed scenes and landscapes.

The hotels were similar, as was the service, sometimes with a predominance of a slightly different ethnic type, which he wasn't able to always note. Sometimes women differed, ordered for them by the companies they were working for, the dishes and alcohols with which they celebrated the success of a transaction were slightly different.

He collaborated with businesses located in specific buildings at specific addresses, in which working people of flesh and blood also produced material goods. However, when he returns to those times and undertakings, he only remembers a series of digits on a computer screen, luminous, numerical symbols that interpenetrate and replace in a two-dimensional world. Sometimes screens reflected faces. He hears the personal outpourings of someone after a larger dose of alcohol or cocaine snorted in the elegant bathroom next door, always the same confessions of those who had trouble with other people. People are disruptive, though supposedly predictable they can be surprised, and it's not known why an algorithm has not been invented for them. They deceive each other, betray, suffer, no one knows why, sometimes they wonder why they do what they do, although the answer is so trivial. In the end they fall asleep alone, although sometimes right next to each other, entwined with each other or touching, they dive into separate worlds that are governed by different, unknowable rules.

He met many people. He did business with them. He ate meals, drinks alcohol. He talked and argued. He played tennis, squash, went to the pool and gym, sometimes he went skiing. And these individuals are so different at the time, with perspective, they became some common entity and Adam had problems assigning a specific scene to a specific person, and individualities went away, lost themselves in common words and situations.

During those eight years he met several women who also overlap with each other and he did not always remember with whom he experienced that moment of elation, and with whom he experienced something else. Until Nancy, with whom the relationship lasted for over a year and promised to be more lasting, than previous women: Doris, Ella, Janet, Molly and a few others, they merged from this view over time into a hybrid, although they could be so different. Where they really?

On several occassions he went on vacation to Europe, the Caribbean, and Africa. The images from there however are confused with television images, film stills, and photographs. Only a few durable experiences remained, which he knew for sure that they are his.

He only remembered Russia differently. And September 11th 2001.

***

He could say everything about memories of that hot day in New York, except that they formed a consistent and orderly whole. The morning was still clear, even exceptionally clear, struck in the memory, he recalled - how many times was it - when they were wondering if inside the hermetically sealed, air-conditioned room they sitting on the twenty-third floor of the R&B office twenty-nine streets north could have heard the first explosion, a blow to one of the two skyscrapers of the World Trade Center, the pride of New York. A workday so disturbingly ordinary began less than an hour earlier, exactly forty-six minutes, as he was to find out later. Work was beginning, although the planes were already taken control of, aimed at targets in New York, the curtain rose and the next installment of the global tragedy began when they were finishing their coffee in white plastic cups in the office on the twenty-third floor, which they set aside on their desktops, staring at monitors and tapping at keyboards. And then their tame space was shaken by a slightly muffled, distant sound of an explosion. This is how everyone will remember it with whom he will talk so many times, so many times reconstructing those moments together, as if their precise reconstruction would change something, affect the past, and thus their present. However, even if they didn't even hear the sound that would become the turning point of their memory, something began to happen, tension broke between them, the first telephones rang, someone started talking about a plane colliding with the skyscraper, someone said that it looked like conscious action, someone identified, that it's about the Twin Towers, actually one of New York's two largest skyscrapers. Someone mentioned terrorism. They began to slide out of their boxes, exchanging more and more amazing hypotheses, not knowing if they were falling victim to a large-scale joke, sometimes joking, though their words and gestures were lined with ever-increasing tension. The telephones rang, and the bands of anxiety spread, enveloped, seeped into fear. Loud TVs were suddenly turned on everywhere, the information was choking, contradicting itself, rushed unconsciously everywhere.

Everything was still uncertain and even Albert Armstrong began to chase them back to work, stating that the accident should not be an excuse for laziness, while on TV screens, repeatedly showing the catastrophe, a second plane crashed into the skyscraper stuck motionless next to its smoking twin.

This time, even if the explosion could be heard in their closed, air-conditioned office, it was drowned out by screams and heavy sobbing billowing up its inside. The blow tore apart New York's day. They were running down the stairs. He didn't know if anyone dared to use elevators, he didn't know if they worked. Outside, in the hot city an inferno started. All the sirens of the world were wailing, all the horns, all the alarms came out, from the cacophony only sometimes hopelessly and desperately the clink of phones and human voices escaped. Residents ran south toward the burning towers. Subway tunnels spasmodically threw out more streams of human. It wasn't known whether the subway was being evacuated, whether people were running away in fear of an explosion, or whether an attack had also happened there, as some of the escapees shouted. Every now and then explosions were heard, and it seemed, that they were the next acts of terror, aimed at removing New York from the Earth. But the city defended itself, opposed the chaos. Policemen pushed cars from the middle of the streets, blocked them to open space for the fire trucks, ambulances, finally their vehicles. They built paths of order in the depths of confusion.

Adam ran with a expanding group. He heard conflicting information around. Sometimes he stoped in a crowd halted in front of a display with a large screen on which they were shown, their surroundings, and reality multiplied as if the passage between an infinite number of parallel worlds was opened. On the screens the Pentagon burned after it was hit by a different plane. On the tunnels of the avenues, he could already see the twin towers in clouds of smoke sometimes pierced with tongues of fire. And suddenly his legs placed him in the middle of the street on their own. He felt that he was growing into it along with others, in the human crowd watching how the New York skyscraper sank in slow motion into the ground, disappeared and everything became lost in a cloud of black smoke. The crowd mumbled, mixed. Some of the people ran away as far as they could from the epicenter of the catastrophe, colliding with those who stood as if embedded in the pavement, and with those who, like Adam, after a moment's hesitation start to march towards the fire and smoke.

The explosion of heat, noise, fear and helplessness melted the day into an endless moment. He wasn't far away when the second skyscraper collapsed. The monstrous human figures emerging from the smoke, covered with dust, carried terror. But city officials surrounded the chaos, fenced the areas, organized a rescue.

Adam remembered this day as a collision of the elements that unleashed destruction while those who face it restored order. Together with others, he participated in a rubble removal campaign led by the police. In the heat, clouds of choking fumes and dust fell from the sky, while groups of citizens cooperating more and more smoothly with each other, he cleared hot pieces of debris until the late night, when paralyzing fatigue fell on him and his neck muscles changed into those unable to carry out the next endeavor, stiff and sore bindings. So, he broke away from the work and distanced himself from it, seeing how through the fog of people with frantic eyes, sometimes crying, who try to hang photos everywhere of their loved ones who are laughing with faces that do not understand anything.

New York is his city, just like his city was Warsaw. Its inhabitants unite, transform each other, becoming one body. Firefighters, policemen, paramedics, volunteers evacuate people from the burning towers to the end, to the last breath of hope and even then, when they didn't even have it themselves, when they went to almost certain death, counting on that they'd still be able to help someone. People can survive only because they save others, he thought semi-consciously, returning on foot through the lit floodlight, choking in the smoke-and-pain night of the city that had become his city.

It took many days for the work in their office to return to the previous norm, if it ever returned, and they wondered if life in their city would returned as well. It was only a coincidence that the headquarters of R&B wasn't located in the World Trade Center. A few accidental decisions on the mid-level board meant that they didn't find themselves in the trap burning under their feet, from which the only escape was through clouds of black, painful smoke into the hot sky. Only a coincidence saved them. If they were saved, if they didn't die along with those in the burning towers on the eleventh of September.

Several of Adam's office friends lost friends or family members that day. He walked with them to Ground Zero, the fenced site of the catastrophe, he looked at photos and read recollections.

And later, as soon as he'll realize that he's in the area of ground zero, and time permits, he'll appear even for a moment to watch the wound in the body of the city grow over, heal. He'll remember Warsaw. The one before September 1939, which he thought he remembered, or at least her paintings come back to him like memories, and those later on, which could never be the same again. Like New York. Only that September 11th lasted many months in Warsaw, maybe even years.

***

Adam learned of the great, yet enigmatic undertaking in Russia as soon as he arrived at the R&B headquarters. It was propriatory information, because employees told stories about a powerful investment in Siberia only in private conversations. They bid on confidential information and details and a special degree of selection inaccessible to others. R&B was to mediate negotiations between the American Texmobile group and the Russian company Nieftsybir to become a shareholder in the consortium they were to set up. Its goal was the exploitation of huge new oil fields in the Far East. However, information on this topic was imprecise, shrouded in mystery and resembled rather sensational stories from such exotic and therefore unreal lands.

A few months later, a representative of the board asked Adam about his fluency in Russian. He definitively declared outright perfection. It was likely that the matter concerned Siberian investments, and participation in them not only opened great prospects for the employee starting his career but brought a breath of great adventure. Adam began to polish his Russian, which, it turned out, he remembered quite well from school. After a few months, it seemed to him that he was indeed approaching his declared state of mastery. Nobody however offered him participation in the Russian venture, which in the company rumor mills still looked exactly like they did after Adam's arrival in New York. In the following months, he decided that it's a kind of myth that embellishes the everyday existence of the environment, and from the elements of information processed by the desires, fears and hopes of team members it grew into a dream of proportion that far exceed reality.

A year and a half after arriving in the United States, Board Member Mike Taggart invited Brok to the office. Sitting across from him, Adam studied the bald head and deeply grooved facial features of the legendary personality of the company curiously. Taggart was the youngest and busiest member of the board. He participated in all the riskier activities of the company. He personally looked after ventures in Brazil and Panama, China and Indonesia, South Africa and Nigeria. Luck never left him. It was said that he didn't get tired and never slept. He was referred to as "the youngest", although his age remained a mystery and it was impossible to find him in any company papers, let alone any information scattered on the internet. He looked much younger than the other board members, but employees said that since he first appeared in the company, which means many years ago, no one saw any change in his appearance. Adam could confirm that for eight years, when he saw Taggart, from when he arrived in New York to the moment when he talked with him, leaving for Poland, he didn't even notice a shadow of the passage of time on his swarthy face, not a single new wrinkle, a trace which age leaves on ordinary mortals. The movements of the small figure remained equally elastic and youthful. It was hard to tell if Taggart was forty or fifty years old.

Then he stared at Adam carefully. Black pupil fissures controlled an egg-shaped skull with disturbing, pointed ears that stiffened against the windowpane. Next, flying over the glowing sunny bay, the planes marked the horizon

"You're probably guessing. It's about the Russian adventure. We've been watching you from the beginning. You know the language and, moreover, as soon as the shadow of opportunity appeared, you began to work on it. This is more important than your slightly inflated" Taggart nodded with a smile "qualifications in this field. Peter Hick will acquaint you with the matter. You have to fly to Moscow in three days.

***

Between the boxes and boards with names and surnames that were raised up by those waiting, the computer made printout of the name Adam Brok stood out. The board was held erect in hands of a man in a navy-blue uniform. However, when Adam finally broke through the dense and disordered crowd of the airport and reached out his hand in greeting, it was energetically grasped by the hand of a balding man in an elegant dark-cherry suit and a pink shirt, who slid out in front of the man with the board.

"Aleksander Stiepaszyn" a full set of teeth reveals itself in a dazzling smile.

The driver of a large Mercedes could find a gap in the string of vehicles, which seemed not to be there, and slid in with the accompaniment of a chorus of horns. Despite this, the ride from Sheremetyev to the center of Moscow took them nearly two hours. Stiepaszyn had time to inform him that he had reserved a table in a pleasant environment, where experts from Texmobile and Nieftsibir were already waiting for them. He hoped that after refreshing himself at the hotel, Adam would still have the strength to eat a business lunch with them. He suggested the real attractions to a pleasant environment was not until the evening.

The restaurant was supposed to resemble a tropical garden. Plant walls insulated its individual parts from each other. The small space around their table surrounded by palm trees and flowers meandering between them created a sense of intimacy and security. Adam drank vodka to free himself from the severe sense of unreality, which was caused probably by the time difference, causing his New York afternoon to transform into a Moscow night, and sleep on the plane melted down to three hours. The Texmobile employees probably thought that it was their duty to keep pace with him, for the hosts it was obvious. After a series of toasts, Adam decided it was time to start controlling himself. He realized that it was too late for his newly-met American colleagues to show this awareness, who continued their increasingly unconscious toasts. Stiepaszyn, who had managed to cajolingly transition to 'you' with Adam, from time to time from English, which he operated flawlessly, switched to Russian.

"It's good that you're Polish. We Slavs are able to communicate better. I like Americans, their directness, optimism...but still our temperament...maybe it's a shared historical experience?" Adam tried not to start laughing. He didn't answer that they had tested the same experience from both sides of the barrel. His host looks solidly drunk. He leans towards him with a strange smile. "Anyway, I think it will be easier for us to communicate. Your bosses understood this. So let's drink to agreement?"

"The best agreement is between us, and I must be careful, I think I'm already drunk," says Adam. Forced by Stiepaszyn, who somewhat ambiguously explains that he can count on the care of the hosts, he just wet his mouth in a shot glass.

"And do you like girls? Young girls" After trying another toast, the host leans over him. Adam tries to watch the situation even more closely.

"Of course."

"That's good." Stiepaszyn embraces him. He looks as if he has trouble keeping himself on his feet. "Because we invited our young interns. Get to know each other. We have really nice girls here."

As if though an invisible sign, into the restaurant's office a few young, and despite the dim light Adam immediately discerns, attractive girls slide in.

"We're not going to have fun in an exclusively men's group. Our young employees really wanted to meet the American guests" announces Stiepaszyn and like a drunken boss distributes girls between guests.

"This is Masha" he brings a laughing blonde towards Adam. "Have fun."

"Do you speak Russian?" Masha's happy. "Because I know English, but it's easier for me in Russian. Are you American?"

"Not entirely. I work in New York."

"Oh, how good you have it!" Masha's childishly happy. "I'm also going to go to New York, to America."

"But what for?"

"What do you mean what for? Because...because everything is there... And...and you can meet Brad Pitt and Angelina Jolie, and...I'll also be an actress." Masha claps her hands. She's amused by the thoughtlessness and ignorance of the interrogator. From beneath the makeup a child's face comes to life for a moment.

"Listen, how old are you?"

"And how old do you want me to be?" She asks flirtatiously. The smooth face of the doll begins to fit the make-up.

Adam looks around and doesn't know if he sees or more imagines how the barely developed bodies of girls sway under elegant high-heeled costumes, and the surprised faces of thirteen or fourteen-year-olds slide out from under strong makeup.

"How old are you really. I ask: how old are you really" he says emphatically, realizing that he firmly grabbed the girl by her hand. However, she misinterprets his gesture. Trying to gently release her wrist from the strong grip, she brushes the back of his hand with the fingertips of her other hand.

"Give it a break. After all we're not going to talk about my age. For you I will be as old as you want."

Adam approached Stiepaszyn. As he looked around the room with the expression on his face of a man who doesn't really knows what he sees.

"Who did you bring here?!" Adam lets out a firm controlled voice. "These are clearly underage girls."

"What, would you prefer older?" asks Stiepaszyn with barely perceptible irony. He no longer looks so drunk.

"After all, you know this isn't the point. What's going on here? This is criminal."

"You're exaggerating. What, did she show you her documents?" the host threw out undisguised mockery. "A pretty girl...or maybe you don't like girls? You should've said. We're tolerant here."

"I want, for you to ask these girls to leave."

Stiepaszyn's eyes narrow. For a moment he looked at Adam with a sober, evil look only to burst into jovial laughter.

"Even if I wanted to, I can't. The girls are adults and their new friends...See for yourself" he pointed with a movement of his head at Roger, who was kissing a delicate girl on her neck, his hands grab her buttocks slipping away. For a moment Adam wanted to still make a row, but fatigue falls on him as thick as the air in the restaurant.

"Will you call me a taxi?" he asks Stiepaszyn.

"But ...", the host begins to escalate the issue again, but stops his eyes on Adam and pauses. "Alright." The man in livery is next to him. "He'll walk you to the car. You're tired. I understand. I hope everything is fine between us" he notes, winking at Adam and distances himself back to the guests.

Brok spent the next days working and wandering around the city. He refused Stiepashin's invitation to go to nightclubs twice. After three days, Adam was presented with another representative of Nieftsibir, a young man in glasses with a thin, silver binding, Vasyl Drużynin. Together, they went to the Trietiakowska Gallery, where Drużynin guided him with expert knowledge. Standing in front of the *Bojarynia Morozowa*, Adam thought about his mother. The fierce face of the woman chained to the sleigh and blessing the people with the forbidden gesture of two fingers could not resemble her more. He scolded himself in his spirit for juxtaposing religious fanaticism with the tenacity of the one who gave birth to him, although at the same time looking at the boyarina, he asked if it was only about fanaticism. Something familiar shone from Morozowa's face. He thought again that it was unfair for it to be him to be walking around the Moscow galleries. This reflection often made itself heard in him when he saw the more or less famous museums of the world that his mother never saw and would never see. He remembered her passion for painting and his moderate interest because of her. It was her who hung St. George on a wall in his room, a reproduction of a fragment of Rublów's painting, and she told about icons, which now, he thought he did not remember, but now watching them in the Trietiakow, he recalled himself word for word. It's thanks to her that he'll watch the paintings very carefully and trying to remember them, transfer them into words, he'll be telling her about them in his spirit.

Drużynin also took him on a few hiking trips that would bring Moscow closer to Adam. During the first days, Brok independently got to know the city center a bit. He wandered around the Twerska at night, amazed at night jewelry stores, elegantly dressed women sipping beer straight from bottles on the street and wasn't surprised at the dingy backyards hidden behind luxurious gates. He looked at Red Square, St. Basil's Cathedral and the queue to Lenin's sanctuary. He walked around the Kremlin several times, trying to recall the history of the city he remembered from a past incarnation. Now Drużynin was telling him about Moscow. In the church of Christ the Savior, he knelt and prayed. He lit a candle in front of the icon of the Mother of God. Then he looked at Adam observing him.

"Yes, religion is returning," he said thoughtfully. "This shrine was rebuilt five years ago. You know, Stalin blew it up. But how long will it take to rebuild religion?"

He flew to Nadarsk in ten days. It was only the first reconnaissance, but Adam decided that one should see their Klondike with their own eyes, from where they would go swimming in the black gold of Siberia. The flight with a stopover lasted over eight hours. They stopped in Novosibirsk for almost an hour, where the plane was refueling, and they ate a meal with a few shots of vodka and straightened their bones. All the data, which he once again consulted with Texmobile and engaged in separate conversations with specialists from Nieftsibir, confirming what he had already learned in New York In Southeast Siberia, huge oil fields stretch to the Sea of Okhotsk. However, geological conditions mean that the investment, which in the future may turn out to be a gold mine, requires considerable expenditure, especially taking into account the condition of the local infrastructure. The whole venture could cost up to three billion dollars, although specialists assumed that it could be cheaper by even more than half a billion. Annual gains at the current price per barrel promised a sum of between two and three billion dollars.

Representatives of Texmobile and R&B calculated that the risk would pay off with a thirty-year license and a fifteen percent share. Adam learned this before leaving in a secret conversation, which was proof of the deep trust, as Taggart confirmed, who invited him after working hours and stared into him from behind the desk, when the lower part of his face was decorated with a warm smile. Officially, R&B demanded an eighteen percent interest on behalf of itself and Texmobile. Nieftsibir agreed to a thirty-year concession without any particular resistance, but for now only offered thirteen percent. In negotiations, the Russians laid out unusual opportunities, and the Americans raised the elements of risk. Both sides once again analyzed every detail of the project, each point of the contract and held their positions.

"It is a pity that you're employed in R&B" mused Drużynin. It was already night and after a long walk they were resting in an elegant cafe on Arbat St.

"Why?" Wondered Brok.

"Although..." Drużynin continued, as if he hadn't heard the question, "there's virtually no reason for you not to take other assignments. Right?" The face behind his glasses focused in thought.

"Actually..." Adam began, to gain on time.

"We've gained trust in you. And we really need a consultant from the outside who would realistically assess our capabilities...These are serious matters, so we understand that they must cost a great deal. We don't hold back where it's not worth holding back."

"I still don't know what you are talking about..." Brok asks, who's beginning to understand.

"It's about our capabilities. Ours, i.e. Nieftsibir's. Someone as impartial and competent as you are could evaluate what we can really gain. Of course, we have different business estimates, but we know that this isn't all..."

"Tell me specifically: what do you mean?"

"But I'm saying it. It's about how much we should gain in agreements with Western companies. Such a somewhat abstract, non-specific quotation could help us a lot, and we pay depending on the value..."

"Listen, I have a feeling that something's wrong here" Adam decided to stop the dangerous talking. "After all, I work for a company which you're negotiating with. Any abstract quote, as you say, would be more than a clue to you, and from my perspective worse than disloyalty."

"Don't exaggerate about this loyalty. Business is business."

"Exactly. Rules apply."

"You're not interested in the valuation of such consultation? Just abstractly."

"In the sphere of business, I don't move between abstractions. What do I need this knowledge for?"

"Well I get it. It's a shame. It was a business conversation. I understand that we're separating it from our personal relations."

"Sure," snorted Adam, who couldn't hold back a pinch of irony. "Nothing personal."

The next day they flew to Nadarsk. It was the beginning of August and the stunning Siberian summer continued. The city grew out of a taiga, which looked like an airport almost reminiscent of a temporary military structure. Still in the first half of the twentieth century there was a settlement here. The city was created by people from the gulags, who had to settle in the area after leaving the camp. Paper and petrochemical plants were established, which processed oil from Sakhalin, and especially a wood industry center.

The end of the eighties was the death of subsequent plants, there was longer and longer interludes before they received salaries and pensions. It was then that two characters appeared who gave the city a new life: Anatoly Menuch and Boris Ilchenko.

Legends were told about Menuch. He was reportedly thief in law, a member of the criminal elders. When times began to change, Menuch, as was said, left the professional mafia. After leaving the Gulag he had to settle in Nadarsk, so he made the city the object of his expansion. Slowly, he began to control state-owned companies, guaranteeing directors markets for their illegally sold products. When he began to be known and influential, another person appeared in the city: a young, elegant, well-educated and refined, important member of Komsomol, Boris Ilchenko. How two such different people could meet and connect, remained a mystery to this day. Their stories were different, but none provide satisfactory answers. In any case, Ilchenko and Menuch not only met, but created a long-lasting and profitable duo for both sides.

Ilchenko came with a project to expand the petrochemical plant, but above all to create a trade center in Nadarsk relatively close to China. This is how the Eastern Trade Company was created, in which both entrepreneurs participated, although almost no one knows, and in any case, it isn't officially known on what basis they could control enterprises which they are not, at least formally, owners. Brok got to know Ilchenko quickly and spent a lot of time talking to him. He knew Menuch less well.

He saw him for the first time at an official party. From then on he remembered him. A short, disproportionately wide shouldered man with a gorilla-like attitude that a tailor-made suit couldn't hide. His long hair unsuccessfully tried to mask the lack of an ear. Outside the black, probably dyed beard, it was difficult to capture the smile of thick lips, but his eyes were extremely busy. More impressive were the moments when they froze, leaving Menuch staring into space seemingly to forget about reality.

Nieftsibir has existed for a long time and made used of the deposits on the coast of the Sea of Okhotsk. A few years ago, when the first reports of oil deposits hidden beneath the Khabarovsk Krai appeared, it turned out that this company had the drilling and exploitation rights. At the same time, it was revealed that Boris Ilchenko was the new president of the management board. Its ownership structure in the last decade had become extremely vague and complicated, which, as Adam noted, surprised no one. It combined state ownership with regional (oblast) shares and private shareholders. No one has ever been able or willing to explain to Brok the company's structure. One thing was known for sure: the most important people in it were Anatoly Menuch and Boris Ilchenko. If Ilchenko's role could be explained by chairing the board, then the principle of Menuch's influence remained inscrutable.

The Nadarsk's Center consisted of dirty and cracked prefabricated buildings. They gave the city the character of a dying termite mound. Uncleaned, streets were full of debris and the pavements and roadways were full of cracks, and wooden pyramids from sticks signaled the entrances to man-holes, whose covers were stolen, as was now more often the case with flagstones. The heavy lumps of empty factories partly covered up with plywood, with the empty frames of windows were the most conspicuous element of the urban landscape. Fading and blurring but still visible under scribbles, graffiti and dominant damp patches on the walls called for "socialist competition", threatened "imperialists", promised "eternal peace" and "socialism forever."

In the middle of the city, on the vast square stood the People's House, a large, irregular building looking like a caricature of the Palace of Culture in Warsaw, or rather its Moscow prototypes. The cracked, ten-story chrome pyramid, peeling with paint, lichen of dirt, and scars in places where communist symbols were hurriedly removed, seemed like the specter of a bygone time. Commissioned in the early seventies, it was the seat of the party and regional authorities, it housed a sports center, swimming pools, gyms, an ice rink, a large hall, as well as a cultural center with a theater and cinemas, as well as a university. The building began to decay after a few years. A design error required a major renovation, but the authorities postponed it for the future, subjecting the People's House to ad hoc repairs and strengthening. They proved to be insufficient. At the end of the eighties, load-bearing structures collapsed in the left part of the building. A few floors fell. Fortunately, only seventeen people were killed. Many found themselves in the hospital. One after another, all institutions moved out of the People's House. Currently, it was a habitat of drunkards, drug addicts and homeless people, it was home to youth gangs, and was avoided by ordinary citizens and militia. In his car-walking tour of the city Brok approached the People's House. He looked into unrecognizable rooms through openings of windows that have long been broken open. The sports hall was known by the rusty hoops once hosting baskets. Sprouting bushes grew out of the empty and cracked bottom of the pool. Moss and undergrowth broke through the walls of the People's House, gnawed at it, and ripped it apart.

The city stank, especially squares full of dog and human droppings. Drunks slept on the few unbroken benches, sometimes thrown to the ground with laughter and kicked into movement by groups of teenagers. Herds of emaciated, stray dogs wandered around searching for food and avoiding people. Usually, broken bottles, plastic packaging, rotten fruit and vegetables were everywhere, and plastic bags, scraps of newspapers and paper flew in flocks with every gust of wind. Garbage bins were also stolen, and those that managed to survive, fastened with rusty chains to the storefronts, were taken inside overnight.

Adam looked at the city mainly through car windows. The hosts were surprised by his desire to walk, when they realized the guest's determination, offered a car, desperately protesting against an independent stroll. In truth, in the very center of Nadarsk Brok got out and walked along a dirty street for some time, causing the interest of residents, some of whom seemed to be sobering, looking at him in stupor, but the uninvited car accompanied him all the time and until finally a group of children circled around Adam demanding money, he decided to get inside, sheepishly admitting that his hosts were right with the urging of all their might to advise against walking around the "old" part of the city, from the late fifties and early sixties.

Then, in the nineties a new Nadarsk began to grow. Large, glazed, adjacent complexes of the Eastern Trade Company, Nieftsibir and several smaller companies dominated. Not far away, close to the forest line, there were elegant walled estates surrounded by walls and fences provided with security towers. The shopping center, in which there were a few hotels, formed an almost separate town. A bit further, there was an infinite, chaotic district with many works under construction, large villas and buildings of unspecified purpose.

On the first day Brok met with Ilchenko. An elegant man looking more than forty years old, he was engagingly polite and spoke perfect English.

"From your perspective, we're at the end of the world" he began, then continued, interrupting Adam's insincere protests: "Because we're indeed at the end of the world. But the end of the world can become its center. Your country, America, even two hundred years ago...Yes, yes, I know you're not American, but I think you'll slowly become one. Work builds a man. Well, going back to what I said: one hundred and fifty years ago, even New York was the end of the world, and one hundred years ago, Los Angeles didn't exist. And what? Of course, we have offices in Moscow, but it's from here, from Nadarsk, that we'll run the largest oil venture in the world. Doesn't that excite you?"

Ilchenko talked a lot about the charm of the area.

"You won't find such forests in the US or anywhere in the world. An ideal place for hunting. And full freedom." Ilchenko beamed. "Even conventional hunting is great here. But I suggest something more exciting. Hunting from a helicopter. You probably haven't even heard of such things."

"From helicopters?" Adam was indeed stunned.

"What, do you think it's inhumane?" Ilchenko guessed Brok's reaction. "Sir, these are just presentations. Hunting is aimed at killing animals. It doesn't matter if we are lurking in position or with battue or with helicopters. Please don't imagine that we're going to massacre animals with machine guns. Do you think it's easy to hit with a rifle from a helicopter? It is much harder than from previously prepared position, aiming from a bulkwork at an unsuspecting animal. And from the helicopter, by the way, we can still admire the taiga. I guarantee you: an unforgettable experience. So what, are you in?"

In the bright room that was offered to Adam as a temporary study, sat a young, beautiful and extremely elegant woman. She was smiling endearingly. She stood up at the sight of the host.

"I'm sorry that I burst in without invitation. I'm your translator. Irina Zorow." Surprised, Brok took the hand stretched out in his direction.

"But I don't need a translator..." he began, realizing that he didn't want to say that.

"Yes, I know you speak Russian no worse than I," she stopped him with a gesture and smile, "but...Nieftsibir hired me as a translator." You can, of course, protest and send me away, but...I think I can be useful as...I know...something like an assistant. I'm suitable to it. I'm enterprising, oriented in the local relations and... honestly. I really care about this job. As far as I know, there are a few Americans with you who do not speak Russian. Maybe I'll be useful to them? But you are the most important, you're the boss and you'll make the decision." Her green eyes continued to laugh even though she spoke her topic very seriously.

"I'm not the boss, but of course I have nothing against your presence, I mean, I wanted to say..." Adam is surprised to discover that he's embarrassed "I'll be very pleased, and you...will definitely be useful."

***

Forests filled the horizon. Rippled. They shimmered with shades of thickening green, to drown in black and in a moment to brighten in red tones, to flow in brown, leafy waves. The helicopter descended, dove. The pilot showed something to Ilchenko, who in turn nudged Brok's arm. Deer with long bounds ran through the clearing. Once again, checking the strength of the harness fastening him to the chair, Adam took the rifle lying at his feet in both hands. When the cross in the crosshair stuck in the neck of the deer, he pressed the trigger. The animal rushed on. This repeated several times, until finally after however after many pulls of the trigger the deer fell on its front legs. His head crowned with horns tossed into the grass, from which he desperately tried to tear himself away. His hind legs kicked the ground violently, throwing up pieces of turf. Brok fired time and time again. The helicopter hung almost motionless above the animal. It seemed to Adam that the bullets were reaching their target, but the deer were still alive. Finally, after another shot, he stretched out on the grass, motionless.

"Zuch!" Ilchenko patted him on the back. Brok wanted to puke.

That evening in the elegant Nadarsk Club he got drunk. Ilchenko raised the first toast.

"For the well-being of our guest, who with his first shot hit the beautiful deer." The host raised his shot glass up. "What shots they were!"

The president beamed. Adam had the feeling that there was mockery at the bottom of his smile. The faces of the hosts, smiling and kind, could laugh at him. Even in Irina's green eyes, flames of mockery danced. Only the Americans, who didn't understand anything, were full of appreciation and sincerely envious.

"You're lucky," Roger began a conversation with him. "With your first try and such a trophy. It must be an impression. From a helicopter. Like in a war. I have to arrange something like that for myself somehow."

"Yes. You're right. It's a sensation."

Adam was drinking subsequent shots to chase away the images of the day and the suspicions haunting him. Beyond him, the hosts were exchanging glances of understanding, they seemed to be having fun at his expense.

"Mr. Brok's deer hasn't been prepared yet. Of course, you'll receive it in due time. And especially the main trophy. Great deer horns." Ilchenko raised another toast: "So for the horns! For your horns!" The toast was greeted with laughter and applause. "And now I invite you to taste the best Siberian venison. As I mentioned, it will not be Mr. Brok's deer meat, but equally worthy."

"You've won a beautiful trophy!" Irina smiled charmingly at him.

"It's not like that..." Adam was having trouble expressing thoughts that mixed sensations and alcohol "I shouldn't have...I shouldn't have participated in it, I shouldn't shoot..."

"What are you saying? After all, it's a beautiful experience" Irina smiles brightly.

With the last flash of consciousness, he decided to return to the hotel. Irina walked with him and they probably made out outside the hotel, in the elevator and in front his door, after a few attempts, he finally opened the door of the apartment but at the last moment she slipped away as he tried to push her in. He didn't have the strength to chase her. He burst into the room and in his clothes fell on the bed. He dreamed that he was a deer chased by armed people in a helicopter. He couldn't run away.

The next trip to Nadarsk was scheduled for mid-September. Negotiations seemed to be stalled. Taggart calmed them down by phone and called for cool blood. "It's a moment to hold your ground. Whoever takes the first step will give a signal of weakness."

Brok pressed for him to be transferred to Siberia. It was there that the heart of the undertaking was beating and there the final details of the contract could be made more precise. He couldn't hide from himself that the main reason for his certainty could be Irina's green eyes, which returned to him more often than he could have imagined earlier. They called each other every day, and Adam had to fight with himself, so he didn't do it more often. In conversations, they didn't return to the drunkenness preceding his departure to Moscow. Brok was ashamed of his behavior, of which he didn't remember much. On the phone, while still maintaining a slightly playful tone, he described how much another meeting meant to him. She laughed and answered equally casually. Finally, he called her, triumphantly announcing the date of his arrival.

"I'll be waiting," she said in a characteristic, serious tone, in which however the fires of irony were smoldering.

From time to time, it occurred to him that Irina was a luxury prostitute hired by the company to control him. However, she didn't go into his room, he convinced himself, realizing that such a refusal could be treated as an element of tactics. "In this way, every behavior of the woman can be interpreted as an element of a complex strategy," said Adam, charmed by her, questioning the skeptical arguments of his opponent. After all, she could simply be a beautiful translator, which for a company such as Nieftsibir (not only for her) mattered. Would this state of affairs mean that Irina tolerated his advances because of the amount of the contract? How far in that case can Brok go then? The only salvation against the endless loop of questions, doubts, self-accusations and self-cleaning was not to think about the matter. Only that Adam wasn't able to not think of Irina.

She was in the team waiting for him at the airport. In the evening, they sat in a cafe to which he invited her by phone, already there, unable to avoid the hostile warmth of the hosts. Irina watched him with an inscrutable smile.

"It's not particularly interesting here. Especially for you" she said suddenly. "It's after all an imitation of America. This new Nadarsk. And you could find such interesting things in the old one."

"Have you been there?"

"I've only heard of these places. It's such an alternative world. If you want, ask Furcew, head of security for Bori...I mean Ilchenko."

"You speak of him by name?"

"I speak of him that way. Like everybody. This is the style. That supposedly he's ours and a modern president. Nobody says Tolia about Menuch."

"So, you know Menuch too?"

"Not at all. I've never seen him. Only everybody talks about him. It's hard to say that I know Ilchenko too. Several times as a translator I involved in conferences with his participation, and then in receptions organized on those occasion."

"You were his translator?"

"About two times."

"But he clearly speaks English fluently."

"Then ask him. Maybe he recognized that in some situations...anyway, I don't know." Irina didn't look confused.

When she refused to enter the hotel with him, to which she escorted him, a few hundred meters from a cafe in the shopping complex, he felt uncomfortable.

"Maybe I'm abusing..." he began uncertainly. She ran her fingers over his forehead, which she had kissed earlier.

"You're not overusing anything," she said, almost affectionately, sliding out of his arms, moving smoothly away and leaving him in a state of complete confusion.

Nieftsibir rented the most luxurious Nadarsk locale for this party. Then for the first time Adam saw Menuch.

"I'm glad," the character murmured, extending his hand to him. Vivid eyes pulsed in the crude bearded face.

"Yes, yes, we're happy" he repeated staring closely at Brok "such a big, capitalist, that is, I meant to say, American company" he laughed indistinctly "we'll definitely get along. Here, gold flows underground. And we'll get it."

"Irina told me that you were interested in Nadarsk's attractions." The large, shaven-bald man leaned into Brok's ear. "If so, I can lead you. Because you know... There are not just such official, elegant locales..." The face of Ilchenko's security chief had something Mongolian in him. "There are also interesting things in the old town. I'm just warning you. It's for men. With strong nerves."

"So, when can we head out?"

"Whenever you want."

"What about now?"

"We can't go right now. But in fifteen minutes."

Brok realized that his testing questions were a determination. Everything happened so quickly, so unbelievably, that Adam began to wonder if he was under an illusion. Fifteen minutes probably really went by, when Furcew appeared next to him again.

"Are we going?" Adam heard a whisper, but the head of security was already in the next group of people, from where he only gave him fleeting gazes.

Brok apologizes to the accidental interrogation and followed Furcew. He meets up with him in the parking lot, where Irina was standing next to a Jeep Grand Cherokee and a broad-shouldered, bald man unknown to Brok.

"You said, that this is for men."

"Yes..." the surprised chief of security confirms, and following Adam's gaze, he laughs. "Irina? I wish many..." He doesn't finish.

"This is all weird," says the stunned Adam to the woman.

"It's nothing," she says with her characteristic smile. "I can only go there with you."

Snuggling in the back seat, Irina hugs him tightly. That, which happened next would be remembered by Adam as a kind of figment of his imagination, which he didn't know if it really happened.

The front of the old factory was painted colorfully, despite the floodlights illuminating it, which barely shined out into the night. Entering the parking lot, the driver leaned through the window to the characters standing by the booth. The barrier rose. Someone joined and lead them, bypassing a large queue waiting before the gate outside the building. Inside, the noise that had already reached them repeatedly, exploded with a deafening roar. From all sides the rhythm of the sharp background music of guitars and drums attacks them. Adam didn't even know if it's just speakers or if he hears a few clashing motifs played in different rooms. The flashing of the lights seem to be in tune with the shouts of the crowd, which encouraged something in the interior. Furcew moved away with one of the gatekeepers. He came back a moment later.

"Now we can go through. Here are some suggestions. We can start with the most, how to say, folk. But there is also a lot of money here."

They push through the crowd to see in the center of the round arena the interlocking and struggling with each other shapes. Clean shaven men in dark suits and with gold chains on their necks scream to each other and show something on their ringed fingers. Here and there young women equally excited and loud can be seen. A high whine breaks through the human screaming.

"Great, I lost!" Someone is breaking through to the center. "Let me take my dog!"

Whistling can be heard, but someone helps the unfortunate owner, someone beat the victorious Pitbull with an open hand on the head.

"Well, let go, let go now!"

A man carried a dog that tried to raise its falling head. In the spotlight you can see streams of blood that cakes on the arena.

And again, the noise increased, turning into a scream. Two dogs were tearing towards each other. A huge, shaggy Caucasian Shepherd tugged on a leash held by two men. On the other side, not reaching even half its height, the fangs of the Pitbull settled on a small, muscular torso and short legs. Adam found it hard to believe that even the most combative Pitbull could pose a threat for a mountain giant.

The owners took off the leashes and the dogs charged each other in a bright spotlight ring in the center of the arena. The Pitbull disappeared under the shaggy dog's body. Everything gets quiet and even the rhythmic crash of the speakers was not able to fill the vacuum. Strange munching and grunting were heard. The shepherd's body, which was hide by the opponent, was torn by violent spasms. Then a long, ghostly moan penetrates the room. The Caucasian collapses on its side, exposing its chest and the Pitbull immersed in it, which tore and bit into it more and more deeply its muzzle covered in black blood. Irina squeezed Adam's shoulder. He didn't see her, immersed in the twilight, face. The shaggy dog's body was shaken by death contractions. The crowd was overwhelmed with euphoria. Its roar drowned out the speakers. The Caucasian became still. Its opponent tugged at him a moment longer, then to let go, raised its head and looked around with a surprised mouth. Brok felt nauseous.

"Let's go from here" he doesn't know who he's addressing these words to, but Furcew answers.

"Sure! There are more interesting things. There are people fighting here" he indicated the neighboring room. "Do you want to see?"

"Can I get something to drink?" Adam motioned through his clenched throat. Irina hugs his shoulder. Through the silk of the dress he felt that the woman's body is being covered with sweat. Her face drowned in darkness and only her eyes shine with a green glare.

"Of course. Kola will take care of it. What do you wish?"

"I vodka. And you?" he turns to Irina.

"The same" the woman replies in a slightly hoarse voice.

"So what? Are we going to see the fights? Kola will find us."

Brok follows Furcew, somewhat automatically grasping with his other arm Irina's hand woven under his arm.

In the middle of the room, two men are entwined with each other in a cage. The noise and excitement outside contrasts with the slow moves of the characters on ground.

"It's not a very interesting moment for those who know little about this" explains Furcew. "Yemielianov is on the bottom, but he caught his opponent in the guard and that one can practically do nothing with him. Yemielianov is good."

Kola appears with a bottle of vodka and two glasses. At the bottom of each lies a few ice cubes.

"And you?" Adam asks Furcewa, pointing to the bottle, surprised at his own directness.

"I'm on duty!" Furcew laughs. "Like Kola."

"What duty? After all we came to see the attractions?"

"But my duty is to protect you two. That's why I have to be sober."

Brok wanted to deepen the conversation but gives up. He drank a large dose of cold vodka to the bottom, realizing that he isn't even waiting for his companion, who's rocking the unfinished liquid in her glass. The wrestlers in the cage are struggling violently. The wrestler on the bottom throws his opponent, breaks away, and struck his forehead on the face in front of him. Blood spurtted, the opponent fell to his knees and then a precisely measured kick from half a turn hits his temple and knocks him to the ground. The crowd howls. In the flashes of the spotlights Adam sees shimmering faces. The animal-human physiognomies distorted in the screams lose their features and outlines. Slavic, Caucasian, Kalmyk and Chinese faces blend in the howl. They're shimmering with the incarnations of animals. People-dogs, people-wolves, people-monkeys. Infinitely plastic faces lose their identity. They're only passion and infatuation.

"Didn't I tell you so?!" Furcew announces with satisfaction, pointing to Yemielianov, who raises his arms in a gesture of triumph. "Nothing like our good old sambo. Even Brazilian jiu-jitsu can't hide!" the head of security is pleased. "And Yemielianov isn't just a nobody. Are we waiting for the next fight?"

"We're going," Brok hears his own deaf voice.

"You have to, if you have to," reports Furcew with disappointed subordination. "It'll now be love," he adds in a more cheerful tone.

In the middle of the room, in a large bed, two copulating couples resemble the wrestlers in the next room. The sweat on their bodies in the light of the colorful reflectors is lustrous multi-colorfulness, characters move spasmodically, panting heavily. The crowd cheers, yells fouls and commands, throws out litanies of insults. The men on the bed exchange women and continue their rhythmic exertions. Around the same as before, sparkling with excitement and screaming physiognomy.

"Nice bets also go on here" Furcew explains matter-of-factly. "And over there," he points with his hand, emerging in the light of lamps women next to pipes "there they can be won. Anyway, you can win everything here. Or lose. Roulette, black jack, poker. Whatever you want. There's also a separate room where you can buy and rent girls and boys..." he suspends his voice, but because no one continues, looks towards the bed-ring.

A heavy character turned away from the bed, where now two men took care of one woman, and the other on all fours helped them as much as possible. The man looked intensely at Irina, who's squeezed Adam's shoulder. Furcew's head bends lazily towards the intruder. In the noise, Brok can't understand the words, but the man turns and walks away.

"We're returning," Adam decided, drinking another dose.

The Jeep left from the hotel after the polite goodbyes to Furcew and Kola.

Adam embraces Irina and enters the lobby. Without a word, they rode the elevator and found themselves in the room. Irina looked at him with that all promising smile, and Adam constantly heard the roar of the audience cheering for animal-human wrestlers. In the twilight of the room they danced, exchanged images from previous hours. The strange condition caused Brok to not even feel a trace of the uncertainty Irina has raised in him so far. He embraced her, began to undress her, and she helped him, adapted to his expectations.

***

"I am the secretary of President Leonid Losiew, well, please do not pretend that you do not know who this is about, the President of Amkom. Can you talk now?"

"It's good that we can finally talk" the phone sounded in a metallic voice. "It's good that they send those who understand languages here. So, listen, sir. I am Losiew and would like to talk about your business interests. It would be best if you come to me, to Irkutsk."

"You will forgive me, but I'm busy," Brok struggled to stop, so as not to interrupt the conversation.

"You must don't understand. Are you a representative of Texmobile and R&B?"

"I represent R&B, which also deals with the Texmobile projects in Russia. But your company probably has nothing to do with it."

"You're mistaken. You will need to start negotiating with us now. And it won't be bad for you. I won't say that we'll agree to your eighteen percent for thirty years, but it may turn out..." the interlocutor suspended his voice "that we'll agree for more. Of course, under the right conditions."

"You'll excuse me, on this subject I speak with officially delegated representatives of Nieftsibir. I'll have to end this conversation."

"Wait a minute. You still don't understand. The situation in Russia has changed. Don't you know?"

"We're not interested in politics. We're businessmen. Goodbye sir."

In the office, he asked Gurchenko about Łosiew.

"Certainly, I've heard of him." Gurchenko's eyes fell on Adam. "A bit weird character. He appeared on the market relatively recently and certainly has good connections. He's quite aggressive in business. Why are you asking?"

"Someone told me about him" Brok dismissed the question.

He was sitting by the huge window of the cafe that overlooked the inner square of the mall and was waiting for Irina. He was worried about this romance, his own commitment, the constant desire for the presence of a person he did not trust and did not even harbor special illusions. However, when she appeared, he forgot all doubts, found justification for every ambiguous behavior, explanation of every imposing suspicion. Was it just because she was beautiful, that he was experiencing exhilaration with her that he didn't know before and was he sure that her erotic ecstasy wasn't fake? Maybe because she's a real professional - the skeptic whispered in him - and in every relationship, indeed, in every dealing she can put maximum passion, and the object has no meaning to her, and this should be used to explain the authentic gestures of tenderness she could manage.

Adam didn't really know anything about Irina. She escaped his questions. Sometimes she only confessed her erotic experiences, which became part of their sexual game, but it did not advance his knowledge of her. He also defended his memories from her and, above all, separated his professional activities from their meetings. Sometimes it occurred to him that he was rude, dismissing her, never really too insistent with questions about work. She didn't seem to notice it. The affair with Irina suddenly became the most important thing. Because besides that...Adam was sitting at the end of the world and sentenced to inaction waiting for no one knows what. And what's more, he dreamed that this situation would last, last forever. Any solution would involve a change in his status quo, a departure, and therefore a likely parting with the woman from here, and Brok didn't even want to imagine that. When later, long afterwards, he'll recall to himself the months in Nadarsk, he'll understand that he was happy then.

He once confided to Irina that he has feelings of closure:

"We're in the largest country in the world. In the endless spaces of wild nature, and we spend our time over a few square kilometers, which we cannot very much leave."

She offered him a trip to the taiga and from then on, they would leave in an all-terrain vehicle, which Irina arranged. It was already autumn, the taiga swelled with mature colors, and even started bare patches here and there. Cold winds could penetrate to the bone, but the woods were wild and delightful. An alien and inconceivable beauty, Brok sometimes thought.

They were returning through old Nadarsk, which looked like a disgusting ulcer on the body of the taiga. Small patches stretched out before the city. They were made of lopsided cottages, made from anything, no different from slums. Rags, pots and old clothes were drying on the fences. The irregular beds of cabbage, cucumbers, onions and potatoes adhered to the enclosures.

"If someone drove over this misery with a steamroller, he would have aesthetic merit in heaven," he once misspoke as they drove along a bumpy road next to the gloomy landscapes of plots.

She turned away from the steering wheel without her usual smile. She clenched her teeth.

"And would deprive those people of their livelihoods, would it? But esthetes like you don't care" the tone of her voice and expression put Brok in much more astonishment than words.

"And how do you know about that? And since when are you interested in this?"

"Since when?" There was no trace of her usual cheerfulness in her voice and face. "Since I was born here. And since, especially at school, we ate only what we grew on our plot. At that time, I was interested in it. Not now, but when I hear such..." she pursed her lips and Adam had the impression that he was hearing an unspoken curse "when I hear such things, damnation hits me."

"I didn't know that you're from here."

"If I were from anywhere else, what would it change? This is Russia. And that's why people like me so badly want to break out and forget about where they were born. And they don't like it when someone forces them to bond with those with whom they no longer feel it." Irina tried to warm up her angry tone, to tone it down with irony, but it was an artificial procedure.

Brok tried to improve her mood. She laughed, joked, but he felt that a wounded and angry woman was lurking underneath, which he had not noticed up until that point.

Their affair was slowly becoming a public fact. Adam's Russian associates, however, treated it either very discreetly or as something obvious, which turned out to be the same. Americans saw their relationship more clearly. During a party, when Irina moved away for a moment, following her with longing eyes, Roger summed up the matter as usual:

"You really are lucky."

Adam began to laugh, unable to hide his satisfaction.

Therefore, when Ilchenko invited him to his dacha, using the plural, Brok was not particularly surprised, although he made sure:

"Us? You have in mind..."

"I had in mind you and Irina, but if...it's after all an invitation for you..."

"Thank you in my and her name."

The dacha was in the taiga thirty kilometers from Nadarsk. On one side, was up against the forest, and on the other, a garden surrounded by a high wooden fence, inside which two handsome Rottweilers ran, adjacent to the beaten road. The house was a large, one-story house. Ilchenko was driven by Kola in the company of Furcewa. An off-road Toyota driven by Irina followed them. There was nobody in the house. Ilchenko had just divorced his wife, and his personal life was at a bend. That in any case, that was what was said in the company, and the president hasn't show up with any women lately. The divorce was associated with closer unspecified problems over children. Kola and Furcew, who also stayed at the dacha, disappeared somewhere into its depths. The three of them sat by the decorative fireplace, in which a fire was stirring, warding off the already at this time penetrating chill. The night stilled outside the windows, and Latin music played by the speakers, whose host turned out to be a devotee of. They partook in bourbon, Ilchenko's pride, for whom it was specially brought from the States. Tasting it theatrically, the host told them about American alcohol, waved an epic bourbon before them, falling into greater elation. Adam liked the drink, although he probably couldn't appreciate its subtlty, while Irina in delight supported Ilchenko's story. At the bottom of his picturesque relationship, Brok sensed a trace of bitterness.

"You know, not much has changed in our country. It probably must be this way" Ilchenko noticed suddenly. When asked, he did not fully explain: "Well...I mean communism. I have nothing to complain about. I'm making a fortune. But I already started doing it in the Komsomol in the eighties. We talk so badly about that system, but after all we were the ones who made it and we made careers in it. Has so much really changed? Alright" he calmed Brok's protests. "It was different for you. You were our colony. No offense. I can agree that our Polish-speaking governors who held you by the face and threatened you with our tanks were pigs and traitors. But we were at home and governed ourselves. Communism was stupid. But this is just..." Ilchenko sought the words "ideology, ritual, talk, and life went its course. It was our country. At one point it was necessary to get rid of this ideology, because it weighed too much, but did relations change so much? Capitalism, communism, just words..." Forgetting about the ritual, Ilchenko poured into himself a large dose of bourbon that he had in his glass in one gulp. "Somebody has to rule, somebody has to listen. And there must be space for doing business. Only this much and just so much."

About a week later, in the early afternoon, Ilchenko burst unannounced into Adam's office.

"We need to talk in private. It may be at my dacha. Only this time without company. Do you agree?"

It turned out that the invitation is for now. Reluctantly, staggering over the phone, Brok canceled the meeting with Irina, who, as usual, understood everything and agreed to everything. Adam felt a little hurt.

"Without company" meant in the company of Kola and Furcewa, who, however, disappeared as usual as soon as they arrived at the dacha.

"These negotiations are taking too long," the host, clearly nervous, began.

He's changing, Brok thought. The suspense in him can be seen pushing up in the business of life, because this is probably the business of his life, he wondered. "Whoever takes the first step will signal his weakness," He recalled Taggart words. Has this moment now truly come up?

"It's time to stop the talking and get to work. The oil is waiting" Ilchenko was feverish, drinking another dose of bourbon. "You want too much, but so be it. I'll give you eighteen percent. So be it" he repeated and only then did Brok believe.

This wasn't a success; this was a triumph. He knew about it. He didn't even want to imagine bonuses and promotion. It was just the beginning of his great career. It was also a radical change in his situation. The prospect of a return to the States soon. Should he offer Irina a trip together in such a situation? Thoughts tangled with each other, but the original feeling of triumph dominated. Adam decided anyway to defend it at all costs.

"That's good," he tried to speak calmly and dignifiedly, although he noticed that he also emptied his glass of bourbon in one gulp, not even knowing when. "I also thought this all was lasting too long. I'll forward your offer to the States and I think that we'll be able to sign the contract soon."

"Hola, hola" Ilchenko stopped his enthusiasm "I said that I think your expectations are excessive. I accept them because I know that the good of the enterprise requires it. But I'll have to convince the management board and shareholders. And it'll cost me a lot. I've already calculated it." Ilchenko calms down and looks at Brok with a calm, cold look. "Forty million dollars. Non-negotiable. I give you three days. Sink or swim."

Wait a minute, wait a minute..." Adam tries to save the wobbly construction of success "how do you imagine this? We're supposed to transfer this to your account?"

"Are you kidding me?!" Ilchenko is outraged. "In one day, I will create a company to which you will pay the money. As a fee for something. You refine the details. You also have to do some work."

This time they did not stay overnight and returned after drinking another symbolic glass. Immediately upon his return, Brok informed Taggart's assistant that he was waiting for a call. Night in Nadarsk was late morning in New York. Taggart called back in less than an hour.

"Well, everything's gone to shit," he said after hearing the report. "After all you know that we're not Europeans. In our country, paying a bribe even abroad is a serious crime. We don't have access to European operating funds..." Taggart dreamed.

"But without it everything is lost. It's clear to me now" Brok continued his previously thought-out issue.

"It also coming to me slowly..."

"You started talking about European companies."

"Yeee…"

"There's a problem securing investment. We could've rented an American company, we could a European one. I met some Englishmen in Moscow. They could take it on. This is a costly operation. I don't know if they could do without the help of a local company. I think that the work of such a Russian company could be valued at forty million. The English have a choice: either get a good contract or not. What do they care if they sublet a local company? All in all, we're still paying for it anyway. And it pays off for us." Brok finished his statement and hearing the silence on the other side of the phone, he immediately added: "I was talking about Englishmen whom I met, but they may be French or Dutch, anyone can find them. I care about finishing negotiations with Nieftsibir."

"Well, sonny..." a deep gasp came from the other side of the globe "hardly anyone surprises me at all. You've done it. Congratulations. They can be English. Handle it. I have no suspicions. And finally, next to congratulations, one piece of advice from the old uncle. Make sure that your personal affairs don't affect your business. Beautiful women...also have to live on something and it's hard to blame them." Brok feels cold at the back of his head and growing cold rage.

"I'm an adult and I don't want anyone to interfere in my personal affairs. Unless they affect my professional behavior. Only then I would ask for justification."

"Oh, Adam, give it a break!" Taggart is nothing but tenderness. "I know you realize it but forgive a debilitated uncle a little. The obvious repeated once more only gains in value. Take care of the English now and finalize the venture. We have full confidence in you."

The next day he agreed with Ilchenko that the order for the English would be entered into the contract. He telephoned Timothy Clark in Moscow. The speaker was interested in the offer, and although Brok didn't explain everything to him, he had the impression that Clark senses that which is unspoken. After all, he has already spent two years in Russia. They made an appointment in two days in Moscow. Ilchenko guaranteed a plane, and Irina was glad as a child to visit the capital. "Finally, we're going to Moscow!" She repeated.

In the hotel lobby, Adam was stopped by a smiling young man in the company of two powerful figures.

"Mr. Brok, I finally have the luck to meet you. As they say here: small world... Will you give me a few minutes? I am Pyrjew, Georgij Pyrjew, a representative of Amkom, of President Losiew" the man spoke fluent English, although he put the saying in Russian.

Adam hesitated. Pressure irritated him, which could be considered an attempt to intimidate, he was interested in what the interlopers wanted to propose. Pyrjew looked like he was guessing his dilemmas.

"You'll forgive the form of the invitation, but it is only because a few hours ago we arrived from Irkutsk especially for you and we waited in the hotel...You didn't want to come to us, you didn't even want to talk to the president by phone, that's why I came. This is of course a request. If you are disturbed by my... friends...we can send them out."

"All the same to me."

"That's great. Let's sit."

"But only for fifteen minutes."

"I'll try to summarize."

Pyrjew ordered a whiskey, he became worried that Adam didn't want anything, and nodded sadly.

"It's a shame you don't take us seriously. But we're not offended. The president is not offended. You don't know Russia yet. This is a serious enterprise that you're negotiating without us...It's not feasible without us, and with us it may turn out to be even more lucrative."

"I'm sorry, but who are you gentlemen? I know, I know: Amkom, an important company in Irkutsk, but how does it relate to Nieftsibir? Therefore, I repeat again: you are wasting your time. We are a honest company and we only talk to officially designated representatives of the company that are is our counterparty."

"Honest talk...a honest company..." Pyrjew mused. "And do you know why Ilchenko is so important? You say: he's the president. But why is he the president, who elected him? And who is Menuch and why is he so important? Who is he in Nieftsibir anyway? You don't know that."

"And I don't have to. I negotiate with official company representatives. Its internal structure may not interest me."

"For sure. Only are all of Ilchenko's proposals so official? And everything happens exclusively in this way? He is the president, but he may not be. We say here in Russia: there was a man, there is no man. If, until now, for unknown reasons, the most important figure in Nieftsibir was Menuch, then it may soon be president Losiew. You say: I'm not interested in politics. But this is Russia, you can't ignore it here."

"We're wasting time." Brok got up. Pyrjew got up as well, and behind him, as if pulling on a spring, two seated at some distance figures.

"Pity you don't want to talk to us. It's a shame for the venture. I hope you can still be persuaded. One piece of advice. Don't bet on Ilchenko like that. He's a former operative."

"Son of a bitch!" Ilchenko jerked. "They're pretending that they're the Petersburg mob. You know, those strongmen from Putin. But they'd only like to be." The President drank some bourbon. He'd been drinking a lot more for some time. "I won't hide it. They have their contacts. But I have mine. They want to take over Nieftsibir and therefore the contract should be signed as soon as possible. If we sign it, we'll guarantee our position. Nobody will touch us anymore. Understand?

Tomorrow you are flying to Moscow."

"It's a shame that you didn't tell me about this earlier," Taggart's New York sigh flared into the Siberian night.

"How could I know that they are not ordinary conmen who want to roll something up for themselves in a big deal, and don't mean anything. I still don't know that anyway. We can't worry about them..." Adam interrupted. Irina stood on the threshold of the bedroom. He went out to the living room to make phone calls, when she dozed off tired from love, but now she was standing and looking at him. They looked at each other for a moment. The smile on Irina's face froze."

"What's going on, what did you stop?" Taggart was asking.

"Wait a minute. We'll be able to talk in a moment, '' Adam said loudly and clearly.

Irina grimaced in a fake smile and returned to the bedroom, closing the door behind her. She pretended that Brok's behavior did not affect her, but she regained her humor only on the next day on the plane. She was happy, and Adam was surprised how much he could enjoy her joy.

The conversation with Clark was a success. The Englishman understood everything and accepted everything. Now it was necessary to complete the formalities and transfer the money. On the way to the hotel Brok turned on his cell phone. He had seven text messages from four sources: "Ilchenko was shot".

He called Drużynin.

"Yes, this is unfortunately true. They shot up his jeep. He probably got at least seven bullets. They also killed his driver and bodyguard. There is confusion in the company. I'll contact you as soon as I know something" ended the upset speaker.

Irina was waiting for him in the hotel. "Now do you know?" She asked coldly. Adam thought that without this special smile she lost her uniqueness and became one of the many pretty women walking the streets of Moscow. Information on the killing of Ilchenko appeared in news services. From the photo on the screen appeared a familiar, smiling, face. Then came a Jeep Grand Cherokee chopped up by bullets with a crushed left front side of the body. 'Transaction of life' rang in Brok's head. He looked at Irina. Her face didn't change and didn't express anything.

"There's confusion in the company. The appointment of a new president is underway. Actually, you have no reason to come" explained Drużynin.

The cool autumn light filtered through the large windows of the hotel restaurant. Adam sat alone. Irina hurried into the city after breakfast. "...and I don't want to disturb you now in your serious professional matters," she said goodbye. This time her sarcasm was devoid of warmth. Adam was pleased. He wanted to be alone. The previous evening, he felt her strangeness extremely strongly. And even sex with her, which he initiated quite reflexively, seemed extremely automatic to him and didn't give him particular satisfaction.

His cell phone rang, displaying an unknown number.

"Expressions of condolences, Mr. Brok. Don't you know who is speaking? It's me, your humble investigator from Nadarsk, actually Irkutsk, the one who spent a few hours hopelessly on a plane to shake your hand. Georgij Pyrjew, is your humble servant. It's sad what happened to Ilchenko. But I warned. Now you will have to start again..."

"You know what..." It wasn't until that moment that Brok controlled his anger which made him unable to speak, "it's good that you called. I now have your number in my phone that I can associate with a name, if it is a real name. In any case, the name of the president you are referring to is true. The police will have something to busy themselves with."

"Of course, it will. But why are you insulting me and doubting my name? After all I gave you my business card. Everything's in the best order. But you're right, the police will have to deal with this. You want to testify. Rightly. I can help and provide good criminal officers in Moscow. Because such ordinary police in Russia... you may have heard...does not always work as it should..." Brok pressed the red button.

After a few minutes the phone rang again. Seeing the unknown number, Adam angrily silenced the case. He thought it was Pyrjew again. A moment later Drużynin called.

"Pick up. Menuch will call."

"Mr. Brok. I think we should talk in person as soon as possible" Menuch's hoarse voice reminded him of his figure. "We'll get you a plane. Can you come today?"

Adam decided. The conversation with Taggart the previous day confirmed the obvious. He would have to wait and examine the new state of affairs. It was three o'clock in the morning in New York now. He'll have to make the decision on his own.

"You decide for me and make me get ready within an hour," Irina's voice was full of resentment and animosity.

For a moment Adam thought he could've arranged the date with her earlier, but he remembered the importance of events.

"You know it doesn't depend on me. I have to go back to Nadarsk. I could leave you here, but I think it's more convenient for you if I take you by plane. I won't be able to later."

"Certainly, more convenient," her voice was colorless and distant.

"Remember: we're leaving in an hour. You can't be late."

She entered the hotel room in fifty minutes with a dark face and a large cardboard box.

"Could you ask your...people to wait fifteen minutes longer? I have to pack, I should shower and change."

"If it's fifteen minutes..." he replied, not wanting to give in to pressure too much.

"You know" he heard from the bathroom "you treat me like a toy, like a thing. You make it clear to me at every turn. Is that what you want?"

He entered through the ajar door. Irina stood naked in front of the mirror and was doing her makeup. Water droplets shimmered on her body.

"Do you really think it's time to play out melodramatic scenes? They shot your employer, if the contract of the century hasn't collapsed, then it's swaying, which would revive the whole of Southeast Siberia, which is the purpose of my stay in Russia, and you complain that I have the wrong attitude towards you. Can't we postpone this conversation?"

"You're making excuses" she turned to him with one painted eye for a moment "that's how you've been treating me from the beginning. We've been spending almost every night together for six weeks, and we're not talking about anything serious. You keep me at a distance from your affairs, although we both know that our future depends on their development. Sorry: your future. For I am only an attraction during hard work, a night rest for a warrior. You keep telling me that. Right? At first you might've been afraid...you should have told me yourself! You were afraid that I was...well, who? A prostitute, someone pays me for sleeping with you, should I report to him? So, I stayed away, I was the peak of discretion and restraint, but it turns out that this is your method. Did you want to show me my place? And you didn't think that I know this world better than you do and I could just help you, advise...help, because...you should know why."

She put the eyelash brush in the bottle of mascara. She scooped up the makeup items from a glass shelf and poured them into a transparent plastic vanity case. She reached for the lace underwear hanging on the arm of the chair and stood naked for another moment. He looked at her perfect proportions, at the wonderful body and felt nothing. He thought he should embrace her, kiss her, but made no gesture. It was already too late. She was putting on the dress and it was necessary to hurry.

"What could you advise me?" He asked when she was finishing getting dressed.

She looked at him with something in the realm of hope.

"You're asking when we're leaving" she smiled sadly "so I'll tell you in two sentences, because we don't have time for more. Don't rush. Something dramatic is happening, but I don't think you can influence it. Wait it out. Then it could be your time. Sudden movements can only spoil the situation."

"And that's all?"

"All within a few seconds. I could explain the facts to you for hours. Before that I would however have to know them."

During the flight to Nadarsk they almost didn't talk. It turned out that Drużynin was flying with them.

"When we arrive, the name of the new president of Nieftsibir should be known. Only does it matter?" He wondered sadly. "You'll talk with Menuch. He'll probably explain the matter to you."

They flew into the coming night. At noon, it began to grow dark, and immediately after a sudden darkness fell. Drużynin was chatting with Irina. They sipped drinks from time to time - Brok refused - and the alcohol clearly improved their mood. They pretty much flirted, though Adam could not see in Irina the joy he was used to. He felt jealous. He wasn't able to join the conversation. Too many things awaited a decision, too many tasks demanded being solved, and too many puzzles to surround him. He felt helpless.

"So I'll go now," Irina said, getting out of the car in front of Nieftsibir's office and making an indecisive gesture.

"Where are you going?" He asked. Irina began to irritate him even more.

"To my place, it's already late," she answered uncertainly.

Drużynin offered his assistance, and Irina, after almost imperceptible hesitation - looked at Adam, who looked elsewhere - accepted the offer. Brok said goodbye with a hand gesture as he entered the building. He didn't spend much time in it.

Menuch sat in an armchair in the lobby, chatting with Furcew.

"We're going to a calm place," he said in greeting. Two figures rose from the couch further on.

They got into an off-road BMW, Furcew next to the driver unknown to Adam. A jeep followed them with four men inside.

"And what's with Kola?" Brok asked.

"He died," Furcew muttered grimly. "At that time he was Ilchenko's driver.

"And you were lucky. You were somewhere else then" Menuch croaked with a strange intonation.

"After all I couldn't be with him all the time! I wasn't his personal bodyguard; I was only a commander..."

"Well exactly," Menuch started laughing grimly. "Who would've thought you were responsible for him? But after all we know that it was different. Let's give it a break!" He silenced Furcew, who was preparing to answer.

After entering the gate, they went down a winding staircase, underground. Brok didn't even read the name of the place, which flickered imperceptibly at the next door. The narrow corridor separated into insulated small rooms insulated from each other. Menuch ordered a bottle of vodka and appetizers - Adam also wanted to drink - and the waiter provided them with everything in a flash and disappeared as imperceptibly as Furcew with the bodyguards.

"I hope you don't intend to back out right now," Menuch croaked. "It's a good time for you. As if you organized it all yourself. I'm just joking," he said in a burst of laughter, waving his hand in Brok's direction, who didn't feel like denying anything. "Okay then. You've waited it out. We'll sign this contract on your terms. Even without these additional clauses, which Boria probably demanded" he again deleted a possible reply of Brok with his hand. "It doesn't matter now. Let's drink so that the earth is light to him, that the tar does not burn too much, that the devils are in a good mood. They'll probably like him. Who wouldn't like him there." They tapped shot glasses and drank. Menuch took a piece of whole-wheat bread and inhaled its aroma deeply. "I have this from the old days," he excused himself, biting a slice. "Although it's now also a snack, not only bread that I could only once dream of." Suddenly, Menuch's face began to remind someone of Brok, although he didn't associate with any person he knew."

"Do you understand, what I mean? They want to show you that those from Irkutsk rule here. That they can do anything. But they can't. They want to intimidate our people. But they will not succeed. Because I'm not of the shy type" Menuch chuckled. "Everything will be decided in the coming days. If we sign this contract, Moscow will understand that we are able to make this investment and will shun the boys from Irkutsk. It'll will start talking with us. If not, our gentlemen from the capital will withdraw and from their Olympus will look at our struggles to finally choose the stronger one. A war will begin and God knows who will win it." Menuch winced at his thoughts. "That's why I drink for the contract. I drink for peace, although all my life is war. But I've had enough fighting. I'd like to leave something behind." He laughed again, as if mocking himself. He leaned his heavy head on his big fist. "So what? Will we get along? You'll never get better conditions!"

"I'll try," answered Adam, who was suddenly overwhelmed by the burden of the matter. "I'll try to convince headquarters. They may want to wait a bit." They drank again.

"Remember, tomorrow is the decisive day. That is why we appointed a new president so quickly. Okin will be waiting for you in the office tomorrow. We'll sign it and be wallowing in oil. I would give you something" he waved his hand at Brok's objection again "but what to give you? Actually, you have everything. A beautiful girl..." Menuch paused for a moment, driving into Adam the screws of his eyes "youth and such a career ahead of him ... After all, it's not proper to give you a suitcase of dollars."

"If you don't calm down, I'm leaving and there'll be nothing of the deal!" Brok finally got his voice back. "Do you want that?"

"Don't get heated." Menuch's beard was trembling in hidden laughter. "And if there is a gift, so as to remember Russia? For example, an apartment in Moscow? A little apartment for ten million, completely finished. How do you say: lege artis? So, no one says anything. You buy it for a loan from our bank. Everything would be OK. I give you a promissory note and you pay off the loan whenever you want. Even according to our laws you're OK and nobody could do anything to you...I think I coincidentally have a contract here." Menuch places a black briefcase on the table.

"This is my last warning" Adam takes on a calm and steady tone, although he is already tired and therefore increasingly drunk. "If you don't stop, I'm leaving, calling Taggart and we're breaking off negotiations..."

"Give it a rest already. Don't you understand jokes?" Menuch is shaken by laughter. "With us, gifts are human and natural, but I see that in your bureaucratic world...Well, tough luck. Maybe we'll give you something as a souvenir after all of this. Then it wouldn't even be polite for you to refuse. Okay, okay, these are just promises. Loosen up a bit. Drop into Okin as soon as possible. I'll be there. You see, Adam..." Menuch is serious "we should stick together..."

"Why not?" this time Brok is smiling.

"I'm serious. I'm serious this entire time, but this time especially. Do you know why...should we stick together?" Menuch stares into him.

"Is there a particular reason?" Brok doesn't accept the serious convention.

"If you really don't know, if you can honestly tell me you don't know what I'm talking about, then it's fine."

"Well let's return to business."

The deep night of the Khabarovsk Krai, afternoon in New York, unconscious associations dance in Adam's brain. However, he dials the special number of Taggart's from a cell exclusively intended for conversations with him and hears the voice of his assistant as usual: "Wait, we'll answer soon."

"Tell the boss to call back soon, because I'm going to pass out, and this is an urgent matter." He doesn't know if the assistant passed his pleading tone, but Taggart calls back after ten minutes when Brok is shaking under an icy shower that hurts but it seems that he comes back to life for a moment.

"And that's why I think this is really our chance" ends Adam, who probably managed to report the conversation with Menuch. "If we sign the contract, we'll maintain the status quo. This seems to me to be our last opportunity. And it's very beneficial..."

"I understand you, but we're not going to interfere in their conflicts, it always comes back to bite us..."

"But..."

"It's decided. Tell them that the procedures in our companies, however, it will take some time. Let them wait."

"How long?"

"However long we'll need them to. A week, two weeks. If nothing happens, we'll come to an agreement."

Adam still had enough sobriety of intellect to hide a cell designed only for connections with Taggart. He called from the one he used for other conversations. He called twice in a row.

"It's you?" he hears Irina's distant voice.

"And who were you waiting for?"

"Do you know that it's already two?"

"But do you know that I can't sleep without you?"

"You woke me up. How are you treating me?!"

"Like a person I can't stand to be without. I'm sorry, come, I'm begging you. If you don't want it, I won't even touch you. I miss you so much..." Silence grows on the other side of the phone. "I can send a car or a taxi from the hotel for you, just come..."

"Send a taxi. I'll be ready in half an hour."

Adam called reception and passed the information a few times to a sleepy porter. He had to scold the receptionist fro him to really wake up. He told him to repeat the order and only then hung up. In order not to fall asleep, he took the bottle from the bar. He put on a jacket and went out onto the balcony. The temperature dropped close to zero. The hazy moon rolls its irregular circle along the distant wilderness. The cold glow of the stars is the call of other worlds. Adam isn't there. There's a figure on the balcony asking hopeless questions to anyone, which are unrelated to anyone or anything. Alcohol heats him up but does not calm down. The tenant heard a rustle at the next door. He opened it. In front of him stood a dazzling woman, who he embraces without a word, slamming the door with his foot and doesn't start, nor did he bring her to bed. She defended herself a bit. He repeated some irrelevant words, but she finally embraced him, accepted him, and gives in. She must give in.

Brok rose with a slight headache. In the shower he tried to wash off the weight of the previous day. He returned to the room and watched Irina waking up. The telephone rang.

"When will you come over?!" Menuch asks.

"Unfortunately. I came to an understanding and explained the matter, but in large corporations the procedures take time. You have to be patient."

"What are you telling me about corporations...I explained it to you. You seemed to understand. We're a bit like in a besieged fortress."

"I understand, but I can't change internal rules. This is about two firms. R&B is a representative of Texmobile, which extends the whole process."

"Are you fucking kidding me?! Remember...You're not the only company in the world." Brok with difficulty stops himself, from exploding in laughter.

“Come on. After all we know that both parties care about the contract. It’s only a few days.”

“But…Alright. Come. We’ll talk.”

“Unfortunately. I’m busy today. Anyway, I would have nothing more to say. Everything is going well. We accepted your proposal. Now the formalities just need to be taken care of. I guarantee, it’s a matter of days, well, at the most weeks.”

“I understand,” he hears, Menuch’s gloomy grinding laughter. “See you soon.” The conversation ended. Adam sees Irina’s gaze full of questions.

“See,” he says lightly, “I listened to you after all. I decided to wait.” The woman’s green eyes fill with light.

“Really?” she asks somewhat childishly.

“After all, you heard.” Adam was confident and pleased. He didn’t think about the specter of the escaping contract that haunted him yesterday. Everything was possible today.

“So maybe...” Irina begins hopefully “maybe we can fly to Moscow, even for a few days? I didn’t have time to buy myself anything. You asked me to come back immediately...You took me out of the store, I didn’t have time...”

“But Irina...” Adam smiles forgiving “you’re still about this Moscow. Waiting doesn’t mean tangling at the other end of Russia. After all, it may turn out that I’m needed at any time.”

“Well, yes,” Irina agrees in a resigned tone. “But if...” she suspends her voice, “if the contract burns out, or you sign it, that…that means you’re returning to the States. Yes?” Her eyes are deprived again glow.

“Why deal with such hypothetical matters? It’s not known when we’ll sign this contract, it’s not known whether I’ll be needed for something here or whether I’ll participate in the implementation of the investment...” Adam said things he hadn’t thought of before, when the finalization of the transaction seemed to him synonymous with a return to the States. Now he didn’t believe so much in what he told Irina, but in the way he pushed away thoughts of the future.

“Does that mean you could stay in Russia for years?” Irina stares at him with a strange, changing face.

“Who can know that? In my profession?” Adam feels he’s fooling around, but he keeps going. “Such far out planning is worth nothing. Experience has taught me...”

Irina snorts with laughter. She rolls on the bed, laughing loudly.

“Experience has taught me...my extensive experience,” she parodies his lowered by a few octaves voice. “What experience do you have? How old are you?”

“If only you knew, I have a lot of experience, although maybe not so many years. I’m twenty-seven,” he admits, embarrassed by Irina’s questioning look.

“And I’m twenty-five. We’re peers. And experience...” Irina interrupts herself and stops laughing. “Never mind. Everyone was surprised that Americans were sending such a little shit to pilot such a serious contract. Sorry, that’s what they said. Then the opinions about you changed a bit. They said you’re a sharp guy. But you still don’t understand what’s going on here. But you wouldn’t understand if you were thirty years older.”

“And you? You’re from here. Do you understand?”

The woman looks at him carefully.

“Maybe a little, just a bit, but not quite...”

“Then finally tell me what’s going on! You were supposed to advise me, help me...”

Irina wonders. She breathes deeply, gets up from the bed and takes cigarettes out of the purse thrown next to the bed. She lights it, not remembering their arrangements, and anyway violated by her, although never so ostentatiously, she inhales, covers with smoke.

“New people want to take over Nieftsibir, people from Irkutsk, Losiew. Those like them had appeared before but kept losing. They’re somewhere in the taiga. Those from Irkutsk have support from Moscow. A lot has changed since Putin came. New people come and start to rule. Those from Irkutsk want to take advantage of this wave...Are they really that strong? Ilchenko had his arrangements in Moscow, Menuch has them too. All in all, nobody knows who is stronger. This is playing out now. That’s why I told you not to mix up in it and wait. It’s the experience of this country. We wait and then join the stronger one” she laughed joylessly. “It’s you who became the catalyst of the matter. Legends about your venture have already spread around Russia. Those from Irkutsk know that it’s now or never. Maybe those from Moscow as well. You know, you can talk to Furcew. He just looks like a dumb bruiser. He is a cunning guy.”

“And loyalty?”

“Loyalty?! What a word that is?! And how do you think that Menuch and Ilchenko gained their positions? Loyalty? Fuck! After all they never counted with anyone. It would be funny if they counted on someone now.”

“And you?”

“Me?”

“What are you doing in this world?”

“I’m a certified translator. Should I show you the papers? I live among them, so sometimes I earn on the side like everyone else. They pay me for some information, observations. And that’s all. And you thought what? That I’m a whore?” Irina puts out the cigarette on the floor. Her long eyes glisten with rage, she brushes away her tousled hair from her face.

“Did you also convey information about me?”

“Information? About you? What again? Don’t overvalue yourself. What would I inform about? Say it yourself. What did I know? What I know? Did I probe you to find something out? Was I begging you? Each of them knows more about you than I do!” The woman jumps up and goes to the bathroom.

“Come on,” Adam calls after her. “I didn’t want to offend you. We needed such a moment of honesty.”

Menuch called in the evening.

“You don’t want to drop by? We are in office.”

“I told you. I have work and I wouldn’t have anything new to say.”

In Menuch’s sarcastic croak, Brok hears tones of resignation.

The day has passed, no one knows how. The tension made it impossible to focus on anything. Adam walked around the apartment, almost tripping over Irina. They went for a walk, drank a bottle of wine with dinner in a restaurant. Then they made love, although none of them seemed to have a particular desire to do so.

When, after a short nap, he woke up and saw her naked body next to him, he felt bewilderment and then surprise that he felt nothing. Aversion began to build up in him. He needed loneliness.

The next day went by similarly. Menuch phoned in the morning. The resignation in his voice seemed more palpable. Irina suggested a short trip to the taiga.

"This is the last time before winter. The forest doesn't want to sleep yet, it's still defending itself. It can be extremely beautiful then."

But Adam wasn't in the mood for sightseeing trips. He felt that he shouldn't move from this place. He waited. In the afternoon, Irina went out, agreeing to meet with him imprecisely at night. He was pleased.

Sitting over the whiskey in the empty hotel lobby, he saw Furcewa. They looked at each other. The bodyguard came over.

"Can I?"

"But of course. I was just about to invite you." The bodyguard makes himself comfortable in the indicated leather chair. "You're not protecting Menuch?"

"There's no need. They're sitting in Nieftsibir all the time. It's a fortress. No stranger will slide in there."

"You're not organizing the defense?"

"I've already organized it. I'm not needed there." Furcew drinks coffee from a porcelain cup in small sips.

"I see that you still stay away from alcohol. Are you on duty?"

Furcew laughed.

"Maybe. Maybe I'm protecting you."

"And do you think I'm in danger? What would be the point of assassination on me?"

"No, of course that's not the point. Maybe...maybe I'm making sure you don't do anything stupid."

"What stupid acts?"

"You know...I'm kidding. None of us can do anything. One has to wait until the case reaches a turning point."

"And you say so...Well yes...It seemed that Menuch was resentful towards you in relation to Ilchenko."

The security guard leaned in the armchair and stared at Brok.

"His partner was killed. It's no wonder he's looking for guilty parties."

"And you? You have nothing on your conscience?"

Furcewa's slanted eyes narrowed even more.

"Do you want to offend me?"

"Of course not, I'm not suicidal." A kind of satisfaction appears on Furcew's face. "Do you know Irina well?"

"You certainly know her better. But I met her many times. You understand it yourself. If you work for one company, paths intersect. As if you are interrogating me..."

"What are you saying? After work, in the evening we kill time, chatting up a bit, please don't be offended, it's a provincial city."

Furcew smiles.

"For me it's the center of life. And Irina is a really intelligent girl."

"And beautiful."

"Of course, beautiful." Furcew seems surprised by the need to repeat the obvious. "You know, we...I with her...understand each other. We're from here. We have such a wise, though vulgar saying: you won't jump your ass higher. Do you understand?"

"Sure. We have a similar one."

"Oh, I forgot you're not a real American. This, perhaps, and you should understand more. Tomorrow is also a day and in a few days it'll happen. And everything will return to normal, although it will be different normality."

In the evening Menuch called. The conversation shrank to a few short sentences. Only Menuch's voice was more screeching. Irina didn't come to the hotel. Adam couldn't recall to himself who was to call whom. He thought that he'd rather be alone. He called Taggart.

"Mr. Taggart said that you have to wait" stated the secretary.

The next morning, Walery Krupin, a board member of Nieftsibir, was shot. The killers were waiting for him outside his house. They blocked his car and packed a submachine gun magazine into Krupin. His driver was also injured, but nobody finished him off. Brok saw all this on the southern news service. He related the events immediately on Taggart's answering machine. He sat thinking about the situation when Irina phoned.

"You haven't spoken to me, and now this. I'm getting upset!"

"Don't make scenes. I thought that you were supposed to call. I'm on the side of this entire row. If that's what you mean, I'm fine. I'm waiting as you advised."

"So maybe we can meet up?"

"I can't right now. In this situation, I should probably go to Niefsibir."

Brok decided. He was not in a hurry, however. He went after lunch around two o'clock. He realized from this distance that something unusual was happening outside the company headquarters. A crowd filled the street. OMON officers in camo uniforms, balaclavas on their faces and with weapons ready to shoot surrounded the building, preventing entry. Adam squeezed through the crowd. After a short, violent exchange of words, the commanding officer of the platoon approached him and stated that they were carrying out security measures and there's not the slightest chance of entering the building. The noise increased. A group of officers was leading out a number of handcuffed characters and was loading them into large, barred vehicles. It seemed to Adam that he saw Menuch's figure among them.

It was only in his room, watching the TV services, that he could understand what happened. In a group of figures escorted with their hands bound behind their backs, Anatoly Menuch was indeed walking with his swaying stride. He stared hard at the camera for a moment, into Brok's eyes. In his gaze, the distortion of his thick lips were barely visible from beneath his beard, the expression of mockery of his own fate loomed in his face. The commentary explained that a series of killings had accelerated law enforcement activities against a company that had been under surveillance for some time. The murders are treated as internal squbbles in a company in which a dangerous and unjustified influence was gained by a dangerous criminal, a multiple, long-term prisoner of numerous prisons, Anatoly Menuch. He tried to take control of Nieftsibir's board and, perhaps, the killing of its members was serving this purpose. The power struggle intensified in connection with a large investment in the exploitation of new oil fields in Siberia, which was to be carried out by a consortium with the participation of the famous American company Texmobile. Menuch was arrested at Nieftsibir's headquarters, as well as the newly appointed, after the assassination of its previous chairman, Sergei Okin, and a group of people associated with Menuch.

Someone was knocking on the door. Irina was clearly nervous.

"What do you intend to do?" She asked after casual kisses, lighting a cigarette and sitting in the armchair.

It wasn't the right time. Brok felt that the venture was slipping out of his hands, and the reality he seemed to be controlling was contorting to him with Menuch's mocking smile.

"I don't have a clue!" He snapped back. "You have the rare gift of asking the wrong questions at the most inappropriate time!"

The girl's lips trembled. She tightened them.

"You don't want to see that it's my life too. You're dismissing me, and after all I should decide about me..."

Brok has the impression that for the first time he saw tears in Irina's eyes. He starts to feel sorry for her, but the more he's sorry for her, the more she becomes a stranger, indifferent, and his pity is only a reflex caused by someone else's pain, compassion for any living being. That beautiful woman who ironically ruled the world was no longer sitting in front of Adam. She fascinated him, maybe he even loved her, while that scared, hardly inhibiting tears can only arouse pity. The face that looked for help lost its beauty, mysterious unusualness. That Irina could cheat, play with him and remained impenetrable, aroused admiration, this one - provokes compassion and the same amount of irritation. Adam forces himself to overcome this unpleasant feeling, embracing Irina. He strokes and kisses her head trying to calm her down.

"Honey, but I don't know what's going to happen. We both don't know this. I'm in the middle of absurdity. It's impossible to predict how the situation may develop. Please, let's postpone this conversation even for one day."

Irina lifts her head. She looks at him with painful tension.

"Does that mean...does that mean that you are thinking, considering..." her voice and expression are almost begging for these few words: to ensure that they can be with each other, that in any case he'd want to be with her, if he can't say, that he loved her. Such easy words, Adam thinks, but he won't say them.

"Give it a break, we'll talk as soon as we know something" he repeats.

Irina stared at him as if translating what he said into what she'd like to hear. She tires him. Suddenly she jumped up and shook herself off.

"I got too emotional," she says in a completely different tone, and with the words "you'll let me, get myself together" disappears in the bathroom.

Brok is surprised and pleased. The phone speaks in the voice of Drużynin.

"We have to meet, it's really very important. I can arrive at the hotel in fifteen minutes."

When they hang up, a different woman was now standing in the bathroom door. It was almost that Irina that he met three months ago.

"I understand that the whirlwind of responsibilities is taking you away. So, I'll give you friendly advice. All this doesn't look good, and yet it may be beneficial. All's well that ends well" she quotes, recalling her philological education, and laughs. "I think everything has fallen apart and now it'll be easier to come to an agreement. This is the conviction of a person who knows this world a little." With a smile she sends him a kiss and goes out.

"You must be surprised by what happened. We're all surprised. Nieftsibir, however, still exists and wants to develop. Especially after these shocks. The investment that we're going to make with you is our priority. We want to start it as soon as possible and sign an agreement with you as soon as possible." Behind Drużynin's wire glasses his eyes are cool and precise.

"You say as if you represent the board. Meanwhile, the president was arrested, the most important figures..." Brok tries to sort the situation out.

"Those are former figures. A new board is being formed. I was offered to take part in it. I agreed. An official composition will be announced tomorrow. And I have the right to act on its behalf."

Brok, who just before thought that now little could surprise him little, is amazed.

"I'm a bit confused" he starts to gain time. "After all, two members of the board were killed, including the president, and the new president, members of the company's authorities were arrested, its gray eminence. And you speak as if everything was in the best order. I don't know if those who were leading at Nieftsibir will withdraw so easily..."

"You mean Amkom, president Losiew? We came to an agreement with them. In the coming days everything will be formalized."

"Well, after all its possible...you can be afraid that they had something to do with...at least with the murder of Ilchenko..."

"How do you know that? Rumors, all rumors. If you want, we can ask Furcewa. He's in the hotel. He's here. It's such a strategic place." Drużynin laughs amused at his wording. "He's a bit better oriented at the criminal aspect of recent events. Do you understand? Experience. Menuch was spreading rumors that Amkom was behind the murder of Ilchenko and Krupin. In the case of the first, suspicion falls on him himself, in the case of the latter...God knows."

"You know, you've surprised me with all of this..."

"I can guess. I have a suggestion. Let's go to Moscow tomorrow. The new board of Nieftsibir will be appointed. We'll meet with Losiew and we'll come to an agreement with regards to cooperation, and maybe more, maybe merger of these projects. Someone, say, very important can guarantee the whole matter. He can responsibly announce that the company is clean, and the few people who have tried, say..." Drużynin is staring at Brok intensely "say, act outside the law, have been eliminated. The short-lived chaos is over and will be symbolically closed along with the selection of a new board and the signing of a contract with your company. What do you say?"

"I understand that I should go to Moscow..."

"We'll take care of the whole matter. Once and for all! Everyone will be interested. So what, are we going in the morning?"

Irina called him two hours later.

"Are you going to Moscow?"

"Yes. The situation demands it."

"And after?"

"That depends. After all, we don't know how it'll develop..."

"Should we say goodbye?"

"Give it a rest. You like such things…"

"Melodramatic ones?"

"I didn't want to say that…"

"But you did."

"Maybe it's not about melodrama. We're in the middle of some game..."

"Us?"

"Honey...You know everything. And only I don't know anything about you."

"And did you want to find out?"

"And did you want to tell me?"

"I also don't know much about you either. I have the impression that you don't know much about yourself."

"Give it a break. You're starting to philosophize."

"That's how we are. Russian people. Maybe we're sentenced to it?"

"Maybe you only think that? Stop with this fatalism." On the other side of the phone he heard laughter. It didn't sound happy.

"You chose a good moment for this type of sermon. In other words: have we already told each other everything?"

"I'll call you from Moscow. Then we'll explain everything to each other."

He never spoke to Irina again. That night, before flying to Moscow, after a precise recount of the state of affairs, Taggart told him that most likely the interests of R&B and Texmobile in Russia would be closed. Adam expected nothing else. In Moscow the evening of the next day, he received information for him to return to the States. He booked a flight. He deleted Irina's number and entered the command to reject her phone numbers. At night in the hotel bar, over shots of vodka, he tried to clear the images associated with her. He tried to poison every shared moment; to imagine that every one of their bursts of passion was the result of a cold calculation that someone else had planned for Irina. He applied the unconscious faces of women he saw during the dog fight to her features. He decided that he'd forget. Memory, however, was not obedient. For years Irina's face returned to him, the brightness of her eyes, the intense feeling of her presence, veiling everything with the passion, which she was able to awake in him. Unexpectedly, she filled his thoughts during closeness with other women who seemed only a pale copy of her. With time, the memories of her faded, but yet they still accompanied him. Even now, six years after he last saw her.

CHAPTER 9

"At my place?" repeated the his son. His father looked at him with an indefinite expression on his face, under which the pain seemed to be growing. "Nothing especially interesting. I've made a lot of money, I've lost a lot lately, but I still have a lot left. I earned myself a position. I traveled a bit. That's all."

"All of that in eight years?"

"Yes. Weird, right?"

"Yes..." His father didn't ask more but looked at his son in suspense. "I have two more matters for you. Important matters. I mean...there are more matters. However, these are the most important for me now."

His father leaned down with difficulty and took out two items from the bedside cabinet. The one that catches the eye is a notebook. A special notebook: thick, old-fashioned, with wooden covers closed with a metal, tarnished lock. It resembles a casket from childish stories. The second object was an ordinary, brown, cardboard folder. His father handed them them in turn: first the notebook, then the briefcase.

"This is the diary of my uncle Jakub. Written in Russian. And this is my translation. I know you know Russian, but it's a difficult language. I sat over it for a long time. I smoothed this translation, chiseled it out. Although it wasn't a pleasant job. You'll see for yourself. In my opinion, this is a ready-to-print book. When I decided to go into surgery...when I found out I had to go to surgery, I took this diary with me. I wanted to give it to you. I want someone to do something with it. At first it wasn't possible to release it. I translated the diary after the fall of Communism. I even wanted to release it through the 'Republic', but they wouldn't agree. Even Goleń was convincing me to leave it alone. And I...I don't agree. Anyway, I got this diary from my father. It's like a commitment. I'm guilty of not having published it yet. This is another serious fault that weighs on me...Not the most serious...because it's precisely about the second one...I'll have to ask you again. Your mother... she didn't tell you?" His father looks into his eyes. His pupils barely glow in the crevices of time. A hand grabs Adam's, who remembers Klein. He tries to oust this memory, but it comes back and lasts.

"Father...you've asked me this enigmatic question many times before. Finally say what's going on, because I don't remember anything special. I would've told you anyway."

"Yes. That attests nicely about her. A lot of things attest nicely about your mother. Only this way she leaves me that, which is most difficult. Well, but I earned it myself. You know, what I tell you, what I have to say, once didn't seem so important to me. I almost pushed it from consciousness. But that can't be done. Nothing can be permanently forgotten. Now it's the most important thing for me. The most important between us. Between you and me and between me and your mother. But between you and me..." his father doesn't stop, breathes heavily, closes his eyes. "I'm so tired. I have a request for you. I'll tell you something now and you'll leave. You'll calmly think about it. Tomorrow you'll come to me...or won't as you wish." His hand silences Adam's protests. "Just take Jakub's diary. I did not live up to this task. It passes to you. Now, what I have to tell you." His eyes open in front of Adam's face. His jaws tighten under the skin of his cheeks. Fingers tighten on his son's wrist.

"I signed to cooperation with SB. From sixty-eight to perhaps seventy-seven, I was registered as a secret collaborator. I tried to be decent, but...then I disentangled myself. And now, please, leave. If you want, you'll come tomorrow. I'm exhausted. Go, Go!" The hand that had just released Adam's hand makes neither a gesture of farewell or of begging, pointing to the door.

His son got up. He should probably say something, but he doesn't know what. Instinctively, he takes the briefcase and notebook. He stopped. He looked at his father as if he wanted to add something. He once again made a gesture of farewell and his son left, it takes him a very long time to leave, although he would like, he really wants to find himself somewhere else already, find himself in a different place. Forget the hospital, his father, the city, this country.

***

"Why didn't you tell me?!" Adam realizes he's screaming at his mother. Her face is unmoved. She looked at him. Lit a cigarette. It's night. Endless autumn night at home on Koszykowa Street, in the kitchen, which the trees look into. His mother sat over a glass of barely drunken tea. "After all you found out, you clearly must've found it in the files of the Institute of National Remembrance that they gave you... And nothing, you didn't even mention it to me? Since when did you know this?" Adam tries to control himself, speak calmly.

"Since when? This was almost five years ago. Do you remember how we talked about Stawicki, "Stawrogin"? I not only found out about him from my files. Next to the less significant ones, I found reports of a certain "Kurtz". I'm unlucky with these literary gourmets!" his mother laughs at night." They weren't particularly important. The snitch didn't describe anything significant in them...I'm sorry..." his mother interrupts, looks at Adam in confusion. He grimaces insincerely.

"There's nothing to talk about."

"Well, it struck me that the denunciations are so meticulous. Nothing important and a lot of unimportant details. As if...the author wanted to write as much as he could so as his audience wouldn't get suspicious. And this is from the late sixties. Such a specific time. At that time, we were running something along the lines of an open house. It was hopeless, we hid in our social excesses. After seventy everything changed, even our guests. And this...author was still reporting, he knew such amazing details. They weren't important but showed how well he was oriented in our lives. He had to have been at least a regular guest, and I couldn't identify him, nothing matched...if he was a guest...When it occurred to me, I thought that

I was a pig. I was thinking about myself the worst things, and at the same time I couldn't free myself from this suspicion. It was like an obsession. I fell asleep and woke up with it. I dreamed about it. More and more details suggested it...and I was sharper myself. You know what I even expected from these suspicious? Funny. A priest shouted at me for being suspicion. I filed a claim for declassifying codenames... And they finally came. I learned about Stawicki earlier. Papers from the Institute of National Remembrance only confirmed what I was sure of before...Never mind about him, although it hurt unexpectedly, but your father? What should I tell you? It was as if he had left me again. I began to study his reports and their history. I did the deepest literary analysis" his mother made a sound that's supposed to be a laugh but doesn't resemble it. "I fought between accusation and purification, I blamed myself. I attacked myself for bad intentions, and soon for lack of courage. It was a foretaste of hell" she interrupted. She drew in a deep breath. She drank tea. Calmed herself down. Looked at her son.

"Now I can tell you. I now have distance to it. Although not entirely." His mother's face contorts uncomfortably." I'll try in any case. Your father wrote reports from autumn of nineteen hundred and sixty-eight to seventy-seven. We found a report from an officer from seventy-seven that declares that TW "Kurtz" refuses to cooperate further. There is also a description that the said TW had been reluctant for some time, and had recently joined the party, which complicates the matter. You probably don't know, that since fifty-six, there was a ban introduced that prohibited the recruitment of secret collaborators from among party members without the consent of their party superiors. The party was protecting itself against attempts to control it by the security apparatus as it was under Stalinist times. An attempt was made to circumvent it. Party members were recruited as experts, so-called "personal sources of information", as intelligence or counterintelligence agents, and in the PRL they operated interchangeably with the SB. With time, this ban was increasingly ignored, and since martial law it remained only on paper. But in seventy-seven it was still taken seriously. Through acquaintances, I even received a correspondence from a higher level, in which officers recognize that with "Kurtz", who has been reluctant recently, and now relied on membership in the Polish United Workers' Party, cooperation needed to be dissolved, especially since he'll be more useful in his official role. 'He'll be more useful'...they wrote. I never told you, but your fathers joining of the party was like a flash of thunder to me. I was just starting my activity in the opposition. I was never able to forgive him. Now I'm beginning to understand that he joined the PUWP to disentangle himself from cooperation with the SB. He had good intentions. Do you understand how fucked up this all is? I've accepted his joining party, because I learned that thanks to this he was removed from collaboration with the SB?!" His mother clenched her teeth, lights another cigarette. "So this is how your father disentangled himself from secret cooperation. It can be said that he led it reluctantly. A lot of details, few hard facts. All in all, he can be defended at the Last Judgment...What was I supposed to tell you?!" his mother threw it out almost aggressively. "That your father was a...TW? I thought about it so many times, if I thought you were coming over to me about it and I...I'm helpless. I waited until he told you. I was going to remind him about it, but I couldn't. I waited; I was fighting with my thoughts. If he didn't tell you, then…I don't know myself. But he did it. Now it's a matter between you and him.

CHAPTER 10

Adam couldn't fall asleep. His mother has already gone to her room and probably wasn't sleeping either. For a moment, Adam wondered whether not to go out, go for a walk around Warsaw at night. He thrashes around the room. Finally, his gaze fell on two items he brought from his father. An old-fashioned notebook with wooden covers and a brown cardboard folder. He reached for the notebook.

After opening the wooden wings, were ordinary, slightly yellowed pages written in Cyrillic, in slightly faded navy ink, he was disappointed. They resembled an accounting record or a notebook of a Russian cotton merchant from a hundred years ago. Where's this merchant from, Adam thought for a moment, reminiscences from Prus? A few deletions were blurred so that it was impossible to decipher them. Half the first page occupied fragments of *The Twelve* by Blok. Adam reached for the cardboard folder. His father quoted them in the translation by Seweryn Pollak:

Jakub Brok's diary

All around - fires, fires, flames...
Over the shoulder - rifle straps...

Revolutionary equal your step!
The enemy's gaze follows you closely!

Grab your rifle, crush the fear inside you!
We'll shoot a bullet at Holy Russia -

In the ancient,
Cottage-like,
Corpulant!

Eh, without a cross!

[...]
Where's Kat'ka? - dead, dead!
Shot through the head!

Are you alright, Katia? – You're not even twitching...
And lie on the snow, you carrion, lie! ...

Revolutionary equal your step!
The enemy's gaze follows you closely!

[...]
Like a hungry dog resides on a corner
The bourgeois – the silent sign of a question,
And the old world tucking in its tail,
When a homeless dog stands behind him.

[...]
- Butt out, you importunate
I will tickle you with a bayonet!
The old world, mangy dog
Die, get lost-or I'll cudgel you!

[...]
- I'll still catch up to you anyway,
You'd better give up and surrender!
- Comrade, it will be bad,
Get out, or else a bullet will greet you!

Crack-crack-crack! - but only the echo
The shot sounds within the walls...
Only in the snow with a long laugh
The gale was beginning to wail...

Crack-crack-crack
Crack-crack-crack

...they march, they march with a heavy step -
The hungry dog follows after them,
In front - carrying a bloody banner,
Behind the gale an invisible
And for bullets unreachable,
With a light step over the snowy
Through the pearl-like heap,
With a wreath of white roses on her temple,
In front - Jesus Christ is walking.

He started reading.

It's strange to start a diary with a quote. But for me it's not a quote. I knew Blok's *The Twelve* by heart. Now all that is left in my memory, which I wrote down. Then, when I read this poem in the first half of 1918, it seemed to me that Blok wrote it for me. It was during the fighting in Ukraine and someone showed it to me, gave it to me. I don't remember the circumstances. It doesn't matter. If I were a poet, I'd write just that, and when I tried to arrange what I had to say in my mind, or rather not so much arrange, when I was imagining this all , when I tried to justify what I was doing, my choices and projects, precisely such images came to life in me, similar rhythms were heard.. "An old, filthy world." We were supposed to cleanse it, wash it in blood, so that this truly human one would finally be born, and this was supposed be the second coming, of the kingdom of man. And this Christ, who led us...

I'm a Jew. But I lost my faith in the moment, when my parents and siblings were being murdered, they were killed like dogs, for nothing, for being Jews ... No, I haven't lost my faith. I began hating our God, the God of the Torah. I cursed him. Still long after that at night, when I would wake up, shaking with fear, and I couldn't fall asleep, only blasphemy calmed me down, which I whispered to God, the worst that I could think of, sophisticated insults. My blasphemies were like prayers.

At Uncle Abram's the service was Christian. In Poland, Catholic and in Russia Orthodox. At the time I didn't even know that there's a difference. I saw that the church buildings are different and the prayers also, the ritual, but I thought, that it's a difference between lands and their cultures. A few women who served at my uncle's tried to convert me. The last one who wanted to do it was named Ksenia and was my uncle's lover. I fell in love with her. She was statuesque, beautiful. She sang wonderfully and for me was the embodiment of female beauty. I was probably sixteen then. Ksenia told me about Christ. Naively, but maybe that's why it seemed to me, beautifully. Or maybe because I was in love with her?

In any case, Christ was haunting me. Faith in him was somehow crossing out that God of the Torah. I knew that Christians don't think that way, but for Jews ... Choosing Christ was renouncing the faith of one's ancestors ... I couldn't become a Christian, but this Christ ... Besides, after all I lived in Russia, and in Poland, but mainly in Russia, and this means something, and since when I escaped from Kurów, from that night when my family was murdered and only us: me, Józef and Adam were saved ... I lived mainly among Russians, some Poles. Jews rarely appeared in my uncle's company. But I saw anti-Semitism constantly. Even among our servant's jokes, when they thought we couldn't hear them. However, I quickly started reading newspapers, being interested in what's happening around me. I started going to junior high school. Anti-Semitism flowed through every pore of that world. The Union of the Russian People called for pogroms. I was sixteen when in Kiev Mendel Bejlis was taken to trial, being accused of ritual murder. I didn't want to believe, that it's possible, but it was. The old world wanted to have blood-drinking Jews. The Black Sotnia was supported by the conservatives, monarchists, the Tsar's circle. Bejlis was acquitted, but ... for everything I somehow blamed the God of the Torah. I didn't want to be a Jew. I hated anti-Semitism even more because it wrote me in to return to the community, from which I had cut myself off and didn't think about returning to. I cultivated a disliked to these passive, praying human plants uprooted like weeds and aren't even able to even oppose it. Those thoughtlessly imprisoned in tradition, which condemned them to the role of sacrifice, as if Isaac's sacrifice was to repeat endlessly, and only the angel didn't appear ... Uncle Abram was different. And that's why I admired him, loved him ... before I started to hate him.

To the point. And so I had to understand anti-Semitism as an element of a broader evil, a symptom of a rotten world. I had to write it into wider, going beyond Jewish matters, phenomena. And this Christ, Christ-revolutionary ... I've heard about it before I read it with in Blok. But, *The Twelve*, was a revelation. I was twenty-three years old. I knew we wanted to save the world, but by reading this poem, I thoroughly understood what I had only previously felt. We're carrying a new covenant. And therefore, we're allowed everything. We're not allowed only one thing. We're not allowed to hesitate, getting bogged down in bourgeois sentimentality and mawkishness.

Were we religious? Can one stop being religious as if being touched by a magic wand? After my family was broken up, I didn't stop believing in God. I stopped believing Him. I started to hate him. But we had to do something with our religion. We were looking for "Godly humanity." "Man is the head of organism that is the world" - we were able to repeat. The more we believed in a "real" man, not alienated by socio-economic conditions, all the more we hated his pathetic caricature that we encountered every day. The less it was worth to us. In *Religion and Socialism* Łunaczarski designed a socialist religion, Gorki did the same, and so did others. They spoke about god-creating. Marx was to be a scholar but also a religious prophet at the same time. Socialism will transform the poor, alienated individuals into a harmonious, reconciled with the world, humanity. Humanity.

And Błok? Over three years later, after writing, *The Twelve*, it turned out he had to go abroad for treatment. They could save him there. The doctors repeated this. And it was true. Gorki bombarded Lenin, Łunaczarski appealed for the release of Blok. He wrote: "this is the greatest living poet of Russia. " Łunaczarski got involved so that Blok could get a visa. I read the reports of our agents. Błok confided why he didn't write anything for the last three years. He claimed that the world became speechless, and he lost faith in human wisdom. "But maybe the world has died?" He asked. "But I've died for sure," he said. "If he died, then why save him?" Asked one of ours. We burst out laughing.

I laughed and thought: why does this matter, this poet, who not even so long ago named the world for me, so indifferent to me now? But these three years of revolution and civil war was far more than one life.

Due to principal we blocked visas in such matters. In cases of such strong support as Łunaczarski's, we deferred. Efficiently. The visa came the day after Blok's death.

But I should probably sort this out. For myself. Otherwise, I won't understand anything from this, neither I, nor anyone else. If there will be someone else and if this is understandable. Another year is ending, the twenty-eighth year of this wretched century. Not even twenty-eight years and so much evil, an ocean of suffering and destruction. I'm thirty-three years old and I don't believe in anything anymore. I only know that I participated in the worst things that were done on the earth. And that's not all. I know that that's not all. From this hell which we created, demons will still swarm out. Blood will flow in rivers. I know all this. Stalin gained full power. I don't think that those he eliminated: Trotsky, Zinoviev, Kamenev were going to be much better than him. All of them are responsible for the immensity of crimes. As I. The difference is that Stalin is more effective and unscrupulous. He'll be more consequential. I don't even want to imagine where this will lead him. Now he's preparing a trial for the peasantry, as well as with the majority of the inhabitants of Russia. I had a foretaste of what's going to happen, what's going to happen on much larger scale. I remember the requisitions I took part in, torture, humiliation of people so that nothing of them remains beyond the desperate desire to survive. Mass executions of hostages, women, children. Pacifications of revolts and poisoning entire villages with gas. The great famine in 1921, in 1922. Cannibalism. Mass suicides of the peasants. Stalin knows what he's doing, and nothing will stop him. Collectivization will be the extermination of a large part of the nation. And it won't end there.

Trotsky, Kamenev are fools. Although supposedly so intelligent. They kept human reflexes. They broke and trampled everything, all the rules, all human superstitions and for years they were immersed in blood and filth, and yet they want to believe that some rules were in effect. They imagined that they would be applied to the Bolsheviks, or at least their elite. Traditional virtues were supposed to be exercised among them: truthfulness, gratitude, loyalty ... as if how and in the name of what?! After all these are superstitions! What's rational about them? We're to build a rational world, a kingdom of reason ... Down with superstition! It's Stalin who's smarter than an intellectual like Trotsky. "Gratitude? It's a kind of canine disease", he said. After all, we're just the tools to build a perfect world. Trotsky declared that he submits to the reason of the party ... So, if Stalin turned out to be the reason of the party, he shouldn't have any grievances. Spit on them! I feel that Stalin will kill them all, and I won't feel sorry for them just like for myself. We've earned this! They're like children. Stupid, cruel children who naively cling to adults. If it turns out that there is no asylum and the party will crush them like others, there'll be any humiliation to which they wouldn't go to.

It's not about them. I see that Stalin will now have a free hand, and this is the worst part. He doesn't nourish any superstition, so he has no scruples. He'll want to speed up the construction of hell, our paradise. He's going to kill his opponents or those, who he sees as such, or those who could become them, or ... He's going to kill. He's going to destroy that which is left.

A lot of time went by before I understood all of this. Probably about six years. Six years since I stopped killing. I shook myself from the chaos and started thinking. And although I still participated, I will participate in abominations and crimes, it's however not the same as then, when we drowned the country in blood and cruelty. Especially for me, behind the desk, when someone else carries out my plans. Slowly, step by step, defending myself against this, I began to comprehend what I took part in and what we did. And gradually I began to understand that this period of calm, when we don't kill massively, it is only temporary. I see how we're preparing for the next act of the revolution. We make files of suspicious groups. For what? It's unknown. We're preparing a camp system. There are thirty-five thousand people locked in Solovetsky alone. A slave's job costs nothing. Stalin and his associates are already planning how to build modernity on this. Stalin thinks practically, he is even very intelligent in this respect. And he'll use his full intelligence. He understood that the cheapest is human material. We'll raise the pyramid of the Soviet Union from it. If only Lenin had survived, we'd be doing this under his supervision. Solovetsky is an experiment. A successful experiment. It turns out that one doesn't even need to particularly exert himself. All you have to do is give power to criminals and they'll take care of everything. They'll make hell for the other prisoners, and we're going to account for them like an economic enterprise. They'll provide us with everything we want. So, I didn't kill, but I did participate in the preparation of subsequent mass crimes and I cooperated in minor ones. This perspective isn't too refreshing.

Young people who came to the party in recent years, brought up by the revolution, were impatient to begin. Their fingers itched. They'd like to experience what we've been floating in for years. They'd like to take our places. Everything becomes clear. These aren't just feelings. The OGPU, our former Cheka, is already in a state of readiness. Barely half a year ago the Shakhty Trial took place. Accusing guilt to these fifty-three God fearing engineers and technicians, I'm sorry: "vermin" was a prelude. For a moment I was even surprised. Why condemn sacrificial professionals and why didn't anyone prepare a better justification? But after all it's exactly about this, to not worry about appearances, and everyone could be convicted. This is supposed to be the norm, and everyone is supposed to understand it.

Then similar trials sprang up. A whole series in Ukraine. Hundreds of people in managerial positions. We're preparing the next operation. We, because I'm a functionary of the OGPU. For now, a few, maybe ten percent, I sentenced to death. The economic dimension of the enterprise is important. Because this, our state, rational economy doesn't function as it was supposed to. So, the big heads at OGPU came up with "new special construction offices". We call them the greys. There, all types of convicted specialists: engineers, technicians, scientists, will work for the good of the Soviets. In conjunction with physical slave labor in the camps, we will create a whole big industry and extend the scope of OGPU's rule. Mnieżyński has a good head on his shoulders.

From the beginning, our madness had a practical dimension. During a banquet, still in the early twenties, when the commandant of the camp in Kholmogory boasted of drowning sailors from Kronstadt and how he personally broke them, another showed off his practicality. "Nothing is wasted with me," he repeated, "and that's how it should be everywhere. We chase the bourgeois to the basement and tell them to undress. We set them up facing the wall. They're naked like pig carcasses. I divided the people. Three shoot them in their necks, two neatly throw loops on the necks and them still convulsing dragged them out and threw them onto a pile in the corner of the basement, two with shovels cover the blood trails with dirt, one sorts and folds the clothes. And soon after we lead in the next ones, until the end. Everything like clockwork. I checked with a regular slaughterhouse. We do it much more efficiently. We just throw away the meat." He laughed. Everyone laughed. Actually, why do we waste so much meat, after all it's superstition, I thought. We tried not to waste other things. At that time, however, these were activities on a small-scale, somewhat improvised and, although effective, it's somewhat on the sideline. Now we're building the foundation of a whole industry.

And we started with the propaganda. Hardly anyone knows better than us how important it is. "They have a guaranteed indomitable, lethal hatred of the working class and the working people of the entire world," I read in the 'Pravda' about the accused before the commencement of the trial. Their lawyers announce that they're unable to defend them. The commander's footsteps were heard.

But I was most struck by the statement of the 12-year-old son of one of the accused. He asked for his father to be executed.

So that's how things are. And I? I shouldn't be alive. I don't deserve it. The only thing that I can do is warn, try to warn those who might read this and draw some conclusions. That would be the only benefit that I'm still alive. I was thinking lately about suicide. Actually, I've been thinking about it for many years, but recently extremely intensely, and I'm not ending myself probably just because I should leave something, a warning that maybe somewhere, someday will lead someone away from following in my footsteps. This is unlikely but...

Or maybe I'm not committing suicide out of fear? Amazingly, I'm discovering my caution lately. I didn't start writing until I came up with a hiding place for this notebook. In truth the very idea of a diary, a real diary, is tempting fate, but I try to keep all possible precautions.

Why am I really writing? Maybe to ultimately settle accounts with myself? If I name all the evil, all the dirty things I did, if I'm able to, without deceit write about my entire journey, so what? Will it justify what I did? Ease the burden of guilt? It's nonsense. And yet I have to do this. I once read; I don't remember whose it was, that an excess of discussion can kill morality. I won't discuss it anymore, although in my case to refer to morality is mockery. However, I know that I should describe it, describe my life, which appears to me completely not like mine, and ... this must be enough. That must be enough for me. I'm not actually describing my life. I don't have a life. There's the story of one of the commissioners of the All-Russian Extraordinary Commission for Combating Counter-Revolution and Sabotage, in short Cheka, and now the United State Political Board, OGPU.

Then I have to escape from here. Escape, to warn those whom I can, my uncle whom I hated, but whom, after all, I love. Only do I really love someone? Do I love my brothers? Whether I'll be able to love someone at all? It is very doubtful. But I have to escape to try to warn someone. Anyway, I neither want nor can live here. I'll have to kill myself or others will kill me. Anyway, they can kill me when I try to escape. It's also a solution.

I was eleven when my family was murdered. My father, mother, six-year-old sister and brother, a baby, even our dog. Our father told us to hide in the forest, to his wife and children. I was the oldest, he instructed me to watch over them, but my mother returned with baby, and Golda ran after her. The fact that I neglected to look after her, weighed heavily on me. What chance did I have? But my father told me to watch over them, and the fact, that I couldn't stop my mother, is understandable, but my little sister...

The next day we were found by - me and my two younger brothers - Uncle Abram, a trader. In the beginning he took us to Pinsk. Later we moved to Warsaw. I was fifteen when we settled in Petrograd. Yes, then it was still St. Petersburg, but never mind. And we didn't settle, but stopped, as my uncle used to say, who wanted to develop awareness of the temporariness in us, the sense of the fragility of the order that surrounded us. "Every certainty is an illusion and a source of danger," he proclaimed.

On vacation we went to the countryside. I remember hungry children, impoverished peasants, their parents. I made friends with someone my age, Sierioża. The next summer, when we arrived, he was dying. Earlier, his mother and newborn baby died. His father became a drunk. Sierioża and his siblings had nothing to eat, they were wandering around. He was the oldest. He still had three siblings. Two others died; he fell seriously ill. I begged my uncle to help him. "It's too late. He won't survive", he said. I hated him for that, especially since he preached to me later a sermon that we could only take care of ourselves and our loved ones. He was tough and brutal. Life made him that way. He kept a short leash, and they were afraid of him and obeyed him. They even had a kind of respect for him. He treated women like objects. He took them, and when he got bored of them, he threw it away. Maybe not so much threw. He pushed them away. I remember the story with Ksenia. Her desperate crying, almost animalistic whine. This cry woke me up. I went out into the corridor. I didn't know what to do when I heard Adam, my youngest brother, he was seven years old then. He was knocking on Ksenia's door and asking her what was wrong, almost in tears. She asked him to leave. She was trying to calm down. The next day I asked my uncle about it. "And what are you so insistent about this Ksenia? Adam, and now you. Has she twisted your minds?" He laughed joylessly as usual. "I sent her away. And it's not bad. I equipped her well." I hated him, especially since I was in love with Ksenia or it seemed to me.

The world was hideous, filthy, and my uncle who personified it was absolutely disgusting to me. He didn't care about the suffering of others at all. I couldn't stand that village. Rivers, forest, ponds where you could swim. Butterflies. Large flocks of multi-colored butterflies. White clouds floated in the sky, changing shapes, and one could lie on a meadow, watch them and almost be happy, be happy until the moment thoughts came. The peasants were dirty and emaciated. Most were shriveled and lame. They seemed to be a different, less successful species of man. Their hungry children ... They could beat those children, beat them terribly. They beat their wives and animals. I once saw a dog rip apart a cow's udder. The owner tied him to a fence and began to beat him with a wooden stake. That whining ... I couldn't stand it, I threw myself to help, I pulled the stake out of the peasant's hand. He was an adult, stronger than me, but he was afraid of me, though probably not me, he was afraid of my guardian, or rather there was this fear in him, class fear burned out by history. I remember his look: evil, full of hatred. We stood facing each other and I didn't know what to do. I said something conciliatory, something about the dog. The peasant was silent, as if he did not understand, and only looked with hostile eyes. I dropped the stick. I walked away. I heard a terrible whine from afar. He beat the dog to death.

Uncle treated this all indifferently. In any case, he didn't show feelings. He didn't show feelings at all. When I told the story about the dog, he looked at me ironically. "The animal would've a chance if you didn't interfere. Then the peasant had to kill it. The dog paid for you." He nodded his head at me. "You've become soft. You can't stand the pain or the injustice. Maybe it's also my fault? I isolate you all too much from the world. And in the world, there is and will be pain and injustice. And either you can handle it, or you'll lose. And you'll make yourself and others suffer." I hated this vile tone of the whinner. I've seen evil and injustice everywhere. Ever since they murdered my family. This was my second birth. I remember little about what happened before. And then? I saw hunger, misery, despair. I met my peers in the countryside. Several times I entered their huts, cramped, dirty, bug-ridden and full of smoke, so that I immediately began to choke. The hosts laughed. The odor was terrible, the smell of animals they kept inside, hard to name smells and piercing everything, biting the nostrils and eyes tobacco smoke smoked in rolled newspaper. Through its thick suspended matter, it was difficult to see the corner with icons and at some places, a decorative stove. And less than ten years was enough for me to understand how much those peasants, whom we later drove out of their huts had to miss them. At that time, however, I saw an animal existence and I was ashamed, because I felt, I was somehow responsible for it. My prosperity grew out of their misery.

I met unhappy people who weren't able to manage. They were everywhere. In Petrograd, I saw magnificent palaces next to starving beggars, emaciated children ran after luxury carriages. Juvenile, anorexic prostitutes begged for the interest of fat men with diamonds on their fingers. Hell, I thought, this is what hell looks like. Yet still, I didn't know what hell was.

My uncle swam in this reality like a fish in water. He was getting rich, winning. Over time I realized that he has no conscience and a dark, criminal past. Actually, it didn't affect me. That world was poisoned to me, and a criminal was more honest than a bourgeois exploiter. Hatred for those who were angry at someone else's injustice and misery was in me. It was growing.

I recently learned that my uncle was even doing business with revolutionaries. Also, with us, Bolsheviks. Actually, I could've guessed earlier, when I was still living with him, but then I rejected all such suspicions. My uncle's dirty paws couldn't defile the pure idea of the revolution. Could I really think that way?

I was fifteen when I read Czernyszewski's novel, *What is to Be Done?* It was a revelation. I don't know its literary nature. I got the book from my middle school friend, Wieniaw Kaługin. He lent it to me solemnly, handing it like an initiation scroll. He warned that this reading was unusual. After reading it - it took me two nights - I understood what I had only felt before. The world was arranged in a clear order. To this day, I remember the names of the heroes: Lopuchow, Kirsanov, and Viera Pavlovna. They were guided by intelligent egoism. That, which I couldn't name before, but I understood it perfectly. One doesn't need to be ashamed for following your own needs, you only need to harmonize them with the needs of others. Even love turns out to be simple and neither marriage nor past relationships cannot stand in the way. If Ksenia and my uncle read Czernyszewski ... But it wasn't these characters that aroused my greatest recognition and willingness to imitate. They were people, the way people should be. There was however someone else there. Someone special. A higher nature. One of those few able to direct what will come because I was sure it would come; a disaster must come that will cleanse the corrupt world. Rachmartov was capable of transcending ordinary human weaknesses. He devoted himself to creating a new order. And such an action - I knew - gave satisfaction that nothing can compare to. The trivial pleasures of the senses, pleasures of temporal existence were for ordinary people. The revolution can be carried out by unique spirits, those, who are capable of devoting themselves entirely. Its they who will lead others, awaken better inclinations in them, unleash dormant, noble human potential. Nothing will be possible without them. That is why later I accepted the concept of Lenin's party relatively easily. It was supposed to be a Communism of people carved as if out of metal, a team of tools that melts into one will. That was later though. Then, after reading, *What is to be done?*, I realized that you have to transform yourself into a revolutionary, subject to iron rigors and discipline. Everything must be subordinated to the revolutionary calling: you need to precisely plan your daily routine, reading, physical exercising, and even diet.

Then nothing influenced me like that anymore. *The Twelve*, by Blok? That was something else.

After arriving in St. Petersburg, uncle sometimes took us to the theater. I remember Chekhov's performances, whose hopelessness shocked me. Gorki went even further. Everything was being confirmed. I read everything as one big confirmation. The world was unbearable. It had to be changed. The literature was supposed to prove it, or it should be thrown away. I read, *Crime and Punishment*. Raskolnikov was weak and stupid, I thought. I started reading *The Demons*. I resigned.

Trying to incorporate the ideal of Rachmhetov, however, I had to go for some concessions. I didn't last very long on the nails though. Together with Kaługin, we began to look for revolutionary contacts. It wasn't that difficult. There were junior high social democratic groups, to which people from the outside, and students appeared. It was through them that I came across more serious adult groups. I've already heard of Marxism before. Then I found out that the foundation of social science was finally built as solid as the Euclid axioms. I decided to explore it, so I wandered through Plekhanov's, *Contribution to the Monistic Understanding of History*, and even tried to break through, *Das Kapital*. I didn't understand much, but enough however to recognize that we have the authority of science and economics behind us. If human knowledge and rationality itself is with us, then who is against us? Deep theory, however, tired me then. From, *Materialism and Empirical Criticism*, I concluded that all traditional philosophical disputes are hair splitting at best. They only prevent the implementation of the revolutionary project. And so, they're not natural, but reactionary. They defend the existing order. And philosophy should be of the Party, for there can be no gap between thought and action. Thought is to serve action, because our task is to change the world. After all, I've read the *Theses about Feurbach*. Thought was to develop the technology of this change.

Sometimes readings fell into my hands that were confusing. I remember Piotr Zaiczniewski's brochure, which was already many years old, but referred to our times, and spoke directly about ... killing. In order to establish social democracy, the tsarist team would have to be killed. We're going to butcher them like the pigs they are, we're going to slaughter them wherever we overtake them, wrote Zaicznewski, and I felt a shiver of disgust and excitement. I recall to myself Raskolnikov's ax. Yes, you had to chop off the old world, and yet this seemed sick. "Whoever is not with us is against us, and for the destruction of our enemies all methods are allowed," Zaicznewski proclaimed. I struggled with this simple and difficult to accept truth. I desired action.

It was at the end of middle school and the beginning of college. I had an argument then with Kaluga. After dozens of endless meetings and discussions which didn't lead to anything, after this intelligent chatting, Hamleting, rolling over the same things without any conclusion back and forth at the next meetings, I had enough. I chose the Bolsheviks who didn't get bogged down in the endless liberal talk of Mensheviks and Social Revolutionaries.

Kaluga became a Social Revolutionary. He composed something about humanitarianism, theorizing. He justified his weakness. Lenin convinced me, the assumption that the revolutionary consciousness must be brought to the working class by an organized group. I had no illusions about workers that were in Russia at the time. They were barely refined peasants, those I remembered from trips with my uncle to the countryside. Intimidated, primitive, cruel. It was necessary to pupate them, to free another man in them. You had to change the world to enlighten it. Lenin's, *What Is to Be Done?* complemented Czernyszewski.

I enrolled in the St. Petersburg University history and philology department. History has always been interesting to me, but it has become a bit of a shameful passion. College stopped being important. They were to be and were only an addition to my revolutionary activity. That's why my Uncle Abram's jokes on this subject were extremely good tempered. "Do you want to learn fairy tales about King David and King Ivan?", he laughed. "And when did history teach someone something? And how could it teach?" At the time I thought of him as a simpleton. Today I agree with him. I replied to the remark: "You're right about the traditional approach to history uncle. They're fairy tales. We however treat them differently. We use the scientific method." "If you have such a method", his uncle was having even better fun, "then why study ancient history? It's enough to reach for it and you'll know everything about everything." Actually, uncle is right, I thought then.

Real disputes with him concerned something else. He wanted me to help him in business. It was probably his most absurd idea, although he seemed to be realistic. I told him to be careful because I would hand over his estate to the party. He laughed but a little uncertainly. However, the quarrels between us were more and more serious and I was the one who provoked them. I couldn't accept my uncle's life, I couldn't, even silently, agree to it, especially because it was thanks to him that I was swimming in abundance.

Quite quickly I assured myself how unimportant college is, although during them I agitated a few people. In the beginning I joined a social-cultural circle. It was called "Omphalos" or navel. Not coincidentally. I met with them a few times because I was looking around in all more or less organized surroundings. I tried to spread the idea of revolution to each one, and groups created a greater chance. Not in this case, however. They were cultural jesters wanting to be considered sophisticated. "About culture cheerfully" - that was their slogan. They wrote parodies and organized parodical meetings. When I got there, their boss, Nikolai Bachtin, was reading his work "Omphalos Epiphales" (Apparitions of the Navel), a parody of symbolists. Probably. I once read some poems by Briusow, some Frenchmen, Blok wrote similarly, so I recognized the object of derision. In the perspective of my, our fight it seemed so trivial and barren ... I wasn't capable of bearing these jesters. Just like the "academics" who believed that politics should be left outside the university. Beyond that there were, however, some political groups there, mainly Social Democrats of various kinds. An extremely wide corridor ran through the university building, we called it Nevsky's Prospect. Political debates occurred there, and sometimes more than debates. Although I didn't take it seriously, I got caught up in the arguments, which at least ended in fist fights two times.

My uncle didn't interfere in my life. As a guardian, I couldn't fault him anything. He left me freedom and tried to help me in everything. That was however unimportant. He was my class enemy. He exploited human poverty and misery.

Later, I began to suspect that he had some special gift. A type of intuition? I didn't believe in intuition. So how could it be rationally explained that in the spring of 1914 my uncle moved to Switzerland with my brothers to take refuge from the war? After all, it was impossible to predict the date of its outbreak. Archduke Ferdinand didn't even go to Sarajevo yet. Was it so obvious that Switzerland would be an oasis in the midst of the murderous turmoil? From a later perspective, everything was arranged in a series of only possible and predictable, consistently resulting from each other events. Why however, weren't those wise ones there then, who would prophesize the inevitable and consequential course of history? On the contrary. The big heads, geniuses of those times joyfully signed death sentences on themselves and their world. That what would happen couldn't have been reasonably foreseen. Nobody could've been able to. Only, are we at all capable of rationally predicting anything?

It was February 1913. St. Petersburg became the stage of a huge spectacle celebrating the 300th anniversary of Romanovs. A dazzling, impressive performance. Could anyone in the countless crowds filling the squares, streets and churches of St. Petersburg suppose that in four years the dynasty would end, and the history of Tsarist Russia would end? I don't think anybody, and certainly not me, even though I wished this for old Russia with all my heart. Wealth and power paralyzed. Well and people ... Endless streams, a human sea applauding the tsar and the dynasty. The crowd fell to their knees before the royal procession, humbling themselves before God's anointed one and his retinue. Defilades of the army, colorful processions, carriages and cars, those on horses and pedestrians, everyone paid homage to him. Almost every square, every park became the place of a concert or fair, or one and the other, so as during breaks to roar from cheers of honor to the tsarist family. The windows of the palaces sparkled, and the audience heard the sounds of dance music through them, to which aristocrats danced at countless balls. The night was filled with previously unseen ballet of lights, fireworks, pyrotechnics, splendor of colors. Widespread admiration for the ceremony became enthusiasm for the monarchical order and its apex, Nicholas II. Everything graced his power.

I knew that we wouldn't give up, but there was a group of us, few against a stupid nation and a system of violence. How many more years does one need to fight despotism which has settled on a large piece of the globe, in order to break even its foundations? Do we have a chance to live to see it? I was asking myself then with hopelessness. How many years will it take for all this to fall? It turned out to be, that four. In five years, in a dirty basement the tsarist family and the former monarch will be shot and stabbed.

Despite my uncle's persuasion, I didn't go to Switzerland with him. It was in Russia that I was supposed make the revolution. Uncle gave up. He left us freedom. And he tried to look after us as best he could. He supported me financially until the February revolution, and even later he would send me money through various messengers until, when I sent him a message that I'm passing it on to the party and for him not to do it anymore.

Just before his trip to Switzerland, we had a big fight. I reproached him that people suffer because of him. I was insulting him. In Zurich I visited him and my brothers only once, in 1916. I really came as a link between the St. Petersburg organization and Lenin's group. I also visited my family, which ended in an argument. I actually anticipated it. In the end uncle said that it's thanks to him that I'm not in prison and that he made my secret trip to Switzerland possible. From what I learned later, he collaborated with Okhrana then and with us, and God knows who else. Besides maybe I'm not fair. He worked with us and he had some contacts with Okhrana that facilitated these actions. I think Lenin didn't condemn him for that. On the contrary. Uncle's arrangements guaranteed him power and money, which in turn increased his power. He had a lot of money. He never bragged, so he probably told the truth in Zurich then.

Anger blinded me. I didn't want to know. I gave my reason and my mind to the service of the Party and lived in a world of beautiful illusions, as the saying goes, that is, I was lavishly lying to myself. I screamed at my uncle. He seemed indifferent, although my declaration that only the party mattered to me, and that family ties mean nothing next to it, probably touched him. He ordered me to leave and not return until I change my mind. And then he gave me a lot of money. I handed it over to our organization in Switzerland.

I write too much about all of this. About trivial matters. As if I was scared to start writing about why I reached for the pen. That's probably true. This isn't easy.

These few days of February 1917 changed everything. From protests due lack of bread, to the soldiers' rebellion and the capturing of the arsenal. Nobody directed it. It's the leaders who tried to keep up with the events. I spent those days in ecstasy. I marched with the crowd towards the hedgerows of police and army. I clashed with them. I withdrew, sometimes fled from Cossack charges only to advance again. After capturing the arsenal, I armed myself. Together with soldiers and civilians armed like me, we fought the already dispersed police and few army units. Soon it came down to chasing the snipers from the roofs who were shooting at us like ducks. Quite quickly we realized that we have to climb up the buildings ourselves if we want to be effective. Petrograd was ours. A group of workers was rolling the large, gloomy head of Alexander II, removed from a statue, along the ground.

These days were extraordinary. I felt one with the crowd, a cell of the living and fighting body of Petrograd. My anger, tension and joy was multiplied many times over. I was rising in euphoria. We were all close with one another and there were no strangers. We exchanged gestures and smiles as if we had known each other forever. Restaurateurs, cafe owners treated us for free, we all tried to help each other. People greeted each other, crying out, "Christ has risen!" "Russia has risen!" - others replied. For this short time I forgot about ideology. I stopped thinking. I let myself be carried away by the rhythm of the events, their madness.

Almost immediately, however, something disturbed our ecstasy. Drunk soldiers and workers who didn't interrupt in the beginning, they quickly started breaking through the widespread enthusiasm. It's wasn't just vulgar screams that I've tried to accept, sometimes even repeating them. Drunk, they were capable of shooting at anything. I was a witness, how they injured several fellow rioters. They aimed at richer windows. I saw teams that were breaking in and leaving laden with various goods. That I was still able to bear, although I heard from the flat screams of people, who were abused and beaten. They were bourgeois, guilty by their own fault. I saw, how a crowd threw itself at captured policemen and for a moment through the common roar broke through the inhuman scream of those being murdered. They deserved it, I told myself, overcoming my nausea. Once I saw a group of armed, drunk civilians and sailors surrounding an older, well-dressed couple. They knocked them down, they probably wanted to force them to eat something straight from the pavement. It was, it seems, horse droppings. They were beating them. I didn't know what I was supposed to do. I walked away. Maybe not even because of fear, although I had little chance. I explained to myself that these workers and sailors were right. They were brutal and boorish, but they were the wrath of the people against those who preyed on their harm without even thinking about it.

Drunk, joyful soldiers were taking joyrides throughout the city in requisitioned cars. They sat with rifles mounted and bayonets straight out so that the cars looked like huge porcupines, and rushed through the streets, shooting in vivat or wherever they were, until they collided with some obstacle or ran out of fuel. Abandoned, partly crashed cars could be seen everywhere. Heaps of unremoved rubbish grew in the yards. The city was starting to stink. It was more and more dangerous. Fighting with a plague of crime, people lynched captured thieves. The crowd beat them and drowned them in the sewers.

Still, despite everything, Petrograd lived in euphoria. Strangers began to discuss on the streets and crowds gathered around them joining the general conversation. These were debates about God, democracy, and Russia. I remember one that was caused by a passerby who thanked God for the revolution. Someone replied that the revolution is proof of the non-existence of God. And it started.

A few hours in the cold and falling dusk the growing group, and then a crowd, wondered if God is real and what results from that, and above all, how to reconcile God's goodness with the evil of the world. I referred to science a few times, but my voice probably didn't sound very convincing. "Student," said an elderly, rather poorly dressed man with a beard, "did science ultimately explain something?" It just names our mysteries differently." They snorted at my concise lecture on scientific socialism. I was amazed at how great ignoramuses' people could be. On the other hand, I was built up with an emotional, but it was a non-aggressive debate.

"You state: God would have to be evil to tolerate the evil of the world. And I'll reply to you, that he's infinitely good, leaving man freedom!" said young man, trying to break his shyness and stuttering.

"Then why did he make it so evil?!" someone shouted.

"He gave him free will to choose. But if man forgets God, he'll fall into Satan's clutches! "

"Don't talk about the devil. Fairytales for children. It's the conditions that make a person evil, and not a demon. Now that we have set him free, the era of God-man is coming." A small bald man shouted excitedly.

Later ... So much time, one can't believe, that only five years have passed, I organized such public discussions myself. Only then they had nothing to do with spontaneity. But let's try to stick to the chronological order.

I joined the Red Guard, which was growing rapidly. Lenin arrived in April. His theses awakened excitement. Even many Bolsheviks were shocked by them. Lenin called to a new phase of the revolution: crossing the stage of bourgeois parliamentarism and transferring all power to the soviets, which seemed a questioning of the Marxist doctrine of the inevitable order of the succession of historical eras. I was fascinated by precisely that. We could subordinate the world to us and bend even the iron laws of dialectics to our will. I saw how chaos was accruing that should be controlled. People's deeply justified hatred had to be harnessed into building a new world. Then will come the era of brotherhood too beautiful to think about in advance.

We took Lenin from the Finnish Railway Station to the Kshessinka Palace. Earlier, as a member of the Red Guard, I took part in its taking over. A strange, asymmetrical building next to the Kronwerski Prospekt with a corner octagonal tower didn't fit as the headquarters of a workers' party, but maybe precisely because of the contrast it was the right choice? – Its owner, a prima ballerina, was apparently the tsar's lover, petty and nervous, she shouted something to Szlapników, she was explaining something incoherently about diamonds, which she gave for some purpose. "But my lady, the people are forgiving. Nobody is driving you away. If you find a corner, you can still live here. "

We were standing around in the street in front of the villa, armed men laughing uproariously. Above us in the cool of the day vapor rose. Someone suggested that she should be hugged in her corner. The proposals went further and further. She looked at us and began to squeeze through the cluster, paving her way with a small suitcase. I didn't completely know why I was ashamed for a moment.

I met my former friend, Kaluga. He asked if I was still a supporter of Lenin. He looked at me ironically. We argued.

"So what? You want to give up parliamentary democracy and give away power into the hands of the soviets. Those feral people who plundered and destroy Petrograd? "

"Precisely yes. That's anarchy and it doesn't look nice. But birth doesn't make a good impression either, especially for dandies from good homes. The people vilified and humiliated all their lives retaliate. In this way they regain their dignity. When they become owners and masters, they'll change, just like the peasants who destroy the manors of lords but take care of theirs. Their energy will be the foundation of the new order", I was getting feverish and shouting.

I was discussing then without a break. Even with Bolsheviks who were afraid of Lenin's boldness. Kaluga was not convinced. We parted in anger. I didn't meet him again. Four years later, we dealt with the Social Democrats and Mensheviks. We arrested them by the thousands. I was in Petrograd at that time and I got a list which had Wieniedikt Kaługin on it. I instinctively thought I had to check if it's my Wienia and what had happened to him. Deep down, however, I knew that it's about him. I stopped thinking about him.

I had the impression that the chaos in the city is growing. Petrograd was swollen like a huge ulcer and was waiting to be cut. The offensive on German the front collapsed in blood and mud. Rebellions and desertions were more and more common. Soldiers from Petrograd didn't want to go to the front. The moment seemed perfect for revolution. Soldiers of the first machine gun regiment refused to leave and threatened to overthrow the Provisional Government. Subsequent units declared the same. I had constant contact with the Bolshevik military organization and although I wasn't a soldier, I became almost a member. I was an agitator among soldiers. We pushed on the Party authorites. But the Central Committee wasn't ready. Apparently, Lenin left somewhere. Without waiting for the consent of the Party authorities, we called on the soldiers to take to the streets and overthrow the Provisional Government.

Everything was weird. We called for going out into the streets against the Council, strictly prohibiting this type of demonstration, in order to give all the power into its hands. At a concert in the People's House, which was to bid farewell to soldiers leaving for the front, Trotsky spoke. He carried them away. He called for the transfer of all power to the Petrograd Council. The next day, I saw an inscription on the wall: "Down with the Kerensky Jew! Long live Trotsky! "

I was coming back from debates with confused soldiers who finally chose the Interim Revolutionary Committee. As its emissaries, we went to military units and factories. In the afternoon I was in a crowd of soldiers and armed workers who took control of the center of Petrograd. There was confusion for some time. In the heat, clouds of dust. There were no leaders. Nobody knew what to do. Some began to shoot at the "bourgeois" hiding fearfully in the houses, and then at the windows of the houses from which people were leaning out. Finally, we managed to lead the crowd to the Tauride Palace. Along the way, we were attacked by troops loyal to the government. Chaotic firefights were taking place. Nobody directed anything, it wasn't clear who was who. Everything looked unreal and only the moaning wounded being carried away by their colleagues and the corpses that someone was trying to clean up brought back a sense of reality.

Our opponents were in the definite minority, they were retreating, scattering. Evening was approaching when we arrived at the great, dirty yellow building of the Tauride Palace. We stood in a large crowd not knowing what to do next. We demanded authority for the Council, but the Council was debating inside and didn't expect anything from us. The Provisional Government hid and there was not even anyone to arrest. Someone was shouting, someone was speaking, but the helplessness was getting worse. A rather accidentally organized delegation broke into the palace, passing on the position of "working masses who are concerned about the behavior of the Council," but this didn't go any further. Along with a large group, I entered the great Yekateryna Hall, where the deliberations of the Council were going on. Nothing was coming of it. The Council debated as before and we turned into an audience listening to some not-so-clear speeches. Finally, with the coming of night we started to disperse.

The next day, a storm was rising over the city from morning. It was stuffy and restless. Closing stores and shutters, Petrograd waited. On to deserted streets groups of soldiers and armed workers began to go out, to whom the Bolshevik agitators distributed leaflets and the new issue of "Pravda". A newspaper with a mysterious white stain on the front page, just as the leaflets it called for a demonstration with the aim to establish the powers of the council, but it wasn't clear what that would mean. Meanwhile, a flotilla of boats, barges and ships was moored by the Mikołajewski Bridge, carrying sailors from Kronstadt, for which we waited in suspense. They were the true, armed arm of the revolution. Their sight, however, probably surprised not only me. Many of them brought with them rather vulgar-looking girls in low-cut tops and high heels, and although they were fully loaded with weapons, they seemed to have arrived for a great party. The image was completed by orchestras, which in truth played revolutionary songs, but it was rather an atmosphere of a party, not a revolution.

We marched to the Kshessinka Palace. On the balcony Lenin appeared, greeted by a great applause. He said that he believed in the coming advent of the soviets and disappeared. It was hard to consider these few words a speech. Even I was deeply disappointed, and I could discern my spirit all around.

We headed to the Tauride Palace again. Again, we were attacked by units located on the roofs and upper floors of the Liteyniy Prospekt. Panic and chaos began. Everyone was shooting, but hardly anyone knew to whom and for what. The crowd was fleeing, leaving the dead and writhing in pain wounded on the pavement. I can't say if we chased away the attackers or went a different route, in any case, the demonstration was brought in order and the orchestras began to play again. Perhaps the because of the tension these events caused, as soon as we entered the rich neighborhoods, demonstrators began to shoot at the windows, smash the vitrines of shops and locales, breaking down doors and also breaking into residential houses. A pointless firefight could be heard, as probably no one was attacking us and a large part of the demonstrators began to plunder the city. Soldiers and armed civilians rolled out of the "captured" houses covered with the strangest objects.

Finally, we managed to reach the Tauride Palace. We didn't have leaders, but the crowd was coming together, getting bigger and bigger. Tens of thousands of armed people surrounded the palace and ... no one knew what to do next. And then the storm exploded. The gates of the heavens opened, and streams flowed from above. In the blink of an eye we were soaked to the skin. And the flood continued. Some, stunned by the rain and aimlessness of our actions, began to shoot at the palace. Panic seized everyone. Escaping, people were falling over and were trampling others. Those left headed to the palace. We broke into the closed building through the windows. A representative of the Council appeared on the representative's stairs to calm us down. One of the workers put a knotty fist under his nose. "Take power, you son of a bitch, if they're giving it to you!" he screamed. A group of people said they were arresting the Council representative. It was probably the Social Revolutionary Chernov. Some of the concerned protesters burst into the meeting room, calling for his rescue. The confusion reached its zenith. Trotsky intervened, who pulled representative Chernov out of the car and led him through the crowd. In the meeting room, an excited worker broke onto the platform. Brandishing a rifle, he threatened that the working class would not tolerate betrayal. He ended his speech with an exclamation: "All power in the hands of the Soviets!" The chairman of the Czechidzew Council asked him not to disturb them in that case in their work and gave him the text of the resolution. The confused worker left. The disoriented demonstration began to disburse. Wiriness and rain completed the feeling of helplessness. We were still trying to figure out how to keep the city's focal points in our hands. We were deciding who would defend what. We already knew that units of the Provisional Government were coming. At night they began to gather around the Tauride Palace. The sailors retreated. I was in the group that was supposed to defend the Kshessinka Palace.

Then for the first time I saw Alos Biezmiena, a young sailor with a charming face who will play an important role in my life. At that time, however, he was only one of us. Wet, tired we placed guards and slept inside on what anyone could. I don't remember the next day well. And then the soldiers of the government came. There were many more of them and they surrounded us. They threatened that if we didn't give up, they would kill us and destroy our headquarters. We could still defend ourselves; there was several hundred of us armed men and we had a lot of ammunition, but the hopelessness was overwhelming. The revolution is over. Nobody fought. Only sometimes we heard the sounds of single gunshots. We surrendered.

I spent less than two months in prison. At first, we were afraid that they would execute us, and with us the rebellion would end. We'll be the Petrograd equivalent of the Paris Commune. Something different was however happening. Kerensky was afraid of the monarchical coup by Kornilov, so he didn't want the left to have anything against him. Some weird games were going on up top, in which we were a stake, though we didn't understand what they were about. Finally, they started releasing us. I already knew that the revolution was only slightly delayed.

I immediately joined the Petrograd Revolutionary Defense Committee which was soon renamed the Military Revolutionary Committee. I once again went to agitate soldiers and call them to revolt. Once we were surrounded by a group led by officers who demanded the authorization of the Council. It was clear that we were acting against their decisions. They wanted to arrest us. With difficulty we broke through the group of disoriented soldiers. I understood then that it's necessary to jump onto the back of the torpid Council and drive it into the land of revolution. Earlier however it'll be necessary to subject it to our whim and that could be done by only us, the Bolsheviks. In truth the Committee was officially an organ of the Council, it was us who really ruled it.

Finally, the final act of revolution was coming, and we had leaders or rather a leader. This time Lenin was determined. The light brown, large Smolny Palace was our headquarters, and although Lenin was hiding in the city from the beginning of October, his orders went to Smolny, from where they were passed on. After July, the Institute for Nobly Born Women became the seat of the Petrograd Council. I probably will always remember a paper sign saying that room 36 is the seat of the Central Committee of the Bolsheviks. The whole palace resembled one great station, through which crowds passed despite armed guards, who meticulously checked passes at the outer gate. Human masses camped in the long, curved, dimly lit corridors. Among the piles of newspapers plainly armed men usually sat or reclined, many in soldier's uniforms. Garbage was everywhere, and the air was thick with shag tobacco and the smell of urine. In the dining room, a crowd of workers and soldiers swarmed, who pushed to get to the pots, to fill the mess bottles with soup or tea.

When Kerensky announced that he was sending the greater part of the Petrograd garrison to the front, we already knew that we had won. From that moment, the Military Revolutionary Committee could direct soldiers against the government. It was us, the commissioners, who had become commanders in the army. Not for everyone. Most were passive, but they certainly didn't want to defend Kerensky. After a vague intrigue of the head of government, which resulted in the arrest of

Kornilov who was adored by most of the staff, troops up until that point loyal to the government were disoriented. The officers hated Kerensky. And in the city, the hero became Trotsky, who doubled and tripled himself, speaking everywhere and everywhere arousing enthusiasm. He talked about the suffering of the soldiers and poverty of the workers. The new Soviet power was to remedy this, forcing the rich to share with those in need.

Actually, only Lenin knew that power had to be seized before the Congress of Soviets that was about to take place. Even Trotsky didn't understand him. It was only after October that everything became clear, but before...

When I watched Eisenstein's movie *October*, I wanted to laugh. A precisely organized and exemplary bloody uprising. In fact, everything was just the opposite.

At night, we took over government posts, from where we chased the soldiers away. There weren't any fights. They retreated without trying to resist. The Smolny Palace illuminated as never before was now the officially visible from a distance seat of our staff. Units equipped with machine guns shielded it in strategic places. In the morning we took the main points of the city without a fight. Only the area of the Winter Palace remained in the hands of troops loyal to the government. We chased away the parliament, which was debating in the Mariinsky Palace. It wasn't known why however, in order to finally seize power, we didn't immediately attack, as planned, the Winter Palace, where the government resided. Hours passed, the cold northern wind was cutting through us, and nothing was happening. With a group of soldiers, I came to the Peter and Paul Fortress, which was supposed to shell the government headquarters. It turned out that menacing looking cannons weren't able to fire scrap. New guns were brought. However, the ammunition in the fortress didn't suit them. The search for the right shells dragged on. The troops surrounding the Winter Palace were to attack the moment a red light was lit on the fortress. However, the red lights were lost somewhere, and the Bolshevik fortress commander who set out to get them also disappeared. He returned later at night, explaining that he fell into a swamp. The lantern he had obtained turned out to be weak, almost invisible from afar, it was impossible to attach it to the mast and, above all, it wasn't red. Finally, the signal was given by the cruiser 'Aurora', firing a blank cartridge. It only had those kind. In any case, the bang was immeasurable. A little later, the cannons of the Peter and Paul Fortress were finally able to be fired. They hit almost exclusively in the Neva, but it was effective, especially since the soldiers all around the palace began to randomly shoot at the palace. And finally, late at night, almost without resistance, we took office of the government and arrested its members. As I was told later, during the "heroic" siege of the Winter Palace, Petrograd lived as always. The theaters, cinemas, cafes, clubs and restaurants operated, public transport functioned, and passers-by despite the cold walked around the Nevsky Prospect. No one noticed that a "great" revolution had taken place.

Time later appeared to me like a nightmare in which it wasn't known what results of what and why it happens after another. Maybe in this way I want to escape from it, forget it. And so, let's try to even harder recall it to ourselves month after month, how much it'll be possible, if at all possible.

In December, along with the Red Guard led by Vladimir Antonowa-Owsiejenka I went to Ukraine. We were supposed to pacify The Don Cossacks, who under Ataman

Kaledin, declared independence and made an alliance with the emerging Volunteer Army of Alekseyev and Kornilov. I spent most of the subsequent three years of civil war in the steppe. We stopped at villages, towns and cities, we fought for them and in them skirmishes and even battles, but human settlements grew out of the steppe, which we had to constantly traverse on foot, on horseback and by rail and without end chase always the same distant horizon.

The Steppe went on forever and changed only with the following seasons. When we arrived there, it was already hardened from the frost, barren. Then it was cut through by ice and covered in snow. Over time, the white desert began to melt, soften. Snowstorms and thaws arrived. The Steppe turned into a slushy puddle in which people fell to their ankles and horses waded through with difficulty. Spring erupted suddenly. The grasses grew almost before our eyes. The Steppe became green and bloomed, gushed with fragrances, indulged in the sun, which unexpectedly turned out to be too much. Its storm choked people and plants, which curled and turned yellow. Steppe dried up, changed colors, filled with red turning brown when autumn storms came. And again, the ground became boggy, difficult to pass through, until the first frosts that cut it down, turned it to cold and dead infinitude.

The weather didn't change just one thing. Constantly on the horizon smoke accompanied us. Vapors from burning villages, settlements, farms, towns. Its bitter odor bit through the smells of the steppe, poisoned us. Sometimes we saw burning human settlements, orchards and fields, we ourselves often set them on fire, but the smoke was like a phenomenon from another world, it became independent of fire, as if the Earth itself emitted it. It marked the line of the horizon.

We walked quickly forwards. The Cossacks retreated. Once in a town whose name I don't remember, like most of them, we surrounded their unit, which defended itself stubbornly. When they realized they had no chance, they started waving a white flag. Our unit was commanded by a former boatswain, a powerful man, Semyon. I was a commissar. "Drop your weapons and come out!" - We called. – "we'll spare your lives!" They came out. There was at least fifty of them. We tied them up and locked them in a yard under guard. We had to move quickly to hit next town, some twenty verst. It was the center of a Cossacks' grouping. Our unit was one of the few that was coming up from different sides, but, as planned, they were to attack at the same time. We wasted more time than we thought on an unexpected battle. We didn't know what to do with the prisoners. In the town we wanted to leave only a few seriously injured people. We gathered in a few and looked at each other. "There's nothing to talk about," Semyon muttered, "they have to be killed."

I was as if paralyzed. With difficulty I got it out of it: "We can't ... After all we promised ..."

Semyon snatched a revolver furiously and shoved it under my nose. "Smell the bourgeois seed! And such a person is a commissar? Why can't we? Because we said something? And what would've they done? For them to be spared, our comrades have to die?! If we don't arrive on time, they may die. A commissar has scruples? Then I'll kill you! "

"Give it a break," said Alosha. "The commissar hasn't gotten used to it yet. This needs to be sorted out quickly. We'll put a comrade with a Nagant behind each one and finish the matter. Then we'll chase the locals to bury them. Are you going with us?"

I was walking as if in a dream. I knew that I should, that I must. I can't leave them to do the dirty work that needs to be done. We entered in a large group. The prisoners who were sitting on the ground with their hands bound, probably realized. They started screaming and throwing themselves around. It was short-lived. In the enclosed room, the roar drowned out the screams and the smoke covered everything. I don't know by what miracle I missed a sitting man from a distance of a few centimeters. He tried to get up with a bloodied head. I shot a few more times. He fell with a skull split open like fruit. His brain and blood splashed me. I felt smoke, blood and human brain in my nostrils.

This was a strange war. It occurred mainly around railways. We arrived by train to subsequent stations, already firing from the wagons. The Cossacks withdrew and we occupied the city. Not always. When we thought we had taken another one and started to deploy, a counterattack came. Some of our men crumbled and ran away. We barricaded ourselves at the station and were shooting back. The Cossacks took a house nearby, from which we made the field hospital. Alosha hit me on the shoulder, showing me something. The bodies of our wounded were flying out the windows, but they weren't reaching the ground. They hung in the air, twitching on the ropes. The Cossacks were hanging them. We heard joyful cheers. We thought that we wouldn't last long, when another train with ours arrived at the station. They had a tachanka. Under their fire we counter-attacked. The Cossacks didn't hold out. We chased them around the city, when behind another fence I saw a collapsed Cossack on the ground, trying to get up. I ran to him with a revolver and he was lying on the ground looking at me wide open eyes. His breasts rose spasmodically. I stood above him motionless. Alosha came over to me. He looked at me and sighed, and then, almost applying the rifle at the wounded man's forehead, fired. A red pulp remained from his face.

"Eh you... Commissar ... we won't win a revolution with people like you. You explained it to me yourself. And you know, how many of these" - the sailor showed already unmoving corpses – "you'll have to kill, so that they don't kill us? So that they don't kill the revolution? If we're going to hesitate, we'll lose. And then ... what's all this for? Then their death would also be senseless" - Alosha with a wide gesture encompassed the city– "and our death."

Alosha was from there. From the Don. He wasn't a Cossack, however. He was a non-resident, a peasant. He whole-heartedly hated Cossacks. He said that nobles had never treated peasants worse than the non-resident Cossacks. He wanted to escape from there, and that's why he became a sailor. He was returning as someone else. He told me that he only wanted to find himself in that kind of role here. From December, when we arrived in Ukraine, Alosha was flooding me with questions. He told me to explain to him, or actually tell about Marxism, which, he confessed to me, knew only from slogans and brochures. He proudly stated that a few months earlier he had read his first book: *Spiders and Flies*. "It's like in Marxism, just simpler," he said, touched. "Spiders are exploiters, flies the working people. So, what can we, flies, do? After all, by their very nature, spiders will kill us. We have to kill spiders." He told me that Marxism feels rather than understands, but he believes that thanks to me he'll understand and explore it. He stared at me with bright, trusting eyes.

We were conquering Taganrog, Rostov and finally Novocherkassk. The free

Cossacks ceased to exist. Kaledin committed suicide. In Taganrog, the defending Junkers capitulated on the condition of their release from the city. After laying down their arms, they marched out the main street. The soldiers seemed to be annoyed that they were walking out in orderly lines. They began to contrive things. Someone shot. One of the marchers staggered and fell to his knees. Then the shooting began. The compact line fell apart. The terrified Junkers tried to run away and hide. The guards pursued them, fired at them close up or finished them with bayonets. Hunting began in the city. I walked a little unconsciously as far as I could from this bloody chaos.

Alosha caught me. He laughed. "What's going on?", He was asking. "They're after all defenders of exploitation, capitalism and monarchy. They're the spiders. We have to kill them so that we can be free. We must kill them!"

The hunts continued. "Come, come!", Someone was pulling me by the arm. Semi-conscious, I realized we were approaching a complex of red and squat factory buildings. "It's a glassworks. We caught a lot of officers. We're going to burn them in the oven," he burst out laughing. I pulled my arm out and left.

At night, Alosha came to my quarters. He got vodka somewhere. Initially we drank from the bottle without a word.

"Why are they tormenting them?", I started to throw out. "Let's assume that they must kill them, but why torture them earlier?"

"Why? Alosha was surprised and looked at me with a clear gaze. He drank and thought for a moment. "Maybe for them to be afraid. Those others. The more they're going to be afraid, the less they're going to rebel, and it'll be easier. The war will end, fewer people will die and building can begin. You after all say this. And maybe they must torment them to get rid of the softness that interferes in the fight. You yourself must get rid of this intellectual softness or return to the books." Alosha laughed specifically. Then he began to tell me how they drowned their officers in Kronstadt. "Earlier they used to beat us for anything. For nothing. They had distain for us. We were afraid of them. We thought that they're different creations from us. Those that pain and fear don't reach. And then, when we stripped them naked and stabbed them with bayonets, they whined like animals. They asked not to kill them. They kissed our hands and shoes," said Alosha with a vengeful smile. I didn't want to hear it and I wasn't able to stop it. Something strange was happening with me. Disgust neighbored with excitement. At times I had the impression that I was going out of my mind, I'm no longer myself, and that, what's happening around me isn't real nor concerns me. I tried to theorize my ideas. But they were falling apart.

In Rostov, we imposed penal taxes on the bourgeoisie. We took everything from them. We looked for those who supported the whites. And we took hundreds of hostages. I don't know who came up with this. For the first time I participated in such an action. Then hostage-taking turned out to be a permanent revolutionary method. Just like concentration camps. When I found out, what we're going to do, I asked Volodya Fomicz, our commander, about the meaning of this undertaking.

"We're going to hold them in our grasp. Oh yes", he said, smiling widely, and clenching his fist.

We surrounded elegant neighborhoods and pulled out the fathers of families. Children were crying, women screaming and sometimes tried to stop us, but a shot at the ceiling or the wall next to them was enough for them to give up. They sat down dazed. Guardsmen threatened families with bayonets and butts, sometimes they couldn't help themselves to not strike. I tried not to see it.

After a few days, Fomicz summoned us, a few commanders and commissars. "I've received order, we're killing them! Are we naming soldiers or using volunteers?"

"Wait, who did you get that order from?" I asked. Others looked at me with strange faces.

"And what do you have to that? Do you want to spread anarchy here? I received the order from the commander. Ask him why?" He paused for a moment and added: "This is war after all! When you shoot at your enemies in battle, do you wonder who's guilty? Here as well! This is a civil war, and the bourgeois are our enemies. When they give in, humble themselves, the war will end, and we'll have peace. What? Do you think I'm having a pleasant time? I don't want to return home?"

They agreed that volunteers would carry out the executions under our supervision. "And you, Lord Commissar? Will you take part in the action?" Fomicz mockingly turned to me.

We put them up against the prison wall in tens. A platoon of twenty soldiers fired the salvo. We finished off those who were still alive with revolvers. One had to lean in. From up close look at the throbbing bodies, pulsating brain jelly and the eyes covered up with cataracts. Sometimes shoot. At such a distance, the bullets crushed the skulls. Subsequent tens of people were coming up, stupid with fear or trying to say, explain or just simply shout or cry. I thought this would never end. And after all there wasn't that many of them. Two hundred? Not more than three hundred.

In Novocherkassk, a local worker reported that there was a white officer hiding next to his house. Alosha came to me with this. I took a few people and the worker led us to the attic door of a multi-story house. The host didn't open up, so we broke in. He ran up to the window, but two men stood under it with rifles aimed at him. He didn't even look very scared. He was unarmed. He said over and over that he didn't know what was going on. He said he was a teacher from Voronezh. He even behaved quite arrogantly during the interrogation. He annoyed me with his self-importance. He looked almost mockingly. "Oj, would you give me a smoke, comrade," he drawled with a hint of irony. I was sitting on the other side of the small table. I jumped up with a threatening gesture, although I didn't know what to do. Then Alosha, who stood silently and motionless a few meters away, so that it was possible to forget about him, spun around and hit him on the head. I heard a groan, a smack of the lips, and the interrogated one fell together with the chair. The sailor was holding a revolver. He jumped up to the person curling on the ground and began to kick him rhythmically.

"You officer bitch! You'll stop wanting to joke? We'll knock it out of you!" Each word was accompanied by a blow with a shoe and butt. I don't know how long it lasted. The moans became a whine. Finally, Alosha grabbed the chair and his hair, in the blink of an eye seated the interrogated one on it. That one, hunched over held his hands over his face. Blood dripped from between his fingers. "So what? Will you interrogate him?" Breathed Alosha, calming his breath and looking at me.

"Surname, first name, officer's rank, unit", I drawl out, trying to speak calmly and clearly, although it came to me with difficulty. The man mumbled. I told him to repeat. He repeated. He was an officer but, as he said, he recognized it was a defeat, and therefore didn't go with the others. He deserted. He said he didn't know if there were others in the town.

Alosha beat him again. Then, together with a soldier he called in, they ripped off his fingernails with a knife. The officer howled in pain but in the intervals repeated his story. I was petrified. It was Alosha who ordered him to be escorted to the basement. "He's probably telling the truth. So what, Commissar?", he looked at me reproachfully, "will you always leave the dirty work for us?"

I interrogated a Jew who traded with the whites. He asked us not to beat him because he'll say anything anyway. He probably did. He explained that he traded with them as he would trade with everyone. He told about the chaos with other peoples. About the disputes of Alekseyev and Kornilov and the coterie that were forming behind their backs. Officers fought for positions consistent with their rank, civilians tried to gain positions in the army that would support them, without forcing them to participate in military operations. Tensions and animosities led to losing the fighting goal. I was collecting information. I noted. I asked about specific things. We were already tired. And then the man opposite me asked:

"And what are you doing this for?" I became speechless from surprise. "After all, our world is ending. Have you seen? It's burning? This is now the end. God has turned away from us. And we will be like crazy animals only capable of killing." I recalled to myself a madman who was shouting something and singing, walking through the streets of Petrograd at night. He cried that God was gone and the end of Christianity and the end of Russia is coming." I dismissed the Jew. A few days later, Alosha told me that they shot him shortly afterwards.

We requisitioned food from the Cossacks. This was accompanied by the screams of women, crying children and the grim silence of men. The Germans were coming, and our commanders decided that it was necessary to scare the Cossacks more. During the expedition, in which I didn't participate, a few churches were looted, and several priests were impaled on poles in front of their believers. Participants told about it. The stories get mixed up in my mind, just like the battle scenes. Then we began to retreat and lose city after city. We backed away, by our necks. We escaped.

We fought on the Volga. Summer was starting.

I woke up and leave the hut which we occupied in the steppe. I see Alosha, as he jumps on a horse in only his underwear. He melts into it. They float over the waking steppe, in the grass that almost reaches up to the horse's stomach. Alosha laughs and waves his arms. He rides bareback, but he looks like he's attached to an animal. I recall to myself the picture: an Athenian Ephebos mounted a horse. Brought forth from my memory, it comes to life before me. Steppe into infiniteness and offers only order.

Unexpectedly, I thought about my father. He rarely came back to me. My mother even less often ... I actually don't remember her words, and if I recall them to myself, I feel them more than I hear them, they are more a caress than a speech. She diminishes our names. She laughs to us. I remember her laughter, less her words.

My father showed me the world. He said how much could be read from the forest, from the steppe, from the sky and clouds. At night he recognized the stars and constellations. He led me out of the house and showed me the sky, saying that it was "the book of heaven saved for us". He explained: "It's God who wrote it and spread signs for us throughout the world. We must grow up, to understand them. Everyone can achieve this, but not everyone does. If we understand heavenly words, we attain wisdom. We understand the world and feel happy in it." The horizon, sky, grandeur of existence. Maybe I always remembered this? Maybe always under my impression my father's voice was heard? For a moment, when I saw the distant silhouette of the galloping Alosha, I forgot about the revolution and about that, which surrounds us, I immersed myself in the painting. But it was only a moment.

After the assassination attempt against Lenin and the announcement of the Red Terror, I decided to join the Cheka. I was already immune to death. Even executions ceased to have an impression on me. I actually didn't torture the prisoners, but I could beat them, and if I suspected that they were hiding something important, then by all means I ordered to draw out testimonies from them and assisted in interrogations. I didn't like it, but sometimes, when I saw the mask of dignity and pride falling down from the faces of those tortured, how they lose confidence of anything, they lose the face, they considered theirs, all poses and faces, how they humiliate themselves, hopelessly trying to avoid suffering, reduced to a whine of pain and fear, I felt vengeful satisfaction. I dreamed these scenes and they persecuted during the day, they returned in intense memories and I had to relive them again and again, but I was able to recall them to myself with a strange, alien type of pleasure.

I told Alosha about my decision. He asked for the reason. I explained that the internal front is the most important, eliminating not only counterrevolution, but all its possible future fires. The sooner this is done, the less people will die, the less suffering and devastation there will be. The faster the country will begin to revive.

"You have to go through hell for a new world to be born. And I can't avoid this. This may be more difficult than the fights that we have behind us, but I also have to take this weight on my shoulders" I said, and I myself was surprised at my own pathos. That's why I quoted Alosha. "I can't leave the dirty work for others," I stated, looking at him. He was looking at me with bright eyes from which I couldn't read anything.

"I understand. I'll go with you".

We were going together with army units. We took and shot hostages en masse. We terrorized the population. I was as if in a trance. Those years I was as if in an amok, which didn't let me really think, feel, understand. Only sometimes did I unexpectedly realize that the last events that I can recall actually happened a long time ago. I unconsciously tried to recall later events. My memories were raging, they didn't want to be put in order of occurrence, and I needed hours to realize that from the last thing I remembered, weeks or months have passed. And it took me even more time to reconstruct forgotten events and words.

I only told myself – I understood this now - that I was thinking and acting in accordance with my will, and I was like a mechanism set in motion. That, which I called my thoughts were only reactions to situations and, sometimes, an answer to the questions that someone was asking in my head. The answers were simple, as if someone had prepared them for me.

In February 1919, we took Kiev. When we entered and saw from a distance the golden domes of the Orthodox churches, I felt elation. We were reaching the heart of Rus, the place of its unfortunate birth. We will let its history flow through another trough, just as in time we'll let through new troughs rivers as large as the Dnieper, I roared.

And we started making history. We made lists of hostages to arrest. Pretty soon I realized that these lists were made according to denunciations. Almost everyone who was mentioned in the piles of denunciations brought to our offices was sent to prison. I explained to my boss that the vast majority of the anonymous letters served to settle personal accounts and being led by them, we lock up l people inadvertently. Small, cunning eyes bore down on me from a fat face.

"After all, I know," he replied, smiling. "When we take thousands of hostages, we can't discern who's who. We use class criterion. Do you remember what comrade Lacis said?" He solemnly raised his fat finger and straightened his stout figure. "We don't fight with individuals. We're eliminating the bourgeoisie as a class. We're not looking if the accused fought against the power of the Soviets. We check what class they're from, what origin they have, their profession and education. We're not bringing justice; we're sweeping away enemies. He puffed back and nodded. "A denunciation isn't bad. The authors must refer to some justifications. It's even less accidental than our usual arrests." He smiled and licked his lips.

Everyone knew that he liked to personally torture the interrogated. He and his subordinates showed a lot of creativity in this. Traditional methods, which they used intensively, were not enough for them. They introduced new ones. The interrogated was chained to the wall, they put a pipe with a rat inside and applied fire to its end. The terrified animal tried to get outside, biting and tearing the body of the interrogated. The prisoners were threatened that they would be buried alive and locked up for a long time in a cramped chest with decaying corpses. Some were actually buried alive. I saw people led out of the Cheka cellars who were throwing themselves about and babbling like mad people. Maybe they really went crazy. I tried not to think about it.

At one point I noticed that I was drinking too much. I began to control myself. I had to be sober. Although I couldn't always be. I had to oversee executions many times. People were brought to the basement, ordered to lie face down and shot in the back of the head with a revolver. To save time and effort, another group was put on the corpses of the previous ones, and this was repeated several times. People struck by fear almost didn't defend themselves, just moaned or prayed, said something unrelated when they were pushed on the still quaking and bleeding bodies. When the prisoners pulled the corpses out onto the prison yard, loaded them onto carts and trucks to be taken away and buried, the Chekist pointed out to me that the floor level of the basement had already managed to rise in recent weeks from the clotted blood and dry brains.

I remember little from those times precisely. Disordered scenes pass before my eyes. As an intellectual, I was ordered to interrogate a well-known professor of Kiev University, who allegedly cooperated with whites. I saw that he was afraid but was trying to preserve his dignity. He answered questions accurately and comprehensively. Clearly, he had nothing on his conscience. He didn't deal in politics. He looked at me in suspense and suddenly decided.

"You'll forgive me, but I also wanted to ask you something. You're an educated man, an intellectual, after all it's visible. You must discern! That, which is happening ... ", he hesitated, "what you are also doing, takes us back to the barbarian era, to wildness!"

"You are wrong," I replied, as if I were waiting for this question. "We, we're actually leading man out of the age of barbarism. You didn't even notice how many people had to suffer so that you could busy yourself with your philosophy at the university. This will change. These are the convulsions of being born again." I don't know what they did with him.

A workers' rebellion broke out in Astrakhan in March. It was about food rations and the arrest of some Menshevik or Socialist leaders. The local Cheka opened fire on the demonstrating workers, but their forces weren't enough. A regiment of soldiers summoned to help, joined the workers. Together they chased out the Chekists and occupied the city. It began to smell like counterrevolution.

I came along with reinforcements. We surrounded the city and blocked it all access points to it. Crowds of workers and soldiers occupied the streets. We started from several sides and immediately started shooting with machine guns and cannons that we brought with us. The crowd broke up and fled. Smaller groups of soldiers and armed workers defended themselves at several points, but we surrounded them methodically and fired until they gave up. All of those from the streets, each quarter surrendering, from houses, from where shots sounded, we chased to prisons: to cells, basements, and when they were no longer fit in there, crowded densely, into the yards between walls. Prepared barges waited on the Volga. We filled them with prisoners. We ordered them to lug stones from nearby quarries. Then we tied them up again and with stones strapped to their necks pushed them into the river in groups. There weren't enough stones, but they were tied up, so probably no one survived anyway. We entered basements, told them to lie down and shot them in the back of the head. When the basements were already full, we began to kill them in the prison yard. We killed thousands of them.

When after two days in the evening, the head of the local Cheka, Atarbekov, invited us I thought it would be a reception after completing the task. We staggered because of fatigue. Indeed, there was vodka and an appetizer. We raised a few toasts and then Atarbekov said: "We killed several thousand workers and soldiers. They betrayed and deserved it. But this doesn't look good. Why are workers rebelling? The bourgeoisie encourage them! Starting tomorrow, we have to go after the bourgeoisie who organized the White Guard conspiracy. Soldiers and workers were only cannon fodder." He laughed.

We were supposed to sleep and get to work the next day.

In the morning we entered a quiet, rich, merchant district. One-story houses with balustrades. Soldiers, Chekists broke into them and dragged out the men, they also robbed what they were in the mood for. Nobody cared about it anymore. In the beginning, the captives were rounded up in groups and driven to prison. There was no reason to lock them up. We shot them immediately in the prison yard under the wall. It lasted for a few days. Towards the end, no one wanted to escort the men pulled out of the flats to prison, anyway there was no room for more corpses. We killed them before the walls of their houses.

I met Atarbekov again a few months later. At Moscow's order, I went to Astrakhan to check the local branch. There were complaints about robberies and banditry. Atarbekov met me and was happy at first, but when he heard that I came for an inspection, he darkened.

"Alright, I'll show you our papers," he said almost defiantly, "but tell Dzerzhinsky that I won't let myself be controlled. We're not making a revolution just so some lords from Moscow could rule us." He looked at me ironically from head to toe.

I noticed that he looks weird. His eyes glowed unnaturally. Then I realized that that's the effect of cocaine. The Chekist assigned to us croaked bluntly and led me to "files". Chekists usually didn't look too nice, but even against them Atarbekov's team stood out. I've never seen such intensity of animalistic distorted muzzles. They looked at us so grimly that I wondered if a four-man inspection wasn't too reckless. Others probably thought the same. I saw this even in the watchful gazes of Alosha. There was almost no documentation. Sometimes a list was encountered with crosses and a notation: "Shot at the order of comrade Atarbekov." When we were entering our quarters, one of the Chekists invited us on behalf of the commander.

A group of them stood in the study, surrounding a few girls with torn clothes and wild gazes. There were bottles and platters with meat and vegetables on the table.

"So what, comrades, will we reconcile?" exclaimed Atarbekov. "After such work one needs to have a good time, there's vodka, and the bourgeoisie girls will finally come in handy for something. "

I peaceably appealed to my duty and led out my people chased by growling of the locals, and in a moment bursts of laughter and screaming women.

After a few days I realized that they not only drink all the time, but also use cocaine, which has become more and more common among Chekists. It was amazing how suddenly it became available, just like morphine. Cocaine also helped me for some time. After taking it executions became fascinating, I participated in them as in a gruesome, but thrilling spectacle. Only the hangover after it was greater than after alcohol. I gave it up, however, not because of that. I decided that I needed to control what I was doing. Therefore, I also stopped taking morphine, after which I didn't feel a similar elation, but I was more confident, relaxed and everything became easy. Only once, when I overdosed, did it overcome me. I was lying half-conscious and my blood vessels were swelling in me, taking my breath away, I couldn't urinate.

One of the comrades joked that communism was already visible in availability to drugs. Earlier the elite used them, today they're available to every Chekist. "And Chekists aren't an elite?" Someone asked consciously. We stopped laughing.

We tried to make contact with Atarbekov's team behind his back. We were to prepare a complete report. They talked reluctantly, although in time Alosha in particular managed to get along with them. They began to treat him as one of their own. They complained about the hard and responsible work.

"Because it's the bourgeoisie who need to be watched. Catch their conspiracies, and here comrades send an inspection team to us", one growled, looking at me meaningfully.

"We also do what they order us to do," said Alosha. "If they ordered you, you'd also go, although you'd feel stupid watching over your comrades. Well, wouldn't you go?" That one reluctantly agreed, and then began to dwell on the recalcitrance of the local bourgeoisie

"We're already thinking: we've broken their necks and they're still alive. There's not a day where someone doesn't have to be gone after. Some head smashed.

Without that powder I want to puke from the sweet smell of human blood," he finally wheezed grimly.

"And I can't fall asleep if I don't kill someone," croaked another who had been listening in silence up until that point. I wondered if it was just a joke.

I later found out that they arrest people and even torture them for ransom. I made a report.

"You're thinking about this, huh?" asked Alosha. "And after all these thugs are the weapon of revolution. That, which they're supposed to do, they do well, although they steal and don't care about discipline."

We fought Denikin's army and the Cossacks accompanying it. We retreated before them and they conquered city after city, area after area. And they organized Jewish pogroms everywhere. The Jews who fled from them joined us. They told terrible things about rapes, tortures. We were doing the same, but it's us who were fighting for a new, good world, they were exclusively motivated by anger.

We saw the glow of burning towns and settlements. Sometimes pogroms were done by ours as well. The madness instilled in people made itself heard. Why should I think particularly about the fate of Jews, I asked myself? These are atavisms, myths about blood connection. When we win, the Jews will cease to exist, they'll dissolve into the international sea of a new people. But I couldn't not recall to myself the night from before thirteen years ago.

We retreated constantly. Apparently, it was the same on other fronts, although it was difficult to say something certain. We heard that Kolchak was defeated in the east, but Judenich was approaching Petrograd. And finally, in October, after a series of battles, supported by the Latvian Brigade and Budyonny's cavalry, we broke Denikin's front. From that moment, the whites began to retreat, and we were riding on their backs. The Red Army was recapturing Orzel, Kursk, Kharkiv, and we pacified cities. We were capturing the whites, their allies and those who could be their allies or seemed to us to be them. We imprisoned, interrogated and executed them.

I think in Kharkov that I saw how drunk Alosha with a few of ours in a similar state, was pushing a group of terrified girls into the office, they probably weren't even twenty years old yet. "These are bourgeois girls, we're taking them to be interrogated," Alosha croaked in answer to my furious questions. I took out my Nagant and ordered them to be released. Alosha's face narrowed into a hostile grimace. He sobered up suddenly. "You're going to shoot at us because of bourgeois girls? Because what, they're too noble, to give us ass? Us who risk our lives every day for the revolution? If we destroy thousands of peasants, there are no individuals, only class, and if we want to fuck some bourgeoisie girls, a knight wakes up in the Commissar? You're going to defend their virtues? And what's this?" Alosha laughed, although his face was angry. The Chekists who understood nothing, croaked to the point of being sick. "Lower your weapon, comrade," Alosha said more calmly. "They'll be fine. They'll experience pleasure with the working class." I put my revolver away and left.

The retreat of the Whites turned into an escape. We couldn't keep up with them. Even then, the Cossacks were still carrying out pogroms. Steppe was burning before us. In one of the cities the local Jews were chased into the synagogue, they nailed up the door and set fire to it. When we arrived, the site of the fire was still smoking. Human remains were lying around in the ashes. The remains of hands that were trying to grasp something, bizarrely curved legs, black, deformed heads.

In a deserted town we caught up with a group of Cossacks, who organized a party for themselves in the building of the local post office. They were drunk, they ran away blindly, few escaped. From a few we didn't kill immediately we learned that they thought we were a few days away. Alosha interrogated them. I watched for a moment. We were in a hurry. He didn't have time. He began to gouge out the eye of one of the prisoners with a knife.

It was probably a Jewish town. There were terribly chopped and disfigured bodies everywhere, which dogs were jerking on. A few naked, eviscerated women were nailed to the wooden wall of the post office. On the fences writhed impaled children. Many were still alive. We had to finish them off.

At the beginning of 1920, I came to Petrograd a bit by accident. I haven't been in it for over two years. It was completely different than the one I remembered. I recognized the city with difficulty. It seemed that the inhabitants escaped from it. The dirty, cluttered with piles of rubbish, streets were empty. Skinny characters rarely and fearfully slipped through them. The silence was only broken from time to time by the roar of shots. Dusk was approaching. I wandered the streets aimlessly. The destroyed, crumbling buildings resembled tombs in a forgotten cemetery. Stories about the birth of Peter's city returned to me. Marked out in the wetlands by the sea, its foundations were made with the bones of its builders. A ghost town in which human will tried to control the elements.

I didn't see people. There were no people. This was a city of the dead. I was one of them. I've never experienced such a dominating feeling of my own death.

Still in the winter they threw us on the Volga to pacify the Kazan, Simbirsk and Uficki Governorates, where the peasants rebelled. These images will repeat themselves. We enter the village; we're looking for men. We interrogate the women and children. We scare, beat, murder. We burn villages, kill peasants. We surround the villages in which they're hiding. We go in line and shoot them like ducks. They're not really dangerous. Almost exclusively they have pitchforks, scythes and axes. Their old rifles aren't particularly dangerous. I no longer paid attention to comrades raping peasant girls.

In autumn, we "de-kulaked" the Cossacks. An end had to be put to the Cossacks, otherwise they would always be a spark of rebellion. We burned Cossack villages, took all the belongings from their inhabitants and in part handed it over to other villages. We killed their animals and sent the meat to cities and the army. We shot some of the men, especially those we suspected of taking part in revolts, some were deported by trains under escort to the Donetsk mines. We wanted to send them north, but for transport reasons it proved impossible. The families of rebels, women, children and the elderly we locked up in concentration camps. I escorted one transport. In the surrounded by wire camp on the steppe, a lack of guards could immediately be seen. The rest were composed of barely put together, sinking into the mud, huts. Women, elderly, children roamed unconsciously, sinking down to their calves in the ground and falling over. Some were sitting, lying or crawling in the mud. These were the sick. It was often impossible to know if they were still alive, especially since there were already many stiff corpses on the ground. Sometimes only up close could the movements of the chest and eyeballs be seen. The more conscious showed us with their lips. They were hungry, desperately hungry. A few women and girls came up to me indicating that they wanted to eat, with fingers touching their stomachs, thighs, breasts and deathly smiling. I've never seen any prostitute in this state. The commandant shrugged with his shoulders in response to my questions. Supposedly, he didn't have enough food, and the corpses, which I pointed out in fear of the plague, he couldn't get rid of fast enough.

I wrote a few reports to my superiors and directly to Dzerzhinsky. I didn't get any answer.

The Cheka's work began to be organized and bureaucratize. We drew up an almost complete list of those executed and arrested. We subdued the chaos, although this gave rise to further problems. We established the number of hostages shot for any acts of terror. After killing one of the heads of the local Cheka in ambush, the numbers of hostages to kill were sent out. One of the Chekists, laughing, told about how in a town, which he came to settle accounts with, a random group of patients were executed to complete the allotment.

In late autumn we went after Wrangel in the Crimea. Troops arrived from the Polish front and the Whites couldn't face us anymore. They fled in the direction of the sea, defending themselves desperately, and we followed them like a horde of wolves hunting a herd. We closed the Isthmus of Perekopski, we tightened the loop on the throat of Crimea, so that the only escape was by sea, and step by step we combed the area. Sometimes I was struck by its beauty. We came to the mountains from the steppes, which rose laboriously, showing off more and more different vegetation, to fall sharply towards the sea shimmering with pale light. However, there was little time left to admire Crimea. We did surveys to track down everyone who fled here with the Whites. We checked everyone. Those who hadn't lived here earlier were shot or imprisoned in concentration camps. We reached Sevastopol a little after Wrangel and his men left by ship. They took a course to Istanbul. Not everyone could however escape.

In the beginning we executed the dock workers who helped them escape. Then we started hunting. At that time, we didn't use files yet. We combed house after house, basement after basement. Those, who looked like soldiers or officers, or could be them, we hung on sycamore trees on the main avenue of the city, Nachimov Prospectus. Soon there was already no room on the trees, and we hung the next ones on lamp posts. I speeded up, I kept walking ahead, all the way to the edge of the sea. Greece once stretched this far, Greek sailors arrived here and founded the city, I recalled to myself. I was thinking about the clear order that the Greek colonists introduced, about their cities imitating cosmic harmony. However, I had to go back to the center of Sevastopol. There was no one on the streets beyond us Red Army soldiers; beyond our screams, laughter and shots nothing else could be heard. Hanged men swayed everywhere in the wind.

In the winter when I returned to Petrograd, I thought that a time of calm was approaching. I was wrong. There was hunger and unrest in the city. Food rations for workers had been lowered. They chose their representatives and called for a general strike. They called for the overthrow of the "Bolshevik dictatorship." Rallies of support were organized for them in some army units. Something was starting and one had to react quickly. We knew that we were going to shoot into a manifestation of workers. I don't know if they knew. There were a few dozen dead left on the streets and many wounded. We broke into factories and arrested the ringleaders. However, the demonstrations did not end, and troop units joined them. Street clashes and arrests continued. The tension rose. And then the Kronstadt garrison rebelled.

Despite the riots, we were still controlling the city, but we were asking ourselves what would happen when the rebellious sailors arrived. Will this be the beginning of a new, this time anti-Bolshevik revolution? These fears also plagued our leaders. Trotsky arrived in Petrograd, followed by special units commanded by Tukhachevsky. The iron drug addict ordered to take sailors' families living in the city hostage and dispose of the counterrevolution. The pacification of the city took us two days. We arrested over two thousand people. Petrograd froze.

The sea was frozen. It was possible to attack across the ice the island on which lies Kronstadt. Throughout the day, artillery shelled the fort. At night, the soldiers wrapped in white sheets ran toward the citadel. We, Chekists, with machine guns occupied positions in the rear. We shot at anyone who tried to turn back. The soldiers ran in dense battle order and fell just as densely under the fire from the fort. Flashes of shots lit up white shadows on which red patches blossomed. More and more densely they were stumbling and falling on the ice. Soon, even we started shooting, because large groups of people gone mad under fire began to turn back under our barrels. After the first series of bullets we forced them to attack again. Tukhachevsky threw the next units on the ice, but some of them stopped, seeing what was happening. They stood to the side, so we didn't shoot, especially since the attack broke down completely and it was in our direction that crowds of white-dressed, terrified, ghostly soldiers rushed.

We received an order to surround and disarm those who refused to attack. Every fifth one we ordered to go to the side to the separate unit that was being formed. That was Trotsky's order. We arrested them and led them to the waterfront. There, we shot them with machine guns and finished them off with revolvers. Tukhachevsky spoke to the others. He said they would be here until they conquered Kronstadt. Every cowardice, every act of betrayal will be punished with death. However, those who stand out in the inevitable victory will be rewarded. "They don't have a chance!" He shouted, pointing to the citadel. "In place of everyone killed ten new ones will arrive. How long can they defend themselves surrounded by a country of Bolshevik's, by armies, that have defeated a counterrevolution and intervention?!"

An ovation was even raised by soldiers from decimated regiments. It was cold. Then came reinforcements from far away consisting mainly of Kyrgyzs and Bashkirs.

Every night, Red Army soldiers sneaked several times from different sides under the fort to attack, or maybe simulate an attack and retreat under massive fire. They left more dead and wounded, but the attacks continued. On the ninth night, the tired defenders let the massed units approach near. When they realized, it was too late. The storm broke into the fortress. During this time, we pacified the uncertain units of Petrograd. We surrounded the indicated groups, disarmed and arrested. We entered Kronstadt after it was conquered.

Everywhere the killed and wounded were collected. In the fort, guarded by soldiers, groups of prisoners sitting in the snow looked at us in suspense.

We had information from local communists as who the ringleader was. We fished them out of the groups and shot them on the spot. In the hundreds. The rest were arrested. A few thousand of them were shot later. Most were sent to the camp in Kholmogory, in the north, near Arkhangelsk, on the river Dvina. They were joined by those who managed to flee to Finland but were lured back with the promise of amnesty. Convincing them was a complicated operation, one of the first such, exemplarily carried out by our reforming institution. During some binge drinking in Moscow, the drunk commandant of Kholmogory boasted that he came up with the best way to eliminate enemies of the people and traitors. "It's a shame to waste bullets on them", he assured. "I drowned them in Dvina. Stone on the neck and into the river. We also threw in those from Kronstadt. Sailors like to swim!" He laughed, delighted at his joke. "Few of them remain. Supposedly, such tough guys. And they softened like wax with me. I have special ways for such people." He was almost tenderly smiling at his thoughts.

We sent others to the Solovetsky Islands.

I participated in the first phase of this operation, and then I was sent to the Tambov region to suppress Antonov's peasant rebellion. I never returned to Petrograd. In the Tambov region I again met Tukhachevsky. The suppression of this rebellion was similar to the earlier pacifications of peasant riots and the scenes from them get mixed up in my mind. Something however distinguished this offensive. First of all, it was better organized and probably not only because, the rebellion was more serious.

We surrounded the next villages. We arrested families, in which the men were not there, and we gave those two days to return. Then we transported the families away and confiscated their property. Soon we had a network of informants. For the most part, we forced cooperation by arresting family members as hostages. If a family did not help us, as we expected, we killed hostages or sent them to hastily organized concentration camps. Sometimes we sent them further north. We often took hostages from each family. We shelled rebellious villages with artillery, burned, deported in full. We shelled many of them with poison gas. That gave the best effect.

I remember the first time we entered such a village. The gas didn't leave any trace. The air seemed unusually clear and trembled in the heat. It was calm, unusually calm. Approaching the houses, in the beginning we saw the corpses of birds, animals, and finally human bodies. It even made an impression on us. Maybe because the corpses showed no signs of injury, no blood on them, maybe except the red foam that solidified on the dead lips. The corpses were strangely twisted, corpses of mothers were squeezing in their embrace dead children, sometimes people held on to each other as if trying to help themselves. Suddenly I realized that silence was swelling, rupturing eardrums and nobody has the courage to interrupt it. Then a young officer, Pimen, spoke up. He spoke in an unnaturally loud soprano.

"There's nothing to be so sorry for them for!" He called passionately. "They've managed to do worse things. In my vicinity, they not only burned the manors, but cruelly murdered the families who lived there. They didn't do anything bad to them."

"Do you feel sorry for those from the manors?", Bogdanow, a Chekist who was walking by me, leaned in his direction. "Lords? " Pimen looked confused.

"Not them. I say the peasants are no better. A group of ours not far from here was ambushed. Those, who survived, the peasants buried headfirst in the ground up to their thighs. Based on their leg movements, they judged who was stronger and would survive longer. They made bets. I know this for sure. I checked".

Bogdanow looked at him for some time. "He's one of those officers, that joined us. Like Tukhachevsky. Maybe because that they don't like peasants? If they didn't like the bourgeoisies the same way, that's fine, but if ... they need to be watch", he winked at me.

In the camps, in which thousands, deprived often of even clothes, peasant families were cramped, typhus and cholera broke out. The guards watched over them from the outside, sometimes throwing in leftover food. I don't know how many could've survived. The peasants were in the snare. Entire families were capable of committing suicide. Often, the fathers killed their children and wives, and then themselves. This could be recognized, because the children and women were stabbed or chopped with an ax, and the men hung themselves on makeshift rope. When we found several dead families in subsequent villages, it occurred to me that it was also a kind of epidemic.

This wasn't a good year, although the war was over. Hunger in the spring had begun to reap a deadly harvest. In truth requisitions were halted, but the earlier one deprived the peasants not only of food, but also seeds for sowing. Almost everyone was starving. In the beginning, they ate farm and domestic animals. Then all possible plants: grass, weeds, bark from trees, moss. The stronger tried to escape to the cities, they reached the railway stations, where they camped in desperate throngs and stench, unable to go further.

We blocked them. We were to stop all hunger migrations; besides, the Bolshevik authorities didn't recognize the existence of hunger until July. The stations were besieged even more and more unconscious from hunger people in rags full of vermin. Some didn't have the strength to move. Lingered in the waiting rooms, corridors, platforms. They laid in the roads. They were falling ill to typhus, whose epidemic was spreading almost as fast as hunger. Many were dying away. Corpses were laying among the still alive. The services couldn't keep up with collecting the corpses. They were picked up together with the dying onto carts, so filled up, that the emaciated horses dragged them with difficulty, and they were thrown into huge pits. They were buried and new ones were dug. It was impossible to keep up.

Many times, we walked through dead, empty villages where the silence was as heavy as after dropping poison gas. Cannibalism was rampant. People ate the dead bodies of their loved ones and then looked for other corpses. They were capable of digging them out of their graves. When we entered an almost extinct settlement, in one of the cottages a pair of peasants of an indeterminate age was quartering a human body. Next to them were chopped off heads and limbs. They tried to fight us when we were taking them. They weren't afraid of us. They were worried about their food. In another settlement we came across a mad woman who was boiling a fragment of a human corpse. She asked us not to take it. "You're Bolsheviks!" She called out. "It's just meat. They're already dead, and we can survive. Leave us this meat." I thought she was right, and that we yield to superstition, trying to protect human carcasses from being eating.

The hungry were capable of hunting children to eat them. They sometimes killed their own or ate the bodies of those who died of hunger and disease. The Chekists from a neighboring group told me about a band of feral teenagers who attacked weaker and sick adults, especially women. They killed them with knives, sticks and stones, and then tore them apart. Unexpectedly, terror awakened inside of me. What have we led to - I thought. But some voice began to explain to me that these are just the last obstacles. A rational economy will conquer hunger and feed everyone. Only that for now all around maundered human skeletons. They stretched out their hands to us with insanity in their eyes.

When I was recalled to Moscow, I felt almost happy. There, however, it turned out that I was to participate in the arrest of members of Pomgo, a social committee to fight hunger, which organized huge foreign aid. The Americans in particular have fed millions of hungry almost the entire year. Lenin was furious but couldn't refuse help. However, when it turned out that the Americans are providing help outside of Pomgo, almost all its members were imprisoned. As usual, Gorki got himself out. The authorities couldn't tolerate independent activities developing under their side that could take any form. We thought we'd have to execute them. I felt a kind of compassion. I was angry with myself. I was beginning to get too soft. However, the images of those dying from hunger were returning to me and I couldn't help thinking about those who were helping them. They dedicated themselves, they wanted the best. I overcame my tenderness rather quickly, but when it turned out that through the intercession of Nansen, the members of Pomgo were only exiled, I felt relief.

The decree of February 1922 on the confiscation of church treasures for the cause of the starving was a masterpiece. We assumed that its author was Trotsky, and even those who didn't like him, this time they spoke about him with appreciation. We knew that one of the church superstitions is the dogma of the sacredness of liturgical vessels. Handing them over for secular purposes would be sacrilege. The church must therefore oppose the law and we're going to enforce it. For the sake of the hungry, we will deal with the church. In truth, Patriarch Tikhon declared that the Orthodox Church would collect money for the hungry of the value of sacred vessels and would hand over other valuable items to them, but I don't think he even got an answer. It's us who have the newspapers and information centers in our hands. His proposal never reached the wider public, who learned that the Orthodox Church is stingy with its treasures for starving people.

I knew, we knew that the trial with the Church must come. We were even irritated that we've been waiting for it so long. In the provinces, often on our own initiative we took care of the clergy. But the authorities were delaying. And the church wasn't just independent. It was an ideological enemy. Communism and the Church couldn't be reconciled. One could even believe that Christ is our prophet, that he proclaims the era of God-man to dethrone an inhuman God functioning somewhere in the afterlife. But this God couldn't be removed from the church. He was looking at us and judging our actions from every place. So, when the February decree appeared, we immediately understood its consequences and with satisfaction we realized that the time had come.

The scale of resistance surprised us, however. The faithful were capable of guarding the churches day and night to prevent the taking of valuables. Crowds came. They were not even scared off by shots. In Shui, a few hundred kilometers from Moscow, a crowd chased away a group of Chekists and Bolsheviks. It was only after a few days that the intervention of military units using machine guns restored a somewhat order. The authorities were stunned. The action was stopped. For a week. And then Lenin spoke about convalescences in the villages. His memorial was secret, and therefore only known in the Politburo. Only verbal orders made their way to us, its consequences.

Show trials about the black-plot conspiracy and coup d'état began. We never believed in bourgeois law. Now we were making trials like their parodies. We directed everything. These were great performances. Sometimes there were several thousand spectators in the halls. They were all supposed to be actors, including the accused. It didn't always work out. Our options, however, were limited. Not all lawyers and defendants let themselves be intimidated, and we couldn't use more serious coercion. Too many eyes were looking at us. All in all, it usually ended the way we wanted anyway. Prepared sentences were passed. Those destined for execution ended up against the wall, and those who were supposed to be sent to prison or exile were there. Those, which we couldn't kill officially, we suspended their priestly functions and we supervised them in seclusion. There we killed them silently.

This was the official scene. In the back we got a free hand and directions that we already knew before: no mercy, strike the neck of the Church.

We confiscated the sacred tools as ostentatiously as possible to desecrate, humiliate every temple. The faithful had to see that God was helpless and His servants weak. We reacted with strength to every attempt at resistance. We shot whenever the opportunity arose. We killed clergy, the friars and nuns, when whatever pretext showed up, or without a pretext. We've arrested them in the thousands. Some Chekists, especially in the provinces, they gave off steam by tormenting and torturing the clergy, raping nuns. The Living Church eagerly supported us. Clergymen from this group were our witnesses at trials. They testified what was needed. They lied that giving away sacred vessels doesn't violate any prohibitions. They became indignant at the church's insensitivity to hunger. They talked about the hierarchy's contacts with emigration, about its hostile attitude towards the Bolsheviks. They privately denunciated about everything, they were pointing out who should be eliminated, found the weak that could be seduced, bribed or intimidated. I knew that their role could not be overstated, but I couldn't free myself from the disgust that I felt for them. I scolded myself for that and that's why I engaged in conversations with them even outside my business needs.

"You're doing well", I told to one of the more zealous ones after I finished my business conversation, when I took out a bottle and glasses. "You're good," I repeated. He Beamed. We drank. "But humanly, don't you feel sorry for them? They're at last like your old ... comrades. "

He looked at me in surprise. "That's how it should be done," he said with conviction. "We must renovate the church. You're renovating Russia. These people don't understand. They may even be decent, but for the good of the Church and for the good of Russia they must be removed. It's difficult, but it must be done. The comrade understands. "

I put the bottle away and shook his hand. I thought about it. He looked like he believes in what he says. Do we always believe in everything we want?

"And you know, the priest you talk to so often, Yegor, was still in the Black Sotnia at the beginning of the war", said one of my comrades, looking maliciously at me.

I worked with the League of Militant Atheists and organized debates for them under the title: "Does God exist?" We exhibited two debaters, and the hall became a court. Both interlocutors were prepared by me. One was our officer or a young activist from the Union. I preferred the officer. Young activists got fired up, left their roles, talked nonsense, which I sometimes had to correct as a spectator from the hall. The officers kept saying what was needed. The priest, who was the other side, was provided to me by Chekists. He was supposed to be already ready. I didn't ask by what method they achieved it. I usually recognized it. There's an intensity of fear visible in the eyes and gestures that can only be achieved through torture.

At first, the clergyman was to convince the room of the truth of his person. He preached, blessed and introduced himself truthfully. He began: "You can see that God exists, because the world is good." Even the favorably disposed to him crowd began to murmur. Then he declared that one must suffer for the Lord's glory, and hunger is good because it's a punishment for sins. Pressed by our man, he admitted that they don't know hunger in the Church, but they must have the strength to pray for sinners. He claimed that the Lord always heard his prayers and that the holy vessels did miracles. When he was asked to give an example, he was fidgeting more and more, and finally fell on his knees terrified and asked that the people would forgive him for the fraud because he himself doesn't believe that God exists. That was the most important moment and the most credible. The clergy really were dying of fear.

During the next performance, I realized that something was going wrong. After the established start, the priest began to say something different. I stared angrily at him, but he glanced at me. Others called to order by my gaze couldn't take their frightened eyes away from me. This one, however, when asked why there's evil in the world, if God is good, only bowed his head. "Is man good?", He asked. "Can a man be good if he doesn't have a good Father above him? If a man who believes is so evil, then how evil will he be when he stops believing?"

The terrified officer mumbled something. "And maybe precisely then he'll become better!" I shouted from inside the room.

"And why is that?" Asked the priest. He straightened up. He was now a different person. I didn't recognize him. "Those who believe, believe even though, there's nature. And you?" He was turning towards me. "Do you at least know who created nature?"

I felt it would end badly when our man spat out like an automaton: "Nature created itself". The audience fell over from laughter. I nodded. Several officers surrounded the priest.

"We have to make sure that nothing happens to our debater", I said. The journey passed in silence. He was trying not to look at me. I saw fear biting into a stooped figure. I felt sorry for him. I felt angry with myself and great fatigue. I needed to get myself together. We entered the office in a group of four.

"And what good did that do you, priest? I asked. He put his arm around his head. "Take care of him", I said.

Gloomy Ivan moved closer to him, raising a sinewy fist. "And what will come to you, cleric, from this? Well, what? Will God save you?" The fist dropped. Grigori came up to him. It stuck. I heard a drawn out, hopeless groan. I went out.

I participated in scattering a crowd at the synagogue. We gave it to the Bund members. We beat people who weren't defending themselves, we dragged them along the ground, arrested them. I felt almost elation. We spat in the face of the old God, humiliated and killed him.

I looked at the rabbi who was sitting in front of me in the office at Lubyanka. He was torn up and beaten, but he didn't let his gaze down.

"What plot are you talking about? After all you know it is ridiculous. If you'll work on me for some time, maybe you'll choke out of me that I work to the benefit of the Japanese, but what good is it for you?" I was tired. It truly wasn't necessary. I waved my hand.

"We'll exile you." I couldn't read anything from his face. Maybe because of the beard covering it - I thought stupidly.

"Then I'm lucky. You're not going to kill me? Should I thank you? "

"There's no need to. I didn't do anything for you. You mean nothing to me. "

"We mean nothing to you?"

"You don't exist for me. I understand that you refer to Jewishness."

"Do you think that identity can be thrown away like clothing? It's not possible. You can run from it, fight with it, argue, but it'll always eventually speak out in a strange way. These Bundists ... How stupid they are. They'll pay for this. After all, when they'll carry out their job and destroy all synagogues, then you'll also throw them away on that... how do you say? Dustbin of history?

"I don't know what you're talking about!"

"I'm talking about responsibility. Do you think you can escape it? But it always comes back. Sometimes in a weird form. Yes ...", he thought, "Trotsky made the revolution, and the Bronstein's will pay for it ... but ... the Trotsky's also ", he added after a while.

It was around that time that Mienżyński offered me a job in intelligence. When I entered his office, he was reclining on a small sofa. He rose, however, and though with difficulty, he came up to greet me. He apologized for having to lie down during the conversation. "Comrade understands. Spine, disease ... ", He smiled shyly under his mustache. He suggested that I bring a chair close to him. Everything in him, except maybe the mustache, was unusual for this place. Courteous politeness, delicacy, an elegant suit with a vest, tastefully well-matched tie and cufflinks. Only then did I recall to myself when I saw him for the first time. I saw him from time to time. Three years earlier, he became an important figure in the Cheka, the Plenipotentiary of the Department for Special Tasks. And yet, despite the unusual appearance, he was hardly remembered. He seemed a blurred reflection of the place, a figure made of smoke. Now a scene from the October Revolution, five years earlier, came back to me. I dropped in to Smolny's for instructions. Running through, I heard a piano. A long, hunched figure was leaning over it, Mienżyński. He was probably playing Chopin. The strangeness of the situation paralyzed me for a moment. In the fever, that was ruling, I forgot about it right away. Now I was seeing him in front of me in the office on Lubyanka, where instead of giving instructions to me, with an almost shy tone he made proposals to me. When I reported that I had accepted them, he smiled.

"But I'm really asking you." Once again, I confirmed my consent. "You meet very few people like you here. You've been downright created for foreign intelligence.

I have been following your career and I'm impressed. Only when I observe people like you do I have a question, which I shouldn't ask, but ... Will you let me? "

"Here you can ask any question."

He smiled. "Witty. So I ask: why did you report to the Cheka? "

"For the same reason as you, comrade, like everyone here!"

"Well yes, of course. But beyond that ...", unexpectedly, he touched the top of my hand almost imperceptibly with his fingertips; I instinctively withdrew my hand. "People still have individual motives. Nothing wrong with that. We're still just human. And so, some want to achieve freedom. To cross everything that previously limited them. Not feel bound by your transgressions or even beliefs. To continuously exceed oneself. This is also a revolutionary attitude ... Do you agree? "

"I don't know if I understand, comrade. We transcend ourselves, integrating ourselves into the collective, into the party. "

He pointed his long fingers in my direction. He played with them and displaying their aristocratic shape. "So, you say that you're integrating yourself in our Chekist collective." At the bottom of his smile a tinge of mockery might loom, but the tone of his voice was still almost shy. "You've been downright created for foreign intelligence. I think that we could not only cooperate well, I'm sure of it, but becomes friends. Sometimes I would like to talk to someone about poetry, for example. I don't know if you know, I wrote once ..."

Of course, I saw. Before the revolution, he published probably a novel and poetry. He functioned then in the circle of a well-known decadent and homosexual, Kuzmin. Everything was known in our circle. In exile, Mienżyński published some political texts. In one he wrote that Lenin was a political Jesuit, who takes from Marxism what's comfortable to him, and he only wants power. Since a copy of this article had reached us, it had to have reached Lenin. However, he didn't display any interest in this type of news. He didn't deal with people, and therefore with what they said about him. Exactly the opposite of Stalin. As far as I know he has everything that anyone has at the very least mentioned about him written down. He probably doesn't have to anyway. He remembers everything.

"Unfortunately, I don't know about poetry and I don't read it. However, I understand that we'll have a lot of contacts. You oversee the foreign section ..."

"Well yes, we'll definitely have ... I'm so happy. Oh well, responsibilities ... You'll have to excuse me comrade ..."

We've seen each other many times, but we've never had a similar conversation.

This was the year in which the Cheka was disbanded, to be replaced by the GPU, christened at the end of this year as the OGPU. We thought it was just a change of name, but it turned out that matters were going further. Our service began to become even more bureaucratic. We threw off the leather jackets. Repressions were to be limited; the rule of law strengthened. Dzerzhinsky himself appealed for caution and moderation, although he suggested that this was only a stage. We were supposed to treat applications for trips outside the country more liberally. The Chekists grumbled. "Are we to be like tools, which are thrown away when it fulfills its task?" - they asked. But they adjusted. They changed their style, although it came to some with difficulty. Everything was fit into the context of the NEP. The new phase of Bolshevik power.

The first news of the New Economic Policy didn't make a great impression on me. It was obvious that the requisitions must be ended. Famine could destroy the country, not only the village but also the city. Free trade was needed until we don't build a rational supply system and for that we needed time. It was the same with crafts and even small production. I think that those of us who were thinking about it treated these solutions like me, as a tactical retreat during the war. However, the NEP continued. I didn't care. I got completely involved in the work of the foreign department. We penetrated the ranks of the emigration. We threw nets at the most dangerous people. We created fictitious resistance organizations that made it possible to catch them beyond the border or lure those into the country, which we wanted to get rid of. That's how we hunted down Sawinkow.

The clergy were the last ones that I killed. In any case personally. Then the bureaucracy began. Reporting on tamed terror. It's as if I was waking up for a long, very long time from a tiring nightmare. With difficulty, it's hard to break free from the dreamy reality and only after some time, we gradually begin to associate that there is another world around. We wake up slowly and painfully, although the nightmare lasts in us constantly.

I was still working for the system, but I was beginning to understand that we had organized hell, not to revive our land, but to corrupt it. We've violated the human world so deeply that it must be rebuilt from the most trivial dimensions. People need to be allowed to work, trade, scrape together things. Thanks to this they can last and even develop somehow. This was the NEP. But those who organized hell do not want to return to normality. This did this to control life and death. They treat people like clay from which any shapes can be kneaded and justify themselves by making it a better grade. Some don't justify themselves at all. They know they are created for power. Others, or perhaps the same, they hated themselves for what the revolution has done with them, and they want to take revenge on others. They recognize that the revolution has unveiled man the really is, so they want to humiliate him, to torment him. They still desire to make a revolution. And we're preparing the bureaucracy of terror that is yet to come so that they can rule.

It took me a long time to understand this. For many years I would wake up and gradually began to recognize that, which surrounds me, what I participated in and continue to participate in. Although I was running away from the truth, I desired to close my eyes, not see, not admit even to myself to that which I was doing, who I was. I twisted out of it using Marxist tricks, intellectual games that could justify everything, and above all ourselves. Painfully, in sleepless nights I conducted this confession before I didn't decided to put it on paper. Because only when I write this, do I begin to really understand what we were doing and what I was doing.

Maybe the last act of awakening that made me write down of confessions, was a meeting with Alosha Bizimana.

A few months ago, he accosted me. Probably only because I saw him from time to time, I could still recognize him. He gained a lot of weight. From the ephebos who mounted a horse bareback on the steppe above the Volga became a bulky, heavy man. The bright eyes went out, immersed in his bloated face. Only sometimes they regained their former splendor. That's how it was then when he stepped in my way on the Lubyanka stairs.

"Jakub, Commissar ", he began, laughing, "we somehow don't see each other. Our paths diverged. And I've missed you. Come to my place. I'd show you my home, family. I already have two children. They're sending me out of Moscow. I don't know for how long. Don't despise the invitation of a cordial friend."

Maybe it was in Kharkov when he was dragging girls into the office and I did nothing to oppose it, maybe a little later or earlier, but our paths indeed diverged. I don't know which of us first began to distance ourselves from our former comrade. Oh, we each moved in our own direction and passed each other with increasing indifference, even though our routes crossed constantly.

I wasn't naive enough to believe in his cordiality on the Lubyanka's stairs. I was no longer naïve at all and didn't believe in anything. But he intrigued me.

Indeed, he had a nice apartment. He advanced and overtook me in our new hierarchy. He had a three-year-old daughter and a son of less than a year. The wife was pretty, gentle and smiled sadly when her husband praised her attributes. She strangely didn't fit him. She looked after the children and brought more food. There was soup and pelmeni's, and immediately a bottle of Armenian cognac.

"And what do you think, intellectual? I'm also being educated! And I know what's good to drink. Have you ever drunk such a cognac? A special delivery from the Caucasus." We already ate the main dishes and Natasha set a plate of cold cuts and pickled cucumbers on the table. The bottle was running out. The host stared at me intensely.

"Who would have thought? Such an intellectual ... and ... idealist. And not a coward, he can even fight. And you didn't go too far. And I, an ordinary boy, not even a Cossack, non-residential from Don, I'm higher. And this is just the beginning. See, this is a real revolution! Just why not you? Maybe because you've always been a little saint. You see? I'm learning. I even go to the theater. Natasha! Another bottle of the best! So well, I think ... you were haughty. That everyone sees. Maybe your tribe is like that. Like Trotsky. Just like him you showed that you're better, and therefore you never had real friends ..."

"Are you saying this to me?" I interrupted for the first time, "my dearest friend, with whom I shared one groundsheet and jointly stuck my neck out?"

"Look at him!" He laughed playfully, threatening me with a finger. "He's going to imitate me. Ah yes! You were capable of sharing ... although not with everything. And you stuck out your neck too. Only I wasn't your friend, but ... how to say ... adjutant. Yes, you taught me a lot. I should be grateful to you ..." he hesitated and looked at me with a crooked smile, "and if I'm not so much, it's because you didn't do it to me. You wanted to be important. Mold me. And when I started thinking and acting my way, you stepped back. I wasn't now just independent. I could teach you a few things. Because you're a theoretician. And when I already understand, when I already understood, what you were teaching me, I was able to bend it to life. You told me about classes and about the fact that we are ... well ... a product of class relations, and faith in the individual is a bourgeois superstition, and you wanted to treat those individuals with kid gloves. Once you even put a revolver up against my nose ..."

"And do you remember why?"

"Sure! Feelings woke up in the heart of the Commissar. So, we could kill bourgeoisie girls but not fuck them beforehand? It wasn't about that. You wanted to be the better one. You've never been honest. You even lied to yourself. Beautiful words. Even if you pushed your paws into blood, there were justifications. And blood is blood. And power is power. Well, don't take offense with me for honesty, dear friend." He raised a glass of golden liquid. He had a cucumber in the fingers of the other one. "Let's have a toast. For friendship!" He smiled contrarily. His eyes glowed with light from years ago. "And friends can tell each other everything. Right? So, for friendship and for the revolution!" I clinked glasses with him. "Because you probably don't think that the revolution is over?" He looked at me closely. "That the NEP will always be, and the new bourgeois will get richer. No, we won't let that happen. The revolution needs continuation. You know that anyway. Theoretically. Or maybe not only? That Mienżyński ... A good boss, and he talks about you as if he was in love." Alosha was looking at me from narrowed eyelids. He seemed drunk just a moment ago, now he looked sober. "Mienżyński ... That's a head. Maybe even better than yours. Forgive me ..." I waved a hand dismissively. "You had a chance with him. You could've made a career. Why didn't you used this. Well, say it. "

"I don't care," I told the truth. I didn't want to say anything else. I didn't want to talk at all.

"Well, precisely, look ... Can one be liked, one like you? You say, as if you wanted to offend me. You're above career, profit ... A little like this Trotsky. But the quails he specifically orders to be delivered to him. And us? You're just that way? But you're now ending. Lenin was replaced by Stalin. It's not worse. He will lead us. Trotsky is the past ... He had his merits, but the more time passes, the smaller they are." He laughed. The second bottle was running out. The world was shaking, Alosha was smearing up before my eyes. I had to get a grip.

"I'll go now".

"Exactly. Did you get offended? Won't you still drink with me? In the Russian style? Till the end! You can sleep at my place. If you want, I can even share Natasha with you. We are like that. And she's pretty. Intelligent. I saved her. She's grateful to me. She must be!" He laughed uncomfortably. "Well yes. Your time is ending. Now we're taking matters into our own hands. Oj, we'll take care of the bourgeois, kulaks, intellectuals, with ..." He looked at me and waved his hand. "You're still useful on the foreign front, but our children will also know languages. Then we won't need you. "

I patted him on the shoulder: "Well exactly. I'm going! Disappearing". He still wanted to stop me, but I was decided. From the other room, Natasha's terrified look was saying goodbye.

And well. Actually, I should end on this. I've written everything. Actually, I've written little. I recall to myself so many matters. So many sins that I didn't even try recall to myself, so many crimes, so many terrible things that I personally committed. I'm not capable of describing them. The most important I've done, however. I probably did. I've confessed. Those who are going read this, if such will be and these won't be Chekists, may not want to believe. I'll just say that I didn't write everything. Many, even worse things, I didn't even try writing about. I wasn't able to, I didn't have the courage? Maybe this can't be described.

It's night. I only write at night. An even worse time is coming. Will we ever be able to get up again? Are we capable of believing in it? Maybe God cursed us? Just like in the Yom Kippur liturgy. God wants to destroy the treacherous people and only Moses saves them. But now there is no Moses. Maybe there is no rescue? I have to finish. I don't know what to write. I don't know what to think.

CHAPTER 11

"So, you came." His father looked at him in suspense. Adam laughed. He thinks his laugh didn't sound real. He sats down next to the bed.

"I'm here, what did you think?"

"I didn't know what to think." They're silent for a long time.

"Do you know the Bible well?" His father suddenly became curious. "Your mother was probably suggesting it to you. She's becoming more and more of a church goer recently."

"Somehow I'm not in the mood to talk about my mother with you."

"You're right," his father backed down, "I'm sorry. I started unnecessarily, but I just wanted to ask you if there isn't a parable in there about the prodigal father. As if it was made for this moment. It's not the son, but the father that comes to the son and the son forgives him ... or not." His father tried to joke, but it didn't sound good.

"As far as I know, there's nothing in the Bible about prodigal parents, unless it's about the first ones. Maybe nobody thought about it then, that it's the son who could judge his father's life.

"You see how it's changed. And have you looked into my uncle's diary?"

"I read it. And maybe that's why I'm a little sleepy."

"A shocking reading. Don't you think? Compared to this, my confessions will be so small ..."

"Fortunately."

"Yes, you are right, but there's importance in it.

"Fortunately, this is not the case with us."

"Yes, although some people miss it. I translated my uncle's diary, so I remember it very precisely. For a long time, he couldn't start it, circling around the topic, I have the impression that I'm beginning to understand him only now.

"How am I supposed to help you?"

"Ask, it'll be easier for me."

"So how did this all start?"

"It was sixty-eight. Your mother didn't want to make a trip to Vienna. I wanted to run away, we wanted to run away, my father and me. Only I couldn't go without Zuza. I loved her very much. They arrested me on t he street. They took us to Rakowiecka. I was so scared of them. They were screaming at me. You know, the first time I found myself there for interrogation, in the spring, they also offered me collaboration. They didn't actually propose, they shouted, demanded ... I don't know myself how I got away. However, in autumn I wasn't able to. The circumstances were different. They summoned me in the spring. I was somehow prepared to go. This time they took me from the street, took me to prison and it looked like I wouldn't get away so easily. I'd stay at Rakowiecka for a longer time. They told me in detail about our plans for departure, about my father's contacts in Vienna. How did they know so precisely all this? They threatened to sentence us for espionage, my father and I. I believed them. Everything was possible then. They played good cop bad cop with me. And it worked. There were a few bad ones. They were the ones yelling at me and threatening me. There was one good one. He offered me a common solution to get out of a dead end. It's weird. I recognized this tactic and yet I succumbed to it. I knew they were playing me, and I treated them like people. Was it really impossible that one of them wanted to help me? I was very scared of this place, of them ... I don't want to repeat this over and over again, and I'll have to. Fear is the reason for my fall, the driving force behind what I did. Does this justify me even in part? I don't think so." His father stopped, and then started imitating someone: 'If you sign, we'll have a reason to release you. Otherwise we simply won't be able to. The mills of our bureaucracy will begin to grind. You're a sociologist, you must understand. You won't get out of a trial.' I still exactly remember his words to this day. Now I know that he was well prepared, they were prepared for a conversation with me. They had my psychological profile, they analyzed methods. I thought about it, but it wasn't until recently, it wasn't until I understood, that I wouldn't be able to shirk away from the responsibility. For thirty years I tried not to think about it and ... I was succeeding. And then ... Like an idiot, like a small child, I asked him: Really? Would they be able to release me then?!" His father snorted contemptuously. He looked at his son, who thought, that his father really saw a mirror before him, with whom he finally wanted to make amends.

"Concerned ... the concerned UB confirmed it. I thought: I'm intelligent, I can play with them. With just my signature I didn't do anything wrong. Being intelligent ... I signed. I left semi-conscious and on the street after some time I explained to myself that nothing had happened. A signature alone means nothing. I didn't tell anyone anything. For a moment, I considered if I shouldn't talk to your mother. However, I was ashamed, and I explained to myself that it was only a signature ..."

"They caught me on the street about two weeks later. They roughed me up in the car. They were going to beat me. I was ... Well what am I going to tell you? I was sure it would end badly. And it ended badly. The good one came in the study. He stopped the bad ones. He put the paper in front of me and told me to write. He ordered me to recount the statements of various friends, those who left and those who stayed. I wrote. I told myself that it didn't matter to those who left, and to those who stayed ... I tried to censor myself, write less important things. He got on me a few times, it turned out that he knew well about some of the harsher statements I wanted to skip. I came to the conclusion ... no, that's not it... I didn't come to any conclusion. I panicked, reacted, believed that he knew everything. I wrote everything. That our friends really said. He made an appointment with me in two days. And they let me out. I was walking unconscious down the street. Eh ... I won't play introspective." His father fell silent, tired. Breathed heavily. Closes his eyes.

Through the thin, wrinkled skin with brown spots Adam he notices his father's other faces. Those from years ago. He felt moved and resentment simultaneously.

He wanted his father to finish and he knew that he had to hear everything out. Unexpectedly, the words of his great uncle, Jakub Brok, come back to him. Those with which he accused himself, he was frightened this night from the pages of a notebook with wooden covers. His peer was addressing him through the abyss of eighty such fraught years. He was giving him a message with which Adam did not know what to do. His father opens his eyes.

"I asked you to ask. He was directing my secrets, actually my testimony. And after all I have been preparing this statement for you for years. Since I understood that I cannot hide the past, I can't run away from it. Maybe I even started to arrange my confession earlier, yet even under Communism it seemed unrealistic for anyone to find out about ... my collaboration. I tried to justify it to myself, but for that I had to go back to what was, to what I wanted to forget. My uncle's diary would not leave me alone. If he confessed to all of these crimes, he committed ... after all he didn't have to. But they were such loose thoughts. Flashes, convulsions at night and morning dreams. Until communism collapsed. But even then I believed that I would succeed, and nobody would find out. Nobody, especially you. I experienced moments of panic: when Wałęsa came to power, when the Olszewski government began to operate... But these were short moments. Then I calmed down. Somewhere at the very beginning of the nineties, Goleń started conversing with me. He supposedly left politics, but he was an important figure in the background 'Don't worry. For a few dozen years you have peace,' he said only that much, and I knew what he was talking about and I was grateful to him. He was wrong. The calm lasted for less than ten years, although ... He was in close relations with Bogatyrowicz, he probably overestimated his influence. But first things first." His father stops again. Breathes deeply. Rests.

"Then the routine began. In some measure regular meetings with my "leading" officer. That's what it was called in their jargon. Probably at the second meeting, he put an envelope with money in it before me on the table in the café,. He ordered me to count it and confirm. I scolded myself. He said that work should be paid for and that I have nothing to say. I took the money. I signed a receipt. Then I took it without fuss. I thought about the strategy. I would write a lot and abundantly, but about bullshit. I will overwhelm them with details and psychosocial digressions. We lived weirdly then. We ran an open house with your mother. In other words, as the saying goes today, we partied endlessly. There was nothing to do. Our apartment on Koszykowa Street had become a center of artistic and intellectual Bohemia. All in all, talking and alcohol. I described it all in endless elaboration. I wrote about our discussions, intellectual performances and fascinations, the art of conceptualization, happenings, a new wave in literature and cinema, total and poor theater, and God knows about what else: free jazz, counterculture, phenomenology, neopositivism and Wittgenstein, fascinations of Buddhism and Taoism and the search for hippies. The leader scolded that I'm wasting their time and overwhelming with talkativeness. He gave me wings. It seemed that I was letting myself be led like a child again. Being proud, I outraged that the reports would be incomprehensible without any specific details. He was convincing and, without enthusiasm, exclusively pro forma, told me to specify: who was talking about what and how exactly he spoke on a given topic. I thought that I could write that. None of those things was forbidden, it really wasn't about politics. Oh, such elitist talk. I began to treat these reports as a somewhat onerous, but indifferent duty, which a bureaucratic state was imposing on me..."

"My peace fell suddenly when one of our circle, a regular at our apartment, Bartek, was beaten by the Police and arrested. A talented sociology student, he quit it away just before graduation despite the persuasion of teachers and friends, including me. He became one of the first originators of the hippie movement in Poland. I cited a few of his statements in the report that I gave just before this event. It seemed completely harmless. Oh, quite a naive demonstration of escapism. The leader acting casually – he looked bored - asked why Bartek didn't join the army when he quit his studies. I lied, saying I don't know. Bartek told me how he arranged to be categorized as unfit, by simulating neurosis. Less than two weeks after my report, he was accosted on the street by policemen, beaten and accused of resisting authorities. He sat in prison for three months, his category was changed and he went into the army for two years. Nothing was heard about him. I don't know what happened to him or what his last name was. I only remember his first name. None of us were particularly surprised by this matter. Bartek wore long hair, dressed eccentrically, to some extent he was asking for the intervention of the police. It was like that then. This coincidence just wouldn't leave me alone. I even asked the leader. He shrugged his shoulders. He said he didn't care about some funny hippie and had nothing to do with his case. He almost didn't remember that we were talking about him. I believed him. I wanted to believe."

"In the summer or fall of seventy another member of our informal group, visual artist Wiktor Czerniak committed suicide. Nothing about him indicated this type of tendency. He was full of life, witty, talkative, but I started to remember that something had changed in his behavior lately. It didn't seem to indicate anything. At the end of the year, drunken Marian Balcerak dragged me into the corner for a frank conversation. 'We've got a snitch here,' he said straight to my face, holding my shirt. I sobered up from the response. However, I quickly realized that he suspected nothing. He was telling this to me accurately, because he had absolute trust. He argued that something had to be invented to track the snitch. 'They summon me constantly. I don't know what to do. They know everything about us. Recently, they threatened to make a case for repeated attempted murder. Do you remember the case?' I remembered. Shortly after Czerniak's suicide Balcerak turned on the gas at our place. He was drunk. I don't know if he was just playing with this thought, but he explained that such a collective death would be the greatest protest against what's happening in Poland. He imagined himself that Czerniak's suicide was an act of protest, senseless, because it was a single one. Maybe he only played with such a possibility? It was Zuza who caught him turning the gas on. She got angry. None of us, however, took this seriously. Maybe because we didn't take Marian seriously. Probably unfairly. Later ... anyway, this has nothing to do with it. I described it in the SB report as an idea for a happening, an absurd party. Now they used it against him. It wasn't just suspicions. I had proof. Meanwhile Marian was cornered. "How do I supposed to get out of this?' He repeated. 'I won't be their snitch, even if I end up like Wiktor!' I didn't know what to say to him. He considered ideas on how we could find this 'fucking snitch' and what to do with him. My next reports had a few sentences. After the second time my leader became furious. I remember it. It was in Rozdroż. 'Are you fucking with us?', he hissed. 'No. I don't want to bore you anymore', I answered. Unexpectedly, he changed his style. He was sharp and unpleasant. 'You don't want to cooperate?', he finally asked. 'I don't want to!' I replied. 'And you know that's impossible? What do you think, that this is a club you enter and exit when you feel like it? We'll release information that you are an informer and are responsible for the death of Czerniak. You finished him off with your denunciations. And we'll lock your father up on espionage charges. You already saw that we have a dossier. And we'll take care of your wife too. We thought about bringing a case against her as early as sixty-eight. Everything is ready'. What can I say? I returned to collaboration, although more carefully." His father stops from time to time. He's resting. Maybe he's considering?

"I try to be as honest as possible. But after all we perfectly know how difficult it is. Our intelligence is an adaptive organ. It justifies our interests. Harmonizes our order of values with our actions. That's why I try to avoid introspection and comments. I'm telling you that the UB officer was threatening me with my father's trial and some harassments toward your mother. He also said, I forgot to add, that I could say goodbye to side jobs for the 'Republic'. I was afraid for my family, but really, I didn't believe in my father's trial, I didn't think they could do anything to your mother. That they could chase me out of the "Republic" was certain. I don't want to say that it decided about my compliance. I was afraid, so fear decided. General fear."

Adam sees how much each sentence cost his father. He wanted to tell him to not tire himself anymore, that he said that which is most important, affairs have passed and ceased to matter, but he could choke it out of himself. His father clenched his teeth as if he was overcoming pain. He closed his eyes and said without opening them:

"Now, when I can't really do anything else, I wanted to understand though. Reality caught me and made a prank of me. I've been a pragmatist all my life. I suspended the question about the absolute truth. I knew that somehow, we had to organize this world, but we organize it in so many ways ... Reality as such, independent of us, is a myth, I thought. And now it's gotten me. The fact that I have to explain it all to you ... and I know somehow, in the end, as hard as anything in my life, I know that I'm not allowed to hide behind the intrusion into my head and onto my tongue with justifications. Only now, before my death, I know for sure that what I did, was wrong, and I was only lying to myself that I could minimize the costs. I don't know if I led to Wiktor's death, but it's possible. I think that I turned the SB's attention to Bartek, so I probably led to the breaking down of his life. I don't know, characteristically, I didn't want to know how the story of Marian Balcerak ended. How much more evil have I done that I don't realize? Somehow, I did it consciously because, despite fooling myself, I knew all of these events, that I was breaking the fundamental norm. I told myself, that abstract norms are fiction, and I can control the consequences of my actions, I appealed to the ethics of consequences and ... I only understood all this now, when I was forced, I felt forced to tell you the truth. And so, there is some truth beyond our intellectual games. Is true understanding not the reason for change? Alright, but let's get back to the specifics." His father opened his eyes and looked at Adam, as if surprised by his presence.

"December exploded and I was hoping that something would change. And it changed. The Lead officer. This new one had a long conversation with me in which he argued that we think similarly. He and his environment in the SB look closely at various shortcomings of our reality and wonders how to deal with it. How not to let the December massacre happen again. He imagines our partnership as thinking together about what and how to improve in Poland. Of course, within the limits of reality. But for this they need to gather information, if only to convince their party authorities. I almost believed him. I wanted to believe in it so much ... I was careful though. Then I got a full-time job in the 'Republic' and we changed our lifestyle quite fundamentally. My collaboration also had an impact on this. I no longer wanted to endanger the crowds rolling through our apartment, or maybe they disgusted me because of my arrangement? It doesn't matter: The partying ended. But the leader began to ask about the 'Republic'. Even when I was only working with it, the previous leader demanded coverage on this topic. I said I got a sponsorship from Bruno Klein. I decided that it wouldn't hurt him. About the rest I talked and wrote in terrible generalities. I did know few of them, but however more than I tried to present them. As a full-time employee, I couldn't quite uphold this version. And the Leader pushed. So, I wrote about them. I tried to write what they said officially anyway, but it wasn't enough. The new Leader was polite but tough. He wouldn't give up. I came to the conclusion that in the case of people such as Goleń or even Niecnota or Pieczycki I can speak. The fact that they want liberalization of the system, especially its economy, was an open secret, so I gave myself a dispensation. It was too easy even with regards to people like Niecnota ... Let's stop moralizing. I also tried to record statements that seemed to me on hand to the SB, and, as I thought, couldn't harm the authors. So, I reported complaints about the lack of discipline and private sighs about putting an end to anarchy, mainly in the economy, anti-church or even anti-Catholic remarks. Then I realized that even with this information I would give them instruments to work with. During some binge drinking, Niecnota complained to me that they were constantly summoning him to the SB and they wanted to make him a consultant to fighting the Church. He would gladly have helped to destroy the Church, but this mode didn't suit him. He was really concerned: where do they know so precisely his private statements from." For a moment Adam's father looked at him, he looked, like he's wondering what to tell him. Is he truly saying everything, Adam thinks, and will I ever be able to believe him completely? His father broke some obstacle, frowns and continues.

"I could no longer reduce my ... collaboration to routine. I knew too much and only occasionally for some time I managed to push my second life into my subconscious. I wanted to leave as often as possible. Like a child, I hoped that I wouldn't have to meet my leader. And indeed. He waited patiently for my return. I kept getting out of them, arranged meetings less often and wrote less, but I wrote and took the money. That just bothered me the least. I explained that I had no contact with people from the 'Republic'. I explained that my lifestyle meant that I don't know anything about anyone, and I can only write sociological analysis. The Leader understandably agreed, but then it always led to questions about what my friends said about these matters and what another one said. And it continued this way. And to be honest, I don't know how long it would've lasted if it wasn't for your mother. This is paradoxical. Your mother confided to me that she was working for the opposition, that she's a collaborator of KOR. I was shocked and scared to death. I was afraid for her, for you, for myself, of course, for us. Anyway, I'm not able to reconstruct my condition. I ran out of the house in confusion. I went out to drink. And suddenly I understood that in such a situation I had to cease collaborating. It wasn't rational. After all, I could explain it to myself because I was constantly doing it and justifying my status, so I could prove that my role would take suspicion away from my wife. But all this was just too much. It occurred to me that they would catch Zuzanna, and my agency would be used as blackmail. I understood that I had to accept her choice. And then it occurred to me that I would bring the matter to Goleń. We agreed to meet in private. I told him about it for a long time. I tried to be absolutely honest. He listened calmly. Sometimes he would ask questions. He asked if I had denounced on him and 'Republic'. I confirmed I had. He patted my shoulder. 'The only way out is joining the Party. As a member you'll be able to request that they unregister you. If they resist, I can help you. Otherwise I can't do anything.' He started laughing. 'You always refused when I offered you membership. Now you have no choice.' I joined the party. The UB officer who was leading me complained, but he gave in and agreed to my resignation. I didn't have to resort to Goleń. In some ways I did it for your mother. And that was the beginning of the end of our marriage. Alright, alright ... '' His father stopped him with a gesture. "I know what you're going to say. About Kalina. But I think that if our relationship was in good condition, I wouldn't have left your mother. Never mind. From then it began to break down. I couldn't after all explain to her why I joined the party. And that's in addition exactly when she got involved in the fight. She thought it was another act of conformism on my part, and even more, something like betrayal." He fell silent, tired. His son sat in silence.

"Only that this still isn't everything. Do you know Aunt Ala's case? They made her a scapegoat and she sat in prison for about two years. It wasn't political matter, or rather not directly. There were no non-political cases back then. In any case, the state was not directly involved, only an influential network. You could count on ... The organizer of the whole scam, personnel manager at Ala's plant, a certain Rojek came to talk to your mother. He suggested that Ala take a plea and he'll arrange a suspended sentence for her. Ala was already in custody. Your mother was outraged, you know her after all. And then this Rojek, I think he was also a UB officer, made an appointment with me. I began to say that we couldn't agree to the conviction of an innocent girl and that the 'Republic' could get involved in this case ... He looked at me dismissively. At one point he took out a paper and set it in front of me. This was my declaration of collaboration. Then he started counting how much money I took. It came out to quite a lot. He quoted some of my tastier reports. And finally, he returned to Czerniak's suicide. 'Stupid matter', he mused. He looked at me coldly and thoroughly. 'If you try to do something in the 'Republic', we'll announce these revelations about you.' 'How?' I asked unconsciously. 'There are many methods,' he answered matter-of-factly, 'but the simplest thing today is to pass them on to the opposition. We can also publish a leaflet on this subject ourselves and turn up the matter. I warn you, though I don't care about your efforts. Nobody will take care of the case anyway. It reaches too far. I just feel sorry for this girl. If you make trouble, she'll stay in prison. Otherwise, she may still be released. And the whole matter will dry up somehow. And that's all I have to say to you.' He went on and I was left with confusion. I tried to suggest to your mother that Ala confess. This was vile but I saw no other way. Your mother of course didn't agree. I deceived her, that I was making an effort, acting ... I did nothing. Once again, I was lying to your mother. Finally, I talked with Goleń. After a few days, he replied that the case was untouchable and I could only write something without names and specifics, a story about a girl who doesn't know what she got into and is suffering. I wrote such an oddity, probably mostly to have an alibi in front of your mother. I don't know myself why Goleń published it. And then ... you know what happened. And this Rojek is today ... I don't know if it's not the most important shareholder in the private television station ABC. Fate turns strangely."

***

Adam immediately liked Artur Rojek. The president was direct in the American way, without a hint of conceit, which could be provoked by a fast career. He wasn't much older than Adam, and already became the head of large private television company. Adam's sympathy was based on solid ground of reciprocity. Admittedly, the sentiment that Arthur – they immediately went to 'you' - felt to him, was due to Brok's position, of which he was well aware, but now he understood well that people are interested in each other for some reason, especially if they had the right task and little time. However, the authentic attitude of his new friend captivating. The fact that, as Adam thought, Rojek liked him, and so he really liked the person whom he should like, testified well about him. Above all, however, Arthur was genuinely enthusiastic, which meant a lot in Adam's eyes.

"I am very happy that we're going to do this project together", Arthur beamed already during the course of their first meeting. They were sitting in his office on some floor of a large building that ABC built. Rojek had invited him. He wanted to show off his possessions. Large spaces, glass, marble, trees and fountains inside, vegetation attached to the walls. It was transparent and clear. As in America, Adam thought. "You don't have to correct me", Arthur overtook the reply, which Adam didn't even want to deliver. "I know we haven't signed the contract yet. But I'm sure we'll come to an agreement. Do you know how can be done here with your companies money? Digitization is coming. There is a great offer of thematic channels. The best, new programs. You understand how much television like this means, and it's not just about the money, although money is a good measure of success. But television changes consciousness's, changes the world. And in Poland we still have a lot to make up for after communism, and especially after our, not particularly happy history. We not only let one understand the world, we introduce it to our viewers, we introduce them to Europe, we taught them modern civilization. We can provide them with everything and it's not just about teleshopping. We are a vanguard and who knows if not the main factor in the modernization of this country."

In addition to enjoyable meetings, Adam had to break through the company documents. It wasn't so transparent and clear here. There were entangled ownership matters. Mysterious shareholders from the Bahamas, large debts where it wasn't always known why they were incurred.

Adam's time was torn between meetings about ABC, conversations with experts, document studies and telephone conversations with Taggart on the one hand, and regular, though never particularly long - since his father got tired quickly

- hospital visits. Not much time was left to talk with his mother, who was also busy with her own affairs. After his second visit and his father's tale, Adam waited for questions from her. They didn't come, however. He decided himself.

"Don't you think you should visit him?" They were sitting in the kitchen at breakfast. Adam did the shopping, for which his mother was clearly thankful. Now in the kitchen she looked at him without saying a word from above a plate of white cheese and a slice of bread with butter and tomato. She pushed back the plate and lit a cigarette, not noticing her son's faces and grunts.

"I'm deciding," she replied.

"Do you realize he's dying?" Adam asked, unnecessarily, as he thought, stressing the words so that they sounded like an accusation. His mother puffed on her cigarette and looked at him defiantly.

"I do realize. And what about it? Actually, why would I forgive him? He ruined my life. So what if he also ruined his own? And above all I don't wish, that you judge me!"

Adam with difficulty refrained from an angry response. Surely this wasn't the first time he realized that sometimes he can't stand his mother. They didn't really talk before he left.

***

"You're not saying anything." His father sat on the bed. Adam had the impression that he looked better that day, as if he had more strength. "You don't talk about yourself and leave me with filling this silence. I told you the most embarrassing episode of my life. You didn't even say a word." His father looks at him somewhat questioningly, but his son is still silent. He tries to gather his thoughts, but he's unable to choke anything out, that would make sense.

"You know, I can't really find the words. I even have trouble with my thoughts. You have to give me more time."

His father looks at him in silence and finally sighs in resignation.

"I should understand you. I also don't really know how to comment on this all. I don't want to imagine what it would mean to me, if it happened to my father. Only that couldn't have happen to him ... How did it happen that I didn't grow up with him so much?" He stops.

Adam was most afraid of these pauses. They required that he finally said something, take a position. He fell into a panic. Fortunately for him, his father couldn't stand silence. Adam realized that he's speaking differently than ever before. He threw out broken sentences with difficulty, as if the words hurt his throat. He got tired and from time to time his son wanted to stop him, tell him to give it a break, but at the same time he realized that he shouldn't do it, and all he can do is listen to him, try to understand...

"When I told you all this ... I understood that this isn't the end. I even felt a kind of relief, but ... suddenly for me myself it turned out that I still constantly have something to tell you and myself and ... I have to do it. You are the person, whom I love ... the most. Maybe the only one I love. And I have to tell you this? Maybe that's why? In fact, I need to formulate this for myself as well. Only now, when

I confessed this all, did I begin to comprehend my experience. I realized that this was just the beginning of understanding. Earlier ... If there was no scrutiny and the Institute of National Remembrance, if I had not been forced, I would never have told you about this. This matter, this so important, though nasty part of my life, it wouldn't have gained meaning for me. I would've push it into my subconscious, denied its importance. After all I remember the nineties. The inspectors were evil, and I was their innocent victim. Yes, I signed something, reported something, but in fact I didn't do anything wrong to anyone, and in any case, I didn't want to, and so I was the most hurt, I repeated to myself, they forced me ... Only because of what happened, something results and in terms of this knowledge I have to think about other things. In how much was I wrong? Were we wrong? Was it nothing? I'm still lost in all this ..." His father wondered. "It's weird. I can say I won. My environment won ... the "Republic" ... It's us who set the measures today and your mother is in the margin. Let's name things by name. An even further margin. And she'll be pushed there more and more. Just strangely I don't enjoy it, not just because, I still have feelings for Zuzanna. A string of paradoxes ... I have to admit this to you as well. Actually, my whole life I thought I was smarter than your mother ...", he pauses. He looks at his son helplessly.

Adam realizes that his father's intellectual superiority over his mother always seemed obvious to him. Just like his own, he must add before himself.

"I read more smart books than of her – the irony is all too visible - I know a lot more theories, formulas, even facts, but she was right in assessing reality, and I was almost always wrong. What am I supposed to say? I am reminded of the Zen parable. At the beginning, man sees mountains and valleys, but when he however is on the path of enlightenment, he realizes that these differences are only an illusion ... The next phases of enlightenment reveal subsequent aspects of this illusion, they allow to see, that everything is one, and next, that it's nothing, but finally, when true enlightenment comes, man sees the mountains and the valleys again. Therefore, reaching enlightenment is a spiral movement, because a man who sees mountains and valleys at the end is not the same as in the beginning. Along the way, however, gaining elements of knowledge, he moved away from true understanding before, finally, he understood everything. But who manages to come to real enlightenment? So, we constantly come across pseudo-wise men who turn out to be infinitely dumber than those who naively perceive the world as it is. Of course, this is contractual naivety because ... And by the way, why am I telling you a Zen story? After all, this wisdom must be contained in many texts of our culture, certainly in Jewish Haggadah's, but I don't recall anything now, maybe only Pascal ... why don't I remember anything ...", his father broke off and stared at something with unusual tension.

Adam turns around. His mother is standing in the doorway. She walks up with a light step to the bed. She's smiling.

"So now what? It's only us again", she says, looking up close into the eyes of her husband. Then he looks at her son. "Only that now we're not the first and last people."

Adam said goodbye. They didn't stop him.

CHAPTER 12

The ABC anniversary banquet fundamentally changed Adam's lifestyle. Rojek advertised it as something special. And so it was. The huge hall on the ground floor of the television building was full. An orchestra played discreetly, liveried waiters carried elegant appetizers, champagne, white and red wine, there were platters on long tables of the most diverse kinds of prepared meats, cheeses, fish, seafood, vegetables and salads, on the neighboring tables towered edifices of cakes, pastries, biscuits and gourmet treats; a separate table was occupied by a composition of sushi. The staff filled in every barely visible gap that appeared on the countertops. Next to silver cauldrons cooks kept watch, serving dozens of dishes, from traditional Polish to exotic Chinese, Thai and even Ethiopian cuisine. Bartenders invite people to multi-storied shelves filled with all possible drinks. Upon request, demonstrating circus like skill, they made the fanciest cocktails, which they offered in unusual abundance. The elegant crowd undulated, vibrated, circled under the overwhelming pressure of the difficult to understand but palpable forces. The subdued lights changed almost imperceptibly color and tone, shimmering in the glass, they extracted subsequent characters from the anonymous crowd. On large backstage screens, the crowd gathered in ABC multiplied infinitely. The cameras took close-ups for a short time and moved away, focused on a new object of interest, only to not long after move on. Everyone who got there was supposed to be the hero of the event, even for a moment.

"All of Poland is here!", Rojek enthused. "Well, maybe not all, but all valuable ...," he looked at Adam carefully, "I wanted to say: all significant representatives of it."

Surprised, Brok saw many faces he remembered from his early youth, and even from their apartment on Koszykowa St. Rojek showed him around, introduced him to guests and guests to him, explained who is who, disappeared for a while and then Adam saw him again elsewhere, where he was chatting and joking, only a moment later to be found in someone else's company, who absolutely must meet Brok, and Brok him. He was just introducing some minister to him.

"Mirek is the brain of this government, and it is a unique cabinet. I will leave you two for a while, because you will certainly have a lot to say to each other."

"I'm glad that such a significant company as R&B wants to get more seriously involved in Poland." The minister sipped whiskey, carefully watching Adam. "I'm not betraying a secret when I say we need capital, but we're also creating unique conditions for this capital. We're such a second Ireland ... I'm sorry," he caught himself by the head, laughing, "I was thinking about that Ireland before it went bankrupt. You understand. Never mind. We're a modern government and we know how important television is today. Television today is more than television. TV and sport. After all, television must have something to broadcast," he laughed at his joke. "Some underestimate the importance of sport. And sport isn't just a healthy society. It's a satisfied society. And television disseminates knowledge about this and generates the correct, in regards to sports, attitudes. Football is the most important. We build stadiums for young people, eagles. This will remain after we're gone."

"Am I mistaken, are you the son of Benek Brok?" A well-kept a man of his father's age was looking at him from behind his glasses. Adam recognized him. He was a well-known journalist of the 'Republic', a television presenter, Sławomir Pieczycki. "I'm very sorry, but from what I understand, your father isn't doing too well. I have to visit him. He had an operation, right? I heard that it is, unfortunately, cancer and advanced?"

Adam confirmed it. Kalina joined them with an older couple, who Brok recognized as the Podlecki's.

"I visit Benek. It doesn't look good. It's good that his son came to him all the way from America." It wasn't known if there's recognition or irony in Kalina's voice.

The Podlecki lamented about Benedict and promised that in the nearest time they'll pay him a visit.

"Fortunately now, his wife is with him, my mother" Adam declared, looking at Kalina. For a moment in their circle, consternation prevailed. Kalina's face was unmoving.

"What a great party," noticed Podlecka.

"I feel the new Poland!" Her husband picked up enthusiastically. "We've crossed the divisions. It's only a pity that Władek didn't live to see it."

"That's true," Pieczycki agreed. "We're talking about our former boss, Władek Goleń," he explained for Adam's sake. "A very worthy character. It's a pity. But on the other hand, he avoided the nightmare of this so-called fourth Polish Republic. You're from abroad. You didn't live through this. But I can assure you that as long as I live and I've lived for a long time, this was the worst period of Poland that I remember."

The rest of them expressed their approval for this judgement.

"Really?" against himself, Adam asked doubtingly.

"I'm speaking most seriously," emphasized Pieczycki slightly chastising him. "What was happening! Times of contempt, hunting people. You know that even the creators of ABC, a man so distinguished in Polish business-like CEO Jacek Rojek, some grim case were beginning to be mounted from the time of martial law. As usual, he behaved very dignified and refused to appear at the prosecutor's office. There was a scandal. Authorities issued a protest letter. I had the honor to sign it as well, just like Julita, Jurek and Kalina." The Podlecki's radiated with dignity and satisfaction, Kalina seemed indifferent. "Fortunately, there were elections soon and the party of reason won. PiS prosecutors backed down, they tucked their tails between their legs, withdrew their accusations, only ...," he looked at Adam with sudden embarrassment, "...never mind. What's important is that the case is closed. It wouldn't be possible today. It's obvious to all intelligent people that our main task is to prevent the recidivism of the so-called Fourth Polish Republic. Well and get rid of that president, who shames us before the whole world."

"In general, this opposition should be delegalized and another one should be appointed, a decent one. It's funny, too, that it would seem that people from that side created such a successful government," interrupted Podlecki.

"I don't understand you!", Pieczycki grimaced. "That side, our side. Those are old divisions, from twenty years ago. That side is PiS. Do you want to say that Bogatyrowicz is that side?" He pointed to the approaching retinue surrounding the editor of the 'Word' with a glass in hand.

"You're right," Podlecki mitigated. "Even the Church isn't on that side anymore. Priests such as Archbishop Korytko, who anyway, I saw here, are in one of us in an obvious way. Anyway, the most important thing is that we meet in a similar group, people feeling responsibility for the country thirty years ago and today.

"Founding father," Brok hears the voice of Artur Rojek and sees a gesture indicating an approaching Bogatyrowicz, "and it's in such a deep sense. We wouldn't be here without him. Do you all agree?" The people of the 'Republic' nodded with conviction. "I'm sorry because for a moment I'll have to kidnap our guest." Rojek took Brok under his arm, and when they were a few meters away, he stopped and looked at him carefully. "I think you should meet my father. What do you think about that?"

Adam hesitated. He remembered his father's words, uncle Stach's funeral, his mother, then he realized that he's actually at work.

"It's fine," he confirmed.

Arthur began to beam. His father stood a little to the side, in the company of those people who are staring and catching every one of his words, who moved out of the way and withdrew at the sight of them.

"I'm very happy to meet you. And that it's precisely you who represent R&B," the tall man's voice was nice and moderate, just as his handshake. Arthur was already pulling Adam into the crowd.

"And these are the most outstanding representatives of our legal profession", he gestured with emphasis. "Mrs. Jolanta Biesiada, judge of the Constitutional Tribunal, and now the Supreme Court, and there are rumors that ..." Artur lowered his voice, "I'll say however ... is it true that you are to become the next Commissioner for Human Rights?"

"Mr. Arthur ... That's very unlikely. Anyway, I don't know if I would agree, maybe Marek?"

"And this gentlemen, is Marek Pietrzak, current judge of the Constitutional Tribunal, and Zenon Karczmiarz, a famous lawyer, former minister. Are you not returning to government again?"

"It's not for me anymore. Tiring, not very lucrative and with limited opportunities. The current government understands anyway that it's impossible to govern everything, therefore it makes more sectors independent. Making the prosecutor's office independent is a good step. The independence of the court prevents all these judgements and caused, that these essentially political processes against Jaruzelski or Kiszczak aren't continued realistically. I don't like the fact that although they're formally going on ..."

"Zenek, don't be a maximalist", Biesiada interrupted him. "Thanks to this, all kinds of fools are shut up. An independent Court. The End. Period. I agree it's indecent to pull such people like President Jaruzelski, minister Kiszczak or even ordinary people ZOMO officers into court, but the judges behaved properly and accepted all dismissals. This is however, as you noticed, politics."

"You praise this government and I could agree with your opinion. But this law limiting the retirement privileges of former SB employees, however is a scandal. And that the Constitutional Tribunal has accepted this ...I opposed it, of course, but the majority..."

"Mr. Marek, my father accepted it humbly, he probably won't protest", Arthur said with a modest expression. Everyone broke out in laughter.

"Adam?" Brok heard right next to him.

It was older man whose head was surrounded by thinning, completely white hair, who only after a while he recognized as Krzysztof Markus, a quite frequent guest in their home in the early nineties. He was accompanied by three women, whose figure he had a hard time attributing to likenesses from his memory. It was Danka Brak and Agnieszka Pelikan. The third, much younger one, who Adam didn't know, held Markus's arm.

"I'm sorry that I'm saying this, but I saw you as a child, and then as a young man ... I was friends with your mother then. She was beautiful. We all loved her."

"However, you've stopped visiting us some time ago."

"Well, yes ... relations between me and your mother somehow broke apart."

"Please don't tell me that she threw you out."

"Of course not. I don't want to judge your mother, anyway. I don't want to judge anyone at all. I never commented on the fact that she signed a loyalty paper..."

Brok was gripped by anger. He'd want to whack that old face.

"That, which you're saying is insinuation, vile insinuation!" He's not finding the words and clenches his fists. Someone is taking his arm.

"Adam, calm down", it was Agnieszka Pelikan.

Brok abruptly calms down. He sees the terrified face of the younger women. Markus is surprised.

"You misunderstood me sir. I said that I don't judge ..."

"Vileness is saying that my mother signed a loyalty paper!"

"Oh, Adam!", this time it was Danka Brak. "We understand, that you're defending your mother. We're not attacking her. Well, but we cannot negate facts. She signed it and that's it. We're not saying, that it's important."

"And I say that she didn't sign it."

"Adam", Brak tries to speak calmly, although this comes to her with difficulty, "she confessed herself, it was printed in the 'Word'. What, in that case did she sign during martial law?"

"She signed ...", Adam became lost. He can't exactly recall to himself the conversation with his mother. He remembered that she signed some irrelevant stupid things ... "She signed that she would obey the law. And that's it!"

"Well, Exactly. That's what the loyalty paper was. It was about accepting martial law! We knew that this shouldn't be signed!" Brok sees Agnieszka's evil face. "And we didn't sign it!"

"Give the young man a break", Bogatyrowicz is nearby. "We don't judge children for their parents' faults. And that's how we differ from them!"

Brok is helpless and doesn't know what to say.

"That's not right ..."

"I told you this was a misunderstanding," Markus continues. "I'm not judging your mother. Let's give up this game of marking the guilty. I condemn exactly this!"

"The truth itself speaks through you, Krzysiek", laughs Bogatyrowicz. "From the beginning this was a method of low-political game. And now when we face dangerous populism ..."

Brok is grateful to Artur, who leads him out from between these people. Out of the corner of his eye, he discerns looks, smiles, which they exchange, leaning in towards each other. At this point Igor Stawicki triumphantly enters among them.

"Adam, my student", he hears and feels arms wrapping around him. Sławek Mucha hasn't changed much. His facial features have become more strongly carved, his wrinkles deepened, his figure and face became even thinner, so it resembles more so a dervish from the pages of the *Fairy Tales from a Thousand and One Nights*, which had occurred to Brok at their first meeting. "I'm glad to see you. And in this role. Yes, yes, I've heard about your career ..."

"You know each other? You surprise me. You come from America and you know all my guests. And do you know, that Mr. Sławek is a gray eminence of the current government?"

"Mr. Artur is exaggerating. Oh, what an advisor. But I must admit that we found ourselves around this government. There's also Igor", Mucha pointed to Stawicki immersed in conversation with the company that Brok left just a moment ago, but seeing his gaze, backs off. "Fine. I understand. I'm not explaining to you that all courts have cleared him from suspicions of collaboration ... But I understand. These are family passions and from this rationality is as far away as possible ... Alright, alright. I won't say anything more."

Arthur, who exchanged a greeting with a passerby, wasn't oriented to the situation.

"Adam, do you know one of our greatest intellectuals, Igor Stawicki?"

"Oh I know, all too well!" Rojek looks surprised, but now his face forms into an expression of understanding. "OK. Everything's right."

"Reality doesn't exist! Philosophers discovered this already a long time ago. Only our perception of it exists. And this is what we should be guided by. This is what the post-politics, which we live in relies on." The small, little man spewed out statements, gesticulating and hypnotizing the circle surrounding him.

"This is Olaf Nok, the most outstanding specialist of dramatic marketing in Poland, but really he is the gray eminence of the government, and maybe even more." Arthur whispered in Brok's ear.

Meanwhile, Nok was dismissing the protest of a young man who questioned the post-political nature of the current era.

"You can't be offended at that time. You have to adapt to it. Postpoliticality means that we hand power over to professionals. So, it's progress, just as progress is delegating treatment to doctors and construction to engineers. In the same the way progress is dramatic marketing over narrative marketing. This is marketing of the fourth generation. We translate reality into spectacles, and we pass it on to the voters in this form. We dramatize it into a few fundamental clashes. Elementary conflict of white with black, good with bad, backward with modern. So, there are specialists in governing and those who can translate this tedious practice into a spectacle in which roles were already cast. And the current government can understand this, which means that it's more modern and better prepared to rule than its predecessors. Please note that I suspend any judgment here. Impartially, as a professional, I describe the state of affairs."

"Olaf, as always, is right. This spectacle is like football", he interrupted the minister with another glass in his hand. "Let's stop with ideologies. Professionalism counts."

Adam, who also drank a little, couldn't help himself. He turned to Nok:

"Excuse me, but you were speaking about how there is no reality. In the following sentences you precisely described to what reality we're sentenced. Don't you see the contradiction here?"

"But dear sir", Nok spread his hands as if waiting for this question, "this is an issue from a bygone era. Do you want to impose the iron laws of logic on me, just how recently the iron laws of dialectics were imposed? But I won't let someone set me up this way. Your ideological formulas limiting us I contrast with a world of an infinite number of possibilities. And I ask you all: in what world do you prefer to live?" The applause from those present was an unequivocal answer. "Professionally governed voters have the right to a spectacle. They have the right to have fun. The performance must last and we organize it. Because we are professionals. And our government understands this."

"That's right," confirmed the minister solemnly.

Suddenly Adam is fed up with this banquet and these people. They're connected by something, which he isn't able to name it. Someone or something animated them, set them in motion, but changed their features, gave a similar grimace, shook them with identical giggles. Among them similar to each other, though such different faces, which they didn't see, because they are just slipping past, Brok notices someone else. Gray eyes look at him, a familiar face smiles. Gaj hasn't has changed at all, though they haven't seen each other for almost four years. Nok, the minister, Artur and all the other guests drifted away and became a blurred, babbling background.

"I've been looking for you for so many years ..."

"And I was waiting for you."

They were saying something. They congratulated each other their meeting and their appearance. They were leaning towards each other. Adam was looking at the woman and thought he came here just for her. Her smile confirmed this thought, gave it confidence.

"I work in PR, she said. "I quit journalism a long time ago. We often work with Olaf. He's a great professional."

"Really?", Brok marked his doubt. She started laughing.

"Don't confuse academic debates with life, I mean, I wanted to say with PR. Forgive me, but Olaf played you. And that's what he wanted. And you attacked him with some comprehensivnesss."

"Drink? Maybe I could buy you something?" Adam asked, he wasn't in the mood to discuss the rules of thinking with Gaj.

"You can't buy me anything here. Everyone who gets in here, already has everything for free", she laughed again. "I've had enough. Actually, when I was talking with you about your mother's case, I already had enough. I stopped believing in journalism. Cheating people. Although in PR I don't lie to anyone. We prepare reality for the receivers and we don't hide it. We only come up with nice names. Work is booming. Those in power understood that governing is marketing, and we have a lot of orders. Don't look at me like that. This is what democracy is about. For them to choose you, they have to like you. And we take care of it professionally. Well and we earn really well from it."

Adam stopped being interested in the world whirling crowdedly around them. He introduced himself automatically a few times to someone who came up to Gaj. He noticed that Artur approached them but withdrew with an understanding smile. He was embracing her and she wasn't protesting.

"We've known each other for so many years, and I still don't know where you live", he decided finally. She smiled at him with an understanding smile.

"And would you like to see?"

"Of course."

"When?"

"Now"

"So let's go" she said naturally.

Standing in a small queue to the locker room, he noticed the minister Filip Madej next to him in an embrace. He lectured, taking no heed of the audience.

"We also once believed in ideology. We now believe in football. Communisms, conservatisms, republicanisms, isms, isms. One liberalism, that's what. Everyone for themselves their own way. And together we can play football. There's rules there. And the rest ... Only effectiveness matters. Sports fields need to be built..."

CHAPTER 13

Benedict Brok died six weeks later. During this time his son managed to fall in love and fall out of love with Monika Gaj.

In the morning after the party at ABC, he woke up after only a few dozen minutes of sleep and noticed that Monika is waking up at the same time. She smiled, as if his presence in her bed was the most obvious thing in the world. They snuggled closely to each other that same moment. 'We wasted so many years', it circled around Adam's head when he was immersed in her, and the thought that he would never want to leave her body, were the last words to reach his consciousness. Gaj jumped up from the bed however, in conjunction with the metallic calling of the alarm clock at exactly seven o'clock. He stared at her nakedness, bustling around the apartment silhouette with pleasure and disappointment.

"Must you go now?"

"My first meeting is at eight-fifteen. I can't cancel it anymore. But if you want, we can see each other tonight. Want me to leave you the keys?"

"Then I'll go as well, and in the evening, of course, I'll come."

Gaj lived on Jerozolimska Avenue not far from the Hotel Polonia. She bought and organized a large, spacious apartment earlier this year. "I'll probably be paying back the loan until I die!" She said, laughing as usual. The minimalist style in the apartment made it look uninhabited and prepared for a photo shoot. Big graphics and photographs on the walls were also transparent and empty. There are a few abstract images. A large reproduction of Edward Hopper's *Nighthawks* was above the bed. "Of course, I can't afford to hire an interior designer yet. And that's why I arranged it myself so that it looked like the best stylist did it," she joked. The only element that didn't fit in there, next to Adam, was a cat, who was hanging around him restlessly.

When he walked to the apartment on Koszykowa Street through the cool, autumn, barely awake Warsaw, he tasted individual memories that he laboriously extracted from delights that melted into the night. He was happy. Only near the house did he remember his dying father and single mother, whose specter hovered between those gathered in the ABC building.

His mother sat in the kitchen contemplating over tea and a cigarette.

"How was it?" Her son asked.

She looked at him with an unreadable expression.

"Strange", she replied, and hid in the smoke.

"Krzysztof Markus was once our guest," Adam reminded himself. "What's happening to him? He stopped coming..."

“Did something happen? Why are you asking about him?”, His mother disrupted from her thoughts looked a little numb.

“Nothing. I saw him briefly at the banquet at ABC.”

“Aha, actually he should be there. He has to solicit…”, His mother collects her thoughts for a moment, “I could tell you about him. I wondered…It took some time, before I understood, what had happened, what had happened to him and why he so equivocally severed our friendship. I liked him, I valued him, and I have to admit ... that break-up hurt me. Not just that one anyway. It’s unusual, I realize that for me free Poland is a series of break-ups. It started already during the Polish People’s Republic when your father dumped me”, she laughed sardonically, “but then ... I subsequently walked away from old friends, but not in a normal, age-appropriate way, when we sailed away to our own affairs and relaxed social contacts. I parted in anger, with growing reluctance, which changed old friendships into animosity. I’m left with only a handful of good friends from the editorial office and I don’t know who else. In moments of doubt I wondered whether the fault didn’t lay on my side. I analyzed, searched, but didn’t find any. It’s really about a few simple rules and elemental loyalty, which I try to stick to, but after all it’s not like I’m always sure ... I’m struggling ... and, unexpectedly, an ally comes from the most unexpected side, that agrees with me. Your father,” His mother paused and was immersed in her thoughts.

Only after a longer moment did she remember about her son’s presence.

“You asked me about Markus. I can talk about him because it’s a very demonstrative story. Even in the early nineties we agreed on everything. He was in favor of vetting, de-Communization, he demanded a settlement of the past and transparency in public life, although he was in the Democratic Union and then the Freedom Union and in my opinion attacked the right wing a little irrationally. He was an MP. This was very important for him. This was very important for all of them. After years of being poor, unemployed or having miserable jobs ... Markus was a warehouse worler and this was his greatest professional achievement in the PPR, and so after years of misery in the opposition, they suddenly became, well ... maybe not the masters of this world, but its absolute elite, legislators, themselves somewhat above the law. They pretended these splendors didn’t matter to them, but I saw, how they were changing under their influence. After years of vulnerability when it wasn’t known when and for how long the prison doors would close behind them, and even if something worse wouldn’t happen, fear grew among the bravest. I knew something about it because I experienced it myself. A parliamentary position beyond everything else gave a sense of security and confidence. Suddenly they were someone completely different. Under fifty they could start their lives afresh. And they did. Krzysiek left his wife. He was an important MP, a face on television, he started to pick up girls and finally found his Małgosia. And here was suddenly a shock. The elections, two thousand and one, the UW doesn’t get into parliament. Something that was supposed to be certain and obvious stopped it. What to go back to? Who could Markus be at fifty-five and what is he supposed to live off of? He didn’t want to be a warehouse worker anymore, and anyway probably couldn’t be. And also, Małgosia is here, who expected help in her career. She finished some kind of college in Mazuria, where Markus started, she was his assistant. And now? Colleagues from the ‘Word’ stretched out a helping hand, they’ll print a few banal articles, but that’s about it. What more could they do anyway? But there are after all people who understand. Supposedly on the other side, but only in politics, because in life they are very loyal. They know that you have to help yourself. From the beginning, from the Round Table they propose civilized relations. Post-communists? What post-communists? After all they were never communists! From the beginning, they promoted civilized democracy. We argue on the parliamentary forum, but we help each other privately and, God forbid, we don't dirty ourselves with bringing up the past. No people are perfect, everyone has something on their conscience, it's not allowed to open Pandora's Box, organize a Polish hell, you have to cooperate, instead of arguing, building consent. That's why brawlers should be kept away, who could spoil everything and serve the people, information which they aren't ready for, without restraint, so that they would develop indigestion. You have to exclude the stupid from the public life who appeal to abstract principles and destroy the delicate matter of politics. Civilized people should come to understandings, and then they can even argue in parliament, in reasonable proportions, of course. Former comrades understood the need for cooperation, without it they wouldn't have achieved anything. They may have disliked each other, even raised pigs, man is only human after all, but they recognized joint interest perfectly. And that's why they'll help Krzyś, found himself on a board. His colleagues also. They will allow him on a few supervisory boards, which in total with a few additional side jobs will allow them to survive, and they'll get his girlfriend a good position. Poland is after all not such a small country and some well-paid jobs can be found in it. Krzysztof recognized that the actions of the democratic winners are rational. In short it's a pity that his intellect was being wasted unproductively, and Małgosia is a talented girl. However, if former opponents are so rational, and their actions bring in overall a benefit to the country, because what else is using the potential of the best, then you probably need to revise your attitude towards them. The settling of old history, obsessively searching for the truth, supposedly hidden somewhere in the past, neurotically tracking the synchronicity of politics and business, as if it was nowhere in the world, all of this not only loses its meaning, but reveals its destructive character. Such actions can be turned against the most honest person who in these strange times had to make choices, not always compatible, well, maybe not with the law, but with the conventions that commonly apply, and which ... we know how conventional they are, though we can't say that publicly. It's difficult in this situation to be friends with the advocates of such activities, their attitudes besides are a typical example of resentment. When we look at them closely, we discover in them a solid foundation of hatred, how else can you explain a vicious desire of persecuting those who simply succeeded? Whew!"

His mother gave this speech in almost one breath. As if she was preparing for it. She took a deep breath.

"I think I explained why Krzysiek doesn't visit me anymore. Not only that anyway. He wrote an article about me in the 'Word'. An unpleasant one. Noting that he doesn't want to judge me, he judged me very intensely. And additionally he carried out a psychoanalysis of my person, all derived from my famous loyalty paper, which has perhaps already become the most famous symbol of oppositional denial in the PPR."

"Aren't you exaggerating?"

"My dear. It's not just the large number of pieces on this topic. I already function almost proverbially as "the loyal one". In the reactions on the internet, under each of my pieces I always find quite a large group of entries dealing exclusively with my betrayal. Many times, I wonder what it meant. Are former UB's or their successors still so well organized, or do just plain, unsure of their own individual asses, desired at all costs to incriminate the one who threatens them? But for them to want it so bad? And in a herd? Anyway, Krzysio Marcus didn't fail to deduce my attitude from this complex of betrayal. Not judging of course", his mother stopped.

Now, of course, she'll light a cigarette, her son thought. She lit it.

"Well and there's still one more matter worth you knowing about. I don't know, if it refers to Krzysiek. After the fall of the Communism it was a strange time. Apparently, some kind of absurd PPR-era law formally functioned, but really it frolicked around. Oppositional bare-asses were landing on important positions. Former officials and officers, who trembled in their chairs, and sometimes not only that, wanted to bend the heavens for them. They proposed many combinations that usually enabled in the beginning the acquiring a good apartment. You don't realize how valuable of a good it was then and how few had such luxuries as we here on Koszykowa. And you have to live somewhere. Some of my old friends without money, suddenly became owners of very good apartments, some even of a few, or houses. Maybe they didn't break the law at all, having them, maybe they just bent it a little. Or maybe a bit more. Such people, by nature of things, become less willing to judge the past their fellow man. And sometimes it wasn't just about apartments. Although almost always these were only leftovers from the State's table. The real business was made by "comrades", but ... a decent apartment and shares in a company, which they arrange until their deaths are also not to be held in contempt. I don't want to continue ... I was analyzing it at one time ... I wasn't filled with optimism. That, what happened to those nonconformists, fighters, although not only with them ... In my publishing house, in the 'Portico', I had a boss, his name was Łukasz Alski. You don't have to remember him."

"But I remember"

"Well he was a typical representative of a large group of people. Actually a decent man, but intimidated. Maybe I'm exaggerating. He was, how fairly decent people in the PPR were. Not long before the creation of Solidarity he dismissed me from work. He were forced to do it by UBs. He didn't know in general that he could refuse them. Besides he probably couldn't if he was going to keep his position. But when he took me back after August, he was genuinely happy. At first, I was suspicious towards him. Over time I became convinced. He didn't throw me out during martial law, even though they pressed him. If they had taken to him more harshly ... he himself confessed to me, but what can we demand from people? He was on our side and was trying to help us. We began to like each other. After the fall of Communism he still visiting me. Then he stopped. I met him by accident a few years ago. He was even happy and invited me for coffee. It turned out that he was still working in the 'Portico', actually in that, what's left of it. Privatized, combined with another publishing house, it now mainly publishes photo albums. Alski fills a definitely more subordinate position than before there, although they left him the title of director. 'They'd remove me if not for the fact that I am in the 'Ordynacka',' he said nostalgically. "You're in the 'Ordynacka', I was amazed. He explained to me that he still managed to get into the Socialist Union of Polish Students, and so it's understandable that he joined the association of its former members. For me this wasn't obvious, but I didn't delve into the matter. The new owner of the publishing house, of course a former party activist, is also in the 'Ordynacka'. I didn't want to say anything, but Alski started it. Clearly, he didn't feel right. 'Are you blaming me?' he asked, although I didn't say anything on the matter. And he began this mantra, which I could no longer bear: that I'm constantly stuck in the past, that I want to account for the past without end, and people are helping each other and he's happy that he ended up in the 'Ordynacka' because there are decent people there who want to do something together. In this never I doubted. 'Ordynacka' was created just for this. You know, it's the lobbying club SUPS. And finally, he told me that he was watching with concern what we do in 'Renaissance'. Apparently, we're 'waking demons'. 'You're creating anti-intelligence attitudes, and when we have this kind of intelligence that we have, and we need to be delicate with it,' he stated pompously. I didn't want to argue with him and parted apparently as it should be, but I know, that he won't invite me for coffee anymore. And so, a man who rebelled in the Polish People's Republic, was forced to return to that system in the Third Republic. Well yeah..."

"Mom, I have to run. I have a meeting in my office. Can you finish this for me later?"

"What's there to finish? Everything has already been said."

***

Adam spent the nights at Gaj's place. At first, he informed his mother, then he stated that he was moving out, he doesn't know himself for how long. His mother expressed no surprise.

"You're an adult. I see, that you met someone."

Adam's days were actually additions to his night. He walked around half conscious and had trouble sorting out his affairs both those that concerned R&B's entry to ABC, as well as contacts with his father.

When he finally broke away from Monica, he swam into the dimmed light of her apartment and realized that it was almost midnight, he was reminded that for the past two days he not only hadn't visited but didn't even reach out to his father. He felt sudden shame.

"I haven't seen my father for two days", he threw into space.

"That's probably not that long?" Gaj said, sitting on the bed and fixing her hair.

"My father is in the hospital. He's dying."

The smile on her face died.

"Why didn't you say? You must go to him immediately!"

"It's twelve o'clock at night. If something was happening, my mother or the doctors from the hospital would've notified me."

"It really is shameful!" She said extremely seriously.

She lit a cigarette. She fought with the addiction, in which Adam, who didn't tolerate tobacco smoke, and was still condemned to it on Koszykowa St., gladly helped her, but from time to time she gave in.

"I came here for him..."

"I thought to do a big business merger ..."

"That was only later, they coincided."

"You're a good son, though you've forgotten yourself, a little from my fault ..."

"I forgot because of you but a good son? His? This is the wrong criteria. He wasn't a good father, he left us, when I was ten years old. My mother raised me. In truth, he wanted to have the best relations with me, and it was I who relaxed them, but it all begins with his leaving ..."

"Don't dramatize. This is the norm today. There are people everywhere with divorces. There probably aren't others. I've already stopped believing in one relationship. I'm not a model myself in this respect. People have right to self-realization ..."

"And your family…"

"My family? That means…"

"Are your parents divorced?"

"No, of course not, you've really stumped me", she laughed. "Only that my family ... It's getting harder and harder to believe that this is my family. I visit them less often, in any case because of a lack of time. I like them somehow, but that's not enough. I'm a completely different species to them, and they understand me less than my kitty. Anyway, I'm not sure if I comprehend them, or rather I'm sure that I comprehend them less and less. Strange people in a strange world with strange views."

"And what's so annoying about them?"

"Annoying? Well, maybe a little bit. Their naivety. This uncritical faith of theirs, their orderly and closed world ..."

"And where are they?"

"In the provinces. Doesn't matter."

***

They fell apart again into separate bodies - which night was this, as Adam struggled to remind himself - and tired, touching each other gently, with difficulty they returned to the shores of reality. It was late after midnight, and they weren't sleepy at all. They went to Praga, where, as Monika said, Warsaw's night life moved to. The place was covered with great photographs and graphics, which were often constituted of somewhat processed photographs, gave the impression of theatrical scenery. Their regulars deepened them, ostentatiously playing out their performances. An chirping group of gays parodied those that enter; two girls were kissing and fondling, cheered on by the company around them and photographed passionately by a young man running around them; another group was laughing itself sick at the noise of spoken and unspoken issues - dilated pupils, unnatural timbre of voices and not entirely coordinated movements informed of an additional source of their excitement. Gaj knew everyone here, or maybe everyone was behaving as if they have always known each other. Very quickly Brok became a part of the group as well, though he didn't feel it.

"Do you want some speed?" Monika whispered in his ear, who within a few minutes had already managed to go to each group, fraternizing with everyone and for a moment participating in the games they played.

"Give it a break, you're enough for me"

"I just took a little bit to get even more turned up and not pass out in an unexpected moment."

They were in yet another identical looking pub. They returned after about two hours, caressing each other and kissing in the back seat of a taxi, promising each upcoming fulfillment. At some point, already at home, Gaj moaned:

"You're killing me. I'm starting to become more and more unconscious at work. I don't know what I'm doing."

Brok thought that he could say the same.

Among the things he brought to her apartment, Gaj became interested notebook with wooden covers. He explained, that he didn't actually know why, but in his rare free time, he compares Jakub Brok's original and father's translation.

"And what is this diary about?"

"It's a terrifying text. My great-uncle was in the Cheka. He murdered people ..."

"So why do you read it over and over?"

"I'm trying to understand."

"What's here to understand? People can be evil."

"But he wasn't evil. Vice versa. He wanted to eradicate evil ..."

"Well yeah, it doesn't always turn out for us", said Monika.

Adam thought she was joking, but she was probably already thinking about something else. She was playing with the cat.

Trips to the city, most often to Praga, happened every few nights for them. When they were in the pub they visited most often he stopped his gaze on Hania, a very young, pretty girl he met a few nights earlier, he felt Monika's attentive gaze.

"Do you think she's cute?"

"Not as cute as you."

"Well I think she's cute. I'd gladly sleep with her."

"Are you kidding?"

"Not at all, but with you."

"Have you done this before?"

"What?"

"Well, with a woman?"

"Sure. And you with a man, no?

"No."

"Oh well, your problem. Are we going to hunt for Hania?"

Monika quickly enough proposed a further introduction into the erotic to Adam. It was at her request that they went to pornographic sites together downloading pages and videos to do it while they were watching sex, participating in a virtual orgy. They often imitated some scenes. Gaj gladly became someone else. She disgraced herself ecstatically. Sometimes they used a mighty artificial penis. When Gaj took it out for the first time, Brok didn't refrain from asking:

"Why is it purple?"

"It's so disgusting that it turns me on," she laughed.

A few nights later they agreed to meet with Hania and her boyfriend. Gaj determined that she and Hania would come an hour earlier for a woman's chat.

"He tagged along. What could I have done?" Explaining Brok's presence. They each took four shots in half an hour. Gaj set the pace. "Come on, we'll prank your boyfriend. We'll bolt, then we'll make a big deal out of how we had to wait for him elsewhere." Hania was uncertain. "I guarantee, it'll do him well. When you want make fun of him? After the wedding?"

On their way they were supposed to stop at Gaj's place. Hania had never been to Gaj's and the offer of trying something special that Monika keeps at home, made an impression on her. As Adam noted, Gaj was well known in this world. She impressed. Closer acquaintance with her was ennobling. He sat with Hania on the couch, and when Monika disappeared in the kitchen, he began to kiss his neighbor. The surprise caused a lack of resistance, and when she began to break free, out of the corner of her eye noticing Gaj entering, in the blink of an eye she was by the couch and began to unbutton her pants. Then everything happened so fast and unconsciously that Adam had problems with a reconstruction of events. Hania stopped putting up any resistance and agreed to everything. Soon she seemed as aroused as they were.

When they sat naked and exhausted on the bed after, Adam had the impression that Hania couldn't believe what had happened. He had trouble with it himself. Only Monika looked relaxed and confident in herself.

"Was it good?"

"Well ... yes ... yes ... of course" Hania tried to adjust to the convention.

"So now call your boyfriend. It's indecent to hold a man in uncertainty for so much time. That cell ringing in your purse it's probably him." Gaj gave commands in a nice tone.

Hania looked stunned.

"What ... what do you have in mind?"

"Well of course not that you tell him about what happened. This will be our sweet secret. Tell him, in accordance with the truth, that we agreed to meet an hour earlier alone, because we wanted to talk about ours matters. Our relationship, mine and Adam's, is going through a crisis. It turned out that it's even worse, I had a fight with my partner, and you had to drive me home, take care of me. You understand: an abandoned woman at the edge of a break-down. I confided in you; I was hysterical ... That's why you didn't answer your cell phone. Assertiveness, remember. Get offended if he offers any doubts. You sacrifice yourself; Samaritan, you were doing a good deed, and your insensitive boyfriend only thinks about his time. Alright now, get to the phone."

Hania talked a little unconsciously while getting dressed. Her boyfriend even offered that he'd pick her up. She explained to him that it was impossible. Saying goodbye to them with calf eyes, she smiled uncertainly.

"Phew, finally out of our hair", Gaj sighed and lit a cigarette. "I deserved it. It was nice entertainment, but then ... you had to get rid of it get her as soon as possible. I did it well, don't you think?", Monika demanded praise.

"Indeed, very skillful."

"What did you think. You're dealing with a professional. And now we can take care of each other", she said, smashing the embers in the ashtray.

***

His father insisted on taking his seat at the table. Adam had to help get him out of bed and sit down, slightly irritated by his elderly stubbornness. Finally, his father leaned on the arm of the armchair, wincing a little in pain, and he looked at his son almost proudly.

"I've decided to tell you something important, although I'm not really able to, it all sounds so pathetic ... that's why I had trouble with it, I was holding myself back ... But I must however overcome my own resistance ... Only now I feel how these ironical meeitngs bind us ... You'll listen, poor man, to the next bit,."

His father took a deep breath.

"My confession allowed me to cross some barrier. I got rid of fear, even obsession, that the truth about me will be revealed. I told your mother this already more calmly. She knew everything anyway. Well, maybe almost everything. And now I have a feeling that I'm starting to understand something or at least I'm trying to. I won't be entangled in subsequent self-justifications, false perspectives ... Maybe indeed ... the truth sets us free ... or maybe it's all only in the face of death? The fear of it frees me from other fears? Somehow I must try to face it."

His father frowns in a strange grimace.

"Do you remember Klein, his unwritten work about fear? He wrote them near his death. Desperate, animalistic agony, fear of which commands to sell off all dignity. He really wanted you to be with him. Suddenly you became almost his foster son ..."

"I know, he even promised to leave me his things."

"He also mentioned this to me ..." His father pauses, and wonders. "I suppose that I'm still alive only thanks to you. Spare yourself those polite denials. Your existence gives mine meaning. And you were born only thanks to your mother. I remember, when she first mentioned about a child, I weaved some nonsense that we face death alone, and offspring are the self-illusion of immortality. Well and I'm standing in the face of death ... This abyss makes my head spin and I don't know myself what I'm afraid of ... if it's just instinct ..."

His father paused. He was tired. Adam is also exhausted. The long-lasting lack of sleep caused the murmuring voice of his father to almost put him to sleep. He was drowning in the waters of illusory death. He didn't want to listen to this. He thinks of Gaj, of her body, that when he sinks into her again, he'll forget about everything and overcome time. He falls asleep. He wakes up in a heartbeat with remorse and even greater aversion to his father, who absolutely wants to share his death with him, just like earlier he put the burden of his guilt on him. Adam tried not to think about them, they were suppressed anyway by the elation with Gaj, but the confessions of his father make him sleepy, they even poison his passions. Now his father's death will poison his life. Some malicious gnome in Adam's head says that euthanasia wasn't a bad solution: people should die alone without burdening their loved ones with it; they should refrain from confessions, especially those like his father, to whom he owed nothing , the father, on whom the existence of a son was forced on his mother.

Adam wanted to hunt down this whispering gnome, break its neck. Shame restores him to reality.

"You look sleepy. Let's arrange for next time", his father says and with difficulty, but independently scrambles out of the armchair. He seems not to notice the clumsy gestures of help from his son and slowly climbs onto the bed. He didn't respond to assurances, after all he hasn't finished that, which he wanted to tell him and misinterpreted Adam's behavior, which was the expression of concentration... "I'm also tired and want to sleep," he cuts into the explanation, closing his eyes.

His son stood over him humiliated and helpless. Finally, he shakes his hand. He feels a weak grip. He lasts another moment in silence and leaves. Suddenly he stops being sleepy. He goes to the first bar he sees and drinks one vodka, then another.

He's a little drunk when Gaj returns home.

"You couldn't have waited for me? She calls with a joyful rebuke, cuddling and hanging off of him.

"It's about my father," murmurs Brok.

Monika makes a thoughtful face, but still showers him with kisses. She begins to unbutton his pants. For the first time Adam isn't in the mood to have sex with her. He tries to delicately move away, but Gaj doesn't give up. Finally, he pushes her away firmly. The woman was surprised.

"Has this depressed you that much?"

"What do you think?"

"I thought I'd let you forget."

"But I don't want to forget!"

"I don't understand you too well. From what you've told me, it's a hopeless matter and you can't help. You can visit him."

"Exactly"

"But you are no longer with him. What will remembering this over and over again do?"

"Older people die. It's sad but natural."

"I don't understand you too well. We're supposed to forget about them when we lose sight of them?

"No, they should be remembered, but without exaltation. Moderation. That's what my lover told me who taught political philosophy."

"You're telling me about moderation?"

"Depends on what. Not in what happens to us ... We have happiness." Gaj moves forward again. She puts her hand on his thigh. "This something special. This is real life."

Brok moved away with obvious irritation.

"This is starting to tire me. Sometimes we should get out of bed!"

"But we do leave it." Monika looks at him surprised and probably a bit resentful. "We go to clubs, meet people ...We can go to the cinema ... Do you want to?"

"No." Adam's trying to calm down and understand his state. "I'm sorry, actually I don't know what I mean. I must go to my mother. I haven't seen her for a long time."

"And I was so looking forward to it ... I was thinking about you all the time at work, about us ..." For the first time Brok had the impression that Gaj is a little uncertain. "I had trouble concentrating, seeing clearly. And here is a new commission and a proposition from Olaf ... I wanted to sleep so badly. Fortunately, some white powder helped me ..."

"Shouldn't you be careful with that?!"

"Give it a break! A teacher has been found. I'm capable of controlling my life!" Now Monika looks angry.

"And what is this new commission? You never tell me about your work."

"And you talk about yours? But I can tell you. Do you want a drink?"

Adam doesn't want one anymore, so Gaj just makes gin and tonic for herself, telling him about a commission for a large fuel company.

"During the previous government they slapped a terrible fine on it. Hundreds of millions. They didn't keep mandatory reserves ... It doesn't matter. The new government canceled the fine. And everything would've been all right if this guy from the 'Courier', Przemek Luty, hadn't gotten involved. He wrote about the matter and it caused a scandal. I mean, no ..." Gaj tapped her head. "The first article on this subject was in your mother's 'Renaissance'. Only nobody treats those publications seriously. But if the 'Courier' got involved ...I mean, we don't know if it got involved. Maybe this is a single action of our priceless Przemek? We must find that out. Whereas, my idea itself is obvious. Because despite being weary," Monika looks at Adam tenderly, "I designed a strategy ... In any case its foundation." Gaj proudly finishes her drink. "We don't defend the decision of the current government; we only mention it casually. We are pounding at the previous government's decision. It was it, oppressive and uncomfortable for their business, it refers to methods appropriate of communism. As a result, it will be it costs the state a lot, because in the final instance the state must lose. You have to stigmatize the irresponsible decisions of politicians that will have unpredictable consequences, blah, blah, blah. With the 'Word' we'll get along. It'll write everything to take care of the opposition. In ABC we have already agreed discussions on how this fine could've undermined the trust international business to Poland. Now we're looking around for experts who'll write to the 'Courier'. I've already commissioned the preparation of a draft. In points I specified what's going on and our specialists this will translate this into proper economic-legal jargon. We'll send it to journalists and the company spokesperson. Tomorrow he's supposed to have a press conference. And Podlecki will write about this in the 'Republic'. With him the only trouble is that because he doesn't know anything, he transcribes the texts sent to him too literally, only decorating them with his rhetoric. But readers won't notice anything anyway." Gaj is picking up momentum, beams with satisfaction.

"And how is it really?"

"But I'm telling you."

"I'm not about that. I'm asking, who's right in this dispute?"

Gaj stops, makes another drink, looks at Adam carefully.

"You know what? You're surprising me! That someone with your American experience can ask such a question? First of all, not only does this not interest me, but I shouldn't even be dealing with it. I am a professional like a lawyer who defends his client. And I should only deal with his rationale. Secondly, probably overall there's no answer for that kind of question. Some are right, others are right, they're both right, they have their own interests, their own explanations. If they're able to present them properly, and that's what we're for, they win. And that's it."

"Aha."

Brok didn't want to, and probably wasn't able to enter into a discussion with Gaj on this topic. She however looks at him tensely and without sympathy.

"All in all, you took advantage me. You took advantage of my weakness to you. I shouldn't talk about this, especially to you. You're negotiating with ABC, and I'm telling you about the secrets of our joint ventures."

"Alright, alright, I've already forgotten about it. You know we're having a weird time talking today. I should go now."

Gaj looked at him in amazement. When Adam threw on his jacket, she exploded.

"You shouldn't go! Stay. I've been thinking about you all day. Only that allowed me to function ... All day. I've been hot for you all day. And you're just leaving?!"

"You're tired. We're both tired. Let's take our first break from each other in almost three weeks."

"No! - Gaj grabbed his arm. "I don't want any break! Stay! Please ..." She looks as if she's going to cry.

Adam was determined and Gaj's behavior only strengthened his resolve. He must use force to free himself, go out into the corridor.

"Get the fuck out!" He hears behind him along with the slamming of the door.

***

The sight of him clearly pleases his mother. Her face brightens, but after a moment, it again falls into sad reverie, staring into the night behind the glass.

"Has something happened?"

"It's I who should ask, since you came to me at this time. Alright, alright! I don't blame you. I came back from your father's. This isn't good. You know, he even said interesting things. It's a pity that only now. When it's too late."

Adam wanted to talk with his mother about this, but he knows he's not able to. He recalled Gaj's statement to himself.

"Someone told me that the scandals written about by you guys are ignored by the public opinion and it's only when someone else writes about it, that they start to live."

"That's true. Maybe not always. Sometimes we're able to introduce something into public circulation. But rather rarely. Recently, the most famous case, to which his article in the 'Currier' dedicated Luty ... is about the withdrawal of an almost half a billion złoty fine for a fuel company by the current government... it was written about earlier, and to be precise, by us. Nobody was interested in it. Luty didn't even refer to us. Hieronim called him. He was explaining himself a lot. He's a decent guy, he probably really didn't read. This says even worse thingsabout us", his mother laughed.

"But I don't understand something here. After all such information had to appear in the media, on news services ..."

"Of course, that it appeared. Specifically expressed, on the economic pages. For example: the government accepted a company's appeal against a decision imposing a fine for non-compliance with fuel storage and protection regulations ... Who'll read this? And if at the opportunity the amount of the fine isn't even mentioned, which can be explained by the fact that it doesn't exist after all...", If it's not translated into an understandable language and didn't expose the matter, then it doesn't exist ..." his mother stopped. Adam's cell phone rang again. It was Gaj. He turned the phone off.

"But in that case, you know ... I feel stupid asking ..."

"Ask!"

"What's the point of your actions?"

"And what's the point of yours, beyond that you earn a lot of money, which gives it meaning in a radical way? I don't know. We have these few dozen thousand readers who get information from us. It's practically sure that a lot more because this information is spreading. And what's the point? I don't know. I believe that I should."

His mother was saying something more, but Adam stopped hearing. The world was running away from him. He apologized to his mother and headed for his room. He barely managed to undress. With his last look, he noticed that it wasn't even eleven. He then fell into a long dreamless sleep.

After more than ten hours, he woke up rested for the first time in several weeks. He listened to Gaj's voice messages. In two first asked for a phone call. In the last one, clearly drunk, she insulted him. He didn't call back.

His father told him about the family. Adam asked him about this. It turned out, that his father learned the most about his grandfather from Jacob's diary. He didn't know much about his father, Adam's namesake, either. He recalled though about the third, middle brother.

"Józef had a fiancée in Germany. He told about that she was wonderful like Brunhilda and that they we're connected by a very passionate romance. It started to break down. What the reason was, I don't know and neither did my father, his brother. Maybe the Nazis coming to power? In any case, my uncle, whom I can't remember, although he supposedly played with me, came to the university in Freiburg, where he worked earlier, he was Heidegger's assistant, in order to take his things. There was a Nazi student rally in the yard. Suddenly he noticed his ex-fiancée in the crowd, and she saw him. She started screaming terribly: "He's a Jew! Jew! Catch him!" Not knowing exactly why, Józef rushed to escape. They chased him for a long time, but he escaped. Maybe they didn't want to catch him yet? My father told me about that when I was in my teens. It stayed in me. As if I survived it myself, as if it was my fiancé, stirring up an anti-Semitic mob against me. This resided in me next to my recollections from the wardrobe. How many similar memories do my friends have who to this day are afraid of each unknown group, crowd, and collective of people? They're afraid of Poles. How many of them founded their worldview on this precise fear?

***

That night Adam slept at Koszykowa Street. He didn't reach out to Gaj, though the need to hear her voice, see and touch her was overwhelming. At times it seemed to him that he was not able to resist her, he'll have to call Monika, ask her for forgiveness or simply go to Jerozolimski Avenue. The more he decided to master this disturbing passion. In his dreams an animal haunted him, which from up close turned out to be a crazy crowd of characters without identity.

The next day before noon Gaj called.

"So, then, you held out longer than me?" She asked, almost jokingly, though with a hint of resentment. They agreed that Adam would come over to her place after visiting his father.

His father was in bad shape. He was injected with strong drugs that suppressed the pain, but intoxicated him. But his father wanted to talk. He wanted to talk with his son, or rather to him. He caught Adam by the hand, and Adam with a kind of internal contraction felt the weakness of his embrace.

"I'm like Klein, huh?" Glossy eyes stared into his son. "And so much I wouldn't want to. Maybe death must strip us of our dignity?" he asked, his eyes teared, becoming lost in the crevices of his face, they were rolling over in search of other worlds. He fell silent.

Adam wanted to free his hand already, when through a space of suffering his father started talking again.

"Apparently, you have to try everything, we hear. Right? What nonsense! Death, you can't try your own death, you can't learn from it. But can we learn from other people's experiences? Books of the dead were written and maybe ...", his father said something else incomprehensible. Adam tried to listen to him, but he realizes it is just delirium and the nurse made it understood that the best he could do now was leave.

"I'm sorry", says Adam right after opening the door, seeing a naked outline of Gaj's silhouette before him, "I'm going back to see my father and it doesn't look good. So, forgive ..."

The woman is beautiful. On her naked body she has a thrown on translucent dressing-gown. She smiles at Adam and gently advances her hands in his direction. And then everything happens on its own. They fell asleep for the first time briefly somewhere around two o'clock, the next time before dawn. A metallic sound hits them in the head and brings reality back. It's Warsaw, it's November, in the apartment on Jerozolimski Avenue. Next to him, a disheveled woman is trying get up from the bed.

"Fuck, and today we're supposed to analyze Olaf's project!"

The next night around twelve they went to a pub in Praga. Adam wasn't pleased. The regulars there were upsetting him more and more. The clamoring company in the custody of always the same gestures and faces. He recalled a scene from a few days ago to himself. "The ninetieth anniversary of regaining our own dumpster", read the inscription at the entrance to the neighboring pub. Brok realized that the anniversary of a national holiday had just passed. Inside, caricatures hung on the walls referring to it. The largest one above the counter showed a drunk and naked woman stretched out on a bed in the shape of a cross. All around there were bottles and brats crawling around. "The martyrdom of a Polish mother", the caption proclaimed. An already heavily drunk company was organizing an adventure.

"We are going on a pilgrimage to Piłsudski Square!", someone was announcing.

"With a procession," another corrected.

"Who will let herself be crucified? We're going to carry her in the form of the Polish mother."

"Crucify yourselves a teddy bear!" One of the women yelled out.

A giggle went through those present. Someone was laughing at them.

"Let's go!" Adam decided.

"Does this annoy you?" Monika, who looked like she was having fun, was surprised. "Alright, as you like."

The characters from the pub are still playing out the same spectacle. That night it exceptionally annoyed Adam. Maybe because he almost wasn't able to talk with his father. He discovers With surprise that he's looking forward to these conversations more and more. He begins to think of what he has heard so far as an introduction to something important. It seems that his father has a secret to tell him. Reflecting on this, he tries to separate himself from the characters around him, sinking into another drink.

A small man approached them in the company of a young man. Olaf Nok kisses Gaj and exchanges a friendly welcome with Brok.

"You're somewhat gloomy?", she says.

"I have a sick father."

"Your father is dying," Gaj says seriously. "I'm sorry that I call things by name, but it's probably not a secret.

"That's sad. I know something about this. My parents died. But nothing we can't do anything. One has to reconcile with this."

"Adam spent entire days with his father ...", says Gaj emotionally, stroking Brok's head and provoking fury, which with difficulty he managed to control, "and he shows this death on the outside."

"Your father is suffering a lot?"

"Yes."

"It's terminal cancer", Gaj explains, and Adam's rage blazes in him with another flame. He finishes his drink and orders another.

"It's bleak. One has to suffer senselessly here."

"What are you trying to say?" Adam's anger is directed against a man with the last name Nok.

"That, sometimes this last episode of life comes down only to suffering which they cannot allow us to shorten due to religious nonsense ..."

"And would you like to be able to decide about someone else's life?"

"Not about someone else's, but about my own. I wouldn't want to suffer senselessly...why are they taking away our freedom to choose?"

"Whose? Of those dying or of their family? Now you're playing with this thought, because the prospect of death still seems unreal to you. And reality ... I imagine older people who shouldn't be suffering anymore..."

"You're annoyed. That's understandable. But in that, how do you say, is a bit of truth. I also spent a lot of hours next to my dying father. To his suffering I added my own", Nok says it almost as a joke.

"Maybe that was the last chance, which you didn't take advantage of?" Brok throws in his face.

Nok looks at him interested. Gaj is concerned. Adam drinks another drink. He has the impression that alcohol isn't working on him.

"What do you have in mind?" Asks Nok, slyly smiling.

"Maybe you would've learned something important, something that you would never have known."

"From my father? You're joking! That was a softie, but he neither understood me nor our world."

"Or maybe it's you who didn't understand him? Maybe you just think that we're living in such a whole new world? Maybe without understanding the old we're not capable of grasping the new?"

"Wow, wow, what a dialectic", Nok smiles, discussion is his element, "and from under it emerges myth of ingranation. You see Luiz", he says to Luiz, on who's smooth face, was arranged in a smile that nothing could be seen. "But I'm more attracted to the idea of the imagining of breaking out, of emancipation. Do you remember Adam, Gombrowicz's 'Synczyzna'? That's a project! That's a challenge! Create our world anew every day. Our fathers, honest townspeople from Prussia, who wanted the best; social workers from Żeromski's book who sacrificed themselves so that science and progress, would die. Today we are already further on. In the Gombrowicz era! We live in a fluid reality. We've lost permanent reference points. And this is our chance. We don't have to commit or sacrifice. We fulfill ourselves and in this way we're building our world! We're liberating ourselves!"

"We're liberate?! Whom and from what? You say: 'Synczyzna'? I don't know Gombrowicz that well, but it seems to me that this project remained as a name, or worse, a phrase ..."

"Oh, Adam, Adam!", interrupts Nok. "Gombrowicz was a prophet. Do you remember the Operetta, *Albertine*, nudity, love, youth? This is our era, right Luiz?" His companion's glassy eyes are reflecting the pub's lights.

"Gombrowicz died almost half a century ago. Then there was Mrożek's *Tango*, but even ... Klein sadly told me that towards the end of his life even Gombrowicz was falling into metaphysics, and his interpersonal church ..."

"You knew Klein, Bruno Klein?", Nok inquires excitedly.

"I knew him. The inter-human church fell apart, maybe because, my father said this, that it was founded on nothingness. You say: youth?", Brok leans towards Nok. He stares at his face from a few centimeters away. He sees or he thinks he sees folds, wrinkles, the sagging of aging skin. "And how old are you? Fifty? More?" Adam beings to speak louder. He knows that with these words he can touch the interlocutor the most strongly and that's why he raises his voice. Shouting: "Do you know how funny your simulation of youth is? Youth? Look in the mirror and you'll see a grim reaper ringing with his teeth."

Gaj grabs Brok by the arm, terror is painted on Luiz's smooth face, Nok's face stiffens in a nondescript grimace.

"Let's go already, let's go!", Gaj pulls Adam to leave.

"Why?!", Brok releases himself. "I'd still like to talk with this creator erudite. Do you know Gombrowicz or just a few phrases which you sell in this marketing theater? Answer, after all everything supposed to be a marketing trick. Nudity?! A good idea! Let's take our ideas apart. Let's peel them like onions. What of them will remain, master of analysis? What going on?", Once again he has to get away from Gaj's intervention. "Why can't I speak in a way that's free, emancipated, naked. You,

Master Nok, admirer of Gombrowicz and nakedness ... I have an idea: come, let's undress together! Well, come on!" Adam tears off his jacket, pulls off his sweater, tries to tear off his undershirt when Gaj grabs him by the arms.

Nok gawks at him with a stupid expression on his face. A big man approaches them from the bar.

"All right", Gaj speaks in a persuasive tone, "You had your fun. You insulted my friends. You made a scene. But even here you can't do everything. Let's get going before they kick us out"

Pushed by Gaj, in an undershirt, Brok goes to leave. He grabs a glass from the nearest table and drinks it with gusto.

"I emancipate myself from conventions!" He calls. "Let's be free!" He drinks another one.

The company at the table falls silent and stares at him in amazement. The flavor of alcohol contorts in exotic aromas. Adam hears Gaj apologizing to someone while she tries to pull the sweater over his head. Brok puts it on and rolls out into the cold night. The lights are pale and the city unreal. The street is empty. It's a nice change. There are no parrot-like characters that look like a series of duplicate reflections, he didn't hear words, which were unable to survive the sounds carrying them. Monika says something incomprehensible. A few kilometers from here his father is dying, who still hasn't entrusted his secret to him, an incantation, which could show him the way. There must be signs in the city that lead to it, allowed him to ask the question. A car stops next to them, and Gaj pushes him into it. They drive through the flashing abysses of streets. Sometimes Brok wonders what city this is. This could be New York or Moscow, or even Nadarsk, especially that Irina is sitting next to him. However, it turns out that it's Monika, who pays driver and helps Adam get out of the cramped vehicle. Then they're already at her place. Gaj participated in the fight against the disobedient clothes, which tried to slip away and confuse his fingers. Finally, completely naked, Brok falls on the bed, which splits apart, kidnapping him into the vortices of an unknown night.

That morning, Adam woke up with a splitting head. When he got out of the bathroom, Gaj looked at him with a mixture of anger and admiration.

"Well, you're even more picturesque than I thought. What you said yesterday, it didn't make sense, but an impressive load of expression."

"I don't remember very well, but it seems to have made some sense. Certainly, more than the talk of those harlequins, with particular emphasis on the chief marketing clown, I'm sorry ... do you have eggs?"

"You will have to eat something at a restaurant. And don't insult my friends! You don't know Olaf. He's eccentric ..."

"He's eccentric? He's the embodiment of banality!"

"You're a fool. All people are either stupid or banal to you."

"Not everyone. Just your friends."

Gaj, who's about to leave, stops in front of the door. She has a angry face. She's silent for a moment.

"Think about what you said," She throws out and leaves.

Over scrambled eggs and tea in the restaurant of the Hotel Polonia Brok tries to organize the events of the day, or rather the previous night, and plan the matters of the coming day. The Office, the *ABC* papers, consultation with an expert, telephone to Taggart and a visit to the hospital. Each of these things seemed impossible to do.

His father felt a little better. Only this "better" didn't reach the level of even a few days ago. Also in better moments the pain struck out through the thinner and thinner skin, tugged on the increasingly diminishing physicality. Father was disappearing. There was less and less of him. Recently, however, Adam had the impression that he took up another fight with his illness. He decided to read the experiences of his life, contrast them with death, and break out of pain and weakness.

"The attempt to die is overwhelming us," said, or rather whispered his father. "Klein, Klein is proof of that. Such an intellectual, independent thought. But was it really independent thought? He didn't understand that we cannot individually stand up to death. We must refer to concepts and experiences that transcend us. Maybe collective, consolidated in institutionalized experience, which infinitely surpasses us, allows us to come to terms with finiteness? Is there such an experience? I, now, a neophyte on his deathbed, maybe I'm only trying to revive dead myths for myself? I only know how wrong I have been up until this point. I stand with empty hands. I, an advocate of self-creation, was a slave to a wardrobe in my childhood. Wardrobes in which they hid me during the war. I never ran away from it completely. I come back to it every night. It's the only thing I have other then you, and you only exist thanks to your mother. I was afraid of having children, you were the act of propitiation and now you are for me ... Do we live in times of breakthrough? Am I supposed to believe in some God? Do I have time?"

Speaking exhausts his father, but he is determined to continue. He wants to entrust something to his son. He speaks with closed eyes through clenched jaws, reporting on the state of his search...

"We want to forget about death. We even succeed. We go along the equilibrium, which is life, not noticing the abyss around. We're afraid of dizziness. We even succeed. We build technological prostheses, justifications, progress, the like, maybe it's necessary ... We talk over our fear, we almost forget about it, but after all it always exists in our dreams. And us? And we're unable to carry the tragedy and we begin to live in a farce. I've lived in a grotesque world and I was like that. My environment ... deformed people who didn't understand themselves or the community in which they lived. Images of pretentious stupidity, and they consider themselves as the highest development, the elite of the nation. After all, I was smarter than them, I thought over a bit, even if only Weber or Simmel. After all I was supposed to be a scientist. If it wasn't for Communism ... I didn't become one. I could even somehow defend that miserable positivism that we practiced in the 'Republic' in the seventies. Maybe even that what we were doing in the eighties would have some sense. But we were paying too big a price. Especially in the eighties. We validated things that were really bad, we built up the justification for surrender, vileness. Your mother understood this perfectly. People from my environment, we pulled ourselves and others down more and more ... Was Goleń different? I owed him a lot. He helped me as much as he could. He was a demiurge of that world. He focused on a political career in a bad time. With all the consequences of it. And those others? How could I let myself be reduced to their level? My father saw it. He didn't like it, I felt it. And yet ... how could I in my daily life disregard that, which I had learned? Maybe it's normal? Rationalization, equalization of cognitive dissonance, adaptive functions of reason, which will justify every deviltry ... All doubts I evaded by talking over them, that Poland is such a special example, premodern ... Reality must've admonished me. But will I, at the price of pain and shame, discover some meaning? Maybe it's just my desperate desire, escape from senselessness, from Klein's fate?"

Adam thinks his father is finished now. He froze on the bed for a moment. His waxy face with eyes closed is only enlivened by the suffering caused by cramps. But his father wants to speak. He's struggling. He opens eyes and through clenched teeth, as if with internal anger, as if he wanted to prove something to himself, his body, he forces a confession...

"Now, when I'm trying to put my life together, think about it, understand it ... I recall to myself what your mother told me about painting. Why do we love some paintings and want to look at them, and others, although they don't seem to be different at first glance, don't arouse interest? She explained that something more than light caught at a given moment of the day shines through these exceptional ones, it's permeated by a different unreachable one for us on a daily basis, quality. I loved her and didn't understand how keen she could be. She said the same applies to literature. Stories about everyday events become extraordinary and language becomes a medium. I listened but I didn't hear. Nicely said, I thought and didn't wonder what. Now it's returned to me and I think it's the same with life. Maybe it's this way with your mother's life. And with mine? Did something shine through it? A light that could justify it? Is this light? 'Beauty is only horror at the beginning', it was somehow like that with Rilke, that's how I remember it. Something that overwhelms us, stuns us, begins to awaken terror. We're not capable of understanding ... My life? Does it mean something, or do I just want it to start to mean something?"

***

After leaving his father, Brok called Gaj. He desired her and the more the lust tired him, the more he felt angry at her. He tersely asked if he could come by. Her affirmative answer sounded similar. She was waiting for him, sitting in an armchair and playing with the cat. She looked at him coldly. Almost without a word, he took her in his arms and carried her to bed. He didn't know if they were making love or fighting. It was only fatigue and a short nap before dawn that threw them onto the ground of reconciliation. In the morning for a few minutes, before Gaj didn't rush off to her affairs, they even showed affection to each other. However, something was changing between them.

"Shall we repeat the scene with Hania?" Monika asked the next evening.

Adam is surprised, but the memory provoked by the question excites him.

"Why not?"

"So in an hour, okay? I made an appointment with her initially. If you didn't want to, then I would've canceled", she explains in answer to his silent question.

Hania came on time. She smiled a little uncertainly. But already through the door, she was taking the coat out of her hands, Monika took everything into her own. This time things are even more obvious, and Hania devotedly fulfills the role of their desires. After everything is done, she rose, smiling, and confidently begins to dress.

"Wawrzec is waiting for me. I'll let him know it's over." They looked at her. "I'm attending an informal seminar on the subject of marketing, and it's unknown when this session was supposed to end", explained Hania, laughing. "I informed him. It's already late. I have to run to the subway." She blew them kisses with the ends of her fingertips.

"And maybe next time we will invite them both?", ponders Monika, probing him with her gaze.

"Would you like to?"

"And you?"

"My benefits would be moderate."

"You don't have to remind me of your radical heterosexuality. Don't say, however, that you don't see new possibilities also for yourself in this arrangement. Don't be trivial. So come on, say it. Are you in the mood for it?

Brok feels another wave of excitement. His hesitation however is imperceptible.

"For now, no."

"Would you be jealous? I accepted that you're in the mood someone else..."

This dialogue begins to irritate Adam.

"What do you want to say? That you were a passive victim? I don't know who of us was more in the mood for Hania and who took advantage of her more!"

"Don't get angry." Monika laughs relaxed. "Oh, we're playing with opportunities. Come to me."

***

Entering the hospital, Brok thought that he's living in three separate worlds at the same time, each with a different smell, color and rhythm. Each of them comes down to a specific place. Monika's apartment immersed at night, whose extension was pubs, to which they sometimes went; then work spanning between the R&B office, in which he has a separate office, and the ABC headquarters, and finally the hospital, which leads to his father's isolation room. From the fourth world, which was housed on Koszykówa St. and was his mother's domain, he's distanced himself lately.

He thought about it when he saw her sitting at his father's bed through the ajar door. The man lying there had his eyes closed. They were silent. Unexpectedly his mother put her hand on his father's hand. His father opened his eyes and surprised, shook his head. She withdrew her hand and froze in the previous position. Standing in the doorway, her son looked at her bent forward back. His mother noticed him and straightened up.

"Look, Benek. I have to visit you to meet my son. I've not seen him for more than a week", she was saying lightly, but her face wasn't cheerful. "Well, but I'll leave you now."

Adam felt ashamed

"I'll visit you. Alright?"

"Don't make promises to the wind," she said as she left.

Up close he can see a movement on the face of the person laying. His father is fighting pain and weakness falling on him. He prepares to say something to his son. He gathered himself long before he spoke.

"Have you read Uncle Jakub's diary?"

"But I've told you, I've read it."

"This is a very important text for me. I'm wondering why. Is it only because it shows who a person can become, and from family? A man led by ethical maximalism and disagreement with evil? Such an interpretation could be suggested to me by colleagues from my circle. After all, they still mark the Bolsheviks, revolutionaries, who always turn out to be their opponents. I did the same, although something wasn't right. We're always fighting the threat of yesterday, while it's taking on new forms ... Is it not necessary to understand anew the confession that my uncle left me? Klein's theories of fear come back to me. Every order for him was to solidify into authoritarian forms. Fear to it was supposed to be a healthy impulse. Just what in return? The 'Word' community are the children of Jews who renounced Jewry, of communists who thought that they'd transgress national identities. Today, their children who negated communism can recognize themselves and only unite in their fear of Poles. Is this not a caricature of identity? And are we supposed to be afraid of every form of authoritarianism? Is my uncle's diary not also a tale about an attempt to throw away identity, declaring war on God, and therefore on his order? It tells how the project of the human kingdom ending. We believed that we could be equal to gods, as our forefathers. How did this end? If we want to be equal to God, as it was with Jacob? We fall into Satan's clutches. H ... he is much more cunning than us. And today? Pride doesn't have to wear the leather jacket of a Czekist... Fear is bad, binds, enslaves, although it allows survival. But maybe there is a form of fear that allows us to survive as people? A metaphysical fear. A feeling that there is something that infinitely transcends us, in which we are, and we are not at the same time. Only in this dimension our choices take on weight. They mean something. Violation of the rules becomes sacrilege ... I'm tired, God, how tired I am. I don't know how long that I have been preparing to tell you this and I can say only this much. That's all."

Already in the hospital corridor, Brok telephoned Monika to inform her that he would spend the night with his mother. She reacted unexpectedly violently.

"You can't! I've been waiting all day for you!"

"You've been waiting?"

"And what do you think? All day I've only thought about, that I'd see you. Go to bed with you..."

"I'm sorry but I have to go to my mother's."

"But your father is sick, not your mother."

"Calm down!"

"Drop in for at least an hour, for a bit, I can't stand it without you!"

"Unfortunately..."

"How do you treat me? Do you decide everything? And I, who am I? Just an ass to fuck?!"

"We end up at this ..."

"Wait ..."

Adam turned off the phone. He fought with himself not to go to Gaj's. Her words irritated him as much as they aroused him. However, he went to Koszykowa St.

"You came."

His mother breaks out of her melancholy for a moment. Soon however she returns to it, it immerses into her, just like the cigarette smoke filling the apartment. Adam begins to explain himself, but his mother waves a hand.

"Your father tells me strange things", she suddenly announces. "He treats me almost like a fulfilled person. Maybe with him, but ... you probably see yourself, how it is ..."

Unexpectedly, his mother bursts into tears. Her son doesn't see her often in this state and maybe that's why he doesn't know what to do. He begins to repeat some senseless comforting words. He embraces her, but his mother frees herself and disappears in the bathroom. She returns a few moments later with a calm face on which the traces of the recent attack are not visible.

"I don't like to fall apart," she almost snarls, "but in whose presence can I do it in if not yours?" She snorts something like laughter. "Bearing this is one of your filial duties." She hesitates, puffing on the cigarette, she looks at her son and begins to speak: "On his deathbed, your father accounts for his entire life. Downright literature. But is that it? You're really grown up now. So, I can tell you the truth, almost the whole truth. I didn't like your father. Of course, I'm talking about the time when he left me, though it wasn't good before either. I wanted to dislike and discredit him. But of course I remember what was good in him, which meant that thanks to him I was able to be happy like never before. Perhaps what I love about him the most, was what was in of his father. Maybe something bad is happening with us? We're dying. Maybe because we are afraid to look into the eyes of death? That's what your father said. There's constantly more and more of the world built by us and less of us. I'm worse than my parents. Your father was worse than his. I hope you'll overcome this fatalism.

***

Adam didn't speak to Monika for a few days, although thoughts about her filled every moment of his existence and made it impossible to focus on anything else. Even at his father's bed, he saw her gray eyes, felt her touch. The more this passion haunted him, the more he disliked its subject, the women, Gaj. This time, however, he called first. He asked if he could come over, although he had the keys and fought with himself to not go to Jerozolimski Avenue.

"I don't know myself ...", he heard the other side of the phone. "Maybe you should come over. We can finally set something up."

She was tapping at the computer keyboard and didn't even look at his direction. He came over and started kissing her hair, neck. She gave in to his caressing, purring like a cat, and suddenly turned around.

"You bastard! How did you figure this?"

"I explained it to you. I need to devote some time to my mother."

"You just don't have it for me. You should warn me. And today...today I can't."

"Why?"

"I have my period."

"Before it didn't bother so much."

"But now I have to prepare a project for Olaf. Stay with me but give me a break. After all I'm saying..."

After all that, she looked at him with squinted eyes.

"Although you're satisfied, and I'll have to do it at computer."

"I won't sleep either," said Adam, and that was the last thing he remembered. When he woke up it was already daylight and Monika was bustling about the apartment.

"I must finally supply this fridge so that we can have a decent breakfast to sit down to", she murmured. "There's no bread. So, there will be biscuits, there can be white cottage cheese, tea for you and coffee for me."

Reluctant, she began to explain the nature of the commission.

"I can't precisely tell you. This is a governmental order. Important politicians have made a big deal out of it. Their bosses are sure that even with us it won't be possible to quite hide it under the bushes. A strategy has to be devised, I've told you. The situation is easier for us. The media will buy everything that's against the opposition. This state of affairs must be maintained. You need to permanently glue the image of the mohair's on them, party of the past, parochial and xenophobic, which brings us shame in Europe. Especially those young, like Pavlov's dogs need to be fixed with a few simple associations. Government: young, dynamic, with perspective; opposition: mindless, backward, in one word: embarrassment.

"And this works?"

"If this is done by professionals and they have the right means ... Olaf, who you don't like so much, theorized this. By the way, you hit him on point. He appears to be much younger, but he is, I believe, forty-two years old. It is difficult to count how much money and time he consumes to keep his youth: massage and beauty salons, special diets, extracts from ginseng and unknown organic substances, some kind of oriental methods, acupuncture, God knows what. And you hit him with fifty. You couldn't hit him anymore harder. He walked like he was poisoned. He circled around me and waited for me to tell him that it wasn't true. I maliciously didn't notice him. But then yesterday, casually, I said that he looks great, I thought that he would cry out of happiness. But he's the best specialist. Gombrowicz is an inspiration for him. 'Their public opinion needs to be destroyed', he always says. The world is a game of mouths and looks. Whoever chases another into a corner with their expression, whoever humiliates him and ruins his public opinion, will win."

"Of course, I'm not going to ask you how this relates to reality."

"And rightly so!", Monika smiles ironically from above her coffee. "Because this precisely is reality! To be means to be perceived, like this one philosopher said."

"I didn't know your champion was Berkeley," Adam replies in a similar tone.

"Don't show off. What does it matter, what his name was and who he was in general? I'm talking about the obvious. This is how the human world is."

"Well, but you're talking about the scandal."

"Yes."

"That means, there was one?"

"Well, there was."

"And you what?"

"And we're precisely here to cover it up. Teach its perpetrators what to say. Assess who cannot be defended and who's not worth defending. Bring out an absurd matter about the competitor from the past and inflate it to monstrous proportions, then claim that they expose this new pseudo-scandal to hide their own iniquities.

Announce that individual cases shouldn't be dealt with, but the mechanisms etc. I'm not going to be selling you our art for free, because this is art ..."

"Well, but you ... you don't mind that corruption exists?"

"Of course, that it bothers me. I don't take or give bribes, well ... outside absolute necessity. It bothers me that people aren't honest, that they don't keep their word, they're not ...", Gaj is irritated and is getting more and more wound up. She looks at Brok with anger. "Alright, I know what you want to say. It's as though I'm helping the corrupt ones. It's not like that. I don't help in corruption. I build image strategies. I advise on how to defend reputation. And you? Do you check the morals of those with whom you do business? Do you know who work with? And so, buzz off. Leave the judging to the judges. I especially don't like those who bring up the past, and if their past was brought up, such things would come out that oh wow. You're also such a saint, the true son ... I'm sorry, I wouldn't want to make personal or family insults ..."

"Well, do it, do it if you can!

"If you want to, then I can. Surely you know the uncompromising nature of your mother is explained that she broke under martial law. I wouldn't want...

"And I don't want to hear anything from you anymore."

He dressed hurriedly and threw things into a travel bag. Gaj ran up to him.

"I'm really sorry. I let myself be provoked. Forgive me. It was absolutely unacceptable ..." She tried to embrace him.

Brok broke free, left. He waved his hand at a passing taxi when he sees Gaj coming out of the gate.

"Adam!" He still hears.

The taxi moves off and he doesn't look back. He's not in the mood to give up the opportunity.

***

His father was semi-conscious. His mother was looking at him with apprehension. Later together, they followed his facial contractions, the involuntary movements of his body. His father spoke some words that couldn't be understood.

"He received very strong drugs. You certainly won't be able to communicate with him until tomorrow. And then ...," the doctor spread out his hands.

In the corridor they met Kalina. Adam explained the situation to her. Kalina came over and gave her hand to her mother, who shook it, looking indifferently at its owner. In his phone, Adam found a few missed calls from Gaj and a few of her text messages. He replied: "My father is dying. Please, give me a break. "

The next day he canceled the meetings and came with his mother to the hospital in the morning. His father looked a little more conscious. He smiled at them.

"It's nice to see you together," he whispered.

Then he said something else, but they couldn't understand his words. He seemed to be burning out. He was moving less and less. He was collapsing into numbness. At one point he awoke. His hands were pulling away from the quit with difficulty, they were showing something. He was whispering. They bent over.

"I have to ... I have to ... tell you ..." he froze and only the movement of his chest indicated that he was still alive. His eyes closed. He died after a few hours.

CHAPTER 14

"Mom, couldn't you try to smoke less?" He said instinctively.

The apartment was thick with smoke. The cold November night which came unexpectedly, discouraged opening the window. A group of his mother's friends from 'Renaissance' had already said goodbye and they were alone. They returned from the funeral a few hours previous. The two clearly separate groups of its participants didn't mix with each other. Those from the editorial office of the 'Republic' surrounded Kalina and expressed their condolences while members of the editorial board of 'Renaissance' crowded around his mother to express their sympathy. Standing next to his mother, Adam was the only one that everyone came up to. Those from the 'Republic' also gave their condolences to his mother at that time, some gave her their hand. Kalina also came up to them. She kissed Adam on both cheeks and squeezed his mother's hand, saying something into her ear. His mother looked as if she was somewhere else. When they started pouring soil onto the casket, Gaj showed up. She looked very attractive in black. She kissed him and then, when in response to her questioning gaze he pointed to his mother with his eyes, she came up to her and giving her hand, as a friend of her son's, she expressed her sympathies.

"Call me when you get yourself together," she whispered into his ear and left.

"Why should I smoke less? You want to encourage me to lead a healthy lifestyle", his mother laughed. Adam opened a window. November settled on them with a dark moisture.

"You're touching ... I don't have much left if anything ... first your father left me and now he died. I don't even have anyone to blame for my fate. This country, my country ... Sometimes I'm overcome by disgust and sometimes despair. This is how we've organized our free country, for ourselves, this pseudointellectual mob. What do I have left? A few weird friends, Hieronim, is devotion incarnate and should perform a responsible function in the state, and is ... You're all I have left, but you left."

His mother puffed on a cigarette and raised a glass of red wine. He looked at the smoldering heat through the almost black liquid. Then she lifted a colorful, shiny weekly from the table counter.

"Here's the issue of 'Republic' in part, devoted to your father. I managed to flip through a little of it. There's an introduction by the editor-in-chief who explains, why Benedict Brok was such an important figure for the magazine, and thus also for the country. At the funeral the editor-in-chief personally handed me this copy. He writes this like your father has always been the mainstay of common sense and moderation, opposing the madness on both sides, even in those difficult times of martial law. You already know that there were two extremes under martial law and the 'Republic' was in the middle. There's a series of quotes from your father's articles. After the talks we've had lately, I can be sure that he wouldn't be happy with them. Maybe it's good that he didn't live to see them. Well ... he couldn't, this is an edition due to his death."

"Maybe you'd leave here? I'm really doing well, and I could easily arrange things for you in the States. That would be a gesture on my part. We'd be together."

His mother looks at him intently.

"Do you really conduct your offer seriously? Recently you offered me a trip to Florence. That was very nice, but I refused. But to the States? What would I do there? You asked what the point is of what we do at 'Renaissance'. The answer is: huge. If we only hit a few dozen thousand of our readers ... or if there was only ten times less of them or even fewer, it would still make great sense. In old novels, castaways throw a letter in a bottle into the sea, hoping that it will reach the right person. It always does. This is how it is in old novels. But maybe they're smarter? On his deathbed your father confessed to me that in this battle that was our life, I was right. All in all, I can agree with him" she laughed dry. "I just don't understand why it was happening that way. Maybe he was too smart. I followed a few rules and obvious truths. He could always find such elaborate interpretations ..." His mother fell silent and looked at a tree that's barely visible through the kitchen window.

Adam remembered the question that has followed him for some time but keeps forgetting to ask it.

"You didn't say anything about Tadek. When I was here before, you were preparing an investigation…

His mother looked at him surprised.

"Ah yes, I forgot ... You weren't in Poland. I don't actually have anything to brag about. I acted as I told you last time, when we were together. Finally, the IPN dealt with the matter properly. Two years ago. It was still, according to legal jargon, 'a case under investigation'. Only the results of such an investigation allowed me to make these allegations. They questioned Andrzej Molnar ... remember? A snitch from Solidarity, today the owner of a large publishing house. All my guesses were confirmed. He was assigned to watch Tadek's every step. I was comparing the dates. It wasn't much after Tadek's conversation with his girl's brother-in-law, a UB agent, who while drunk told him about their agents in Solidarity. Then Tadek started his own investigation. When Molnar notified the ministry that he was going to Gdansk with Tadek in a few days, that same day, Lt Col Rojek was temporarily assigned there. And when they finally arrived, Molnar got time off. He could calmly return to Warsaw and for the first time in a few months have no interest in Tadek. So, it's no wonder that the next step was summoning Jacek Rojek to submit an explanation, the main shareholder of ABC, who was earlier its president, and even earlier an SB colonel. And here this Jacek Rojek officially announces that he wouldn't appear before the IPN and will not agree to be the voluntary victim of a witch hunt. In the Institute of National Remembrance, there's a regular prosecutor's department, and the prosecutors working there don't differ from others. So, Rojek announced that he wouldn't respect the decision of the justice administration. It was a perfectly prepared strategy. He wrote a letter that was probably printed in all the media that he wouldn't give into harassment, whose aim is the subordination of the government to big, independent private television services. Everything was in this letter. About that the Institute of National Remembrance has proven that it works on political orders, and the Fourth Republic of Poland is a police state that breaks the backbone of the media and business. Of course, the whole bunch of the politicians in authority for the Third Republic fired up in protest, which was more or less a repeat of Rojek's theses. All of those who normally tell about, how Poland is a country that follows the rule of law, and every most absurd sentence is a revelation of justice to them, this time congratulated Rojek for breaking the law. I'm not in the mood to talk about, what was happening, but you can guess. Until now Rojek's case is cited as the greatest disgrace and compromise of the Fourth Republic of Poland, and what kind of authority the president-colonel had become, isn't worth talking about. The prosecutors from the IPN backed down. They could've in truth, in accordance with the law, sent the police to bring Rojek in, but I don't know who would've dared to do so in such an atmosphere. There were elections soon anyway. Opponents of the Fourth Republic of Poland won, and the case was killed. I was still collecting all the information and wrote about Tadek's story in 'Renaissance'. I wrote that Rojek blocked the murder investigation. He sued me. In the justification of the sentence, I found out that I suggested his involvement in the murder and acting against the exposure of the murderers. Meanwhile, I just described the facts without adding nothing from myself. We appealed, but I must admit that the editorial was terrified. I was as well. The bankruptcy of the magazine hung in the balance, not to mention the humiliating formula of apologies in which I had to submit for terrible slander. Anyway, various journalistic authorities, and others, said it was a good opportunity to put an end to the infamous existence of the center of hatred and bias that is 'Renaissance'. The 'Word' never devoted so much time to us as it did then. And suddenly the gracious gentleman reached out his hand. Rojek's lawyer said that it would be enough for his client if I wrote that I didn't want to associate the chairman with the death of my brother, and he'll withdraw both the sentenced fine, as well as the humiliating formula of apologies. Our lawyer said that we don't have any chance, we'd be defeated in every level of court. All of our lawyer friends confirmed this. In such an atmosphere and with such courts ... I told you, what kind of situation we were in, the prosecution was pursuing us and would pursue us for other cases. The editorial team decided. I agreed and I ..."

His mother paused, pursing her lips in a strange scowl.

"Maybe I didn't tell you about this because I was so ashamed? Although I don't know what else I could've done. Aha, and one more matter. When we signed the settlement, Rojek's spokesperson asked for a word with me. The president obliged him to forward the message that he had withdrawn only to put an end to this senseless war. Rojek believed in my intelligence, related to the snitch, and so he knew, that he understood, that he could destroy 'Renaissance' and me as a journalist. He didn't want to do it because he had no grudge against me and thought that it's finally necessary to close old stories and bury the war hatchet. He is reminded that from the beginning he proposed how to help my cousin. The lawyer repeated this clearly, not knowing what it was about."

His mother became lost in thought and stared into the night.

"And so, Rojek forgave me, I admitted that he had no connection with my brother's death, though I know this isn't true. Tadek's case has been closed and no one will ever be held responsible for it."

"And you want to live here?"

"Yes. I want to live here and even do something."

"Actually I could think about it myself. But ... after all you know, that I do business with Rojek's company."

"I know."

"And it doesn't bother you at all?"

"It bothers me."

"Why didn't you tell me about it?"

"Because you're an adult and you make decisions yourself. I can't push you. Anyway, I don't know if my feelings should play any role. If it's not you, there'll be someone else. I settled with him myself. But I haven't yet reached the level of Ala, who's devoted to him."

"You can't advise me anything?"

"I can't."

***

Adam met with Artur Rojek in his study day the next day. Dark clouds were gathering outside the windows, and he exposed room suddenly cast into shadows.

"I'll have to withdraw from our venture. Personal affairs."

Artur's face became serious.

"I was afraid of that. My father warned me."

"And so, you understand why. My decision will not have any impact on R&B. I'll hand over my entire, and you can believe me, impartial report. The last thing they'll be interested in, is my personal motivation."

"It's not quite like that. Capital may not have nationalities, but capitalists on the contrary do. They treat you at R&B like on of their own, for them we're exotic natives. They're always going to believe that the worst from their team is better than the best from ours. That's why we need you to stay. We got along well. We were broadcasting on the same frequency. I'm not my father just like you're not your mother. It is up to us to end outdated wars. My father understands this. He knew this from the time of the Round Table and earlier. He wanted to with ... I'm sorry, with the opposition, in which your mother was, get along. Recently he withdrew from the case won against her and the claims against her paper. He explained to me about the beginning of your ... I'm sorry, my mistake is emblematic, of our family conflict. Do you know, that your aunt works for him? Ask her, if she has had any issues?"

"I know. Your father took care of her, he just earlier put her in jail!"

"Give it a break! He wasn't the one who decided who went to prison."

"But from the arrangement...

"Yes, he was an SB functionary and he's not proud of it. He took part in ugly matters. But that was that system from which luckily got out of. We're lucky. Our parents' generation wasn't. Let's not be children. Sorry, don't be outraged, just listen. Your father was in the 'Republic'. I'm the last one who would blame anyone with this. But after all this was a publication of the Communist authorities. For Goleń it was a political trampoline. The SB was an instrument in the hands of the authorities, in his hands. Were the people in the 'Republic' not involved in that system? Let's finally give our parents a break. You know that this television is big project. Look at this from the perspective of the country! How much can be done for it from here."

"I'm sorry, but I've already made my decision. I'm backing out. I'll finish that, which I started. Then I'll pass it on to my boss and leave."

"I know your father's funeral was yesterday. Anyone would be shocked. I'm asking you for one thing. Hold off on your decision. If you want to maintain it ... after all I don't have the resources to force its change."

From his office Brok emailed Taggart another file of documents and their analysis. Their fears were confirmed. There are not always clear and logical movements hiding behind a shiny façade. Part of the money was leaking out. The beneficiaries of the last, unsuccessful purchases of ABC were joint-stock companies with a very complicated chain of shares, at the end of which was a company registered in the Cayman Islands, owned by Jacek Rojek and his partners. Adam ended the analysis with a statement that he's withdrawing from the venture. He wanted to close the activities associated with the investment in ABC as soon as possible and transfer his analysis into the hands of his successor.

Taggart's reply came after a few dozen minutes: "Don't make any important decisions. I'll be in Warsaw in a week. Then we'll ultimately determine everything. "

Dusk was already falling. The days of the late November were getting shorter. Brok called Gaj's number. He was thinking about it since yesterday.

"I've been waiting," he heard.

"I'd want to ask you one thing. Did you prepare the defense strategy for Jacek Rojek two years ago?"

The handset on the other side fell silent. The silence grew. Finally, he heard Gaj's voice, which he couldn't recognize.

"Are you only calling for that?"

"I would like to find it out. It's important to me."

"I won't talk about this topic!"

"But I'm not asking for details."

"Why is this so important to you?"

"I would like to find out if he came up with it himself ..."

"You've got to be fucking kidding! A major shareholder of the big private television service, the president, in a deadly emergency relies on his intuition ... and it even works out for him so well. You have an imagination!"

"So, show off. Did you come up with it?"

"A single person never comes up with such things. But I'm not going to talk about this with you. What's possessed you?"

"Me? Nothing. The past has caught up with me."

"Just forget about it! When will you come to me?"

"I don't know if I'll come at all. Probably not."

On the other side of the phone, silence began to grow again. Gaj's voice sounded like a whine.

"Why?

"Too much to say, it'd be best not to say anything. Such affairs are ending."

"But why? Give me at least one reason! After all it was so extraordinary..."

"Monika, I'm extremely tired. Let's give it a rest. This isn't for the phone."

"Exactly! Come over. We will try to come to an understanding ..."

"I won't come. That conversation has no point. It's unnecessarily to have. Goodbye."

"But ..." He hung up.

Monika called him many times that evening, but he didn't answer. She began sending text messages. Pleads for any type of contact were mixed with insults. Over time, there were more and more insults. Around eleven o'clock after a longer break, another text came: "Come! Something terrible is happening! If you don't come, you'll be responsible. " He smiled ironically and deleted the text. The stream of messages stopped. The silence of the phone was finally beginning to worry him. It was almost twelve when he called. Gaj's phone was off. Brok decided to call a taxi and went to Jerozolimski Avenue.

Something peculiar was happening in the apartment. In the space, which wasn't usually a mess, individual, random items made him worry. The silence was overwhelming. Already from a distance Monica's naked body could be seen on the bed. Coming up, he almost stepped on the big, purple penis left on the floor. The packages of pornographic cassettes were all over the floor near the bed. Standing next to the bedside table was a three-quarters empty bottle of vodka. Several packets of sleeping pills were lying on the table. The cat was running around the room like crazy. Gaj was laying with her legs spread out. He ran over, grabbed her by the shoulders.

"What's with you!"

He put her on the bed. She was limp in his hands. He grabbed the phone, when she opened her eyes.

"I'm drunk," she said, quite soberly.

"Did you take this?!" He shouted, pointing to the packaging lying on table. He shook her violently. She hiccupped.

"I didn't. You can check. I was supposed to commit suicide", her swollen face was slightly reminiscent of the Monica, he knew; her gaze with difficulty was coming out from under her swollen eyelids "...but before I wanted to feel good. I prepared the pills, but I was drinking the whole time. I was already drunk. I lost the purple cock somewhere. I wasn't able to find it ... and these pornos. I didn't have the strength to clean them up. This is stupid though. Strangers would come and all around these ... gadgets. What would it look like? And what do I look like! I postponed death. I won't escape it. Because I have to kill myself. You don't love me, right?" Monika begins to sob. Her naked body shook to the rhythm of internal spasms. Adam embraced her. He wonders, why he feels such indifference. Above the bed Hopper's characters each look in their own direction. Gaj spasms more and more rapidly. She throws out through her tears: "God! I'm fed up with being independent woman. I want a normal life: husband, children. For fifteen years I took steps so as not to get pregnant. Now I tremble with fear that I won't be able to ..."

"Give it a break, Monika. Everything will be alright, you'll see. You'll definitely develop a new life strategy. You're after all a professional. Right?"

Monika closed her eyes. Her body calmed down.

"But will you visit me again?"

"Everything will be alright, sleep," said Adam.

Monika slowly sinks into the torn-up bed. She froze. She began to snore. Brok left. On the table in the living room he left the keys.

***

Taggart received him at a late breakfast in Bristol. He stopped there after flying in from New York two hours earlier. On a silver tray there's bread, cottage cheese on a porcelain plate, the same kind of jug with coffee and cup. With a silver spoon Taggart eats an egg from a silver glass. An egg-shaped, bald skull reflects the white light from behind the window.

"I have a problem with you, Adam. You did your job very well. Your reports are exemplary. You have prepared everything properly and ... you want to back out."

"Mike, these are personal matters. Nothing to do with work."

The metallic face rises from the tray.

"And you're saying this? I'm going to pretend I didn't hear. Otherwise I would have to fire you. We're not interested in your personal matters, but if they interfere with work, then you're unfit for the job. Could you have surely not known about this? You stand at the threshold! You were supposed to take this step and truly find yourself among us. Among those who create the world. For our part, you'd be the one to drive this business to Poland, the region, Europe. That would be your pass to enter among us. Only this isn't just work anymore. This is a responsible duty, twenty-four hours a day. After all it's not about just some, even big money. None of us is capable of spending what he earns. It's about something ... definitely much more. We've watched you for eight years. You've passed all the tests. In Russia you didn't let yourself get corrupted, and that's difficult. In truth, you took advantage of the lady which Nieftsibir sent you, but nothing resulted from it, and we're not prudish. You are very talented, Adam, and I like you. After all I knew you had a family history with him; what's his name, with Rojek, but you agreed, so everything indicated that you're fit for the job. And maybe because of these events you're especially up for it. And now, suddenly ... maybe you Adam, you just don't have luck. In Russia, you didn't succeed, not of your fault, but ... no luck. Now ... It's I prefer to work with those who have even less talent but more luck. This crisis shows that even such a seemingly controlled world can slip out of your hands. Control needs to be increased. Otherwise it's not known what'll happen. Chaos will rule without us. That's why we're throwing out nets. Television is a basic thing. We have to watch it. We don't care if our Eastern partners were communists and fascists. In the gentleman's club they're going to have to behave like gentlemen. Otherwise we'll get rid of them. But those to whom you'd join must have trust in each other. They need to know what's most important to you."

Taggart pauses. He finished his cottage cheese, followed it with coffee. They're found in an almost empty hall. In the corner, obscured by a newspaper, sat a man. A few tables away, a couple freezes above their cups. The air has the tone and consistency of coffee with milk. Opaque light pours in through the window. Taggart slightly changes the expression on his face, and Brok wonders whether it's a shadow or an illusion of a smile. "Your father died. This must've affected you. Everyone has the right to a moment of weakness. Think it over. Until tomorrow evening. You take up this enterprise, or we part ways. It's cold here."

***

Adam borrowed a car and went to Niemir. His mother refused participation the journey. He hadn't been in the countryside for many years. He turned after Wyszków onto a side road. The forest, somewhat cut through by autumn, was dark and gloomy. The earth has already hardened from the cold. The village emerged from the forest suddenly and unrealistically. His uncle's family received him enthusiastically, although they didn't recognize him immediately. With them and one of his cousins - the other had moved to Warsaw, just as the two girl cousins - Adam sat until evening, drinking a bottle of vodka, which he brought, and then another brought by hosts. They ate minced pork chops with potatoes and cabbage prepared by his aunt. They talked about their lives. Adam talked about places he went to and the things he's done. His aunt and uncle complained about hard times. Soon after dusk Adam went to a small room prepared for him. He immediately fell into a heavy sleep. He dreamed that he was walking through a snowy wasteland, not far from the forest. He notices the horse-drawn cart and a man lying on the snow. He comes up close and sees a familiar face smiling at him. The lying man points his eyes at the raven who stands nearby in the snow. Adam stares at it in suspense, but the crow flies away.

When he awoke, dawn was rising. Throughout the night an exceptionally thick and heavy snow fell. Adam headed for the forest. He broke through drifts, sunny clearances between the trunks of pine trees shimmered in the snow. Images of his childhood were returning to him, games in the forest, in which he took on subsequent roles in search of his identity. He had the impression that there are more memories and he remembered things that didn't happen to him, unfamiliar, and yet unfamiliar faces, words, whose meanings he guessed though, not entirely clear, suggesting a continuation of the scene. The clouds were running above the tops of the trees, they were sliding down lower, hooking on them. The wind picked up. The light of the sun was moving away. A clearing covered with white snow opened up. Adam fell on his back facing the sky. He was laying deep in the snow. He paused. The trees were moving restlessly. Between them above himself he saw something dark. A large bird slowly circled over him. Only when it flowed down to the ground a few meters from his head, did Adam realized that it's the crow from his dream. He looked at it intensely. But the crow flew away.

ABOUT THE AUTHOR

Bronisław Wildstein (born in 1952), writer, journalist, currently a columnist for Rzeczpospolita and the weekly Uwazam Rze. He graduated in Polish at the Jagiellonian University in Krakow. In the 1970's he was an anti-communist opposition activist. He was the co-founder of the Student Solidarity Committee in Krakow (1977). In 1980 he participated in the founding of Solidarity and the NZS in Krakow. Martial law found him in the West. He was the Co-founder and in 1982-87 editor-in-chief of the monthly magazine, *Contact*, published in Paris. He published in the emigration and underground press. He was the Paris correspondent RWE: 1987-90. At the beginning of 1990 he returned to Poland, where he performed the functions of, among others, director of Radio Krakow; edited "Zycie Warszawy "; deputy editor-in-chief "Life"; president of TVP; journalist of "Rzeczpospolita" and weekly "Wprost" and many other periodicals. He has worked in broadcast radio and television. He was decorated with the Officer's Cross of the Order of Polonia Restituta.

Look for more books from
Pike & Powder Publishing Group, LLC
and Zmok Books – E-books, paperbacks and Limited Edition hardcovers.
The best in history, science fiction and fantasy at:

visit us at www.PikeandPowder.com & www.wingedhussarpublishing.com

or follow us on Facebook at:

Winged Hussar Publishing LLC

Or on twitter at:

WingHusPubLLC

For information and upcoming publications

**This publication has
been supported by the
©POLAND Translation Program**